What Lies West

A Novel of the American Frontier

LaDene Morton

iUniverse, Inc.
New York Bloomington

What Lies West
A Novel of the American Frontier

iUniverse books may be ordered through booksellers or by contacting:

iUniverse
1663 Liberty Drive
Bloomington, IN 47403
www.iuniverse.com
1-800-Authors (1-800-288-4677)

ISBN: 978-1-4401-9084-1 (sc)
ISBN: 978-1-4401-9085-8 (ebk)

Printed in the United States of America

iUniverse rev. date: 12/02/2009

To Robert, and Roger

Part I
The Trail

1

Thank God the spring rains is over. Only thing worse than this chokin' dust is the mud. The lanky man at the reins of the wagon had tried for the better part of the morning to make it from the river landing to Westport. Now, only a few lousy feet from his delivery, he was stopped dead in his tracks by the horde around him. "Dang fools!" he cried, to no one but himself. "God dang fools!" he hollered, this time to the man in the covered wagon in front of him. But it was no use. Behind that wagon of fools was another, and another.

The driver considered his options. It wasn't as if he was hauling barrels of nails he could just chuck anywhere. His delivery was neither crated, kegged, nor boxed, but appareled in blue silk and adorned with black lace. A young woman sat straight and proper in the wagon next to him, a matching parasol shielding her from the morning sun, and only her coal black curls and a slightly daring neckline revealed. The driver look around for an open railing where the horses could be tied, then realized the crowd would keep them penned for the short time he needed. He jumped down and pushed his way through to one small storefront, leaving the woman alone in the center of the throng, like a queen bee in her hive.

The driver didn't notice the missing sign above the door as he went inside. He knew the store well—Clark & Morgan's, Overland Outfitters. But today, when others were enjoying land office business, the shelves in Clark's were nearly empty, and not a soul was in sight. He looked around, then called out, "Miz Clark! Are you about?" With silence his only answer, he mumbled in frustration, then headed back to his wagon.

The young woman was sitting just as he had left her, but now holding a kerchief over her face, trying to keep out the dust. Without a word, he grabbed her trunks and carried them to Clark's door. On the return trip, he stepped on the wagon hub and, without so much as a beg-your-pardon, scooped the woman into his arms. She gasped, but he was carrying her through the crowd before she knew what had happened, and without ceremony, set her on her feet inside the store. "There you are," he said flatly, then left.

****

Lina Clark was outside behind the store. She had spent the previous hour standing in front watching the same crowd the driver fought getting to town. Out of habit she trained her shopkeeper's eye on them, trying to guess what they would need. Then she remembered there was no point to it now. The sight of them only reminded her of her circumstances. So she had retreated to the quiet of the small shed out back to count inventory. She was only twenty, but today her worries made her feel much older.

Lina kept chickens in the shed, too, and they were clucking for attention. "Here you go, darlings. Last meal for the condemned, I guess." Lazily, she tossed them some feed. *Time to get back*, she thought.

She was studying the ledger book she held as she walked back into the store, but a flash of bright blue caught her eye. A young woman covered in blue silk and dust stood folding her parasol and checking her reflection in the door glass. "Something I can do for you?" Lina asked.

The woman turned. "Yes, you may." She wore a look of solid determination and utter confidence. "You may tell me if what that lout of driver said is true!"

Lina moved behind the counter. "Driver?"

"I told him I was to be met by a Mr. Clark, but he told me that Mr. Clark, the proprietor of this establishment, is deceased. Is that true?"

Lina nodded. "You had business with him?"

"He was to transport me to California!"

Lina laughed. "Not very likely, miss."

"My name is Josephine Paul. And why do you find that so amusing? Mr. Clark is…I mean… was, an outfitter for the overlanders, was he not?"

"Yes, but you must be mistaken. Ephraim had no plans to transport anybody anywhere. Perhaps it was another outfitter. There are several here in town. Why don't you…?" Before she could finish, Josephine Paul reached inside the small bag she clutched, took out a letter and thrust it toward Lina.

Lina took it. She recognized the handwriting and poor spelling. It was addressed to Josephine Paul of St. Louis.

> *Miss Paul*
>   *As you have reqwested, I will be pleased to secur you*
> *a place in the joint stock company I am forming headed*
> *for California. Please make shure you arrive in Westport*
> *by the first of May as I espect to be departing near that*
> *date. The cost of membership is two hunderd dollers.*
> *Very truly,*
> *Ephraim Clark*

"Dear Lord," was all Lina say. She closed her eyes and rubbed her brow.

"This is the same Mr. Clark?"

"Yes," Lina answered weakly.

"Then, I am sorry for his passing, but I have arrived as instructed, and I expect to join this company regardless."

Lina looked up to see that same damnably determined expression. She laid the ledger down, and leaned into the counter. "Miss Paul, there isn't any company. This was just another of my husband's pipe dreams."

"Your husband?"

"Yes, Mr. Clark was my husband. He died a week ago. Lost everything at poker, got stinking drunk, then fell off his horse coming home and broke his neck."

"Then, I would assume that as his widow, his responsibilities are now yours. Your husband promised me passage, and I feel that promise now falls to you."

"You can assume what you like. It won't get you west. Didn't you hear me? He lost everything. The last of our money, this business. The only reason I'm here today is to make sure his creditors get a clean accounting. I'm sorry for your troubles, but the best thing for you to do would be to turn around and go back to St. Louis."

"That's out of the question. Perhaps you could help me locate another company."

Lina considered how to answer this question. She moved out from behind the counter. "Miss Paul, I have to ask why you want to go to California."

A bright smile came to Josephine's face, deepening her already considerable dimples. It was a practiced expression, Lina could plainly see, and no doubt designed to charm a gentleman, but Lina couldn't resist some of its charm as well. "I intend to move west to take advantage of opportunities there."

Lina smiled, "I assume you're not referring to farming?"

"Indeed not. Farming is an unnatural calling for a woman. It claims youth and beauty, and asks for sacrifice disproportionate to reward. No, I plan on making a great deal of money from the gold fields of California."

The miners, Lina thought, not a bit surprised. "Then let me speak frankly. The wagon companies are a mixed lot. There are plenty of miners, to be sure, but just as many settlers. It's nothing to me what you think of them. My concerns are for what they'll think of you. Let me ask you something. Did you contact any other companies before you wrote my husband?"

"Yes, but no one else replied."

"And you mentioned you'd be traveling alone?"

"Yes."

"Well, there you have it. None of those other outfitters want to risk upsetting the other members. I've no particular quarrel with your scheme, although I think it's risky, and probably not thought out properly. But I understand why no one would transport a woman traveling alone clear across country in the company of mostly men. Scandalous behaviors cause problems, Miss Paul, and intended or not, you can easily find yourself the subject of some contention among the group. Anyone putting together a company wants to avoid trouble of any kind." Josephine listened carefully, and to Lina she looked confused, so she added, "Perhaps you really should reconsider going home to St. Louis, Miss Paul. St. Louis is a big city. There must be opportunities for you there, where you worked before."

Josephine blushed, which struck Lina as out of place on that face. In a half whisper, she said, "I didn't work anywhere before. You see, I, well, I haven't yet…"

"You mean you're not really a whore?" In Lina's surprise, she blurted out the word that had been in her mind all along, the one word she had until now worked so hard to avoid. "I'm so sorry!" she said, "I shouldn't have said that, or said it that way, or…"

Josephine wasn't bothered. "No need, although I daresay there *are* more flattering terms. But how can I explain?" She looked around the store. "Did you work here before your husband passed?"

"Yes."

"Do you like it? Do you have a talent for it? Well, I have a talent, too. The rush to California seems like the perfect opportunity to earn more. Much more. Surely a woman of business like you can appreciate that."

Lina laughed. "I suppose I never thought of it like that."

"Josephine. Please, you must call me Josephine. And your name?"

"Carolina, but folks call me Lina."

"Well, Lina, are you certain you can't help me find other passage?"

"I'm truly sorry. It isn't that I refuse. I simply can't think of a single company that would have you. Like I said, it'd probably be best if you returned to St. Louis."

"I'm afraid that's impossible. I've been dismissed from my father's house. He has washed his hands of me, and I of him. There is nothing for me back there."

"Then all I can offer is a room. There are no other rooms in town, so I would advise you to take it. At least that'll give you some time to figure out what you want to do. But the room's only for two nights. After that, the creditors will be taking over the business."

"Thank you. You're very kind."

Lina rose, walked to the door, and bolted it. "The afternoon's nearly gone anyway. I still have all day tomorrow to finish up here." Lina started up the stairs.

"What about the trunks?" Josephine asked, still standing by the door.

"Leave them there. If you want them up here, you'll have to haul them up yourself." Josephine looked bewildered. Lina decided she was clearly born to the breed that was use to considerable accommodation, so she added, "If you're determined to make your way to California, you'll need to get used to taking care of yourself. Sometimes, it'll be your strong back and not your feminine wiles you'll need." Josephine looked at Lina, then left the trunks behind and followed her up the stairs.

****

Lina had lived in this small space above the store for nearly half her young life. It never felt like a home, although she wasn't sure what a home should feel like. She was ten when she and her father moved in, just after they got to Westport. "Westport! Why, the name alone sounds like the place for me!" her father said back then. Her father, Thomas Morgan, followed the flow of westward migration all his adult life. He started in Kentucky, and somewhere in Illinois he met Lina's mother, Eleanor. Lina had only the vaguest memory of her, for she died when Lina was only three. Young Tom Morgan was a hard worker back then, but never very shrewd. He was always at the losing end of opportunity. He followed the settlements as they sprung up along the Missouri River, the last merchant to arrive, and the first to lose his shirt.

In Morgan's eyes, the chance to move to Westport was a stroke of good fortune. He would be partnering with someone for the first time,. Ephraim Clark had offered a fair price for half his business. It took everything Tom Morgan had, but he gladly paid it. Lina could clearly remember the day the partners hung the sign over the store. Her father seemed bursting with pride. For the next six years, Lina lived the most stable life she had ever known. She worked with her father in the store. It was a solitary life, but it seemed to suit her. She loved her father, and was particularly good at keeping the books, so she felt needed. Besides, she didn't consider life held other choices.

Ephraim Clark might have had a going concern at some time, but not by the time Tom Morgan became his partner, and never after. It took all the hours in the day to work hard enough just to keep the doors open. As Lina took on more chores at the store, both men took on fewer responsibilities. At first Lina didn't mind. Her father might be a dreamer, but he was a kind man who tried his best, and she felt she owed him that much. Although they were poorer than when they arrived, Morgan remained optimistic. "Westport is a growing place," he would say to his daughter almost nightly. "Coming here was the right thing to do."

Tom Morgan never left Westport. Three years earlier, he had died suddenly. The doctor said it was most likely his heart. Lina was barely seventeen at the time, but had no place to go. Her father had no relatives that she knew of. She never met her mother's family, and didn't imagine they would think kindly of the sudden appearance of the child of an unwelcome union between a daughter they grieved for and the man who stole her away.

So Lina stayed in Westport, in the small store working alongside Ephraim Clark, and living with him in the rooms above the store. Soon, though, tongues began to wag. A young woman and a man older than her father living under one roof without benefit of marriage raised eyebrows all around town. Ephraim suggested the marriage as a convenience for both. Not knowing what else to do, Lina agreed. Fortunately she had no expectations for the marriage, for none were fulfilled. The wedding was without ceremony, the wedding night without subtlety. At first, they worked together during the day, and at night Ephraim would drink and gamble. The harder Lina worked, the more time Ephraim spent away from the store, until finally he was gone nearly every day and every night. She was forced to work even harder to keep ahead of the debts Ephraim seemed to accumulate so easily. But if the whiskey and the late nights kept him out after she went to bed, leaving him to pass out on the small cot in the kitchen, so much the better. She could stand this drudge of a marriage, as long as there were no children. The whiskey made that near to impossible, so Lina said a quiet thank you each night for the whiskey.

That gratitude gave her more than a little guilt when whiskey ended up as Ephraim's undoing. She knew she had not wished his death, but she also knew she had never really tried to stop him either. The guilt went away when she fully understood the sorry state of affairs in which Ephraim had left her. She was not just alone and penniless, but homeless, in debt, with no friends, and no idea what to do next. Worry replaced guilt. Deep within her, a sense of panic had started that felt like the first echoes of thunder before a storm.

By contrast, the woman who was Lina's unexpected guest seemed quite calm, despite her own uncertain future. She was nothing short of cheerful as she watched Lina prepare supper, asking all sorts of questions and barely giving Lina a chance to answer before another was asked. Lina welcomed the silence that came as they ate. Then she became aware that Josephine was studying her.

Discovered, Josephine answered the unasked question. "I'm a bit surprised by your demeanor, Lina. As a recent widow, you seem less than despondent."

Lina shrugged. "My husband was no damn good, plain and simple. He was a terrible businessman, and then there were the schemes. Always something to make a fast buck, just like this letter he sent you. But since no one else has shown up asking about it, I'm guessing that plan petered out, too. Thank God you didn't advance him any money." Then suddenly, she asked, "You didn't, did you?"

"No, thankfully. My finances were fully intact. When my father showed me the door, he placed a thousand dollars in my hand, and said, 'Here you are. That's all you should ever need from me. Leave here forever, and do not ask for more.'"

Lina laughed. "A thousand dollars! Why, that's twice what most come west with. But I suppose it doesn't matter, if you can't find a way to travel." She started to clear the table. Josephine made no move to help.

"What will you do now?" Josephine asked. "Have you any prospects? Perhaps there is some other fellow whose eye you've caught?"

Again Lina laughed. "Hardly!" she said, dropping the plates in a bucket of water. "Most fellows who come through here aren't looking for a wife. A wife's just another mouth to feed. The farmers already have families, and the miners are seeking fortunes, not wives." She pulled her sleeves above her elbows and plunged her arms into the bucket. "Besides, I've been married. It's a bad trade for a woman, if you ask me. All that worry and doing without, and no say-so over yourself.

No, I've been taking care of myself for a long time, even when I had a father and a husband. I guess I'll just keep on."

"How?" Josephine asked.

Lina stopped, staring absently at the plate in her dripping hand. She had been asking herself that for days now, and she hadn't come to a satisfactory answer. She glanced over her shoulder to Josephine, then started on the plate again. "Well, there are a number of businesses here. Freighters, I mean. I know that trade. Perhaps they could use an experienced hand." But the words were spoken without conviction. She had already asked around town, and no offers were given.

"Working for other people seems a little like marriage to me, Lina. All the hard work and sacrifice, with few rewards. The only appeal it might hold is constancy, if one wants that sort of thing."

"And what's wrong with it? I've lived hand-to-mouth. A little constancy sounds rather nice." She took a cloth to the pile of clean dishes.

"Perhaps. For a while. But, tell me, year after year you've catered to these people who head west. Didn't the thought of going there yourself even seem appealing? Or at least intriguing?"

"Intriguing, yes. Practical, no." Lina dragged the bucket of dirty water to the window, and with a quick glance below, poured the contents onto the street.

"Why not practical?"

Lina took a chair across from Josephine. "So many things to consider. You have to come prepared. You need a wagon, and at least four good oxen. Six would be better. Enough food for five or six months, and that's assuming you can find game along the way. There'll be long periods without water, without grass for the livestock. You may come down with cholera, if last year's any measure. A lot of folks won't make it at all."

"But consider the reward if one does, Lina. Adventure and fortune. What could be better?"

"Well, adventure, yes. More than you bargain for, maybe more than you can survive. But fortune, that's another matter. If you mean those miners out there, I imagine they'll end up poorer than they came. Most of them are as green as the day is long."

"I agree. To pin one's hopes on any one of them would be folly. But some men will be making fortunes out there, and ultimately, they'll spend those fortunes on providing themselves with the comforts they lack," Josephine smiled slyly.

"Like the charms of a lovely companion," Lina added.

"Or a good meal, or a good night's rest. Whiskey. Perhaps a bath. Or just the simple things of life—the sort of things you sold here." Lina looked at Josephine, who still wore the same, knowing smile. The smile made Lina take a step back.

"Oh, no! Not me. No! Thank you, but no!"

"Just consider it, Lina. I have seen, as have you, how sudden changes influence the fortunes of a city. St. Louis has become a real city over the last fifty years. My father and his fat friends became wealthy from sending easterners here. People here become wealthy sending them further. There will be fortunes made in California, Lina, and not just by the men who find the gold."

"If I couldn't make money here, what makes you think it'll be any easier in California?"

"You very likely have made money. But your husband wasted that fortune for you. Are you going to be content to wait here for another man who'll show so little regard for your hard work and talents?"

Lina was listening to Josephine, despite her herself. She walked to the window and stared down at the nearly empty streets. She considered all the wagons that had come through that day. How far would they travel before they found themselves needing something, something she might have? And once there, they would need even more. Unconsciously, she came to form a vision of herself somewhere out west, with her own store, making her own life.

As if reading her thoughts, Josephine was suddenly beside her, whispering in her ear. "What have you to lose, Lina?"

What indeed? A life no better than what I have. "Oh, Josephine, if I came with you, what would that get us? We'd be two women traveling alone rather than one."

"My dear, we would be two women traveling *together*, which is an entirely different matter, wouldn't you agree? And with your expertise and my capital, we could outfit ourselves amply."

"But we would still have to find a company that would take us."

"Will that be difficult?"

Lina sighed. "Honestly, I don't know. I suppose it's possible a company might have us. Of course, we'd need a team, too...."

"So you agree," Josephine said delightedly, "it is possible!"

"It is *possible*, yes," said Lina. She led Josephine back to the table by her arm, pushing her with just a little too much force back into the chair. "But there is one consideration beyond my control. You."

"Me? I'm quite certain I don't know what you mean." She tossed her head dismissively.

"Very well, Josephine. It's time to talk straight again. As I told you, it's not my concern what you intend to do in California. But until we get there, or until we strike out on our own, you would have to refrain from setting up shop. There'd be no plying your trade on the road. Not if you want my help."

Josephine pretended a little pout. "I don't see the harm. If *you* have an opportunity to make a little money on the trip, why shouldn't I?"

"Because your kind of trade is likely to get us left behind. If we go, and I say only *if*, we'll need those other folks a hell of a lot more than they'll need us, my supplies and your charms notwithstanding." Josephine shrugged her shoulders. "In fact, it goes further than that. You'll not only have to promise not to ply your trade on the trip, you'll have to sacrifice. Those pretty dresses you've brought, for instance. There are far too many, they'll take up too much valuable space in the wagon. You'll have to get all your things into one trunk." Josephine started to protest, but Lina stopped her. "There's no way around it. The wagon has to hold food, tools, everything. Goods a lot more important to our survival than those fancy dresses. And the hardships won't stop there. It'll be hard work, harder than anything you've ever done, and at the end of the trip you'll feel more like a farmer's wife than you care to." Lina was watching Josephine closely, searching her face for any sign that the realities she was describing would change her mind. She saw no such sign.

"If I do these things, will you promise to come with me?" Josephine took hold of her hand.

"I'm not sure I can pull it all off, getting what we need—the company, the oxen...."

"Oh, I have no doubt you can do it!" Josephine jumped from her chair and threw her arms around Lina. "You will find a way, I am certain. Oh, now, why the frown? In a few days' time, we'll be off! Away from this sad, tired Missouri. To California!" Josephine went to the window and looked toward the western sky, a dreamy smile on her lips. *It's as if she can see the future from here*, Lina thought. She joined her at the window, hoping to see what Josephine saw. But try as she might, she could not.

2

Lina was in a dither that had kept her awake much of the night. Yesterday she had been resigned to let tomorrow take care of itself. Then this silly woman had been dropped in her lap, and somehow Josephine's problems were now Lina's. Even worse, she had set Lina's brain on fire with talk of heading west. Sleepless hours deep in the night were spent trying to talk herself out of the notion, but something kept pulling her back to it. Only when she finally gave into it, and started working out the details in her mind did she finally fall asleep. But an hour later the sun was up, and so was she, eager to get started.

Bang! Lina threw open the door to the room where Josephine slept. "Coffee's on. Wake up." That was as warm a greeting as Lina could muster. The coffee was poured and waiting at the table before a sleepy-eyed Josephine emerged. "Good morning," she said drowsily, rubbing her eyes as she walked to the table.

"Are you awake?" Lina asked. "Because we have to talk before I leave, and you've got to remember everything I tell you."

Josephine yawned and stretched, relaxed as a cat in the sun. "Where are you going?"

"Drink up. I need you awake." Lina sat next to Josephine, watching every sip she took, thrumming her fingers on the table. Josephine was halfway finished with her cup when finally she said, "Very well, you have my full attention."

"I need two hundred dollars."

"Oh really?" Josephine took another sip. "For what purpose, might I ask?"

"You might ask, but I'll not answer. Listen to me. It is better for a whole lot of reasons that you know as little about what I need the money for as possible."

"Well, Lina, you're asking a great deal on faith. After all, by your own admission you are a person who is about to lose not only all apparent assets, but your livelihood as well. What would prevent you from walking out the door and never returning?"

"Not a thing, Josephine. You're absolutely right. I could easily take your money and you'd never see me again. Of course, I could have taken the whole thousand last night, the way you sleep like a hibernating bear, but I didn't. If you don't trust me, take your dilemma elsewhere. I'll be no worse off than I was yesterday."

Josephine considered that. "Very well. Two hundred dollars. Is there something else?"

"Yes. And this is as critical as the money. I need you to stay here, all day if necessary. You can't leave, not even to go downstairs."

"But what possible difference could that make?"

"I've got some errands to attend to around town. I'm going to have to stretch the truth, and not just a little bit. But there's no choice in it, if I'm to make this work. I have a feeling you're the chatty type, given the chance. So I must make sure you don't have that chance. Hell, even the sight of you is likely to raise questions it's best to avoid answering."

Josephine watched Lina as closely as she listened. Even when Lina had finished, she said nothing. For a moment, Lina was sure Josephine had realized she had made the offer in haste, and now had changed her mind. Whether she admitted it or not, she had already started to bank on this scheme, and the idea that Josephine might reconsider put a knot in her stomach.

Finally, Josephine walked to the bedroom and returned with two hundred dollars, which she placed in Lina's hand. "Don't worry, I'll stay here. All day, if I must."

Lina took the money from her, squeezing Josephine's hand for a mere moment. With a smile, she headed for the door and had started down the stairs when she called back up, "By the way, if I haven't returned by midnight, then I *did* leave with your money."

****

Lina's list for the day was long, and at the top was the matter of oxen. She needed at least four, but would prefer eight. Oxen would be hard to come by and cost dearly. But there was no good substitute. Mules couldn't pull a wagon long distances over hard terrain. Horses were too expensive. Then there would be provisions. After running through an account in her mind last night, she reckoned she had most of what they would need, right here in the store. But there were some items she would have to buy. Then there was the matter of finding a proper company to join. Likely as not, there would be several at the encampment no matter when they arrived, but that was chancy. Finally, all the two women owned between them would have to be sorted and packed, leaving behind all but the most necessary items. These, along with all the other provisions and equipment, would have to be loaded into the wagon. Tonight, after dark.

But that was tonight, and none of that would matter if she didn't get what she needed today. And first and foremost, what she needed were those oxen. Her best chance was Sam Johnson, a blacksmith just two doors down, and as close to a friend as anyone she could think of. Mercifully, Ephraim had not died owing him anything.

Inside the smithy's, Johnson was already pounding away. With the sun still low in the morning sky, it was dark inside, and other than a little sunshine streaming in through chinks in the slats, the only light came from the glowing embers of the furnace. Johnson stood at the bellows, each stroke by his thick arms stoking the fire. Lina took a quick glance at the livestock on hand. Four oxen, plus two horses and a mule. The horses were Johnson's, and she had no interest in the mule.

"Good morning, Sam."

Johnson looked up only long enough to see who had come in, then returned to the bellows. "Mornin' Lina. You're up early." Then, remembering, added, "I guess you're closing up shop today, eh?"

"Tomorrow." Lina paused a moment, afraid to seem too eager. "I was wondering, Sam, if any of those oxen are for sale."

"Yeah, matter of fact, two of 'em. Why?"

"I was hoping to buy them."

"What would you be wantin' 'em for?" It was clear from his tone that his question was born of neighborly curiosity, not suspicion. Still, she would have to tell the same tale everywhere she went, so she told what she'd rehearsed last night.

"This couple from Indiana showed up yesterday. They had written Ephraim, and for some reason they figured they could just show up and he would have everything ready for them. I explained the situation, but I couldn't help feeling sorry for them. They're so green, you know? So I told them I'd try to help."

"Why not just send 'em down to Pickens' or Dobbins' place?"

"They sold everything to come this far, and barely have enough to buy what they'll need. Those two'll gouge them, you know they will. I'm just trying to help them stretch their dollars."

"This is your lucky day. I had some folks show up yesterday, wagon falling to pieces already. Gonna take me better part of a day to fix it, too. The one thing they were thick with was oxen, so I took a pair in trade. Kinda like you, felt sorry for 'em, I guess."

"How much do you want?"

"I'll let ya have 'em for forty. Probably get lucky to get that much for 'em in a day or so. Pickens' been expectin' a fresh herd for a week. More'n a hundred head. The town'll be lousy with 'em soon enough."

She handed him the money. "I'll be back to get them later. I thank you for your help, Sam."

As she left, Sam returned to his work. "Don't worry, Lina. Things'll work out. Always do."

Well, I've had my first bit of luck today. Perhaps it will hold, she thought as she headed toward Pickens' place. If what Johnson had said was true, perhaps she could afford to buy the second team from Pickens. Still, she detested the thought of dealing with the man. Of all the merchants in town, he was the one to whom she owed the most. Ephraim, continually finding himself low on inventory, cash, or both, would stock his own store from Pickens' reserves, and Pickens charged handsomely for the favor. He had run other men out of business, and the way she saw it, he'd done the same to Ephraim. There were other people in town Ephraim owed money to, but they took it in stride. If Ephraim was too far in arrears, others quietly cut him off. Pickens had encouraged Ephraim's debt for his own gain.

The Pickens operation was the largest in town, fully twice as large as hers, and with a livestock pen attached. It was widely held by people in town that last year Pickens made ten dollars for every man, woman and child who headed west. Folks believed it because Pickens boasted as much to anyone who would listen. Nearly every day he could be found out in front of his store, glad-handing everyone. He was a master of publicity, and had even managed to get his operation mentioned in some of the guidebooks that circulated back east, enticing folks to go west. Pickens' self-proclaimed goal was to make certain that every settler that passed through did not consider he had really seen the west without a stop at J. Pickens' Overland Emporium.

Lina stepped inside Pickens' store, and right into the path of the clerks who were feverishly moving stock from one side of the store to the other. Crates and kegs were flying open, their contents crammed onto the endless shelves. *Pickens gives himself airs, trying to make this place so fancy*, Lina thought, but she knew she was a bit jealous, too. Pickens' store was more than just an outfitters. He carried all the usual fare, but also the rarified items, like canned butter, fine silks and laces, the best Colt rifles and elaborately tooled saddles. While most settlers were smart enough, or tight enough, to stick to the necessities, the last chance at a little luxury was often more than some could resist. Pickens stood surveying the fracas his mere presence seemed to generate. When he saw her coming towards him, a smug smile came to his thin lips. "Well, Mrs. Clark. What an unexpected surprise. Here to settle up?"

"I have until tomorrow to do that, and I intend to take it."

His smile vanished. "Surely you aren't thinking of asking for more time?"

"No. I won't need more time. Tomorrow will do nicely. I've come about buying some oxen. Four of them."

Pickens laughed so hard that it rose above the din of the room, and everyone stopped momentarily to look his way. "Sell you something, Mrs. Clark? Can I believe my ears?"

"Yes, sell me something." Lina was working to keep her anger contained. "You've done it often enough for Ephraim."

Pickens was still laughing as he said, "Correction, Mrs. Clark, I *advanced* your husband cash or goods, not sold, which is the very fact that brings you to where you are today."

"But I have cash!" she blurted out, then immediately realized the foolishness of it.

"Oh this is too good, Mrs. Clark. You want to pay me for four oxen today, when I can wait until tomorrow and have both the money and the beasts! I'd be a poor business man to take that bargain!"

"The cash isn't mine," said Lina, slightly more contritely. "I'm trying to help out a couple from Indiana that showed up late yesterday. They were expecting Ephraim to outfit them."

"Then send them over. J. Pickens will be happy to accommodate them."

"Yes, I'm sure you will. Happy to take every cent they have left." Lina was almost beginning to believe in this imagined couple, and that she was their defender.

"Well, then, send them elsewhere. Or send them back to Indiana, for all I care." Pickens was no longer laughing. "I have no intention of selling you a single potato, let alone four oxen, even though by mid-morning I'll have more than I can sell for weeks. It's time you gave up, and the sooner you realize this, the quicker I can claim what's owed me."

He would not change his mind, she knew, and at this point she wanted nothing more to do with him. But just leaving did not seem enough. She started to leave, passing the counter upon where the large jars filled with penny candy sat. She grabbed the first jar she saw, opened it up, and took a piece, tossing it in her mouth. "Put it on my tab," she said flippantly, walking through the door.

As soon as she was outside, she spit the foul thing on the ground. *Horehound!* She despised the bittersweet molasses taste. Now she was angry with herself, and with Pickens. She had wanted to make one last jab at the old man, and her desperate impulse with the candy backfired, making her feel like a petulant child. She was walking towards Dobbins' store, intending to buy oxen there, but her mind was still on Pickens. *That man doesn't need my pittance, and what's more, he doesn't deserve it. That's his problem, he's just got too much of everything to appreciate it. And every day, the boats up the river just bring him more. More customers, more money, more livestock....*

Suddenly, Lina switched directions and headed back toward her store. The street was really teeming now, and it was only mid-morning. Lina had to dart between wagons as she crossed the street. Finally, she reached the planked sidewalk, then veered around the back of the buildings to where her own horse was tied. She hastily threw on the saddle, mounted the horse, and rode north toward the river landing.

****

People came from all directions to Westport, but every day during the season, the road most traveled was the road between Westport and the river landing where steamboats delivered shipments of settlers, livestock and cargo. It was four miles to the river, a trip that usually took her an hour. Judging from the number of wagons headed south, she figured a steamboat had arrived early this morning. When she reached the landing, she saw her guess was right. The passengers and wagons had disembarked, and the crew was well into offloading the livestock. A quick count told Lina there must be more than a hundred head of oxen. Pickens' oxen. She stayed on her horse, away from the crew, sizing up the situation. The oxen were herded down a ramp toward a holding pen. A Pickens man would no doubt arrive soon to take them back toward town. Lina remembered Pickens said he was expecting them around mid-day. The Pickens man might be here anytime. She would have to act fast.

Lina spied a fellow loitering near the pen. She watched him for a while. He spoke to no one, and no one spoke to him. Lina knew most of the folks around here, and she had never seen this face before. She almost wished she had brought Josephine with her. A woman like that would be handy to have in creating a distraction. But her own limited wiles would have to do for now. "Hello," she called as she rode up to the young man. She judged him about her age, twenty perhaps. He had a shock of dull brown hair, and a long horsey face that was covered by a wide, open grin. His skin was tanned, and he wore the clothes of a rider, with spurs on his boots and leather chaparrals over his pants. "Are these yours?" she asked demurely, pointing toward the oxen.

"No, ma'am! I prefer horses ma'self." He removed his hat and kept his grin focused on her. "These fool animals is dumber than rocks."

"Then whose are they?" Lina dismounted and joined him at the rail.

"Heard somebody say they's goin' to a fella name of Pickens. I'm just watchin'm, killin' time, so ta speak."

Lina smiled at her luck, to find he had no business with Pickens. "How many do you suppose are in there?" she asked as coyly as she could.

"Oh, I know for a fact. Stood here and counted 'em myself. There's 'zactly one hundred twenty."

"Really?" she said. She looked around her for a watchful eye. When she knew they were alone, she leaned in toward him, and, in almost a whisper, said, "I say there's one hundred sixteen."

"Oh, no ma'am! I counted 'em twice!" he said.

Lina reached into her pocket and removed twenty dollars. The bills caught the young man's eye. She smiled and took his hand, pressing his fingers around the money. "No," she said slowly, and deliberately. "I think there's one hundred sixteen."

Without looking at the money, he took his hand from hers and slipped the bills into his shirt pocket. "Ya know, ma'am, now that ya say it, I think you may be right." He grinned, and casually slipped off the rope that held the gate closed. Without a word, he walked in and cut four head from the herd. Gently and quietly, he clicked his teeth and urged them from the pen. Just as casually, Lina mounted her horse. When the oxen were out of the pen in front of her, she looked down on the young man and smiled. "Good day to you."

"And to you, ma'am. Nice doin' business with ya."

****

Somehow, her luck did stay with her that day, and she managed to secure everything they needed without raising suspicion. From Pickens' prime competitor, Jed Dobbins, she bought the last of the goods. The young man who helped her there recognized her, but asked no questions.

As to the matter of a company to travel with, Lina had resolved herself to taking her chances at the encampment, for she knew no one to ask without some questions being asked. But as she was leaving Dobbins', she noticed a flock of handbills tacked to the building, and a cluster of folks standing about reading them. She was about to pass them by when she heard someone mention a company looking for members. She shouldered in among the group. "What company?" she asked to no one in particular.

"Goes by the name of Granby," said the voice she had first heard. The man stabbed his finger at a leaflet that stood out among the others for its fancy lettering and a coat of arms stamped at the top. *Granby Joint Stock Company*, it said. The piece was wordy, full of flowery speech, all of which was meant to entice anybody and everybody to join, for the sum of one hundred dollars a wagon. Lina glanced through all that until she found what she was looking for—a date. Tomorrow's date. The date the company planned to leave. She snatched the leaflet off the nail and headed home.

It took the whole evening for Lina and Josephine to prepare to leave at first light. First, they each went through their clothes. Ephraim's two shirts, undershirts, socks and drawers, his shoes and boots were all carefully packed, only because they were the most practical clothing either of the two women had for the trip. Lina had a few simple dresses like the one she was wearing, which she also packed, along with a pair of pants that had been her father's.

Lina was pleasantly surprised that Josephine had spent much of the day going through her own trunks, and had reduced her pile so that it would fit into one very large trunk. Still, most of her clothing was completely unsuitable for the trip, so Lina gave her two ready-made dresses she had bought for her at Dobbins' store.

"These? You expect me to wear these?"

"You'll wear these and be glad for them, at least for a while, until we're well on the trail. Save your other things as long as you can. And keep them out of sight."

The household goods were easily packed into one wooden crate. Blankets and bedding went into another. Then they dragged their luggage, crates and boxes downstairs to the dark, empty store.

"Tonight we're just going to try to get everything loaded. Tomorrow, and later on the trail, we can get everything arranged in such a way as to make full use of the space." Lina had pulled their wagon behind the store, hoping they could pack unnoticed. It took a long time to get everything lashed, stacked and stored within the wagon, because Lina had to do most of the heavy work. Josephine tried, but being unaccustomed to physical labor, she seemed only willing to carry the smallest, lightest bundles. But she worked without complaining, a trait Lina much appreciated after her long day.

Nearly everything was loaded, and the two had just sat down inside for a short rest, when outside they heard the sounds of a horse approaching at a fast clip. The hoof beats stopped in front of the store and Lina heard boot steps along the wooden sidewalk in front, followed by a sharp rap on the bolted door. A man's voice called, "Hallo there!"

The two women stood silent. Lina's mind was racing. Perhaps someone had seen her today, and figured out her plan, and now here was one of her creditors to keep her from running out. The man's voice called out again, as he knocked on the door. "Anybody about?"

Then the sound of boots moved away from the door, and everything was silent again. After a minute of this quiet, the two women looked at one another and, in unison, sighed. In a whisper, Lina said, "Let's get back to work and get this done." With Josephine right behind her, Lina headed toward the wagon, but as she stepped outside she stopped so suddenly that Josephine bumped into her. Standing by the wagon was a young man, the same young man she had bribed to get the oxen.

"Hello again! You happen to be Miz Clark?" he asked, clutching his hat.

"Why do you ask?" Lina pulled herself up to full height and made her voice sound as imposing as she knew how.

"Oh, I asked after you at the landing. Fella gave me your name, said you ran this outfitter's store. That was just what I was lookin' for, so I came to see ya. Figured if anybody in town'd be likely to do me a favor, it'd be you." His grin made Lina uncomfortable. He had something on her, and now he wanted something in return. *But what?* The young man kept looking into the store, behind the two women, but they didn't move from the spot.

For the first time, Lina noticed the two pistols he wore. "What do you want?" she asked.

"Name's Parker, ma'am. Henry Parker from the Arkansas Territory. Pleased to make your acquaintance." He held out his hand to her. She didn't take it, but he still felt welcome enough to push past them and come inside the store. Lina and Josephine followed him closely.

"Mr. Parker, you come riding up here, in the middle of the night, barge into my store armed, so what am I to think? I don't know you from Adam. What is it you want?"

"Oh, I'm sorry, miss. Here, let me put your mind to rest." Henry reached for his guns and Josephine gasped. Seeing her reaction, Henry moved more slowly, purposefully. He took his two pistols between finger and thumb and laid them so carefully on the store counter they might have been snakes. "Here, miss, you can see my weapons is out. I don't mean you ladies no harm. I was just hoping maybe I could join up with your group."

Lina pushed the pistols away to add distance between them and Henry Parker. "Well, I appreciate that, Mr. Parker, but I can't help you. I've been helping Miss Paul here, because my late husband made a promise to her before he died. But that's all. If you want I can direct you to where the companies are camped. Perhaps there you could find a company for you and your family."

"Family? No ma'am. Just me."

"Where's your wagon, then? Your supplies?"

"Well, ma horse's outside. Got me a rifle, two pistols, bedroll, canteen. Cain't think a nothin' else. Like to travel light."

"You'll travel dead, Mr. Parker, without any food. How do you expect to feed yourself?"

"I'm a fair shot. Figured I could scare up some game along the way. And what I cain't shoot, maybe I could barter for."

"Barter? With what?"

Henry looked at Lina, then at Josephine, and then his grin grew bigger. "Well, ta tell ya the truth, when I came lookin' for ya, I wasn't 'zactly sure what I'd need. I got a little cash, as you know," he said, patting his shirt pocket. "I reckoned I could buy a few things off ya, maybe get a good price. But now I'm here, I think maybe I see another way." Henry looked around the empty store. "Couldn't help but notice your wagon out there. All loaded up and ready to go. Looks like ya figures to head west yourself. I'm thinkin', why, I wonder? Been my experience, folks loaded up at night figures to slip out early. Folks what slips out early usually trying to avoid bein' seen. And folks whats trying to avoid bein' seen's usually runnin', either from the law, or from their bills. You two lovely ladies don't figure to be in trouble with the law, so…"

Still the women gave no answer, so Henry continued. "Then thar's those oxen out there. Seems to me I heard somethin' bout some being

25

cut from a herd down at the docks earlier today. Might be folks in town want to look at them animals 'fore they disappear." Henry laughed a deep, good-natured laugh. "So, what we got? Two ladies, maybe tryin' to slip outta town, under false pretenses. Perhaps that's reason enough to invite me along."

Lina was furious. "Mr. Parker, if you think you can blackmail me into helping you…"

Henry seemed shocked. "No ma'am! No way would I suggest such a pernicious act as that. No, ma'am. It just seems to me that if I'm right, you two might have need for a protector. Like I said, I'm good with a gun. I know my way around a wagon team, too. I don't shirk chores neither. When the wagon busts, or beans is gone and somebody's gotta find game, I think you'll be right glad I was around."

Henry had struck a chord with Lina. Wagon repairs were one problem even she hadn't considered. Fixing a wagon was too great a chore for two women.

"You can see the sense of what I'm sayin', cain't ya?" Parker was grinning again. "Ladies, I swear to ya both, on my mother's sacred grave, ya got nothin' to fear from Henry Parker. I give ya my word that if ya let me tag along, and share with me what ya got, I'll do for ya whatever I can."

Lina still had reservations. "You're a bright fellow, Henry. Coming here and sizing up the situation. Well, I sized up a few things myself. Seems curious to me that a capable young man such as yourself," Henry beamed at the compliments, "is in such a hurry to leave. You wouldn't perhaps be running from something yourself, would you?"

"Ma'am, ya got me dead to rights there. I'll tell ya the truth. I *am* runnin', but what I'm runnin' from ain't no problem for ya. I ain't killed nobody, nor stole from nobody neither. Just a bit of a brawl, ya might say. A diff'rence of opinions."

"Well, surely then, it could be straightened out."

"Yes, ma'am, I reckon it could, eventually. But it'd just keep me from gettin' outta town, which is what I been tryin' to do, and what them what's lookin' for me probably want me to do anyway. See, I been trying to join up with the Army. My plan is to follow the wagons to Fort Laramie, where I can join the Cavalry!"

"So you'd be traveling with us only as far as Fort Laramie?"

"Yes, ma'am. I figure by then, well, maybe the worst of the trip'll be over. If ya gets there and still needs help, I'll see ya get as far as ya want. If ya don't need me, then I'm free to go. Either way, you'll have safe passage that far, and I'll get out west, which is what we both wants."

Lina looked at Josephine, who hadn't made a sound since Henry Parker entered the room. "Would you wait outside, please?" Parker took his hat and walked out the door, looking expectantly over his shoulder. When he had left and Lina had shut the door behind him, she spoke in a whisper.

"Josephine, I'm inclined to accept his offer. How do you feel?"

Josephine looked at the two pistols on the counter. "Are you sure we can trust him?"

Lina laughed. "This morning you couldn't trust *me*! Now you're asking if we can trust *him*? I don't know. But I say let's give it a try."

Josephine smiled. "Very well. You're in charge."

When Lina opened the door, Henry Parker was still leaning against the door frame. His confident smile told her he already had her answer. "Henry, you've got a deal. Make yourself at home out there, and keep an eye on the wagon while you're at it."

"Thanks, Miz Clark. Ya won't regret it, that's a fact. You too, ma'am." He nodded again towards Josephine.

"Henry, let's get a few things straight between us before we go any further. You're right, we're heading out first thing in the morning, hopefully with as little notice as possible. It's like you said. There's no worry in it for you. And just for appearances, let's let other people assume we're family. So from now on, call me Lina. We'll call you Henry. This is Josephine, Josephine Paul." Henry quickly wiped his hands on his shirt and took Josephine's outstretched hand.

"Please ta meet ya, miss."

"No more formalities. Remember, we're cousins. From now on it's just Henry and Lina, and Josephine."

"But Josephine's too high falutin' a name for family. Don't sound right. How 'bout I just call you Josie?"

Lina looked at Josephine. Josephine wrinkled her fine brow and flipped her dark curls back. "Josie," she said, listening to the sound of it. "That sounds fine. Josie it is."

"Just one big happy family, I reckon," said Henry.

3

Lina rode through the last hours of night, heading west toward the mission where they were to meet. Last night, on the basis of a handshake, she and Henry sat down to confab on a plan for leaving. Henry suggested they leave separately. "Anybody sees you ridin' outta town in a loaded wagon gonna jump to the right conclusion." So Henry and Josie would leave first with the wagon, and Lina would follow an hour later.

That morning, there was a final rush to make room for Lina's chicken cages, a last minute inspiration. Eggs could be valuable as a bartering chit, and if that didn't work, the chickens would make for fine eating. The birds made a terrible ruckus, so they were quickly shoved into the wagon. There'd be time later to fit them in properly. Before the squawking woke the whole town, the wagon headed out.

Lina found it was hard riding in the dark. The road was rough and hilly, with several creeks to cross. Too little sleep had left her brain weak, too weak to keep her thoughts from drifting backward in time and distance. She felt a loneliness that more than once brought tears to her eyes. She remembered her father, and was suddenly seized by the urge to go back one last time to the place where he was buried. She tried to put thoughts of him out of her mind, but they could not be stopped. So she gave into the memories, and said her final goodbyes to him in silence as she rode west through the dark.

Among all that she remembered about her father, one memory came back, a night she had long forgotten, and now could not be entirely sure that her tired brain remembered rightly. She had been quite small. She heard angry voices coming from another room, as she lay in her bed in the dark. Some fellow her father owed money to, no doubt. Then there was silence, and then her father scooping her up in his arms, and into a wagon, and the two of them leaving in the middle of the night. *It's the same as then*, she told herself. *I learned to run at my father's knee. And learned to lie, too, I guess.* She felt disgusted, not only with him but with herself. She had to face the fact that up until now, much of her life had been based on lies. Her father's hopeless dreams, her marriage of necessity, this escape to the west, even the fact that she claimed to expect no more of life than what she had been handed, all were lies of one breed or another. Some had been carefully, even lovingly constructed, and none were intended to harm. But they were lies no less. And she was sick of them. *Well, no more*, she decided. *When I cross over into that territory out of Missouri, that'll be the end of the lies.* But there would still be the tale she would have to tell about Josie, and the one about the three of them traveling as cousins. She swallowed hard. *Alright, then. Just those two. After that, no more. As soon as I can, I'm not going to be afraid to tell the truth any more.*

****

Henry joined them just as the sky was turning light. Lina took the reins of the wagon, and Henry rode his horse as the three pressed on. An hour later, the woods through which they rode started to thin, revealing the first patches of prairie. Just as Lina had hoped, with the light, the distance from town, and a little distracting companionship, the knot that had been in her stomach most of the morning was starting to loosen.

Suddenly, Henry let out a loud whoop, and rode ahead across the open plain at full speed, just to the top of the next knob. When he reached it, he pulled his horse up, tore his flop hat from his head and waved it wildly. Then, just as fast, he rode at full speed back toward the wagon, then past it and finally coming back to round the wagon twice before pulling up alongside it. He was too winded to talk, but he was grinning from ear to ear.

Henry's eagerness was contagious. Lina laughed as she called to him, "Henry Parker, don't you be wearing out that horse of yours before we've started. Then you'll want mine, and I can't spare her."

"Hell, Lina, that nag of yours'd never do for a cavalryman." Henry's animal, the horse he called Traveler, was a beauty, a palomino with a blaze on his face.

Henry's whooping woke Josephine. Lina was amazed at how Josephine could sleep in the rolling wagon. *If only it holds*, she thought, *she might make this trip after all.* "I'm hungry," said a drowsy voice from the back of the wagon. *Oh, dear God,* thought Lina.

****

Lina knew they had arrived at the camp before she could see it. Henry was riding ahead of them again when he reached a ridge and stopped, then stared straight ahead into the valley below. When the wagon reached him, Lina could see what he saw. The wide flat valley below was filled with wagons, a thousand wagons or more, scattered in clusters around the fields—dots of white canvas gleaming in the afternoon sun like a field of cotton. Among them, wisps of smoke carried the scents of a hundred cook fires across the spring air. The camp was still too far to see people, yet the whole scene fairly quivered and hummed with activity. When Lina looked over at Henry, she saw a light in his eye she feared meant he was just about to take off at a gallop.

"Henry, take the wagon, head it over there," she said, pointing to the north side of the gathering. "I'm going to go see about this Granby Company."

She half expected to hear an argument from him, but he just grinned. "Sure thing, Cap'n!" he said, with a mock salute. Henry tied his horse to the wagon and headed off.

Lina's mare moved slowly through the wagons. "You know where I can find the Granby Company?" she would ask as she rode. The answer was always the same. A laugh, a nod of the head, and then they would point west.

It was hard to say where one company ended and another began, so crammed together were all the wagons. Then she came up to a crowd listening to a man standing on top of a wagon. As she came closer, the crowd broke up, slowly revealing not the wagon she had supposed, but a carriage, its enclosed body made of glossy black wood. The driver's seat was high in the front. It was an aristocratic rig, and it looked delicate next to the common wagons. Except for its wheels.

Someone had the good sense to remove the rig's original wheels, and in their place, mount regular wagon wheels. The effect made the whole contraption seem preposterous. On its door was the same crest that was on the handbill she carried. Lina had found the Granby Company.

Standing on the step that raised the driver to the seat was a stocky fellow of middle years, with ruddy hair and a complexion to match. He had a long waxed mustached, and hair slicked back with macassar oil. He wore an unfamiliar looking uniform, striking with its red jacket and a whole host of ribbons. Below this man, standing next to the coach, were two other men. The white man was tall, powerfully built, with a full black beard and a broken hat shading his eyes. His wore a well-tanned buckskin coat that hung to his knees and was cinched at the waist with a broad belt. Beads and feathers hung from his hat and his belt, and at his side was a rifle. He stood rock still, but Lina could see his eyes follow her as she approached.

In contrast, the Negro at the mountain man's side stared at Granby in silent obedience. He wore a crisp white linen jacket that made him seem all the darker, nearly the same ebony as the coach. But he looked more dignified in his simple white coat than the red-haired man did in his fancy uniform. This man, she assumed, must be Granby's slave.

Lina had seen very few Negroes. Missouri might be pro-slavery, but the truth was few people she knew owned them. Lina thought the notion of owning another person outrageous. Taking this presumption into account along with the ridiculous carriage and the odd collection of men before her, Lina felt uneasy about this company. "Are you Granby?" she asked of the red haired man.

With one eyebrow raised, the ruddy fellow looked down to her and said, "Madam, I am Granby. Colonel John Gordon Granby," he said, with an unmistakable English accent. The black man held out his hand to assist Granby's descent, but in a single bound Granby jumped to the ground.

Lina dismounted. She shook his hand firmly. "Sir, my name is Carolina Clark, and I was told you might have room in your company for another wagon."

"Indeed, madam, I do. As you can see," he said, motioning to the collection around him, "we are a small caravan. Plenty of room for another, provided of course, you have the fare. But all in good time.

Follow me." He headed off among the wagons. Lina followed, leading her horse, with the big man and the Negro right behind.

Granby led her to his tent. It was not large, but no doubt more comfortable than trying to live out of that absurd coach. "Smith, see to the lady's horse," he said. Lina handed the reins to the big man and followed Granby inside. The Negro followed too.

The tent was decorated with an exotic flair. An ornate rug covered the bare ground. A small carved table with two matching chairs stood on one side, displaying a fine porcelain tea set. The only other piece of furniture was a cot. The cot itself was commonplace, but hanging over it, suspended from the ceiling of the tent, was a canopy that hung all the way to the floor, completely encircling the bed. It was made from cloth like a spider's web, so light and airy Lina could see clear through it. The Negro held the chair for her to sit, then Granby sat opposite. "Tea, Miss Clark?" Granby asked, but Lina shook her head. The Negro poured tea for Granby, then left.

Granby sipped, then opened the conversation. "How many wagons will you be taking?"

"One."

Granby eyed her carefully over the rim of his teacup. "How many persons?"

"Three."

"Family?"

Lina paused. "Yes."

"And are there any gentlemen in your group?"

"Yes, one. Why do you ask?"

"I am accustomed to contracting with the leader of each wagon group. Normally that person is a gentleman. If that is the case here, then I would prefer to have him present for this conversation."

For all his polite language, the fellow's starched manner was wearing thin with Lina. "Sir, I am traveling with my cousins. They are newly arrived to the area, whereas I have been living here for some time, and am more familiar with the nature of our journey. So I am assuming the role of responsible party. I have come, sir, prepared to pay what I understood to be the rate of one hundred dollars per wagon. We have one wagon. Are you interested, or should I ask around elsewhere?" Lina rose, prepared to leave.

Her small outburst did not ruffle him in the least. He took another sip, then set the cup down. Immediately, the Negro appeared and handed him what appeared to be a ledger. "As to the fee, it is one hundred dollars per wagon. We are bringing with us one hundred head of cattle, which, should conditions warrant, will be made available to the company for the duration of the journey. However, each party is responsible for supplying the bulk of its provisions. I assume you are adequately outfitted? Food stuffs, munitions, those sorts of things?"

"Yes."

He opened his ledger. "You have one wagon?" he asked as he began to write.

"Yes."

"Livestock?"

"Apart from the oxen, two horses only."

"And your destination?"

"California."

"You're not planning on prospecting, are you?"

"I intend, that is, *we* intend, to operate a general mercantile somewhere where opportunity presents itself."

Granby smiled. "Well, at least your goals are more attainable than most of the others who'll be making the trip. And as you possess what is obviously a determined nature, I predict your success. Please enter the names of your cousins, here."

Lina took the ledger and beneath where Granby had written her name, she added Josephine and Henry's names. When she returned the book to him, Granby eyed the names. "Three cousins, all with different last names?"

"I am widowed. Our mothers were sisters," Lina replied quickly, but she could not look him in the eye.

"Ah. Very well, then. Nothing left but the formalities. We travel under my authority, but with the guidance of Smith, the large, surly fellow you saw earlier. His instructions must be followed to the letter. He is here to keep us on course, and to help keep order. I like order, Mrs. Clark. I expect each member of this company to behave appropriately, refraining from unnecessary violence and vices. Transgressors will be dealt with as appropriate, including banishment from the company. Is that clear?"

"Yes." Lina handed him the money.

"There is an established order for the cortege. Smith will show you where to make camp tonight. We leave tomorrow at first light." He stood. "Have you any questions?" She shook her head, and he motioned her to lead him from the tent.

Once outside, Granby looked around until saw Smith, who was talking to a group of farmers. At Granby's wave, he came to the tent. "Smith, show Mrs. Clark where her party may camp tonight. Good day to you, madam."

After Granby left, Smith looked down at her. "I seem to recollect seein' you before. You from around these parts?"

She nodded. "I'm from town. My husband used to have a store there."

Smith creased his brow in thought. "Hmm. Clark was your name, you said. Ephraim Clark, that your husband?"

"Yes, was. He died a few weeks ago. Broke his neck coming home drunk."

Smith shook his head, and continued walking. "That's how I knew him. From the saloons. I'm sorry, ma'am. Your man was a drinker, that's a fact, and he had more hare-brained schemes than sense. But I never had trouble from him." Smith looked down at her as they walked side by side. "This here trip one of *your* hare-brained schemes?"

Lina chuckled. "Maybe, but I don't think so." Then, with determination, she said, "No. No it isn't."

"Well, if ya ask me this whole notion of folks movin' all the way west is one big fool-hardy scheme. I been all over and there ain't but a handful of places one man can make a living, let alone whole families. But I just get paid ta get ya there. I'm nobody's nursemaid. Well, here's your spot."

Talking to Smith made Lina feel more certain. She gave him her hand, "Nice meeting you, Mr. Smith."

"Smith, ma'am. Just Smith." He touched the brim of his hat. "Dawn tomorrow, ma'am. Be ready." Then he left.

****

Afternoon was moving toward evening by the time Lina found Henry and Josephine, and they brought the wagon to their designated place.

When they were settled, Lina called the three together. "Henry, go do some scouting for us. Spend some time getting to know this company. But don't offer anything about us you don't have to. I told Granby we were cousins on our mother's side, headed to California. Try to keep it to that for now. We'll get the wagon ready for tomorrow."

When Henry left, Lina jumped inside the wagon and began moving boxes to the open end. She and Josie worked for a while in silence. Lina could see Josie was little help, but she wanted to keep her busy, so she continued directing her in small tasks.

When Josie finally spoke, though her words were said casually, they caught Lina's attention right off. "You're remarkably good at this lying."

Lina was deep inside the wagon. "I beg your pardon?" she asked, as she came to the gate and looked down on Josie.

"I said…"

"I heard what you said! What the hell did you mean?"

"That you can be quite duplicitous when it suits you."

"Well, that's a fine sounding word! You've got quite a number of airs, don't you?"

"It's a simple statement of fact. When we met two days ago, I was as direct with you as I could be concerning myself. I never hid who I am or what I want. You were the one who insisted on secrecy. At the time, I couldn't imagine you'd be able to pull it off. You seemed very much a straight-laced sort of person. But I can see now I was wrong. You've quite a talent for telling a tale. I suppose that'll come in handy."

"Well, think what you will about what I've done, but it's only for your sake I did it, not for my own. The simple fact is you don't do much to disguise your intent. You dress too fancy, and you wear too much paint. No doubt this company is filled with gossips and prigs who will be more than happy to jump to any conclusion they like. If I've lied, it's only to protect that well-upholstered hide of yours," Lina went back to her work and said no more to Josie until the wagon was finished.

Lina was pleased with the results. She had made a cozy little spot for them among the sacks and boxes. And as a special favor, Josie was given a box to keep a few of her personal items handy, which pleased her. As for the more suggestive clothing and the face paint, Lina cleverly made certain those things were buried beneath other boxes, thus avoiding temptation. She also found handy places to secure all the tools, wagon parts and equipment they would need at the ready. She even found a way to tie the chicken cages near the back, where they could be easily reached, and where they would be downwind.

"What's fer dinner? Walking around all those other fires gave me a powerful appetite!" Henry had returned.

"Well, get a fire started, and I'll fix something."

"With what, I'd like ta know. Dintcha bring no wood with us?"

Damn, she thought. *Wood. Of course.* This place was so heavily camped that all the available wood was long since picked off. Henry wagged his head, and mumbled as he headed back through the wagons. "Little miss know-it-all." His mutterings irked her, but Lina swallowed her retorts.

Lina started to unload the kettle and spider, but Henry returned before she had finished. In his wake was a large bosomy woman in pale calico, her sunbonnet hanging behind her. Her hair was nearly as pale as her dress, a combination of dusty brown and gray. She possessed a generous smile, and round cheeks with an apple-polish shine. "Lina, this is Mrs. Olmstead. Ma'am, these are my cousins, Carolina and Josephine." Lina reached forward to take the woman's fleshy hand, but Josephine merely peeked out from within the wagon. "That's her family there," Henry said, pointing to wagons some fifty feet away. "Mrs. Olmstead's invited us over. Says we can use their fire if we want."

"Thank you kindly, Mrs. Olmstead. We'll be over directly." Lina took the woman's hand again, more vigorously now.

Mrs. Olmstead kept hold of Lina's hand, her grin still firmly fixed, her button eyes still shining. "You have chickens!" Mrs. Olmstead said enthusiastically.

"Oh, yes. Yes, we do."

Hesitantly, the older woman continued. "Would you sell us eggs? For my children, you see. We have eight."

"Eight children! Why, certainly, Mrs. Olmstead. Let me bring you a couple for the use of the fire."

"Thank you. Please, come over to the fire. You are most welcome."

The Olmsteads were pleasant folk. As Lina cooked at their fire, she watched them prepare their wagons for the morning, and ready their children for bed. She spoke briefly with Ulmer Olmstead, and learned his wife's name was Greta. They were of German stock out of Ohio, and both still spoke with the thick accent of their homeland, but their children spoke with the flat sound of native Midwesterners. They traveled in two wagons to accommodate all of them. The oldest, two tall, muscular boys, Frank and Herman, were just a bit younger than Lina. They had four playful sisters, from six-year-old Trina, up to shy but sweet Louisa, not quite fourteen. Then there were the two youngest boys, Max, a sharp-eyed boy of four, and three-year-old Lukas. By the time Lina finished cooking, there were Olmstead children sleeping everywhere—under wagons, inside wagons, beside wagons, even in a makeshift hammock strung between the two wagons. Lina whispered a goodbye and thank you to the Olmsteads, and headed back.

Lina struggled with the heavy iron pot, and nearly dumped its contents on the ground before Henry got up to help her. "Serves ya right, not rememberin' wood."

"Serve *you* right, if I were to spill it, for want of your helping."

Lina spooned some of her stew onto three tin plates and passed them around. All three of them were hungry past reason, which explained why Henry cleaned his plate before he spoke. "Well, I can see right now that I'd better take on the cookin' chores. This ain't got no taste to it at all." Yet he rose to get another helping.

Lina protested. "You don't seem to be turning your nose up at it." But as she took another fork full, she realized he was right. It tasted like leather in a sauce of hot water. She turned to look at Josephine, who was picking at the food in front of her indifferently. Suddenly all Lina's energy left her. "Very well, I'm too tired to argue. If you think you can do better, the chore is yours."

Henry spent the rest of the evening sharing the information he had gathered about the company. His impression of the group was that they were of two sorts, and impossible to mistake one type from the other. The miners traveled light, their single wagons loaded only with basic provisions. Their wagons were often decorated, not ornately like Granby's coach, but crudely, with banners and flags proclaiming their adventurous spirits and their local pride. 'Fortune Seekers,' 'Bound for Glory,' 'Michigan Miners, 'Hoosier Spirit.' The settlers' wagons were usually crammed with children, and heavy loaded with the stuff of building a life—seed and hand plows for planting, bibles and books for teaching, quilts, coffee mills and rockers to fill houses only imagined.

Henry counted thirty-two wagons, including their own, representing about a dozen parties. He guessed there were a hundred people all told, split almost evenly between settlers and miners, with one family of missionaries thrown in. "I asked what I could, but folks is still a little closed-mouthed. Guess everybody's careful about showing their hand."

"Why do you suppose they signed on with Granby?" Lina asked.

"Oh, that I found out. Folks mighta been shy of talking 'bout themselves, but not that funny little bastard! It's like it was for us. Granby was their last resort. Miners who showed up not knowing their backside from a bump on the ground, farmers findin' themselves without others they was ta meet up with, that sorta thing. Ssh! Here comes that popinjay now." They looked up to see Granby, Smith and the Negro moving toward them. Granby stopped at nearly every wagon to shake a hand and pass a word or two, before moving forward. The mismatched trio had the look of a curious little parade.

As Granby came near, Lina rose and walked toward him, anxious to make a good impression. "Colonel Granby, I'd like you to meet Mr. Henry Parker and Miss Josephine Paul. My cousins."

Henry rose, wiped his hand on his trousers, and thrust it eagerly at the man. Lina knew the grin Henry wore might break out into a laugh at any moment, so she hurried the Englishman toward Josephine. Josie rose, gave a quick little curtsey, and held out her hand. "And this," Lina said, pointing to the tall man behind Granby, "is Smith, our guide." Smith shook Henry's hand, then moved quickly toward Josephine. Henry was impressed with the large man, and kept his eyes fixed on him. But Smith was staring at Josephine. "Ma'am," he said simply, as he took her hand, and gave her a nearly full-toothed smile.

"And this is…" Lina started to introduce the Negro, but realized she didn't know his name.

Granby looked around then realized who she meant. "Oh, this is Bartolomé. He, uh, *works* for me." When Lina shook Bartolomé's hand, she could see it caused Granby discomfort. Bartolomé shook her hand lightly and quickly, but said nothing, and never looked her directly in the eye.

"Well, it'll be an early morning," the Englishman said. "I suggest we all get some rest. I bid you good evening." The three men continued to the next group of wagons.

When Granby was out of earshot, Lina whispered. "'Works for me.' Ha! Why doesn't he just say he owns him?"

"Oh, the other folks I talked ta had a lot ta say on the subject. Said Granby goes to great lengths to assure everybody that he ain't now and ain't never been no slave. Granby picked him up somewhere in the West Indies, so they say."

"What about Mr. Smith?" Josephine asked, failing to disguise her curiosity.

"Oh everybody's real high on him. Granby claims he's trapped and traveled all over the west. Most said Smith's the only reason they agreed to travel with that crazy Englishman."

"Now listen, you two," Lina said. "Granby made it very clear that Smith's the man to listen to. That means, Henry, you do as he tells you. And Josie, well, you just remember what we talked about. Granby was quite explicit. 'No violence or vice.' That's what he said. Be pleasant, but keep away from both Granby and Smith."

"Lina, my dear, I am not to blame for the fact that men find me attractive. And just remember, a pretty woman can barter a smile like any other commodity, but without depletion." She turned with a flounce, hopped into the wagon, and pulled the gate up with a bang.

Lina was already moving her bedroll into position, readying for sleep, but Henry had not moved. "What the hell you two snappin' 'bout?" Lina didn't answer, and a long silence followed. Finally, he said, "Well, I'll be damned. She's a...."

"Stop." Lina pushed her hand against his lips. "She's your cousin, that's all you need to know."

"*Kissin'* cousin?" Henry laughed.

"Hardly! Ssh. Quiet, you idiot." Henry stifled his giggle, but it barely held. When he finally had control of himself, he climbed into his bedroll, stretched out at an angle to Lina's. After a while, when he was sure Josephine was asleep inside the wagon, Henry whispered. "I can't believe you're bringin' a whore!"

"I'm not bringing her. She wanted to go, landed on my doorstep, and expected my husband to have everything ready for her. I explained the situation, about him being dead, about how women like her can't take out alone. And before I knew it, she had me agreeing to come along. That's when you showed up." Henry said nothing, but he rose on one elbow and faced her. She propped herself up enough to meet his gaze. "Look, I don't care if she is or isn't. I've burned too many bridges to go back."

Henry's eyes grew softer. "I know. Me too. Ain't no goin' back now, huh? Don't worry Lina. We're all gonna get there." Then they both lay back on the blankets. Lina fell asleep with a million bright stars over her head.

4

The soft bellows from the cattle stirred Lina from deep sleep, but the wood smoke and bacon smells of breakfast fully woke her. She climbed out of her bedroll, nudged Henry with her boot, and slapped the side of the wagon to rouse Josephine. "Rise and shine. This is it!" Inside the chicken pens she found five eggs. She shoved the eggs and a skillet at Henry. "Go to Olmstead's. Give them a couple, then cook the rest for us. Hurry, now." Then she climbed into the wagon where Josephine was struggling to get dressed.

"Ouch," Josie cried, feeling an elbow to her rib. "Watch yourself. There's not room in here for you too."

In the end, both women managed to change into suitable attire for the trip. Lina chose a pair of Ephraim's trousers to wear with her own shirt, though the pants were so big she had to roll up the cuffs and cinch the waist considerably. She added her father's hat. Josie wore one of the calico dresses. Seeing her in it, Lina realized it would take more than calico to draw attention away from Josephine Paul.

Henry returned with the eggs, and they each ate one straight from the skillet. Then the two women took to the wagon, and Henry to his horse, and they moved into position.

Smith rode up, all business. "Try'n keep a distance between you and the wagon ahead of ya, but don't lag, neither." Then, looking at Henry, he said "Any problems, you come lookin' for me. Don't waste time tryin' to handle it yourself." Then he left.

Lina kept their wagon in pace with the one in front of them as they moved. Suddenly she realized they weren't positioning any longer. They had started. She flicked the reins, and the wagon lurched. Josie must have been unprepared, for Lina felt a thud behind her, then heard a grunt.

The notion of a single road west was a myth, Lina decided. Here the trail was a river of ruts running in all directions, crisscrossing itself, trying desperately to sort itself out. She was glad it was not her job to do the sorting. She had to trust in Smith, and trust in the road that it knew where it was going. The low-lying but steady line of hills and valleys they followed made for a jostling ride. Lina was used to riding in a wagon, but Josie held on for dear life. Lina's backside might have been tougher than Josie's but her arms were not used to this constant battering. She looked to the weeks and months ahead, trying to imagine this same routine day after endless day. She despaired of being able to last.

Late in the afternoon, the caravan entered a wide valley, cut through the heart by the little Wakarusa River. On the other side, the wagon ruts that had meandered all day came together and led them through a pass to the south of one small mound, cast in blue shadows by the late afternoon daylight. On the other side of that mound, the world was suddenly different. Before them lay open prairie, the only trees lined along the river. A carpet of wildflowers ran to the horizon. Golden daisies, bright blue bachelor buttons, scarlet paintbrush and brown sumac glowed in the sharp low light of the setting sun. Soft cattails and thorny purple thistle bent in the soft breeze to touch gray heather and green grasses. Only twenty miles from home, and here was a sight Lina had never seen, a world about which she knew nothing. The west was meeting her with open arms filled with a tempting bouquet.

Their first night's camp was on that prairie. They were almost the last wagon in Granby's train, behind the Olmsteads, and ahead of one other wagon. A young couple, Andrew and Sarah Reed, were traveling with a brand new baby boy, little Harry. Henry had gone over to check on them that night, and came back with a report. "All hepped up about it," was how Henry described Andrew Reed's enthusiasm for the trip. But it was Henry's opinion that Mrs. Reed, a petite, blonde woman, whom Henry described as "'bout the purtiest girl I ever did see," was not as excited.

As suggested, Henry took over the cooking chores, and he did have a talent for it. It was just after dark when they finished eating, when a single gunshot broke the peace. Lina and Josie jumped, but Henry stood up calmly. "Smith told me 'bout that. It's the signal he gives every night, when it's time for the evenin' meetin'. I best be gettin'."

Henry started towards Granby's wagon, but Lina caught him. "I put my name in as head of the family. I'll go." Henry started to argue, but Lina gave him no chance. She walked off without another word.

All but two of those who gathered were men. The other woman was a stringy, pinch-faced woman of forty or so, whose dress and demeanor were so plain that Lina figured this must be one of the missionary contingent Henry spoke of. The men stood in small groups, talking casually. Lina stood silently on one side, the pinch-faced woman on the other, both ignored by the men around them. Granby climbed on top of his coach and rapped it loudly with a walking stick.

"Everyone! Your attention, please!" The chatter turned to mumbles, then silence. "Smith has asked that we gather here each evening to discuss the next day's travel and to assign duties. Smith?"

Smith came forward. "Won't be goin' much farther tomorrow. Gotta cross the Kansa River, just a few miles north. There's a ferry, for those with the fare. Usually a few dollars. Ferry's run by the Potawatomi." At the mention of the Indians, some grumblings were heard. "You best get use to Indians. Gonna see a lot of 'em the further we go. Most of 'em consider you as much a curiosity and you consider them. Some'll wanna trade with ya. Only time folks has trouble with Indians is when they wanna argue or fight 'em. Do that, you'll lose every time. But that's further down the road. If the thought of Indians bothers ya, shouldn't oughta come." There was restrained silence, then Smith continued. "If ya don't have the jack, ya can try and ford the river yourselves. Might be this time of year it's low enough, might not. When we get to the river, we'll see what's what.

"Everyone shares in the sentry duties. I know that's a hardship for the smaller groups, so you with big families, if ya got extra men, I'd be obliged. Need four men, two-hour shifts each from now 'til sunrise. That's sixteen men a night. Who's volunteerin'?"

Several men raised their hands. So did Lina. Smith gave each their assignments in turn. When he came to Lina, he looked her straight in the eye. "Sure ya wanna do this? What 'bout that young buck travelin' with ya?"

"I'm sure Henry'll take his turn in time. I'm on for tonight."

"Gotta rifle?"

"Two. A Hawken and a Sharps," she answered proudly, hoping he would appreciate such weapons.

He did not, particularly. "Can ya fire it?"

"Sure." Lina could fire it, she just wasn't sure she could hit anything.

"Bring the Hawken. Sharps won't do no good in the dark, if ya can't see where you're aimin'. Take the ten to midnight shift." Then he went on to the next volunteer.

When Lina returned, Josephine was cleaning up from supper, and Henry was stretched out on his bedroll. He sat up when he saw her coming. "Well, Cap'n? Ya get our marchin' orders?" He found her insistence on being the leader more entertaining than exasperating.

Lina told them of the next day's plans. Like some of the others, Henry had some misgivings about the Indians. "Seems kinda backwards to me. The gov'ment hires soldiers ta make sure they don't bother settlers comin' through. Then they expect us ta trade with 'em. Wish they'd make up their minds."

Lina didn't care about the Indians. She had other concerns. "Henry, you ever taken a wagon across a river? Without a ferry, I mean?"

"Well, no, but…."

"No 'buts'. We'll take the ferry. We can't afford to lose our one wagon in a bad crossing." She ran her hands over her tired eyes and felt the weariness in her arms from the day's ride. "Let's get some sleep. I stand watch at ten o'clock."

Frank Olmstead woke her two hours later. He showed her where to stand watch, then left her in the dark silence. Her eyes strained to make out any landmark, any tree, any figure in the deep black night all around her, but she could see nothing. All Lina knew to do was to fire a signal shot if she saw a threat. She didn't worry about staying awake. Fear kept her awake. She knew the only intruder might be a coyote with a nose for beef on the hoof. The real creature she feared was Smith, of letting him down, of not doing her sentry duty as well as the men. After her shift, her eyes ached from straining to stare through the dark. Once Herman Olmstead came to relieve her at midnight, she headed straight for her bedroll.

****

Four gun shots at four o'clock signaled the hours of sleep were over. Henry started the fire and cooked breakfast while Lina and Josephine dressed. After eating, Lina and Josephine repacked the wagon, while Henry washed up. Everything had to be ready by dawn.

Smith rode up. He gave a big, bright grin to Josephine, but spoke to Henry. "Ride the rear. Any problems, come see me." Then, as a concession, to Lina he said, "That alright with you, ma'am?" He didn't wait for a reply.

Henry was pleased to have his first command. He mounted his horse with pride, sitting a little taller, casting his eyes a little farther. When Lina and Josie were ready to go, he said, "If ya need me, ladies, just holler." He was off to his post.

"We'll walk today, Josie," Lina said. Josie rolled her eyes but Lina added, "We've got to get used to walking, and we need to keep an eye out for wood." Lina stepped inside the wagon and pulled out her father's hat, and tossed it to Josie. "That'll help." Josie held the hat in front of her, eying its possibilities. It was just a simple straw hat, but the way she set it on the back of her head, it might have been the latest Paris fashion. Lina looked at her with awe. *At least her vanity is warranted.*

As the two women walked, they flanked the team. Lina, in the lead with whip in hand for the oxen, walked easily. Josie was not as practiced. She walked with her head down constantly, trying not to trip in the ruts of the trail, and all the while looking for stray pieces of wood. Twice, she was so focused on the ground beneath her that she drifted away from the train at an angle. Lina had to call her back, and so now Lina had to keep an eye out for wood *and* for Josie.

By late afternoon the company reached the ferry crossing. Lina was disheartened to see a long line of wagons ahead of them. As the wagons pulled up together, Henry came riding toward them. "Makin' camp. We'll ferry tomorrow." He said it with the same perfunctory tone Smith used. *Fooled yourself into thinking you're somebody important, haven't you, Henry Parker?"* she caught herself thinking.

At that night's meeting, Smith explained. "The ferry can take four wagons at a time. But it takes an hour 'cross and back. The company ahead of us'll finish up first in the morning, then us. Any luck, we'll be across, all of us, by nightfall. If not, then first thing next day."

The sour-looking woman from the night before spoke up, directing her comments not to Smith but Granby. "Tomorrow is the Sabbath! You gave us your assurances the Sabbath was to be strictly observed on this journey."

Smith answered. "Ma'am, if you want to hold services in the morning, there'll be time before our turn comes. But if we don't cross that river tomorrow, some other company takes our place, and we could end up two, three days behind. I ain't losin' that many days 'cause of the Sabbath."

"The Lord says we are to rest on the Sabbath."

"Rest if you want. I'm taking these wagons across. Step out and lose your turn. I won't wait." Mrs. Whittier gave up and left.

Sentry shifts were assigned for the night and Lina was relieved she didn't have to take another. She was tired, and planned on sleep as soon as the company meeting was over. But as the group dispersed, Smith caught her arm. "Miz Clark. I 'preciate how you're the leader of that little band of yourn. But that young Henry, he's handy. I'm askin' you bring him to these meetin's so he knows what's what."

"Of course, Smith. I'll tell him." She knew he was right, but she was not happy about it. Henry *was* a handy fellow, and Lina was already guarding him jealously, like she did her chickens and eggs. "But remember, Smith, he's part of this family, and if we need him, his first responsibility is here."

"Right enough. But, everybody's gotta pull together now. The road'll get tougher by the day, and you never know who your friends'll be."

It would be afternoon before their turn would come, and there was much to do. The oxen had to be unharnessed and moved with the other livestock. All the gear that hung from the sides of the wagons had to be stowed inside, so that one wagon took only the space necessary on the small raft. Everyone hurried to finish preparations so they could find a spot along the riverbank to watch the ferry at work.

Lina was fascinated with it. The Kansa was not as big a river as the Missouri, which she knew so well, but it was wide and fast enough, and she was glad not to have to ford it. The raft was made from large timbers, and was tethered to ropes that stretched across between two trees on opposite banks. Four at a time the wagons were pulled on board. A handful of Indians supervised the operation at each end, and another group walked about collecting the tolls. Usually they were paid in coin, but sometimes folks offered goods in trade. Apparently they accepted clothing, tobacco, food—anything that caught their eye. The bartering went smoothly for the most part because Granby himself accompanied the Indians among the wagons to make certain each wagon paid.

As she had vowed, Mrs. Whittier organized a Sabbath service. Her husband, the Reverend Whittier, led the service, but it was Mrs. Whittier who was possessed of the fervor. She was missionary born and bred, determined to reclaim every soul within reach. She made the rounds to each wagon trying to shame folks into coming, if they weren't already inclined. She succeeded with nearly half the company, including Lina, who saw it as a distraction from the long wait. Henry was busy with Smith, and Josie stayed at the wagon. It was that day Lina learned Josie was a devout Catholic who preferred to keep her own observance with her rosary. The Whittiers were Methodist. Methodist missionaries were famous, even notorious, for their determination to convert all Indians, and Mrs. Whittier did not waste her first encounter with them. She rounded up a collection of Potawatomi not involved in the ferrying business, mostly women, children, and a few old men. The congregation gathered under trees along the river bank. Mrs. Whittier had the Indians herded to a spot at the back, segregated from the company members. The Indians didn't notice the slight. They had not come to be converted. They were curious about these settlers.

Reverend Whittier started full of fire and brimstone, and held everyone captive with his talent for oratory. The white congregants sat politely silent. The Indians, too, were transfixed, and those who understood English appeared to be whispering translations to the others.

Then Mrs. Whittier led the group in song, selecting 'Shall We Gather at the River?' as an appropriate choice. The choir was less than heavenly, and the result was a sad cacophony. The music, if it could be called that, sounded so strange to the Potawatomi that they burst into laughter. Soon many began to wander off. As their ranks thinned Mrs. Whittier spotted one old man at the back drinking from a bottle of whiskey. Abruptly she stopped singing. Mrs. Whittier marched directly through the crowd to the old man. She grabbed the bottle from his hand just as he brought it to his lips. She had turned the bottle upside down and was pouring most of its precious contents on the ground when a brown hand snatched the bottle from her.

The Potawatomi who had left the service looked back when the singing stopped and saw what Mrs. Whittier had done. One Indian had rushed back to stop her, and now was yelling at her in words none of the whites understood. Mrs. Whittier argued back. "No whiskey!" she said, pointing to the bottle in his hand. "No whiskey!" She said it over and over again, yelling at the top of her lungs as if her yelling would overcome the language barrier.

Smith and Granby charged into the middle of the group, though Granby let Smith lead. "What the hell's going on here?" Smith hollered. Soon Smith, the Indian, and Mrs. Whittier were yelling all at once.

"Mr. Smith, it is the mission of our church to bring redemption to these savages. I cannot in good conscience stand by while the Indian weakens his mind, body and soul with this detestable potion. And I most *certainly* will not tolerate it at my service!"

"You've no right to destroy his property, ma'am. He got this whiskey as payment for the ferry. The way they see it, you've robbed them, and they want to be paid. Or they want justice."

"Payment! Justice! Mr. Smith, would they ask payment for their eternal souls? Would they ask justice from man, or from God?"

Smith glared down at her. "Neither. They want payment for their ferry, or justice for their wrong. You're the one who's destroyed their property. You tell me. Which will it be?"

Mrs. Whittier held his stare for a long while, and everyone around them was silent. Then she walked back through the congregation to the front of the gathering and picked up a small tin plate sitting by her chair. She walked silently through the crowd, passing the collection plate. The people up front, feeling both cornered and coerced, threw in a few pennies. But when those in the rows behind saw Mrs. Whittier's ploy, they got away from that service in a hurry. Within seconds there was no one left, and Mrs. Whittier's collection plate held only about six bits.

She was flushed with embarrassment but resolute as she presented Smith the offering. He looked at its contents, smiling. "Appears you're still a mite short," and then laughed. His laugh was so easy that it let the others standing around, both whites and Indians, join in. Mrs. Whittier's usually ashen face went from a pale pink blush to a deeper red, as if she might burst. "Here ya go. This should make up the difference." He tossed two bits into the plate. Mrs. Whittier held the plate out to Smith, expecting him to take it. But he stared right back at her. "Go ahead. Pay the man." She held the plate out to the Indian, but her face registered nothing. The Indian smiled, took the coins, and walked away laughing.

Lina was back with Josephine when Henry came bounding toward them. "Hey, ladies! The Olmsteads is taking a picnic lunch over there by them trees. They wanted us to join 'em. I told 'em we wouldn't miss it for the world! The Reeds is comin' too."

Josephine was elated. "Oh, how wonderful!" she said, jumping down from the wagon.

"Now wait," Lina said. "I'm not sure that's such a good idea. What if…"

"What if what, Lina?" Henry asked. "What are you so all fired 'fraid is gonna happen? The Olmsteads is nice folks, the Reeds, too. You'd know that if you bothered to spend any time talkin' ta people."

Josie looked up at her pleadingly. "Lina, please. I promise. You won't be sorry." Then she grinned. "I'll behave."

Lina looked at the eager faces of Henry and Josie and found she lacked the heart to say no. "Very well," she said, which immediately brought a holler from Henry and a giggle of delight from Josephine.

The picnic spot was a cool, shady place. It was a lovely spring day, the billowy clouds casting great islands of shadow as they floated eastward. The breeze was soft, making the damp smells that rose from the river almost sweet. Henry made introductions all around, and very quickly, under the guidance of Mrs. Olmstead's motherly hand, the picnic began. Appetites were high and the conversation was spirited. No one asked a single question about them or their "family," nor did anyone seem to take particular notice of Josephine. Lina was grateful for that, but it didn't shake her resolve to keep an eye on Josephine.

Lina sat back and watched the casual friendships being struck that day. Mrs. Olmstead, with her teeming brood, stood as a mother figure to the group. Greta Olmstead seemed particularly struck by the unsure Mrs. Reed, and encouraged her to bring her Harry over so that he could be cooed over by her daughters. Harry was happy to be passed from girl to girl, and his little feet never touched ground all afternoon. Lina found she most enjoyed talking with Andrew Reed, even if he was a bit starry-eyed. She admired his education. Josephine enjoyed Andrew Reed's company as well, and apparently not simply because he was a handsome man. It was obvious to Lina after listening to the two chat that Josephine's education had been considerable.

It was obvious that Frank and Herman Olmstead already admired Henry. He was only just a bit older than them, but possessing skills they hoped to acquire on this journey. He told stories of his home in Arkansas and of places out west he had been. Most of those places were not so very remote, for Henry had not traveled much further than where they stood that afternoon, but to the Olmstead boys these places were as remote as Persia. Ulmer Olmstead stayed just a step apart, saying little to any one person, but keeping a fatherly eye on them all. When the meal was over, Olmstead left the group to go down to the river and watch the ferry operation. In no time, the other men joined him. As they watched, the men talked about the ferry. They discussed, as men do, every facet of the operation—how it must have been built, how it would be maintained, the division of labor, and speculation as to how to improve the process. But as they walked back to where their families were seated, they were in agreement on one thing.

"Pretty damn clever," Henry was saying. "This is a nice piece a business for these Injuns. 'Spect they're makin' a pretty penny."

"Ya, it is dangerous work, though." said Ulmer Olmstead. "Hard work, too. A neighbor back home, he ran the ferry. Each year he must rebuild the raft, many times."

"They're not at all like I imagined them," said Andrew Reed.

"The ferry?" asked Henry.

"No, the Indians. They seem, well, sort of, tame, I guess. I suppose spending time around the settlers coming through, they're less, uh, savage?" He made the statement a question, looking for confirmation from the group.

"Savage?" Lina asked, laughing, although no one else in the group found Andrew's notion funny. They looked at her, with questions in their eyes. Without thinking, Lina spoke frankly. "Oh, I'm sorry, but it just seemed odd to me. I've been around Indians all my life." Her audience listened closely. Lina struggled to explain. "Well, surely, Mr. Reed, as a teacher you're aware that the Potawatomi, like so many tribes, were sent here from the east by the government. We're far from the first white folks they've seen. They've been trading with whites for a long time. They're peaceful by nature. They feel as threatened by other tribes as they do us."

"Threatened? How?" asked Sarah Reed anxiously. Her husband immediately moved to her side, as she cradled the baby. She was, as Henry had noted, a pretty woman, and seemingly sweet of temperament. But her voice was as thin as her frame, and her white blonde hair, pale blue eyes and fair complexion added to her look of frailty.

"Now, sweetheart, Mrs. Clark didn't mean to alarm us."

"Of course not!" Lina said. "I only meant that the Indians are like us. Just trying to make their way out here. They're wary of strangers. They want to protect their homes. I suppose that as long as we're merely passing through their lands, they'll have no reason to trouble us."

"I only hope you are right," Mr. Olmstead said. "If they are as you say, then I know we will sleep better and travel easier. So much to worry about on this trip. One less thing would be welcome."

"Well, I certainly hope so, too," said Sarah Reed, faintly. "I must admit, your words are a bit of comfort, although I can't say that I would agree that these people are the same as us."

The conversation was interrupted. "Excuse me, folks. Henry, Mr. Olmstead, can I have a word with you?" It was Smith, who'd come up from the ferry.

"Of course," said Ulmer Olmstead, and the men stepped away to talk. Though she couldn't hear them, it was apparent to Lina by their expressions Smith had come to ask something important of them. The younger Olmsteads were quite animated, but Mr. Olmstead seemed to be holding steady. Then, with a stern look and a reassuring hand on the shoulder, Smith convinced him, and Smith, Henry, Frank and Herman walked away from the group. Mr. Olmstead and Andrew returned to the ladies.

"They're getting ready to take the livestock across the river," Andrew told them faintly.

Sarah Reed moved straight to her husband's side. "Andy, you aren't going with them, are you?"

Andrew Reed put his arm around his wife's thin shoulders. "No, sweetheart. I told him I couldn't. I don't know anything about herding cattle." The Reeds' devotion to one another was uncommonly apparent. They were never out of sight of one another, and when together the glances they exchanged, the tone of their voices, the gentle touches they shared, all spoke their deep affection. But that also revealed an anxious dependence on one another. Sarah Reed seemed perpetually worried, and while there was much to worry about, her worries were endless. No reassurance on the part of her husband seemed to help. Andrew had but one worry, and that was Sarah, who required all his energy and nearly all of his attention. Still, it was clear he wanted nothing more than her happiness.

"What was the argument about?" Josie asked.

"Oh, no argument," said Mr. Olmstead. "It is only that I did not want to spare both the boys. I volunteered to go, but the boys insisted. So filled with the adventure of it, they are. I hope I have done the right thing."

When the picnickers had gathered their belongings, they stopped just long enough to watch as the Granby Company cattle herd came over the ridge and started toward the river. The herd, like the company to which it belonged, was small. Still, one hundred animals moving as one created an awesome sight.

The two herds had been combined, but not intermingled. The oxen were larger, more powerful than the cattle, and their horns posed a hazard to the cattle. So Henry, Frank Olmstead and two other fellows unknown to Lina worked the cattle at the rear, while Smith, Herman Olmstead and some others were working the oxen at the front. The low bawls and bellows of the animals rose as they neared the water, and their movements were unsteady. Herman Olmstead and another fellow rode into the water, near the front of the herd, urging and prodding them as they moved. As the first oxen started into the river, they hesitated, confused and insecure in the soft muddy bank of the river. One balked, on the left front flank near Herman. He rode up to it, trying to direct it into the river, but the frightened beast turned around, and tried to move back up the bank against the stream of the livestock. Herman moved closer, and it was then the force of the herd was upon him. The ox made a quick turn to avoid being forced under by the drove, and its horn caught on the leg of Herman's trousers. Caught, the ox became more frightened still, and pushed hard against the horse, knocking Herman from the saddle. Before there was a chance to get to him, the rest of the herd moved into the stream and over the young man, crushing him beneath the weight of the herd, and drowning him.

****

So it was that young Herman Olmstead from Pennsylvania, on the edge of a new life, but less than a hundred miles from the edge of the frontier, became the first casualty of the Granby Company. He was buried on the southern bank of the Kansa River. The service was held that evening, just after the final ferry crossing of the day. Smith had convinced the Potawatomi to stop with just one group of wagons left. The Olmsteads, the Reeds, and Lina's wagon were to be the last, along with the Whittiers. Because of the Sabbath service, the Whittiers were behind in getting ready, and Smith had threatened again to leave them. But after Herman's death, Mrs. Whittier insisted they stay to help the Olmsteads give Herman a proper service. Smith felt bad about the boy's death, so he agreed, hoping the service would provide some comfort. The Olmsteads insisted on their own service, however, but thanked the Whittiers for their words of solace and their presence at the grave. The rest of the company, having already crossed with their wagons, could not return for the burial. Granby had already made camp beyond the river's north bank, but Smith was there. The Potawatomi were there, too, standing once more on the periphery.

Herman was wrapped in a sheet, placed in a hollowed log that the Potawatomi helped prepare, and lowered in the grave that Henry and Smith dug in the same spot where they had all picnicked that afternoon. The Olmsteads were remarkably stoic. Although Mrs. Olmstead and the older girls wept, they wept silently, and managed to sing in full voice with the hymn Mrs. Whittier led. When the brief service concluded, the group walked back to their wagons in silence. Smith trailed them, and was stopped by one of the Indians who motioned to the grave and said something to the guide. After everyone was back at their wagons, Smith came toward Mr. Olmstead. "They wanted me to tell you," he said, nodding to the Indians as they walked away, "they will protect your son for you." Ulmer Olmstead only nodded.

5

"It's the cholera," Lina said. She sat on a flour sack outside the wagon in the twilight, trying to catch a cool evening breeze. "Talk of the cholera has the whole company on edge. Folks are staying to themselves. I haven't seen the Reeds since we made camp."

Josie talked Henry into dragging down a trunk so she could sit too, but more comfortably. "I say it's the heat. It's insufferable out here with no hope for shade. You won't even start a fire because it's too hot to cook. A company of hungry people are understandably disagreeable."

"Smith won't let us start a cook fire. It's too dry and windy."

"Then, if you won't feed me properly, then the least you could do is allow me a cool bath in that little creek. I won't get lost, if that's your worry. I can see the banks from here."

"No, it's the cholera again. Folks are convinced that creek is tainted with it. A lot of people died of it coming through here last year. Word spreads. Whether it's true or not, we shouldn't risk it. Besides, it's only a few more days."

"A few more days until what?" Henry had been stretched out across the wagon seat all evening, and he hadn't spoken a word. Henry, so usually lively, had grown increasingly quiet over the past few days. Figuring him unlikely to worry about something like disease, Lina assumed he was tired as they all were from another long day under the relentless sun and wind of the prairie. But when Lina looked up at him, he was standing, looking down at her with nothing but worry on his face.

"Ft. Kearney. Surely Smith told you. There'll be safe water there, and for you Josie, a chance to clean up a bit."

Henry slumped like a spent man on to the seat. He sat there staring off into the last of the evening's light. A ruffle of air came through, too light for a true breeze, but enough to make the ladies sigh with small relief. Behind them, the sound of little Harry Reed fussing and crying in small starts floated beneath the chirrups of crickets at dusk.

"The sound of a crying baby doesn't help raise spirits. Mrs. Olmstead said he's teething," Josie said.

Lina stood. "Perhaps I have something that will make us all feel better." She reached beneath the wagon seat and brought forward a small box. One of its lid hinges was broken, and it was badly scratched and covered in dust. "It's a music box." She lifted the lid. Inside, the glass that covered the movement was cracked, but beneath, its mechanism was still intact, the intricate brass workings gleaming. "I found it scavenging for wood. Henry accuses me of being a pack rat, but I've managed to find us plenty of firewood from other people's castoffs. But this isn't for kindling. I just like it because it's pretty." Carefully she turned the crank until she could turn it no more, then flipped a switch inside the case. Short, bright notes rushed forward like a bubbling spring, then slowed to a trickle, then a drip, then stopped.

"What's the tune?" Henry asked.

"Josie, do you know it? I've never heard it, either. But it's pretty." She paused to listen, but there was only silence. "And I think it's quieted Harry."

"It does make me feel cooler. Play it again," Josie asked.

Lina cranked the handle again, and a second and third time too. Lina agreed, it did help, but in the end, Harry's teething pain must have returned, for the three of them had to settle for the soothing tune heard over the muffled mews and sobs of a fussy baby.

****

The next morning, when the Reed's wagon failed to pull out with the rest of the company, it was assumed that the baby was fussy again. But the Reeds' wagon was almost out of sight behind them when Henry rode past Lina. "I'm gonna see what's up with 'em," he said, and hurried back toward the wagon now sitting alone on the prairie. Lina stopped their wagon, as did the Olmsteads, shortly after. The rest of the company maintained its plodding pace.

Mrs. Olmstead walked toward Lina as she stood alongside their oxen, her eyes fixed on the Reeds' lone wagon in the distance. Mr. Olmstead came forward, too, and Josie. The sun bearing down on them from the cloudless sky made a blur of everything except the bright white canvas of the wagon. Through the rippling heat they saw Henry riding as fast as he could toward them. "It's Sarah," he gasped. He tried to say more, but couldn't.

"Cholera?" Lina asked, and Henry nodded.

"We must go to her." Mrs. Olmstead was already moving back toward her wagon when Lina caught her by the arm.

"No. Your family's depending on you. You can't risk your health. Or theirs."

"We can go to her." The voice was Josephine's.

Lina looked at Josie, stunned. "Are you certain you want to?"

"I have some experience with this." She said no more, and the hard look in her eye said she was not to be questioned.

"What do we need?" was Lina's only question.

"All the medicines we have between us. All the water we can spare, and any extra linens." Mrs. Olmstead returned to her wagon to get their medicines, while Josie and Lina searched their own wagon for what they could take.

Everything was wrapped into bundles, and tied to the two horses. Lina turned to the Olmsteads. "Stay here in case there's anything else we might need." She looked to Henry. "Do we have everything?" He didn't answer her directly, but he took the shovel from their wagon and tied it to his saddle. She knew what Henry was preparing for, but she wasn't ready to put words to the thought. Henry helped Josie onto his horse, and then took the saddle in front of her. Lina mounted her horse, then they turned the horses toward the Reeds' wagon, riding side by side.

Approaching the wagon, they called out. "Andrew! Sarah!" the two women called as they got off their horses and started for the wagon. Henry remained outside. He had already seen enough. He knew if they needed him they would call.

Lina reached the wagon first. She saw Sarah Reed lying stretched out on a thin pile of blankets, and Andrew crouched next to her holding her hand. The pretty young woman was gone, replaced by ghastly vestige. She laid soaked in perspiration, her face flushed with fever, staring unaware at the wagon bonnet above her. The blankets beneath her were drenched with waste and retch. Sarah lay so still she might have seemed dead but for the slow blinking of dull eyes.

Suddenly, as if gripped by unseen hands, Sarah began to convulse, and a hoarse scream broke over her parched lips, taking more energy than she seemed capable of.

"Dear God, Sarah! Tell me what to do!" Andrew cried as he tried to hold her, to still the convulsions by force of will. But the spasms ran their course, and in a few moments, Sarah lay limp and motionless once more. Andrew began to sob, dabbing at his wife's hollow face with a dirty scrap of cloth.

Gently, Josephine pushed past Lina to climb inside. "Andrew," she said calmly, over and over until he finally heard her. Even so, he could only gaze at her blankly. "Andrew, we're here to help Sarah. Is that alright?" Gently she tried to take the towel from his hands.

"Let Josephine help," Lina said. Finally, Andrew turned to look at Lina. "Come on now, leave the wagon for a moment. Let us help her." Andrew backed away from his wife, right out the back of the wagon, but his eyes never left his young bride. He stood on the ground below looking up into the wagon, helplessly.

Lina climbed out with him. "Andrew, where's the baby? Where's Harry?"

Andrew answered flatly. "Under the wagon."

Lina found him there, sleeping. "Andrew, when did Sarah take ill?"

"Yesterday evening, after supper. She complained of a headache. I slept with the baby under the wagon last night." Andrew finally looked at Lina. "She said it was a headache."

"Andrew, I'm going to have Henry take the baby to the Olmsteads." He looked at her suddenly, frightened. "Just for a while. Sarah can't take care of him. You know Mrs. Olmstead will be good to him." He gave the slightest nod, then once more turned his attention to the wagon.

Lina carried the baby to where Henry sat astride his horse. "Take him to Mrs. Olmstead. Tell her I don't think he has the fever. Not yet, anyway. And tell them to get moving. We'll be here a while, I guess." She looked back at the wagon. "I don't know what else to do," she whispered. Henry took the basket, but placed one hand on top of her head. When she turned to look at him, he gave her a smile that tried its best to reassure her. Then he turned and rode back to the Olmsteads. "Come back as soon as you can!" she called after him, and he answered her with a wave.

When she got back, she found Josephine had stripped Sarah of all her clothes, and had thrown them out on the ground, along with all the dirty linen. "Burn it," she told Andrew, pressing a bottle of matches into his hand. Slowly, he began to drag the filthy pile away from the wagon. But when he tried to light the match, a palsy struck his hand, then he broke down in a heap next to the pile, sobbing uncontrollably.

"Take those linens and soak them in water," were Josie's instructions to Lina. "But don't waste it!" As she searched the bag that held all the remedies they brought with them, she whispered, "I doubt we can do much more than treat her symptoms. But if we can keep her from more dehydration, perhaps...." Lina tried to get her to drink some of the water, but every attempt resulted in more retching. The only fluid they managed to get past Sarah Reed's lips was a little laudanum. She could not swallow a dose, so Lina poured a little on a rag and Josie placed the moist corner in Sarah's mouth. The elixir dripped into her throat slowly, and it seemed to ease her convulsions. For a time.

By mid afternoon, the laudanum had lost its effect. Sarah's convulsions came more frequently each time. There was little conversation between Lina and Josephine, only enough words to do what had to be done. Lina felt the stale air of the wagon closing in on her. Frustrated and tired, she whispered, "It's so damn hot in here, Josie! Let's take this cover off, get some fresh air in here! Won't that help?" Lina started to move toward the laces that held the bonnet in place, but Josie reached over Sarah to touch Lina at the waist, and shook her head. "That won't help. There is nothing to do but wait." The words had still not been spoken, but the fate was finally named. *Nothing to do but wait.*

"Go outside. You need the air," Josie told Lina. When she shook her head, Josie said, "Go check on Andrew."

Henry was sitting by Andrew, yet had not been able to console him, for Andrew was still on the ground sobbing. When he saw Lina come out, though, he tried to regain himself. Weak with his own despair, he crawled towards her, hope and fear together on his face. "She's sleeping, Andrew." He pulled himself up, and went over to the wagon. Josephine crawled out to make room for him, and Lina, Josie and Henry stood, waiting.

Suddenly, they heard Sarah's voice, thin and dry. She had pulled herself upright, and was staring straight into her husband's eyes. "Why? Oh, Andrew. Why?" But no answer came, nor would Sarah Reed have lived to hear it. She closed her eyes, and fell limp into her husband's arms. Andrew began to sob again, holding her and rocking her back and forth.

In time, they managed to convince Andrew to let them take care of her. Henry started digging, while the two women wrapped Sarah in a sheet. Henry carried her body to the grave. In a short service, Josephine said the rosary. Lina hoped Sarah would have liked the effort. It had been no solace to Andrew. He sat at the end of the wagon, lost.

"Andrew, you've got to listen," she said, taking him by the shoulders to get his attention. He looked at her, but every muscle in his body was limp. "You've got to come with us, now. There's nothing more to do here. We'll burn these things, and then we have to catch up with the company as quickly as we can. You need to be with your little boy, Andrew." Her words had started out stern, but her tone softened when she looked into his eyes and saw a hollow sadness.

"Mrs. Olmstead has Harry?" he asked.

"Yes, Andrew. Remember? I sent him to her when we first got here?"

"Oh, yes. I remember." He looked over toward the grave. "That's good. Mrs. Olmstead will take care of him."

"Yes, she will, for now. But he needs you Andrew. Let's go."

A light came to Andrew's eyes. "I want to make a marker for her," he said simply.

"That's a fine idea, Andy," Henry said. "How 'bout that headboard ya got? I'll help ya."

"No!" Andrew shouted, his jaw set, his eyes on fire. "I'm her husband! It's up to me!"

"Okay, Andy, fine. We'll wait for ya, then."

The outburst seemed to have roused him, and finally, he looked at them, clear-eyed. "No, I've kept you long enough. Go ahead. I'll see to this and be behind you shortly."

Lina and Henry took the reins of their horses and, with Josie beside them, started walking in the direction of the trail. Lina was already thinking ahead. The Granby party was nearly a full day ahead of them. She calculated that if they traveled well after dark, with luck, they might catch up with the company tomorrow. They walked in silence, but from time to time each looked over a shoulder to the small wagon. Andrew had placed the wooden headboard by the grave, and stood next to it for a long time. When Lina turned around next, she couldn't see Andrew at all. She stopped, searching for some sign of him. It worried her. *He should be moving out by now.* Henry and Josie stopped too. "What's the matter?" Henry asked her.

She didn't know. She could only shake her head. Then she saw first a flicker, then the whole wagon bonnet swallowed in flame. Immediately Henry and Lina were on their horses, driving them back toward the wagon with all the speed they could muster. Their hearts' pounding matched the horses' hooves on the hard packed earth beneath them. Now the whole wagon was on fire. Then suddenly a single rifle shot rang out, and the life of Andrew Reed was over.

In the end, they chose to let the wagon burn itself out. They got there in time to get the team away from the fire, and Henry had managed to get Andrew's body clear, too. There was nothing left to wrap him in, so they dug up Sarah and wrapped them together, hoping it was enough to keep the coyotes away. Henry helped the Reeds' team to their wagon, and they headed off to meet up with the Olmsteads.

Lina told the story as briefly as possible. The memory of it had left her with a feeling of desolation beyond words. The Olmsteads were hardly curious for details. Mrs. Olmstead sat quietly, cradling the sleeping Harry Reed. She looked at Lina, eyes moist, but the question she dreaded asking would not come.

"You should keep the baby," said Lina.

"But they had family, perhaps," Mrs. Olmstead said. "The baby should with them go." Mrs. Olmstead searched each face for confirmation.

"I never heard 'em talk 'bout where they was from, let alone any kin," said Henry. "If there was any clues, they're ashes now." The words summoned a vivid picture that brought a momentary silence.

"I told Andrew we had sent him to you. He said he knew you would take care of Harry. Those were his words, I promise," Lina said.

Greta Olmstead said nothing, but turned to her husband with pleading eyes. Ulmer answered softly, "It seems God's will to me, somehow." Greta looked down on her new son just as he smiled.

****

They tried without success to catch up with the Granby Company the next day, but Lina knew they weren't traveling as fast as they might. The blazing sun drained them of what little remained of their spirits. Then, the second day on their own, they noticed a small band of Indians behind them. All day they watched the Indians follow them from a distance, traveling a mile or so parallel. Still feeling the weight of the duties with which Smith had charged him, Henry reminded everyone of what Smith had said about encountering Indians—to mind your business and let them mind theirs. When they stopped to make camp, the Indians stopped, too.

The Indians stayed there as the settlers went about the evening's chores. Then Frank spoke, his voice straining to stay calm. "They're coming," he said.

Three men, one old, two not quite yet fully grown, had ridden up within a hundred feet of their camp. Greta herded her children into the wagon, while Ulmer slowly reached for his shot gun. "Steady," Henry whispered.

The Indians stayed calm. They rode in a slow, wide circle around the wagons, eyeing them carefully. When they came back around, the old man took a blanket that lay in front of him across his horse, and held it out toward Ulmer. Ulmer looked at the man, then reached out for the blanket, and with a nod, said "Thank you." Then one of the young men took a bundle that hung from his pack, and handed it to Mrs. Olmstead. She looked at her husband and took the parcel.

Unwrapping it, she found a leg of venison, a rare treat. She, too, thanked the Indian. Then the whites and the Indians sat staring at one another, waiting. Finally, the Indian who gave Ulmer the blanket said to him, simply, "Swap."

The word didn't register with Ulmer, who looked to Lina and then Henry, eyes wide. "He wants you to trade with him," Lina told him.

"What could I trade?"

"Anything. Clothing is good."

"But there is nothing we can spare." With so many children, and limited room for provisions, the Olmsteads could spare neither shirt nor shift. "Greta, we must give these things back."

"No," Henry said evenly. "Takin' 'em back now would be like insultin' him."

"Then what are we to do?" Mrs. Olmstead, said, a quiver of fear in her voice.

"Swap," the Indian said again, this time looking at Lina. Lina's mind ran through the choices available. She, too, was reluctant to give them any of their clothing. While bacon or biscuits could be eaten in place of venison, there was no good substitute for a warm shirt or a good pair of boots. Then she remembered Josephine.

"Josie, give him one of your dresses."

"My dresses?" Josephine had scarcely moved since the Indians had first approached.

"Yes. Your dresses. *Now*, Josie."

"I'm not giving them one of my dresses! What need does a savage have for such a thing?"

Lina figured this was no time to argue. So she headed toward the wagon. But Josie followed her inside the wagon. Lina started flipping through the contents of Josie's trunk, then grabbed a dress. "Here, this one."

"No, not that one!" Josie grabbed it from her. "You can't have that one." She clung to it wild-eyed. "Not this one."

"Oh for God's sake, just give me something."

"Here." Josie threw one at her, made of dark red silk and far more stylish than the green one she guarded so ferociously.

Lina took the dress to the old man. He considered it in amazement, held it aloft for his two companions to see. They all smiled and seemed satisfied with the trade. Then the old man looked at Lina and said again, "Swap," pointing to the articles he had given the Olmsteads and holding up two fingers. He pointed to the dress and held up one.

"He wants something else," Lina said, looking around to her friends.

"Well, you'll not give them anything else of mine!" Despite the apparently desperate situation, Josephine was determined not to give in. *Apparently, she'd rather see us all murdered or worse than give away another piece of her precious wardrobe*, Lina thought. She glanced around. She couldn't ask the Olmsteads to give up anything, although she wanted to. But she had just saddled them with another child. She thought of her own possessions, then inspiration struck her.

She crawled back within the confines of the wagon. Soon, she returned with the music box she had salvaged on the trail. She opened the lid and turned the crank. As the box began to play its tinny tune, the old man seemed even more pleased. He took the box, looked at the mechanism inside, held the box to his ear, and then passed it to the young boys who seemed equally intrigued.

"Swap?" Lina asked.

"Swap," he agreed. They left without another exchange, as quietly as they had come. For a few minutes, as the little company watched them leave, they could hear the music box's faint tune as it drifted on the prairie breeze.

The encounter with the Indians seemed to rouse the group. Conversation became livelier than it had been in days. The children asked endless questions about the Indians, and the adults talked reassuringly about how they would soon find Granby—and Smith.

"We've been keeping pace, I'm sure of it. That means that they can't be more than a day ahead of us. I expect they'll lay over at Fort Kearney, so we should be able to meet up with them there." This was a comfort to everyone but Henry.

"How can you be sure? Maybe they'll press on, skip the fort altogether. Maybe we should, too."

"It'll be a good three weeks or more before there's another chance to stock up. And at Kearney folks can make repairs. But even so, *we* should stop at the fort. We need to rest and restock. And if we miss the Granby Company, maybe we'll find another group to travel with.

I think we'd all feel better not traveling alone." The Olmsteads quickly concurred, as did Josephine. Henry said nothing, then wandered away from the fire to stand watch.

Getting ready to bed down for the night, Lina found Josie inside their wagon, carefully folding her dresses and placing them back in the trunk. She had pouted through dinner, and Lina supposed she did owe Josie a word of thanks. "I appreciate what you did, Josie, giving them that dress." Josie said nothing, but merely turned her back to Lina and kept working. Lina decided to help, hoping that might improve the mood. The dress Josie had so stubbornly refused to give up lay crumpled to the side, so Lina picked it up and started folding it. Then she heard a clinking noise within the folds of the fabric.

Josie heard it, too, and quickly snatched the dress from Lina's hand. "Give that to me!" she said, but as she pulled, the dress caught in Lina's hand. Both women heard the unmistakable ripping of fabric, and the sound of coins dropping to the floor. Lina looked down. Gold coins lay scattered around their feet.

"What's this?"

"What does it look like?" Josie said, scooping the coins in the apron of her skirt.

"I thought you told me all you had was a thousand dollars!"

Josie quickly inventoried the money. "I told you my father gave me a thousand dollars. You didn't ask if I had other money, and I didn't offer."

"Well, this is funny!" Lina laughed. "What an interesting turn. Josephine Paul, always quick to pester me about telling the truth."

Josie opened a small box she took from the trunk and dropped the coins inside. "Oh, this is silly." She closed the trunk and sat down on the lid. "You make up a silly story that we're cousins, the three of us. It's laughable, and unnecessary. As for me, I don't care what people think, but I do prefer to keep some particulars to myself. Given the choice between a lie and a secret, I prefer a good secret. A well kept secret is its own treasure, to be shared when it benefits the holder." She smiled.

Lina shook her head. "Josie, you've got a strange way of looking at the world. Very well, then. Keep your secrets. But be careful *where* you keep them," she said, pointing to the trunk where Josie stashed her treasure, "and keep them safe."

A few hours later after everyone else was asleep, she went to take the watch from Henry. She could just make out his shape thanks to the last flickering light of the night's fire. He was crouched quietly, facing west. He made a poor sentry that night, for Lina had no trouble slipping up behind him, unnoticed. "Hey, there!" she whispered when she was right behind him.

He swung around at her at the last moment, too late to have stopped an attacker, human or otherwise, but the way he snatched his rifle made her jump. "Easy, Henry!" Lina said, taking a quick step back. "It's only me." At the sound of her voice he turned back without a word, and went on staring into the night. "I'm here to relieve you," she said. "You can go catch some sleep now."

"I'd like to stay a bit longer, if you don't mind," he said. They sat together quietly for a long spell. Finally, she heard him sigh, and then he said, "Lina, we cain't go to Fort Kearney. Least ways, I cain't."

"Why not?"

"I'm 'fraid to."

Lina chuckled. "You, Henry Parker? Afraid? Don't be silly. I can't imagine you being afraid of anything."

"I'm afraid of jail."

"What are you…" Lina had laid a hand on his shoulder, but he pulled away so abruptly she stopped talking, and waited for him to speak.

"I lied to you, Lina. Well, I guess it warn't so much a lie as I didn't tell ya everything. But some of it was a lie, and now it's come back to me, just like lies always does."

"Henry, you're not making any sense. What did you lie about?"

"I ain't Henry Parker."

His words stunned her. In the short time of their trip, Lina had felt increasingly unsure of herself. She had started out so confident she could handle this trip. But a dozen little things had made her start to doubt that, a doubt that had found its full measure with the deaths of Andrew and Sarah Reed. She had come to rely on the Olmsteads. They were so constant. But she knew she could only rely on them so much, for they had themselves to look after. She had never been accustomed to relying on others anyway. But she realized now the one person she had allowed herself to depend upon was Henry Parker. He was a wild boy, perhaps a bit too rash, too taken with adventure. But where she and Josephine were concerned, he was as steady as they come.

"Who are you, then?" she finally asked.

"Clay Parker. Henry was my cousin." That was all he offered.

"Henry, um, I mean, Clay, or…oh dear." She wanted to ask more, but speaking his name, the name she knew him as, just reminded her how unsteady she now felt. His face was in shadows too deep for her to look him in the eye, and he didn't help by keeping his head down, by staying so quiet. He spoke quietly too, and Lina had to listen closely.

"Here's the whole account. I joined the Army last year. I told you that much. Right away, they sent me off to Fort Scott. But, hell, I joined up to see the west. Fort Scott ain't more'n a stone's throw from home. Nothing to do but ride patrol for a bunch of traders running back and forth to Santa Fe. One night, me and some of the boys got ta drinkin'. Then we got to drinkin' some more, and 'fore I knew it, we was good 'n drunk. Somebody started a fight. I don't know who or even what it was about. I just remember jumpin' in with the rest. 'Fore I knew it, I'd hit me an officer. An officer, God damn him! Didn't look at his stripes 'fore I hit him. I just hit him." Henry, or Clay, lowered his head, slowly shaking it in disbelief. Then he went on.

"The Army, they take that hittin' officers real serious. Put me in the stockade 'fore I had a chance to sober up. Next thing I know, I been court-martialed and was on my way to Fort Leavenworth. That's where they send the military prisoners. They was goin' to lock me up for ten years. *Ten years*, can you believe it? Ten years, I'd be an old man, too old to join the cavalry. In ten years, won't be no west to go see. I just couldn't stand the thought. So I escaped."

"How, in heaven's name?"

"Them boys takin' me up to Leavenworth warn't a whole lot older 'n me, and not a whole lot more predisposed toward officers. Anyhow, they unshackled me when we got to Westport, while they was gettin' fresh horses. I gave 'em the slip, and stole one of the horses. I got an aunt 'n uncle lives just south of town. Henry was their boy, died when he was little. They gave me some money, and told me 'bout some of the freighters that put companies together. That's what I was lookin' for when I found you."

Lina's thoughts jumped in all directions. She wanted to wring the fool's neck, but she had to ask herself why. After all, Henry hadn't done anything in lying that she hadn't done herself. But Henry's lie might get him arrested, taken away from her before she was ready. Then where would she be?

"There's something I don't understand. If you're afraid to enter Fort Kearney for fear you'll be spotted, what'll be different about Fort Laramie? For that matter, why go back in the Army at all?"

"It's all I ever wanted to do. Since I was little, and first seen them boys ridin' off. Stuck in a little mud hole in Arkansas, what else was there to dream about? Ridin' was the only thing I was ever any good at. Far as Fort Kearney's concerned, it's just a little too close to home, I guess. I figured by the time we got to Fort Laramie, wouldn't be no chance of anybody recognizin' me."

"God damn it, Henry...Clay...oh, God damn it! What the hell were you thinking?" She allowed herself the outburst. It made her feel better, but it changed nothing. Henry sat like a scolded child. She hated seeing him like this, but it made her feel better to know he felt bad.

Lina stood up and walked off into the darkness of the prairie to think. She was gone for several minutes and it was quiet all around them. Henry must have lost sight of her, for she heard some worry in his voice when he cried out for her. "Lina?"

"Be still! I'm thinking!" Her patience and her energy were failing, just when she needed them both. Here was this boy—really a man who acted like a boy—dropping these problems in her lap. It annoyed her terribly, but it reminded her of a fact that was all too inescapable. *You can't rely on anyone, anyone at all*, she thought. *Just yourself.*

Finally, she surfaced from the cloak of night. She came right up to him, and spoke to him like a reprimanding mother. "Alright, listen to me. From now on, as far as I'm concerned, Clay Parker is dead. Henry Parker you said you are, so Henry Parker it is. You're not to say a word about this to the Olmsteads, to Josephine, to anybody, do you understand? When we get to Fort Kearney, you're to stay as far away from the fort as possible. I don't care what you do, or how you explain it away, just stay away from the fort. Ride off into the prairie or go to hell for all I care." Henry looked down at his feet, out of shame she could only guess. "But they won't take you back to prison, not if I can help it, at least until we get to Fort Laramie. If anyone recognizes you there, then to hell with you." She tried to sound indifferent, but she didn't feel that way.

"Lina, I'm awful sorry. Guess I didn't think this thing through."

She couldn't yet tell him everything would be fine. She wasn't sure it would, and she was still too angry. But she knew there was nothing to gain by talking about this further. She laid a hand on his shoulder and said, "Go get some sleep Henry. I'll take over here."

6

At the distance of some miles, the only evidence of Ft. Kearney was the American flag hoisted high on a standard and snapping in the stiff, straight wind of the plains. The fort itself was hidden behind a blanket of wagon bonnets, more wagons than the camp outside Westport by two. It was a welcome sight to all of them, made more so by the rider they could see coming out to meet them—Smith.

There was much waving and whooping among the group when they saw him, and Henry rode out to be the first to greet him. Smith never varied much in temperament, but he smiled broadly as he neared the wagons. "Good to see you, folks. Good to have you back. Ulmer, Miz Olmstead." He tipped his hat to her, then looked to Josie and did the same, though Josie provoked a special response. "Ma'am. A pleasure." He looked around. "The Reeds?"

Lina shook her head.

"All of 'em?" he asked in surprise.

"Andrew and Sarah. Mrs. Olmstead's got the baby. Andy's wish."

Smith shook his head. "That makes six of ours. But we seem to be through the worst, for now. Follow me, I'll lead you in."

"Are we going straight to the fort?" Henry asked. There was a quiver in his voice that, fortunately, Smith took for excitement.

"Not yet, son. Ride with me while I lead you folks to the other wagons. I'm advising everybody to take stock of repairs to be done and supplies they need before they head to the fort. Prices here are high, but they'll only be higher down the road."

That evening at supper, Henry was full of news Smith had shared with him. Smith was of the opinion the Indians they had encountered were Pawnee, and sent his compliments to all for cool heads and quick thinking. There had been no further outbreaks of cholera within the company, nor any reported around the fort. This was a relief to everyone. The company was set to leave the day after tomorrow, delayed a day because so many families had wagons to repair. Knowing their time near the fort would be short gave Henry some relief. There would be a dance the night before they left, which promised Josie some relief from the monotony.

Lina was consumed with entirely different matters. As soon as Smith had mentioned that goods at the fort were going for a premium, her shopkeeper instincts took over. There was an opportunity here, she knew it. Already, within the Granby Company word had spread of her chickens, and she had made a little money from the eggs, and taken a few things in trade, which she then sold or traded again. It was all very informal, but it was exactly the business she needed to keep their finances intact.

Now here was a real opportunity to stock up on critical supplies, at the best prices to be found for the rest of their travels. But with less than twenty dollars to her name, Lina's ability to capitalize on the opportunity was limited, until she remembered Josephine and her clinking dress.

As usual, Henry had gobbled his supper in short order. Lina ate hers at a moderate pace, but Josie had a habit of picking at her meal like a bird. Lina set down her empty plate and watched Josie pick at each morsel with a delicate stab of the fork. She seemed to be in a pleasant mood, so Lina decided to take a chance.

"Smith said prices at the fort are high," she started, straight out, "and getting higher the further west we go."

"Mmm," Josie nodded before she swallowed. "Well, thank heavens we have you, Lina. You were very clever to bring all these extra supplies, I must say." It was a gratuitous compliment, Lina knew, but it gave her the opening she had hoped for.

"Yes, and you know, we've made a bit of money off those supplies. Not enough to put us ahead, but a start. I only wish I'd brought more."

Josie stopped paying attention to her plate, and turned her focus on Lina. Slowly, she set the plate on the ground beside her. Until that moment, Lina had every intention of asking Josie straight away for more money. But something in Josie's expression made Lina stop speaking. Henry must have sensed a brewing storm, too, for he turned over to watch, propping himself on one elbow. But Josephine surprised them both when she finally spoke. "Lina, dear. Why don't I give you some more cash and you can buy what you think we'll need? Would that be a help?"

Lina was so surprised at Josie's offer, she could hardly find words. "Why, yes! Thank you, Josie! That's just what I was going to ask. I think it's a good plan. I can use some of the money I've already, I mean *we've* already made, and then…."

"How much do you think you'll need?"

"Well, I suppose another hundred would be good. Two would be better."

"And how much do you suppose a new wagon would cost?" she asked casually.

"Oh, I don't think we'll need another wagon, Josie. We can get everything I'll be getting in the wagon with a little effort."

"That's not why I asked. I assume you'll be putting what we buy… what *I* buy, in that rolling emporium of yours. In fact, my dear, I simply insist on it. And to give you as much room as possible in that miserable excuse for a coach, I'll be taking all my possessions out, and putting them in my *own* wagon. That is why I asked."

"Now, wait just a minute," Lina started to say. Henry was doing a poor job of concealing his laughter. Josie wore a grin so innocently full of delight in herself that even Lina had to smile. "Now, Josie…."

Josie stood her ground. "You won't talk me out of this, Carolina Clark. You can use the money you've made so far any way you like, but if you want any more money from me, then I insist on having my own wagon. How much did you say it would be?"

"Two hundred. Maybe more."

"Very well. Let's see. Two hundred for my wagon, and another two for your enterprise. Is that it, then?"

"Yes."

"Well, that shouldn't be a problem." Josie smiled and rose.

"But I can't guarantee what kind of wagon we can get for that money, Josie. You have to understand. Mostly what they have at the fort are cast-offs, broken down pieces of junk. But I'll get the best deal for you I can."

"I'm sure you will, my dear," Josie said, as she picked up her plate and scraped the last bits of food into the fire. "I'm going with you. If you want my money, then I come attached to it."

Lina looked to Henry, but he was still laughing. But he was less amused the next morning when Lina commandeered his horse. "Hey, what the hell am I supposed to do? Stay here all day?"

"That's exactly what you're to do, Henry Parker. Stay here with the wagon," Lina said as she saddled her own horse.

"But what if Smith needs me to...."

"I've already spoken to Smith. He said he could get along without you for one day. Oh, don't look so disappointed. You're not that indispensable, you know," Lina said. "Besides, with any luck, this won't take long."

"Well, if you're gonna steal my horse, then you gotta be the one to ride him, Lina. I figure Josie ain't all that good with horses, and he's a might spirited for the likes of her."

"Poo!" Josie said, emerging from the wagon. "I've been riding as long as you have, Henry Parker. Longer, for I'm older. Although it doesn't look like much of a horse to me," she said, as she mounted his palomino. With an ease born of practice, in one single move she rose in the stirrup and wrapped her leg around the pommel. "Are you ready?" she asked, looking down at Lina.

As they started for the store, Lina gave Josie her lecture. "Let me do the talking when we buy the wagon. I have more experience with trades like this, and there's no sense paying more than we need. Also, be on your best behavior, as far as the soldiers are concerned. And try not to say much about the three of us to anybody, particular anyone in uniform."

"Because of Henry?" Josie asked casually. "Henry's in some sort of trouble, isn't he? As far as the Army's concerned?"

Lina was stunned. "Damn him! I told him to keep his mouth shut."

"Henry didn't say a word. He didn't have to. Any fool could see he's been anxious about getting here. I don't have a clue about the particulars, though. Not that it matters."

"It's hard to put one over on you, Josephine Paul," Lina said.

"No, my dear. It's impossible," Josie said, smiling.

The store actually sat outside the post proper, but they rode directly past the fort on the way. It had been built only a couple of years earlier, but if this was the best the Army could do, Lina despaired at what they might find as they traveled further out. It had been built as a way station and a source of protection for the emigrant companies, but it hardly looked prepared for either task. Fort Kearney was a collection of sod huts, completely overwhelmed by the stock companies that surrounded it. As a stronghold it was laughable. There was no battlement, no enclosure to keep Indians out or soldiers and citizens protected.

When they reached the store, Lina handed the reins to Josie. "Wait here. This shouldn't take me long. When I'm done, then we'll go see about the wagon." She nodded in the direction of the livery next to the store. Then she went inside.

Lina was right. The whole transaction took only an hour. The supply officers were happy to find a customer with ready cash. Lina was proud of her investment. She bought every basic supply she could afford, and with money still in hand, another wagon wheel, and some corn for her chickens. Even a bolt of plain muslin. All that was left was to get Josie's wagon, come back and load up, and be gone.

When she stepped outside, she didn't see Josie anywhere, and immediately began to worry. But before her imagination could run away with her, Josie came riding up on the seat of a fine looking wagon, Lina's mare and Henry's horse in the harness. She waved when she saw Lina and pulled the team to a stop.

"What do you think of it?" she asked with a satisfied grin.

Slowly, Lina walked all around the wagon. It looked brand new. She looked up at Josie with suspicion. "How much did you pay for it?"

"One hundred."

"I don't believe you!" Lina climbed up so she could scrutinize the inside. "It doesn't make any sense. Why would the Army sell this wagon for one quarter of what it's worth, when good wagons are in short supply, and everything else they sell around here is so high?" Josephine was smiling. "Oh, no! Josie, you didn't."

"Of course not! How ridiculous! Where? When, I'd like to know? Carolina, be reasonable."

"Then, explain it!"

"I was restless waiting for you. I thought there could be no harm in looking at the wagons, if I was going to buy one. And there was the nicest young soldier at the livery. We struck up a conversation. He comes from Cincinnati, a beautiful city. My father took me there once. Before I knew it, he was insisting I take this wagon. I looked at the other rigs he had, and while he didn't have many, I did think it seemed the best of the lot."

"Well, that it is," said Lina quietly, looking intently at something behind Josephine.

"This just goes to show you, Carolina Clark. There are lots of ways for a woman to do business, provided she's willing to employ the full arsenal of her charms."

"And is this something that charming young soldier gave you for your arsenal?" Lina asked.

"What?" Josie turned around toward Lina, only to see her pointing at the place right behind the seat. She leaned over and peered down into the dark recesses of the wagon at a long box. "What is that?"

Lina lifted the lid on the box. Inside was a load of rifle ammunition. "Oh, heavens!" Josie squealed. "Do you suppose someone forgot and left it there? Should we go back and return it, do you think?"

"I don't think so," Lina answered. She closed the lid. On it was stamped, *Property U.S. Army.* "Josie, I think we'd best get our supplies and head back. Quickly." She climbed onto the seat next to Josie and took the reins from her hands.

"Why? What's the hurry?" Josie asked.

"Because, dear Josephine. If I don't miss my guess, this wagon is the property of the U.S. Army. I'm thinking that charming young soldier pocketed the hundred dollars for himself. In other words, the Army likely will consider this wagon stolen. But if we don't take it, you're out a hundred dollars. So let's just get our supplies and get out of here before anybody notices."

"Yes, let's do," said Josephine, happy for once to follow Lina's lead.

****

"Well, now! Looks like I've fallen into fine company, now that the Army's after the both of you, too!" Henry said that evening. Josie wasted no time in telling him the story of her new wagon on their return to camp.

"Henry, I don't know it's fair to say the Army's 'after' us." Lina's reprimand was weak.

"I don't know what else ya'd call it," Henry replied. "All I can say is, sure hope we don't have ta go back into the fort for anythin'. We done run outta people to go that ain't crossways with the Army." He cackled at his own joke.

"Henry, please," Lina pleaded softly. Josie was settling herself in her new wagon, and Lina was trying to arrange all the supplies in hers. But Henry's needling kept drawing her attention away. Henry had taken off his shirt and was shaving, in anticipation of the dance that evening.

"Now here's an idea!" Henry offered. "The three of us could be outlaws!" Ridin' the west, runnin' from the law…."

"Oh, honestly, Henry!" Lina snapped.

"Darlin', 'honesty's' got nothin' ta do with it!" From inside the wagon came the music of Josie's deep laughter.

"You two go be outlaws if you like. As for me, I've a different life in mind," Lina said.

"And what would that be?" Henry asked, wiping the soap from his face.

"Oh, you know," she answered, but hesitantly. "To find some place in California. To open a store and make a living."

"You mean you come all the way out here just to live like you did before?"

"The difference, Henry, is that now I'll be working for myself, with no one to account to but me."

"Hmm. Well, if you say so. Seems an awful waste of a chance to me, though. Seems to me like you could make more of your life than that." Henry shook the dust out of his shirt and slipped it back on.

"It'll be an honest life, that's for certain," Lina answered, as she lifted a box into the wagon.

As he finished with the shirt buttons, Henry looked out across the wagons around them. The sounds of voices mixed with the music of fiddles had started somewhere out of sight, the first signal that the evening's festivities had started. "We got a real luxury, ya know, the three of us. We come out here for differ'nt kinda reasons than these other folks. Folks like the Olmsteads, they're good folks. But they're just headin' ta Oregon ta do pretty much what they always done. That doesn't make much sense ta me. All the hardship, losin' a son, just for a differ'nt patch of dirt. Then there's them gold rushers. Now, I'll grant ya that sounds like real sport, workin' the gold, maybe strikin' it rich. But what'll most of 'em do if they make it? They'll head back ta wherever it was they came from and live the same sort of life they was leadin' for they left. Now, the three of us, we come out here ta be differ'nt people altogether. Ta live as we please, and no goin' back. Me, I wanna be a soldier. And you know what? I can see that life plain as day. I could describe it to ya 'round the clock. Sleepin' under the stars, breakfast on the fire, spendin' the day ridin' patrol. Fightin' Indians, makin' expeditions out in parts where white folks ain't never been before. It'll be a grand life. And Josie's the same, ain't ya, Josie?" Josie had left her wagon and joined them.

"Oh, yes indeed. I can see it clearly, too." Josie had been inside her wagon getting ready for the evening. "I'll have only the nicest clothes, the loveliest place to live. It'll all be quite elegant. And while I'm working, I'll have the company of all sorts of interesting men. I can think of nothing more pleasant than spending my days indulging in the finest life has to offer, and my evenings indulging myself in romance." Josie spoke with no sense of shame at all.

"So, Lina. What do you see, when you look out there?"

"Out where?" she asked, looking about.

"I meant out there," Josie said, with a quick nod toward the west. "Ahead of us, way into the future? What do you see? For yourself?"

"I honestly don't know," Lina whispered. "I wish I did. Seems like it would make this trip easier, somehow."

"Well, keep lookin', girl. You'll find out eventually, I reckon," Henry said. "But tonight, I ain't lookin' for nothin' that's any further than the sound of them fiddles. Josie, you comin'?" Henry grabbed Josie by the hand and they skittered away. They were gone, but Lina called out, "But we haven't finished loading the wagon!"

****

Lina finished the chore by herself, and would have spent the rest of the evening feeling more than a bit put upon. But as she prepared to bed down for the night, she heard the celebration. She knew Henry was right. There was more than four months travel still ahead of them, and already she was tired, but not from the strain of the day. She had always worked hard, and she was learning that the constant walking and working made her stronger. But her mind was weary.

The sounds of a fiddle screeching out 'Old Dan Tucker' came to her, mingled with the laughter and singing and talking of dozens of people. She remembered how the music box had cheered her the last time her spirits were this low, and suddenly she needed to join the party, to laugh and sing and talk for just a while, without a thought as to what would happen tomorrow. Quickly, she drew a little water and splashed it over her face and ran her comb through her hair before she took off in search of the dancing.

When she arrived, Lina was struck by something she had not noticed before—the sense of community within the company. She hadn't realized how familiar others in the group had grown with one another. Lina saw she was losing a valuable opportunity to get to know these people, beyond a passing nod or the opportunity to sell them some eggs or sugar. There were the Olmsteads, chatting with another family that Lina did not know. Over there was Henry, in the midst of some of the miners. Henry, who at Smith's instruction had ridden the full length of their caravan, now knew every member of the company. And in the center of it all was Josephine, dancing to the tune of the fiddle. The smile on her face brought more light to the circle than the camp fire.

Lina felt alone, an outsider. Then the sound of her name made her turn around. She hoped to see a friendly face, but it was Granby calling to her. He marched toward her most deliberately, wearing a scowl.

"Mrs. Clark! I understand you have purchased an additional wagon."

"That's right."

"Then you will be so kind as to remit to me an additional one hundred dollars before our departure tomorrow morning." Granby saw her shocked expression. "You do remember, Mrs. Clark, our discussion when you signed on? One hundred dollars per wagon. Those were the terms."

"But Colonel Granby," she stuttered, "We haven't got an extra hundred dollars." *Not an extra hundred to spare,* she thought. She had forgotten this detail.

"And yet you could afford another wagon."

"Colonel Granby," she started, forcing herself to remain polite. "Others in the company have lost a wagon. Doesn't it all come out on balance?"

"Irrelevant, Mrs. Clark. The fares were calculated on the expenses of managing a certain number of wagons. The expenses were fixed at that point, even if the number of wagons were not."

His reasoning was so illogical, Lina was losing her patience. "Well, I can't pay you what I don't have, Colonel Granby. Perhaps if you could wait until we get a bit further down the road, and I've had a chance...."

"No exceptions, Mrs. Clark. How would you expect me to maintain order among the members of this company if I began arbitrarily permitting some members to follow the rules, and others to disobey?"

"Rules? Rules?" Lina started shouting. "Colonel Granby, you've been playing fast and loose with the rules since we started. Yes to the Sabbath, no to the Sabbath. No liquor allowed, but yes if it's kept out of sight," she waved frantically in the direction of the miners. Her voice was rising and folks nearby were starting to listen to the conversation. "Why I've half a mind to...."

"Lina, dear, what seems to be the problem?" From nowhere, Josie appeared at Lina's side. When she looked around, she saw Henry standing beside her, too, and was suddenly aware of the faces of the company, and the quiet all around them.

Lina collected her composure, and lowered her voice. "Colonel Granby here is asking that we pay another hundred dollars for the additional wagon we bought today. He wants it before we leave tomorrow, or I believe he intends to cut us from the company."

"I'm within my rights," Granby postured, and looked to the crowd in the background for a challenge. None came.

Josie gave Granby her sweetest, most dimpled smile, and said, "Perhaps, sir, if you could just give us a little more time...."

"No."

Josie had tried her only weapon—her charm. It hardly ever failed her, and never with a man, and yet even Lina could see that in Granby, she had met her match. Money was the only thing that would charm Colonel Granby. Josie's jaw set square, and her eyes turned hard and cold.

"Very well," she hissed. "The wagon in question is mine, not Lina's. I'll pay you. Tonight."

Granby was already smiling, but Lina interrupted. "No, Josie. It was me that wanted the extra supplies...."

"I insist," she said, still glaring at Granby. Then a slight, sly twist came to her lips, giving her a grin as hard as her voice. "It'll be my pleasure."

"Very well, madam. Shall we settle the matter now?"

"Certainly. But not with you."

"What?"

"Colonel Granby," Josie said clearly, for all to hear. "I do not like you. You are a pompous little bully. I may have to pay what you ask, but I won't deal with you. Have your man Smith meet me at my wagon. I'll give him the payment. But not you." Josie didn't wait for Granby's agreement. She walked back toward the wagon.

"Fine! I'll do that!" said Granby, heading the other direction.

"Come on, let's go," Lina said to Henry, as she took a step toward Josie. But Henry caught her arm.

"I know what you're thinkin', Lina. That this is somehow your doin', 'cause ya had the notion ta get them extra supplies. But it was Josie that decided ta get the wagon. So let her do this. You do a lot for us, Lina. Let her do this thing." She couldn't think of a good argument, but still she would have tried, had not Henry said, smiling, "Let's have us a dance, huh, Lina?"

He didn't wait for her answer, but grabbed her hand and pulled her into the dance, which had resumed behind them once Granby left. Before she knew it, Henry had her dancing a sort of addle-pated polka. When the music stopped, Lina collapsed in exhaustion on a nearby stack of full flour sacks. She held her sides, trying to stop laughing. Henry held his sides in desperation for his lungs, crouching on the ground before her. "Damn, Lina. Didn't know you could dance!"

"Dance?" She laughed. "I never danced before in my life!"

"I don't believe you."

Lina shook her head. "Never."

"Didn't that husband of yours ever take ya dancin'?"

"No."

"Ah, I know your foolin' me now. Cain't believe a man wouldn't want to take a girl as pretty as you dancin'."

Lina was surprised at Henry's unaffected flattery. Without realizing it, her whole demeanor at once took on a coy and modest aspect that Henry found charming.

"How 'bout before him?" asked Henry.

She shook her head. "Besides," she teased, "I'll wager there aren't that many girls you've danced with. What girl in her right mind would have you?" She gave him a gentle nudge at the shoulder.

Henry laughed. "You got me there." He was looking at Lina in the warm glow of the camp fire, her face still flush from exhaustion, wisps of red curls framing her face. He was taken with an urge to kiss her, right there and then.

Lina looked at him, and saw something of his feelings in his eyes. Part of her wanted him to kiss her, to know what the kiss would be like as much as anything. She had never been kissed for fun. She had never been a flirt, certainly not with the coquettish talents of Josephine. So she had never flirted with a boy to get him to come around. She just waited for the boys to approach. If a boy waited for her, he would wait forever, so several had given up, more than Lina knew.

But for all her curiosity about kissing Henry Parker, her responsible nature won out. In public, their familial relationship could not be compromised. In private, she worried anything between them might affect all their plans. The intimacy could not be risked. So instinctively, she moved to change the tone of the moment.

"Henry Parker, you've fairly worn me out. I think I'm ready to head back. Stay if you like."

"Ah, c'mon, Lina," Henry said with a wink. "Just one more?" She smiled and joined him for one last dance, then another and another. By now she was truly exhausted, and when the fourth dance was over, she pleaded with him to walk her back to the wagon.

They met Smith along the way. Lina decided he must have enjoyed the dance too, for there was a noticeable bounce in his step and a smile on his face. He nodded at them as they approached.

"I trust Josie's settled our accounts with you?" Lina asked.

"Yes, ma'am. Everythin's squared away." He started to walk back toward the circle, but stopped just long enough to make one last comment. "No need to take a watch tonight, you two. See you at first light." Then he kept walking, whistling all the while.

7

It was late May, a time on the plains when spring might just jump back to grab a bit of winter's chill or race ahead to the blazing heat of summer, all in the course of a single day. This morning, the sun rose through clear skies, but it failed to light the distant western horizon. A stout wind from the west kept heads down all morning, then calmed in time for the noon respite for water and food. The heat kept folks quiet and slow moving. So when a loud cry came out from among the company, everyone looked up. It was one of the green young prospectors. "Look," the fellow was shouting and pointing toward the west. "It's the mountains!" Folks stretched to see what he saw. "There," he called, "over there. See the white peaks?"

Smith saw them clearly. White foamy clouds lay along the horizon, but the sky below them was so dark, it gave the illusion of mountains. "It's a storm," he said. "Good sized one, too, I'd say. Keep moving."

In the wide, exposed prairie, the wagon train was an easy mark for the weather, and by now Smith had taught them how to prepare. Twice before, huge rain clouds moved in from the west and drenched the wagons inside and out. The wagon bonnet might provide shelter from sun and wind, but it was useless in the rain. Weeks of heat and wind had left most cracked and torn, and even so, once the canvas was soaked the water would puddle on top, and soon the drips inside were as persistent as the rain outside. The tar so carefully applied to the wagon box to make it possible to ford rivers now turned it into a bucket. Blankets, clothing, flour, gun powder, anything left unprotected would be soaked and take days to dry out. And if the storm brought thunder and lightning, it spooked the livestock, making them dangerous if corralled and prone to stampede if not.

Their one advantage was time. Even a fast moving storm could be spotted a full two hours before it hit. They kept their eyes fixed on the gathering clouds. What had first appeared as snow capped peaks became a towering thundercloud, stretching the full horizon. Faint lightning pulsed within the bank, and the sky was near black beneath the clouds' billowy white heads. With another passing hour, they could smell rain. The wind died, and the still air was stifling hot. Then it picked up, blew in cool, then chilly gusts. The clouds changed color. Green, the unmistakable sign of hail.

Suddenly, Henry came riding hard toward Lina and Josephine. "Smith says to start pulling in the wagons. Take the yokes off and let the oxen loose, but keep the horse tied to the wagon. When I get finished down the line, I'll be back to help." Lina tried to hurry the oxen, but they were always slow, and now they, like the horses, had picked up the scent of the storm. She found her place in the formation, then ran back to help Josie, who was at a loss when it came to moving her team in any direction other than forward. With the wagons in place, the two women freed the oxen from their yoke, then jumped in Josie's wagon to try to protect what they could. Then they heard Colonel Granby outside, yelling.

"Herd them in, I tell you!" When Lina look out, she saw he was yelling at Smith. Each was on horseback, but Granby had a long barreled pistol drawn. Smith was collecting the oxen and moving them away from the wagons. Other men on horseback had joined in, and Lina could see Henry was part of that crew. The oxen were moving slowly to the south, away from the wagons. Smith was calling short, sharp directions to the men, ignoring Granby completely.

"Herd them in, God damn you!" Granby moved between Smith and his men, forcing Smith to face him. "I'm ordering you to herd the cattle inside the wagons, man!" Granby shouted one last time.

Smith's face was set like stone, but his voice was full of fire. "Herd those cattle inside the wagons and you'll have a stampede on your hands. I told you these stupid beasts'll run in hail. And while I don't give a good God damn what happens to them, or you, I'll not have these folks and their rigs trampled in the rush. We'll get your God damn cattle back later. Now get out of my way!" He finished his tirade in such a roar that everyone within ear shot, and most particularly Colonel Granby, were left standing, jaws dropped. They had never heard Smith utter so much as a 'no sir' to Granby. Everyone understood Granby was largely a figurehead, but he had never been publicly challenged. Granby looked around at those who had witnessed the scene, and drawing himself up as fully as the squat little man was able, he rode his horse back to his carriage.

The wind blew hard and cold just as the first drops of rain began to fall. Suddenly, Henry was there, getting down from the horse. "Get out of there!" he shouted to the two women.

"But the rain has started, and we haven't…." Lina began to argue.

"To hell with the rain. It's the hail." He lifted them one at a time out of the wagon, almost against their will. With a hand at the back of each waist, he pushed them beneath the wagon, then followed. "Looks bad. If that ice is big enough, it'll rip that bonnet to shreds. Stay here." Henry climbed out from the shelter of the wagon, and then ran off, hollering to the others to hide beneath their wagons, just as the hail began.

Lina could only see the storm build from ground level. The first rain drops were large, hitting the hard, dry earth around them with a dust-muffled thump. She watched the rain collect in little puddles that grew by the second. Then the drops began to bounce, no longer drops at all, but nuggets of hail the size of a spring pea. She heard the icy stones strike the bonnet, louder and louder as they grew from pea to acorn. Faster and faster they fell, until the ground was white with them, like snow in a desert. By the time they were the size of walnuts, the noise was deafening, but Lina could still hear people screaming and the horses squealing.

Under the wagon, the two women clung to each other. Lina kept quiet, but she squeezed Josephine with all her might. Josie tucked her head beneath her friend's arms, trying to block out the sound, and she shrieked every time thunder cracked.

Then came the horrible ripping sound of the wagon bonnets. The hail would open a gash, and the wind would catch the tattered edges and widen the rend. Across the way, Lina could see one wagon where the canvas was gone, and the family that had climbed inside for shelter was now completely exposed to the storm.

As quickly as it had started, the hail stopped. The lightning and thunder faded toward the east, but the rains continued to pour. By now the shelters under the wagons were quagmires. Lina looked down to see her knees and elbows sunk into the mud. She patted Josephine. "It's over. Let's get up before we drown under here."

Despite the continuing rain, folks were beginning to look around. Some were checking on the state of their wagons, others on their animals. But most just stood around in a daze, eyes fixed on the sky and the passing storm above them, or at the ground and the hail at their feet.

As suddenly as the storm itself, Josephine's fear vanished. "Grab the buckets!" she called as she scrambled from beneath the wagon. Lina followed her, but by the time she was out from under, Josie already had both buckets in hand. "Here," said Josie, thrusting one at Lina as she took off. Lina watched as Josephine headed out towards the open prairie. She began to gather the largest chunks of ice into the bucket. Lina suddenly understood. So did many others, or perhaps they had the same idea as Josephine, for soon the prairie was covered with people, mostly women and children, gathering the hail stones like wild fruit. When a bucket was filled, it was returned to the wagon and another was taken, if there was still one available. Otherwise, folks were gathering hail stones in boxes, blankets and hats, in the apron of their skirts, whatever way they could manage. As they harvested the stones, the air was filled with laughter, as everyone scampered to get the best pieces. The hailstorm, for all its havoc, had provided the company with ice water that day, and fresher water than the Platte for several days more.

Finally, even the rain stopped, and the ice remaining on the ground was too small to be gathered. The company regrouped inside the wagon circle, surveying the destruction, and comparing hail stones for size. Smith appeared, and as always, took charge of the situation.

"Well, I guess that does us for today, folks. Men, I know ya got repairs, but we gotta find them oxen. I need every last one of ya that's able to come with me. Ladies, see to yourselves as best you can.

Hopefully, we'll be back 'fore nightfall." Smith started off as the able men scrambled to their horses.

"And the cattle!" The sound of Granby's voice boomed from the middle of the crowd. "You'll damn well bring my cattle back before you do anything else!" Smith turned without a word, but Granby was unrelenting. "I've had enough of your insubordination, Smith. You'll do what you're told or you'll be dismissed."

Lina expected another blow up from Smith. Instead, he merely laughed out loud. "You want them God damn cows so bad, get 'em yourself. We'll get to 'em once we got the oxen." The men rode off.

****

In a fluke of good fortune, the hail proved something of a boon for Lina, who made a tidy sum selling scraps of the muslin she bought in Fort Kearney to be used for patches. A few provisions were lost, a few minor injuries were suffered, but all the cattle and oxen were reclaimed, and the storm was the topic of conversation every night for a week. Folks were beginning to feel as if they had tasted the true west. The west could be a lonely forbidding place, yet it was bigger, broader and livelier than their imaginations had ever dreamed. They were impressed with the enormity of the place, and humbled by its raw power.

But small beauties also caught the eye. One evening she found Greta Olmstead sitting by the fire, writing in a small book, with most of the smaller Olmsteads asleep beneath the wagons around her. Lina sat next to her and whispered, "A letter home?"

Greta shook her head. "My book. I write in it every day."

"Really? What do you write about?"

"What happens each day. Remembrances."

Lina smiled. "I don't think I'd need to keep reminders. I'm not sure I'll ever forget this trip."

"Oh, but you will forget." Greta closed the book and laid it in her lap. "Trust me. I am older than you, and so many things have I forgotten. I wish I could remember more."

"I can't believe you'd want the reminder of…" Lina stopped herself, afraid to put words to the memories, but Greta did not seem afraid. She even smiled as she spoke.

"Oh, I will never forget our dear Herman, nor how we lost him. Nor our dear Harry, and how he came to us. Those are not the memories you lose, Lina. The small moments that make up our lives, that is what we forget. For me, it is how the children are growing. How beautiful this country is. I doubt we will ever come through here again. At least I pray not. But I see God's work all around me, and I want to remember that, too. The way the wind blows across the grasses, the small birds and animals that live here, how pretty the wildflowers look in the morning light." She saw Lina's smile. "You see, you have those memories, too. You should write them down, Lina. You will be grateful someday you did."

While Lina noted with interest the subtleties of nature that Greta had spoken of, what she saw with more interest were the small changes within the company. The group worked together better. Bickering was rare. Folks were more determined than ever to reach their destinations. And if bonds between the families were strong, bonds within the families were stronger. Her own circumstances were a testament to the shift. Lina and her two 'cousins' were becoming close. When she started out, her only thought was to leave Westport with as much as she could, as fast as she could, and to start over somewhere, somehow. Josephine had been the trigger for the enterprise, and Henry simply made it easier. Each made an unspoken pledge to do their part, and that was the sum of her expectations of them. But now the silence of the daily walk was ample opportunity for Lina to consider both Henry and Josephine more fully.

To Lina, Henry Parker was a contradiction. Most times she thought she understood him well enough. *He is just what he seems to be, a boy with wild notions of adventure. Hard to take that too seriously. Still, he's stayed when others would have left.* There were families among the company that had hired single men as hands to help make this trip. Several had abandoned their employers before the trip was barely begun, taking with them the wages they had been paid in advance. Lina realized Henry had no reason to stay with them now that they were well on the road. He could easily have ridden off towards Fort Laramie or any other outpost, to join up with the cavalry. But he stayed.

This much Lina would have said to anyone, even to Henry himself. But she had other thoughts of Henry that only the solitude of the walk would permit. Since that night of the party outside Fort Kearney, Lina felt an attraction to Henry Parker. *He can be a charmer when he wants, with that easy smile of his. The men seem to respect him, and Smith seems to trust him.* Lina didn't know what to make of that. In her experience, charmers were always slick, and altogether unreliable. She had little practice with reliable sorts of men. *Men are either dreamers, charmers, wastrels or bullies.* But she knew she was being unfair to men like Ulmer Olmstead. The fact that there were men like him, too, men who could be sober, faithful and dependable was apparent, even to Lina's skeptical eye.

So with Henry as the object of her supposing, she began to imagine what it might be like to really have a man in her life. Not a weakling like Ephraim, nor a simple dreamer like her father, but a dependable, decent man, like Henry, who treated her well, and fairly. She tried to imagine the Olmsteads as a young, courting couple. She was curious about this partnership between a man and a woman, for that was how she saw the Olmsteads—as partners. *Henry and me, we make a good team when it comes to the work. And I have to say, he's pleasant company after a long day.* For the first time in her life, Lina considered the possibility of marriage as something she might want to do, not something she felt she had to do, as she had with Ephraim.

But I'm not in love with Henry, she reminded herself. She remembered back to the Reeds, the longing and devotion she saw between them. Love made them weak, she decided. Sarah Reed was too weak to keep her husband from a journey they had no business taking on, and Andrew Reed was too weak to finish the journey without her. Lina also supposed, somewhere deep within her, that her own mother must have been weak, too. Why else would a woman follow a hopeless fool like her father? Then she would look at the Olmsteads and wonder if she was right. Perhaps there was another kind of love, a more sensible love, a love more suited to her.

Lina didn't carry the idea of an infatuation with Henry far. Henry was as resolved as ever to follow his dream, and for the first time, Lina found herself starting to dream her own dreams of life out west. She was making a success of her trade, and in the weeks since Fort Kearney, she had earned back nearly half of what she had spent there. She liked the independence her income gave her, and the more success she had, the more she wanted. Still, she could not help but wonder. Sometimes at night, when she and Henry lay on their bedrolls, she found herself wondering about the physical side of a relationship. More than the act, she wondered about the tenderness and, she guessed, the pleasure of it, both of which had been lacking in her brief marriage. There were many questions she wanted to ask Josephine, but she felt too shy and awkward to broach the subject with her.

If Henry was a puzzle to Lina, Josephine was a revelation. Lina remembered how Josie handled Sarah Reed's cholera, and she had to admit Josie was capable, and steady. Lina still found her a curiosity, unlike anyone she had known, and Josephine's motives were a complete mystery to her. But despite all they had been through together, there remained an emotional distance between the two women that Lina couldn't figure out, as if Josephine, like Henry, had been hiding her true self all along.

****

The trail had at last crossed the slow, fetid Platte River, and started heading northwest. The road was imperceptibly rising. The company might not have noticed the rise, but they knew the wagons were loose at the fittings, shrunk by the dry air, beaten by the constant wind. So when the company came to Ash Hollow, they were in for a grueling day. The descent into the hollow was nearly straight down. "Past the perpendicular," Smith had called it. But the reward was great. A good grazing pasture for the livestock, and the first fresh water in weeks.

After a hard, slow day of lowering each wagon down the ridge with painstaking care, the company made camp early. Lina and Henry attended the evening meeting, where Smith was telling tales of the trail ahead, and answering the concerns of the company. Lina felt a tug at her sleeve and turned to find Mrs. Olmstead behind her. She leaned in and whispered in Lina's ear. "Come with me, please. It is Mrs. Frick." Mrs. Olmstead slipped back into the darkness among the wagons toward her own, and Lina followed.

When they were away from the gathering, Lina asked, "Is she ill?"

"It is her time," Greta replied. But her meaning was lost on Lina, until she gave her the sort of knowing, secretive look shared between women. "Her time," she said again. Now Lina understood. Mrs. Frick was about to give birth.

Lina had never been around a woman giving birth, and the sudden realization that Mrs. Olmstead expected her to help paralyzed her. "I know nothing about this!" she pleaded. "Please, isn't there someone else?"

"You will be fine. Just do as I ask. I know everything there is to know." Greta smiled at Lina, and Lina felt relief. *Certainly, if anyone here knows about babies being born, it's a mother of eight.*

"Alright," Lina said. "What do I do?"

"Get any linens you can spare, and bring them to the Frick's wagon." Suddenly, Lina heard a cry followed by a moan coming from the Frick's wagon. Eyes wide, Lina looked quickly at Greta. "Do not worry. Everything is as it should be. Now hurry along." Mrs. Olmstead patted Lina's arm, then went to the Frick's wagon.

Lina climbed into her wagon and began rummaging for linens. There were few, but she thought Josephine might have some. She climbed out and headed to Josie's wagon. She started to crawl inside when she heard a whimper. Josephine was curled up tightly on the little mattress. Lina fumbled in the dark for a match to light the lamp. In the glow, Lina saw the trembling Josephine, holding her hands over her ears and rocking back and forth.

"Josie? Josie?" Lina leaned over her, trying to pull her hands from the side of her head, to make her listen. When she finally looked up at Lina, Josie's eyes were wide with terror.

"Make it stop. Make it stop," Josephine pleaded over and over again in a whisper.

"Make what stop, honey? What is it?"

"Make her stop. Please. I can't bear to hear it."

"What? Oh, you mean Mrs. Frick? Why she's just having her baby, that's all, Josie."

The words Lina had meant as comfort brought a look of panic to Josie's tear-stained face. "I know!" she moaned. "I can't bear to hear it! Make it stop!" Josephine began to sob, softly but uncontrollably.

Outside the tent, Lina could hear Mrs. Olmstead's voice calling. "Lina, hurry!"

Lina was torn. Mrs. Frick would not be kept waiting, but whatever had Josephine so distressed was not to be denied. Lina fretted about leaving her in this condition, and for another moment or two she hesitated. She gathered Josephine in her arms, and held her. "I'll make her stop, honey."

Just then, Henry appeared outside the wagon. "What the hell's goin' on in there?"

"Ssh!" she snapped at him. She searched for a blanket, then laying Josephine back on the mattress, she tucked the blanket about her. Josephine seemed calmer, but her tears persisted. Lina climbed out of the wagon.

"I don't know what's wrong with Josie, but Mrs. Frick over there is having a baby, and Mrs. Olmstead needs me to help. Go tell Smith you can't do your watch tonight, then come back here and see if you can't help Josie. I'll be back as soon as I can." She gave him no time for questions, already running toward the Frick's wagon.

Inside, Mrs. Frick was stretched out on a thin feather tick. Mr. Frick held his wife's head in his lap, so that she was propped up. He held her hand in one of his, and with the other daubed the sweat from her forehead. But he was calm. This was not their first birth. Mrs. Frick was between pains when Lina arrived. Greta took the linens Lina offered, then dunked them in the bucket next to her. "Lina is here now, Mr. Frick. You can see to your other children." Mr. Frick seemed relieved to be asked to leave the wagon, but reluctant to abandon his wife. He squeezed her hand and gave her a soft kiss on the brow before he left. "Lina, hold Mrs. Frick's hand, dear." Lina came to Mr. Frick's place to hold the depleted Mrs. Frick in her lap.

The next few hours were among the most frightening, anxious and thrilling Lina had ever known. She kept her eyes fixed on Mrs. Olmstead, who went about her work calmly and deliberately. Greta Olmstead would chat with Mrs. Frick as if the two were having a polite afternoon visit over tea. With each new contraction, Mrs. Frick would nearly choke on the urge to scream or cry, until she could hold back no more. Greta calmly continued her chatter, occasionally interjecting some little direction. When the spasms were over, Mrs. Frick would join in the conversation as if nothing out of the ordinary were happening.

When the baby finally arrived, it came in a torrent of blood and muck unlike anything Lina had ever seen. Awash in the stuff, the wriggling creature was unrecognizable as a baby. But Mrs. Olmstead picked it up and began wiping it. She ran her finger inside its mouth, and the baby cried. "You have a son!" she told Mrs. Frick, and held the baby up for her to see. Then she laid him on the warmth of his mother's stomach. "Hand me that knife," Greta said to Lina, nodding toward a box to her left. She handed her the knife and watched as Greta Olmstead pinched the cord, then cut it and cleverly wrapped a rag as a bandage around the tiny baby's body. For the first time in hours, Mrs. Frick released Lina's hand and reached for the infant. He was healthy and strong, already crying. Lina looked down on the mother as she held her child for the first time. Mrs. Frick began to cry and laugh simultaneously with assurance at the sight of the baby. They all laughed and cried a little, a sort of communal sigh of relief.

As they walked toward their wagons, Mrs. Olmstead declared, "Well, now you are an experienced midwife!" and she hugged Lina tightly.

"It's a wonder to me, Mrs. Olmstead, that women have babies at all, let alone more than one!"

"And what choice do we have?" she answered, smiling. "It is what it means to be a wife, to have a family. Someday, you will see." She reached to brush a small tear of fatigue and relief from Lina's cheek. "Get some rest now, it is very late." Then she left.

Suddenly, Lina remembered Josephine. She rushed toward the wagon, and found Smith standing beside it. His cold black eyes followed her as she came toward him.

"What are you doing here?" Lina's tone was urgent. The sight of him worried her.

Smith leveled his gaze at her, and said calmly. "I came to see to Miss Josephine. Henry's on watch."

"I asked Henry to look after her!"

"And when I got here, I sent him away. I thought it best."

The evening's work had taken its toll on Lina, and her exhaustion shortened her temper. "You? Who are you to say what's best? This is a family matter!" She was beginning to believe her own lies. Not Smith.

"Ha! Family indeed. Well, if you care to know, your 'cousin' is sleeping fine now. Mostly she just needed a little company, a little distraction." Smith started to leave.

In a softer voice, Lina asked, "What was the matter with her? Why was she so upset?"

"You mean you don't know?" Smith was truly surprised. "Huh. Seems maybe your family ain't as close as you let on. Well, I 'spects if she wants ya to know, she'll tell ya. Good evenin' Miz Clark."

Lina climbed into the darkness of the wagon. She expected Josephine to be asleep, but she wasn't. As soon as she lowered the gate, she heard Josephine speak from the shadows. "Carolina?" It was weak and tired, but there was no more terror in that voice.

"I'm here, honey. You alright?"

"Yes, much better now, thank you."

Lina sat next to where Josie lay. She reached out and fumbled in the dark until she found Josephine's hand, then pressed it gently into hers. "Honey, what was that all about?"

Josephine didn't answer at first, but she let out a long sigh. "Oh, nothing for you to worry about."

Lina was suddenly struck by the notion that Smith understood Josie better than she did, for all the miles they had traveled together. She didn't want to stay at arm's length any more. "Please, honey, you can tell me, really you can."

Another long silence followed. Finally, Josie sat up and faced her, although neither could see the other through the darkness. "The reason I left St. Louis, the reason my father sent me out." Another long silence. "The woman in the wagon. The sounds. The memories came back."

"Oh," Lina said, the veil of comprehension slowly lifting. "Oh, you poor dear." She grabbed Josie and held her tight. She could feel her friend hold her tightly too, and sensed just a trace of a sob before Josephine pulled back. When she finally spoke, her thoughts were small fragments.

"The holy sisters took the baby…It was a little boy…I know it is for the best, still…"

Lina gathered her again, then said, "Well, it's over now. You must try to get some rest. I'm just thankful Smith could be here to keep you company." Lina tucked Josie into her bed, and watched her friend drift to sleep before she left. Then she walked through the quiet camp in search of Smith. She found him standing watch.

"It's Lina Clark, Smith," she said softly so as not to startle him. He gave a quick look over his shoulder toward her, then turned back to stare out into the empty prairie night.

"Everythin' back there to your satisfaction?" he asked sharply.

"Yes, sir. Everything back there is just fine. Thanks to you, I understand." Lina was here hat in hand but Smith gave her no quarter. She pushed on. "I owe you an apology. Whatever you said to Josephine must have been right. She's more peaceful now."

"Didn't say nothin' to her in partic'lar. Didn't have to. Just let her have her cry, say her piece, then tried to keep her mind off her worries."

"I gather you understand what was upsetting her?"

"I do."

"I see."

"No ma'am. You'll forgive me, but I don't think ya do see. She told me you'd be worried about my knowin', but there's no reason for it. Far as I'm concerned, Josephine's a fine lady, none better, and that's all there is to it. Doesn't matter what she's done in the past, or what she plans on doin' in the future. You're too worried about what other folks think."

"But I only asked Josephine to be discreet, careful. It seemed to me the prudent course, given the likes of people like Mrs. Whittier in the company, to say nothing of Colonel Granby."

"Can't you see by now anybody worth their salt's got more to worry 'bout out here than what's in the past? Didn't that baby comin' show you that?"

The silence between them lasted a long time as Lina remembered all she had witnessed that night, and in the weeks before. The memories humbled her. "You're right, Smith, and I thank you for saying so plainly."

Smith finally turned towards her. "You're a fine woman, too, Miz Clark. You're smart and you're hard-workin'. You've got just as much right as any of 'em to come out here, live your life the way you want. Let others do the same." Lina said nothing, but his words ran over and over in her mind as she walked back. And for this night, she pulled her bedroll next to Josie's wagon instead of her own, just in case Josie needed her.

8

"A bunch of folks are talking about riding over to that big rock and climbin' it. Tonight. Under the full moon. Don't that sound fine? Wanna go?"

When Henry asked Lina, she started to say yes. But something was different now between them and she wasn't quite sure what she might be saying yes to. Instead, she offered, "Josie should come with us!" Henry might have argued, but when Lina reminded him that Josie had barely left the wagon in the week since the Frick baby was born, he couldn't say no. But Josie was being her usual obstinate self.

"The fresh air will do you good," Lina tried to reason. "It's invigorating!"

"Fresh air? How silly! I spend all day walking. My constitution can barely stand any more invigoration."

"See, Lina? I told you she wouldn't want to come. Let's you 'n me go."

"It wouldn't be the same without her!" *Please, Josie. Please say yes.*

"Hmm." Josie looked from Lina, to Henry, then Lina again. Lina knew Josie had sized up the situation when she smiled so coyly, but she didn't care. She was too happy when Josie finally said, "Oh, alright."

"Wonderful!" Lina said, but Henry seemed disappointed.

"But I've no proper shoes," Josie said, pulling up the hem of her skirt just enough to show her that weeks of walking had taken their toll on her shoe leather.

"My father's boots!" Within minutes, Lina produced them from the wagon. She handed them to Josephine, though they were easily three sizes too big. Josie held them by the laces and wrinkled her nose, then dropped them.

"I'll not wear those! They're disreputable. Besides, my feet would swim in them."

Lina picked them up again. "We could fill them out with wool socks."

"Then do so," Josie said. "You wear them, Carolina, and I will wear your boots! They're only a bit too big for me. I'm sure I'll be much more comfortable in them."

"Fine!" Lina said. Dropping to the bare ground, she hastily untied the laces, matching Josie's self-satisfied grin with her own frustrated scowl. But she paid her back by insisting Henry take Josephine with him on his horse while she rode alone.

The steep ridge into Ash Hollow a week before had been the first inkling of the changing terrain. The soft, grassy hues of the prairie were now replaced by the warm, bright tones of the earth. The trail had passed through strange outcroppings of rock that stood like distant sentinels. With each passing mile the muscular contours shouldered their way out from the surrounding landscape, looming large in the distance for hours. Like a mirage, they seemed what they were not—castles, ruins, a city built for giants. Earlier travelers had given them names that lived in legend. They had already passed Courthouse Rock and Jail Rock, and today they had finally come in sight of the most famous—Chimney Rock, a single pinnacle of stone jutting from a broad, high mound. The rock lived large in the settlers' imagination, and many an overlander had already explored it.

Now it was their turn, but when they reached it, they realized what it would take to scale the rock. The first third of the mound was rocky but uneven enough to be easily climbed. From there up, the broad base was worn nearly smooth by the wind, and was steeper than it looked. The pinnacle itself was beyond reach. Henry took the lead, pulling Josephine by the hand, then Lina. Henry chided Josie all the time, "Come on, girl, pick up them clod hoppers. Almost there! Too late to go back now." When they reached the spot that was near level, Josie plopped down.

"This is where I stop, Henry Parker! If I'm to go any further, you'll have to carry me!"

Lina sat beside her. "I agree, Henry. Go on ahead if you like, but we're staying here."

"Alright for you, then. But I'm goin'. This has gotta be the grandest view in all creation." Henry headed off toward the pinnacle. Around the base most of the rest of the group were resting, while a few wild boys like Henry tried to make an assault on the summit.

As soon as he was out of earshot, Josie said "I think Henry Parker has an eye for you, Carolina Clark."

Lina laid back against the rock. "Don't be silly," she said, her gaze fixed on the night sky.

"I'm not being silly. I know, better than you, when a man notices a woman. And Henry Parker has definitely noticed you."

"So, what of it?" Lina tried to sound indifferent.

"I think you've noticed him as well, unless I miss my guess. Which only makes me all the more curious. If you fancy him, Lina, and he fancies you, then why bring me along? Unless you were feeling the need for a chaperone." The notion was so silly, Josephine giggled.

Lina sat up quickly, and spoke with certainty. "Henry Parker is a fool, a rounder and a bumpkin. I wouldn't have him if he were the last man left. Besides, he's off to join the cavalry. We're headed to California."

"You're right." He's all of those things. But he's a fine start."

"What on earth do you mean?"

"Well, it seems to me someone like Henry is just what you need, for now. It isn't complicated. You have no experience in matters of the heart. Now you find yourself a little attracted to Henry. He may not be your heart's desire, but he has his charms. But without experience, you run the risk of making the mistake made by so many young women—taking the first man that shows an interest. And that would be a shame, considering you've never even been really kissed before."

"Don't be ridiculous, Josephine. I've been married!"

"It didn't sound like much of a marriage to me. Tell me, have you ever had a kiss that made you feel weak? Light headed?"

"That sounds like the ague to me," Lina snickered.

"My dear, if you confuse what I'm talking about with the ague, then you truly haven't been kissed." Josephine paused. "Well, one has to start somewhere, and Henry Parker would make a fine start. Then, when you find a fellow for whom you have *real* affection, you'll be able to compare."

"I'm not certain I ever intend to go looking for such a person. As far as I've seen, men are far more trouble than they're worth."

"Oh, Lina," Josephine said, laughing. "Trust me. There will come a time when you will find a man who will most definitely be worth the trouble, and you'd best be ready for him, lest the chance pass you by."

Just then, Henry returned. His shirt was torn, and his face was scratched and dirty. "Damn," he said as he sat down between them. "That rock is a pisser. Ain't no way up that I can see, leastways not in the dark. Oh, well, it's still a hell of a view, ain't it?"

"It seems a lot of fuss to come sit out here in the dark," Josephine said. "From now on, you two can make these little excursions by yourselves."

"Well, that's an intriguin' proposition, I must say." Henry grinned at Lina, and Josephine smiled. But Lina was not amused.

"It's getting late," she said abruptly. "Let's get back." She headed off down the rock, stubbornly determined to make her own way down, and leaving Henry to help Josephine down by himself.

****

The next two days saw them through Mitchell Pass and beyond. The pass was bumpy and narrow, and the bluff to the north was the highest formation they had yet seen. Its crest was crowned with green grass and cedars, like a perfect, unreachable oasis. That spot held a particular fascination for Lina. *What might it be like*, she wondered, *to sit on that spot? What would you see that you can't see from this tiresome trail? Perhaps whole herds of buffalo, or the great mountains ahead. What else might there be that I cannot even imagine?* She heard Mrs. Whittier one evening speak of the land as possessing all God's terrible might, and that folks should feel meek and humbled by it. But where others felt small and lonely in this broad sweep of land, Lina felt large and strong, as if her own spirit was rising to fill the emptiness. To some, each change in the land was another reason to question their reasons for coming, but for her, the challenges of the land spoke of the possibilities before her.

It had been more than a month since Fort Kearney, and everyone was eager to complete another milestone. But Smith judge Fort Laramie still a week away.

Henry's energy couldn't be contained. He seemed to sense his destiny just ahead like the horses had sensed the coming storm. There would come a time when the party knew the night's camp was just ahead, no more than an hour. In that moment, the sun is low, its heat fading but its brilliance growing. Shadows grow long and the winds die. It was at this golden hour that Henry would abruptly ride toward the west. One minute he would be riding slowly along with the wagons. The next he would take off at a gallop. He would ride out to where he was barely a dot in the distance, and just sit there on horseback, staring. Then she usually heard a shot, and here he would come, just as fast as he had left, game for dinner tossed across his saddle, and a peaceful smile across his face.

This afternoon, Lina was watching him, waiting for him to go. There was a tension in his body in the saddle, a focus to his gaze that told her it was time. She pulled her wagon out of line, then ran to find Josie. "I'm going hunting with Henry. Wait here or follow the others. We'll catch up in an hour."

Lina ran toward Henry, hollering and waving. "What's gotten into you?" he asked.

She smiled up at him, and held out her hand. "Take me with you," was all she said, and all she needed to say. With a smile he offered her his hand, and with one strong pull, she was behind Henry in the saddle.

"Hold on," he hollered back to her, and she had just enough time to throw her arms around him before they were off. After weeks of a wearisome pace, she felt like they were flying. Her heavy braid drummed her back with the sprinting horse's rhythm. Suddenly the horse stopped, and Henry jumped from the saddle. He held his hands out to help her down. They walked to a short rise just above where a thin stream washed out the grasses. The whole of the prairie stretched before them, and the light of the setting sun washed their faces. "This is what I come out here for, Lina. The hunting's just an excuse. I come out here to see this sight. Reminds me why I come west." He paused. "After a long day, when it feels like we're never gonna get anywhere, I come out here. It feels like the whole God damn place belongs to me, ya know? I get ta thinkin' 'bout what it's gonna be like, ridin' all over, findin' adventure, seein' everything there is to see."

After a long silence between them, Henry finally spoke. "Well, Lina? How 'bout you? Figured it out yet?"

"Figured out what?"

"Remember? Back when we was at Kearney, I asked you what you see for yourself out here. Have you figured what you want?"

She considered her answer a long time. "I guess I don't know yet, Henry. Not all of it. I do know I want my own life, made from what I do with it, not just something that happens because I was too weak or lazy to get out of the way."

"Well, that's a start. And I 'spect whatever it turns out to be, you'll do a bang-up job of it." Henry seemed about to say more, then stopped. He looked around the prairie again. "Sure is a big place."

"Sure is," she answered softly. She knew he was looking at her again. She was afraid to look back.

"Lina," he said softly. "Didja ever think 'bout maybe goin' to Oregon, instead of California?"

She chuckled. "Whatever would I do in Oregon?"

"Oh, I don't know. Maybe find a fella. Settle down to some farmin', raise a family."

She looked into his eyes. "I'm not the farming type, Henry. As to the rest? Sure, I've thought of it. It's just that I can't see it. I try to imagine myself like those families back there. And I just can't see myself like them, a passel of kids, digging out some kind of hard scrabble life."

"Yeah, you're right. I think about it, too. I see them families, and sometimes they look so cozy, like squirrels in a tree. And I think, hell, why not? But then I ride out here and look at this country, and I can't say as I'm ready to settle down yet." Henry looked at her again. "But then sometimes I look at you, and I think…."

Lina stopped him. "Henry, you've got your dreams and you've waited a long time for them. You deserve them. Me, I'm just putting my dream together. I'm not ready to give up on that yet." Lina slipped her hand into his. "But I thank you for thinking of me," she smiled. As the sun first touched the horizon, they mounted the horse again and returned to the wagons.

****

"Here we are, in a country where men outnumber women two to one, and still you manage to avoid them. Absolutely astonishing." Josephine had been all curiosity about Lina and Henry's evening ride, but Lina wouldn't take the bait. Finally, on the particular subject of Lina and Henry, Josie fell silent. But on the more general topic of Lina's attitudes toward men, Josie was relentless. Lina felt as though she had opened a hornet's nest when she allowed the discussion with Josie about men. Now Josie never tired of it. Lina tried ignoring her. But this evening she was having no luck moving Josephine from her target.

"It escapes my understanding why you should be concerned with finding me a man."

"Lina, before we left, you warned me of what I'd have to know to get by on this trip, like handling a gun and driving the team. I'm simply returning the favor. Just think of men as snakes."

"I already do," Lina laughed.

"No! What I mean is, one should know what to do in case of snakebite, but the very best kind of advice is the kind which teaches you how to avoid being bitten in the first place."

Josie was beginning to catch Lina's interest. "It seems to me the best way to avoid being bitten by a snake is to never go near one. Which is my policy."

"You can tell yourself that, Carolina, but trust me, you *will* go near them. Someday, there will be a man you'll be drawn to. And I'm here to make certain you know it's the proper sort of man, one who suits you. For example, stay away from weak men, and I tell you that in case your marriage didn't teach you enough. Weak men are drawn to strong women like us. The woman is always the loser."

"And what is the *proper* sort?"

"Strong, obviously. Strong enough to tolerate your independence. And someone sure of himself, who knows his own mind. But not a tyrant. Smart, of course. Not just smart, but clever and industrious. And of course, wealthy is always nice, but wealth can be earned. The other attributes are born."

"And where do I find such a man?"

"Anywhere and everywhere. It's not so much the where as the how. Keeping your head about you, observing them closely, learning how to talk with them, how to flirt with them. The best hunters are those who know their quarry well."

"I do watch them, Josie, and I seldom see the strong ones you talk about. For the most part I see little about them to admire. If they're not lazy, then their ambitions are totally misdirected. Look at the fools in this company. Heading out west where they think they can grab some easy riches. That's a bad mix, sloth and greed. Then there're those who womanize or drink or cheat or run away. And what's left over is just too dull for words."

"Your expectations are high. But how will you ever find this man if you don't make yourself more available. Men aren't like women, Lina. A man would never say he wants a dependable, solid woman. Oh, he may *want* one, but he'd never *think* he wants one. Men believe they want a coquette, a challenge, someone whose attentions flatter them. No matter if he's country boy or city gentleman. They're all moths to a flame. As a flame, I say the fancier you are, the more moths from which to choose."

"Well, there you have it. I'm no fancy flame, that's for certain."

"You may not be fancy, but that's just a matter of a few touches. You're plenty pretty. You simply don't think of yourself as pretty."

"No, I don't."

"I suggest you start."

"Thinking doesn't make it so, Josephine."

"Sometimes it does. If you'd put a little effort into your appearance, then perhaps you'd think of yourself as more attractive. As it is, just look at yourself! It's been weeks since I've seen you in a dress. You wear those pants of your father's, that dreadful hat, and your hair! That hair could be your fortune, dear. Such a color! I've never seen anything like it. So thick, and the natural curls. What I wouldn't give for them. But you do nothing to show them off."

Lina looked down at her clothes. She believed she had achieved a mastery of comfort and practicality for travel. She abandoned skirts when she had tired of having them dragged through mud and thorns. Pants were more sensible. The hair was a matter of convenience. It took time to put it up as Josie had done with hers. Braiding it and tying it off kept it out of the way.

Josie continued. "Let me have a try at your hair." Lina held up a hand in protest, but Josie grabbed her fingers and held them gently. "Come on, dearest, where's the harm?"

"Very well. If this will satisfy your urge and shut you up, let's have it. But none of those silly twists and rolls. Something simple, something manageable."

"Don't give it another thought," said the delighted Josephine. She threw herself into the work. She would grab some hair and hold it up on top of Lina's head, this way first, then that, looking over Lina's shoulder into the mirror before them, squinting her eyes. At last, she began. Josie gathered a few chosen strands from the crown of Lina's head, and began to weave them. Lina kept moving her head side to side, trying to steal a glance. "Hold still, silly, unless you want a crooked braid." Josie gave the hair in her hand a quick tug.

"Ouch," Lina cried. Then she tried touching the braid to get a sense of it, but was met with a slap from Josie's brush.

"Not until it's finished!"

"Hurry up, then." Despite her initial misgivings, Lina was anxious to see the results. "Besides, I told you nothing fancy. Nothing I can't take care of myself."

"Oh, poo. So what if you can't do this yourself. I'm here to help you, aren't I?"

Once the braid moved to the length of hair down Lina's back, Josie's delicate fingers flew through the weaving. She was nearly at the bottom. "Hand me that ribbon. That one, there, the green one." With a quick flip, a few tucks and a finish to the bow, Josie placed her hands on Lina's shoulders and looked down to admire her handiwork. "There! Now that's a thing of beauty!"

Instinctively, Lina reached her hand to the back of her head. "Don't pull at it," said Josie. "If you're careful, it could last several days. Here, let me show you."

Josephine took the large hand mirror and held it behind Lina. Lina took a smaller mirror, and with the two reflections, was able to see the back of her head. "Oh, my!" She could scarcely believe she was looking at herself. Josephine had fashioned an elaborate series of braids which pulled Lina's hair up and over her ears, toward the back of her neck.

At the nape of the neck, all the braids became one long twist down her back.

"You're pleased and surprised, I can tell. Perhaps from now on you'll take my advice." Lina kept staring at this unfamiliar reflection in the mirror. Her face was brown and freckled from days in the sun, and she knew she was dirty from the trail. Still, she had to admit, it was a pleasing face, and quite possibly a pretty face.

Lina looked into the mirror at Josie. "Thank you," she said simply.

Josie squeezed her shoulders. "Don't mention it, honey. Someday, this beautiful hair of yours will catch the eye of a special man. And when it does, you can thank me then."

9

Broken wagons, broken bodies or broken spirits—the journey was taking its toll on everyone. They questioned decisions, challenged authority, made unreasonable demands. Some wanted to rest, others argued for speeding up the pace. All that united them now was their impatience to arrive safely at Fort Laramie, and soon. Lina was the only one who dreaded reaching the fort. Henry would stay there, and Lina and Josephine would be on their own.

Henry had talked of little else for days. This night he was captivated by the fine regimental jacket he would soon be sporting, with its fancy yellow braid. "Yellow," he told them, over and over, "that's the color of the cavalry. Probably get a new rifle, too," he'd said. He droned on so that finally Lina snapped at him.

"Henry Parker, I don't want to hear another word about the cavalry. We'll be at Fort Laramie tomorrow, but for one last night, they'll be no more talk of it!"

They had a plan to ride together to the fort, under the guise that Lina might need his help loading supplies. But Henry was going in to enlist. This might be their last chance to ride together. *Last chance.* The words kept running through her mind. But when she awoke that morning, Henry was already up and gone. She looked around for any sign of him, but he had taken his bedroll, the razor he kept tucked in a corner of her wagon, everything. Her heart sank. She dressed as fast as she could hoping to catch up with him. Then she saw him, standing by the Olmstead's wagon talking to Frank, his horse saddled and ready beside him. She led her mare over to them.

"I thought you went off and left me," she said, her heart still pounding.

"Not yet, I ain't." He looked at her and said, "What's got you so worked up this morning?"

"Wanted to get a jump on those other folks at the post store, that's all."

"If you say so," Henry chuckled. "Well, Lina, what say we go see this fort." He jumped on his horse and took off like a shot, but not so fast that Lina couldn't catch him.

Fort Laramie was a real cavalry post, not as raw and new as Fort Kearney. It had a more orderly look to it. There were frame buildings and a parade ground in the center. Soldiers were everywhere, and Indians too, and settlers milling about among them.

"Will you be going to enlist right away?" Lina asked quietly.

"I reckon so. No point in puttin' it off." When Henry saw the look in her eyes, he added, "Tell ya what, I'll go to the command office and find out the reg'lations and routines. You go check out the store. I'll meet ya back here in an hour or so."

Lina went to the store, but it took only a moment to see there was no need to stay. Just like Fort Kearney, everyone was trying to sell what they had, so they could buy what they needed. Only now they were even more desperate. For Lina this was a mixed blessing. If her customers couldn't afford Army prices, that left the market to her. But it would be a market without cash, and she had no more use for castoff family heirlooms than the Army.

When she left, she went to wait for Henry. She didn't know how long it would take him to enlist, and she didn't want him wandering off without her. There, directly in front of the building, was Granby's coach, with Bartolomé standing beside it. But no sign of Granby. A constant stream of soldiers flowed in and out between the parade grounds and the main door, which stood open. That seemed enough of an invitation to her to go inside. It looked cool and lovely inside the dark hallway, away from the high morning sun. She smiled and nodded at Bartolomé as she entered, but he seemed not to notice.

She stood in a long hallway that ran from the building's front to its back, where another set of doors also stood open, creating a nice breeze through the corridor. On either side of the hall were two closed doors.

Though she could hear muffled voices behind them, she had no idea which room Henry was in, but the Army had been kind enough to put a bench in the hallway, so she sat down to wait.

Slowly she became aware that she could hear bits of the conversation in the office next to her. And she most certainly recognized one of the voices as Granby's. He was laughing, and the other man, whom she presumed to be the post commander, was laughing too. A young soldier came through the main door and headed straight for the door next to her. He entered, but left the door open so now Lina had no trouble hearing the conversation.

The young soldier said, "Sir?"

The unfamiliar voice said, "Sims, report back here with a detail at 1300 hours. You'll be heading out to pick up the cattle Colonel Granby has sold us."

"Begging your pardon sir? How many? I mean, how many men will I need?"

"Eight."

"Yes, sir." Then he left, closing the door behind him.

The smell of cigar smoke followed the soldier out of the room, and lingered in the hall. Lina heard more laughing, and the clink of glasses. She jumped up, and almost barged into the office, when suddenly Henry appeared through another door.

"Lina! I thought you were goin' to wait…"

"Ssh!" She grabbed him by the arm. "Be quiet. We've got to talk." She dragged him outside to where the horses were tied.

"Ouch! Let go my arm. Damn, what's got you so riled up?"

"Just answer me something, Henry. How many men does it take to mind the cattle herd, Granby's herd."

"Six, eight."

"Damn! I knew it! That sonofabitch."

"Who?"

"Granby. I was waiting for you in there, when I heard Granby in the commander's office."

"Major Anderson's his name."

"Fine. Major Anderson's office, then. A soldier went in and the major ordered him to take a detail out to bring in the cattle Granby just sold him. He didn't say how many head, but he did say the man would need eight men. That must mean he sold them all our cattle!"

"Lina, that can't be right. If Granby sold the Army all them cattle, that don't leave none for the company."

"That's right Henry. And since he said those cattle were part of what we paid for when we joined on, then he's stealing from the company."

"Then we should tell the Major. Can't imagine the Army'd wanna be buyin' stolen cattle."

"Hmm. Maybe…. I hate to take a chance on what the Army's priorities might be. That many cattle would feed a lot of soldiers, and since they're the only law around here, if they decide to keep 'em, we're sunk. Think, Henry! What can we do?"

Henry scratched his chin. "Hmm. Depends. How much time you think we got?"

"I don't know," Lina said. Then she looked up and saw Bartolomé and the carriage. "But maybe he does."

She put forth a big smile and walked toward the carriage. "Good morning, Bartolomé. Lovely day," she said. Bartolomé only gave her a quick nod. No smile, no glance.

"I was wondering if I might ask a favor."

Bartolomé looked puzzled. "A favor, miss? Of me?"

"Yes, Bartolomé. You see, when I came in this morning I didn't think I'd be buying anything from the sutler's store. But as it turns out, I did find a good deal on some…" she tried to think of something plausible. "Some beans. And since I didn't bring our wagon with me, I was wondering if I could impose upon you to take the sacks back to camp for me?"

Bartolomé looked flustered. He kept looking over his shoulder toward the building. "I..I..I don't know miss. You would have to ask Colonel Granby, miss."

"Of course. And I will, but could you just tell me what time you expect to head back to camp?"

Now the man was more agitated than before. "The Colonel said we wouldn't be heading back to camp. He told me this morning we would be heading east when we left the fort."

"Thank you, Bartolomé." She went back to Henry, who had heard the whole exchange.

"Well if that don't tear it!" Henry shook his head. "Okay. Here's what we do. Stay here, and if I don't make it back in time, do what you need to, but don't let Granby leave the fort if you can help it."

"Where are you going?"

"To find Smith," he answered as he jumped on his horse. Then Henry was gone in a cloud of dust.

****

Lina stood outside in the heat and the dust, trying to keep an eye out for any sign of activity from the major's office, and on Bartolomé and the coach. But with each passing minute, she spent more time looking over her shoulder toward the gates to the fort, hoping Henry would return with Smith. She didn't know what they would do at that point, but having Smith here would make her feel better. And she certainly didn't know what she would do if Granby tried to leave before Smith and Henry returned. The image of throwing herself in front of his coach kept coming to her, as ridiculous as that notion was.

She never had to find out. She heard the sound of a wagon, and here came Henry, Smith and Frank Olmstead on horseback, ahead of Ulmer Olmstead in his wagon. And sitting next to Ulmer was the unexpected figure of Mrs. Whittier. The men's faces were hard but calm. But Mrs. Whittier looked fit to be tied.

As they tied the horses, Lina came up to Smith. "What are you going to do?"

"Let me handle it. Come along if you like." With a long, certain stride he walked toward the major's office, the rest following close behind.

He knocked but did not wait for a response. He opened the door. Granby was still sitting across the desk from Major Anderson, glass in one hand, cigar in the other. Smith didn't pay him any attention. "Major," Smith said. He walked toward Anderson, hand extended.

"Why, Smith!" said the Major, shaking his hand vigorously. "Good to see you, man. How long has it been?"

"Major, we need to speak to you about a matter concerning this man," he said, with a quick nod towards Granby.

Granby interrupted. "Major Anderson, this man works for me." Then he leaned in close to Smith, and whispered, "Smith, whatever this is, let's go outside and settle this between ourselves. Like gentlemen."

Smith ignored Granby, except for the quick look of disgust he gave him. Major Anderson looked at Smith, then Granby. Granby seemed uneasy, as if he might bolt any minute. "Very well, Smith. Come in. Everyone, come in."

"Major, I don't have time to listen to these people's complaints. I have other business to conclude. If you'll excuse me…," and Granby started to walk away.

"I will not excuse you," said the Major. "You have business with the United States Army, sir, and if you want that business completed, you'll stay and let these folks air their concerns. Besides, Granby, you seem awfully quick to dismiss their request. That in itself makes me curious." Granby stood for a moment, hesitating. But the Major would not be denied. "Sir, I insist."

Granby sat back in the chair. "Now, sir," said the Major, addressing Smith, "what is this matter you wish to discuss?"

"It has come to these folk's attention, Major, that Granby here has just sold you some cattle."

"That's right, Smith. One hundred head, I believe, though we'll see the final tally when my detail brings them in this afternoon."

"Major, you should know those cattle belong to the members of the company."

The Major looked surprised. "Granby, is this correct?"

Granby shook his head and grinned smugly at the company. "Read your agreements. Nowhere in that contract does it award ownership of the herd to you."

"You said the cattle would be there for us," Ulmer Olmstead spoke up. "All the way to Oregon, you said. Now you are going back east, and leaving the cattle here. You lied to us."

"Back east? How did you know…"

Mrs. Whittier pointed out the window toward Bartolomé and the carriage. "That's what your *slave* out there told Mrs. Clark!" She spat the out the word like poison in her mouth.

Major Anderson looked outside at the man, then turned to Granby. "Slave? What is she talking about, Granby? Am I to understand you're transporting a slave?"

"Damn him!" Granby sputtered. "I'll teach him to..." Then he looked around the room. All eyes were fixed on him. He turned suddenly cool.

"Think what you like everyone, but the matter is concluded. Regardless of what you thought, the cattle were mine. Now they're the Army's. And yes, I'm headed east. You've made it this far, I'm sure you can make it the rest of the way." He took a long puff from his cigar. "Oh, and Smith? Your services are no longer needed."

"Well, that's the funny part," said Smith, who by now was grinning from ear to ear. "Seems a peculiar thing happened this mornin'. Mosta that herd wandered off, all but about twenty or so. Ain't a single sign of 'em anywhere."

"What!" bellowed Granby. "Why you stupid... Oh, I see. Wandered off, did they? Well, then, the Major will have his detail go find them!"

Major Anderson was smiling as broadly as Smith. "I'm afraid I can't do that. I suggest you read *your* contract with the Army, Colonel. It calls for the delivery of the cattle. If I have to send a detail on a cattle drive, they've hardly been delivered, have they?" Anderson laughed.

Granby turned beet red. "Then I demand you pay me for the twenty cattle that haven't 'wandered away!'"

Major Anderson stopped laughing. He leaned across the desk and looked Granby squarely in the eye. He spoke in the practiced tone of a military commander. "No. You aren't going to get that money. You're going to get in that buggy, without that Negro out there, and you're going to head back east before I have you thrown in the stockade."

Granby stood. "You're going to deny me of my property? By what right? There are no laws within this territory or this post that prohibit me from owning a slave."

"There are no laws sanctioning it either. And as far as that goes, this command *is* the law of this territory." Anderson looked at Granby, then said, "Sir, I come from abolitionist stock. I can't abide the notion of slavery. And as long as I'm in command here, I won't sanction it. You won't be allowed to leave here with the Negro, Granby."

Granby was still in a rage. "Incomprehensible!" he sputtered. "I'm to be deprived of my assets without adjudication or recompense. I'll be discussing this with your superiors in Washington upon my return, Major. You may count on it!"

"That is your prerogative, sir. Now, I believe this concludes our business. Leave this fort immediately before I decide to charge you with defrauding the United States Army." Granby threw a hot glance at the Major, and at Smith, then threw down his cigar and stormed out. Through the window they watched the exchange between Granby and Bartolomé. Granby threw a bundle on the ground at his feet. He was yelling at Bartolomé, but no one could hear what he said. Bartolomé looked confused, and seemed to be pleading as Granby climbed into the driver's seat that had always been his. As Granby drove off, Bartolomé reached down and picked up the bundle, then just stood there.

Major Anderson turned to Smith. "Will you ask that man to come in here, please?"

The man Smith brought into the Major's office acted lost and frightened. His head was down and he looked at no one.

"Mr. Bartolomé, Colonel Granby has just relinquished any claim he has on you. You're free to go."

Bartolomé looked at the Major meekly. "I do not understand, sir. I was supposed to drive…"

"Yes, but that's all changed. You are free to go." Anderson smiled. "You are free."

"Free to go where, sir? Where would you like me to go?"

"Anywhere you want," Anderson said.

Bartolomé looked at Smith, at each of them, hoping someone would give him instruction.

"Come with us," Lina said. "He can come with us, can't he?" she looked to Smith.

"I guess he can if'n he wants to. You want to, Bart?" Smith knew the man better than anyone there, and Bartolomé seemed to recognize something of a friend in him. "You could go to California, maybe. Or Oregon. How 'bout it?"

"He's got no wagon, no provisions, nothin'" Henry said. "How's he gonna get by?"

"I tell you what, Smith." Major Anderson reached inside his desk. "If there are any cattle you'd be willing to sell out of the company's herd, the Army will buy them, on one condition. You give the money to this man so he can have a proper start. Why, I'll even throw in a wagon and team." He took a slip of paper from his drawer and scratched a note on it. Then he looked at Henry. "I hear you're a new recruit. That right, son?"

Henry gave his first official salute. "Yes, sir, Major. Henry Parker. Joinin' up tomorrow."

"Well, permit me to press you into service a bit early. Take this over to the sutler's, and he'll see Mr. Bartolomé gets everything he needs." He turned to the assembly. "I'm sorry for the misunderstanding, folks. Let me know if there's anything the Army can do for you before you leave tomorrow. Good luck," he said, then turning to Bartolomé, he added, "Good luck to all of you."

****

Smith had stayed behind at the Fort. He said he had some business of his own to attend to. The business didn't take him long, for they were barely on the road back to camp when he came riding up behind them, the Olmsted wagon in the lead, then Bartolomé and his Army surplus rig, then Lina and Henry on horseback.

"Are we still leaving tomorrow?" Lina asked.

"You are. I ain't."

"What do you mean?"

"You heard. I don't work for Granby anymore. Truth is, he ain't yet paid me a nickel." He roared with laughter, adding "He sure as hell ain't gonna pay me now! Like I give a tinker's damn."

"But what about us?" Lina was frantic. She knew she was acting selfishly, but she didn't give a tinker's damn either. Henry was leaving her, and now Smith, too. Soon, it would be the Olmsteads. And the worst of the trip was still ahead of them.

Smith took a plug of tobacco from his pocket, and biting some off, he chewed slowly. "That's what I was doin'. I talked to Anderson. That's what the gov'ment put these soldiers out here for—to give folks safe passage. He said he'd put together a detail to get you as far as the trail splits. But after that, you'll have to figure it out on your own." He spit, then wiped the tobacco juice from his beard with his sleeve.

"Figure it out on our own?" Lina said quietly.

"There's more. I made sure Anderson put his best men to the job. That's why Private Henry Parker, here, he's been assigned to that detail."

"Oh, that's wonderful!" She looked to Henry, who was beaming. That was all it took. Lina's spirits buoyed as fast as her heart had sunk a moment ago. A small reprieve, a little while longer to consider how they would manage without him, that was all they would need, she told herself.

"Thanks," Henry said to Smith. "I won't let you down."

"But what about you?" Lina asked. "Will you go back to Westport?"

Smith chewed, then spit again. "I got me an Indian woman in the Bitteroots probably wonders where I been. Think I'll go pay her a call."

"What about him?" Henry said, nodding toward Bartolomé in the wagon ahead of them.

"Don't know. He'll have to make his way same as everybody else. Maybe you could keep an eye on him." Then Smith rode on ahead.

The company decided a little merriment was called for to send Smith on his way. Lina didn't join in. The sound of the fiddles and folks clapping and laughing did make her feel better. Despite the accommodations Smith had made for them, she still felt uneasy, but if the whole camp had shared her mood, she would be despondent. So she appreciated that others were having a good time, even if she wasn't quite up to it herself.

Josie and Henry had gone with her blessing. She sat quietly by the fire drinking cold coffee and looking at the stars, trying to solve a problem she didn't yet have—what they would do once they reached Fort Bridger and lost Henry for good. Slowly, a strange and delicious scent wafted by her. Everyone had long since finished supper. *What could this be?* She looked around and saw the flicker of a campfire just beyond the edge of camp. As she walked toward it she could see Bartolomé crouched beside the fire, stirring something in a pot.

Bartolomé. Here was another matter weighing on her thoughts. He was the unintended victim of the overthrow of Granby. Until today, she supposed that a slave who was freed would be happy. But since Major Anderson had declared him free, he looked as worried and frightened as she felt. What would he do? What *could* he do? Lina realized she was partly to blame, if blame there was. Of course Henry had relayed her conversation with Bartolomé to Smith and the others. And of course Mrs. Whittier, ardent abolitionist that she was, would use the opportunity to bring the matter up with the Major. But Lina knew she needn't have involved the poor man at all, much less lied to him to get information.

Now here he was, in a company where most of the people would want nothing to do with him, and more than a few would hate him or fear him. He was stuck with them, and they were stuck with him. But he was the friendless one.

"Good evening," she said as she approached the fire. Immediately he stood up, almost at attention. "Please, don't mind me," she said. She sat down across the fire from him. It was one thing to try to be friendly with him, but the truth was that Lina wasn't sure how to speak to him. He, of course, didn't speak at all. He was still stirring the pot, but she could tell he was nervous.

"What are you cooking?" she asked. He looked up. "It smells wonderful, not like anything I've ever smelled before."

That brought a smile to his face. "Would you like to taste, miss?"

She came closer and took a small taste. "Why, this is just beans! But oh, the taste! It's sweet, and, oh a little hot, too!" she laughed. "How did you make that?"

"I'm glad you like it." He dipped in and ate straight from the spoon. He took a second scoop and offered it to Lina. "No, thank you," she said. "I've had my supper."

He ate slowly. Through the silence, occasionally one of them would smile at the other. Every time she thought of something to say it raised an awkward question. She settled on something easy.

"So, where were you born?"

"In the West Indies, miss."

"Had you been with Granby long?"

"He brought me to this country ten years ago. Before that, my family had always worked in the plantation houses."

Here was her chance to have the discussion she had been avoiding. "So, maybe you would like to go back there? I mean, if your people are there."

Bartolomé considered the question a long time. "I don't know if they would still be there, miss. Someone may have bought them."

"Hmm." Of course, she thought, feeling utterly lost at this. "Well, perhaps you could go to California. They say there are a lot rich men there. Maybe they could afford a cook as wonderful as you."

"Really, miss? Someone there might want me?"

"Someone there might want to *hire* you, yes. And until then, why when Mrs. Olmstead and Mrs. Frick and the others find out what a good cook you are, I won't be at all surprised if they aren't over here begging you for your recipes." All this effort to keep the conversation cheery was wearing her out, and she wasn't getting done what she needed to do.

"Listen, Bartolomé...I heard Smith call you Bart. May I call you Bart? Good. I know you've been thrown into this without your say so. And I know I had something to do with it, and I'm sorry. But here we are. I just want you to know that Josie and me, well, we'd be pleased if you felt you could come to us for anything you might need. I'll do what I can, and if I can't, well, we'll try to figure it out together. Okay?"

"Yes, miss." He seemed pleased and surprised, but cautious.

"And I wasn't fooling about California, either. You know you're free to do as you like, and you should think about it. But that's where we're headed, if that makes a difference."

"Thank you, miss."

"Goodnight, then." She walked away at first feeling more than pleased with herself. Then she was reminded of her own worries and uncertain plans, and she hoped she wasn't leading one more innocent soul down the primrose path.

She climbed straight into her bedroll beneath her wagon, hoping it would not take long to fall asleep. She could still hear music and laughing nearby, and Henry wasn't back, so the party must still be in full swing. She was nestled in when she heard two voices. The high one was most certainly Josephine's, the low one somehow familiar, but indistinguishable. She opened her eyes just in time to see a broad male backside crawling out of Josie's wagon. It was Smith. Then Josephine leaned out, clutching a blanket around her.

Then Lina heard Smith say, "Goodbye, darlin'. Take care of yourself." He leaned forward as Josie leaned down, and the kiss they shared was full and deep and long, and made Lina blush. Then he rode off.

****

"Has anyone seen Smith this morning?" Frank Olmstead was at their fire early, with a request from his mother for more eggs.

Lina spoke up. "He's left," she said. "I saw him ride out late last night." She looked at Josephine, who stared back, suddenly aware of what her friend must know. Lina would have sworn she finally saw Josie blush.

"Too bad," said Frank. "We had some news. Last night we all got together and chose Pa to lead the company. He's sort of senior man here. Sorry you weren't there, Mrs. Clark, to vote. Hope that's okay with you."

"Of course, Frank. That's wonderful news!"

"But that wasn't what we wanted to tell Smith. We voted on a new name for the company. 'Smith's Sojourners.' We're gonna paint it on our wagon now that we're going to be in the lead. Well, the Army will be in the lead, I guess. But there it'll be."

"That's a wonderful idea," said Lina. "I think he would have been pleased. Wouldn't he, Josephine?" She gave Josie a quick wink.

"I'm certain he would," said Josie, smiling. Nothing more about Smith was mentioned between them for a long time.

10

The road was moving upward now, not into the mountains, but between them, like a snake in the sun, a long, curve across a broad, faceless plain.

The company was tired. Tired of the drudgery, the sacrifices, the worry and the wondering. Most of all, tired of one another. What weeks ago had seemed a lark was now an endless struggle with the natural forces that gave life to this formidable country. But nature couldn't be argued with, persuaded or defied, so they bickered among themselves. They were lucky to have chosen Ulmer Olmstead to lead them. He was a stern but fair-minded father to the company. He preferred people to resolve matters on their own, but was not timid about getting in the middle when called for, and he was in the middle more and more.

Lina tried to stay out of the fray, but it was impossible. With the trade she relied upon, there were always disputes. As she predicted, cash was scarce and folks wanted to trade for what she could provide. No one seemed happy with any deal she struck. Some had accused her of gouging, or shorting orders. Others had quite simply refused to deal with her, suggesting openly that, rather than profiteer, she should provide goods at no charge to those in real need.

"And will you be giving your crops away, once you reach the Willamette? Or the gold you expect to find, will you ask less than a fair price?" This was her response, and to her good fortune, Ulmer Olmstead openly supported her in these disputes, but privately he cautioned her.

"Remember," he had said, "these people are your only friends here. It is best not to provoke them." Because of her respect for him, she took his advice to heart, and tried to strike a balance in her dealings, and mostly, when it came to some of the more contrary members, she learned just to bite her lip rather than speak.

There was also the business of Bartolomé. As she guessed, only a few people spoke to him at all. Mrs. Whittier came by to convert him, but discovering his was already a believer, she had no further use for him. Josephine's aristocratic upbringing found the news that they would be "looking out for him," as Lina told her, an appalling notion. Then he cooked for her, and Josie said no more about the matter. Henry had also disapproved of Bartolomé traveling with them. But he acquiesced when she told him Frank Olmstead had agreed to teach Bart how to handle a rifle. She played on Henry's guilt, and reminded him that once they parted, she and Josie would need the help.

Lina had seen Henry only twice since they left Fort Laramie. She wasn't sure she liked the Henry she saw now. He was very taken with his new position with the Army, and his new role as guide. But he did little guiding. He was simply one of many soldiers assigned to duty. He did only what he was told. He knew no more about the territory they were crossing than anyone in the company, and less than the soldiers.

Then he appeared suddenly one night, just after supper. He came forward, hat clutched before him, with a pleading look in his eyes, more like the old Henry. "Somethin' sure smells good," he said, through his familiar, lop-sided grin.

"Well, you're just fortunate there's something left, Henry Parker," said Josephine. But she said it with a warm smile, and came up to give him hug. Lina said nothing. She went about her chores, cleaning her plate, storing supplies back in the wagon.

"Got anythin' left for your ol' cousin, Lina?"

She shoved a clean plate toward him, but didn't look up. "Help yourself."

Henry took the plate, then looked to Josie, who shrugged. As he started to eat, Josie said, "So, Henry, tell us about the Army! How handsome you look in your new jacket. Is it as thrilling as you had hoped?" Josephine used all her charms to make Henry the center of attention, and he reveled in it.

"Well, it's a fine life. Course, ain't been but a week, but I can tell already, Cap'n Wayne's takin' a likin' to me. Gives me special duties. I'm the one ta make certain all the horses is tended to at night, and I'm the one ta get them saddled and ready each mornin'."

"It sounds to me like a lowly job." Lina mumbled her opinion as Henry kept talking, but he heard her.

"Oh, no. This is the cavalry. Horses make the cavalry the cavalry, after all." Lina simply gave a little sniff as a response, then went back to cleaning the kettle and the plates.

"And the trail ahead?" Josephine shot her friend a killing glance before she turned her sweet smile back toward Henry. "What has this Captain Wayne told you about that?"

"First we gotta cross the Platte. He says there's a ferry there, and the crossin' shouldn't be too difficult. Then, it'll be time for a decision." He plunged into the last of the stew, stuffing his mouth too full to continue.

The word 'decision' caught Lina's ear. "What decision?"

"Sublette's Cut-off, they call it. Goes pretty much due west, Cap'n Wayne says, then up toward Oregon. Most of the farm folk will be headed that way." Henry took his fork and started drawing a crude map in the dust between his feet. "See, the two trails split here. Take the north fork, that's Sublette's. Go the other way, south of Fort Bridger, what takes people across the Salt Lake Valley, and that's Hastings Cut-off. Both of 'em joins up with the trail to California, but if ya go south and wanna go ta Oregon, ya gotta double back a little here." He stabbed the ground to make his point.

"But why would anyone do that?" Lina asked.

"That's why I came to talk to you and Josie. The Cap'n says some folks break off here, try to find new ways through the mountains. The mountains'll start about here." Now Henry drew a long line west of the cut-off, then drew several more, all of them long and jagged, running north to south. "Pretty soon, won't be nothin' but mountains, and everybody'll be guessin' which is the fastest way."

The enormity of it all began to fill Lina. Until now, Smith had led them along a fairly well-worn path, with few options. Soon, there would be several decisions to make. And she and Josie would have to decide for themselves. Lina wanted someone to tell her what to do.

She didn't want run the risk of guessing wrong. She looked deep into Henry's eyes. It was the old Henry she saw there. "Henry, tell me what you think we should do."

"I'd take the south trail. Two reasons. First, there's no doublin' back, although that traipse across the desert won't be no picnic. Then again, they say there's a desert up north just as bad. The south takes ya through Fort Bridger. It's a decent place to rest and stock up."

Lina looked at him, and saw the young man who had been so true to them all these weeks. She knew she owed him this bit of trust. "Then that's the way we'll go," said Lina. She finally gave him a smile. "Henry, would you care for some coffee?"

****

A late spring storm had turned the trail into a river of mud that some noted laughingly was only slightly smaller than the Platte River itself. The mud sucked at their shoes and dragged at the wagon wheels. The rains weren't heavy, but they were persistent, and by the end of two days, the company was exhausted, filthy, and soaked to the skin.

The ferry crossing they had been walking toward would be delayed. The river was impassable from the rains. Wagons were backed up waiting to cross. Captain Wayne sent word that the entire company was to assemble that evening so he could address them. They gathered as instructed. Ulmer Olmstead was there, and though most looked to him to start the meeting, nothing happened until Captain Michael Wayne came forward.

This was the first time Lina had seen the man up close. She noticed immediately the insignia that marked his rank. But whether in breeches or buckskins, he had the bearing of a leader. He was not nearly as old as she had imagined—probably only in his early thirties. His features were classically handsome, but hard. His entire bearing was military, from his stick-straight posture to the way he addressed the group in a full, rich voice that neatly clipped each syllable.

"The rains have taken away the option of crossing the river here. This is probably best. I've been assessing our condition, and it appears many of you are ill-prepared for that crossing. I suggest you take advantage of the stop to make those repairs. After this crossing, the opportunities will be rare. That is all."

Captain Wayne turned to leave, but several of the company started voicing their objections and concerns. "Isn't there another place to cross?" asked one. "How can I make repairs, when I've no extra parts to make them?" asked another. A third argued, "We can't camp here. There isn't enough grass." Slowly, others started to speak out too, and soon it was nothing but noise.

Wayne stopped, turned, then spoke, in a voice so strong it immediately hushed the crowd. "Gentlemen! I have told you how we will proceed. If any of you are dissatisfied with this course, you may choose to continue where and when you like. You will do so without the protection of this command, however. Those who wish that protection will follow my orders." Then he turned and the crowd parted to let him pass.

Lina didn't care one way or another. She and Josephine had decided to follow the Army, and to follow Henry to Fort Bridger so there was no choice as far as she was concerned, and nothing to argue about. The two women started walking back toward their wagons when they heard Henry's holler.

"Lina! Josie! Hold up!"

The two turned to see him walking toward them with Captain Wayne, waving wildly. They looked at one another. Weary and filthy as they were, they wanted nothing more than to be left alone. But it was obvious by Henry's excitement that he wouldn't be denied.

"Captain, these are my cousins I told ya 'bout. Miss Josephine Paul, and Mrs. Carolina Clark." Captain Wayne removed his hat and bowed a quick, stiff-backed bow.

"Ladies. Private Parker speaks of you fondly and often. He's fairly worn the other men raw talking of your exploits on the trail." When Wayne looked at Lina, he lingered just a moment. "I would not have taken you for cousins. It seems Parker here did not inherit the same fair features which grace the distaff members of his family." Then he smiled at Lina, and the smile came from his coal black eyes, and over his full lips, traced by a pencil-thin moustache. She blushed, she knew, for she felt the heat on her cheek when she tried to wipe a trace of the dirt from her face.

"Heck, Captain. You should see 'em when they're all cleaned up."

Henry's remark was enough to fluster Lina. Immediately she began to fuss at her dirty clothes. Captain Wayne remained cool, said, "Come along, Parker. It would seem the cavalry has more to teach you than military maneuvers. Good evening, ladies."

As they walked back to the wagons, Josie turned to Lina and said, "Quite a handsome fellow, wouldn't you agree?"

"I suppose."

"Don't be coy with me. I saw the way he looked at you, and so did you."

"Josephine, why is it that whenever you meet a man, you're either flirting with him yourself, or insisting that I do so? Never mind. I know the answer."

"Indeed? Well, then, sweet, you are learning. And it's high time, too. I've surrendered any thoughts of you and Henry. He's a sweet boy, but this Captain Wayne, now here is a man!"

The next day, Wayne came by personally to offer them the use of his men should they need assistance with any repairs. His demeanor was courteous but no-nonsense, and hardly flirtatious. Lina tried to make a joke with him. "I think we can manage, Captain, though we appreciate the offer, considering you have taken our Henry."

"He is a soldier in the U.S. Army now, madam, and has important responsibilities. Responsibilities more sacred than kinship."

Lina saw then he was a humorless man, and let the matter drop. According to Josephine, however, this was simply a clumsy male ploy. "Not all men are adept at courtship, sweet. You must learn to read the signals." She had insisted that Lina take Wayne up on his offer for assistance, as a means of encouragement.

"I'm not even certain I'd be interested," she confided.

"How will you know? And surely there is something that needs repair? Why not take advantage of the offer, if for no other reason?"

There was a loose wheel that needed attention, so she sent a request to Captain Wayne for some work. She hadn't expected he would do the job himself, but she had hoped that he might accompany his men. He didn't. "You see," Lina said, when the men left, "I knew you were reading more into this."

But when Wayne showed up that evening to ask if the work had been done to their satisfaction, Lina had to eat her words. She thanked him, complimented the work and said, "We won't be any more of an imposition, Captain."

"As long as we were at rest, it was no imposition, madam." Lina's heart sank a little each time he was so perfunctory, but his curt tone was always accompanied by a smile that Lina found most attractive. And she liked the fact that he was the sort of man who did exactly what he said he would do, and who acted with authority. There was something about his character that made her feel more secure now that he was traveling with them.

She was also beginning to understand Josie's appreciation for a handsome man. Wayne was attractive in all features. Dark, glossy hair, coal black eyes. Lina didn't care for the thin moustache he sported, but it drew attention to the sharpness of his jaw and cheeks. He wasn't tall, but he was well proportioned and muscular, and when atop his horse, he cut a striking figure. She had to admit she enjoyed looking at him.

With all repairs completed, the company finally ferried across the river, grateful to have the muddy Platte behind them. But they had never traveled far from water, and now they were crossing a valley without a river. Wayne assured them the trail led to the Sweetwater River, which in turn would lead them across the divide. But the ground beneath their feet was nothing more than sand, barely held in place by tough, low growing grass, nearly too tough for the teams to graze upon. It was summer now, and the sun rode hot all day and lasted nearly eighteen hours. The sand was quick to heat up in the day, but it was also cold at night. As soon as the sun would set, a chilly wind would race down from the mountains. The same winds stirred the sand and dust each day, making it hard to see. Grit got into everything—scalp, clothes, food, and water. It filled the nose and mouth, it scratched the eyes, and it pelted the skin.

Four days after the crossing, Smith's Sojourners came to Independence Rock. The mountains that marked this valley on all sides were large and foreboding. But here, in a valley that was otherwise flat as a table, sat Independence Rock. Sublette himself had named the place more than twenty years before when his party passed here on the Fourth of July. "It shows we're making good time," was how Captain Wayne viewed the landmark. But to the company, it was cause for celebration. Everyone wanted to stop, as others had done before, to carve their names on the rock. Wayne was determined to keep the party moving at an appropriate pace and at first refused to stop. But Mr. Olmstead exercised his authority as leader to insist that camp be made early that day, and that festivities, while limited, be held that night.

Wayne directed the company to camp, and after all the wagons and the stock were tended to, folks headed toward the rock. It reminded Lina of the night that she and Josie and Henry had climbed Chimney Rock, and she wanted him with them today. So she mounted her horse, and went off in search of him. She found him tending the horses. "Henry, come with us. Josie and I are going to climb the rock. Remember? Like we did at Chimney Rock? Please, can't you come?"

"Only if you allow me to accompany you," said Wayne. She hadn't seen him come up behind her.

"Well, of course, Captain. We'd be honored."

The four of them set off for the rock. They left the wagon and started the slow ascent along a washout that had gouged the rock and provided something of a pathway in this dry weather. Wayne, as always, took the lead. He would walk ahead, and having secured the path, turn and offer a hand to Lina, steadying her as she tiptoed from one foothold to the next. Josephine followed, assisted by Henry, who was less chivalrous in his attentions. Henry had a firm hold on her hand, but he did more dragging than leading. "Step over here, Josie," he would holler over his shoulder, but he barely gave her time to reach the perch before he was towing her to the next. Finally, she sat down in defiance. "Henry Parker, I'll not move another step. I'm tired of your yanking and pulling. If there isn't an empty spot here, then I'll just carve my name over someone else's."

Henry laughed, and sat down with her. "Yep. Just like at Chimney Rock," he called to Lina, who was several feet in front of them with Wayne.

"Like Chimney Rock?" Wayne questioned her.

"Yes. We stopped there, too. Josie wasn't fond of rock climbing then, and it seems time hasn't changed her mind."

"But you do very well, Mrs. Clark." He extended his hand to help her once more, and when he pulled her up to him, they stood close together. She nearly lost her balance, but he scooped her quickly around the waist to hold her fast. It had been an effortless motion for Wayne, but to Lina it felt as if suddenly she had been made as steady as the rock itself. She liked the sensation, but when he looked at her, he looked too closely and too long. She was not used to flirtation of this kind, so she gently moved his arm away from her.

"This will do," Wayne said, pointing to a place on the rock surface that remained untouched.

"Yes, that's fine. May I borrow your knife?"

"Permit me to make the carving for you." Lina felt herself bristle some at his presumption. *Does he think I can't do it?* No, she could hear Josephine telling her, let him do it. Another clumsy attempt, perhaps.

"Certainly," she answered with a smile. Wayne pulled out his knife and knelt down, scratching and digging at the rock. She watched as he scratched her name, "Missus Carolina Clark," and the date.

When he was finished, he wiped his hand across the carving, and said, "There, now you will be here for posterity." She watched his hand move across her name, like wiping the leaves from a grave, and she shivered. Wayne rose and put his knife away.

"But Captain, won't you make your own mark as well?"

He shook his head. "I intend to make a greater mark upon this country than these poor etchings, Mrs. Clark."

"And how do you intend to do that, Captain?"

"In many ways. I intend to be instrumental in the government's dealings with the Indians. In so doing, I intend to rise within the military."

"Worthy goals, Captain. No doubt you'll achieve them."

Wayne was looking at her again, so closely that she could not look back into those hard, black eyes. "And I intend, of course, to fulfill my duties of lineage—to marry, and raise a family."

Lina blushed just a bit at so personal a reference. "Well, Captain, it is fair to say you do not lack for ambition."

"No, madam, I do not. I have never been denied in any ambition so far, so I see no reason that will change."

When Lina looked at him, she saw something in his face that made her uncomfortable. It was not lust, or even love, which she had almost expected to see. It was resolve, and domination, and it was hard and intractable.

That evening when the company returned, there was a dance, a modest one by the standards they had established at Fort Laramie, but heartily enjoyed by all but Lina. Henry had sentry duty, so he wasn't available to keep her company. Captain Wayne stood at the periphery of the festivities all evening, watching, but never joining it. After eyeing him slyly for a while, Lina decided he was watching her most closely of all. Lina found the whole matter unsettling. All evening she expected him to ask her to dance, yet he never did. She hated to encourage Josephine's fancies by confessing her interests, but his whole behavior was too confusing. Finally, she pulled Josephine aside.

"So why won't he ask me to dance?" she asked her, after Josie confirmed her opinion that Wayne was most definitely watching her. "It's like you're always telling me, it's only a dance, after all. But he just keeps staring at me."

"As I've told you, men are basic, uncomplicated creatures," Josie said. "But now that you're paying attention to the elements of romance, let me instruct you on some of the variations on the theme. Men contemplate romance with suspicion—wanting the flirtation, avoiding the entanglement. And whenever a man finds himself on unfamiliar territory, he will rely on trusted methods of action. Now a soldier, such as your Captain Wayne, he will map out a strategy, just as if this were a military campaign."

"A *conquest*?" Lina whispered, in disbelief and annoyance.

"Exactly!" Josie didn't share Lina's distaste for the comparison. "He assumes he has only one opportunity to make the conquest, and so he considers his tactics carefully before he begins."

"I don't think I care for this approach," Lina said, looking over Josie's shoulder to where Wayne stood, still with his eye in her direction.

"Oh, don't worry about the approach, my dear," Josie laughed. "It's the result that matters."

****

The wagons now had the benefit of the Sweetwater River to both guide and sustain them, and compared to the Platte, it was sweet water indeed. The mountains had been with them for weeks, always just ahead on the horizon. Each day the emigrants were certain they would see the trail take some frightening turn toward crossing them, but it never did. Now they realized that some of the mountains they had watched approaching for days were beside them, yet the terrain they traveled remained flat, if slowly rising. They were moving through a valley of such enormity, none had ever considered such a place could be called South Pass.

One evening after dinner, with the entire company assembled, Captain Wayne made an announcement. "Today, we have crossed the divide. There," he pointed to the northwest, "is the boundary of the Oregon Territory." At the sound of these words, a hush fell on the group, and then suddenly a loud whoop from one of the farmers resulted in accompanying yells and cheers from others.

When the clamor died down, Wayne resumed. "I understand your sense of accomplishment. However, you must realize you are only just past the halfway mark of your journey, as measured in days." These words took the last of the festive mood out of the congregation. "In two day's time, we will reach Sublette's Cutoff. Here, most of you headed to the Oregon Territory will break off to the northwest. Those bound for California will most likely head toward Fort Bridger. However, there is a southerly route into the Willamette that breaks off from the road to Fort Bridger."

Ulmer Olmstead spoke up for the company. "Captain, you are more experienced than any man here. Which road would you take to Oregon?"

"Each of you has made the decision to make this journey, and, for better or worse, you are here. Let your own judgments be your guide, then you will have no one to blame but yourselves, and no one to thank but yourselves." Captain Wayne left the company to consider their futures.

In the final tally that night, the company was nearly split in its decision. Of the remaining seventy-five members, forty would be taking the cutoff. Olmstead informed Captain Wayne that night of their decisions. The cattle were apportioned to each group. Captain Wayne made his assignments. Henry was lucky. He was granted his request to stay with Lina and Josie to Ft. Bridger. Lina was particularly glad of this, for the Olmsteads had chosen to take the cutoff. It had been a difficult decision, Greta had told her, but they were lucky in that they did not need to stop for provisions at Fort Bridger. "And the children, Lina. I worry for the children. Every day on this road is a danger to them." So the night before the company would split, Lina, Josie and Greta Olmstead hugged and said their goodbyes. There were many tears, and there would have been many more but Lina resolved not to dwell on her sadness. The well of loneliness inside her had grown deeper and deeper since they left Fort Laramie, and now this evening, it was so deep she doubted she could stand any more. She couldn't allow herself to even think of the time, very soon, when she would say goodbye to Henry.

One full day passed after that evening, and half of another, before the company reached the place where the wagon ruts split. If the travelers had expected more of a sign, more of a ceremony for this momentous place, they were disappointed. They simply came to a place where there were two trails instead of one. Wayne had rearranged the wagons the evening before so that the first detail was lined up for the cutoff, the second followed bound for Fort Bridger. By the time Lina and Josie reached the parting of the ways, the first group had already started up the cutoff, and the Olmsteads, leading that group, were already out of sight. But for as long as she could, Lina kept her eyes trained on the now disappearing chain of white canvas leading off to the west, just as hers headed south. The lump in her throat choked her worse than any dust she tasted, and the tears that rolled silently down her cheeks traced little rivers through the grit on her face.

11

Nearly a week passed before the company reached Fort Bridger. On the way, they crossed the Green River by ferry. Once again, some of the company fought over the delay taking the ferry would cost them. But as they argued, another group, equally determined to keep pace, tried to ford alone. These poor hapless souls—too quick to try, too slow to learn—lost one man, three cattle, and two wagons in the crossing. The debate about whether to take the ferry concluded.

As it was, Lina suffered enough damage using the ferry. Just as it reached the opposite bank, it hit a snag, tipping the ferry for only a moment. Her wagon, poorly secured and off balance, slipped, and was upended. Surprisingly, the wagon itself remained largely intact, except for the wheel, which caught the brunt of the force and split in two. But when the wagon fell, all its contents fell onto the muddy bank of the Green River.

Lina watched helplessly as her possessions floated downstream. As scared as she was, she waded in and gathered what she could. Bart swam downstream to retrieve what had escaped her grasp. Josephine tried to help, but of course would not have even considered diving in the water. She dragged what was salvaged off the muddy river bank. Henry and some of the others righted the wagon and pulled it to dry ground. The Army detail offered no help, as Captain Wayne had not ordered them to. Wayne chose instead to berate the ferry's operator. Lina was angry with the operator too, but Wayne's tirade was so brutal, she ended up feeling sorry for the man. She even started a half-hearted attempt to intervene on his behalf, thinking that perhaps this was another of Wayne's clumsy attempts at attentiveness.

"Captain, thank you, but I have to take some of the blame. The load probably wasn't properly balanced, and I should have…"

"No doubt true, madam. Make certain you attend to those details in the future. But this incident will cost us time—time we don't have."

Lina's equipment was not damaged, and her clothing and bedding were only waterlogged. But half her food stores were ruined. There would be enough left to provide for her and Josephine, but there would be nothing extra with which to trade. She thanked heaven she had not lost the little strongbox in which she kept her cash. She would at least be able to purchase some necessities at Fort Bridger.

Her wagon would have to be abandoned. The wheel was beyond repair. She had no spare, having sold that weeks before. And there were no spares among the company. She and Josie were back to sharing a wagon. Bartolomé offered to carry what they could not.

"I could help carry your things in my wagon, Miss Lina. If I have anything you need, I would be honored to share it." Bart stood on the bank of the river, soaked to the skin and caked in mud. In that moment, he could not have appeared more retched, nor more humble. None of the others had bothered to help in any way. But this man offered what he had. At that moment she knew she had in him someone she could count upon.

The company was fully on Fort Bridger before they realized it, so small and meager was it. The fort itself was a wall of poles, the height of two men, shabbily constructed and held together with a thick slathering of mud. Some two dozen Indian tents were scattered just outside the walls, and everywhere the natives mingled, mostly women and children. The fort enclosure was too small to accommodate the wagons of even one company, let alone the many camped there, so Captain Wayne led them to a clearing where they made camp and set the livestock out to graze.

Officially, the company was now on its own. But the night before they arrived, Captain Wayne announced that he and his men would stay over a day to confer with Jim Bridger himself. Bridger's name was already well known on the trail, and the prospect of meeting so famous a figure had thoroughly excited everyone. Bridger owned this outpost. It was not a military fort, but a private trading post Bridger had shrewdly established at just the point on the trail where he knew the settlers would be in need of provisions. But even though the fort had no official standing with the Army, Wayne and the cavalry understood the important position Bridger held, not only by virtue of this geography, but as a man with a unique understanding of the area, and the changing relationships with the Indians.

Lina understood this better when she first entered the fort. After so many weeks on the trail, the sight of Indians clustered around the fort made the settlers uneasy, if only because of their sheer numbers. Instead of the handful at a time they were accustomed to, at Fort Bridger there were scores. Compared to others they had seen, these Indians looked healthy and fed. Their tidy tents operated like individual trading posts. As the settlers passed in and out through the gate, the Indians called out to them to trade. Lina's mercantile instincts was intrigued. She came toward one tepee and began talking with the elderly squaw who stood outside. More through gesture and expression than words, the old woman showed her the pelts she had laid on the ground before her tent. "How much?" Lina asked, pointing to one good-sized beaver skin.

"Ten," said the squaw, holding up all her fingers.

"No," Lina said. She shook her head and started to walk away.

"No," the little woman shouted back, and when Lina turned around, she held up eight fingers. Smiling, Lina started to walk back to continue the bartering, but a yank at her elbow stopped her.

"Mrs. Clark!" Captain Wayne wore a horrified expression. "What are you are doing?"

"I was curious how much pelts like that went for."

"The practice is unseemly, and unadvisable." He started to pull her back towards the gate, gently but insistently.

"Unadvisable? Whatever do you mean?"

"Mrs. Clark, these people are not to be trusted. One misunderstanding between the two of you could escalate already fragile relations. I must insist."

Lina wanted to argue, but decided to err on the side of caution. So she allowed him to lead her inside the fort along with the other members of her group. At the last moment, she could not resist. "Captain?" she asked with a smile that she knew Josie would be proud of, "do you always get your way?"

Her simple flirtation completely baffled him. "Mrs. Clark, you speak as if this were some arbitrary request. Logic and custom demand that things be done certain ways, that's all."

The inside of Fort Bridger was more disreputable than the outside. There were only three buildings. The largest was the blacksmith's, where a crowd was waiting for a turn at repairs. Another building looked to be for storage. The third, where Wayne led her, was a long building. Inside, there was a crudely constructed bar along one wall, and a few men stood there with drinks in their hands. Adjoining the bar, on the adjacent wall, was another counter, with shelves behind it, serving as the sutler's store. Several tables were scattered throughout, and most of the chairs were occupied. One table in particular, in the far corner, was crowded with people, some sitting, and some standing. In the center sat a gaunt old man, his long, thin face covered by a scraggly beard. On his head was a wide brimmed hat, so large that it looked as though it might fall down over his eyes did not two large, protruding ears keep it secured. The wrinkled skin of his neck fell in soft folds over the frayed and dirty collar of his shirt, over which he wore a heavy woolen coat, matted with dust and grime. But it was his eyes she noticed first. They were small and beady, sunk deep in high craggy cheeks. Their pale blue color was piercing, and gave the appearance that he saw everything around him at once.

The man was decidedly taciturn. He spoke neither loudly nor with tremendous animation, yet the gathering of men around him, as well as a few women, was a rapt audience. But when he saw Captain Wayne, the old man stood up, and the others at the table followed those piercing blue eyes to the man in the cavalry uniform who had just entered. "Captain Wayne," called the old man, without feeling, only recognition.

"Mr. Bridger," said Wayne, as the two met mid-room and exchanged a quick handshake.

"You've made camp, then?" Bridger asked, and Wayne nodded. "Are there many in your party?" There seemed little welcome in Bridger's question.

"Ten wagons." Then he turned to Lina. "Mrs. Clark, this is Jim Bridger, the owner of this outpost. Mr. Bridger, Mrs. Carolina Clark, a member of our party" and then he added, "and a particular friend of mine. Mrs. Clark is traveling to California with her cousin."

"Pleasure, ma'am," Bridger said, shaking her hand firmly.

"The pleasure is mine, Mr. Bridger. I've come from Westport, sir, where you are well remembered."

"It's a full house today, I see, Bridger," commented Wayne as he looked around.

"Cheek to jowl, just the way I like it. How long you stayin'?"

"My men and I return to Laramie tomorrow. The overlanders are on their own, now."

"Join me for dinner tonight. They'll be lots to talk about. Mrs. Clark, perhaps you could join us, too. Always happy to catch up with the goin's on back in Missouri."

****

Lina had convinced the Captain to extend the invitation to Josephine. He was reluctant, but she called upon his manners not to leave Josie alone for the evening. Lina tried to convince him to include Henry as well, but Wayne wouldn't hear of it, saying it was contrary to military protocol for a private to dine with his commander.

In addition to their party of three, there was a Mister Joseph Downie, a trader from California. Accompanying Mr. Downie was a lady he introduced as Miss Cora Peck. Any relationship between Mr. Downie and the woman was omitted from the introduction, and she said little during the evening to shed any light. Mr. Downie was dressed like a gentleman from the city, wearing a fine gray waistcoat, and sporting a slightly worn, but still stylish beaver hat. Miss Peck was dressed well too, but she had a mousy look to her that, unfortunately, her finery could not improve.

Lina was flattered when Bridger asked her about Missouri. "So, you hail from Westport, Mrs. Clark? How fare things there?"

"Thriving, Mr. Bridger. It seems the traffic to the west only increases each year."

"And men makin' money hand over fist, I imagine. Is that bastard Pickens still there?"

Lina didn't try to hide her laugh. "Yes, I'm sorry to say. He's the principal reason for my resettlement. My husband owned a small outfitting shop, and it was Pickens who eventually ran us out of business."

"Your husband? Clark was the name? Ephraim Clark?"

"Did you know him?"

"I recollect such a fellow, although not well. Never much of a business man as I recall. Didn't know he was married."

"We married only a short time before his death this past spring."

"Well, sorry to hear it, ma'am. So what's your plan in California?"

"I'd hoped to start a similar business there, perhaps in San Francisco. But it seems this trip has proved more costly than I had planned. I suppose I'll just wait until we get to California and see what opportunities present themselves."

"An ill-advised course," Wayne said bluntly. "The odds are heavily weighted against your success."

"Why do you say that, Captain?" Joseph Downie asked.

"Because, sir, Mrs. Clark is a hardworking and honest individual. All reports from California say the place is a haven for the lazy, greedy and morally corrupt."

"Well, Captain," Lina said, "it'll be no different than what I've known. I haven't seen nearly so much of the country as you, but in my experience, you find good and bad wherever you go."

Bridger spoke up. "If California's your interest, you should talk to Downie here. That's his territory. Deals in everything between the Rockies and the coast."

Lina turned her attention to Downie, whose attentions were on Josephine. At the mention of his name, however, he turned to join the conversation. "You flatter me, Bridger. I'm simply in charge of requisitions for my employer."

"And what do you requisition, Mr. Downie?" Wayne asked politely.

"Just as Mr. Bridger said. Anything and everything. Captain Barclay, my employer, owns most of the more established properties in the gold fields, as well as several businesses in San Francisco. Everything from lumber to livestock, from household goods to, uh," he paused, "the more rarified entertainments." Miss Cora Peck giggled a most unflattering giggle.

"Well, Wayne," said Bridger, "seems you're alone amongst the merchant class tonight. But then, Laramie *is* a trading post."

"Yes, but let's not forget its chief purpose, Mr. Bridger. To serve as shelter and protection for the overland travelers."

"Shelter and protection from the Indians, you mean. There's a laugh. These Indians ain't no trouble to anyone, least of all your settlers. If anything, it's the Indians that need protection."

Downie nodded his head in agreement, but Wayne looked as if he were about to argue. Lina was content to let the comment pass, but Josephine, in an uncharacteristic outburst of curiosity, asked. "How do you mean, Mr. Bridger?"

"In every way possible, miss. For nearly a decade settlers been coming west. And every year they take more land, break it into farms and plough it under. Then there's the buffalo. Seen many west of Kearney? Used to be ten times as many. White men's cattle eat the grasses, white men eat all the game they can find, take all the wood, leave the Indians hungry and cold. That's why they trade with you. Just ta be able to eat. And then there's the diseases. Any Indians not frozen or starved is too weak to handle all the contagion those wagons bring."

"And still you trade with the settlers, Mr. Bridger?" Lina asked.

"'Deed I do, miss. 'Deed I do. That way I can at least take care of the Indians 'round here. They're my family."

"And you arm them, Mr. Bridger," asked Captain Wayne. "You give them guns with which to fight."

"Fight, no. Protect themselves, hunt game, yes."

"Well, whatever your opinion of these settlers, Mr. Bridger, they are here to stay. And their presence means an unavoidable conflict with the Indians for territory. I consider it the poorest possible military strategy to arm one's enemy for battle."

"The only reason there'll be a battle, Captain is because of you and men like you, who don't know the first thing 'bout the Indian, and have no inclination to learn. But would you rather these Indians just gave up? No sir, whether you admit it or not, you want a fight. You're achin' for one. Well, you'll get one, I suspect, and God help you if you underestimate these people, Captain. Now, if you'll excuse me, folks, this conversation's 'bout ruined my digestion. Ladies."

Bridger gave a short nod, left the table, and disappeared within the building's inner rooms. The dinner guests were a little stunned by his sudden departure, and it was Downie who broke the awkward silence.

"Well, it was an unusual evening, but then, what else does one expect from Bridger? As many times as I've come through here, I always join him for dinner, and I never feel quite like I know the man any better than I did the time before."

"I suggest you not waste your time trying, sir," said Wayne. "Bridger is one of a dying breed, a man for whom progress is anathema."

"Well, Captain, that's not your curse, nor mine, I daresay. We both prosper with progress, do we not? And on that subject, Mrs. Clark, Miss Paul, I wonder if I might have a moment of your time. If it is your intent to locate in California, I have a business proposition that might interest you."

Before Lina could answer, Wayne answered for her, another cause for her increasing irritation with him. "I have a matter of pressing urgency to discuss with Mrs. Clark." He stood, waiting for Lina to stand as well, which she did, reluctantly.

"I have no urgent matters, Mr. Downie," chimed Josephine. "You may discuss your proposition with me, and I will be happy to discuss it with Lina later." She smiled coyly and moved to the seat next to him.

Lina and Captain Wayne strolled out of the building. They walked a long way in silence, through the fort's gate, then out among the wagon camps. In the farthest corner of the campground, Wayne came to a stop. Lina had moved a few feet past him when she realized she was walking alone. She turned back and saw upon his face a most strange look, part deep concentration, part anxiety.

"What is it, Captain?" she asked, placing her hand gently upon his arm.

Wayne had been lost in thought, working on his strategy. But when Lina reached out to him, he saw it as the opportunity he had hoped for. "Mrs. Clark. I realize it is your intention to continue on to California."

"Yes, it is." Lina wanted to sound certain.

"Mrs. Clark…Carolina," Wayne started. Almost as an afterthought, he took his hat from his hand, and held it properly before him. "I must speak frankly. You are traveling to California with no particular purpose. That is a dangerous approach, as I told you earlier. California is a crude and violent place, full of opportunists and frauds. Even a woman such as your cousin would, I believe, be ill-advised to locate there."

"What do you mean, 'a woman such as my cousin?'" she asked him sharply.

"Plainly said, I believe her professional motives are, shall we say, suspect. Regardless, I am certain yours are not. You have shown yourself to be a woman of integrity—hard-working and determined. Admirable qualities lost upon the Californians, I fear."

"Captain, please. You said all this earlier. Do you have something to suggest?"

"I do. Return to Fort Laramie with me. Live there as my wife, and assist me in the pursuit of my command." He said it flatly, and his expression mirrored his tone.

Lina was stunned by this sudden turn. "I beg your pardon, Captain? Was that a proposal?"

"Yes, madam, it was." Lina stared at him, her mind reeling as she listened to his words. "If you consider this offer, you'll see the logic of it. You would lead a comfortable and protected life at the Fort. And I do not expect to be stationed there long. In a few years, I have the promise of advancement and a return to the east, which I am certain you would find to your liking. I come from more than comfortable means, and so I would be able to provide you with a life without complications."

With just that phrase, everything became quite clear to her. Only a moment ago, she had felt confused and anxious. She had wondered if she would be able to find the words to explain. But Wayne had made it so easy. *A life without complications*, she thought, and a sense of calm washed over her.

"Captain," she started, a smile slowly rising to her lips, "had you asked that question a few weeks ago, I might very well have accepted the offer. But now, well, I'm sorry, but I must say no."

"The last few weeks? Madam, I don't understand."

Lina chuckled. "Captain Wayne, you're right. Maybe Josie and I don't know exactly what lies ahead. But the truth is, none of us knows what waits for us. We make plans, we try to be prepared, and we hope for the best. That's all we can do. If there's anything I've learned on this trip, it's that. The trip's been hard, there's no denying that. And for a while, I guess I thought I'd take the easy way and look for something safe, secure. Perhaps that's what gave you the impression that I might be interested. If that's the case, I'm sorry. It was never my intention to hurt you."

Wayne narrowed his gaze, and set his hat back on his head, giving the brim a quick, precise tug to secure it. "Then is no need to apologize. It appears you aren't at all the sort of woman I'd hoped you to be, Mrs. Clark. Despite the practical trappings of your character, you are obviously a dreamer. A widow, young and without means, who still imagines romance in this unforgiving place—it leads me to question your judgment. I should have realized from the outset that any woman who could tether herself to someone with Miss Paul's morals was herself lacking character."

He might have said more, had Lina let him. But when he spoke of Josephine, something in her snapped. The rage that had been building since he began berating her came up through her arm to her hand, and she swung wildly to land her palm as hard as she could across his cheek, to shatter the smug expression he wore. But Wayne was ready for her, and stopped her swing mid-stroke with his left arm, then swiftly grabbed her wrist to keep her from trying again. Without the release she had hoped that slap would bring, Lina's fury rose one last time, and she twisted her wrist from his grasp. His hold on her arm ripped her sleeve from the bodice, ever so slightly exposing her shoulder.

The sound of ripping fabric stopped them both, and in an instant another sound, more furious than the tearing of the dress, broke the frozen scene. A gunshot, and suddenly Wayne looked down at his leg. Blood was running from a hole in his trousers. Wayne looked at her again, and opened his mouth as if to say something, then dropped to the ground with an agonizing scream.

Lina was too dumbstruck to move, but suddenly there was another voice behind her, another hand grabbing her, turning her around. It was Henry. He stood there, his pistol dangling from his right hand.

"Are you alright, Lina? Did he hurt you?"

"I'm fine, Henry. Fine. He didn't hurt me." Then, as the realization of what happened rushed over her, she moaned. "Oh God, Henry! What have you done?"

Before he could answer, a crowd gathered. Through clenched teeth, Wayne hollered. "Somebody get help. I've been shot!" Then Wayne spotted his other private. "Tyree," he barked, "Arrest that man. He has assaulted an officer."

Tyree moved forward to take hold of Henry. Just then, a booming voice came from the darkness. "What in the hell's goin' on here?" It was Bridger.

"This soldier shot me. I'm taking him into custody, to be court-martialed," Wayne answered through his pain.

Bridger came toward Lina. He lightly touched the sleeve of her dress where it had been torn, then looked back at Wayne. "Mrs. Clark, would you care to add anything to this story?"

"Yes. Captain Wayne made unwelcome advances toward me. Private Parker simply came to my defense."

By now someone had arrived to work on Wayne's wound. "Don't be a fool, Bridger. They weren't unwelcome advances. You can tell the type of woman she is, she and her 'cousin.' Damn!" Wayne screamed as the man probed at his wound. "Regardless, that man is a subordinate. I have every right to take him into custody."

"Perhaps, perhaps." Bridger was looking over the scene, deciding the best course of action. "Very well, Captain. If you insist, *I'll* take the man into custody. You have no way to secure him, anyway. He'll be safe enough locked in the smithy's for the night. Tomorrow, we can discuss this. Now that's it for the night. Everybody, back to your wagons!" Henry was led off by Tyree and Bridger, back toward the fort, leaving Lina to stand over Captain Wayne and his attendant. "Captain, I am so sorry it came to this," was all she could think of to say.

Wayne, who had been watching the man work on his leg, turned his head slowly to look up at Lina. "Mrs. Clark, sorry cannot even begin to describe your situation. Very well, go to California, and may you reap the rewards you deserve. But be certain to say a fond farewell to Henry Parker before you leave. His fate will be more unfortunate than any you will find in California. A military prison is where he will spend the rest of his days, if they don't hang him for this."

Lina rushed back to her wagon, and found Josephine just arriving, escorted by Mr. Downie, who greeted her cheerily. "Ah, Mrs. Clark, I'm sorry you missed our little tête-à-tête. But Miss Paul has been the most delightful company."

Josie smiled up at him, and then at Lina. "Lina, dearest, Mr. Downie has a very handsome proposition for us. He has offered us both employment in California. He says…"

Lina interrupted. "I'm sorry, Mr. Downie. Something has happened, and I need to discuss a family matter with my cousin." Downie stood there looking a bit confused. "We'll talk more of your offer tomorrow. Please." There was no mistaking the urgency in her voice, so Downie doffed his hat and walked away.

"Now what in heaven's name could be so urgent, Lina? I think this could be the answer to our …"

"Josephine, it's Henry. He's gotten into trouble, and we have to help him."

"Trouble? How?" Then Josephine noticed Lina's torn dress. With an unexpected anger in her eyes, she snapped, "Did Henry do this?"

"This? Oh, heaven's no, don't be silly. It was Captain Wayne."

"Wayne? I'm surprised. I wouldn't have thought that cold-blooded fish had it in him."

"Well, he did, although it's not as you think. But Henry thought so too, and that's when he shot him. Now he's locked up, and Wayne's going to court-martial him. Oh, Josie, we've got to help him. I have an idea, but it may take every reserve we have. Will you help me?"

Josephine did not hesitate a moment. She nodded, and asked "What is your plan?"

****

After the commotion among the wagons had calmed down, Lina and Josephine moved as silently as they could through the encampment toward the fort. They went straight to the building where Bridger had served dinner. Inside, they found him sitting at a table, enjoying some whiskey, all alone.

When he saw them, he said, "Well, I thought I might hear from you ladies. You come to bargain for that soldier's freedom?" He asked so matter-of-factly that it took Lina by surprise. She had expected to have to work up to the point. But now he was giving her the opportunity to be direct.

"Yes, Mr. Bridger. Let me speak honestly. Private Parker has already been in trouble with the military. He came west with us so that he could join another outfit under a cousin's name. If he is released to the military, they will surely discover that he is already an escapee, and that will go even harder for him. Henry did nothing wrong except try to protect me. If he hadn't shown up, I fear what might have happened." This last was an elaboration. Lina hadn't feared Wayne at all, but it couldn't hurt her case with Bridger.

"Mrs. Clark, if this were a civilian matter, there'd be no question. But it's an Army matter, and as much as I dislike soldiers, particularly Wayne, I can't afford to strain relations with them any more than I have to."

"Perhaps," offered Josephine, slyly, "if it merely seemed an escape? Wayne is wounded, and he has but one man with him. He wouldn't be inclined to pursue Henry out in the middle of unknown territory, would he?"

"Don't be so sure of that. He's a headstrong fella, as you can attest, Mrs. Clark. Still, he might not be able to track young Parker if he left with the help of the Indians. *That* could be arranged."

The faces on the women grew suddenly hopeful, so Bridger was quick to add, "But it will cost you. Parker will have to have a horse and provisions. And provisions for the Indians he travels with, along with weapons. I can't be providin' these things, else I'm worse off than when I started. I need everything I can to keep body and soul together for my people and the others."

"We have money, and goods as well," Lina said desperately. "Whatever you ask, Mr. Bridger. Just help him. Please."

"Fair enough. But there's one other thing you must consider, ladies. Parker will disappear. I'm not sure where to send him, but wherever it is, it has to be someplace that Captain Wayne won't think to look for him. And that means that neither of you will ever see him again, at least not any time soon. In a place as big as this west, the chances of you running into one another again ain't likely. You understand?"

"Yes. Of course. But where will he go?" Lina asked this more to herself than Bridger.

"He can join Smith," Josephine offered.

"Smith?" said Bridger. "You talkin' about the same Smith I know? Big burly fella, sometimes works as a guide?"

"Yes!" said Lina. "You know him?"

"Hell, we go way back. Used to trap together. How do you know him?"

"He was our guide as far as Fort Laramie," said Josephine. "He left when our company split up. We were, uh, friends, you might say."

Bridger broke into an uncharacteristic smile. "Yes, I can imagine. Well, Miss Josephine, where did our friend Smith set out for?"

"He said something about bitter roots," Lina answered.

"The Bitterroot Mountains. He's got people there. Yep, I know the spot. We can get Parker there, don't you worry about it. But after that, he's on his own."

The ladies rose. "Thank you, Mr. Bridger," Lina said, taking his hand. "I'll never forget your kindness."

"Think nothin' of it, ladies. It's a small enough victory, I 'spect, 'gainst the victories Wayne and the cavalry will be chalkin' up, soon enough. Well, let me take you to Parker, so you can say your good-byes."

****

Henry was half asleep when he heard the padlock on the smithy's door jingle in its latch. He jumped to his feet, then remembered where he was, and slumped into a corner. All he could see were two small silhouettes inching their way toward him.

"Henry? It's us. Lina and Josie."

When he heard the words, he stumbled toward them through the darkness. "Lina! Josie! What are you doin' here?"

When he reached them, he took each of them in the folds of his arms, and held them close on either side. But Lina pushed away quickly. She knew they did not have much time. "Henry, we've talked to Bridger, and he's going to help you escape. Some of his Indian friends will help you get away from here. We think we know where Smith went. They'll take you to him."

"Bridger? Smith? What are you talkin' about? How did you arrange it?"

"Well, uh…" Lina searched for a lie Henry could live with, but instead, Josie spoke the plain truth.

"We bribed Bridger. We paid him to help."

"Paid him? You hardly have anything left. Damn, Lina. I cost you everything, didn't I? What an idiot I am!"

"Henry Parker, you stop that right now! After what you've done for us, why I'd have paid anything to help you. I can't stand the thought of them taking you to prison, Henry."

"We haven't much time, you two," said Josephine. "I'll go keep a watch by the door. Say your good-byes quickly." Then she threw her arms around Henry's neck and kissed him on the cheek. "Take care of yourself, Henry Parker. Don't let anybody tame that wildness in you. It's your best feature. Oh, and when you see Smith, tell him… well, just give him my regards."

"Sure thing, Josie. Take care of yourself. Don't break too many hearts out there in California." Josephine left them standing together in the dark. Henry spoke first. "Lina, I'm awful sorry things turned out this way."

"Henry, don't be silly, you did what you thought was right. Wayne wasn't trying to hurt me, but he sure made me mad. He deserved it."

"Yeah, he did, didn't he? He's an awful bastard, and I ain't sorry one little bit about him." He was quiet, and when he spoke again, his voice was softer. "I'm sorry about us, Lina, you and me. You know, there was a time, back there on the trail, when I coulda kissed you. Things mighta turned out all different if I had."

"Henry, I know." It touched Lina's heart to think that with all Henry had before him, it was this missed chance he regretted. "But Henry, it's for the best. You'd have still wanted to live the wild life out here. And I would have still wanted to find a place for myself. It's just the way things were meant to be, I suppose. I knew how you felt, just like you knew how I felt, but we stopped ourselves anyway. Hell, it may be the only smart thing we did on this whole trip." And the two of them laughed, just a little.

"But let's make a promise," Henry said, all seriousness again. "No more regrets. Let's promise to never let another chance slip through our fingers."

She could hear the sorrow in his whispered voice, and it was breaking her heart. "I promise," she whispered back.

Her answer seemed a comfort to him. "I'll never forget you, Lina. And it'll be a comfort to know you're out there in California, livin' the life you want."

"And I'll be able to imagine you, Henry, living the life you want. Free, out in the open. With memories like that, Henry, it's better than living forever."

Then he kissed her, the kiss he had always wanted to give her. It was sweet, soft and warm, not filled so much with passion as with tenderness. It was short, but long enough, and when they parted, Lina placed a hand on his cheek, and choking back tears, she said. "Goodbye, Henry Parker. Take good care of yourself." Then she left. Josie led her out of the fort. When they reached the wagons, Lina climbed inside and dropped, exhausted, onto the small mattress. She began to sob without end. Josephine climbed in next to her, and she held her close and stroked her hair until finally Lina fell asleep.

It was well past sunrise when Lina woke the next morning, and she could hear the sounds of the morning routines outside. When Josephine appeared with a fresh cup of coffee, it was a welcome sight. Lina felt horrible. *This must be what you feel like after a good drunk*, she thought. Her head ached, and her face felt swollen. But soon, the hot, strong coffee started to rouse her. She found the strength to change her clothes, then to climb out of the wagon to freshen up.

Josephine had said nothing to her yet, but once Lina was out and about, it was time. "Sit down, darling. There are matters we must decide."

For once, Lina was content to let someone else give direction. "Alright," she said after one more sip. "I'm listening."

"Good." Josephine sat down next to her. "Lina, I don't blame you, not one tiny bit, for helping Henry. It was the right thing to do, and I'm glad we did it. But paying Mr. Bridger has depleted our already minimal reserves. Neither of us wants to be in desperate straits when we arrive in California. Wayne may be a scoundrel, but he's right about our chances. But Mr. Downie has made us a proposition that I believe, given our current situation, offers our best prospects."

Josephine paused to make certain Lina was paying attention. Lina nodded, and Josie went on. "You may remember he mentioned he works for a gentleman, a Captain Barclay, who operates all sorts of businesses in California. Well, after you left, Mr. Downie told me more about his employer. It appears this man, along with a few others, have virtually sewn up all the businesses that service the miners in the gold fields. The gold is already playing out, he told me, and most of the best claims are being sold to these same businessmen. So the miners work for them, you see." She looked around at the wagons. "Mr. Downie says most of these fellows coming now won't make a nickel, and anyone attempting to start a business won't be able to compete with the big interests."

"Oh, no," Lina said. "Then what can we do?"

Josie smiled. "Mr. Downie has offered us both employment. I know we had hoped to be able to work for ourselves. But we must be practical. This way, we can make enough money to get back on our feet."

"And this Mr. Downie, he understands what you…what we each intend to do?"

Josie nodded. "He does. And he said there is no problem finding work in our respective occupations."

Lina wrinkled her brow. "Mr. Downie seems to say a great many things, Josie. You don't suppose he might be pulling the wool over our eyes, do you?"

"Of course I've considered that possibility. And I wish I could tell you I am certain he is not. But I see no other way to get to California. We can't stay with this group. I suspect both our reputations are in question after last night. Besides, these fools don't have a leader, and whatever uncertainties Downie might present, I feel most certain we'd soon be in dire circumstances with the others. Frankly, dearest, I don't see that we have any other option."

Lina was forced to agree. She was still tired, her head still hurt, and now, too, her heart. But any energy to argue, to even reason out another course of action seemed beyond her present abilities. "Alright, Josie. It's a good plan. Thank you." Then she really looked at Josie, as a memory came back to her of the night before, of being held and comforted. She took Josephine's hand in hers.

"Josie, thank you. I'm so happy you're here. I don't ever remember feeling more sad or alone than I do today. If it weren't for you, I don't know what I'd do."

Josephine beamed, and put her arm around Lina. "Oh, Lina, don't fret. We are sisters, now, after all we've been through. You're much stronger than you think. Everything will work out for the best, you'll see. Here, I've some good news to tell you. Captain Wayne and the other soldier have already left. It seems Bridger himself broke the news of Henry's 'escape!' Evidently he put on a real show for the Captain's benefit. Bridger came running into the Captain's tent, accusing him of absconding with the prisoner! When Wayne finally got the story from him, he insisted they both go looking for Henry. So Bridger sent Wayne off in the opposite direction he sent Henry, then he volunteered to cover the other way. Wayne and that soldier took off, and you could tell every stride of that horse was sending a horrible pain through Wayne's leg!"

"But what about Bridger?"

"Well, let's just say he hasn't quite organized his search party yet." Lina laughed, and it felt good. But Josephine turned sober again. "There is one more thing, dear." She reached into her pocket. "I found this tied to the wagon when I came out this morning." Josephine dropped the contents of her pocket into Lina's palm. It was a piece of gold braid, torn from a cavalry jacket. Henry's jacket. Lina smiled, running her fingers lightly along the twists in the braid. She felt a lump rise to her throat again, but just then Josephine said, "Here comes Mr. Downie. Look bright now, and eager. We want to make a good impression." So Lina stuffed the braid into her pocket, quickly ran her hand over her loose hair, and put on her best smile.

12

Lina and Josephine now traveled together in their own wagon, followed by the wagon belonging to Bartolomé. As part of their bargain, Lina asked Downie to include Bartolomé in his offer. She convinced him by promoting Bartolomé's accomplishments as a cook, which seemed to interest Downie. Still, he was reluctant, saying he wasn't certain he could promise the man employment. Bartolomé didn't care. He was grateful, he told Lina, not to lose the company of the only people he knew. Finally, Downie agreed, laughing. "Mrs. Clark, I have a feeling you may be both a blessing and a curse on this excursion. You're insistence on going your own way might be at times a liability, but your stubborn determination to do so is, I believe, an invaluable asset." But it was not stubbornness that made Lina insist. She was desperately clinging to the only reminders she had of happier days on the trail. She needed her familiar traveling companions.

Not that Downie was a poor traveling companion. He was an affable fellow, Lina had to admit, polite in his manners, and steady in his temperament. But he seemed guarded with them, stopping short of a full answer any time he was questioned. Lina wanted to trust him, but her experiences of late made her more than a little suspicious. Downie had promised they would be able to reach the diggings within a month's time. "Oh, it will be a difficult month. You'll work twice as hard as you've worked so far. But I've made this trip enough times to know a few tricks of the route." Downie had a particular reason for insisting on arriving before winter. "In the fall, rain makes the mining near impossible. Most of the miners head down to San Francisco. The diggings close up like a saloon on election day. I want to get there with time to spare, or I won't make a dollar from this haul."

"But, Mr. Downie," Lina interrupted, "if the miners leave, how do you make any money during the winter?"

"We don't make much. Oh, we can keep a crew working on each claim, but production falls way off."

"Then how will you be able to pay us?"

Downie stuttered a bit, then chuckled. "Well, Mrs. Clark, you're right. I'm not certain we will be able to employ you very long. But don't forget, we have businesses in San Francisco. Like the miners, we might find you work there." So, it seemed, the promise of work that Downie had dangled, that Josie had pinned her hopes upon, and that Lina held so valuable was not quite what it appeared to be. She rose from the group without a word, and returned to her wagon. All she could think of was sleep.

The Downie party was only just past Fort Bridger, but Lina felt a world away. As soon as they left the tiny blockade on the bright side of the Green River, Downie's solitary string of wagons headed for the Wasatch Mountains. Crossing mountains, real mountains was inevitable now. *They seem manageable enough,* Lina tried to convince herself, but as it often was in this unfamiliar landscape, appearances deceived. The grade was not so steep, but she soon learned the trail dropped down dangerously into deep ravines crowded with scrubby brush. It was an exhausting, meandering path, requiring twice the effort to go half the distance. The rock was soft underfoot, always crumbling with the turn of the wheels. Each misstep added to the cloud of dust that filled the air—a dust so salty that it burned the hundred tiny cuts on Lina's face and hands, where her skin had been scraped and torn by brambles and rocks.

When they were done with the Wasatch, the wagons rumbled down into a desolate valley. Lina could see now why Downie was reluctant to talk about the trail ahead. She could remember places along the trail where life was hard to find. On the prairies west of Missouri, along the plains leading to Ft. Laramie, for hundreds of miles life seemed sometimes invisible. But it was there all along. Beneath a sea of grass, hidden in the crannies of the monument rocks, wriggling in small currents of flat rivers, or soaring above in the impossibly blue skies, life had been there, all the time. It took the practice of those miles, and a patient eye to find it, but it was there. *Maybe it's here as well*, thought Lina. *Maybe I just can't see it. Maybe I'm too tired to see it.* But nothing Lina could see promised any sort of life at all. Life seemed to have disappeared altogether.

When Lina had agreed to come with Downie, she had neither the capacity nor the inclination to reason any other possibility. Try as she might, she couldn't think of a reason for choosing one path over another. But Josie seemed eager to press on, and confident in Downie's ability to get them there. So Lina acquiesced. She reasoned it was only a momentary lapse, this inability to care what happened to them next. But two weeks had now passed since Ft. Bridger and the numbing fatigue was still upon her. She felt tired, empty inside, and somehow lost. All she could hope was that through the simple act of moving forward, the fatigue would drift away.

From a hundred wagons to fifty, then to two score and now to seven, so the count of their traveling companions had dwindled. Six men, and three women, that was the size of the company. In her thoughts, Lina called it the Downie Company, to make it seem more like a real wagon party. She struggled to keep hold of as much of the past few months as she could. She remembered a time that seemed so long ago now, when she had stood on the edge of the prairie in a setting sun, thinking the world was a fine, grand place, and her soul was big enough to fill it. Now she felt very tiny indeed, and alone. In such a barren place, it was easy for her memories to rush in to fill the emptiness. She remembered that first day they started on the trail, when she had to sneak out of town. She thought of the morning they left Fort Kearney, after she put all their reserves into supplies. She remembered the morning outside Fort Laramie, when she watched Smith ride away for good. Lina had approached each change with trepidation, but each time remained optimistic as to her prospects. This morning, she felt no such optimism. Each evening, feeling fully spent from the effort it took just to move ahead a few miles, she would sit, gazing long minutes into the fire, or out at the darkness around them, too tired for words. It was then that Josie would come to her, slip her arm around Lina's waist, and whisper in her ear. "We'll be there soon, honey. I promise."

That thin promise Lina now counted among her most valuable assets. Among her losses she counted one wagon and its contents. Most of their money, the last of the chickens, and her sweet tempered mare were given to Bridger to pay for Henry's freedom. Henry was lost forever to the wilds of the Bitterroots, and friends like the Olmsteads were lost to the Oregon Territory. But she still had Josie's promise. *If only for Josephine's sake*, she thought, *I'll go to California. This road owes me that much, after all I've paid for it.* Surely there she would find something that would make up for everything she had lost. If only she knew what that was.

****

Lina's shopkeeper curiosity was piqued by the cargo Downie was hauling. Three of his five wagons were piled with boxes, crates and bags. Lina couldn't tell what was in any of them, and she didn't ask. Downie was evasive when it came to his business, and since Lina now considered herself more or less in his employ, she thought better of asking. All she could tell for certain was one whole wagon carried nothing but large barrels. *Certainly it must be whiskey*, she decided.

No explanation was ever given about Cora Peck, either, but Lina could imagine her history as well. Perhaps hers had been the fate Lina had once warned Josie about, a loose woman left behind by an intolerant company. Or maybe someone had died, and she found herself without a man to help on the journey. Whatever her circumstances, Cora seemed content, from what little Lina saw of her. She never spoke to her, although Josephine occasionally passed a quick remark with her. Miss Peck seemed to regard the two other females as lessers, and the distance that created was fine with Lina.

Downie insisted they travel out of the heat of the day as much as possible. Rising before dawn, they traveled until the sun neared its summit, then made camp. Every person ate the noon meal quietly but ravenously before finding shade and slipping into a fitful sleep. Those who slept in the wagons were stifled by the hot still air inside. Those who slept under the wagons might find a breeze, but it was thin, and carried a salty dust that covered every inch of their skin. When the sun's arc started downward, they would set out again. They traveled late, until the dark was so thick they couldn't see. They would make quick camp, drop into their bedrolls after a rushed and unsavory meal, and sleep until one of Downie's men woke them, hours before daybreak. The routine would start again.

This change in their clock was hardest on Josephine. She detested being awakened in what she considered "the very middle of the night." But Lina liked the quiet of the morning. She felt almost rested then, and the air was still cool. She would eat breakfast with Bartolomé, who was always quiet. Most mornings they went about their meal and straight into readying the wagons for the day, without exchanging a word.

The two of them sat some distance apart, the morning's fire between them. Lina had picked at her breakfast, salt pork and beans. Bartolomé could usually make the simplest meal quite tasty, but even he couldn't improve this. The food left her too thirsty, and water was at a premium. Sluggishly, she pulled a brush through her hair, and as she sat, she watched Bartolomé. He was not young, but he had more vigor than a man half his age. His movements were smooth and lively, and there was always the trace of a smile on his lips. Then Lina noticed something quite remarkable. He was humming. Lina watched him for a long time. He worked very hard, yet effortlessly. All the while he continued his peaceful, contented humming—as he gently patted the animals, as he carefully tied the yoke to the wagon, as he meticulously stowed all the gear. Lina noticed, too, that despite the desperate heat, Bartolomé appeared clean and comfortable.

Finally, she spoke. "Bart, I swear you're a wonder. How do you manage to stay in such fine spirits? Aren't you the least bit tired?"

He didn't even pause from his work as he answered. "No, miss. Are you tired?"

Lina laughed. She looked down at her dress. It was rumpled beyond recognition, filthy beyond words, and torn beyond repair. She knew from brushing her hair that no amount of work would make it right again until she had a proper bath, which was certainly weeks away. And she had but to touch her face and look down at her hands to know she was sunburned, callused, and bruised. Every ache in her body gave her his answer. "Yes, Bart," she answered with a sigh. "I'm very tired."

"I'm sorry, then, miss. Is there anything I can do?"

"No, thank you all the same." Lina could only shake her head and smile. She started to go wake Josie, but she heard Bartolomé softly say, "It's going to be a lovely day, don't you think so Miss Lina?"

It was fine for him to be rested and full of energy, but it irked her that he should be so damnably happy, when she felt so dispirited. So she turned sharply back and said, "No, I don't think so. I think it's likely to be another long, tiring, hot, dusty, miserable day. What could be lovely about that?"

For just a moment, she worried her tone had hurt him. He lowered his head and she thought he might be afraid to look at her. Then he bent down, and picked up a small stone near his feet. He rubbed it gently between his fingers, until all the dust was gone. Then he held it out to her, the stone lying flat against his palm.

"This is lovely, don't you think?"

She took the stone. It was nothing more than common sandstone. The desert floor was littered with it. She turned it over in her hand, looked at it closely, then handed it back. "Yes, it's very nice," she said, without conviction.

"Isn't it?" Bartolomé took the pebble back. He rubbed it between his fingers until it looked washed clean. "Why, see how it sparkles! And the tiny ribbon of pink that runs through it. It reminds me of the islands where I came from. Yet this place is very different. Very different indeed."

"Do you miss that place?" she asked.

He nodded. "It was my home, and it was very beautiful. The sea, the sweet flowers, the cool breezes. But I was not always happy there." He continued to rub the stone until its whole surface glistened. "I know now there is much to the world that I never dreamed. Every day since I came to America, I have seen something new. But I think now, I never really saw these new things until I traveled for myself. I want to thank you, Miss Lina. Thank you for giving me the opportunity to see all this for myself."

"You're entirely welcome," she said, smiling.

Bartolomé looked around again, grinning. "Now, each day when I wake, I can hardly wait to see what the day will bring. I want to remember everything." He turned to her. "After all, miss, it is not likely I will travel this way again." Smiling, he held the stone out to her.

"I suspect you will not either. Let this little stone remind us both of that."

She took it. He waited until he was sure she understood. She did. "Perhaps you should wake Miss Josephine, now. We will be leaving soon."

Lina started back toward the wagon, Bartolomé's words still running through her head. "Josie, wake up," she called as she came toward the open end of the wagon. To her surprise, Josie was awake, lighting the lantern just as Lina arrived. Seeing the wagon from the outside, just in that instance that Josie lit the lamp, the wagon itself glowed like a shade on a fancy oil lamp, its light warm and reassuring.

"Well, that's a pleasant change," Josie said.

"What is?" Lina said as she climbed inside.

"That's a smile on your face, sweet." Josie took her hand mirror and passed it to Lina. "Take a look. Perhaps you've forgotten what your smile looks like. I have."

Lina didn't need to see her reflection. "I know," she sighed, "and I'm sorry."

"You brood too much," Josie said as she dressed. She laughed softly. "You know, it *is* funny. When we left Missouri, you warned me not to complain, remember? But if you ask me, a good rousing complaint is better than moping. At least you know what it is that is bothering me! Besides, when I complain, I complain about real inconveniences—the food, the filth, the work. Heaven only knows what's ailing you!"

"It's easier for you," Lina offered. "The reason you set out for California, well, nothing's changed with that. I suppose I should have had more of a reason to go, perhaps then I'd still be anxious to get there."

"Reasons, meanings, purposes—I swear, Lina, you have more philosophy in your soul than an abbey full of Dominicans. Can't matters be just what they are, and have you take them so?"

"I used to be that way, Josephine. Honestly. One day after the next, I had no expectations, and I took what life gave me as it came. But I've changed, I can tell. Now I've had things I never had before—companionship, friendship, and ambitions. But I've lost them, too, and I suppose that's what has me 'moping', as you say."

"Well, that's the way of things. You have something, and then you lose it. Then you have it again. Like a misplaced glove, or a favorite hair ribbon. All the more reason to appreciate what one has, I should think."

"Simple pleasures..." said Lina quietly, thinking back to Bartolomé.

"Hmm? Well, I suppose—if they *must* be simple, although I confess I do prefer the more extraordinary. But yes. Focus on the simple pleasures, Lina. At least until we get to California. Give that brooding little mind of yours a rest."

So Lina did as Bartolomé and Josie had advised. She got up in the morning and said a silent prayer of thanks for the food, no matter how lacking it might be, and always told Bartolomé how much she appreciated his help. She tried to look around this desolate landscape with new eyes—eyes of one who hopes never pass to this way again. Every step was taken in gratitude, as one less step needing to be taken.

It was only a matter of a few days before she had another reason to be thankful. Downie's party was out of the salt desert. The change in terrain was hardly dramatic, but it was sufficient to remind her they were making progress. As the company moved from the desert, through the small stretch of mountains, and down toward the Humboldt River, she fought off once more the feeling of loneliness that plagued her. The trail was littered with goods left behind. But whereas in the early days of the trip, the cast-offs had been luxury items, now they were necessities. Extra wagon wheels, yokes, even food. Worst of all were the carcasses of oxen, cattle, and horses. In places the stench was unbearable.

The Humboldt afforded intermittent pleasures. In this wild expanse, any river, however thin and foul, was welcome. But as days passed the river flowed less freely. Yet there were springs along the way, each a welcomed oasis. They made camp one day near a spring, and Lina and Josie had the closest thing to a bath they had enjoyed for months. With the men present, they kept their clothes on, but took off boots and bloomers and anything else not necessary for the sake of decency, and sat up to their necks in the warm, bubbling water. "I wish it was cooler, but it'll do" Josephine said. She leaned back and let her long black hair float freely on the water. Lina only answered with a long, deep moan, as she felt the water soothe her every aching muscle.

Even Miss Peck joined them, although she seemed less eager to linger. She sat by the side of the pool, dangling her feet and splashing off her face and hands. "What's the matter, Cora?" Josephine asked, dreamily as she soaked. "The water not to your liking?"

Cora Peck wrinkled her nose and shook her mousy brown locks. "It's hardly what I call a bath. When I get to the diggings, I'm going to have a proper bath."

Cora Peck's snit gave Lina something else to be thankful for, and a pleasant diversion from hard times. In the days ahead of them, there would be times when Lina and Josie were so tired from the grind of travel they barely spoke to one another. There would be nights so cold all they could do was shiver, huddled together under every blanket they owned. There would be days when the sun shone so bright that at night their eyes burned and their brains ached. But all it would take would be for one to say to the other, "When I get to the diggings..." and it would give them both a smile. "When I get to the diggings," Lina would say, "I'm going to sit down and have a real meal. Nothing fancy, mind you, but a regular meal, with meat, and bread, and the biggest cup of cool, fresh water I can find." "When I get to California," Josie would counter, "I'm going to find someplace to take a long bath. I don't care if I have to sit in the altogether, in front of God and everybody. I'm going to scrub myself from head to foot, and let the cool water run all over me."

Finally, they reached the end of the Humboldt River. It was only mid-day, but Downie told them to make camp, eat what they could, and meet him after their meal. Downie rarely called a meeting. *Surely*, Lina thought, *this can't be good.*

"Tomorrow we head out across the desert again. Some folks call it the Forty-Mile desert, though eighty is closer to the truth. In some ways, the next few days will be the hardest you've known. And then we hit the Sierras." He pointed off to the west. Outlined in the shadow of the setting sun stood a range of mountains that swept the horizon. "When we've crossed the desert, that'll be our reward, if you can call it that. We have only to cross those mountains, and we'll be within a day or two of the diggings. If you have anything left in you after this desert, those mountains will take it out of you."

A pall fell on the ladies. Not wanting them to linger in their melancholy, Downie continued. "So here is how we'll proceed. Starting now, we'll do even more travel out of the heat of the day. It'll be easier on us, and on the animals. You've seen the carcasses along the Humboldt River. You'll see more in the desert. Whatever we do, we must preserve the oxen. We'll need them to cross those mountains. So if there's anything you have that will lighten your loads—anything at all—I strongly suggest you abandon it now."

"And what about you, Mr. Downie? What are you abandoning?" Lina asked. She and Josie had precious little left to give up, but she resented being asked to make a sacrifice not shared by the others.

"I never carry more than I need. I have nothing to abandon," he answered.

"What about the whiskey?" she asked. She could think of nothing more useless in the desert than a wagon full of whiskey.

"Whiskey?" he asked.

"Yes, those barrels! Couldn't you abandon those?"

Surprisingly, Downie laughed. "The barrels? Oh no! I should think not, Mrs. Clark. Trust me, you wouldn't want me to leave those behind."

Lina didn't argue, but in defiance, she silently decided they would not leave anything behind either. *We can always throw something out later,* she thought.

When the sun began to slip behind the mountains to the west, they started into the desert, and walked well past dark. The moon was full, and its bright white light made the desert floor seem lit from within. Lina thought of the night on Chimney Rock when they sat with Henry and looked at the moon. It gave her some comfort to think that somewhere, the same moon was shining on Henry.

She kept her eye on the moon until it disappeared behind the mountains in front of her. She was tired to the bone, and thirstier than she could ever remember. She longed to stop, but Downie pushed them onward. "At least until the sun is up. If we stop now, we'd be wasting good time."

They were nearing noon of their second day in the desert. Soon they would be making camp, but Lina felt as if she couldn't move another step. All she could think about was water. She and Josie had used the last of their fresh water crossing the salt desert, and since then had made do with the settled, alkali water of the Humboldt. It was bitter to the taste, but they drank it gratefully, but now that was nearly gone. For the first time, she actually wondered if they could live much longer in the heat of this desert.

Without warning, one of Downie's oxen collapsed in its tracks. The other wagons pulled to a stop. Downie and his men jumped down to attend to the animal, but the poor beast was beyond saving. No one said a word, but they all exchanged a look that bespoke the fear they felt. Downie looked around. "No one in sight," he said quietly.

"Were you planning on somebody passing by to help us?" Lina said. "Is that what you were counting on? Or perhaps some miracle?" *I'm going to be hysterical,* she thought suddenly. *But I can't. I can't let Josie see me this way.*

"I never count on miracles, Mrs. Clark. I bring them with me." He smiled broadly, but Lina could find nothing amusing about their circumstances. Downie calmly walked to the wagon full of barrels. He signaled for one of his men to come over, and the two of them lowered one to the ground.

"Whiskey?" Lina laughed excitedly. "Why, yes, let's all get drunk!"

"Not whiskey," Downie said calmly, prying the lid from the barrel. He reached his hand in and let the cool liquid trickled down his fingers. "Water."

"Water?" Josie, Lina, and Bartolomé spoke nearly in unison.

"Yes, water. I've learned enough to know to bring water with me, and to save it until it's needed. There's water enough here to get us to the other side of this desert. I bring it for the livestock, mostly. But water for you, too." Then Downie grinned. "That is, if you care for any."

The women climbed down from the wagons and walked to the open barrel, followed by Bartolomé and Downie's men. Lina reached in with both hands and cupped the water to her mouth greedily. "Water!" she laughed, wiping her wet hands across her dry and dirty face. "Water," she said, laughing.

****

It took another day and a half of steady travel to cross the desert. When they did, the party collapsed at the base of the Sierras to rest, even though it was still early in the day. Lina longed to take just one extra day to rest. She had never felt so tired in her life. But Downie wouldn't permit it. "Not a day to spare," he cautioned. So on they moved.

If the Wasatch were shifting sands, the Sierras were solid rock—a force to be reckoned with. The boulders were craggy and cratered, steep and sloping. And gray. After months of land that was red, brown and yellow, these rocks were cool gray and green. Even more remarkably, trees seemed to spring forth from their very cracks. And not just little trees, but towering pines and firs—huge, mighty, amazing trees. But the beauty was lost on the company as they struggled to move teams and wagons over the rough terrain. Many times, Downie's men had to fashion winches with lengths of rope to pull wagons through crevasses, with everyone throwing their shoulders against the wagons to keep them on a steady climb. Their progress slowed to less than ten miles a day for a week, and the lack of progress made everyone irritable. Exhaustion, however, prevented any complaining.

Then, finally, the company crested a ridge. Below them were gradually descending hills, cast in a rosy glow from the afternoon sun. By contrast to everything they'd seen in weeks, the world below seemed warm and golden, and the air tasted fresh and cool. Far, far in the distance, were other hills, not the equal by any means of those they had just crossed. Even from this height Lina could see rivers running across the valley floor, sparkling like silver ribbons under the sunlight.

Downie came up behind the women as they looked down. "That, dear ladies, is the Sacramento Valley you see before you." He said it with a voice that held both the pride of the owner and the awe of the believer. They looked at him, eyes wide with wonder.

He smiled. "Welcome to California."

Part II
The Gate

13

Lina could recall the moment she first felt the change. The second day over the crest, they made camp perched on a small, treeless shelf on the mountain's slope. It had been a cloudy day, but with the last light, the clouds thinned and she watched them move toward her, then over her and behind her. She inhaled the chilling air, and pulled close the blanket that cloaked her from the gathering night. And she smiled. She looked back at the clouds, and it was as if she was watching the last vestiges of her own veil, floating steadily, serenely toward the east. No doubt about it, her melancholy was gone. *None too soon*, she thought. Where before her thoughts left her brooding and stifled, now all thoughts turned to the life just below, which, compared to the trail just behind them, had become in her mind a paradise.

What Lina saw in the diggings was not paradise, but it was not without its charms. There was no road, only ravines that followed one to the other. This was their path, and it was the gold's path, too. From the jostling wagon, Lina could not see the gold, or even the sandy streambeds. All she could see were the shanty towns—tents and shacks tucked into the little gullies, placed as if they had been thrown there haphazard, and one strong wind from being leveled. It was mid-morning as they passed, the most productive time of the day for the miners. The men at the claims, focused on their work, were oblivious to the rain or the passing wagons—until one of them noticed the females. Lina saw the stunned young man drop his pan where he squatted. The man next to him took notice, then all of them saw them. The miners did not call out, did not whistle, wave or even follow them. They only stared as these angels floated by.

Finally, Joseph Downie stopped the wagons at a camp that appeared only slightly more permanent than the others. In among the lean-tos stood a real building, although its construction was still suspect. Cadged together with mismatched boards, somehow wider in back than front, and windowless, Lina figured it for a shed of some sort. Next to it was a large tent, its canvas sides tied back, revealing rough-built benches and tables within. The pavilion draped over a structure of wobbly poles set loosely in the mud. Adding to that condition the fact that the morning's rain was pooling on the canvas top, Lina felt it would surely collapse any moment.

A sea of quiet, gawking faces surrounded them at a polite distance. Downie chuckled and shook his head. "Ladies, come inside." He led them into the tent. Bartolomé followed, but waited just outside, keeping watch on the men who eyed the ladies so closely.

The room could hold a hundred men, Lina figured. They sat down. "Ladies, I'm happy to announce we've reached our final destination. That is, Mrs. Clark has. I have other accommodations just down the road for you two ladies," he finished, looking to Josie and Cora Peck. Then he noticed the sudden, anxious glance that passed between Lina and Josephine. "Yes, yes, certainly I understand your attachment to one another, but…."

"Mr. Downie, may I speak to you?" interrupted Josephine. "In private, please?" Josephine led him to the other end of the tent. Cora ignored them. She was already eyeing the prospective customers she could see just over Bartolomé's shoulder. Lina was fixed on Downie and Josephine. She saw the determined look in Josephine's eyes and the flirtatious smile she used, a smile Lina knew well by now. Their conversation lasted for many minutes. At first, Downie shook his head, polite but determined. Then Josie spoke for a long time, and slowly Lina saw Downie smile. Josephine charmed him a little more, then Downie nodded his head.

"Very well, then," Downie said on their return. He smiled again at Josephine. "Mrs. Clark and Miss Paul will be staying here. Miss Peck will settle in Long Bar. Mr. Bartolomé?"

Bartolomé turned around. "Yes, sir?"

"Miss Paul suggests you stay here with them. Would that suit you?"

"Yes, sir. Most definitely, sir."

"Fine. Then back to the wagon, Cora. We'll head out for Long Bar in just a few minutes. Come with me, Mrs. Clark."

He led her inside the camp store, the shed Lina saw when first they stopped the wagons. Downie's men had already hastily stacked some of their cargo behind the counter, which was no more than a long board placed across two sets of precariously balanced whiskey kegs. On either side, two men faced one another over a set of scales, weighing gold. The scroungy fellow behind the counter focused on weighing the dust, while the other fellow, an old man, scrutinized the first man's every move. Downie broke the stillness. "Fraser," he said to the man behind the counter, "that will be all. I've found your replacement."

Fraser slammed his fist down on the counter. Gold dust scattered, sprinkling the counter and the scales, and catching the afternoon light even in this dark place. "What the hell?" said Fraser. "I gave up my claim to do you a damn favor and take this lousy job!"

The old man, with whose gold Fraser had been so careless, cackled as he carefully scraped the scattered dust with his knife. "Thank God, Downie. 'Bout time this idiot got run out of here. Maybe now a man'll have a chance at getting' an honest rate!"

Fraser reached across the counter to grab the old man, who dodged him and ran out just as Downie grabbed Fraser. "None of that! I'm sorry you gave up your claim, but it was played out. Go find another one." Downie shoved him toward the door.

"You bet I will," grumbled Fraser. "I'll show every man-jack here. I'll own the lot o' ya before it's over!" With a sidelong glance at Lina, Fraser stormed out.

"I apologize for that, Mrs. Clark, but as I'm sure you've already noticed, there're a number of rough characters here in Babel. Babel— that's what the miners call this place."

"I'm accustomed to rough characters, Mr. Downie." Lina wanted to make certain he knew she was not easily scared off.

"Fine, then, I'll leave you to it." Downie started for the door.

"But Mr. Downie, what do you want me to do?"

"For now, start on the evening meal. Your first customers will be here soon." He was already to the wagon. "Don't worry, I'll be back before then. Good luck!" he said, waving as he rode down the valley.

Lina walked back inside the small store. Josephine was already working the old man. "Mr. Kennedy, would you be so kind as to show Bartolomé, here, the kitchen? We should get started."

"Yes, ma'am. My pleasure," Kennedy said, and he and Bartolomé disappeared in the back of the store.

As soon as they were gone, Lina yanked Josie by the elbow. "What did you say to Downie? I thought for sure he was going to separate us. Did you promise him something I should know about?"

Josie calmly ran her hand across the counter's rough surface, and scanned the shelves behind her. "It could be a pleasant little place, don't you agree, Lina?" Josie was teasing her with the information, but Lina had little patience for this game.

"I think it's a shack in the middle of a muck hole, if you really must know. But that's beside the point! What were you and Downie talking about, your heads so close together?"

"Downie told me on the trail he planned on taking me to that bordello in Long Bar. Well, honestly, I just couldn't see myself working alongside a gaggle of pea hens like that Cora Peck. But I decided I'd wait until I saw what these diggings were like."

"And what did you have to promise him for this favor?"

"That we would make more money for him than if he separated us. I told him that when men had to travel several miles for companionship, it was just that many fewer hours they could spend mining his gold. I told him that by staying here, I can build him a clientele that will also patronize his store, and that by combining that with Bart's talents as a cook, and other ideas you have for making money—you do have other ideas, don't you? Well, I told him men from all around, not just those that work for him, would be coming here to spend their money. And…" Josie added, "I told him I wouldn't stand for you to be left here alone." Then she smiled.

Just then, Kennedy reappeared. "Well, I got your man started back there. Showed him where all the victuals and such is. He's already started on supper."

"Supper?" asked Lina, suddenly aware that it was mid-afternoon already. "How many men? How many meals?"

"Well now, miss, that's hard ta say. Use to be, maybe a hundred a night. Hard tellin' how many'll show up tonight, though."

"And how much do we charge, Mr. Kennedy?" She could almost see the old man's brain trying to decide whether to tell her the truth. "Mr. Kennedy, you might as well tell me the truth. Mr. Downie may be back before dinner is served anyway," said Lina.

"A dollar a meal's what they used to charge, 'fore the last cook went off to stake his own claim. That's been six months."

"Alright, Mr. Kennedy, thank you. Josephine, let's see if we can't help Bart. Oh, don't give me that look. It won't kill you to work in the kitchen once in your life." The immediacy of the evening meal had her gripped by a small wave of panic, until she looked again at Josephine. Impulsively, she came to her and hugged her tightly. "Thank you," she whispered in her ear. "You did well."

"Alright then," said Josie. "Since you put it that way. I guess I can lend a hand this once."

Lina turned to the old man. "Mr. Kennedy, tell everyone the store's closed until tomorrow, and that there'll be an evening meal served here tonight."

****

Downie did return that night, but later than expected. By then, the three newest employees of Barclay & Company had served nearly three dozen meals, with still more patrons lined up and waiting for their chance. From the mishmash of supplies he found in the larder, Bartolomé had fixed a dish sufficiently tasty to keep the place busy. Josie, on the other hand, was of the opinion that it was more than the food they were coming for, based on the salivating stares the women got from each man as they served up the plates. Lina found the attentions almost laughable. Not Josephine. She said little to any of them, but she seemed to be inventorying all of them as they came through.

When he arrived, Downie came through the line with the others, then took a seat at one of the tables where several prospectors who obviously knew the man greeted him. Downie ate his meal, lingered about until the last man was fed, and as Bartolomé cleaned up, he called the ladies over to join him.

"You seem to have taken the bull by the horns," Downie said. "And your fellow, Bartolomé. His cooking has already won over the locals. Now, let's talk about the rest of the operation." He headed for the store, returning with a ledger book, a bottle of whiskey and three glasses. He offered a drink to the ladies, but Lina declined. Josie accepted, and slipped the drink slowly as he talked.

Downie took a stiff swallow, then began. "It's been harder than hell to keep decent help here. If they aren't stealing from us, they're running off to find their own fortune. The last time I was through here, I found the place had been abandoned for more than a month. That's when I asked Fraser to take over." He opened the ledger book. "There are a few basics you'll need to know. The rate of exchange, for one. I keep that recorded here," he said, pointing to a line on the page. "And make note of these prices." He pointed to another line. "All this is variable, of course, based upon prevailing demand, which you will shortly learn can be quite extraordinary here. Everything costs far more than you are accustomed to." He flipped to the back of the book and produced a small key tucked inside a tear in the binding. "We keep the men's gold in a small locked drawer you'll find under the counter. They're skittish about keeping too much of their stake with them, so they leave it with us. Lord knows why, but they think it is safer here, or at least as safe as it can be until I take it back to San Francisco. We charge them five percent shipping."

"And do you charge them for holding their money?" asked Lina.

"Why, no, we don't," Downie responded, then with quick a turn of his head, asked, "Do you think we should?"

"You yourself said it. You're providing a service, like a bank, aren't you? You have the right to charge for that service."

Downie smiled. "Fine!" Then he turned to Josephine. "And you, Miss Paul. I presume you know how to establish yourself? Certainly don't require any direction from me, do you?" He chuckled, a bit self-consciously.

"No, Mr. Downie. I can take the situation completely in hand. I do, however, have a few questions."

"Certainly."

"Well, first, our accommodations."

"Ah, yes, well, that's the unfortunate part. All our past help have been men, so they found places among the miners, or lived inside the store. That probably won't be to your liking, however. Particularly not for you, Miss Paul. I presume you were hoping for private quarters."

"Indeed, I was," said Josephine, with just a trace of disappointment. "However, we can make do. I presume I can make use of the wagons we brought with us, and any other provisions I might need from the store."

"You'll have to pay for any of the store goods you use. I'm sure we can extend you a bit of credit, however," Downie said with a grin. "And I might suggest, Mr. Bartolomé could stay in the store, or sleep in the kitchen. Make himself a tidy little place back there. That leaves only you, Mrs. Clark."

"I'll sleep in the store tonight. After that, as Josephine said, I'll make do."

"Very well. But I wouldn't presume that the men will always be as gentlemanly as they were this evening. I advise you to be careful. Do you know how to handle a weapon? Do you have one?"

"Yes," Lina answered. She still had one rifle she hadn't surrendered to Bridger.

"I shouldn't think it will come to that, but it never hurts to let the fellows know you're to be taken seriously, eh? Anything else, ladies?" He looked to them both. "Then I'll say good night, and goodbye. I should return in two or three weeks."

Lina was pleased that she had Downie's full confidence. She only wished she felt that confident. After seeing the enormity of the gold locked inside a flimsy little drawer inside a flimsier little building, Lina was afraid to close her eyes that night. She made Josie stay with her, locked inside the store. They dragged their two bedrolls into the building and bolted the door. Bartolomé took his bedroll, and his own gun, to the kitchen, just in case anyone tried to come in from that way.

Lina checked twice to make certain her rifle was loaded, and sat on the floor facing the door, the gun not quite resting in her lap. Josie tried to talk her into sleeping, but Lina insisted she wanted to stay on guard for as long as she could.

"Very well, then. Just try not to shoot me in my sleep, if you please. There's lots of work to do tomorrow, and if you kill me, you'll have to do it all without me."

In the morning, Josie found Lina just where she had been all night, leaning against the wall, sound asleep, and the rifle still resting across her lap.

14

One morning, as Lina walked to the stream for water to wash herself, she realized that her life had taken on a new routine with the luxury of being rooted to one place. After months on the move, constancy of place was a novelty. She leaned over the stream, bowl in hand, remembering the little game she and Josephine had played during the last weeks of the trip. All those happy notions of indulgences to enjoy once they made it here—a cool bath, a hot meal—still seemed out of reach, but just. For five days she had turned her attention to the little store and its kitchen, and to the slipshod shantytown that surrounded it.

While Lina and Josie worked to set the store right, and Bartolomé cleaned the cramped kitchen, the old man Kennedy loitered about the place. He bent their ears with what he assured them was necessary information about their new home. Despite the fact that no one had been paying him any attention for the last hour, Kennedy persisted. "The fellas here come ta call this place Babel, like the Tower of Babel in the Bible, on a counta the fact there's so many differ'nt tongues 'round here, can't nobody understand what the hell's bein' said half the time!"

"The folks of the first Babel had committed a crime, Mr. Kennedy," laughed Josephine. "A crime of arrogance—trying to reach the heavens by building a tower, wasn't it? Their punishment was never to be understood. What manner of crime have the folks here committed to be likewise punished?"

"Any sort you might care to name, miss," Kennedy answered without hesitation or apology. "Gettin' ta heaven's 'bout the last thing on these fellas minds. They're here for one thing only—the rock."

"And there's your second lesson, Mr. Kennedy," Josie continued. "For God also punished the builders of Babel because they put the importance of the stone over that of the laborer."

"Well, I can promise you ladies, even if folks here have trouble keepin' conversation with their neighbor, they share a healthy respect for God's laws. It's the only law 'round here. No lyin', no stealin', no cheatin', no killin'. Those laws every man understands. Particular when they know the punishment."

"What is the punishment?" Lina asked.

"Depends on the crime. Liars, cheats, such as that, well, a good knockabout by a couple of fellas usually keeps the card games on the up and up. Ain't had no murders yet, so I can't speak ta that. As to stealin', a man gets beat good and proper, a regular floggin'."

"You just track him down like an animal and beat him? No trial?" Lina asked. Kennedy just shook his head. "Then how can you be certain you're punishing the right man?"

"Oh, ain't hard ta tell. Most fellas knows 'bout what the others got. If we see somebody spendin' more'n he should, losin' at cards, getting' drunker, whorin' more'n usual, we can pretty well take him for a thief. Ain't been wrong yet." The look of horror and disapproval on the ladies' faces genuinely surprised the old man. "Sorry, miss," he said to Lina, "I thought you'd find this a comfort. It's just that your friend here said the worry's cost you some sleep, that you was up half that first night and…"

"Thank you, Mr. Kennedy," Lina said. "I'm certain I'll sleep much better, knowing that there are vigilantes at the ready to avenge any wrong doing."

There was plenty of other worry to keep Lina awake at night, and all of it to do with this pitiful excuse for a store and the money she had to make from it. It was hard enough to sleep as it was. Her old feather tick was flat and filthy. At least she hoped it was filth and not infestation that made her itch all night. When it rained, the roof leaked. The droplets hit the rough plank floor with a muffled but persistent thud, like the steady meter of an old clock marking the minutes she lay awake.

She tried to find comfort in a simple notion. *What is the worst that can happen if I fail?* The answer made her uneasy. She was certain that this Barclay & Company for whom she now worked was a considerable enterprise. If old Pickens could make her life miserable, what deviltry could such important men make for her? *Then I won't give them a reason*, she resolved. *After all, Downie said I was already better than the last fellow, if that's any consolation. If I'm going to lose sleep, then let me lose sleep in thought of what will do me some good.* Thereafter, she put her worry to good work, and earned the benefit of it right away. She saw new ways to make or save money every day, and soon she was more caught up in which idea to try first than worrying if an idea was worth doing at all. The easiest decision was to raise prices, that much she saw right off. *Careful not to gouge anybody, though. We can use all the good will we're offered here.* But Lina couldn't ignore the gold she held for the men in safekeeping. A quick guess as to how much the men stored and how much they spent told her these fellows would pay more. She started with the meal service. Every time Lina rang the dinner bell, the line to be served was longer than the last time. She seized the opportunity; she raised the price by a quarter, and by a quarter diminished the portions. The men still came. It was the same when it came to the store. She never found a price the miners were unwilling to pay.

Lina was learning there was more to running this store than moving its goods. The store was the center of Babel's world, and most of the men didn't miss a day or two without stopping in. The miners came thick as fog the same time each morning. They came early, they said, to stock up for the day. They always lingered just a bit to gossip, to complain, and to joke, before starting the day's work. The loitering made the little store cramped, but Lina liked the bustle. The miners treated her decently. The proof of their trust was that more miners were leaving their stashes with her for safekeeping. She told every new customer about the policy of charging for storing their gold, and again, no one objected. "It's worth it," one of them told her. "Worth it and then some, to know it will be handled fairly." That confirmation meant the world to Lina. Their trust and her curiosity made her look forward to her days spent inside the store. In no time she began to feel at home.

****

Lina had to admit Josephine had been unusually cooperative and agreeable. For more than a week they had worked to bring order to this chaos. All the supplies that Downie brought with them had been shelved. The larder was now inventoried, and they were producing three meals a day for nearly one hundred men. Through everything Josephine had stayed, long past the time of her usual patience. They were still working in the store by day, sleeping on the floor at night. And not once had Josie pressured Lina about her own ambitions.

But this morning, as Lina opened the store, Josephine was already up and gone. She wasn't there for breakfast, so Lina and Bartolomé handled it themselves. Just as Lina was starting to worry, Josephine appeared.

"Well, miss!" said Lina. "I was beginning to wonder what had happened to you!"

"I've been working, too!" Josie said. Her tone was coy, pure coquette, and her small frame bounced on her toes with a child's excitement. "Here, come see for yourself!" Josephine dragged her outside. Two rickety wagons stood there, piled high with scrap lumber. Three men were unloading the boards and handing it off to a chain of fellows who took turns stacking it by the side of the store.

"What's this?" Lina asked.

"We need a place of our own, and now we have it! I went about the claims and talked to the miners. I just asked if they had any spare lumber." Josephine gave a dimpled smile to a lanky young fellow as he walked by with an armful for the pile. "They've been very helpful." He tipped his hat and went back to work. "We found an abandoned shed. Some poor fellow whose claim played out, they said. They spent the morning taking it apart, piece by piece, and bringing it down here. Isn't it wonderful?"

Lina walked around the wagon, sizing up the contents. No two boards matched in any dimension. Some were whitewashed, some were scraps from packing crates, still others were rough hewn.. Still, it was lumber ready for the nail, and while trees might be plentiful here, finished lumber was scarce.

"Oh, this is wonderful, Josie! I suppose we can figure out how to build something that might work."

"I've thought of that, too! These men are going to build it for us!" Sure enough, some of the men were already taking boards from the pile and carrying them to a spot on the other side of the gully. Soon the site was an ant hill of productivity. As they watched the men work, Josie slipped her arm contentedly around Lina's waist and held it there for a while. When she pulled away she gave her friend a quick pat on the shoulder. "Well, if I want this done right, I can see right now I'll have to keep a hand in it. You there!" she called out as she gathered her skirts to cross the muddy gully, "Here, now, that won't do." Lina went back to the store, smiling, knowing the effort was in capable hands.

At day's end the two little shacks were done, and after the evening meal was served, Josephine gave Lina the grand tour. Lina's place was a one room lean-to adjacent to the store. Inside was a bedstead for Lina's mattress, a short cupboard with one door, a small square table with uneven legs, and a wash stand with no bowl or pitcher. On the wall a line of nails were the hooks to hold her clothes. Josephine's cabin was in clear sight of the store. It looked much like Lina's, but there was a second room, so small it could barely be called a room. "That's my dressing area," Josephine said proudly. "See how I've arranged my trunks and things? It gives me a bit more privacy, you know, for when..."

"Yes, I can see that would be handy." *No need to say more*, thought Lina.

By the end of the day, Josephine even had the men make improvements to the kitchen, so Bart would have more room for himself. Some of the men had been hesitant about helping the Negro, but Josephine made it clear to everyone that the favor was being extended to her personally. That sealed it. Whether Josephine flatly told them her business, or the miners had reached that conclusion on their own, it was apparent they understood the incentive in building Miss Josephine her own cabin, and if that meant they'd help Miss Lina and Bartolomé too, it was well worth it. Lina didn't like feeling obligated to the men, particularly given the favors Josephine had implied. So that night, supper was served free to all those who helped.

****

Four weeks after leaving Babel, William Downie returned. Loaded with supplies, the rutted trail up the valley had fought him the whole way, and he was tired. So tired, in fact, that at first, he believed the evening light must be playing tricks on his eyes. But as he came closer to the familiar tent in the center of Babel, he knew there was no doubt he was in the right place. He stepped down from the wagon and was walking toward the store when he noticed Lina sitting beneath the tent, surrounded by a half dozen men. She was dealing cards. Downie watched them play a hand. At the end, Lina rose. "More drinks, gentlemen?" Two of the men held up their glasses. Lina poured the whiskey, then took payment from each of them. She had just sat down again when Downie came in.

"Well, well, what have we here?" Downie asked, delight evident in his words.

"Mr. Downie!" Lina cried, standing up abruptly.

"Boys, I hate to break up your game, but I need to talk to Mrs. Clark. Will you excuse us?" The men began to grumble, but they picked up their winnings and started out slowly.

Before Downie could continue, Lina spoke. "Mr. Downie, I didn't know how you'd feel about me turning this tent into a tavern at night. But you did say if I saw any other way to make some money, I could do so? It just seemed like the men might appreciate a nice dry place for a good game, and a fair game, too, since none of them trusts anybody further than they can throw them. And of course, if they were losing at cards, they had less to spend here, and well, it just…

"Relax, my dear. I have absolutely no problem with what you've done. Genius, really. You're absolutely right. As far as the Company is concerned, they'd like to see us take at least eight bits every time a dollar changes hands. It looks as if you're doing quite well for yourself." Downie poured himself a drink.

"And for the Company, too. I think you'll find the accounts back in order." Without waiting for him to answer, Lina ran to the store, and returned with the ledger. "See for yourself," she said proudly.

Downie scanned the entries quickly, occasionally making a thoughtful noise to himself, and twice, stopping suddenly to look up at her over his shoulder, staring almost in amazement. Toward the end of the book he paused. "What are these entries?"

Lina sat down next to him. "I added some other services. For one, I charge for outbound mail. That's the total figure here. And here's the bar business, and here the money I charge them for dealing cards."

Downie simply chuckled. "Go on."

"Here," she said, flipping back some pages, "you'll see where I changed the pricing for the meals. It seems to be working out well. We're making more money, and using fewer rations. Also, you can see here that a lot more men are coming for their meals. I think Bartolomé's cooking is gaining a reputation." Lina smiled.

"Indeed." Downie said, resting his hand over his mouth, pensively.

"Oh, and I've added a laundry service. I charge three bits for a shirt. And I've started taking in boarders, just for a night or two, newcomers who haven't set up for themselves yet, or who're on their way to another camp and looking for a place to stay the night. I set them up in here under the tent, after the game is over. Ten dollars a night. That figure is here."

Downie closed the book before she had finished pointing. He sat for a long time, silently, with one hand still over the book, and staring across at Lina.

"This is nothing short of a miracle. When I brought you here, I had only hoped to keep from losing our shirts. In four short weeks you've turned this place into a center of commerce!" Impulsively, he leaned over, gave her a quick peck on the cheek, and said, "Mrs. Clark, I think I may love you!" Then he laughed.

Lina blushed, but she laughed too. "I'm so happy you're pleased."

Downie interrupted. "And Miss Paul, has she done as well?"

"Well, to be honest, Mr. Downie, Josie and I haven't discussed it. I can attest to the fact that business seems to be brisk, shall we say. But you will have to talk with her yourself. Right now, however, I think she's…"

"Ah, I see. Never mind, then. It will keep until morning. So, do you have a spare corner to rent me tonight?"

"Mr. Downie, I think we have just the room for you. And I can give it to you with the management's compliments."

Lina woke Downie the next morning with a cup of strong coffee. It was early and the tent was needed for the morning meal. Downie took a quick sip from the mug, then asked, "May I help?" Lina smiled and led the way to the kitchen. After quick instruction, Downie rolled up his sleeves and became errand boy for the two now-experienced kitchen hands. He brought the food from the kitchen, he counted the money, he cleared the dishes, and when it was all over, he swept the floor. Afterward, Lina showed off the improvements made to the kitchen and the store. She showed him her room, and told him how Josephine managed to have the shacks built for them. She finished the tour by taking him outside and pointing toward Josie's own cabin.

Downie looked up the hill toward Josie's place. "Do you suppose Miss Paul is awake yet?"

"I could go up and see, if you like."

Downie kept his eyes on Josie's cabin. "No, I'll check on her myself. Will you excuse me?" Without waiting for her reply, he walked up the hill, then Lina returned to the demands of the store. She lost track of time, but she and Bartolomé were busy with the midday meal when Downie returned. He came through the line, and was sitting by himself when she found the time to approach him.

"Oh, Mr. Downie! You talked to Josephine?" she asked.

"Yes," he answered quietly.

"And you found everything in order?"

Downie smiled broadly, then sighed. "Everything concerning Miss Josephine is entirely satisfactory."

Lina looked at him peculiarly. What had once caused her so much embarrassment was now simply a source of amazement, this intoxicating effect Josephine had over men.

Downie stayed one more night. The next morning, he took with him a list of supplies Lina needed, the outbound mail packet, and nearly fifty thousand dollars of the miners' gold. He also took notes he copied of the accounting from Lina's ledger. "I'm quite eager to share this news with Mr. Haarten. He'll be pleased with what you've accomplished here."

"Mr. Haarten?" asked Lina. "I thought the Company belonged to Captain Barclay."

"So it does, although I daresay Captain Barclay would be happy just to know we aren't being robbed blind here. Captain Barclay is a very wealthy man, and although he likes to make money, he's not much of a taskmaster when it comes to business. That's why he has Haarten. Mr. Haarten was his first mate, and an accomplished seaman in his own right, but in an operation of this size, they neither one spend much time at sea anymore. Barclay has charged Haarten with overseeing the Company's business in California. And I assure you, Mrs. Clark, Haarten *is* a taskmaster when it comes to that business." Downie tucked the notes from the ledger in his vest pocket. "I plan on being back in three weeks. Just keep up the good work, Mrs. Clark. You're doing a splendid job! Absolutely splendid!"

****

Little more than a week later, Downie was back in San Francisco. He had safely deposited the gold at the company's bank, but the supply list and every other chore would have to wait. Haarten would be expecting to see him as soon as he returned.

He stood in the library of Captain William Barclay's Rincon Hill home, the library that served as the main office of Barclay & Company. But it was not Barclay he was here to see. The man seated at the large inlaid teak desk was younger than the captain by a generation, although already his neatly cropped blonde hair was sprinkled with silver. His firmly set jaw and flat grey eyes were fixed on the papers Downie had placed before him. He was tall and lean, and the stiff blues of the officer's jacket he wore showed not a detail out of order. The hands that held the paper were steady, the fingers long and fine. This was Edward Haarten, Barclay's right-hand man, formerly his first mate, and the executive of Barclay's holdings.

Haarten intimidated Downie, but then, he was known to have that affect on most people. The stony silence of the room intensified Downie's impulse to speak. But he knew from experience Haarten didn't like to be interrupted when reading, or thinking, which meant never. So Downie used his nervous energy to fidget where he stood.

"Mr. Downie. Be so good as to take a seat." That was all Haarten need say. Downie dropped into the chair in front of the desk. But he couldn't keep still in the chair, crossing one leg over the other, then switching back, then absently drumming his fingers on the arm of the chair. Haarten cleared his voice and peered up at him. Those eyes froze Downie where he sat.

Haarten closed the papers, then reached over to the humidor that dominated one corner of the desk. Slowly he took out a cigar. He rolled it between his fingers, examined it thoroughly, precisely clipped the end, then carefully lit it. After one long taste of the sweet smoke, he laid it on its tray.

"You've done quite well, Downie. Profits from our mining interests are clearly up."

"Yes, sir. Shouldn't be long before the Company will have control of most of the better claims." Haarten nodded as he absently blew a thin line of blue smoke in Downie's direction. Too anxious to ingratiate himself, he added, "Sir, did you notice the operation in Babel? In particular, sir? I thought you would be most interested…"

"Yes, yes, Mr. Downie. I noticed. The results are impressive. And you are certain her accounts are accurate?"

"Unquestionably, sir. I looked the whole place over before I left. The situation is exactly as it is shown there. By now, no doubt better." Downie chuckled.

"How can you be certain?"

"Well, sir, she did all that in just four weeks. Four weeks! Imagine what that woman will have done in eight weeks! Six months!"

Haarten took another long draw from the cigar, then said plainly, "Perhaps not."

"Oh, sir," Downie argued, worried as always that Haarten lacked confidence in his judgment. "I really do believe Mrs. Clark has the potential to make even more money out of those operations."

Haarten only shook his head, then stood and walked toward the window. The view from here was not what most would call picturesque. But Haarten liked it for it afforded him a view of something he was a part of creating—a city growing boundlessly. Everywhere he looked there were ships, piers, warehouses, shops, and taverns, all earning money. Every day the city grew, and every day Barclay & Company made money. It didn't matter where Edward Haarten looked, for his view always held opportunity. And he had just seen another in Downie's report.

"I have, for some time, shared the same concerns for the Company's interests here in the city that you share for operations in the gold fields. It is difficult to find capable people on whom one can rely." Haarten turned from the window back to Downie. "I am of the opinion that, if this person is as capable as you claim, she could be of even more value to the Company here."

Downie was dumbfounded, and not a little bit angry, although it would do him no good to show it. After all, the money he earned from Barclay was in direct relationship to how profitable the operations in Babel and the other camps were. If he were to lose Lina, he'd be right back where he was before she came—losing money. Still, he had a thought about how such an arrangement might, in a way, benefit him as well.

" I'm not certain Mrs. Clark can be convinced to leave."

"Why not? If it's a question of money, we can pay her better here than what we're paying her now."

"Well, sir, Mrs. Clark has a companion with her."

"Companion?" It was a suspicious word to Haarten.

"A friend. Or a cousin, I'm not certain which. A Miss Josephine Paul."

"And I suppose you think we'll have to offer Miss Paul some employment as well? Very well. We'll find something for her, as a maid perhaps."

"No, sir. What I mean, sir, is that Miss Paul has other talents. Considerable talents, I hear, although of course I'd have no knowledge, myself." Downie was being evasive, for he knew how Haarten would feel about what he was trying not to say. But there was no way around it. "Miss Paul is a prostitute, sir."

Only those who knew Haarten well would have noticed the barely perceptible flinch. Of all of Barclay's interests, prostitution was the one which Haarten wished they could be rid of. He despised whoring. He fancied himself a highly moral man, and while as a man of commerce he appreciated the financial rewards of backing such an industry, he saw what the practice did to the clientele. Haarten considered it a waste of a man's pay and his time, and he held the women responsible. He'd had to drag many a seaman out of a house of ill-repute in his time. Still, Haarten was pragmatic. He knew this business was a part of what made San Francisco an attractive port of call. And it did make money.

"I'm certain we can find a suitable place for the whore."

Downie was relieved. He might be losing the best shopkeeper he ever had, but he was gaining the more regular company of Josephine Paul. It was a fair trade in his mind.

"Very well, Mr. Haarten. I'll make the proposal to the ladies when I return to the diggings at the end of the month. And I'll…"

"Next week, Mr. Downie."

"Excuse me, sir?"

"You'll be traveling up the American River next week, Mr. Downie. I see no reason to put off the opportunity to better our position here, do you? And I'll be going with you. I want to meet this Mrs. Clark myself, before I commit to an offer."

15

Change came to Babel with the rain. For three solid days the rain fell so hard it brought a stop to all activity. Too wet to pan gold, too wet to come out for a meal, or even to come visit Josie. Winter was coming, this rain proved that. The rain was cold, and it was turning to snow higher up. Soon, it might snow in Babel, Lina supposed, and then business would dry up completely.

She worried what would happen when the business did dry up, and if they could wait it out. With every rain, more men were leaving the diggings. Most headed to San Francisco, to spend what little they might have as fast as possible. They promised to be back in the spring, but most would not, and Lina knew that now. Their gold fever had broken, and they would be heading home to heal.

The ones left behind were edgy. They were more desperate. They were men with no home to go to, no sweethearts pining for them. They were the men who spent every penny they made, who always spent every penny, and wasted it. *Men like Ephraim*, Lina thought. They drifted to California, and would stay until someone or something gave them reason to drift elsewhere, someplace that looked like easy pickings. Otherwise, they'd just as likely stay put. But as their money and their whiskey ran out, and with nothing better to do, they grew more troublesome. These fellows, the dregs of the miners, didn't come to the store to share the chatter and gossip Lina had come to enjoy. They loitered. They tried to barter their way to another bottle. Bartolomé would find some passed out in the tent in the morning. Everything that seemed to go wrong—another day of rain, a lost hand at cards, the wrong look from the wrong fellow at the wrong moment—became fuel for a fight. There was serious squabbling among the miners, and with increasing frequency it broke into violence. Most were fistfights between poorly matched foes, but a few times men had been beaten, seriously. Lina became quite good at putting splints to broken arms and wrapping bandages.

One man had died by his own stupidity. He was drunk. When he accused another man of cheating, he drew his knife. The accused, having considerably less to drink than his accuser, knew better than to attack. When the drunk lunged at him, the accused simply stepped aside. The drunk tripped, stumbled to the ground, and fell on his own knife. Lina did not see the fight, but she was called to the scene after the fact to give her opinion as to whether it was a fair fight, or if, as a few friends of the drunk were saying, the man had pushed the knife into their friend and threw him down.

Lina saw only the pitiful man, face down amid the bloodstained mud. *What a senseless death*, she thought. Lina knew the dead man to be a notorious drunk, and seeing no evidence to the contrary, agreed with those who argued it was an accident. That seemed to settle the matter. In any event the friends of the drunk were greatly outnumbered and not prepared to press the point.

She was surprised when all the men insisted that, as a member of the community and a Christian, the drunk be given a decent burial. While he had not been popular among the miners, each man there hoped that should a similar fate befall him, the fellows would give him as much. Besides, a funeral was as good a diversion as they were likely to find in this weather. There would be music, food, and whiskey afterward, and that was enough for them.

It was customary for every man to share in the chore of digging the grave. Those who were not presently digging stood by, waiting on a turn or just finishing one, sharing a bottle and passing the time of day in remembrance of the dearly departed. The hole having been completed, the service began promptly. A miner named Morley, who claimed to have once been a Presbyterian minister from Ohio, led the service. Morley seemed a bit too unconventional to Lina to have been a minister, but the diggings were a strange place, and besides, Morley seemed to have the gift. There had been another funeral she had attended, a man who apparently had died in his sleep, and Morley had done a superb job with his oration.

Today's corpse was lowered into the hole just as the rain stopped. A few thin rays of sun poked through the clouds. With all eyes on him, Morley began. "Fellows!" he said, in a deep, commanding voice, "here lie the mortal remains of our dear departed friend, Howard. I say 'friend,' and I mean 'friend,' for even though Howard was a drunken little sneak, who among us ain't laughed with him, and drunk with him, and swapped a lie or two."

Lina was standing at the back of the crowd, present out of respect to the miners who considered this a required appearance. She watched the men, as Morley's eulogy continued. Their attentions began to flag. She noticed one distracted miner in particular standing opposite Morley at the foot of the grave. At first she thought he was just fidgety, but now she watched him poke around in the dirt with the toe of his boot.

Morley was still decrying the death of poor Howard. "The diggings is a rare kinda place, where man looks after neighbor, for without no families of our own out here, we gotta be family to each other...."

"Color." Lina heard the distracted miner whisper it, but did not understand his meaning. But the men to either side of him understood. He was still looking at the ground, moving his toe through the dirt when he said it. Then he said it again, louder. "Color!"

Suddenly, the men were on the move. Three jumped in the grave, on top of poor Howard, while others dropped to their hands and knees to claw at the dirt. For in digging poor Howard's grave, his dear friends had uncovered another small strike. An unclaimed strike. Unclaimed, that is, except by poor, dead Howard, whose claim was now being jumped by all his friends. The body came rising from the grave, lifted by hands attached to unseen arms. Then a living head popped up. It was Morley the preacher, Morley the great good friend of Howard, taking the body from the grave. The body was passed out of the hole and eventually deposited next to a tree, wrapped in its shroud. Lina turned her back on the scramble around the grave, and started walking toward the store. "Amen," she said quietly, to no one but herself.

****

One of the duties Lina found herself assuming, one with which she was not entirely comfortable, was that of unofficial judge. It seemed whenever there was a dispute of any kind, no matter how trivial, the miners came to her for arbitration. At first she was flattered. She took it as a sign of acceptance, and that the miners must think of her as someone whose opinion held weight. The first matters they asked her about were petty disputes, but soon she found herself as the court of final appeal for matters concerning claims and property ownership. These were weighty matters, she knew, and she tried her very best to be impartial and fair. The men always seemed satisfied with her answers, until one day, when the argument centered on a claim held by some of the Celestials.

A miner called Fortas returned to Babel after some weeks' absence. Fortas had heard of a fellow he'd come west with, who had settled at another camp, and had now died. Fortas thought he might lay claim to some of the man's traps, but everything was picked over by the time he got there. On his way back, he stopped by for a drink on his way to his claim far up in the valley, and then left. But an hour later he was back. He came running and hollering all the way down the valley. Everyone came out to see the source of the ruckus. Fortas made a beeline for the store, all the while ranting in full voice. The closer he came, the clearer his ranting.

"They stole it! Stole it, God damn it, right from under me. Goddamn Chinese! Goddamn yellow sonsabitches. By God, they'll not steal from me!" Everyone seemed to understand Fortas' meaning except Lina. But the cheers and collective hollering of the men made her nervous.

"Wait! Wait!" Lina struggled to be heard. Finally, pushing through the crush of men, she came up to Fortas himself. "What are you carrying on about?" she demanded.

"That's right!" she heard someone say. "Tell 'er! Let her decide." That only fueled the hubbub more, until Lina grabbed Fortas by the sleeve, demanding an answer.

"Alright, alright! I'll tell her." He gave a jeering kind of laugh. "Them God damn Celestials jumped my claim. Took the very best part, they did. They stole from me, and I say we take 'em on."

This was the worst kind of trouble, for it rose in defense of a system the locals held dear. There was a hierarchy in the diggings, a sort of provincial caste system. The Americans considered themselves superior to everyone. They hated the Europeans, but both felt superior to the Negroes. Free Negroes were considered better than the Mexicans, called 'greasers.' The 'greasers' were preferred over the Celestials—the Chinese. And the worst mistreatment of all was reserved for the local Indians.

But there was a particularly strange reason these men hated the Celestials—they worked harder than anyone. A miner would not usually have more than one or two friends working a claim with him, for lack of trust. The Celestials would have a dozen at least, and would do all the better for the extra hands. They worked ceaselessly and tirelessly. When the rains came, only the Celestials kept working when every other miner let the weather defeat him. They were the first to start working each morning and the last to quit. When they could, they moved to claims other miners had abandoned as played out. Somehow, miraculously, the Celestials would find more gold. Perhaps not much, and not of the finest quality, but gold nonetheless. It angered the other miners to see the Celestials succeed where they had failed. As a result, men jealously guarded their claims, even when not working them. A lazy miner, and there were many, would as soon sit and watch his gold wash downstream to another man's claim as he would consider letting the Celestials work it for a fee.

Lina considered this sort of thinking nonsense. But she never shared her views with the miners. It was her opinion that anyone that stupid and pig-stubborn deserved what he got, which was usually little. And she knew, too, that for all the general amity she had come to share with the miners, her defense of the Celestials would not be welcomed. She hesitated to say anything that would alienate her customers. After all, she made little money off the Chinese. They never came to meals, and only rarely came to the store.

"Alright!" she screamed, gaining the men's attention. "Let's see what the map says." Lina headed toward the store. Of all the information Downie left with her, the map was the least helpful. One of the first prospectors in the area had started a map to delineate each man's claim. But the lines marking one claim from another had been crudely drawn, no surveyor being available at the time. The task of identifying claims was made more difficult as men moved about their own claims trying different methods or working different sections of the same stream, for most of the claims were marked central to the miner's initial strike. Finally, as miners came and went in Babel, old abandoned claims were taken over, in whole or part, by other miners. Still, it was the only means Lina had of arbitrating this dispute. She could only hope that in this case, the map would be helpful.

When she returned, everyone turned to head up the valley. "Wait," she called, relieved to see she had stopped them in their tracks. "We don't all need to go. No need acting like a mob, gentlemen." She chose these last words carefully. There were a great many in their number who, at other times and in other places, would not normally be disposed to violent behavior, and she was hoping she could call upon these men's better instincts. Lina scanned the crowd for the faces of some of the men she felt could be trusted to be the most reasonable. "Kennedy," she said, seeing the old man close by, "does anyone here speak Chinese?"

"I do, some," came a soft voice. Behind her stood a man she knew as Simms. "Used to sail the Pacific. Lots of Chinese ports. I know a little of their tongue."

"Well then, you and Kennedy come with me and Mr. Fortas." Kennedy puffed his chest out at his selection.

The four of them started the long trek up the valley. Fortas began his ranting again, calling the interlopers, "God damned yellow sonsabitches." The first time, Lina gave him a swat with the rolled up map. The second time, she stopped. "God damn it! If you can't keep a civil tongue, I'll head back and let the sonsabitches have your claim!" Her swearing silenced him for good.

Fortas' claim was the last one up the valley. Perched just under an outcropping of rock sat a small hovel. In front of it was a cradle, the only visible sign of someone working the claim. "Where are they?" Lina asked.

"Down there," Fortas said, pointing toward the back of the cabin. The four climbed up a small ridge beside the cabin and looked down the other side. There, at the bottom of the hill, crouched around a very small stream, was a collection of Chinese. As soon as they saw Fortas they scampered across the ravine to their own little shack.

Fortas started to move toward them, but Lina grabbed the hem of his coat as he moved past her. "You mean to tell me, you think because they're working down there, they've jumped your claim?"

Fortas looked at her wildly. "Of course I do! This here's my claim. Always been! This whole damn hill! Look at the map for yourself."

Lina rolled the map out on a flat rock nearby. "Here!" hollered Fortas, pointing to a spot at the top of the map. "There it is. Right where we're standin'!"

Lina made note of the place Fortas indicated, then tried to get her bearings in relation to other landmarks. She looked up at the cabin and the cradle, then back down to the map. She studied it this way for some minutes, finally testing Fortas' patience. "Well, God damn it, I'm right!" He was looking to Kennedy and Simms for affirmation. They, however, were looking to Lina.

Lina wanted to choose her words carefully. Fortas was an outraged man, she knew. "Mr. Fortas," she began in as calm a voice as she could. "According to this map, your claim centers at the cradle, at the place you first made the strike. Well, it's my understanding that the custom is to mark the claim out from that point, and the distance from that point is largely a function of the size of the strike. Is that right, Mr. Kennedy?"

"Yep. That's the way it's done." Kennedy was visibly pleased to be included in the arbitration.

"In that case, Mr. Fortas, the claim would only extend about as far as we're standing now. Certainly not anywhere near the bottom of this hill. According to this map, the Chinese are working unclaimed land." Fortas snatched the map from her hand, looking frantically to judge the distance for himself. But he quickly realized there was no point in measuring the distance. The Chinese were clearly beyond the customary boundary for his claim. With no other focus for his anger, he thrust the crumpled map back into Lina's hands, and stomped off toward his cabin.

Lina, Kennedy and Simms stood where Fortas had left them. Lina looked below to the cabin of the Celestials. She could see one of them open the door a crack to peek out, then seeing her and the two men, the door closed quickly.

Lina trudged down the hill with the two men in her wake. She knocked on the loosely hung door. Nothing. She knocked a second time. "*Please,*" she said, knowing she was not being understood, but hoping the tone of her voice would coax him out. "Open the door. We need to explain."

This time the door opened again, revealing a younger man. Lina smiled again, but the man remained completely impassive. She pulled Simms forward. The Celestial took a step back, as if preparing to defend himself. She turned to Simms. "Tell him that it's alright if he works the claim. Tell him it's alright."

Simms stepped forward and began talking to the man. Lina had no idea what Simms was saying, and could only hope he was approximating what she had instructed him to say. He pointed toward where they had been working the claim. The Celestial showed no sign of understanding. Then Lina stepped forward, and gingerly reached for the man's hand. He jerked in surprise, but she tried again, and this time, he allowed it. Slowly she led him back to the stream. Lina reached into the cold water and grabbed a rock. It had no gold in it, at least none that she could see, but she hoped he would understand her meaning anyway. She took the rock and placed it in the man's hand, closing his fingers around it. "Yours" she said, grasping his clenched fist in both her small hands. "Yours," she said again, nodding.

The Celestial looked to Simms, who spoke again. Finally, it seemed the Celestial understood. He smiled, then made a deep bow to Lina. Lina looked toward Simms. "He expects ya to bow back at him. It's how they say everything over there. Hello, goodbye, thanks, welcome. Just give him a bow."

Lina did as Simms said. Then the man returned to the cabin. Lina, Kennedy and Simms started back to up the hill. By the time they reached the top, the Celestials were already back at work on the claim. Lina turned to look toward Fortas' cabin. Fortas stood there behind his place. He had witnessed the whole exchange.

****

Lina went to bed that night feeling quite satisfied with herself. She had managed not only to shut up Fortas, which she found tremendously satisfying, but also to quiet the other miners. Kennedy and Simms had done much of that, for when they returned they were so excited to tell the story of how Lina had dealt Fortas a blow, the men were as happy to be distracted with a good story as a good fight. The tale had raised their estimation of her, she felt quite certain. *Perhaps, with any luck*, she thought, *I might be able to change their minds about these Celestials.*

The sense of satisfaction gave her a sound sleep. So sound, in fact, that when she was awakened from it in the middle of the night, she hardly knew where she was. She sat up in her cot, thinking she had been dreaming. Then she heard a scream—a woman's scream.

Lina jumped from her bed and tore out the door, running straight for Josephine's cabin. Soon her bare feet were freezing and covered in mud. It slowed her, but did not stop her. The night was cloudy and moonless, and though she knew well the path between her door and Josie's, she was having trouble making her way. She tripped, and as she stood up, saw a figure run from Josephine's door up the hill among the trees and rocks. Then she saw the white nightgown. Josephine was standing in the door of her cabin.

When Lina got to her, Josephine was screaming. "Get him! Get him!" But she was sobbing too. Lina gathered her in her arms and pulled her back into the cabin.

Once inside, she made Josephine sit on the bed, then fumbled to light the lantern. She turned to look at Josie just as the light was spilling across the tiny room. Josie sat there with what would surely be a terrific shiner the next day, but was now little more than a small bruise below her left eye.

"Honey, what happened?" Lina asked, as she tried to look at the wound.

"I was asleep. I kicked the last one out hours ago. I woke up and that man was on top of me. It was too dark to make out a face. I screamed, but he had hold of both my wrists. Then I managed to reach his hand with my mouth. That's when I bit him!" And at that sudden thought, she began a nervous giggle. "Imagine that, I actually bit him!"

"Is that when he hit you?" Lina went to the washstand for a cold cloth.

"I suppose so. He struck me with the back of his hand. Before he could grab me again, I managed to push him off the bed. That's when I screamed. He just scrambled from the floor and ran."

The men started appearing at Josie's door. "What happened?" "Who got killed?" "Is it Josie?" "Miss Josie, you alright in there?"

"I'll see to them," Lina said as she stepped outside, closing the door behind her.

"Josephine's alright. She was attacked, and whoever it was gave her a black eye." The men seemed relieved. "He ran up that way," she said, pointing up into the hills. With that, she expected the men would run after the attacker. Instead they just stood there.

"Well? Aren't you going to go find who's responsible for this?" Her question was met with total silence. "Well?" she asked again, louder this time, as if her voice had the power to shake them into action. But still they did not move. Finally, one of them spoke.

"Well, Miss, it ain't like she was killed."

"Are you telling me that in order for you to go after this man, Josie had to be murdered in her sleep?"

"Are ya sure she was asleep?" came a voice from the middle of the crowd. The comment sent a wave of sniggering through the men.

"What do you mean by that?" Lina bellowed, trying to put a face to that impudent question. But it was Kennedy who answered her.

"He means, miss, that, well, after all, she *is* a whore. Maybe this was just one of the boys gettin' a little carried away, ya know?" Lina's eyes widened at what she was hearing, but Kennedy, unaware of the anger he was raising in her, continued. "Anyway, ain't like we'd be protectin' her virtue." Then he quickly added. "No offense meant, miss. It's just how the boys see it."

"Is that so?" said Lina, slowly. "Well, let me tell you how I see it." She looked around to catch the eye of every man she could before continuing. "You asked me today to help you protect one of your claims. I did it. I've done it in the past, too. But now somebody comes down here and tries to jump Josephine's claim!" When the snickers started, she stopped them. "Isn't it the same thing?" she screamed. "She's working here just like everyone else. Somebody comes down and tries to take something from her that he didn't pay for. Isn't that about the same?" Still the men said nothing. "Very well," she said finally. "But don't ask me to help you in these matters again. Ever!" She went back inside Josie's shack and slammed the door.

They sat together until Lina was certain Josie wasn't hurt worse than she seemed, and until Josie finally calmed down enough to go to sleep. She made Josie lie down, then turned out the lantern and sat there with her in the dark. Josie had been quiet so long Lina thought she was finally asleep, until she heard her ask, "It's this place. These men. Please can we go to San Francisco now? I'd feel safer in San Francisco." Her plea was like a child's and it nearly broke Lina's heart.

"Josephine, honey, let's talk about this later. Please try to get some sleep." Lina stayed until she heard the light sound of Josie's slumbering. By then there was just enough light outside that she knew that there was probably no hope she would find sleep herself. She decided to try anyway.

She quietly closed the door behind her, and took only a step before she saw Bartolomé step from the shadow on the side of the shanty, cradling his rifle. She knew without asking that he had been there all night. She looked from the rifle up to Bartolomé's tired eyes and smiled. "Thank you," she said, reaching out to squeeze his arm. She turned to walk toward the store, and he came with her.

"I would have gone looking for the man, miss. But one man alone, a colored man alone…"

"You did exactly the right thing, Bart. Thank God you did. I didn't even consider he might come back."

They walked in silence until they reached the store, and just as Lina was about to go into her room, Bartolomé said, "You ladies should leave here."

Had he heard them talking? "Where? San Francisco? It won't be any better there."

"It cannot be any worse than it is here. You have no friends here."

She smiled. "We have you."

He shook his head. "We have traveled together a long time, miss. Those months on the trail, there were always friends to help keep you safe. Mr. Smith, Mr. Parker, the farmer and his family. Tonight, you had only one old man to stand guard."

"Wake me in an hour, please," she said abruptly, then hurried inside. She felt the cold settle deep within her. It made her feel empty. She climbed beneath her blankets and pulled them tight around her.

Exhaustion won out over worry, and she fell asleep with surprising ease.

When Bartolomé knocked on the door an hour later, she dragged herself from the cot, threw some cold water on her face, tossed on a dress, and was just brushing her hair when she heard the sound of wagon wheels outside, and a familiar voice calling. "Hallo! Mrs. Clark? Are you about?"

Downie had returned. She was excited and relieved to see him. Hang what Bart had said, here was a friend at last. She threw the door of her room open to see him standing there, ready to knock. He was evidently pleased to see her as well, for he took her hand in a hearty handshake.

"Mrs. Clark! Oh, it's grand to see you again. I was half expecting that you'd have left like so many of the others. But here you are, looking fresh as a rose!"

Lina could only laugh, thinking how, if he had arrived a few minutes earlier he would have had an entirely different impression. But it was such a pleasure to see him, she felt almost flirtatious. "Why Mr. Downie," she started, "you'll turn my head with…" Her sudden awareness of the man standing by the flap of the meal tent stopped her from talking. "Oh! I'm sorry. I didn't realize you had someone with you."

Downie gave her his arm and escorted her to the tent. "Mrs. Clark, may I present Mr. Edward Haarten, the manager of Barclay & Company."

Lina made a quick curtsey and extended her hand. Haarten simply stared at her, clearly appraising her from head to toe.

"Mr. Haarten was so impressed with your handling of this operation, he wanted to see it for himself!" Downie meant that to lighten her thoughts, but it made Lina feel all the more flustered.

"Oh, Mr. Haarten, had I known you were coming…"

"I prefer to find things as they would regularly be." His tone was so cold, Lina was certain she had already disappointed the man beyond repair. He moved past them quickly and entered the store. Lina and Downie followed, but not before Downie gave her a reassuring wink and a smile.

For the next hour, Lina followed as Downie showed Haarten everything she had put into place. He spoke about the new businesses she had created, and the way she had increased profits. Downie led Haarten through the store, the kitchen, even the tent, but Haarten showed no interest in any of that. It was the ledger books about which he cared, and he took these with him when their tour had ended, going back to the meal tent to examine them more closely.

Lina took her cue from Downie, who stood while Haarten scrutinized the books. After many minutes of silence, Haarten looked to her. "This cousin, this companion of yours. Miss Paul. Where is she?"

"She was under the weather yesterday, and I'm sure is still asleep. Would you care for some coffee, Mr. Haarten?" Lina wanted to change the subject. She felt like she was making an excuse for Josie, even though she knew she owed none. But there was something about this man that unsettled her enormously. Even though Haarten didn't respond to the offer, she brought him a cup. He took one sip, looked at the cup suspiciously, then set it on the table without drinking any more.

After what seemed an eternity, Haarten closed the book and looked up. "Sit down, both of you." They obliged. Haarten started to take another drink of coffee, then remembering, pushed the cup away. "Mr. Downie brought me a report of your successes here. While he is often prone to unwarranted exaggeration, I see that in this case he has not embellished." No expression accompanied the comment.

"Thank you, Mr. Haarten. I'm glad you're pleased. I have every expectation that we can continue to do better. I have many ideas that even Mr. Downie hasn't heard. Why, just yesterday I was thinking that...."

Haarten raised a hand to silence her. Then he shook his head. "I'm not interested in that."

Lina was confused. Haarten seemed so terribly interested in the ledgers, why wouldn't he be interested in her plans? Fearing he was still displeased, she tried to argue her case. "But, sir, I'm certain I can make even more profit, given the chance."

"I have no doubt you can, and will. But not here."

Lina looked to Downie, but Downie nodded in Haarten's direction. "Just listen, my dear," he said.

"Mrs. Clark," continued Haarten, "you've done a fine job here. But this operation is minor. And, frankly, you've put in more effort than the place warrants. You may have increased profits here by fifty percent, but what's fifty percent of a pittance? For that's what this operation is, in terms of the interests of Barclay & Company. That is why I want you to come to San Francisco and work for us there."

It took a moment for her to fully comprehend his words. "What would I be doing in San Francisco? And Josie?" she asked, looking to Downie rather than Haarten. "What about Josephine?"

"Downie tells me you owned a store of some sort where you came from. We have similar operations in San Francisco. I'm sure we could find something. A warehouse, perhaps. As to your friend, perhaps she would like the opportunity to find a new occupation."

They were interrupted by the cries and hollers of men moving down the valley toward the tent. She ran outside to see the source of the commotion. Several men were carrying another man on their shoulders. As they came closer, she could see it was Fortas they carried. Fortas already had a bottle in his hand, as did several of the other men. They were celebrating. As they came closer, Lina stepped out to meet them.

"What's happened, boys?" she asked.

"Let me tell her!" called Fortas. The crowd turned silent as the two men carrying Fortas set him to the ground. Lina could tell Fortas was drunk, by the way he swayed as he walked toward her. He took a swig from the bottle, then set his eyes squarely on hers. "We caught him!"

"Caught who?"

"Why, the sonofabitch that attacked Miss Josie!" said a voice in the crowd.

"You did? Who was it? Where is he?" She was both delighted to know the men had finally come to their senses, and eager to see the bastard who had attacked Josie.

"Too late," sneered Fortas. "It was that Chinaman what done it. I heard them screams and came out to see him running down to that shack of his. Caught him before he could hide, though." Fortas wore a self-satisfied grin that made Lina cringe.

"Are you sure?" Josephine had said her attacker was a big man. The man Lina met yesterday was barely taller than she.

"Sure I'm sure!" bellowed Fortas. "Didn't you boys see him?" But no one answered.

"Well, then, where is he?" Lina asked.

"Dead." The word struck her like lead.

Kennedy came through the crowd toward her. "They strung him up on the spot, miss. I'm sorry." She could see in his eyes he was sincere. But her heart was breaking over the thought of the man she had only yesterday tried to reassure that everything was fine. She looked at Fortas again, ready to strike him. He was taking another swig from the bottle when she noticed the bandage on his hand. She grabbed it and pulled it down to look at it. He twisted it away.

"What happened to your hand?" she asked pointedly. "Get bit, did you?"

His lip curled in a smile. "Just a bit of a scrape."

At that moment, she knew life in Babel would never be what she had hoped when she first arrived, when everything seemed possible. She looked at the faces of the men in the crowd. They were happy with themselves, contented to be just as they were. There was no more argument in her. She turned away and went back to the tent. Haarten and Downie were waiting outside.

"Mr. Haarten, you have a deal. How soon can we leave for San Francisco?"

16

They left for San Francisco the next morning. That gave Lina and Josephine just enough time to gather their belongings. Josie needed every minute of that time, of course, but Lina had trimmed her possessions to the bare bone. She left behind forever the clothes of Ephraim's and her father's that had served her well on the trail, but took her own clothes, which were not many, and a small box of keepsakes. Among its contents were Henry's cavalry braid and the sandstone from Bartolomé. She gave Bartolomé her rifle. She feared he might need it. He was staying behind. "But only for a few weeks," he assured her.

When she accepted Haarten's offer, she hoped he could be persuaded to include Bart. Haarten flatly refused. "He may come with us, but that's all. Free or not, Mrs. Clark, there are no less than ten thousand men flooding into San Francisco this time of year. He has no chance of finding work."

Bartolomé surprised them all when he declined. "It is time for me to return home, if I can." Downie struck upon a solution that benefitted all. Bartolomé would keep the store operating until Downie's last trip in for the winter. In return, Downie would arrange Bartolomé's passage on a Barclay ship bound for the West Indies when they returned to San Francisco. Bartolomé spoke of going back to find any family he might have. "I would like to have some peace," he told her.

All Lina could do for Bartolomé was to talk to Downie privately. "Joseph Downie, if anything happens to that man before he gets to on that ship, I swear…"

"Mrs. Clark," Downie whispered, "I'll do everything in my power to make certain Bartolomé gets home. But I can't guarantee anything. You understand that?" With a nod toward Bartolomé, he added, "He does." That's when she gave Bartolomé the rifle.

****

They traveled a whole day going through more mining camps. Lina hadn't realized how much more there were to the gold fields beyond Babel. Everything she had come to hate about Babel she saw multiplied twenty-fold. And the sight only served to renew her sense of relief that they were leaving that desperate, dangerous life behind them. The second day they spent crossing the fertile valley between the Sierras and the hills ahead to the west. The sun was bright and the air cool, and Lina felt at peace. She was content to sit under the wagon bonnet on a little crate and watch the valley pass by. Josie said the cool air and the rocking of the wagon made her sleepy, so she napped.

It was mid-day the next day when Josie and Lina first saw water. They were trying to fight drowsiness again when a dazzling reflection lit the shadowy interior of the wagon. They looked out from behind the shoulder of the wagon driver, and saw water all the way to the horizon. "Is that the ocean?" Lina asked the driver.

"No ma'am. That be the bay. Ocean's way out there, past the Golden Gate."

"Gate?" Lina asked, trying to envision a gate that could hold this much water.

"Yes, ma'am. Gate to the gold, you might say," said the driver, chuckling. "Golden Gate's where the land pinches off the ocean, two spits o' land like fingers." He held his large fist up, showing his thumb and forefinger nearly touching. "Bay's a powerful big puddle, ma'am. Can't see the gate from here."

Lina was the first to see the city. She threw her left arm around Josie, and pointed with her right. Just over there, hills rose from the south side of the bay. Steep, rounded hills, dotted with buildings, still too far away to see clearly. And over there, ships waited in the harbor. They seemed so tiny. By now the wagons were on a road that rimmed the bay. They could see the water lapping the rocks along the shore. Gulls swept overhead, letting out long cries that seemed both lonely and thrilling. As she followed the flight of one gull headed back toward water, it led her eyes to a ship, cutting through the deep central waters of the bay. It was at full sail and moving toward them.

The driver pointed to the vessel. "Aye, thar's a bit of luck, ladies. That there's the Penrose, come to take us to San Francisco."

"We have to sail there?" Lina asked.

"Well ma'am, ta go overland, we'd need two more days that way," he was pointing south, "then another day north to get back over to the peninsula where San Francisco sits. This way's faster, partic'lar since we gots this ship at the ready."

The wagons came to a halt at the end of a pier. The driver came around and helped them out of the wagon. "We'll be loadin' the cargo and wagons, misses, and it'll take some time. Yas might want to find a spot to wait."

Lina felt herself drawn to the water's edge. A large rock near the pier proved the perfect perch from which to watch the Penrose maneuvered to the dock. In size the ship was not much larger than a Missouri River steamboat. But its tall masts and fluttering sails gave it a sleek and graceful line, more living thing than machine. On board, a dozen men stayed in constant motion, maneuvering lines and sails as they went. In the midst of them she saw a short, squat man in uniform. He was bellowing, she could not tell what, and pointing, she could not see where.

As the ship neared the pier, the men ceased their respective chores and moved into position. Now she could hear the man in uniform as he called to those on the pier. "Look alive, fellows, tie her fast. You there, watch your line, boy. That's it. Easy does it. Fine job, men, fine job." When the ship was secured, one sailor took a small whistle from his coat pocket, and blew a funny high note that trilled and dropped at the end. The captain of the ship, for surely that was who this man in uniform was, stood on deck by the gangplank as Haarten boarded the ship. The two men saluted one another, then the smaller, older, man, embraced the tall figure of Haarten.

"Welcome back, son. Good to see you. Everything shipshape here?" The Captain absently waved his hand at the assemblage around the docks.

"Yes sir, cargo and passengers are ready, sir."

"Fine, fine. You men, there," the captain called. "Start loading that cargo." He indicated the crates and baggage the men had stacked at the pier's end. Then he headed down the gangplank toward the others. "Downie, you old mule-peddler, how are you?" The Captain came toward Downie, gripping his hand firmly and slapping him on the shoulder.

"Fine, Captain Barclay, and yourself, sir?"

"Couldn't be better, lad. Had to come and greet you myself. Been in port too long, I guess. Needed to get back on ship, even if it was only for this short crossing. And what have you brought me this time?"

Downie leaned in to whisper. "Nearly sixty thousand, Captain."

"That's fine, Joe, my boy. Splendid." Then the captain turned to the ladies. "And these two?"

"Captain, let me introduce Miss Josephine Paul and Mrs. Carolina Clark. They've been working for us up in the diggings." The Captain took Lina's hand and gave it a light kiss. But he looked back to Downie with a puzzled expression. "Oh, no, Captain. I'm suggesting Mrs. Clark for a position in one of our mercantile operations."

"Ah," this seemed to answer the Captain's question. "Well, then, splendid Mrs. Clark. Can always use a good head for figures." Even as he spoke to Lina, Barclay's eyes were already on Josephine. He smiled at her warmly, and he took Josie's hand. "Miss Paul," he said, adding a bow before kissing her hand. "A pleasure to make your acquaintance, indeed." He allowed his eyes to take in every inch of Josephine, without apology.

Josie flashed a dimpled smile. "The pleasure is mine, Captain Barclay. How kind of you to help two enterprising women such as myself and Mrs. Clark." Josephine had launched her assault, and Barclay, like so many men before him, would be no match.

It was a short sail across the bay to San Francisco's waterfront. Lina's curiosity kept her shifting from one place to another, trying to catch a glimpse of the city. The sun was setting through the Golden Gate, a landmark she could now just faintly distinguish through the lowering sun in her eyes. Try as she might, she could not seem to stay out of the way. She was nearly knocked in the head by one sail, and another nearly tangled her up in some rigging. Finally, she gave up and returned to a seat next to Josie. She felt content, and while Josie shaded herself with her parasol, Lina delighted in the bracing wind against her face.

Halfway across the bay, the city of San Francisco started to come into focus. Dozens and dozens of ships were moored near the waterfront, some at anchor out in the harbor, some at the pier. As they steered through the sea of ships, Lina could now clearly see signs of civilization clumped around the base of hills rising abruptly, steeply from shore. There were small shacks everywhere, reminding Lina of the hovels of Babel. But along the waterfront in particular there were large, new buildings, sporting real windows and doors. And people! She could see people everywhere. "I didn't imagine anything so big," Lina said to Josie.

"Nor did I. But this is a real city, almost as big as St. Louis!"

Just then, Downie came over. "Ladies, Mr. Haarten will escort you to your lodgings. We'll have your luggage brought over directly. I hope you'll find the accommodations adequate. I'm certain we'll be seeing one another again soon."

It was a short ride along the waterfront. The streets were lined with brightly lit taverns with snappy, tinny music spilling out into the streets. Then the carriage took a turn down a dark alley, then turned again and stopped behind a row of waterfront bars. Haarten opened the carriage door. "Wait here," was all he said before he shut the door and disappeared inside the back door of a wood frame building. In a few moments, he returned with a woman by his side. She was tall and bosomy, in her forties, Lina guessed, with the brightest red hair Lina had ever seen. *Painted red*, she thought, *and it matches the paint on her face*. The dress the woman wore was just as blood red, full skirted and made from heavy brocade, cut deeply at the neckline. From her ears fell two perfect diamond drops. Haarten introduced them as he helped them from the carriage. The woman beamed at the girls. She had a deep, almost musical voice. "I'm Ada Quincannon. I run this place. Welcome to the Golden West."

"You'll be staying here. I'll have your trunks delivered in the morning," Haarten said to Lina and Josie. Then to Ada, he added, "Captain Barclay specifically requested you offer them 'his' room."

Ada's eyes widened. "If that's what he wants. Very well, ladies, go on in," Ada told them. "I'll show you to your room in just a moment."

When they were inside, she turned to Haarten. "Well, that one's a looker, but the other, she doesn't seem the sort at all."

"She is not 'the sort.' They are inseparable, those two, but Mrs. Clark is here for more reputable work. Miss Paul is yours. She is of no interest to me."

Ada tossed out a laugh. "That's your trouble, Haarten. If you took a little more interest in 'that sort', it might take a little of that starch out of your collar." She turned and went inside.

Ada led Lina and Josie to their room, the last door in a long hallway of doors. After six months of bed rolls and hard packed dirt, the cool clean room seemed too good to be true, even if it was a bit cramped. The room overflowed with ornate furnishings. To the left of the door stood an oak washstand, topped with a hand-painted porcelain bowl and pitcher. Next to it stood a large chifforobe, decorated with carved leaves and flowers, and a bunch of grapes as the door pull. It was a corner room, which afforded it two windows, each draped with heavy curtains. The floor was covered with two small oriental rugs, showing dazzling blues, golds and reds. But the centerpiece of the room was the massive bed. The dark, polished cherry wood made the clean comforter and fat pillows seem all the more white and crisp. The headboard stood eight feet high, and the footboard was nearly as tall as Lina, giving the whole piece the look of an upholstered sleigh. The bed looked so inviting, Lina couldn't resist walking over to gently touch it.

Ada saw the young woman's hesitancy. "Go on, bounce on it, if you've a mind. It's yours for as long as you need it." Ada moved toward the windows and tied back the curtains. Josie took Ada at her word and plopped her backside on the bed. She gave the bed a bounce or two, then let the reach of her fingers draw her backwards until she lay flat on the bed, stretched out like a cat.

Lina was not as quick to settle in. *Business first.* She walked straight over to Ada and spoke. "Miss Quincannon, I'm not certain what your understanding is about how we're to pay for such a beautiful room. We have very little money right now, and won't have, until we start work."

Ada reached for the single straight-back chair that stood next to the chifforobe, placed it beside the bed, and motioned for Lina to sit on the bed next to Josie. "Look here, ladies, there's no need for worry.

I suspect Haarten hasn't told you a thing, has he? I thought not. He doesn't much care for me, or my business. Well, never mind him. Let me explain. I run this place for Captain Barclay. He owns this tavern, like he owns a lot of businesses in town. You understand what those other girls are doing here, don't you?"

"What a silly question," Josie said. "They work in your saloon."

"That's right! I'm glad you said it that way, because that's exactly what they're hired to do. They're here to be good company for the men who come in here, as long as a fellow minds his manners. Anything else they want to do, upstairs, is up to them, but the house takes a cut. We make out alright whether these girls are extra sociable or not. Usually, we take rent out of the girls' pay. But Barclay wants you to have this room. It's his—I mean, he keeps it reserved just for him. He's what you might call a regular customer. And since he owns the place, he gets his pick of the rooms."

Ada paused for any reaction from the two, then continued. "Now it's my understanding, Miss Paul, that you've an interest in working here. That's good news to me. You'll do well here, and we'll do well by you. So there's no charge for the room. Now Mrs. Clark, Haarten tells me he has another job for you. But if you're staying here together, there's no need for you to pay, either."

Lina thought for a moment, then said, "I'll take the Captain's hospitality for now. But I'd rather pay my way, Miss Quincannon."

"Call me Ada. Well, you can take that up with Barclay yourself, then." She rose and walked toward the door. "You're welcome to come downstairs after you've settled in. You won't have any problems, any attention you don't welcome, I promise you that," she added before she left.

****

Edward Haarten returned with all deliberate speed to Barclay's estate on Rincon Hill. Until recently it was the largest, most ornate house in San Francisco, a mansion by current standards. But new homes were springing up everywhere. These modern castles were the residences of the city's burgeoning population of merchants, traders, bankers, and profiteers, each competing to seem more prosperous than the next.

Not Barclay. The house he had built was large, but he had built it as a home, and for entertaining his friends. William Barclay had spent his early years sailing with the best of England's merchant explorers, roaming the oceans for the newest, finest, most exotic imports to be bought, traded or stolen, and he had had a grand life. He left England to take command of a ship trading along the eastern seaboard of the United States, and had mastered one of the first ships that brought men around the Horn in search of fortune in this part of the New World. Barclay had seen the possibilities waiting for the outpost springing up on the shores of the bay, and it was here he chose to make his home. Already a wealthy man both by virtue of inheritance, and now by clever professional dealings, he quickly turned a sizeable fortune into a greater one. He had survived the loss of ships to storms and men to the lures of gold, and had emerged a successful transporter and purveyor of the precious goods needed to fuel San Francisco's growth. He loved the wealth that he created, but he loved more the place he had created for himself in this town. He was less interested in the attentions of the bankers and profiteers than the rag tags along the waterfront. To them, Captain Barclay was a sort of rajah, a bringer of prosperity and pleasure, all meted out with genuine conviviality. He was welcomed in every shop, tavern and whorehouse along the waterfront, those he owned and those he did not. And while the city's new, self-proclaimed aristocracy did not approve of his lower associations, they courted him nonetheless—for his money, if not his society.

When Haarten arrived at Barclay's house, he entered without announcement, as was his custom. Barclay had a man-servant, Jackson, who stood in command of the household, and usually met guests at the door. Haarten regarded Jackson and the rest of the staff with indifference. He considered himself their superior in his service to Barclay, and paid them only minimal notice. Besides, Barclay didn't demand much of his servants in the way of domestic protocol, and Haarten disapproved. He came from an aristocratic background, where servants understood the consequences of poor performance. In Barclay's home there were no such consequences.

Barclay was in his library, lounging in one of the leather chairs that sat in front of the hearth. Haarten knocked lightly. "Sir? You asked me to come?" Haarten entered and waited for Barclay.

"Oh, for God's sake, man, sit down. You're off duty now. Pour yourself a drink." Barclay pointed to the mantel, and several bottles of liquor. Haarten chose the brandy, but there was nothing relaxed about his posture as he took the seat next to Barclay. With meticulous practice he cupped the snifter as he swirled the brandy to warm it. Even the sip he took seemed cautious and measured. He spoke to his employer as Barclay stared deeply into the fire.

"Sullivan and Porter have seen to the cargo, Captain. Downie has made arrangements for the gold. The ladies have been taken to Miss Quincannon's." Haarten took another sip, then asked, "Have you anything else?"

"Yes, damn it, I want you to sit here and keep me company for a moment." Barclay stretched his short legs out before him, and took a healthy swallow of his whiskey. "Tell me about your trip inland." Haarten reported with a clerk's precision on the condition of the camps, and the status of their current yield, all without emotion. Barclay listened, then spoke.

"Fine, Edward. Very, uh, precise. Now…" He straightened himself in the chair and leaned toward Haarten, grinning. "Tell me about your two special passengers, Miss Paul and her friend."

"Downie had them working the store in Babel. Mrs. Clark demonstrates an aptitude for figures. The Company can benefit from this expertise. Good shopkeepers are hard to find, as I've told you before, sir. Women are particularly good, for they usually lack a source of independent means, and so are less likely to chase opportunity. They are more honest and reliable than the men we find, and while they are physically less capable, well, one can always find a fellow in need of a quick dollar who'll carry crates."

"You've a real talent for business, my boy." His glass empty, Barclay stood and poured himself another. "That Miss Paul. Quite a beauty, wouldn't you say?"

"I suppose, sir." Haarten's flat response irked Barclay. He liked Haarten, and relied upon him heavily. The older Barclay grew, the less interest he seemed to have in acquiring more wealth. Haarten always saw new opportunities, however, and he had no doubts as to his loyalty. But Barclay considered it a personal failure that he hadn't been more of an influence on the younger man's view of the world.

"Alright, Haarten, you're dismissed. It seems to pain you to stay here and make small talk with me. You're ruining the affects of my good whiskey. I'll see you at the Penrose first thing tomorrow." Silently, Haarten set down his glass, nodded, and left the old man to stare into the fire, remembering the vision of a beautiful young woman.

****

Josie had wanted to go downstairs, of course, but Lina lured her away with a bath, their first real bath in five months. One entire room upstairs in the Golden West was dedicated to this purpose, which seemed to Lina the greatest of luxuries. The girls took turns—Josie first, then Lina. Ada employed an old man she called Ortiz to help her around the place, and when the girls asked about the bath, Ada sent him running up and down the stairs with kettles of hot water, and soon had the tub filled. The girls added a drop of every perfume they found on the washstand beside the tub. Scrubbing the grime off seemed to take Lina forever, and though the bath made her feel better, she marveled at how it positively transformed Josie. As she helped her friend brush her long black hair, she admitted with a sigh, "Josie, there's no doubt about it. You've a real talent for beauty. I could bathe from now 'til next Sunday and not come out of a bath looking half so lovely as you."

Josie smiled, admiring her reflection in the small mirror above the washstand. She moved her head back and forth, practicing her art. She smiled deeply to let her dimples show, then pushed her lips into a pout, while looking up through her thick black lashes. She held her hair on top of her head with one hand, and used the other to adjust the absently looping curls.

"See here, Lina, you've shown me that a person can make their own way in the world, using whatever talents God gave them. He made you smart, he made me pretty."

"You're very bright, Josie, honey."

"Oh! And you're pretty! You're much prettier than you realize. With that hair of yours, you could be a real stunner, had you any interest in it. But you're wrong, Lina. I'm more clever than smart. Clever enough to use what I've got to get what I want. And now that we're here, that's just what I'm going to do."

17

Their first morning in San Francisco, Lina woke early. She slipped out of bed, and opened the window to look out on the streets below. Everywhere there were signs of a city coming to life, and though the occasional cry or whistle broke the early morning stillness, the scene for the most part played out with quiet vigor.

Lina breathed deeply from the cool morning air. This was the west she had come to be a part of, and she would waste no more time before seeing it. She dressed without waking Josie, but just before she left, she nudged her. "Best get up." Then she went downstairs.

The large main room of the Golden West looked much different in morning light. The acrid mix of stale smoke and spilled whiskey still clung in the air, but the doors were propped open and sunshine flooded the room. The chairs were all turned on top of the tables, and the long mahogany bar was clean and bare. The room was still except for the sound of Ortiz sweeping the floor. At the far end sat Ada, with Edward Haarten, drinking coffee as he looked through some papers.

Ada looked entirely different than she had the night before. The paint and the red dress were gone. Had it not been for the same flaming hair Lina might not have recognized her at all. This morning her face was clean and scrubbed, her dress elegant but simple.

"You're up bright and early." Ada motioned for her to join them by pouring another cup of coffee.

Haarten kept reading, but added, "Early? The morning's half gone, and there's much for us to do."

"Take it easy, Edward," said Ada. "Give the girl time to eat something." Ada motioned to Ortiz, who soon returned with a full plate of breakfast.

Haarten laid the last paper down. "Mrs. Clark, I have need of your abilities in one of our warehouse operations. It is primary to our shipping operations, and has been poorly managed. Most of the men there are untrustworthy, to say the least. I need a smart, reliable person to protect our interests from thieves and embezzlers. It's not a complicated operation, but our losses there affect all aspects of the firm. So please hurry up. Finish that so we can get started." Lina tried to enjoy the last bites, but found it impossible as Haarten stared at her every swallow with blatant impatience. Finally she surrendered. She took one more sip of coffee, and by the time the cup was returned to the saucer, Haarten was on his feet. "That's it then." He stood, and as soon as she began to rise, he took her by the elbow and led her directly through the swinging louvered doors of the Golden West, and onto the streets of San Francisco. "You'll be walking to work each day. It's best to learn the route."

Lina tried hard to keep pace with Haarten, but he was tall, and used his long legs to their full advantage. And there was so much to see. She found she would tarry only a second to study life on the street and he would be yards in front of her. Then she had to run to catch up.

The street down which they hurried had the most fantastic assortment of shops Lina had ever seen. There were grocers and dry goods shops, chandlers and tinkers, gunsmiths, blacksmiths and farriers, cobblers, coopers and wheelwrights. And activity was not confined to the shops. On the street, shopkeepers setting up for the day had to work against a steady stream of hawkers and vendors, carriages, men on horseback, scullery maids, sailors, drunks, a few stray dogs, and everywhere, seagulls.

Abruptly, Edward Haarten stopped. "Here, now. This is the warehouse." They entered an enormous building, a whole city block long. Inside it was one large, dimly lit room, save for a small partitioned space near the front door, where she could see an elderly man fast asleep over a desk. Everywhere else, men were loading, hauling and stacking all types of goods. One whole area was reserved for lumber, another for kegs. *Whiskey or nails*, Lina decided. Over there one corner was devoted to produce, not quite fresh. As Haarten led her through the warehouse, men picked up the pace as they caught sight of him.

Haarten grabbed a box and set it down beside her. He pulled her to stand on it, then he spoke up. "Give me your attention." Everyone stopped. "This is Mrs. Clark. She will be overseeing operations here. Obey her instructions as you would my own. Should she report any dereliction, you may expect the usual measure of discipline. That is all." The men went back to work without a word, and Lina, who felt embarrassed by this introduction, scampered down as soon as she could.

Then Haarten walked to the little office where the old man, now awake, seemed too intensely focused on the work before him. "I must have woken him," grumbled Haarten, taking her aside. "That gentleman is Walter Monroe. He is employed here solely at the pleasure of Captain Barclay. Another of his charity cases. But the man is old and feeble of mind. He's honest enough, I suppose, but he doesn't have to be asleep for the thieves here to take advantage of him. Captain Barclay insists you work under his supervision, but supervision is not a task Monroe is up to. I expect you to take the initiative, to learn the accounts as quickly as possible, to learn the men's work habits, and to stop the hemorrhage." Finally, he led her toward Monroe's office, and entered without a knock.

The older man was on his feet. "Good mornin', Mr. Haarten. How might I be of assistance this fine morning?"

"Monroe, this is Mrs. Carolina Clark. She is here to assist you with all functions of this office. See that she is completely familiar with each account immediately. By week's end, she should be able to run things as if you weren't here."

Monroe obviously had no idea he needed an assistant, for his expression betrayed his lack of enthusiasm. Yet he smiled at Lina pleasantly, then answered, "Certainly, Mr. Haarten. If that is what the Captain wants," emphasizing the reference to Barclay.

Haarten turned to Lina. "Report here each morning, except Sunday, by 6 o'clock. You may leave at 6 o'clock in the evening, provided your work for the day is done. You will be paid the sum of five dollars per day. I'll return before week's end to check on your progress."

Haarten left, but his words still rang in Lina's ears. *Five dollars a day!* She had never made that kind of money. Lina smiled as she stepped inside Mr. Monroe's cramped and cluttered office to start her new, independent life.

****

Haarten allowed himself a little optimism. For weeks he had tried to find a reliable fellow to oversee this operation. But it was the same in every warehouse all over the city. Reliable men were not merely scarce, they were non-existent. So Haarten had been forced to employ a woman, and not even a woman of maturity. This Carolina Clark was little more than a girl by his estimation. But the Babel experience had shown she just might be the answer to his prayer. *If she is*, Haarten thought, *then I can turn my energies to better use.* For Edward Haarten, the better use was anything that served the substantial ambitions he had for Barclay & Company—and for himself.

Edward Haarten couldn't remember a time in his forty years when these ambitions hadn't been his foremost thoughts. Even as a young boy, he was keenly aware that he wanted something other than what his strict New England upbringing afforded him. The son of a Boston banker, he was raised with the kind of affluence that made other young men indolent, satisfied to inherit their father's wealth, as their fathers had before them. To such men, Boston was the center of the world, a thriving commercial city, filled with culture and sophistication, and a safe, certain life.

While his boyhood friends planned their predictable futures, Edward Haarten would go down to Boston harbor. His father had introduced him to the place one day, and after that, Edward showed little interest in anything else, except that which would prepare him for a life at sea. His interest in mathematics was a means to understand navigation. His interest in geography was confined to the world's ports of call. When his father began to notice his son's obsession with the subject, he tried everything to dissuade him, but to no avail. Edward Haarten was a single-minded young man. When it came time for college, Edward announced his intentions to go to sea instead. The senior Mr. Haarten disowned him on the spot, dismissing his son's plans as romantic fantasy. He never bothered to ask Edward his motives, and Edward never felt the need to justify his intent. He took his disinheritance as the price he had to pay for what he wanted.

But there was one price on which he had not counted. There was a young woman, a beauty with pale blonde hair, the daughter of one of his father's most prominent clients. She found him dashing and handsome, and she was the only thing, besides his career, that interested him at all. Their brief romance, like so much of their lives, had been easy at first. But when he told her of his disinheritance, she was astounded that he would put something as seemingly frivolous as his own desires ahead of the plans she had for them together. Without money or position, she lost all interest in him. The rejection shocked Edward. In his simple, straightforward way, it had not occurred to him that he could have been so fooled by her. He promised himself it would never happen again. It never had.

He threw himself into his career, and he succeeded. Each ship he signed on with was chosen for a purpose—to see a new port, to learn a new task, to serve under a particular captain. That was why he had come to Barclay. He knew the man's reputation, and the size of his assets. He saw Barclay building an empire, and he resolved to be a part of that. He followed him to California, and stayed with him through the lean times when the city was starting. Edward Haarten was making himself a small fortune with the money Barclay paid him, and with his own speculations on the side.

But had it been up to Haarten, Barclay & Company would have chosen a place more sophisticated than San Francisco as the center of an empire. There was still that much of the Yankee prude in him, that he had a fervid disdain for the tawdry side of San Francisco life. He hadn't met what he considered a single truly hard-working soul in all his years here. *But perhaps, this Mrs. Clark is different.* He smiled to himself as he thought about her, leaving the warehouse that day. Perhaps, he thought, she was just the person for whom he had been looking.

****

Monroe was a more able teacher than Haarten would have guessed. He understood the operation well, but was too old for the attention to detail the job demanded. Lina treated him with a moderate amount of deference. He appreciated that, so in turn he treated her like a doting student. Monroe showed her the ledgers first, believing this would be the hardest part to master. But she picked up the accounting tasks in no time, and was anxious to learn more. She could tell from the books that some shipments were coming in short, going out shorter, with more frequency than could be accounted for by sloppy bookkeeping. If she was to 'stop the hemorrhage,' as Haarten required, she would need to understand how the shipments moved in and out, and from where and to where. Monroe explained that this warehouse was for Barclay's local shipments. Currently, the bulk of the materials on hand were for construction. There were vast stores of lumber coming in from the north, bricks from Mexico, hardware from the eastern seaboard, and furniture and cabinetry from around the world.

There were also plenty of everyday items. Food, bolts of cloth, cookware, even a few fine rare items like clocks, bathtubs, and French perfume. And liquor. Barrel after barrel of every sort of liquor. In no time, Lina determined it was liquor and lumber that seemed to be what most often came up short on the books. She focused her immediate attention on these, and by the end of the first week, when Haarten arrived to learn her progress, she was glad to have something to suggest. He brought her pay, and then walked her back to the Golden West to hear her report.

"I've already caught a couple of men slipping a few board feet out with other orders, sliding them along the bottom of the wagon, then burying them under other crates or barrels. Also, I've found old boards slipped in with the new lumber, keeping the inventory right. That's just the outbound side, of course. I'm almost certain the loads that are coming in are short as well, but that will take a little longer to figure."

"Good, good." Haarten kept his eye trained on her as the two walked.

"Then there's the liquor. I suspect they're watering it down, probably at night when I'm not there. You might try adding a couple of new guards for the place. Those you've got there now are probably in on the deal."

"And the men? Do they follow your directions?"

"Well, you can imagine some are none too pleased. But evidently your admonishments have sheltered me from any defiance, if that's your meaning. I do a fair job of handling myself in such situations, regardless."

"Yes," Haarten said without mockery. "I suspect you do." They arrived at the entrance to the Golden West. "Mrs. Clark, I'll be visiting with you from time to time. If there is anything you should need, send word for me at Barclay's." He handed her a small white card, imprinted with his name and an address she didn't know.

"Is this also where I might contact Captain Barclay?"

Haarten stopped. "Why would you want to do that?"

Lina felt she needn't share her real motive with Haarten. "Simply to send him a short note of thanks, Mr. Haarten. For the job and the accommodations."

"Certainly, how appropriate. Yes, Mrs. Clark, you may send word to Captain Barclay at that address." He started to leave, then turned back quickly. "But you do understand, under no circumstances are you to visit Captain Barclay there directly."

I'm not good enough, Lina thought. Clearly that was Haarten's meaning—he didn't even try to disguise it. "No need to worry, Mr. Haarten. I won't be dropping in for tea." She turned on her heel and swept into the saloon.

****

The Golden West was open for business. It was the dinner hour and the crowds were just beginning to trickle in. Ada was standing by the bar, painted and primped for the night, talking with her bartender. "Well, you look like you're 'bout ready to bust, missy," she said when Lina come through the doors.

"I feel as though I just might." Lina came over to her, and whispered in her ear.

Ada laughed and squeezed both Lina's hands in her own. "Well, that's a fine haul for a week's work. Got ya off to a good start, I'd say." Lina nodded.

"Ada, do you have any note paper?" Ada went behind the bar to the till, and produced a clean white sheet and envelope. "Thank you. Oh, and Ada, how much do you charge for our room upstairs?"

"Now, honey, like I told ya before. No charge. Captain Barclay insists."

"Then, how much would a room cost, if I could find one?"

"A room like that would go for maybe a hundred dollars a week. But you might find a suitable room somewhere else for much less, maybe a couple of bucks. See, honey, best you keep that money for yourself. Don't be worrying about the room, just now."

Lina headed up the stairs to their room. Josie was inside, changing her clothes. Lina gathered her friend in her arms. "Oh, honey, I miss you. It's hard to believe isn't it, after all the time we've spent together, day after day. You'd think we'd be sick to death of one another. I got paid today, Josie! Five dollars! Five whole dollars, can you believe it? Maybe, if I'm careful, and work hard, I can save enough to find a room of my own. No more living above a saloon, huh?"

Josie pulled herself from Lina's embrace. "It's not so bad here. There're so many interesting people coming and going all the time. Something new every day." She looked at herself in the mirror one last time. Satisfied, she said, "Well, I'm off to work as well!"

Lina held her arm and stopped her. "Josie, you know, here's your chance to change your mind. I was hoping…I mean, I thought after what happened in Babel, you might change your mind. Consider another line of work, perhaps?"

Josephine patted Lina's hand, then pulled it gently from her arm. "I just wanted to change the location, honey. Not the business. I haven't changed my mind." She gave Lina a peck on the check, then added, "But I promise to be careful." Then she left.

Lina sat on the bed, and with a book in her lap to support her, she took the note paper and wrote in her best hand:

> *Captain Barclay,*
>
> *On behalf of myself and Miss Josephine Paul,*
> *I write to thank you for the opportunities and the*
> *accommodations you have provided us. However,*
> *as it is my deepest hope to make our way here, I am*
> *enclosing two dollars as payment for my lodging with*
> *Miss Quincannon. I realize this might not be equitable*
> *compensation, but it is my intention to send you this*
> *amount weekly until such time as I can secure my own*
> *room.*
> *Respectfully yours,*
> *Carolina Clark*

She folded the bills inside the paper and placed them both in the envelope. On the outside, she wrote the address Haarten had given her. Then she headed downstairs again.

The Golden West was filling up by the minute. The piano player clanked out a jangling version of "Old Rosin' the Beau," and the sound of the keno wheel clinked in time to the tune. Scattered around the room, Ada's girls were pressing glasses of whiskey and beer into the grasps of thirsty men. The brightness, the laughter, the jocular mood— Lina did understand Josie's attraction to this life, even if she herself felt out of place here.

"Ada, how would I see this letter gets to Captain Barclay?"

With a nod of her head, Ada answered, "Give it to him yourself, honey. He's right over there. With Josephine." Lina turned. Behind the stairs were three tables, each surrounded by partitions that made them more intimate, but still open to view. In the first she saw the back of Josie's head, and sitting opposite her, the ruddy face of Captain Barclay. Lina made a beeline across the room. She drew a few stares, her plain workday clothes in stark contrast to the bright colored gowns of the other girls in the room. She simply thrust her chin forward with her head held high.

"Excuse me, Captain Barclay." Barclay and Josie sat, heads together, exchanging a laugh. Neither had seen her approach.

The Captain rose immediately, and gave her a short bow. "Mrs. Clark, how pleased I am you could join us. Your lovely companion and I were just about to share dinner. Join us, won't you?"

"Thank you, Captain. I only came over to give you this." Lina handed him the envelope.

He opened it and read the contents. Pulling out the two bills, he said, "Oh, Mrs. Clark, this isn't necessary, really."

"I feel it is necessary, sir. You've given us an opportunity, by bringing us here. Beyond that I can't, in good conscience, take more."

Barclay studied the willful look on Lina's face. "Alright, Mrs. Clark. I accept your payment. But still, I would ask that you sit down and join us for dinner. Surely there can be no harm in that. A simple gesture of welcome to two lovely and obviously diligent young ladies. Nothing more." He held a chair for Lina, who paused a moment, then sat.

"Splendid, splendid!" Just then, the waiter appeared with two large steaks, and placed them before Barclay and Josie. Barclay handed his to Lina, saying to the waiter, "Matt, another one here, if you would be so kind."

Josie plunged into her meal with abandon, and Barclay laughed. "A girl with healthy appetites. A wonderful thing to see." His eyes stayed on Josie, but he spoke to Lina. "Miss Paul has been regaling me with some of the exploits you shared on your trip. Quite amazing, really. I've traveled most of the world, but I've never been more than five hundred miles from the sea. The country you traveled sounds quite remarkable."

"Oh, it was!" Josie bubbled between bites. "Horrible, nasty, places really, but remarkable. I would never have come if it weren't for Lina."

"Really, why do you say that?" Barclay asked Josie.

"What Josie means, Captain, is that I was the more experienced traveler of the two. My father and my husband were outfitters for the western trails, which gave me the chance to learn some about overland travel."

"Ah, so you come from a background of commerce, then. That explains your natural proclivities for business. Edward has told me of your skills. With those talents you'll no doubt go far."

Lina took the opportunity to make her point again. "Exactly, Captain. Sir, I mean no disrespect, nor do I wish you to think me ungrateful. It's simply that it is terribly important to me that I make my own way."

"I do understand, my dear, I do." There was nothing but kindness and compassion on his face. "I've been very fortunate, but I have also worked hard in my time. I understand the gratification of completing such an admirable goal." He motioned with his left hand. "Look around the room, Mrs. Clark. I say with all humility that a good number of the people here, indeed a number of folks in this part of the city, have benefited from my fortune. My own success came as the result of a good many personal sacrifices. Sacrifices that caused me to wonder, once all was said and done, why I had worked so hard. I had no family of my own, no home to speak of. When I decided to stay here, I realized how much my wealth could do. These people, the ones that I've helped, that I employ, they are my friends and my family in the truest sense of the word. They owe me nothing, except a good day's work, and to be happy and decent to one another."

Lina watched the Captain carefully. There was a glisten to his eye as he spoke of these people he so obviously loved. Josie had noticed it to, and Lina saw her smile at Barclay with genuine affection.

"I sincerely hope, no matter what your future may hold, that the two of you will also come to think of me as a friend." He reached across and patted both women on the arm, just as the waiter returned. "Wonderful, Matthew. I'm ravenous. And bring another bottle of port at your next opportunity, young man. Now ladies, forgive me, but I'm simply famished." Barclay thrust into the steak, and Josie and Lina followed suit.

Lina's affection for Barclay began that evening, and it made her proud to think that she was working for such a seemingly honorable man. She felt a kindred spirit with someone who understood why making her own way was so important to her. So she wasn't quite sure what to make of the fact that the next time Edward Haarten paid her, he said, "Captain Barclay instructed me to raise your pay two dollars per week." He eyed her suspiciously. "Did you approach him about additional wages? I specifically asked that you not come to his home."

"I didn't, sir. I promise. He came to the Golden West one evening and I only tried to pay him for my room. I insisted he take the money."

"Apparently, he is insisting you take it back."

"Apparently." She looked at the bills, trying to think of a way to force Barclay to accept it. Haarten could see it on her face.

"Best you relinquish that notion, Mrs. Clark."

"The Captain is evidently used to getting his way, then?"

"Entirely," Haarten answered grimly. "Sometimes even to his detriment."

18

Lina and Josephine saw each other only in passing, one always sleeping during the height of the other's day, or night. So Lina developed a new bond with someone who shared both her interests and her hours—Ada Quincannon. Lina's friendship with Ada grew over morning biscuits and coffee. Ada took an interest in Lina, and often provided sound advice. Early on, she told Lina, "It's always best to ask more than you tell, and to listen more than you ask." Ada followed her own advice, and was particularly tight lipped about the customers of the Golden West. If Lina asked about anyone in the saloon, Ada would stop her. "Best not to carry tales, Lina. Even true ones. Folks around here like to keep their business to themselves."

On more general matters regarding life in San Francisco, Ada was open and friendly, and if there was no time for Lina to roam San Francisco to learn about it, at least she had Ada to tell her stories. But it was Ada's stories of her own life that Lina found most interesting. They shared common experiences. Ada had come to San Francisco from the east, via Cincinnati, then New Orleans and Mexico. Her motivations had started much as Josie's had, though her background was meager, like Lina's. But she had ambition, and by the time she met Barclay in Mexico, she had her own place. "Not as grand as the Golden West," she told Lina, "but a real pearl of a place regardless." It hadn't taken much for Barclay to entice her to come to California. She was one of the many he had set up in business here. But what impressed Lina in particular was the way Ada treated this like a business. Ada paid shrewd attention to the cost of everything, and knew within a penny how much she made on each transaction. She planned ahead, and had ideas for improving the Golden West that she budgeted for, and worked on constantly.

So when Ada Quincannon asked Lina Clark "What now?" even though Lina feigned ignorance, she knew in her gut what Ada meant. It was a question that had plagued Lina after that first week. Though she continued to pay Barclay for her room and Ada for her meals, she had few other expenses. So each week she was able to lay aside a tidy sum. True, it wasn't yet enough for her to feel independent. One small change in her circumstances could wipe it out in a week or two. But for the first time in her life, it was her own money. It was growing, and she didn't owe anyone anything. It was a heady feeling, but it did beg the question—*what next?*

"You've been thinking about it, I can tell," Ada said after Lina's prolonged silence. "So, tell me what you've been thinking."

"Well, at first, I thought I wanted to find another room. Somewhere perhaps a bit quieter. But the truth is, I like it here. And I would miss Josie. Maybe one day I will, but after that, I don't know. I suppose I could afford a new dress, it's just that nice clothes seem a waste down in that dirty warehouse."

"You're right about the dresses. I've been meaning to give you the name of my seamstress, Mrs. Birnbaum. Does lovely work. But that wasn't my meaning. I'm referring to your own ambitions. You do realize, don't you, that Barclay would likely set you up in your own shop, if you'd have an interest. He knows you, and Edward speaks of you favorably, which is about as much as you'll ever get from that one." As she took a sip of coffee, she added, "And of course, Barclay would do anything for Josie."

"Do you suppose? Oh, I couldn't think to ask such a favor. And besides, what sort of a shop would I run?"

"Yes, I do suppose, and no, it wouldn't be a favor. Barclay's generous, but he is a businessman after all. He'd be partners of some sort, as he is with me here. But he's a good partner to have. Not a meddler. And as to the sort of shop, well, it could be anything you'd like. From what you've told me, you've sold everything from guns to butter. On the other hand, this could be your chance for something new."

Lina was dumbstruck. A moment ago she was stumped by what to do with a little extra cash. Now her thoughts were frozen by the notion of so limitless a world.

"Honey, time's wasting," Ada said. "Think about all this on your walk. Better get to work now."

****

With renewed interest, Lina resolved to spend what spare time she had to learn about the city. Six days a week she maintained her routine, but on the Sabbath she walked to every corner of San Francisco. She learned the location of every merchant. She made notes of what each shop was selling. She always stopped to watch new buildings rising up, and she tried to learn something about every ship in the harbor. All her energy was spent keeping abreast of what happened in the city, for in this way she felt she might see opportunities for Barclay & Company, and for herself.

Ada's idea had grabbed her imagination fiercely, and it overwhelmed her. Not that she had a moment's hesitation about whether she was up to the task of running her own store. In fact, she leaped over that notion entirely to be completely undone by the sheer range of possibilities, particularly in San Francisco. With everything growing in every conceivable direction, she wore herself out trying to second guess which might be the best opportunity, only to see the speed of growth eclipse the moment to seize it. Every day she was possessed of a new idea.

She was lounging across the bed one evening after a particularly invigorating scouting expedition, making notes in her little notebook. Josephine, fresh from her bath, watched Lina in the reflection of the vanity mirror. Her brow wrinkled, her hand pressing red marks into her cheeks as it propped up her head, Lina would occasionally mumble something to herself, scratch something out or jot something down, then flip back and forth between pages.

Josephine turned around. "Lina, look at me."

Lina looked up. "Hmm?" She sat up. "What is it?"

Josie walked over, sat next to her, and took Lina's hands in her own. "Lina, sweet, you worry that something might happen to me, and I love you for that. But I worry about you, too. I worry something *won't* happen to you. You work so very hard, but to what end? We're finally here! California! What we worked all those months for! Don't be afraid to enjoy yourself."

Lina leveled a maternal gaze on Josephine. "But I do enjoy this, Josephine. I know I probably seem tired, and I am, but…" Lina stopped herself. She had resolved not to mention Ada's idea to Josie. Josie would say something to Barclay, Lina was sure of it, and she wanted to wait until she had the perfect idea for her business before Barclay was told. "I just enjoy it, that's all."

"But you need to socialize, too, Lina, and since you've devoted Sundays to these excursions around town, you've left yourself no time to have fun. Go on picnics, take a buggy ride, meet people. Maybe even find a beau."

Lina laughed. "I should have known it would come back to that."

"Well, now you don't have any excuse, do you? We're here. We've made our lives. I'm keeping my eye out for you, even if you aren't." Josie gave her a playful pinch on the arm.

Lina laughed. "Oh, is that so? And have you any prospects?"

"Perhaps. Too soon to tell."

"Too soon? When, then?"

"In a few weeks, I should think. But you'll not get a word from me before then, Lina Clark!" They started giggling like the girls they were now too worldly to be any more.

****

Lina had been so absorbed in her work, she had not really thought about Christmas. For her, Christmas would always mean snow. But there was no snow here. Christmas was always cold, and the leanest time of year in her childhood. San Francisco might be grey, but the temperature was moderate. And abundance came in the form of Captain Barclay's party.

Barclay had invited everyone who worked for him, and all the city's reprobates, to a party at his home. Lina surprised herself with how much she began to look forward to the party, but she was concerned about her lack of attire. Every dress she had was only suitable for work, all plain blouses and high-waisted black skirts. The ladies at the Golden West would be wearing their finest gowns. So it seemed a good opportunity to take up Ada's offer of the seamstress. Mrs. Birnbaum was another of Barclay's patronage businesses, but she did not have the same jovial demeanor that most of his partners shared. She was a stern, middle-aged woman, who herself dressed quite dowdily. But her husband was Barclay's personal tailor, and judging by Ada's attire, Mrs. Birnbaum knew how to make a stylish gown.

Lina neither wanted nor could afford a very stylish gown. She was happy to take a gown declined by another client, and altered to fit her. It was a modest design, cut from pale green taffeta, but it was suitable for the occasion. Josie fixed Lina's hair in a beautiful braid, and Ada loaned her a warm wool cape. Lina felt as pretty as she could ever remember.

The feathers and frills the ladies from the Golden West wore made the group conspicuous as they walked to the party that night. The evening had been so balmy they decided to walk to Barclay's house. And, if their finery weren't enough to attract attention, they chattered and tittered all the way there. Even Lina was swept up in their mood.

But when they arrived at Barclay's, they all fell silent. The flock of females stood on the street, looking up at the great house. In later years, San Francisco would see mansions that would put Barclay's to shame, but in these modest beginnings, the city had no finer residence. Although it was only two stories tall, its cupola and five chimney stacks gave it the look of a much taller building. The fact that it was built of brick made it seem massive. It was new, scarcely more than a year old, so that every element of its design was crisp.

That evening, the house seemed a living thing, filled with voices, music and movement. As soon as they entered, the other girls were embraced by old friends, then were led straight to the dance floor. Thank heavens for Ada, who as ever, was keeping an eye out for Lina. "Here, honey, let me show you around." Ada knew everyone there. Everyone called her by name, waved her toward them, rushed over to greet her. And every time someone did, Ada made certain Lina was introduced.

Before long, Lina found herself with a glass of champagne and listening to the pleasant chatter of the group. She was content to stay as she was, on the fringe of the festivities. There was just so much to see! The long room where they stood was set up to serve as the ballroom. In fact, it was actually three rooms, normally separated by ornate pocket doors that created a series of parlors and sitting rooms. At the far end, a band of musicians were playing lively tunes as dancers thrashed about, but most people mingled throughout the house. There was a constant stream of folks moving up and down the central stairs, and while Lina did not yet feel quite so bold as to go exploring up there, she was curious, and having no one in particular with whom to talk, she decided to look around. She stepped out of the ballroom, and into the long central hallway.

Lina had never been to such a party, never even imagined such a party. Everywhere she looked, in the dining room or in the ballroom, vignettes were played out. Every laugh, every whisper, every flirtatious smile or friendly embrace seemed beautifully timed and performed, as much a part of the dazzling affect of the evening as the lights, the music and the food. Even though she felt distant from the players, it seemed somehow right to be so, as if she were the only audience for this comedy.

She found herself standing outside a small room at the front of the house. The door was slightly open, but at first she did not consider entering. Then something caught her eye—a shelf filled with books. After standing there for some minutes, and hearing no sound inside, she cautiously pushed open the heavy door and looked inside. This was Barclay's library.

The room was lined, floor to ceiling on three walls, with books. A fireplace stood opposite the door, making it warm inside, not drafty like the rest of the house. Barclay's desk sat to the left of the fireplace, facing the front windows. Two large chairs, cushioned in leather, along with a small side table, were the only other furniture. She leaned against one of the chairs as her eyes scanned the books. One set caught her eye, a matched set, each marked with a date, and a name. She pulled one from the shelf. They were log books, marked by date and name of ship. There must have been more than twenty. Her eyes started moving from one shelf to another, and onward. *So many books*, she thought, *and all sorts*. Some were literature, some dealt with navigation, or foreign lands, or the natural world. Here and there among the books would be a curio, some strange acquisition from a voyage, no doubt. She found herself drawn from one shelf to another, her eyes hungry to devour the titles, as if reading the titles alone would impart their contents. She had moved around the room, slowly, looking only at the books, when she bumped into something. Next to the fireplace was a large globe, beautifully hand-painted but smudged from years of use. She ran her hand along its surface, touching places in the world she never even knew existed. She turned the globe so she could see America. She placed the tip of her finger at the approximate point where Westport stood. Then, guessing onward, she traced her finger west until it rested on the California coast. She was surprised. It had seemed so far, making that journey. But now, as she looked at the full size of the globe, she realized it wasn't very far at all.

"Are you lost?"

The sudden sound of the voice made her jump. Edward Haarten was standing in the doorway, looking typically stern, but not angry.

"Lost? And would I need a globe to find my way?" Lina laughed. She tried to joke with him, but his expression didn't change.

"I meant were you lost in the house? This room isn't open to guests."

Lina blushed. "Oh, I'm very sorry, Mr. Haarten. I truly didn't know. The door was open."

"The door was only partially open. You chose to come in."

Fine, thought Lina, *if you want the truth, you shall have it.* "Yes, I chose to come in, Mr. Haarten. Did you think I came in here to snoop?"

Lina wanted to leave, but Haarten was blocking the door. He studied her for a moment, then went to the desk, opened the humidor that sat on the corner, and withdrew a cigar. "No, Mrs. Clark, I know you did not. Had it been someone else, I might have." He lit the cigar, then looked at her. "But of you? No, I did not think such a thing."

"I came in to look at the books. So many! I've never seen so many in one place! Do you suppose Captain Barclay has read them all?"

"I suspect he has." Haarten leaned against the edge of the desk, watching her the entire time.

"I think it would be marvelous to have read all these books. So much to learn!"

Haarten smiled coolly. "That," he said pointing to the globe, "is far more interesting, far more educational than a book. Even though it is old, it is rooted in a reality in which I operate—the trade of the world."

"Perhaps you say that only because you're fortunate enough to have read such books. I have not. It would mean the world to me."

"Really, Mrs. Clark? You struck me as an educated woman."

"Whatever education I've had has always seemed lacking. Now I look around and I can see how much there is to learn. But I try to educate myself, as I can."

"It shows." This was the closest Haarten had ever come to flattering her, and something about the way he said it almost made her blush. She was always a little shy in this man's presence, for rarely had she known anyone so completely reserved. She smiled at him, and to her surprise, he returned it.

"Ah, I should have known!" The two turned toward the voice of Barclay, standing in the doorway with Josephine on his arm. "Haarten finds pleasure anathema—leave it to him to find an office at a perfectly delightful party!"

"Well, William," Josephine laughed, squeezing the older man's arm, "I wouldn't be so quick to blame him. If I know Lina, she found her own way in here!" She gave Lina a curiously devilish look, then looked at Haarten and grinned.

The whole exchange made Lina uneasy. "It's true, Captain. I confess I came in here to look at your wonderful library. Mr. Haarten was merely...."

"Mr. Haarten was merely being his usual, sober self, I'm afraid. Now come out, the both of you. I insist! I've gone to a great deal of trouble to make this the finest party in San Francisco, but it's to no avail if each and every one of my friends isn't out there enjoying it to the utmost!"

Barclay and Josephine waited by the door until Lina and Haarten left. Haarten quickly drifted from Lina's sight, but not Barclay and Josephine. She stood against the stairs and watched them. The man was likely old enough to be Josephine's father. Lina had no recollection of seeing the two of them together since that first night at the Golden West, but she realized now that since Josephine worked there, it was entirely likely they were familiar, more familiar than mere friends. For all the apparent delight Josephine took in men, nearly all men, she never was as fascinated with them individually as she was delighted in their fascination with her. But as the couple moved about the room, Josie's gaze stayed fixed on the portly old fellow, and a perpetual smile hung from her lips. And Barclay seemed to dote on her equally. He always seemed courteous and deferential to her, as well as attentive. The two practically glowed in their delight in one another.

Suddenly the room was filled with a lively tune, as guests lined up to join in a reel. Someone grabbed Lina by the hand and before she knew it she was in the dance. Just as the dance began, Lina noticed Haarten watching her from the bottom of the stairs. His expression was intent, but otherwise empty. Then she was lost in a dizzying spin as the dance proceeded. And when at last it was over, and Lina had caught her bearings, she saw Haarten still staring at her, his gaze no less intent, but his expression less than pleased. That disapproving look sent a wave of regret through her, and without thinking, she pulled away from the dance.

19

By the end of January Lina had learned enough about the operation of the warehouse to answer Haarten's concerns. She knew he would be pleased to find that the warehouse losses disappeared once she took over the books. But his satisfaction was not the only reward she sought for all her long hours and hard work.

Each Saturday at the close of business, Haarten would come to the warehouse for a report. He would dismiss Walter Monroe with the excuse that the reports were only to make certain Lina was performing to his standards. But Haarten already knew about her performance. He had eyes and ears around the city, when needed, and through them Haarten learned that she was just as she appeared. Each week, she spoke of what she had learned, what losses she found, what improvements she had made. Haarten concluded Carolina Clark to be capable and bright. And perhaps even a bit ambitious. All were qualities he could put to his advantage.

Lina quickly grew to look forward to those Saturday meetings. They fueled her confidence and her curiosity. She always knew she had succeeded when she would finish, and Haarten would smile. *From him*, she considered, *that's a rare commodity.*

"Mrs. Clark, you've a talent for estimating what the market will bear in the way of a price."

"I have tried to learn everything I could, sir. I spend my free time walking about town, making note of what's sold, what shops have opened or closed. All this helps."

"You see, didn't I tell you as much, that night in Barclay's library? Knowledge is most useful born of experience. Here is proof of it. Ada Quincannon can bend your ear all she likes. But you've put your efforts into learning for yourself. Your own experiences, your own intuitions, combined with your obvious diligence, *that* is useful!"

Lina was still wondering how Haarten knew about her conversations with Ada, when suddenly he closed the ledgers and said, "I want you to look in on the warehouse on Clay Street. It's a small operation. Review its books. Suggest any changes you think appropriate."

"Yes, sir," she said, smiling.

Then Haarten handed her a piece of paper. "I've written here the address of a new shop—a dry goods store that apparently is doing quite well. Barclay & Company is interested in acquiring it. Find out what you can about this place. Learn if it's as promising as I've heard. But be discreet. I wouldn't want it known that we're interested. Might drive up the price."

"Yes, sir. Of course. Is there anything else?"

Haarten rarely gave her more than a glance, so when she realized he was scrutinizing her from head to toe, she felt unsettled. "Yes, there is. Your appearance."

"My appearance?"

Haarten stood up, and came around the desk to her, his face stern. "Look at yourself. You look common. Worse, you look unkempt. Sawdust everywhere. If you're to go about this city representing Barclay & Company, you'll have to have some other attire befitting your position.

"But it's so dirty in the warehouse. I haven't yet saved enough to buy one dress, let alone more. I would hate to spend my money on something that's likely to be ruined."

"This isn't open for discussion, Mrs. Clark. I insist. Please see to it as soon as possible." He turned and left.

****

It would be more than a week before Lina would find the time to go to Mrs. Birnbaum's for another dress, and if she had waited through the fittings it might have taken her another week before the dress was ready. So wearing the dress she'd worn at Christmas, she took the precious opportunity of a little free time the next day to find Wilson & Sons. There would be time for Mrs. Birnbaum's soon, she justified, and besides, if she waited to answer Haarten's questions, he might think she wasn't up to the task. Then she'd lose the very advantage she hoped to press.

When she left early that day, Monroe tried to scold her. She quickly answered, "I'm going under Mr. Haarten's orders," knowing that would end the discussion. Without further regard, she hurried out the door.

In her careful way, she had planned her afternoon. She would go to Wilson & Sons first. Then, depending on the time, she wanted to walk north, toward Telegraph Hill passing through Portsmouth Square as she went. She wanted to see parts of the city she hadn't yet seen, up the hills and down the valleys to the west of the harbor. She wanted to have much to share when next she saw Edward Haarten.

For three months she had seen this man every week, and she was learning how he conducted business. He was meticulous, and kept a clockwork schedule. He liked clean, orderly records. He liked those who worked for him to make decisions themselves, so long as they were the right decisions. He didn't like to be bothered with details, and preferred to get to the point quickly, so Lina would practice her report each time. She learned not to talk when he was studying the ledgers. And she had learned not to ask questions like 'Why?' Haarten didn't like 'why'—it seemed to set his teeth on edge, as if there were mutiny in her 'why.'

The man himself remained a puzzle to her. She had known ruthless men before, and she was sure Haarten was one. Why, she could not say, but there was something about his demeanor that made her sometimes feel just a moment from his anger — anger she felt sure, once unleashed, would be cruel. But as far as she thought the man capable, Haarten was almost generous with her. Hadn't he given her opportunity, shown his trust in her by taking her into his confidence? She knew Haarten was no man for idle flattery, yet hadn't she managed, a few times, to earn that praise, even to elicit a smile from those stern, straight lips?

That smile puzzled her most. She still could not anticipate what would genuinely please Haarten. She knew it shouldn't matter, but it did. Something in her couldn't stop searching for something else in him. What was behind that seldom-seen smile? When she did see it, she searched it for an ease she saw in other men's smiles. *How*, she wondered, *could a smile show pleasure without happiness?* The thought of those lips was followed by a memory of his cold grey eyes, and she knew the answer. Those eyes didn't smile. They showed no happiness. Their light was dull, like a milky moon behind clouds.

Thoughts of Edward Haarten distracted her as she walked through familiar surroundings. But in short time she was in a district she had only seen the night of that walk to Barclay's party. This was the district of the city's new, self-designed aristocracy. Grand houses sat on top of the hill, and all the steep roads around it were lined with new shops providing the necessities of a refined life.

Lina slowed to eye the shop displays. Such displays they were! She marveled that stores could thrive selling such exclusive wares. Lina understood the market of the general supplier—the commodities that people traded in when moving across country, when building a city, or just to subsist. But she suddenly realized she knew nothing of this rarified world, this commerce of luxury.

She also realized how out of place she felt, and how right Haarten had been in correcting her appearance. These ladies wore fine dresses, not work clothes. They were gloved and hatted. She was not. Their hair was done in the latest fashion, hers in a simple knot. She missed the familiar faces and greetings she had enjoyed just a few blocks back. These strangers she passed would not even look her in the eye.

She found Wilson & Sons easily, for it was larger and busier than any other shop on the street. It was a general emporium, much like Pickens' place back in Westport, so much so that she half expected to hear Pickens' boisterous bragging over the din. Here were those same clerks pushing pallets and crates, those same shelves packed from ceiling to floor with everything imaginable. She felt at home.

Lina wandered among the stacks and shelves, taking in every detail. She made note of prices, and how much the customers were spending. Quickly, she estimated this place could be taking in as much as a thousand dollars a day.

She was looking through some yard goods when a conversation caught her ear. Two men stood nearby in one corner. She glanced at them, then returned her attention to the calicos. The younger man she guessed to be the proprietor, though whether he was Wilson or

Son, she couldn't say. He wore a simple grey waistcoat and pants, with garters on his crisp white shirtsleeves. The other man was older by a generation. He had a broad face, and full white hair that hung to his shoulders beneath the wide brim of his hat. He was corpulent, but with the ruddy look of an active man. With his back to her, Lina could not see the expression on Wilson's face, but his tone was decidedly deferential.

"Yes, sir. Very brisk indeed," the one she decided was Wilson said. "Most days are like this. Saturdays are the best. Of course, Sunday, we're closed."

The older man nodded. "The Sabbath must be obeyed. But perhaps in time."

"In time, sir?"

"Once we've got you up and going, if reliable help might be found, perhaps those whose convictions aren't as strong as ours, eh? It's always good to make a little more where we can. So much to be done."

"Yes sir, Mr. Brannan. So, you're satisfied with everything we've done with your investment?"

"Entirely, young Peter. Just keep on as you have. I'll be back next week. Good day, lad."

She left soon after. Lina turned around and took one last long look at Wilson & Sons. Then she started back to the Golden West. A light rain sat in, and she had no parasol, not even a shawl to pull over her. She quickened her step, but not because of the rain. She was hoping to find Captain Barclay at the Golden West. Finally, she was ready to speak with him.

She walked as night fell. It seemed to take forever until she was back to familiar streets. She picked up her pace and in just a few blocks was within sight and sound of the Golden West. As she turned the last corner, she saw the saloon glowing like a hearth, spilling embers of life onto Pacific Street. The rain made the glittering garishness of its lights seemed cozy, and the bright currents of laughter and music from within welcomed her.

But the crush at the tavern's front door sent Lina to the back entry. Once before on a night like this she had tried to come through the front, and found herself pinched, mauled and trodden upon before she could reach the stairs. Entering from the back, she was surrounded by familiar, friendly faces, among them Matt, the cook. Suddenly, she realized she was hungry beyond words.

"What's for dinner, Matt?" she asked as she came up behind him. He gave a quick glance over his shoulder, then a smile before turning his attention back to his cooking.

"Fish. But you'll have to wait a bit, Lina," he said. "It's a wild one, tonight. One of Barclay's ships finally come in. Barclay's entertaining the whole place out there."

Lina peeked through the door that opened to the main room. She had never seen the place so lively. Crowded into every corner were men of all descriptions, drinking, joking, gambling, even singing. Ada, in her finest array, stood at the end of the bar, keeping an eye on all her lovely ladies as they handed out drinks and kept the customers happy.

In the center of the room sat Josephine. She wore a gown Lina had never seen before. Made of a lustrous silk, and trimmed with tiny bows and ruffles. It was a rich, pale yellow, the color of light itself, and for just an instance, Lina thought Josie might be the source of the light she had seen outside. All that light made Josie's dark hair and features all the more dramatic, and this night her hair was studded with small pearls that matched the strand draping down to her bosom.

Josephine held the company of three gentlemen, two more than any of the other ladies in the room. The others girls were prone to laughing too loudly or to drinking too much with the customers. But Josephine seemed genuinely rapt by the conversation. She kept a drink in front of her, sipping it with moderation. The dimples, the turn of the head, the fluttering eyelashes Lina knew so well were all in play, and the three gentlemen were in total surrender.

Then Lina saw Barclay, standing and waving to her from his private table. Lina walked over, and Barclay offered her a chair. "Hungry, my dear? I ordered this fish for Josephine and myself, but it seems she's a little too preoccupied to eat!"

"I'm famished, Captain, thank you," she said as she sat. The two ate quietly for a few moments, until Lina felt the sharpness of her hunger fade. Then she seized her chance.

"Captain, I've wanted to talk to you for some time. That is, I wanted to talk to you, but I wasn't ready. Or I wasn't sure. Oh, but after today, I am sure. And here you are."

Barclay chuckled. "And here I am. What can I do for you?"

"It was Ada's suggestion. You see, she's told me all about what you've done for her, and what you've done for all the others. And now that I'm doing so well, or at least, I think I'm doing well. Mr. Haarten seems pleased, but it's always so hard to tell with him…"

"Lina, really. What has you twisted in such a knot? Out with it girl, before you choke on your supper."

She took a slow breath and then said it straight out. "I'm hoping you might consider starting me up in business."

Barclay stopped, fork in mid air. He looked her straight in the eye for what seemed the longest time. "Hmm," he said, returning to his meal. "What sort of business?"

"That's what I was waiting for, sir. But today I think I found the answer. You see, Mr. Haarten asked that I take a look at that emporium you're considering buying. Wilson & Sons."

Barclay was surprised. "I don't recall that. But then, this might be one of Edward's ideas. He's always suggesting investments."

"I can understand why. It's a thriving business, sir. Catering to the city's finest homes. A general emporium, sir, but with all the nicest merchandise. I think it would make a splendid investment. And, I think I could manage it for you. It's the sort of business my husband and I had back in Missouri. Bigger, it's true, but I've learned so much since I've come to California, sir. About the city, and about Barclay & Company, too. Captain, I'm so very grateful for all you've done for me. For Josie, too, of course. I've worked hard, sir. At least, I've tried. So when I saw Wilson & Sons, I just knew I found the sort of business you might be willing to start me in."

Barclay put up a hand, bringing Lina's speech to a halt. "Lina, first let me assure you that you have done a splendid job. Whether you know it or not, you have a few admirers who tell me this is so. Ada, Josie of course, others too. Even Edward, in his own way, has commended you to me. Not that I can't see for myself how loyal and hard working you are. So on that score, you should have no doubts." Lina beamed at his words. Then he said, "However…" and her heart sank.

"You are young," Barclay went on. "Yes, you have considerable experience, but enough for this, I am not sure. And I would not put you in a position to fail, not for the world. Better to err on the side of caution. Besides, I don't know yet even if I would acquire this establishment. I'll wait until Edward suggests it to make that decision. Oh, see, now, I know I've disappointed you."

"No, it's alright, Captain," Lina said, half heartedly. She laid her fork down, her appetite gone.

Barclay looked at the dejected young woman. "Oh, hang it, madam. I can't stand to make anyone unhappy, particularly a lovely young lady. But Haarten would skin me alive if I took you away from him. He's grown to depend on you, you know. In fact, my most heartfelt advice is to be content for a while under his instruction. You might more easily satisfy your ambitions through that path. I have no doubt he has more in mind for you than your current position. But I will make you a proposition. If you broach the subject with Edward, and he thinks it a good idea, you'll have my blessing. And my backing. How's that?"

"Oh, that's wonderful! Thank you, sir," Lina picked up her fork again. "I'll mention it to him tomorrow."

Barclay shook his head. "Not tomorrow, or for a good while, I'm afraid. We're sailing to Mexico tomorrow. Some new venture Edward has in mind. Won't be back for a month."

The news was disappointing, but as she thought about it, Lina decided it might be for the best. Plenty of time to think the whole idea out, and be ready for any objections Haarten might have.

As she ate, she watched Barclay, who had returned his attentions to Josephine, still seated with her three admirers. "Captain Barclay, may I ask you another question?"

"Of course."

"You're, well, fond of Josephine, I take it?" Given the nature of their friendship, she wasn't sure what term to apply, but fondness seemed safe enough.

But the smile in Barclay's eyes told her that fondness was a pale imitation of how the old man felt. Then he gave her a devilish grin. "Why do you ask?"

Lina nodded toward Josie. "It doesn't bother you, then, this attention she gives to other men?"

"Hmm, I see," Barclay started. "Am I jealous, then? Is that what you're asking?"

"I suppose so."

"No, I can tell you most sincerely I am not." He poured himself a full glass of wine, and leaned back in his chair, resting the glass on his widening paunch. "Look at her, Lina. Isn't she a thing of beauty? Oh, I know she's beautiful, even a blind man could tell that. No, I mean really look at her." Lina and Barclay watched Josephine, as Barclay continued. "I gain nearly as much joy in watching her as I do being with her. So full of life, so happy in it. I could hardly be jealous of those poor devils caught in her spell — I know how they feel. I couldn't begrudge her anything that would make her happy. And the attention of men makes her happy. She revels in it, she blossoms under it. It's a marvel to watch, isn't it, how easily she captures their hearts, at least for a moment? But there's nothing in that talent that takes more than it gets. It's a relationship that suits them both, Josie and those admirers of hers. And besides, whether she knows it or not, I know where her heart lies. That's enough."

For weeks, Lina had been so busy she had hardly spoken with Josephine. For once, the fault was not entirely Lina's. Barclay had just confirmed what Lina suspected—that Josie was now Barclay's exclusive companion, and although she continued to entertain the gentlemen who visited the Golden West, her attentions were limited to conversation and drinking. Anything other than coy endearments was reserved for Barclay alone. *She found herself that rich man*, thought Lina.

The next morning, a Sunday, Josephine rose earlier than usual. She was up and about, but seemed completely distracted in all her morning routines. Lina's own mood was much improved after Barclay's assurances, so she teased Josie.

"What's the matter, Josie? Now that you've caught yourself that rich man you always wanted, isn't there anything left to challenge you?" Lina laughed as she said it, but Josie only stared at her blankly. "Josephine, what's the matter?" Lina stood at the end of the bed brushing her hair. Josie sat upon the bed, in the middle of dressing herself, apparently forgetting what to do next.

For a moment, Lina thought Josephine hadn't heard her, for she rose from the bed and walked lazily toward the window. She pulled the drape back just a bit and stared out across the city. "Barclay's at sea," she said with a sigh. "He left this morning, and won't be back for a month." Josie gave another long, deep sigh.

"Josie, what in heaven's name is wrong? Has something happened?" Lina came up very close behind her, almost whispering in her friend's ear. When Josie turned the two women stood nearly nose to nose. Lina looked into her eyes, and was shocked at what she found.

"Oh my Lord!" Lina had to take a step back. "Why, you're in love with him!" She threw her hand in front of her mouth, but the laugh came out through her eyes instead.

Josie threw her head back, then stomped toward the wardrobe to finish dressing. "Well, of course I am!" she declared as she whisked passed Lina. "And if you weren't so captivated with your own self interests, you might have noticed weeks ago!"

It took Lina a moment to shift to the defensive. "Well, of course, I am very sorry, Josie. I know I have been busy. But Josephine, it does seem, well, funny!"

"You find this laughable?" Josie shouted.

"No, not laughable. Funny, in a different sort of way." Lina approached her cautiously. "You always talked about coming here and, well, enjoying yourself, unencumbered. A rich man, yes, but *love*, Josie? You never talked about love! For me, yes, but not you. It just surprised me, that's all."

"Well, he is rich," Josie said, almost hoping that would answer Lina's questions. Then her face went soft, and she lowered her eyes. "But you're right, Lina. The whole matter has me completely befuddled. Heavens! Just look at him! Nearly my father's age! Round and squat as a whiskey keg. Oh, but he has a wonderful smile. And that laugh of his! He does love to have fun. He's the happiest, most contented man I've ever met. Bright as a penny, too. But not much for industry. Leaves too much to that Mr. Haarten of yours, to my mind. I've warned him, but he just pats me on the cheek. Oh, Lina, he does dote on me so! Sometimes the look in his eyes fairly melts my heart. And there's never been a man that treated me better. He'd give me the moon if I asked, but for some reason, I don't want to ask. Does that make any sense?" Josie had nearly made herself dizzy from all the pacing and turning. She looked completely lost.

"All the sense in the world," Lina said as she came forward to take Josephine's face in her hands. Lina kissed Josephine on the cheek, and hugged her.

****

The month Haarten and Barclay were gone was the busiest Lina had known. Spring was only days away. Everyone was on the move, in and out of port, or heading back to the diggings. Lina was kept busy overseeing her warehouses, and feeling a keener sense of responsibility in Haarten's absence. She thought it odd that for so vast an operation as Barclay & Company, there was no one besides Haarten to oversee its operation. But Barclay trusted Haarten, and Haarten apparently trusted no one. *Except perhaps me*, Lina thought.

She took Barclay's suggestion to heart. She still held hope that she might persuade Haarten to let her run Wilson & Sons. But in the alternative, if working for Edward Haarten would provide future opportunities, she delighted at the prospect. She kept her notebook with her always, and it was bulging with information she was eager to tell Haarten upon his return.

Haarten's ship had already been expected for two days when word came down to the wharf that it had been seen passing through the Gate. Lina had half-hoped Haarten might come directly to the warehouse. She waited the rest of the day for word from him, but it didn't come. Nor did it come the next day, and by the third day, still without word from Haarten, she was feeling uneasy. Perhaps he had some reason to be upset with her, something he heard upon arrival. She strained to think of anything, but there was nothing. Perhaps it was a test, she thought, a test of her patience. In the end, she had to accept the notion that possibly Haarten wasn't as excited about hearing her report as she was to tell it.

Then, without notice, one of Barclay's drivers entered the warehouse. He was standing outside the office door waiting for her attention when she looked up. "Mrs. Clark?" he said flatly. "Mr. Haarten asked that you come to Captain Barclay's. Right away. The carriage is out front."

She did her best to pat herself clean and smooth her hair on the ride over to Rincon Hill. She climbed the steps to Barclay's house and pulled at the heavy knocker. Almost immediately a tall, pleasant man in coattails opened the door. "Mrs. Clark. Please come in." He held the door for her.

With but one foot in the door, she heard him. "Jackson?" Haarten was calling from within the library. "Is that her?" Jackson turned to

Lina and nodded in the direction of Barclay's library. Lina pushed through the half-open door.

The library seemed very different than it had the night of Barclay's party, when the warmth of the fireplace had made the room so inviting. Despite a chill in the air, there was no fire, and the late afternoon sun cast the room in dim shadows. With no other sounds in the house, Lina could only focus on the tick of a clock on the mantel and the scratch of Haarten's quill pen as he worked over his books.

Finally, at no particular moment, Haarten said in a tone as cool as the room, "Sit down, Mrs. Clark."

She took a seat in a chair opposite the desk. Haarten wrote a minute or two longer, saying nothing. Carefully, Haarten closed the books, returned the pen to its place, and then looked up. He studied her steadily for a moment, then said, "Mrs. Clark, relax. You look as though you've been sent to the gallows."

Lina released a long slow breath, and managed to smile. "It's just that I've been eager to tell you what I learned about Wilson & Sons."

"And what would that be?"

Lina flipped to the pages she had marked. "Wilson & Sons is doing a fine business," she started. Then she described everything from her visit—the customers, the sales, and the inventory. She concluded by saying, "I don't know what sort of price Mr. Brannen might ask, but I'd think you'd be able to clear as much as a thousand a day."

"Brannen?" Haarten asked sharply.

"Yes, sir. I overhead the gentleman I assumed to be Wilson talking with a man he called Mr. Brannen. It was clear from their conversation that the place was owned by this Mr. Brannen."

Haarten shook his head, and looking toward the window, said, "Well, that's that, then."

"Sir?"

"Don't you know who Sam Brannen is?" Lina shook her head. "Sam Brannen is the only man in San Francisco to make more money from the gold rush than Barclay. He was the one who brought the news of the gold strike to the city. For months every man who ran to the gold fields bought their picks, axes and pans from Brannen's store in Sacramento. Then he used his newspaper to promote the rush, and from there he's built an empire. I can't begrudge him that. But

239

he imports his own kind to set up businesses all the way back to the Salt Lake." Lina face showed she was still puzzled. "Sam Brannen's a Mormon. An elder in their church."

"Oh, then that explains it," said Lina, and she proceeded to tell Haarten of the rest of Wilson and Brannen's conversation. As she spoke, Haarten's smile grew, and with it a sort of pleasant astonishment.

"Now *this* is useful information, Mrs. Clark. Thank you."

Lina couldn't figure out why this bit about closing on Sunday was so satisfying to Haarten. "If you don't mind my asking, Mr. Haarten, are you going to buy the emporium?"

"No, I am not. Brannen would never sell to me, or to anyone else. But it does tell me how to proceed." Lina fell silent. "You're disappointed? Why, because you thought Barclay might hire you to run that store? Yes, he told me. One of the Captain's weaknesses is his tendency to talk too much while in his cups. It was a long trip to Mexico and back. Plenty of opportunities for him to be talkative. He also told me of the advice he gave you. I concur. Your best course is to proceed as you have been. But your interest in bettering your position is duly noted, Mrs. Clark. Perhaps, in time. We shall see. Now, is there anything else?"

"Yes, sir. Yes, there is." Lina told him of two other stores she knew of, similar to the Wilson & Sons, but in more modest parts of the city. One was in the Russian quarter, and apparently catered solely to that group. For its size, this store did an even brisker business than Wilson's, although their prices were not nearly so high. Another was just off Portsmouth Square, on Kearney Street, and while it was a much smaller shop than Wilson's, it did a fair business and was well situated, drawing clientele from all different parts of the city.

Haarten listened with some attention, but Lina had no sense of whether what she told him was of interest, or if he was merely humoring her. When she finished, he said, "Fine, fine, Mrs. Clark. Just leave your notes. I'll give that some thought as well." She stood and handed him the sheets she had torn from her notebook.

As he took the papers, he looked at her closely. "I see you still have not done as I asked regarding your attire," he said.

"The dresses should be ready soon," she lied.

"Very well, then." He seemed satisfied. "Your ambitions won't get you far if you're unwilling to take my instruction. Good day, Mrs. Clark."

She hurried outside, to let the late afternoon breeze cool her cheeks, which were flushed with anger. The meeting hadn't been nearly as satisfying as Lina had hoped all these weeks in Haarten's absence. To make matters worse, he had concluded by insulting her, whether intended or not. Then she remembered what else Haarten had said, and the sting lessened. He would help her advance, if she were willing. He must have a good deal of faith in her judgment, she reminded herself. It was on this single measure of success that she focused on the ride back to the warehouse.

****

The next day Lina made time to go to Mrs. Birnbaum's to have those dresses made—dresses which, sadly, consumed her savings. Still, she viewed them as an investment in her future. She was determined to prove herself capable of anything that Haarten asked of her. That night, though the revelry continued downstairs, Lina was deep within her soft bed upstairs. She had long since learned to sleep despite the ruckus below, so that was not what kept her awake. It was thoughts of Haarten. Always before she had worried when her fate was in the hands of someone else, particularly someone weak. Ephraim had been weak, obviously. So had Henry Parker, in his own way, and her father, and nearly every man she could remember. Except Haarten. Now she found she wasn't completely at ease with the fact that this one man's approval was so important to her. If Lina had misgivings about trusting Edward Haarten, she decided it was because she was not in the habit of knowing trustworthy men. She closed her mind to the voice of doubt in her head, and pulled the comforter close around her to keep out the cold.

In the weeks that followed, her worries receded as her workload grew. Increasingly, Haarten's errands kept her out of the warehouse. Haarten had even managed to remove Walter Monroe from the warehouse. Lina didn't ask how, for he replaced him with a young, earnest lad named Jack. Jack was adept at the paperwork, and took over many of Lina's more routine responsibilities. Lina hovered over poor Jack, checking his every movement for two weeks before she was satisfied.

Only once did Lina revisit her concerns about Haarten, and only briefly, for it may have simply been a series of uncanny coincidences. She would never know for certain, and without proof, speculation only worried her needlessly. But during one week, three seemingly unrelated bits of local news reached her. A new emporium had opened recently just a few blocks from Wilson & Sons, and was said to be much like it. Business was so brisk there, and the prices so low, they were taking business away from young Peter Wilson, whose own store was rumored to be closing. Then one day she happened by the other emporium that she had mentioned to Haarten, the one just off Portsmouth Square. It was closed altogether, and the neighboring shopkeeper told her the owner had not been able to make his bank note. Worst of all, Ada told her the little store in the Russian quarter had burned to the ground one night, without explanation.

20

By spring, Lina had explored nearly every corner of San Francisco. With so much building going on, there was always something new, though patterns became predictable. Saloons and bawdy houses clung to the shore between the docks and warehouses. Lawyers and bankers preferred the city's new broad streets. Each of San Francisco's hills was an enclave, and within each enclave there were the same array of stores, butchers, grocers, dress shops and the like. And on top of each hill lived the richest of each tribe in fancy homes. Except for one hill, the one Lina had yet to climb.

She knew about the semaphore that gave Telegraph Hill its name. Everyone knew about the semaphore. It was a central feature of life at the docks. By posing its two arms this way or that, the signalman could tell the whole city which ships were coming into harbor. Knowing which ships were coming told those who managed the city's business, as Lina did, what cargo would soon be unloaded.

One Sunday, checking on the shops in North Beach, she walked by Telegraph Hill and decided on an impulse to climb it. She was interested in the signal house, but after making the long, steep hike over a rocky path, she was disappointed to find that the semaphore just looked like a windmill whose paddles were either missing or stuck still. The unexpected surprise was the hill itself.

The hill had been chosen as the semaphore site because of its view of the whole bay, which was impressive. The bay swept to the north and the south beyond Lina's vision, and to the west through the strait and out to sea. Up so high, the wind whipped her skirts like a sail, the sun bouncing off the rippling water was blinding, and the windblown scrub trees offered no shelter.

The top of Telegraph Hill was everything San Francisco wasn't—quiet and cool, with sweet-smelling breezes. It was just what Lina needed. Perhaps it was only that she had been working so very hard for so long. Or perhaps it was seeing how happy Josie seemed now. Lina only knew that she was tired all the time, rarely found anything to laugh about, and longed for something to lighten her mood. At least for this day, she had found it. Those trees might be thin scrubs, but they could still offer a place to rest, to lean back and watch the world go by.

The lure of Telegraph Hill, and a casual offer from Barclay broke Lina's Sunday routine. Occasionally, Lina would join Josephine and Barclay for dinner. The talk was lively, particularly when Barclay spoke of his travels. Barclay was taken with Lina's curiosity, and remembered her interest in his library. "Come to the house and borrow whatever you like. Consider it your personal lending library."

So she did. Every Sunday, Lina would fill her eager arms with Barclay's books, take a light meal, and make the steep climb up Telegraph Hill. Her perch was below the crest of the hill and the signalman's tower, but high enough that she could see the whole stretch of the bay. She would stay all afternoon, watching ships pass, imagining their destinations. She would read for long periods, then fold the book in her lap, close her eyes, and see the stories played out before her.

She treasured those days, but they were not idle. The books were carefully chosen. One must be edifying—history, geography, or perhaps the natural sciences. These topics always seemed more interesting when Barclay spoke of them than they did in his books, but they allowed her to feel justified in her second choice, which was always for pleasure. There weren't many of these on Barclay's shelves, and so she took her time reading each one. They were tales of heroism, romance, and adventure. The good were always rewarded, the villains always undone in the end. Death seemed clean and poetic, and love was always pure and victorious. Lina knew they were fables, but they were a welcome escape from her daily life, like the high, solitary place itself.

Lina came and went through Barclay's house by the kitchen, something she had learned from her experiences at the Golden West. It was always easier to get in a back door, she had discovered. She knew the kitchen folks by name. They knew she worked for Barclay, as they did. They considered her one of their own.

That day as she returned, the kitchen was quiet, and Jackson was nowhere in sight. She was walking to the library when she heard the sound of someone inside. *Probably the Captain,* she thought. Always happy for the chance to see him, she hurried to the door and knocked lightly. "Yes?" It was Edward Haarten's voice.

Lina's mind raced. She wasn't sure whether to be concerned that he would learn she had frittered her Sunday, or that he would notice how disheveled she looked. She prayed he wouldn't ask where she had been as she quickly brushed some mud from her skirt. Lina didn't see the smudge that had made it from her fingers to her cheek.

"Good afternoon, Mr. Haarten," she said, as she entered and headed for the shelves to replace the books, never looking at him. She hoped to be out the door again before he had spoke, but that was not her luck.

"Mrs. Clark." Lina stopped, then turned to see Haarten slowly rise from his chair behind the desk and walk to her. He came close, so close she felt herself pull back just a bit. Haarten raised his hand, then with a single finger, he rubbed lightly on her cheek. "You've brought a bit of Telegraph Hill indoors with you," he said, as he rubbed the dirt from his fingers.

Her hand instinctively went to her cheek. Her fingertips felt the heat of her blush. "How did you know where I was?"

Haarten looked at her, and then walked back to his chair. As he sat, his only reply was a sly smile.

"I went there because of the semaphore, sir. I was interested in it. It's so very important at the warehouse, I thought I might learn something."

He leaned back to consider her for a moment. "I must say, the respite seems to have done you some good. There's color in your cheeks and a sparkle to your eye."

Lina was dumbstruck. "Why, thank you, sir."

Haarten opened another ledger and started reading. "One cannot underestimate the importance of good health and a strong mind," he said as he read. "Not easy commodities in this squalid city."

"I agree!" She sat down across from him. "It's as if I can truly breathe up there." The day had relaxed her, and Haarten's compliments emboldened her to strike up a conversation. She wanted to share her day with someone, and perhaps today Edward Haarten might be that someone. "Such a wonderful view of the bay from up there. The city looks so big when you can see it spread out before you."

"Hmm." Haarten kept writing, but did not seem to mind her, so she continued.

"I hadn't thought of it until you mentioned it, but I do feel invigorated after I visit there. I had no idea it showed," she said, putting a hand to her cheek. "I suppose Josephine and Captain Barclay have been right to scold me for not enjoying my time here more."

Suddenly, he looked up, closing the ledger with a sound slap. "If that is your influence, Mrs. Clark, then I worry that this new habit of yours is a mistake."

"What do you mean?"

"There's a decided difference between a brief distraction from honest work and an indolent existence dotted with sporadic attentions to life's necessities. When one steps off the former path, one can find oneself on the road to the latter in short order."

"Oh, Mr. Haarten, I think you may make too much of this."

"Madam, I assure you I do not. I have high regard for Captain Barclay, but over the years he has changed from a man of considerable ambitions to someone dangerously distracted. All the more so since he started associating with your friend. It's a perfectly ridiculous situation, and one that only serves to make him seem foolish and gullible."

"It seems harmless enough to me."

"I see nothing *but* harm coming from it. For this Company to succeed, the Captain must be taken seriously. Barclay is a very important man in this community, and in many places around the world, something I'm certain neither you nor your friend understand."

"If you are concerned about Barclay's association with Josephine because of her...profession..." Lina was never quite comfortable defending Josephine on this point, but she was provoked enough to try. Haarten would not let her.

"Profession! Those with professions add value to the world. Females like those are parasites. Opportunists. Taking money for appealing to the basest part of a man, leaving him at best poorer, at worst, well… "

"Mr. Haarten, I understand your concerns about appearances, and I can only suppose you have your reasons for not approving of women such as Josephine. But I wouldn't be her friend if I didn't defend her. We've been through a great deal together, and she never failed me, not even once. She's done everything I asked and more. Despite what you think, she is at heart a decent, moral woman. I've never known her to take undo advantage of anyone. She hasn't a malicious bone in her body. She has been both sister and friend to me. I have and would continue to trust her with my very life, and if I thought there was anything that she needed, anything I could do to protect her, nothing would prevent me. Most importantly, let me assure you that her affections toward Captain Barclay are tender and genuine. You have nothing to fear from her."

She expected him to fire another volley against Josephine. He was still angry, and he opened his mouth to vent it. Then, he seemed to check himself.

"Mrs. Clark, I owe you an apology. I was forgetting myself, my loyalty to Captain Barclay, and your loyalties to Miss Paul. Forgive me. I'll not burden you with my opinions on the subject again."

****

Lina banished thoughts of that disagreement with Haarten. She preferred to remember only the loveliness of her day, which she shared in detail over dinner that night with Josie and Barclay. Of course she would never mention that discussion to either of them, though she felt quite certain Haarten's opinion wouldn't matter a whit to either of them. *If they don't care, why should I?* she thought. As it turned out, Josie and Barclay's interests lay elsewhere.

"Lina," Barclay began, mouth half-filled with the steak he was in the midst of devouring, "tell me your opinion of Edward Haarten."

The question came from nowhere, leaving Lina curious as to Barclay's purpose, and careful in considering what response to give.

Barclay noticed her hesitancy. "Now, now, my dear. You know you may speak freely. I value your opinion. Tell me what you think."

"Well," Lina said cautiously, "he's a very good business man."

"Spoken like a true diplomatic!" Barclay laughed, and took a long drink from his glass of wine. "And very true. All Edward thinks of is business, and it pains me to watch him. Truly pains me. The worst of it is, he expects everyone else to be equally singular in their interests." In that moment, Lina knew Haarten must have also spoken to Barclay about Josephine, and the pain it caused the old man was apparent in the tender glance he gave Josie.

"Well, sir, I'm sure he believes he's only looking out for the Company's best interests. And yours, too, of course."

"See there?" Barclay turned to Josephine. "Lina understands the difference between my business interests and my personal affairs. Edward makes no such distinction where I'm concerned, or any of us, for that matter."

"In fairness, Barclay," Josie answered, "if Lina understands the distinction, she is newly enlightened. I've been trying to persuade her since we met that there's more to life than hard work. It must be your influence, my dear, that's given her insight. Your *joie de vive* is positively inspirational."

Barclay lovingly patted Josephine on the cheek. She gave him an adoring smile, and touched his hand. "I only wish I could find something to interest the damn fellow besides business," Barclay added.

Josephine lit up. "I know! We should invite him to join us at the beach! Perhaps getting him away from work and the city would do him some good."

"Splendid idea, my dear, splendid! But do you really think he might consider it?"

"He might be persuaded, if he were to have some companionship of his own." Josie gave the old man a quick wink, and a nod toward Lina.

"Really, do you think so?" he asked Josie. She nodded, so he turned to Lina. "My dear, would you care to join us on an outing to the beach next week? A prospective business partner is coming here, a banker, accompanied by his wife. They're Swiss, never been to America before. I plan to show off our fair city, and thought a picnic at the beach would be just the thing. If I could persuade Edward to come, we could discuss a little business while we're there. But Edward will want to do nothing *but* talk business, and I intend to enjoy the day. You could be a help, Lina, in inducing Edward to come."

"I really don't see how I'd be much of an inducement, Captain."

"Don't be so modest, my dear. You're practically the only person he seems to tolerate," Barclay said.

"Besides," Josephine added. "You haven't seen the ocean yet. We've neither one been in all the months we've been here."

Barclay was amazed. "It's settled then. You simply must come and see the place for yourself!"

Lina was torn. She wanted so much to go, yet she had misgivings about accompanying Haarten any place that involved Josie and Barclay, misgivings she obviously couldn't share. But Josie changed her mind with one word.

"Please?" was all she had to say, while showing that sweet, dimpled smile and those imploring eyes that made everyone acquiesce. Lina agreed.

****

"You never answered Barclay's question, Lina. What *do* you think of Edward Haarten?" After dinner, Barclay decided he had to speak to Haarten straight way and insist he join them on the trip to the beach. Josie insisted she help Lina with selecting her attire. Now she had Lina a prisoner in a chair in front of the mirror, while Josephine played with different ways to arrange her hair in a style that would flatter the dress Josie had selected. Lina was already fidgeting, and now Josephine's questions annoyed her even more.

"I'll tell you if you answer me this, Josie. Are *you* quite certain the only reason you're going to all this fuss is to make a good impression on that banker? Or has this been your scheme since Christmas?"

"Christmas? I don't know what you mean?"

"Don't give me that look, Josephine Paul. You said you had a prospect in mind for me. You said you'd know in a few weeks, but you never mentioned it again. It's all making sense to me now. You've had this bee in your bonnet about Mr. Haarten all along, haven't you?" Lina glared at her in the mirror's reflection.

"I have had no such 'bee' at all," Josie said. Then she rolled her eyes a little. "But what's the harm in trying to attract a man's attention, particularly one as handsome as your Edward Haarten."

"He's not 'my' Edward Haarten, and I have no interest in attracting his attentions," Lina said, as she jerked her head against Josie's incessant pulling.

"Hmm. If you say so, sweet." Josie went back to her work and said no more for a few moments. Then she added, "Still, you must admit, he's quite handsome. Those grey eyes, that tall, striking figure he cuts…" In the mirror, Lina could see Josie's eyes half closed, a shameless smile belying her thoughts.

When Josie opened her eyes, she saw Lina look away. "Why do you blush every time I mention romance?" Josie asked.

Lina paused, then answered softly, "I suppose it's because I don't understand it. It seems like a secret shared by everyone but me."

Josie sat on the corner of the bed, and Lina turned to face her. "Truly, Lina? You've never felt your pulse race at the sight of some man? Never had the sight of one make you feel disoriented, weak in the knees?"

Lina thought Josie made it sound like the most natural thing in the world. But not to her. She shook her head. She studied Josie's curious smile for a moment. "How is it different, Josie? How, exactly?"

"Mmm." Josie purred, and her eyelids lowered to a dreamy loop as she leaned backward across the bed. When Lina sat on the corner of the bed, Josie leaned up on one elbow to answer her. Her words came out slowly, as if with each one she stopped to linger just a moment on the memory behind it.

"When I was fourteen, my Father held a very grand party in our home. He had only permitted me to stay for the dinner. I was too young to stay for the real party. I stood against the wall with my older brother and my little sister, watching all these beautiful people in their handsome clothes arrive at my father's fancy party.

"Suddenly, a soldier entered. I never learned his name, but I can still see him, as clearly as if he were standing here right now. He was very tall, or at least seemed so to me then. He had a powerful build, and looked so very dashing in that uniform. He had coal black hair, and a thin moustache. His features, his coal black eyes, his smile, everything about him was absolute perfection."

"As I watched him, I became very aware of sensations I'd never known. I'm sure I was blushing, but the blush seemed to cover my whole being. It radiated a warmth that made my head feel light, and my heart pound. I completely lost any sense of anyone or anything else in the room. I felt a smile cross my lips that I was incapable of stopping."

Josie stopped, lost in her own memory of the handsome soldier. Finally, her eyes opened and she looked straight at Lina. "That was the first time. There have been a few others since then, and the sensations have remained essentially the same. A man like that has the ability to make my whole being feel alive just with the pleasure of looking at him. It's absolutely intoxicating."

"Is that how Barclay makes you feel?" Lina asked.

Josie wore a softer smile now. "No, to be honest, he doesn't make me feel that way."

"But you said you loved him."

"So I do. I love Barclay with all my heart. For all the reasons I've told you, and more. But it's not the same sensation. Not the same at all. Barclay makes me feel safe and cared for. We talk, and laugh, and sometimes just spend the day like an old married couple. He's very dear, and I'd be lost without him."

Lina still wore a puzzled look, so Josie offered one final explanation. "It would be perfectly lovely, my dear, to have a man who was as congenial to be with as Barclay, and who also made you feel the way that handsome soldier made me feel. But I'm afraid that's impossible."

"Why?"

"It simply is. Men like that soldier, they're inconstant. A woman can't depend on them. Most will steal your heart. *Only* your heart, if you're lucky." Josie's voice drifted. Lina touched her softly on the hand, and gave her a smile. Then Josie said, "I'll say this, sweet. If you ever *do* find such a man, one that can melt your heart and still hold it in his hand, don't let him get away. No matter what."

****

"Oh, hang it man! Can't this wait until tomorrow? You're ruining my exceptionally fine mood." Barclay sat with his feet propped on his desk, trying to decide whether it was the fire in the hearth, the brandy in the glass, or the day spent with Josephine that had left him in such a satisfied state. He decided he didn't care.

"Captain, I've been trying to speak with you for days now." Haarten regularly reported to Barclay, much as he required Lina to report to him. The reasons, however, were different. The practice had started as his duty to his employer, and as a safeguard against the old man ever accusing him of dereliction. As Barclay freely gave him more responsibility, Haarten continued his reports to remind Barclay who it was that was earning him his fortune. More recently, Haarten started using the occasion to monitor Barclay's mental faculties. Over the last few years, Barclay had become easily distracted, and it was difficult to tell whether it was simply due to his boredom with business or perhaps some more significant decline in his capacity.

Then Josephine Paul came into Barclay's life, and since then, Barclay had not wavered in his distraction. It was firmly fixed on Josephine, and almost nothing else. For months, hardly a day had gone by without mention of her name, and certainly no more than a few days before Barclay would visit the Golden West. Once, Haarten commented on Josephine. Never one to stop short of his full opinion, he told the Captain his opinion of "this latest bit of French lace." The reaction he received stunned him—he had never seen Barclay so indignant. Barclay was usually a man who avoided a position in favor of maintaining a convivial tone. This time he was firm. "Mr. Haarten, let me be clear. You're to keep any opinions you may have about Miss Paul to yourself. If I hear another word against her, I'll dismiss you."

It was because of Josephine that Haarten had coerced Barclay to make the trip to South America that winter. Haarten made an excuse that the trip required them both. Haarten hoped that a break in routine would be all that was needed to distract Barclay from Josephine Paul. He was sure that by the time the Captain returned, either he would have found some other bit of 'lace' with which to waste his time, or the inconstant Josephine would be on to another conquest. But the matter was only made worse by the separation. After Barclay returned, the two were even more inseparable, until it had come to this.

"And these matters you've been trying to discuss with me for days. I'll wager they've already been attended to? Am I right?"

Haarten nodded. "Yes, sir. You left me no choice."

"Well, Edward, what does that tell you?" Barclay laughed. "It tells you I trust you implicitly." Barclay rose and walked toward the window. "Edward, I thought we worked this out long ago. You're to earn the money, and I'm to spend it." He chuckled. "Look here, lad. For the first time in many years, I'm truly happy. I'm not a young man, and I'm damned lucky to have found such happiness this late in life. I'll not give it up, no matter what."

Then as he continued, his voice became nearer a whisper. "Edward, I'm going to tell you something, even though I know you won't approve. But dammit, man, I'm nearly bursting with it! I plan to ask Miss Paul to marry me."

Barclay continued to talk about Josephine. For once, it was Haarten who was distracted. That Barclay would marry Josephine was not a possibility Haarten had ever considered, nor one he could allow. For how many years was it now, Haarten's mind was racing to remember, he had built this old fool's fortune. With no one to leave it to, no heirs of any sort, to whom else *could* Barclay leave his fortune but to Haarten? Edward had known all along that the old man could be so persuaded. The groundwork had been laid. But this was something Haarten had not foreseen, and it would mean the loss of what he considered his rightful claim. He would have to think of a way to stop this marriage, there was no question about that. At that moment, Haarten heard Barclay's voice through his racing thoughts.

"Happiness! I highly recommend it. You should give it a go! Look here! I'm planning an excursion to the beach, when that banker de Rutté is here. You see? I do remember what you tell me! A Swiss banker, Haarten! However did you manage that? In any event, he's bringing his wife, you said, so I thought we would take them to the beach. Just the thing—a convivial outing in which to talk a little business, eh? Josephine will be joining us, and she suggested Mrs. Clark come along, for neither of them has ever been to see the beach. You must join us as well. Now, no arguing. I insist."

Haarten started to decline. He never enjoyed these sorts of casual entertainments. Then something stopped him. He still didn't know what he could do to prevent this disastrous marriage, but he knew that in any plans he made involving Josephine Paul, Lina Clark would be a valuable resource. Perhaps there might be something in this opportunity to spend time with her. He would have time before the outing to figure out the details. For now, he needed to keep his options open.

"Perhaps you're right, Captain. It would be wise for both of us to spend some time with M. de Rutté, to discuss business in a more casual setting. Very well, sir. Thank you. I'll come along."

21

The outing to the beach didn't begin well for Lina. With Jackson along to attend to them, Barclay and Josephine, the de Ruttes, Edward Haarten and Lina all crammed into the Captain's finest turnout. The coach was barely adequate for four, and certainly not six when two were as rotund as Barclay and M. De Rutté. Lina sat between Haarten and M. deRutté and opposite Barclay who was flanked by Josie and Mme. de Rutté.

The deRuttés didn't speak English, but they did speak French, so Josie could translate. They all chattered and laughed, oblivious to the heat, the sand, and the constant jostling, except for Lina, who sat silent clinging white-knuckled to the seat. She also gripped in the hope of avoiding any unnecessary contact with M. de Rutté, who had already twice patted her on the knee, and with Edward Haarten, who unnerved her by being the only one of them who seemed to roll naturally with the erratic rhythm of the carriage. Every bump threatened to dislodge Josephine, so she finally gave up and just sat on Barclay's lap. Every bump Lina sent up a prayer that the trip would soon be over.

The moment they crested the last ridge and could see the ocean, the surf broke across the sand in bright rolling waves of foam. The carriage stopped and everyone climbed out. While Jackson and the driver unpacked the day's provisions, the group had its first good look at the shore.

The beach itself was perhaps a mile in length, bounded at the north by massive, jagged cliffs that trailed out in a chain of smaller rocks into the sea itself. Each time the sea crashed over them, towering sprays shot high above, and boiling eddies churned below. Dotted on top of these rocks were what seemed to be smaller, smoother rocks. But when one of those rocks moved, Lina let out a little gasp.

"Sea lions, my dear!" she heard Barclay say from behind her. "Sea lions. Listen to their call." The roar of the ocean as it collided with the shore was deafening, but the cries of the sea lions were louder still—a deep, gritty, mournful sound. "No wonder that sailors fancied these creatures to be mermaids. The siren's call, that's what you're hearing, my dear. Just as Jason and Ulysses and all the sailors since them have heard it. Well, what's for lunch? I'm ravenous!" Barclay turned back toward the luncheon spot, and the rest of his entourage followed.

After they ate, the casual talk about business started, aided by the stores of wine they brought with them. Lina was interested in their talk, but the translating slowed the conversation considerably, and there was no chance for her to be a part of the discussion. Besides, she was distracted by her surroundings. Finally, she stood, and excusing herself, headed back toward the shore.

Shading her eyes with her flattened hand, she peered at the horizon. The sea was boundless, infinite, and ever changing. It moved with a power unlike anything she knew before. Waves broke far in the distance, yet rose again and again, each time larger, each time breaking with more force. Yet here at her feet, it lapped gently at the toes of her boots. She knelt down and dipped her fingers in the water, icy cold though the day was warm. Bubbles of sea foam stuck to her fingers. Just then, the tide surged up. She let out a squeal and skittered backward, laughing as she dodged the water. Shorebirds rushed in to snatch invisible morsels brought by each wave. Then a long shadow crossed the sand next to her. Edward Haarten's shadow.

"Now that you've seen the beach, Mrs. Clark, what do you think?" Haarten was standing some distance behind her, and when Lina saw him there, for some reason she guessed he had been watching her for a time.

"It's indescribably beautiful. But frightening, too. So large and powerful."

Haarten smiled. He stepped closer, and taking her lightly at the elbow, pointed toward the horizon. "See that ship? I've seen thousands of miles of shoreline from ships like those. Sailors love the sea, but when a man has been months at sea and he heads into port, he's eager to leave the shore behind. I couldn't imagine why the beach held such fascination for others. But I must admit, now I understand a little better. I was watching you, Carolina, and I saw this place through your eyes. It *is* beautiful here."

Haarten had never called her by her given name, nor could she remember hearing him refer to anyone so informally. But his comportment was stiff and formal, despite the smile he gave her. She smiled at the thought that perhaps there was something to Josie's notions about this man's interest. She turned and started walking slowly up the beach. She could tell he was following her, and they walked in silence for some minutes. She had picked up a shell and was looking at it closely when he finally spoke.

"Carolina, I have a proposition to make you. One that I hope will please you." Lina turned to face him. "Would you like the opportunity to go to school?"

The suggestion had come unexpectedly, leaving Lina at a loss for words. "School?" was all she could say.

"I realize you are not without some education. Perhaps if you had the opportunity for a bit more, shall we say, cultural exposure, it would satisfy this thirst you have. In addition, I frankly do not see how else you might advance your position without it. In fact, what I will be asking of you in the future demands it."

Now Lina couldn't ask her questions as quickly as they came to her. "What sort of school? Where is it? And what might you be asking of me?"

"I've learned of a woman who came here last year from Massachusetts and has opened a school for young women in Santa Clara, at the southern end of the bay. I am proposing to make your application."

"But such a school would be expensive, wouldn't it?"

"As a matter of fact, it would. I suggest that you attend this school, and when you return we can arrange some sort of scheduled reimbursement from your wages. And since you will likely see an increase in your wages, repayment should not be a concern."

"How long will I be away?"

"For one term, at first, starting in the fall. If you like it and wish to stay longer, we can discuss that then."

"What will I be learning?"

"The usual sort of subjects, I imagine. I understand Miss Ward to be a highly cultured woman. I'm certain she's up to the task of presenting you with sufficient challenges."

Lina turned and looked out to the sea. Of all the possibilities for her future, this was one turn she hadn't expected, hadn't even dared to consider. The prospect was so thrilling she realized she was already starting to imagine it. For once, she let her heart take the lead. "Thank you, Mr. Haarten. I'd be pleased to go!" She offered her hand to shake on the bargain. Haarten took it, but grasped it very gently, and looked straight into her eyes. "Fine, Carolina. Splendid."

****

The summer was a frantic time for Lina. She was to leave in early September, and be gone until Christmas, Haarten told her after the arrangements were finalized. Besides all the preparation for the trip, and the time she still spent working each day, she saved as much of her free time as possible for Josephine. As the days counted down, Lina realized how much comfort she took in knowing Josephine was close at hand. She never missed a chance to spend time with her, even if she had to share her company with Barclay, over dinner.

With only a few weeks to go, the three of them were enjoying a particularly fine evening together. It was a balmy night, and all the windows and doors of the Golden West stood wide open, and a hint of salt breeze in the usually musty saloon raised their moods and their appetites.

"Fine thing, an education!" Barclay pronounced between mouthfuls. "Nothing like it! And no doubt it won't be wasted on you, my dear. You'll put the experience to considerable advantage, I'm sure."

"Well, it would be lost on me," Josie added, laughing. "I couldn't tolerate schooling. I couldn't get away from those Sisters fast enough!"

"That's because the Sisters hardly had anything to teach you!" Lina joked, and then blushed at her meaning.

"Well put, my dear! But then, that's the wonderful thing about this place. Any man, or woman, with the right talents, can come here and make their fortune. Why, look at the three of us! Couldn't be three more different people, and yet here we are, all doing rather well, because each of us is uniquely talented at our avocations. Three rather clever rascals, the lot of us, eh?" He lifted his glass in toast, and the ladies responded in kind.

"Well, I don't know how clever I'll feel once I get there," Lina added. "I'm sure to be the oldest girl there by far. Most girls are finished with their education by my age."

"Poppycock, my dear. I suspect there'll be all sorts of young ladies at that school. So what if you are the oldest? That's no reason to hang your head. You've accomplished quite a bit for a woman of any age, if my opinion counts for anything."

Impulsively, Lina leaned over to the old man, and gave him a sudden peck on the cheek. "It does to me," she said.

"And to me," added Josephine, as she patted Barclay's arm. "Oh dear, if we continue on like this, I'll be teary in no time."

"No tears! I forbid it! This is no wake, my darlings. In fact, I'm going to do everything I can to make this night a celebration! Josephine, I order you to accompany our Lina to Mrs. Birnbaum's, to make certain she's fitted with the loveliest dress ever to be seen in Santa Clara!"

"Oh, Captain, you needn't..." Lina started.

"Tsk, tsk, my dear. Not another word. It's the least I can do. Go to Mrs. Birnbaum's, and when you've finished, stop by the house, and take some of the books you like. That'll boost your spirits! Show up at this school already looking the learned young woman. What do you say?"

"It's a wonderful idea, Captain. Very generous of you. But I really have to be at the warehouse tomorrow, and..."

"Oh, hang that. It's my company, after all. What's the use of having all this money if I can't have some say-so? Don't worry yourself about Haarten. I'll tell him that I've sent you on some business. It's no concern of his, now, is it?"

"No. No it isn't!" Lina allowed herself a guilty giggle.

So it was agreed, and the next morning, Josephine and Lina walked down the streets of the city to Mrs. Birnbaum's, arm in arm. The pair had never strolled the city's streets together like this before. They took their time, stopping at any window that caught their eye, to admire the array of finery. They had chattered most of the way there, but for some time now Josie had been quiet. Then she said, "Lina, I'm simply thrilled for you. I know this is something you've always wanted," she told her, "but I will miss you so terribly."

"Oh, the time will be over before you know it." She took Josie's arm as they continued walking. "But you have Barclay now," Lina said, "and I go with a good deal less worry knowing you will be looked after."

"Ah, but sweet, *who* will look after *you?*" she grinned, then lightly pinched Lina on the cheek.

"Well, right now, I'd say Edward Haarten." Lina expected this to get a smile from Josie, but it seemed to have the opposite effect. Josie wrinkled her nose and looked away. "What's the matter? I thought you were hoping to make a match. Well, I don't know about that, but you must admit, this schooling idea certainly indicates he is looking out for me."

"I've changed my mind. I've decided I don't care for him at all." Josephine was not one to take a disliking to people, but this time it was obvious by her tone that her dislike of the man ran deep.

"Because of how he feels about you and Barclay, you mean?"

"That's just it, Lina. Since the beach, I've sensed a change. He's been very polite the few times our paths have crossed. But it was too easy, this transformation. He may act polite, but I doubt his true opinion of me has changed. And while I'm so happy that you have this chance, I can't help but think there's something he wants from it as well. He's cold, that one. And cunning. Mind yourself around him."

Lina was trying to put her friend at ease. "I know you're the expert when it comes to men, Josie. But I've come to know Edward Haarten, and what you see as cold, it's just his formal nature, I believe."

"Hmm. Perhaps, but I wouldn't depend upon it. You're smart, Lina, usually much smarter than me. But I know when a man is up to something, and I'm telling you that Edward Haarten is up to something. As I said, mind yourself with him."

****

The day Lina took the coach from the city south, Barclay, Josephine and Haarten, as well as Ada and a few of her other friends from the Golden West came to see her off. There were a few tears all around, but for the most part it was a happy occasion. Josephine nearly squeezed the life out of her when they said their final goodbyes. Lina waved to them through the open window of the coach until it was out of sight. Then Barclay and the others walked back to the Golden West to drink to Lina's good fortune.

Haarten did not join them. He walked the distance back to Barclay's home, deep inside his thoughts. Four months wasn't long, he reminded himself. If he was attentive to the details, however, and with a little luck, four months would be enough, just enough.

He arrived at Barclay's house, and went straight to the library, closing the door behind him. He poured himself a brandy, and sat in the chair opposite the fire, stretching his long legs before him, uncharacteristically relaxed. He considered the brandy more than drank it, moving the amber warmth in a precise and rhythmic swirl within the glass. A calm smile crossed his lips. With Lina on her way, he was free to do what next needed to be done.

From the moment Barclay had confided in Haarten his plan to marry Josephine, Haarten had but one thought—how to prevent it. Edward Haarten for too long counted on being the sole benefactor of Barclay's will. It was only logical. Barclay had no other heirs, and no other person had any rightful claim. But a marriage between Barclay and Josephine would change that. So Haarten saw no alternative but to prevent their marriage. Method was the only variable.

From Haarten's point of view, anything he might do was only to protect the true interests of Barclay & Company, which was to say himself. He could no longer distinguish between the two, nor did he try. Josephine and Barclay had to be separated permanently. To do that, all that would be needed would be a temporary separation. Just a bit of time, he reasoned, to convince each of the other's disinterest. But in order to manipulate Josephine, as he planned, he had to also separate her from Lina.

What happened to Josephine was of absolutely no interest to Haarten. He had at his disposal any number of ways of removing her from the picture, as long as Lina wasn't at hand. But removing Lina was not a thing easily done. Barclay knew her, considered her a friend, by virtue of his relationship to Josephine, and would not believe ill of her were Haarten to drum up some excuse for her dismissal from the company. Even if Haarten could accomplish that much, he felt certain Barclay would, out of loyalty, see Lina was taken care of somehow. He had enough friends in the city to secure her any number of positions. And keeping her in the city kept Lina too close to Josephine.

He had considered finding another position for her, what might seem a promotion, for he knew that would flatter her. That was when he was struck by the solution, a perfect solution to all his concerns.. With relative ease, he would soon be rid of any threat to inheriting Barclay's fortune. An aging Barclay would, in relatively short time, be relinquishing that fortune to Haarten. That, too, would be easy enough. Then Haarten would finally be free to run Barclay & Company solely for his own purposes, and to take his rightful place among the leading merchants in the country.

But first, he would need to achieve the kind of social standing he had almost achieved for Barclay, before the arrival of Josephine Paul. He would need to be seen, indisputably, as the most prominent man of commerce in San Francisco, and all that this entailed among the city's burgeoning upper class.

That would require a wife.

A single man was unheard of among that crowd of neo-patricians who considered themselves the city's elite. All the men, young or old, were stodgy, overfed, and each in their own particular way, ruthless. Nevertheless, publicly at least, they were first and foremost family men. Many of their wives were well-bred eastern women, and it was their influence that was bringing some semblance of decorum to San Francisco. By sheer force of their collective wills, these matrons demanded to see the city decked in the finery and comforts of their eastern ways. They brought with them a level of respectability the city hadn't yet enjoyed—respectability which Haarten not only craved for himself, but recognized would be necessary to put him above public reproach.

For Haarten to remain single would only complicate his ambitions. Bachelorhood would serve as an unwanted distraction once these dowagers set their sights on him. He saw with clarity the inevitable, endless parade of marriageable young women they would bring before him. No doubt many of them would be lovely, but he had no interest. Memories of that fickle young beauty in Boston left him with no inclination to marry for love, nor for leaving himself susceptible to the same sort of romantic apoplexy from which Barclay suffered.

No, his would be a practical marriage, to a woman bright enough to be a real asset to him, capable of being trusted, clever enough to take advantage of an opportunity, and with enough composure to handle herself in any manner of situation. But she would also need a certain level of culture, some sophistication. She would need to know how to manage the formal staff of a large household, and be trained in refined arts such as etiquette, entertaining, and such.

Haarten had no prospects that fit this bill. There were some of Barclay's business associates who had daughters Haarten had met at various social events, but none had seemed particularly appropriate. When he was struck at the irony of having to find one woman, while getting two others, Lina and Josephine, out of the way, he saw the answer. Lina was nearly everything he could reasonably expect for a wife. More important, she innately possessed, and actively pursued, the very traits that would be nearly impossible to find in just any woman— her talent for business and her clever mind. If only she were a little more trained in those social skills, and a little more conversant on a wider range of topics that might be discussed casually at a social affair. If only she were a little more educated....

22

Lina stood on the steps of Barclay's house, knocking on the door. It was early November, and she was not expected for another three weeks. She had left the Ward school and would not be returning. She had long wondered what it would be like to see Edward Haarten truly angry, and now she just might learn. She didn't care. All she cared about was Josephine.

Life at Miss Ward's school had been intolerable from the beginning. It was only the newness of the setting, and an insistent belief that the situation might change that seduced Lina from seeing right away how wrong she had been to come. The school was nothing more than a boarding house for gullible young women. There were nine girls total, all sixteen to eighteen years old, except for Lina. She was one of only two girls new this term. The other was joining her older sister there, making Lina the outsider. Not that she cared, for Lina found she had little in common with these girls. They were a giggling, flighty bunch, whose families had sent them there as a display of their new wealth.

But the girls were merely annoying. Lina's deepest disappointment was that this was not the sort of education she had hoped for. Miss Ward ran a finishing school, where young ladies learned the proper way of walking, speaking, and behaving. They learned how to manage servants, how to oversee a gracious meal, and how to make charming if empty conversation with a room full of strangers, provided you all agree to talk about the same meaningless drivel.

Lina was heartbroken. She remained quiet the first week, hoping soon more interesting subjects would be taught. After a month she knew that would never happen. Lina thought of leaving right then, but she realized she would still owe the money. Miss Ward made it clear there would be no refund made for those who left before the end of the term.

So Lina resolved to make the most of this opportunity, whatever that might be. Week after week, she sat patiently through her classes. Social etiquette, personal grooming, domestic management, needlework, painting, musical instruction, diction and elocution. It was tedious, but it did teach Lina something—that many women didn't have enough to occupy their time.

To make up for the instruction she had hoped to receive, Lina devoured the books she had brought with her, as well as those in the school's modest library. These were mostly books of light verse, and some classics, including copies of Shakespeare's plays, which she enjoyed tremendously. And when the opportunity presented itself, Lina would take short walks around the town. In this way, Lina managed to fill her empty time. When the chatter of her classmates became too much, she would take a book and walk a few blocks to a small plaza where she could read quietly. In the evenings, or on rainy days, she was the first to claim a quiet corner of the sitting room for her studies. The other girls considered her a bookworm, and left her alone.

One day, flipping through the pages of a book she had brought with her, she came upon a letter from Josie. It was dated the day she left. The letter was not long, and Josephine's hand was cramped and difficult to read.

> *Dearest Lina*
>
> *I thought I would surprise you with this note, which you will no doubt find right away, for I know Barclay's books will be a great comfort to you. I will miss you every day, dearest, but I console myself with the knowledge that you are following your heart. That is most important, Lina. You must always follow your heart. It is so much smarter than you know. Never permit anyone to come between you and that which will make you truly happy. I have lived by this, and you see now what happiness it has brought me.*
> *Your dearest friend,*
> *Josephine*

That evening, Lina wrote Josie a long reply, crammed with every gossipy detail she could summon. She hoped Josie might write back, but knew it wasn't likely. Lina couldn't remember ever seeing Josephine write to another living soul. Lina sent the letter to the Golden West.

When a letter finally did arrive from San Francisco, it was not the letter she had hoped for. It was from Ada Quincannon.

> *Lina*
>
> *I'm sorry to send you bad news, but Captain Barclay is dead. Robbed and shot, they say. When I received your letter I realized you must not know this, nor that Josephine had moved to Barclay's house. I sent your letter there, but I haven't heard from her since then, nor has anyone I've asked. I thought you would want to know.*
> *Ada*

Lina closed the letter, and without a moment's hesitation, began to pack her things. She was going back to San Francisco to find Josephine. She asked no one's permission, nor did she send word she was on her way. She made her brief apologies to Miss Ward who, understanding such obligations, expressed her condolences and wished her a safe trip. Lina didn't bother mentioning she had no intention of returning.

Lina hadn't appreciated Miss Ward's influence on her appearance until Jackson failed to recognize her when he opened the door. She smiled. "It's Carolina, Jackson. Lina Clark."

"Good heavens, miss, look at you. Every inch the lady." He held the door for her. "But miss, no one mentioned your arrival."

"No one knew. I came as soon as I heard about Captain Barclay." She entered the hall and started removing her gloves.

"Carolina."

Edward Haarten stood in the library doorway. Instead of the familiar uniform, he wore a black suit that made him seem even more somber. She could see he was surprised by her appearance, and she saw a flicker in his eye that typically signaled his displeasure. She didn't care. "Where is Josephine?" she asked flatly. Haarten turned and went back inside the library without a word. She followed him. She shut the door behind her, then waited for his answer.

"You shouldn't have left school."

"Where is Josephine?" she said again, sharper this time.

"I take it, then, that you heard the news of Captain Barclay," he said.

Lina nodded with a sigh. "I sent a letter to Josephine at the Golden West. Ada wrote back. She told me about the Captain. And she said she sent my letter here. But why didn't *you* write me? Why didn't Josephine? None of this makes any sense!"

"Please sit, Carolina, and I'll explain." She did as he asked. "Captain Barclay was murdered. A few weeks ago. Apparently shot during a robbery on his way home. He made it back to the house before he died. There's been no luck in finding the culprit."

"Oh, God," Lina cried softly. She choked back tears as she thought back to the lively old man, her benefactor and friend.

"As you know, I repeatedly advised him against associating with questionable people, frequenting saloons and gambling halls. I told him no good would come from such habits. Regrettably, my prophecy has proven true."

"Was Josephine with him?" The thought that poor Josie might have had to witness this crime broke her heart. "Oh, God, she wasn't…?"

"No, she was not with him."

"But she was living here, as Ada said?"

"Captain Barclay was needed in Vancouver on business. At his request, I arranged for Miss Paul to situate herself here shortly after he left. It was only a matter of days after his return that he was murdered. When I broke the news, understandably she took it badly. So badly, in fact, that I was forced to seek treatment for her right away."

"Josephine is ill?"

Haarten shook his head. "Not her health." There was a long, deliberate pause. "I'm afraid it's her mind." Lina slumped in the chair. "A terrible tragedy." Lina remembered that night long ago on the trail, when Mrs. Frick gave birth, and Josephine fell into uncontrollable anguish. It seemed entirely possible that Barclay's death could cause a spell much worse. Haarten continued. "Out of respect for Captain Barclay, I hoped to be able to attend to her here. But it was soon clear the situation was untenable. For her own sake, and the safety of those in the house, she had to be removed."

"She was *violent?*" Haarten nodded. This development strained Lina's imagination. Before, Josephine had been anything but violent. She had been meek and timid like a wounded kitten. "Where is she?"

"The Wilcox Clinic, a private asylum on the outskirts of the city. A very reputable hospital where she will be well cared for, I assure you."

"I want to see her."

"Carolina, that would be quite impossible. I won't have you subjected to that place."

"But you said it was a reputable institution."

"It is. The best facility of its kind within a thousand miles. Still, the poor wretches housed there are beyond reclamation. It is a sad, frightening place."

"Regardless, I'm going." Lina moved toward the door, but Haarten reached her and caught her by the wrist.

"No." His tone was meant to quash any resistance.

Lina was resolved. She wrenched her wrist from his grip. "Just try to stop me!"

This time he took hold of her at the shoulders. Calmly, he said, "Very well. But I insist on accompanying you. I'll have the carriage brought around."

The two sat in silence the entire trip. Haarten kept his eye on Lina, as if she might leap from the carriage any minute. Lina ignored him by staring out the coach window. She tried to focus on the image of Josephine the last time she had seen her. Happy, laughing, cooing over Barclay. But the image of her inconsolable that night on the trail kept returning. *I hadn't been able to comfort her then, and I wasn't here for her this time*, Lina thought, and a pain went straight to her heart. Hot, sharp tears filled her eyes, and a hard swelling in her throat choked her. *I should have stayed. I could have stopped this.* The recriminations stayed with her, playing over and over in her mind. *Perhaps I can fix it*, she realized suddenly. *Once Josie sees me, she'll be much better. I can take her back to Barclay's. She'll be better then.*

Just then, the Wilcox Clinic came into view. The carriage rode up a long drive, and at the end stood a large new building, freshly painted white. The only ornamentation on the building was the heavy metal bars covering every window.

Haarten opened the carriage door and offered his hand to assist her. She ignored it, and stepped out of the carriage and through the door of the hospital, Haarten following just behind.

The cold sterile smell of astringents and ether assaulted her. The hall was vacant, but the place was alive with sounds of agony. A cacophony of screaming, wailing, whimpering voices emanated from rooms on the floors above her. The sound stopped her cold. "Sit here," Haarten said, pointing to the single chair in the hallway. He walked down the hall and out of sight.

For the endless minutes he was gone, Lina fought to block out the voices. She held her head down, covered her ears and hummed to herself. She jumped when Haarten laid his hand on her shoulder. He had returned with a sullen gentleman in a white coat. "Carolina, are you alright?" Haarten asked.

She didn't answer him, but turned to the other gentleman. "Where is Josephine Paul?" she demanded.

"Carolina, this is Dr. Maxwell. He is the head physician here. He can answer your questions."

"Good. Where is she?"

The doctor looked to Haarten. "Are you certain, sir?" Haarten nodded.

The doctor led them up the center staircase. The cries grew louder with each step. On the second floor, Lina entered a nightmare. She stood at the entrance to a long hallway lined with doors, each with a small set of bars set high. Lina could see hands grasping, flailing through the bars. The voices behind the doors became distinct. One woman was spouting gibberish. Another screamed nothing but obscenities. Somewhere, another woman sobbed pitiably.

The doctor stood in front of the first door on the right, waving them forward. It took all Lina's strength to move one foot, then the other. When finally she reached the door, the small barred window was just above her eyesight. Cautiously, she stood tiptoe to look inside, grabbing the bars in the door for balance.

A woman lay on a cot, her back to the door. She was tethered tightly with straps that bound her arms to her body, and she lay coiled, rocking slightly back and forth, softly humming a nonsense melody. Her jet-black hair was a rat's nest. With her hair tumbling over her face, and her back to the door, Lina could not be certain it was Josephine, but she behaved as Josie had that night in the wagon. Lina tried once to speak, but her mouth was too dry. She swallowed hard, and then managed a low whisper. "Josie?" was all she could summon.

Without warning, the woman let out a high shrill scream that seemed to last forever, then rolled into a giddy laugh and then a frantic sob. Lina recoiled from the door, burying her face in her hands.

"Take me away from here."

Little was said as they rode back to Rincon Hill. Twice Haarten spoke. "I tried to warn you," he said first, and then later, "You must never go back there." Lina said nothing. She tried hard not to cry. He was right on both counts, she knew, but his words could not drown out the voice of her own conscience. *If only I hadn't left San Francisco. If only I had been here when Josephine needed me. If only I had come back sooner. If only…*

He led her into the house, where Jackson and Mrs. Spear the housekeeper greeted them. Seeing her distress, Mrs. Spear tried to comfort her. "I'll make up a room," she said quietly to Haarten, then took Lina's arm and led her upstairs. Lina didn't resist when Mrs. Spear helped her undress and put her in bed, even though it was only mid-afternoon.

****

Lina slept all that day, and late into the morning of the next. When she did wake, she stayed in bed, huddled beneath the blankets, hiding from her own thoughts. She had cried herself to sleep. She remembered when she felt traces of tears beneath her sore, puffy eyes. The tears were gone now. She felt cold and empty inside. The whole world was blank. A lifetime ago, she and Josephine had thrown in together, and Lina now realized that since then, every plan she had made included Josie in some way. Lina always knew there would come a time they'd go their separate ways. But never like this. Lina felt grief, and knew she would grieve for a long time. But last night's tears had cleansed her of her sorrow, and today, there was only emptiness. She had no idea where to go, or what to do.

Eventually, Mrs. Spear came knocking, "just to check on you, miss." She brought coffee, which warmed Lina, roused her, and reminded her she was hungry. "As soon as you're dressed, miss, Captain Haarten would like to see you in the library." *Captain*, she thought. Haarten had assumed Barclay's position. It rankled, but knowing Edward Haarten, it did not surprise. *He would waste no time.*

Inside the library, Haarten sat by the fire with his own coffee. He rose as she entered, then invited her to sit down next to him. Lina sat quietly for a while, occasionally sipping her coffee. As the strong black drink warmed her fingers and stirred her blood, she finally looked to Haarten. "I appreciate your hospitality. I have nowhere else to go. If you could allow me a few days, I'm certain I can find ..."

"Of course. There is no urgency. There is plenty of room here."

"Thank you. And you should know I've decided not to return to school."

"Good. I was hoping that was the case. You're needed here, now. I'm glad not to have to disappoint you. That's exactly what I wanted to speak to you about."

"Then will I be going back to my position at the warehouse?"

"No. You can best serve by helping run this household for the next few weeks. The holidays are approaching, and I plan to host several events. For some of the company's business associates. In this time of trial, it's wise to show our partners they may continue to have full faith and confidence in Barclay & Company."

"But sir, I really know very little about such matters."

"Truly? Did you learn nothing at Miss Ward's?"

Lina had almost forgotten all those silly lessons in etiquette. Then a thought came to her so suddenly she blurted it out. "But then, you must have known. You knew Miss Ward's was a finishing school, not a real school."

"Of course. It provided you with exactly the education I needed for you. I simply didn't imagine I would need it so soon. I wanted you to have more polish, Carolina. As befitting a representative of the firm."

"I see." The news stung a bit, the realization that he hadn't wanted for her what she wanted for herself. But it was a day full of loss. This disappointment was barely noticeable amidst the sadness that filled her.

Edward continued. "I confess this business of running a large household is a new matter to me. And you, fresh from Miss Ward's, no doubt have many talents to offer. There will be plenty to do. I'm not entirely satisfied with the household staff here, but I'd rather have experienced hands during this hectic time. Mrs. Spear and the staff could use some direction and guidance, and I haven't time to see to it."

Lina looked at him, seeing him more clearly than she had since she returned. He had completely filled Captain Barclay's place, in his company and in his home. "Mrs. Spear referred to you as *Captain* Haarten."

He nodded. "Yes. I am Barclay's heir. He named me so in his will. And it was in the best interests of the company that I assume his role in the firm as quickly as possible."

"Full faith and confidence, as you said."

"Precisely."

"And you've assumed his obligations as well."

"What obligation?"

"Josephine's care. It must be expensive."

"Yes, it is."

"We don't want to be obligated, Captain Haarten. Please deduct the cost of her care from my wages."

"That's impossible, Carolina. Your wages are but a fraction of the costs. But don't let that worry you." He leaned forward and placed his hand on hers. "Does that mean then that you accept my offer?"

Cautiously, she withdrew her hand. She felt wary, felt the need to avoid sudden movements or thoughts. If she stayed, she would have time to figure out what should be done. "Very well, sir. I'll stay through the holidays."

****

Everything that made San Francisco feel like home to Lina—Josephine, Barclay, the Golden West, the warehouse—were all gone from her life now. Lina desperately needed to find that feeling somewhere, and at first she thought living in Barclay's house, where she had so many fond memories, might help. It did not. Every day was a painful reminder of how unlike that home the house now was. Except for the familiar faces of Barclay's servants, she hardly recognized the place. Haarten had disposed of most of Barclay's furnishings. "Too cluttered" he told her. The library was the only room that looked as it had before, but its warmth and welcoming atmosphere were gone. She had never been upstairs before, so even her bedroom felt strange. Her window looked out over unfamiliar views, to a winter that was colder, more blustery than the last she had spent here. No, nothing seemed familiar at all.

Even in the quiet of night, in the darkness of her room, where she could pretend she was anywhere that seemed more like home, there was no sense of comfort. She felt like a stranger in her own skin and her own thoughts. No plan of action, no future she could envision seemed plausible. And she could think of nothing to do for Josephine. Haarten made her swear she wouldn't return to the Wilcox Clinic. She was ashamed at how easy a promise it was to keep. The memory of that visit only brought sorrow and guilt.

Perhaps Lina would have been happier if she was as successful in her new position as she had been in her old one. She earnestly tried to be helpful around the house. Except for Mrs. Spear, the staff was obviously uncomfortable in her presence, and treated her with far more reserve and diffidence than Lina was accustomed to. Mrs. Spear was pleasant, but would more often than not relieve Lina of any task she started. "Let me handle that, miss. I've been doing this a good many years. For Captain Barclay." It seems Mrs. Spear still considered herself working for Barclay. Lina, on the other hand, was keenly aware she worked for Haarten. Accustomed as she had been to pleasing him before, she was disturbed to find now she seldom met with his approval. The worst of it was, she knew he was right. She could not shake the fatigue that had been with her since she returned. She couldn't concentrate for long, forgot things easily, and lost things often.

Two weeks before Christmas there was to be a tea, an afternoon affair to show off the house in all its holiday best. Haarten gave her specific instructions on every detail, and charged her with making certain they were followed. But when Lina approached Mrs. Spear with those instructions, the housekeeper dismissed her, saying, "Just leave everything to me, Mrs. Clark. You see to the invitations, and I'll take care of the rest."

She knew she should have insisted, but she lacked the will to argue. She was working on those invitations the next afternoon when it happened. She sat in the cold dimness of the library, scratching out the lettering in her finest hand. "Damn!" she whispered as she tore up yet another piece of the fine linen paper she had been instructed to use. For every note she finished, there were two ruined with sloppy writing, misspellings, or splattered ink. Suddenly, she heard Haarten's voice. "Carolina!" Then she heard his boots as he came down the hall toward her.

"Carolina!" He bellowed again, now standing in the doorway. "Did I or did I not give you specific orders regarding the menu?"

"Yes, sir."

"Then can you explain this delivery from the butcher's? It's fortunate I happened by just as it arrived. From what I can see, absolutely nothing about it is correct!"

"I tried to tell Mrs. Spear, sir, but she insisted…"

"Insisted? *Insisted?* You permitted yourself to be corrected by a subordinate?"

"It's just that she seemed so confident she knew what you wanted."

"She does *not*. She knows what Barclay wanted. She has not the slightest notion of what *I* want. I'd have dismissed her when Barclay died, if I thought I could replace her for the same wages. That goes for the whole lot of them!" He raised his voice purposely at the last, to make certain any staff lurking in the hall would hear him. Lina could hear the eavesdroppers scurrying back toward the kitchen.

"Carolina, this is your sole responsibility. To make certain my directives regarding the management of this house are fulfilled to the letter. Is that clear?"

"Yes, sir."

"From now on, I expect you to treat the staff as subordinates. Be direct in your instructions. Precise. And unrelenting in your insistence for obedience. Do you understand?" Lina nodded. "And be careful, Carolina," Haarten added, pointing to the papers in front of her on the desk. "You're wasting paper. Be neater." Then Haarten left.

Lina was as good as her word regarding the staff. The next morning she went to the kitchen first thing. The entire staff was present and busy at a dozen different chores. Mrs. Spear held the center of the room, calling out instructions in all directions.

"Mrs. Spear?" Lina said, but no one paid any attention to her. "Mrs. Spear?" she said louder this time.

"Just a minute, miss," the housekeeper said without even looking in her direction.

This wouldn't happen to Haarten, she realized, and then it struck her. She had struggled all night to think of how to command the staff's attention, and now she understood. She would treat them as Haarten treated them.

"Mrs. Spear!" Lina spoke in a voice as threatening and resolute as she could make it. Everyone stopped. She looked around the room at the half dozen stunned faces. "Mrs. Spear. Make certain the delivery man takes back the goods you mistakenly ordered yesterday. And you!" she said, pointing to the delivery man. "You're only to take orders that I have authorized. Do you understand?"

"Yes, ma'am," the driver said softly, then he snuck out.

"As to the rest of you, finish here by ten o'clock, and then everyone is to wait for me in the front parlor. I'll be handing out instructions then. Is that clear?" When no one answered, Lina said again, a bit more forcefully. "Is that clear?"

"Yes, ma'am," and a few silent nods were her answer.

"This will be our new daily routine. I'll be managing the household from now on."

From that moment on, Lina had the authority which Haarten demanded of her. But it came at a cost. Even Mrs. Spear was now cool to Lina, although always respectful. Lina lost the only friend she had in the house.

Following Haarten's orders became easier once she realized that all she had to do was treat the staff as Haarten would. She found it easier than she would have thought. Perhaps it was Miss Ward's training after all, that made her feel authoritative. Or perhaps it was only that it gave her the focus and the energy she had been lacking since returned. She discovered a day filled with scrutinizing every detail of every chore that every member of the staff performed left no room for moping, or wondering what had happened to her happy life. It quickly changed her fortunes in Haarten's eyes as well, and in no time she was back earning his praise.

The Christmas afternoon tea went exactly as Haarten wanted, down to the petits fours and lace tablecloths. The dowager wives of Haarten's associates all came, and were suitably lavish in their praise of the beautiful home, its exquisite appointments, and Captain Haarten's gracious hospitality. As Haarten expected, they would tell everyone, including their husbands, that Edward Haarten was a refined and courtly gentleman in the old tradition. As Lina oversaw the day's affair, she noted another affect Haarten had managed. To these ladies, and particularly the daughters who accompanied them to the party, Edward Haarten cut a dashing figure. He was the center of female attentions all afternoon. Lina wondered if this consequence was intended, for never had she seen him this convivial. He was almost flirtatious, and certainly went out of his way to flatter every female there.

Lina had assumed that, like the rest of the staff, once the party started, she could fade into the background. But Haarten had other plans. He insisted they take this opportunity to introduce her to San Francisco society. Further, he decided she should be introduced as *Miss Carolina Clark,,* the late Captain Barclay's ward. He felt this story would give her a legitimate, yet ambiguous role in the household. So she dressed in a suitably modest dress selected by Haarten, allowed him to introduce her, and performed her duties as instructed. Lina found the afternoon deadly dull, but she smiled through everything.

With that modest success behind her, Lina felt more confident managing the smaller, more formal dinner to be held two nights before Christmas. A dozen of Haarten's most important associates came to dinner that evening, held in the full regalia of the dining room. If Haarten had been precise in his instructions for the tea, he was meticulous with the dinner details. He had even gone so far as to tell Lina which guests to engage in conversation, what topics she should and should not discuss, and how to gracefully lead the ladies into the parlor so that the men might retire to the library to discuss whatever men discuss in libraries. In the end, Haarten declared the evening a success, and even thanked her.

With all the preparatory occasions, Christmas itself was forgotten. Even in the slimmest days of her childhood, her father always brought home a Christmas surprise. A peppermint stick, a cornhusk doll, a shiny penny all her own. Last year, she and Josie had exchanged small presents. This year, Lina woke to a nearly silent house. The staff would have the afternoon off to spend with their own families, a rare treat for them. They fixed a lovely meal, but Lina and Haarten shared it in near silence. When the meal was over, Jackson entered. "Will there be anything else, sir?"

"No, nothing," Haarten answered absently, but Jackson remained.

Lina understood. "Captain, I think the staff would like your permission to leave."

"What? Oh yes, of course. Carolina, make certain everything is in order before they do."

Lina accompanied Jackson to the kitchen where she found most of the staff assembled. She entered thinking she would give a cursory check of the state of the kitchen, then dismiss them. She looked around the room at their faces, and saw in each one the look of fear. Were they waiting for the inevitable scolding? Anticipating some last minute chores before she would let them leave? Or was this what remained of their sorrow, their loss at Barclay's passing? A wave of regret came over her, regret that she had estranged herself from people she once might have counted as friends, friends she desperately needed now. "Just a moment, everyone." She ran upstairs to her room and came back with a small coin purse. "I'm sorry," she kept saying as she placed a dollar coin in each person's hand. "I'm sorry. I know this isn't a very happy Christmas. I'm sorry." She wanted to say, "I'm sorry I haven't been kind. I'm sorry we have to work for such a difficult man. I'm sorry I haven't thanked you for all you've done. I'm sorry Barclay is gone." But she knew she still had to keep some of the authority she had worked so hard to earn. Otherwise, they would all feel Haarten's ire.

Of all the parties planned, New Year's Eve would be the grandest. Hearing through the local gossipmongers of the lavishness of the home and its dashing new occupant, all of San Francisco society was eager to attend. More than one hundred guests were expected. As the ultimate symbol of refinement, a six-piece orchestra would play.

Lina spent time downstairs before the party began, making her final inspections. She found Haarten already in the ballroom, doing the same. He turned to see her, delight in his eyes. "My dear, you shouldn't be seen down here when our guests arrive. I want you upstairs for now, so that you can make a formal entrance." He took her hand and held her out before him, examining each detail of her appearance.

"I just wanted to make certain everything was as you wished."

"Of course you did, Carolina. And you've done a splendid job. Everything is perfect. Now run along upstairs. I'll send for you when its time."

She remained in her room for nearly two hours, well after guests had started to arrive. Finally, a new maid, a young girl named Darcy, knocked on her door. "Captain Haarten says you're to come downstairs, miss." Lina checked herself in the mirror one last time, to make certain she looked just as he had instructed her. Haarten had a dressmaker specially prepare a gown for her, made of deep purple taffeta and Irish lace, with ten layers of crinoline beneath, and matching slippers. He had given her pearl ear-bobs, which hung beneath the trailing strands of her red gold hair, which she wore up for the occasion. Edward Haarten hadn't overlooked a thing.

She walked down the hallway to the landing. As she approached the top of the stairs she heard the orchestra strike up a waltz. Haarten was standing at the base of the stairs, looking up. When he saw her, he turned to the assemblage gathered in the main hallway, and announced in a full voice. "Ladies and gentlemen, allow me to introduce our hostess and Captain Barclay's ward, Miss Carolina Clark."

Lina wanted to run out the door. She felt awkward and silly, and couldn't seem to move her feet. She thought if she did, she would surely trip and make a fool of herself. So she focused on Haarten, and found a strange assurance in his eyes. He offered his hand. *If I can take hold of that hand*, she convinced herself, *if I can just make it that far…* She took a step forward, then another, and another, until she reached him. As she took his hand, she smiled with relief. With the same assurance, he linked her arm in his and led her into the ballroom. As host and hostess, they led the first waltz, but were soon joined by others, much to Lina's relief.

The evening continued without incident. They both danced with other guests, and from time to time she would excuse herself to give direction to the staff. On one trip she found Mrs. Spear in the kitchen, where everything seemed to be going smoothly. Lina came to her and said, "Tell everyone Captain Haarten is very pleased," then added, "Thank you so much for all your help." She was surprised to see sadness in Mrs. Spear's eyes. "What's wrong?" Lina asked her.

"It's just…I'm sorry, miss. It's just that it's…different. Not like the old days, with Captain Barclay. But it's not my place to say."

Lina laid a cool hand on Mrs. Spear's sleeve. "No, you're right," she sighed, then whispered, "I miss him, too." The two shared a sad, weak smile, and Lina thought perhaps she found a friend again.

When Lina returned to the party, the guests were clustered near the orchestra. Haarten stood on the periphery, and saw her enter. He stepped forward quickly to meet her. "Come, my dear, it's nearly time," he said as he pulled her into the crowd.

The orchestra conductor, holding his watch aloft, was leading the group. "Ten, nine, eight…" Everyone counted off the seconds together. Couples looked at one another with anticipation, and every eye gleamed with excitement. "Three, two, one! Happy New Year!" Suddenly, Lina felt an arm around her waist, pulling her closer. With the same authority he had led her in the waltz, Edward pulled her to him and kissed her fully on the lips. He lingered there for just a moment longer than he should have. When it was over, Lina was painfully aware that everyone was looking at them. When the orchestra started playing again, and everyone turned their attentions back to the party, she wriggled from his grasp.

****

Within an hour of midnight all but a few guests had departed. Haarten seemed anxious for them to be gone. Lina hoped it was because he was leaving the city the next day and would be gone for a week. *If I'm lucky,* she thought, *I can avoid him tonight. Perhaps he'll leave early, and I'll avoid him all together.*

When Haarten closed the door on the final guest, she started for the stairs. "It was a wonderful party, sir. I hope you're pleased. I'll say goodnight now."

"Carolina, would you join me in the library?" She was bone tired, but knew he would have instructions for her before he left. At least, she hoped that was all this was about.

He did not, as was his custom, walk into the library and wait for her to follow. This time, he held the door for her. Lina stood by the desk, but Haarten came to her, taking her hand and leading her to the fireplace.

"Did you enjoy yourself, Carolina?"

"I suppose so, Captain." She lacked the energy for more enthusiasm. *Just speak your mind and let me go to bed.*

"And the last few weeks, have you enjoyed that as well?"

"Enjoyed it? Well, I appreciated the employment, of course, and I enjoy helping you." *What was he working towards?*

"And you have been a help. A tremendous help. But now I need something more from you."

"Of course, sir."

"Marry me," he said flatly.

Lina was stunned. In a flash she remembered his kiss. "Forgive me, sir. Quite simply, I'm shocked. I had no idea before tonight you had feelings for me."

To her surprise, Edward Haarten chuckled. "Oh, that kiss you mean? That was for show. We wouldn't want our engagement to come as a total surprise." Lina could only stare at him, puzzled. "You are a bright young woman, Carolina. Passably attractive. Since Miss Ward's, you've acquired some social poise. You manage the household aptly. These are qualities I require now, in my new position. Now more than ever, it's absolutely imperative that this household be maintained in an orderly fashion."

"But I could do that for you, without marriage."

He shook his head. "Your position in the house as a 'ward' will only safeguard appearances for so long, and I won't—I can't—tolerate suspicion of any sort."

"I see," she said. "Appearances." Appearances would, of course, be so very important to Edward Haarten. "And these 'appearances' of which you speak? They are more important than your own heart?"

"Marriage is far too important to be left to the heart," he said stoically. "Marriage is just a contract between two people for mutual services."

She searched his eyes for some indication, no matter how slight, that he was masking some deeper, finer, feeling, even if she didn't share that feeling. But she found nothing of the kind.

"Then, I'm sorry, sir, I cannot marry you. I realize I owe you a great deal. But not that."

He showed no reaction to her rejection, but he moved from the mantel to the desk. She waited for a response that was a long time coming.

"I'm glad to see you remember your obligations. I didn't want to have to remind you of your indebtedness to Captain Barclay, and to me. The offer of work, the schooling, Josephine's care." His voice stressed this last so that there was no mistaking his intent. "I know you feel obligated to repay that debt. But it will be financially impossible for you to do so. Miss Paul's care will continue for years to come." His threats slipped their veils as he spoke.

"I'm capable of making my own living, and supporting her."

"In the past, yes. But now?"

"Now?"

"If you leave, what will people think? Particularly when I tell them you were revealed to be an opportunist, no better than those women at the Golden West."

For the first time, Lina saw something to laugh about. "Is that how you'll explain this?"

"That, and more, if need be."

His motives clear, Lina suddenly felt quite calm, and free speak her mind. "I don't give a damn what people say. I never have."

Haarten stood suddenly. He towered above her. She took a step back, and when he spoke, his voice was like low, rumbling thunder. "That's fine for you, but what about Josephine? A word from me and no one in this city will give you a decent job. You'll end up a whore like your friend. And even a whore's wages won't be able to support her in that asylum she's in. You could spend day and night on your back and never make enough."

Hate, fear, anger all came flooding over Lina at once. For an split second she thought if she could only remain calm, she could think of a retort—an escape path he hadn't yet blocked. Then she realized there was no escape path, and that her emotions weren't keeping her from seeing the truth. The truth was, she was completely cornered.

Haarten continued. "My dear, I prefer not to upset you. But you must understand, this is no idle threat. I mean everything I say. I'd like you to accept my offer willingly, but willingly or not, you will accept. There is no rush, however, so take a few weeks to get accustomed to the notion. That's all for now. Run off to bed." He turned his back on her. As she left, she slammed the doors behind her with all the defiance she could muster. Then she ran to her room, and slammed those doors too.

23

Haarten left the city early the next day. From her room, Lina heard the door close and the sound of the coach rolling away. Then, there was a soft knock on her door. "Pardon me, miss?" It was Darcy, the maid. "Captain Haarten left a note for you."

"Slide it under the door, please," she answered. She wanted to avoid everyone, to be left alone to cry and fret and think as she had all night. Lina sat at the dressing table a long time, staring at the letter on the floor. *Would it be an apology, perhaps? Some awkward attempt to excuse his behavior?* In defiance, she left the note there as she considered her situation.

Everything Haarten had said was true. In San Francisco, he could thwart her every attempt to start a new life. She would never be able to care for Josephine on her own. He had maneuvered her into exactly the situation he planned as she suspected he maneuvered all his business dealings, with calculated precision and no remorse. For Edward Haarten, everything was about business, and if it wasn't he'd make it so. She bristled at the notion that she had emulated him in dealing with the household staff, and that this was a quality he valued in her.

An hour later, utterly exhausted and head aching, Lina gave in to her curiosity. She opened the envelope and read Haarten's note. It was only a list of household chores he expected her to attend to in his absence. That was all. No apology, no reference to his ultimatum, nothing at all of a personal nature.

Lina knew at that moment that there would be no further discussion of his demands. She could bring the matter up, but there would be no point. Haarten wasn't a negotiator, nor was he a gambler. He never entered into dealings where he didn't control every move. He never took a chance when he didn't have to. With nothing to barter, Lina was left without a prayer, for clearly there would be no appealing to Haarten's sympathies. He had none.

Since that horrible day at the clinic, Lina had kept Josephine from her mind, except at night when the house was so quiet all she could hear were her thoughts. Now she knew she would have to think of Josie, for there was more that needed to be done than simply saving herself. *I have to be able to provide for Josephine after I've left San Francisco*, she thought. In that moment, for the first time she knew she *would* leave, even if it meant leaving Josephine behind for a time. As horrible as conditions might be for Josephine, Lina had no alternative to offer. The most she could hope for was to free herself, and provide for Josephine's care later. Until then, it would be best to appear compliant. Lina dressed and went downstairs to start her day, Haarten's list in her hand.

****

It happened that Lina returned to the Golden West, quite unplanned. Haarten's list included a routine check on the warehouse. She found Jack happily managing the place as she had done not so very long ago. It was only an ordinary warehouse—rough, dirty, blindingly dim on anything but the sunniest day, and totally lacking in creature comforts. But she missed it. She reveled in the familiar sounds of the men's grumbling, the fishy smell of seawater, the feel of sawdust beneath her feet. In none of the places she had worked had she ever been as content as she had been here. She wanted to linger, but Jack was busy with a new shipment of lumber and she could find no reason to stay.

She had finished her errands for the day, and her time was her own. She didn't want to go back to Rincon Hill. The warehouse had left her with a longing for a happier time. Haarten's house was the last place she wanted to be. She followed the familiar path she once took every day. She headed for the Golden West. It was mid-day, and she thought if she hurried, she might join Ada for a bite to eat.

When she rounded the corner and saw the Golden West, her heart sank. The long row of windows was boarded, and on the door there hung a crudely lettered sign. "Closed."

As she neared, she heard voices inside. Anxiously, she pushed the louvered doors open. Inside, all but a few of the chairs and tables were gone, and there were no bottles behind the bar. "Hello?" she called out.

The door to the kitchen swung open, and out came Ada. Dust powdered her dress and smeared across her cheeks. She carried a broom, which she dropped in her surprise at the sight of Lina.

"Oh, honey!" she called, as she came running. The two embraced, then laughed at the dust that now covered Lina too. Ada reached up to wipe some of the dirt from Lina's face when a look passed between them, and their laughter stopped.

"Ada, I was so sorry to hear about Barclay. Thank you for writing me." They embraced again, then they sat at one of the tables.

"Then Josie didn't write you. I thought she might not. How's she taking it?"

Lina looked down and shook her head. Ada squeezed her hand, then whispered, "Is she being tended to?" Lina nodded, and Ada smiled. "Well, that's some comfort." Abruptly her tone changed. "And I bet that damned Haarten didn't bother to write either, did he?" Ada gave a low grunt when Lina shook her head. "Well, the bastard's not my problem anymore. I'm leavin'. Good thing you came by when you did. Another week, and I'll be gone."

"Gone? Where? Why?" Lina was shocked. She couldn't imagine a San Francisco without the Golden West.

"Haarten, that's why. Fired all the girls two weeks ago. Said now that *he's* running everything, he wants no part of whores. He wanted me to keep running this place for the gambling, though. Strange sense of propriety that one. Poker's fine, but… Well, without the girls, I can't compete. If you ask me, Haarten wanted out of the saloon business altogether. Too dirty a trade for the likes of him."

"I suspect you're right."

"As to where, Oregon, probably. They found gold up there, too. And I hear there's big timber coming out of there. Either way, there'll be lots of fellas looking to spend money. Anyplace like that, I'll find work." Ada smiled. "It's not the first time I've had to pull up stakes. Probably won't be the last either." Ada patted Lina on the arm as she rose slowly. She walked over to the broom, lying where she dropped it. Picking it up, she surveyed the room.

"Had some grand times here, didn't we?" Ada said with a smile. "Now there's nothing to be done but clean out the rubbish. Oh, that reminds me! I've got something for you." She darted up the stairs, and a moment later returned with a small box.

"I found this in your old room, tucked under the mattress." She handed the box to Lina, who set it on the table, then carefully removed the lid. Inside was Josie's Bible and rosary. Lina tenderly picked up the Bible. She clutched it to her breast as she fingered the delicate beads of the rosary.

"Ada, what did Josie say to you when she left?"

"Nothing," said Ada, shrugging her shoulders. "I didn't talk to her. I was out one morning and when I came back, she was gone. Later a boy brought me a note from Haarten, saying Barclay had Josie moved to Rincon Hill. All her things, too. I went upstairs, and sure enough, her room was empty. Except for that, it seems," she ended, nodding toward the Bible.

"And you never spoke with her?"

"No. I half expected to see her come 'round. But I never saw her again."

"I wonder why she wasn't here with Barclay the night he was murdered," Lina said.

"Barclay wasn't here the night he was murdered." Ada said. "I never heard where he was, but he wasn't here."

Something's not right in this, Lina thought. It was hard to imagine Josie would leave these things behind, or not return for them.

"Honey, I gotta get back to work. I gotta be outta here by tomorrow. But I'm so glad you came by!" Ada wrapped her arm around Lina's shoulder and walked with her to the end of the bar. Ada ducked behind the bar to take out a piece of paper. "If you ever need me for anything, or if they ever get that bastard that killed Barclay, get a hold of this fellow here in town, a lawyer. I'd welcome that news, and he'll know how to get in touch with me."

'S. Tunnicliff' was the name on the paper. "I will. And thank you so much." Lina held Ada long and tight. She started to turn to leave, but Ada held her arm.

"There's something I'm not sure you know, Lina. But I'm pretty sure Josie did." She paused. "A long time ago, it used to be me and Barclay, like it was Josie and Barclay. There were others in between me and her. Lots." She chuckled. "So I hold no grudge against Josie, or any of them. But when you see Josephine, well just give her my sympathies, would you? Tell her…I understand."

****

Haarten returned unannounced. Lina found him in the library one afternoon. "I arrived early this morning," was all he said to her obvious surprise, and then turned his attention back to work.

Their daily interaction fell into a routine. During the day they spoke only about the household. Haarten insisted she join him for supper, and then they said nothing. She was surprised that he seemingly took little interest in where she went and what she did. She expected him to be suspicious. Then she realized the staff would report her comings and goings. She remembered how eager she, too, had once been to do anything Haarten asked.

If Haarten was suspicious of her, Lina was doubly suspicious of him. She had suspected from the start Haarten had not told her everything he knew about Barclay's death. After her conversation with Ada, those suspicions grew. Why would Barclay have been out for the evening without Josephine? And where had he gone, if not the Golden West? And that Josephine would leave without saying goodbye to Ada seemed particularly odd. So many questions that might never be answered, she thought. Unfortunately, there was no time to solve riddles. Soon her luck with Haarten would run out, and he would bring up the subject of marriage again.

More than time, Lina needed some place to think. Even when Edward was not in the house, she felt his presence. He dominated the place, and she worried she might leave some telltale sign of her plans for the staff to find. She decided to walk to Telegraph Hill where she had always been able to think. She went to her room for her coat. It was a beautiful sunny day for winter, but she knew the wind on the hill would be brisk.

From the hallway, Lina heard Darcy and the youngest of the household staff, another Irish girl named Annie, talking as they worked.

Darcy was stripping the bed sheets, and Annie was dusting, although mostly talking. Annie was only about fourteen, but she was forthright and lively. "Well, all I know is, me eldest sister's talkin' of goin'. It sounds thrillin', all that way to the Oregon Ter'try, travelin' the sea, and maybe a husband in the bargain."

"What's a child like yourself want with a husband?" Darcy said, cracking the clean sheet as she laid it on the bed. "A world of worry, they are, never doubt it. And how, will ya tell me, can your sister be affordin' such a trip? She's no more than you or me. It would take me two years' wages for such a fare, and only that if I saved every penny."

"See here, it says 'Passage included at no charge'." Annie took a sheet of paper from her apron pocket and laid it on the bed.

Darcy picked it up, gave it a quick glance, and then tossed it back to her. "Ach, it's a pig in a poke, it is. Who knows what devilment these people have for ignorant girls like you? You're better off stayin' right here."

"I agree with Darcy," said Lina. "I don't know why you'd want to marry when you have your whole life ahead of you. Men are nothing but trouble, let me promise you." She walked toward the closet to get her coat.

"Ah, but miss! A husband! And a new life! Why, it all sounds grand to me." Annie stared at the handbill she held in her outstretched arms, as if she could see her happy future in it.

Lina was in no mood to listen to starry-eyed daydreams. She wanted to tell Annie to have better sense than to ever expect anything more for yourself than what you were given. Exasperated, she snatched the paper from Annie's hands and stuffed it in the pocket of her coat. "Girls, get back to work. Tell Mrs. Spear I'm going out."

She had not been back to the hill since coming home, and though it was cold and grey, she felt immediately comforted by its familiarity, by the total absence of anything that reminded her of Edward Haarten. She sat down, closed her eyes, and listened to the wind and the cries of the seagulls.

I've traveled halfway across the country, she thought, *and now, here I am, backed up against the ocean, no place left to go.* She opened her eyes and watched an outbound steamer pulling through the bay. She imagined herself on it, wondering where it might be headed. She closed her eyes again, and imagined the globe in Barclay's library that charted the sea routes. Her mind's fingers traced the lines on the globe leading south from San Francisco. Mexico, Chile, then around the Horn. West to the Sandwich Islands and beyond. North to Oregon Territory, and Russia.

Oregon Territory! Her eyes popped open, and she stood up, cramming her gloved hands inside her pockets, until she found Annie's handbill.

> *Female Emigrants Wanted For Relocation to Puget Sound. Women of high character and tenacity of spirit sought for purposes of possible matrimony and domestic settlement. An imbalance in the distribution of eligible men to women necessitates the settlements near Puget Sound, in the northern west portion of the Oregon Territory, to solicit available and interested ladies to consider this unusual inquiry. Ladies will be provided with comfortable lodgings and afforded every available accommodation. Abundant opportunities for respectable employment. Passage included at no charge. Interested parties may contact Capt. M.D. Riordan, the schooner Bantry Bay, Pier 3, San Francisco.*

She crammed the handbill back into her pocket, and headed down the hill as fast as the muddy path would allow, back to Rincon Hill.

****

Dear God, where is this place? She stood before the globe in the library, turning it until she found it. Puget Sound. Straight up the coast from San Francisco. Lina used her thumb to estimate distance. Perhaps as much as a thousand miles. That could be two weeks on a ship. Two weeks and a thousand miles, surely that was far enough away. And if it was on the coast of the Pacific, wouldn't it be like San Francisco?

In the half-constructed scheme that was already beginning to form in her mind, Lina needed this place to be like San Francisco. It was that very notion that had made the idea seem plausible. San Francisco was built upon sudden fortunes. A place of immediate, and often sizeable, opportunity. Lina understood such places. She had lived in them her whole life, and what she didn't know, Ada Quincannon had schooled her in those mornings over breakfast. She remembered Ada had talked about moving north. Ada saw the opportunity there. And Lina remembered what Ada had said about big timber from there. When Lina started at the warehouse, she had noticed how much lumber Barclay & Company handled. Between the timber and the farming in the Willamette, and the gold Ada spoken of, there ought to be lots of opportunity up north.

Lina realized she was pinning her hopes on a 'pig in a poke,' as Darcy had called it. There was no way to know for certain without arousing suspicions with her questions. She couldn't afford to arouse suspicions. Nothing could tip her hand to Haarten.

All she had was a destination she could only pray would be a safe haven. Now she needed to look out for Josie. When she left, Haarten might just leave Josie destitute as he had threatened. Lina didn't know how quickly that might happen, and so she needed someone here, a confidant, who could keep her apprised if and when that happened. Ada would have been a good choice, but Ada would be gone soon. Then Lina remembered something else Ada had told her.

****

The next morning, Lina walked to the office of Sylvester Tunnicliff, Esquire, the lawyer Ada had mentioned. If Ada trusted this man, surely she could as well. She needed someone who was not beholden to Haarten, and any friend of Ada's surely fit that bill.

As soon as she saw him, she recognized him as a regular at the Golden West, an affable fellow in a threadbare waistcoat, with a fleshy, florid face. His office was above a ship chandler's shop halfway between the Golden West and the warehouse. When she introduced herself, he shook her hand enthusiastically, saying of course he remembered her, and how kind it was of Ada Quincannon to commend him to her. He held the chair as Lina sat. "You're looking well, Miss Clark. Business is good, I take it. And how is that charming Miss Josephine?"

"I'm afraid, Mr. Tunnicliff, that it is because of Miss Paul that I am here. She is not well, I'm sorry to say. Captain Barclay's death has left her inconsolable."

"I'm just stricken to hear that. Such a lovely woman, and so charming." He leaned across the desk, and in his most sincere voice, asked, "How may I be of service?"

"I want to establish an account on her behalf. A trust, I think you call it? It probably isn't necessary, but I'd feel better knowing that if anything were to happen to me, Miss Paul will be taken care of. Confidentially, sir, she's under the care of the Wilcox Clinic, and I'm sorry to say she will be for an indefinite period. It is for this purpose I intend to establish an account at the Page & Beacon Bank. I will make periodic deposits, and the bank will be instructed to provide you access to the account. For your part, you will contact the hospital the first of each month to make certain Miss Paul is being properly cared for. Use the funds to improve her conditions however you see fit. I'll instruct the bank to issue you a stipend for your services each month."

"But, Mrs. Clark, forgive my asking, but why do you need me to take care of this? Surely you can visit her and determine for yourself...."

"It is difficult for me to see her there." Lina did not have to feign a sense of revulsion at the thought.

Tunnicliff immediately responded. "I understand."

Lina bowed her head momentarily to heighten his impression of a woman overcome by tragedy. She raised her head and looked Tunnicliff straight in the eye. "You can appreciate, then, the trust I am placing with you."

"Of course, of course. I'm touched you would consider retaining me for such a personal and important service. You may rely upon me completely."

Lina stood and offered him her hand. "I do already, sir. I will have the bank send a messenger over with the paperwork listing the account and other details."

She left Tunnicliff's with one last errand for the day. At the docks she could surely find someone who knew of this ship, or its captain, M.D. Riordan. Lina did not have to look far. There, docked in a berth off Pier 3, sat the Bantry Bay. As Lina gathered her thoughts, she gave the ship a long, careful look. The ship wasn't much to look at. There wasn't a spot on it that wasn't showing a patch, or needing some paint. Still, the crew was busy offloading its cargo, so clearly someone had confidence in the ship and its captain.

Lina shouted up to the ship's deck. "Hello! I'm looking for Captain Riordan. Is he aboard?"

A sailor came to the gangplank. "Aye ma'am. He's here. He's just not, well, it's just that, um, he's not been on deck yet this morning, ma'am."

"This morning? But it's past midday!"

"Aye, well, that's true, ma'am, but he, I mean we, well, last night we… Uh, I'll wake him, er, get him, ma'am. Come aboard." The young man waited for Lina to reach the deck, then he went below. Lina found an empty keg on which to sit. She waited fifteen minutes before Captain Riordan appeared.

By his look, he could have been a hundred other old salts Lina had seen along these docks. Like his ship, every inch of him needed either a patch or a scrubbing. But he had obviously attempted to straighten his appearance before meeting her, for these were surely his finest clothes, and although Lina could clearly smell whiskey on him, it was mingled with bay rum and soap, and he'd slicked back his thin gray hair.

"Good mornin', missus. I'm Riordan. What is it I can do for ya?" The chipper tone in his voice was forced, and the bright morning sun clearly pained him, for he was squinting so hard it caused his face to gathered in a tight knot around his bulbous nose. He was tall, and his skin was tanned as leather. Despite his age, he had the strong arms of a man who'd spent his life at sea.

"I wonder if we might speak in your cabin," Lina glanced at the men at the other end of the deck.

Riordan winced. "Ah, best not." But he winked in recognition of her concerns. "Let me take you to the wheelhouse. You can speak your mind there." The room was small and cramped, with but one chair that Riordan offered to Lina. He stood leaning against the ship's wheel and absently fingered the grips, worn shiny from years beneath his hands. "Now, tell me, lass, what's the worry?"

"No worry, Captain. I've come about this handbill." Lina held the paper out to him. Riordan quickly nodded his head.

"Of course. You're wanting to make arrangements for your maid, or cook perhaps?"

"For myself," Lina said. Riordan gave her an odd look, but she continued. "I have some questions, if you don't mind. Who is behind this offer?"

"Name's Kincaid. A gent what has business concerns up there on the sound. A mill owner."

"And what is this community, Captain?"

"Well, it's more what you might call a settlement. But there're plenty of 'em up there like it. The place is growing like a weed."

"And when do you depart?"

"The fourteenth."

"The fourteenth? Why, that's only a week away! I can't be ready in time!"

Riordan raised his eyebrow. "Well, miss, it's like this. I haul timber down here once a month or so. Part of this contract they got goin', ya see. So this ship'll be in port mid-month, every month for the next two or three. You can come any time yas are ready." Riordan noticed lines on Lina's brow. "Here, now, no cause for concern, miss. I gives you my personal assurances. These folks up there, I consider each and every one of 'em a personal friend, I do. They're honest folk, and hard workin'. Why, it's a pity you weren't here earlier. Another gentlemen from them parts came here with me, he did. Marr, Robert Marr's the man. A logger by trade. It's his contract I told you about. Perhaps you could come back later and meet 'im. See for yourself what sort of folks these is." Riordan took the handbill from Lina's hand. "It's just what it says here, ma'am. No tricks or schemes." Lina looked at Riordan, then at the flyer again. "Tell ya what. I promises that if you're unhappy, I'll brings ya back to San Francisco any time ya likes."

Lina smiled. Whatever else happened, Lina knew one thing—she would never return to San Francisco. Still, the man seemed honest, if coarse, and his willingness to make this pledge was the only guarantee she would get. "Thank you Captain. You've been most helpful. I'll contact you when I know my plans."

****

It was a starry night, and rather than spend his money at a saloon, Riordan took a bottle on deck to feel the breeze. He could've gone to a saloon, but this way he always managed to find his way to bed. *The older I get*, he thought, *the lazier*. He laughed and took a long taste from the bottle.

Riordan heard someone coming up the gangplank. He turned to see the outline of a large man, framed by the wharf-front lights. "Is that yourself, Marr?"

"It is," said a voice deep and clear, as the man walked up to him.

"And just where is it you've been all day, man?"

"Taking every advantage of this beautiful city, and all she has to offer." Marr stood tall, arms outstretched as if to embrace once more the mistress he had just left. Even in the murky light, Riordan could not mistake the grin on Marr's face.

Riordan chuckled. "Aye, and if ever 'twas a man who knew how to take advantage of a lady, city or otherwise, it'd be yourself."

"Milo, my friend, you flatter me," he laughed, but there was little humility in his laughter.

"Ha! It's the truth, plain as day. You're the most persuasive fellow it's ever been my misfortune to know. Otherwise, how would I have let you talk me inta weighin' anchor permanent like up in that God-forsaken Puget Sound?"

The ship rolled slightly in its moorings, and with a bit of help from the whiskey, Riordan half stumbled as he sat on the bulkhead. Marr gently balanced the old man at the elbow, then sat down next to him.

"Smartest thing you ever did, Milo. Admit it! Why, you've made twice the living you made before."

Riordan grumbled as another drink passed his lips. "Aye, there's truth in that. Still, it wasn't for meself you did the persuadin', now, was it? No, you needed your precious supply line, that's what done it. Some poor wretch foolish enough to promise reg'lar shipment of them timbers of yours. 'Just a few times a year', ya said. Then that scoundrel Kincaid comes along, then that shopkeeper, and before I knows it, I'm stuck with a regular run. Puget Sound to San Francisco. San Francisco to Puget Sound. Me! Milo Declan Riordan, who's sailed every sea, who's rounded the Horn five times! Who's gone whalin' from New Bedford, and…"

"And who now finds himself, in the years of his reward, with regular work, a ship of his own, a woman to come home to…" Marr reached across and took the bottle from Milo's hand… "and friends." He toasted him with his own bottle, then drank.

"Aye, lad. Friends."

Marr handed the bottle back, then stood, stretching. "Well, better turn in. I did a lot of business today, and there's more to do tomorrow. There's a big job coming up. A brewery, they say. We're going to get the timber contract if I have anything to say about it."

"No doubt, boy, no doubt," Milo said. "With that determination of yours, you'll make a fortune, that's for certain. Why, that little mudhole of a town we call home will be another San Francisco before ya knows it!"

"Perish the thought, dear Milo!"

"What? And what would be wrong with that, I'd like to know?"

"People, Milo. Too many people. We have just enough folks at home. Logging is a wild business. You tame the country, the logging won't be the same."

Riordan laughed "Well, you folks shoulda thought of that before you started invitin' folks like me and Meg up to stay!"

"That's different, Milo. We needed you."

"And the women, I guess. You need them, too, eh?"

"Women?"

"Man, don't flaunt your ignorance! The handbill! You've had another inquiry today."

Marr leaned down to wag his finger in the old man's face. "Riordan, you know I dinnuh have a thing to do with that ridiculous scheme!" When Marr was excited, traces of the Scotsman's burr that he was raised with slipped into his speech. This was a topic that excited him, these fool dreams of Kincaid's to civilize the Great Northwest. Riordan only laughed as Marr continued his tirade, gesturing broadly. "Most ridiculous scheme I've ever heard of!" Marr's words rang across the waters, and echoed among the moored ships.

"Shhh.. man!" laughed Riordan. "You'll be raisin' the dead with that boomin' voice of yours."

"Single women have no business up there, Milo. No business at all. You know it as well as I do!"

"'T'aint for me ta say, man. T'is nothin' ta me. I only does as I'm hired ta do. Bring that timber of yours and Kincaid's down here, and fill out the requisitions yas send wid me. And for Kincaid, that means women."

Marr grumbled to himself as he took the whiskey bottle from Riordan's grasp, and helped himself to another swig.

Riordan studied Marr. "What I don't understand is why it sticks in your craw."

"Well, because! Because, dear Milo, it's not a fit place for young women alone. It's raw, and it's wild. It's dangerous and isolated. It's, it's lonely, it's muddy, it's rainy, it's…."

"It's just the way you like it. And you don't want no females tidyin' it up for ya!" He stopped Marr in mid-sentence with the truth. Marr looked stunned for a moment, and then burst into laughter. He leaned forward again, and flashed a smile at his friend, embracing his shoulder in confidence.

"Exactly!" When the laugh they shared drifted away, Marr began to chuckle to himself. "You know, my friend, the only good part of this plan of Kincaid's is watching him squirm," he said, savoring the word. "Each time one of these young innocents arrives, he has to find something for them to do."

"Ya mean there ain't no real work for 'em?"

Robert Marr shook his head. "Oh, a couple found husbands right off, and one's stayed on trying to make a go of it teaching school. And those that married all left. So nothing has come of Kincaid's grandiose notion of building a town. All those passages paid for, and what does he have to show for it? A hole in his pocket."

Riordan stood and stretched his old wrinkled frame. "Well, like it or not, the females is comin'. And if this one today is any measure, it's a changin' breed, they are."

"How's that?"

"Not a domestic, like most the others. She's a woman of means."

Robert Marr stood back and considered this bit of news. "Wonder why a woman like that would want to move to the end of civilization? Say, you don't suppose she's a.."

"Oh no, lad! No, she wasn't the type. Smart, I'll give her that, but no, I don't figure her for no fancy lady."

Marr seemed to consider this faceless, contradictory female Riordan had described. "Since I won't be coming back with you, watch her, Milo. Talk to her. See what you can find out about her."

Riordan nodded. "Well, her plans was indefinite, so I don't know that she *will* be back. She seemed skittish about somethin'. I hope she's got what it takes. A woman like that can have a powerful effect on a place, with her high expectations and such."

"Ah, dear God..." Marr's voice trailed off, and he shook his head.

"Aye, lad. Next thing ya know, there'll be lace knickers hanging from the trees."

24

Lina sat at the writing desk in her room. She wrote notes for herself on small pieces of paper. The slips of paper held lists and numbers. The lists took account of what she needed to do, and when. The figures took account of her assets. The list was much longer than the chart of accounts. She had much more to do than money with which to do it, a fact made worse by the money she had deposited in the bank on Josephine's behalf. That had taken half the money she had managed to save. But two items on the list were finished now. Through Tunnicliff, she could keep an eye on Josephine. Through the Bantry Bay, she had a place to go, somewhere that she hoped, more than knew, would give her a livelihood. With a sigh, she tucked her notes inside Josie's Bible, where she kept them hidden.

Opportunity was next on her list. She would need to be on the lookout for an opportunity to leave San Francisco, without Haarten's knowledge. *And to do that, I'll have to start spending time with him again.* Her stomach clenched at the thought. Each night after supper, Lina would hurry to her room to avoid conversation with Edward. He had a habit of retiring to the library to read or work. She decided if she joined him she might keep abreast of his plans and find the opportunity she was looking for, and her presence might convince him of her compliance, easing his suspicions.

That night, when Haarten left the supper table, she waited a few minutes so as not to seem too eager, then casually followed him to the library. Haarten sat at his desk, reading over some papers. Lina walked to the shelves for a book, something properly literary. She took the book to the chair opposite the fireplace and started reading. She knew she would simply have to wait for a time when he spoke to her. Anything she might ask, or say, that seemed to be eliciting information from him would only arouse his suspicions. Lina settled in for a siege. Not five minutes later, Haarten folded the papers, and with hardly a glance in her direction, rose from his chair and headed toward the door. "Good night, Carolina," he said just before he left the library.

The routine was the same for the next three nights. He said nothing but "Good night." The following night Edward didn't come back to the house until very late, after Lina had gone to bed. The night after that Edward brought a business associate for dinner, and Lina wasn't invited to join them. She started to fret. She felt time slipping away, but she knew she must be patient.

She was rewarded for her persistence the next evening. Again, Haarten left the dinner table for the library. When Lina entered, Edward was standing at the mantel, brandy in hand, waiting for her. She said nothing, nonchalantly browsed for something to read, and then settled herself in the chair. She read for a few minutes, knowing without seeing that he was watching her. Then he sat down next to her.

"I take it that this interest in joining me after supper signals you're over your tantrum, and have come to make amends?" he asked.

Slowly, she set the book to one side. "Partly," she said. "I'm still angry, it's true. But it exhausts me. If you've trapped me, so be it. I'll make the best of it. I don't really see I have any choice, so I suppose it's wisest to learn to get along, Edward."

It was the first time she had called him by his given name, and she could tell he noticed. She liked it immediately, for it made her feel stronger, more equal to him, and with an added benefit that she no longer would have to call him 'Captain', which had always seemed wrong—Barclay was 'Captain', not Edward—or 'Sir,' which she loathed.

"Quite right, my dear." Haarten moved to the desk. As he opened his papers, he said "This is precisely why this is the best course of action. For both of us. Neither of us is well suited to romance. We neither one are capable of that much dependence on another human being, nor are we willing to let momentary distractions of the heart deter us from what we really want." He picked up his pen, but before returning to his work, he looked up at her again, and smiled, almost fondly, saying, "You see, Carolina, we really *are* quite a bit alike."

With his head now bowed over his work, Haarten did not see the look of horror on Lina's face. That he would compare them appalled her, but though she wanted to argue their differences, she found she couldn't. From his perspective, she realized, they were alike. He didn't know her at all, and she was just beginning to know herself.

After some time, Haarten rose from the desk and came to her, a paper in his hand. "I have some matters that need your attention." She glanced at it, but there was nothing unusual about the list. Then he handed her an ornately lettered card, an invitation. "That banker Whittaker and his wife are giving a ball Friday next in honor of the Mayor. Many important people will be there, as will we. Please make certain you have proper attire. If you need something, from now on go to Madame Bonaface, not that Birnbaum woman. Madame Bonaface is the seamstress of choice, I've been told." He walked toward the door. "I'll say goodnight. I have an early day tomorrow, and in fact, a busy week. I'm sailing for Mexico on business, aboard the Rosalea. I leave at first tide the morning after that ball."

✲✲✲✲✲✲✲

Lina hardly slept at all that night. Here was the opportunity she thought she would have to wait for, but far too early! That this chance would so perfectly coincide with the departure of the Bantry Bay seemed almost fated. Then again, to leave that soon gave her only a week to prepare, and she still had no idea of what she would do once she reached Puget Sound. Waiting for another opportunity might be disastrous. Any number of things could happen between now and then that might keep her from ever leaving.

Lina wanted to get up, light the lantern, and pull out Josie's Bible so she could look at her list. But light seen from under her door might draw the attention of Edward or Mrs. Spear, who was living there now as chaperone. Her mind was racing, and she needed to think clearly. She could see the list in her mind's eye. Where and how had been answered, and tonight, when. Josie was accounted for. That left only two details—the scheme of getting to the Bantry Bay unnoticed when the time came, and the matter of cash.

She had already decided she needed cash, or something to barter with, as a matter of contingency. If she found the situation in Puget Sound not as Riordan portrayed it, or for any reason she needed to leave there, she would not be back to San Francisco. Riordan's offer of return passage would be of no help. She couldn't afford to find herself stranded there, friendless and broke. Most of her money, three hundred dollars, had gone to Josie's trust. She planned on sneaking some from the household account. Under the circumstances, she felt no compunction about stealing from Edward, but she wouldn't be able to take more than perhaps twenty dollars or so. If she had something to barter or trade, that might be as good as money. She thought back to all her past money-making schemes, and wondered which might work in a world and a place she could yet only imagine. Her thoughts drifted as sleep finally took her, when her thoughts and dreams became one. In her dream she was walking along a street searching for something. Josephine was somewhere near, and in her dream Lina knew Josephine had whatever it was Lina was looking for.

Lina opened her eyes to a late morning, seized by an idea her dream had given her. She hurried to dress, and opened her door. She stopped, listening for the sound of anyone upstairs. Then she quietly made her way down the hall toward Captain Barclay's room.

Barclay he had been dead for months, but the room looked as if he had only just left this morning. It was a dark, masculine room, crammed full of books and mementos gathered over a long life. In the corner were two well-worn trunks. Lina didn't recognize them, but she knew no other place to look. She reached for the clasp of the larger and gave it a twist, but it was locked. "Damn," she whispered.

"Is there something I can help you with, Miss?"

Lina turned quickly to see Mrs. Spear in the doorway. Her heart raced, but she stayed calm. "Yes. Would you know if these trunks belonged to Miss Paul?"

Mrs. Spear walked over to stand between the trunks and Lina. "No, miss. These are the Captain's. Captain Barclay, that is." She laid a gentle hand on the trunk Lina had tried to open, then looked to her and asked, "Does Captain Haarten know you're in here?"

"Then perhaps you can tell me where Miss Paul's trunks are?" Lina had not answered the housekeeper's question, and judging by the silence, Mrs. Spear might not answer hers. The two women had come to some understanding over the holidays, but that didn't change the loyalty Mrs. Spear had to this household. Interminable seconds passed before Mrs. Spear spoke. "Is there some reason in particular you think Miss Paul's trunks would be here?"

Lina chose her words with purpose. "Edward told me the Captain asked that Miss Paul be moved here while he was away." There it was! Mrs. Spear had blinked, and the faintest trace of puzzlement came to her face. "So of course I assumed her things were in this room," Lina finished.

Mrs. Spear was choosing her words carefully, too, for Lina saw her move her lips to speak, then stop, more than once. Then, she said, "Oh! The cellar! I'd forgotten. About that time, some trunks were delivered, on instruction from Captain Haarten. He said they were to be stored in the cellar. I gave them no further thought. Could those be them, miss?"

"Let's go see."

Lina followed Mrs. Spear down the stairs, through the kitchen, and out the back entrance to the cellar door. It was a small, spidery space, but the trunks were sitting right inside the door. Lina recognized them immediately. "There they are," Lina said, and mostly to herself added, "I wonder why he didn't have them taken upstairs for her?"

"What's that, miss?

"Nothing. Have someone bring them upstairs to my room, would you, please?"

Lina ran ahead to make space in her room for the delivery. Mrs. Spear came with the boys who carried the trunks, scolding them all the way. "Watch the banister there. Don't drag it! You'll mark the floor. Careful with that corner!"

"Thank you," Lina said to the boys as they left the two women standing over the worn, dusty trunks in the middle of her room.

"If there's nothing else, miss. I'll leave you to them."

"Nothing. Thank you." Then, just before Mrs. Spear left, Lina asked, "Did you speak with Josephine when she was here?"

"No. I never even saw her. I presumed she went straight to the clinic."

Lina closed the door behind Mrs. Spear. The sight of the two trunks she and Josie had hauled a thousand miles was comforting, but she had no time to languish in sentiment. With a sharp twist of her wrist, she unlatched the first trunk and flung open the lid.

She knew in an instant that Josephine hadn't packed this trunk. The contents were obviously thrown in with no regard, something Josie would never do. *Whoever packed this*, she thought, *was in a terrible hurry.* She was in a hurry herself, so she began to plow through the layers of dresses crammed inside. These dresses were all new, dresses Lina had often seen Josephine wear at the Golden West. They were beautiful, but were they marketable? Lina laid them across her bed, straightening each one as she went. The bottom of the trunk was filled with small boxes of combs, ribbons, hat pins, and beads. *Those are worth something*, Lina thought as she greedily piled the boxes on the floor, to be culled through later.

The second trunk wasn't like the first. Josephine had packed this one, but not recently. All the dresses and keepsakes that Josie had saved from the long trip west were here. The blue silk dress she was wearing the first time they met, the green dress Josie fought so hard to keep from the Indians. Hat boxes, glove boxes, and a woolen cape. Lina picked up the two dresses and the cape. Within the folds of fabric she heard a muffled jingle.

Lina laid the clothes on the bed, then pressed her hands against them until she found the source of the jangling. A pocket inside the green dress had been stitched closed. She snatched a small pair of scissors from her sewing basket and clipped the threads. A dozen gold coins spilled out. She scooped them up and counted them. Nearly three hundred dollars! *Good girl, Josie*, Lina thought. *Good girl.*

With all these clothes strewn about, it seemed a good time to consider what she would take for herself. A few of Josephine's dresses, her combs and beads, and the rest might be bartered or sold. There would be little of her own clothing that she would take. Haarten had paid for everything she owned now. They were his possessions, not hers. But she would take the black skirts and white starched chemises she wore at the warehouse, and her boots and her coat. She took the contents of her keepsake box and threw them into her sewing box, along with Josie's Bible, and her coins neatly tucked in the lining. She would only need a fair-sized portmanteau to hold everything, and she could pack that quickly and carry it by herself. But there was nothing to pack yet. It wouldn't do to have a bag packed and waiting.

She hid those clothes of Josie's she would be taking in the back of her wardrobe. Everything else was folded neatly back in the trunks. Later, Lina would have them returned to the cellar, with the explanation that she had simply wanted to make certain Josephine's belongings were secure.

Now the only question that remained was the escape itself. Tomorrow, Lina planned to send word to Riordan to expect her early that morning. She could only hope that Edward would be true to his word and leave the house early. She wouldn't be able to pack her things until that night, after they returned from the ball. Everything else would have to be left to chance. There were only so many details she could control.

****

The Whittaker's ball was the most opulent social event of the year, and more popularly attended than even Haarten's New Year's Eve ball. Cornelius Whittaker did not owe his popularity to his stunning personality. His demeanor fit his gaunt physique. He was laconic and humorless, and by comparison made Edward Haarten seem gregarious. Cornelius Whittaker was popular by virtue of his profession as the city's wealthiest banker. Several banking fortunes had come and gone in the city's brief life, but if ever there was a man born to hold onto a dollar, it was Whittaker. Any other popularity he enjoyed was granted him through his wife. Eugenia Whittaker was a garrulous woman who was the only one who could squeeze a nickel out of her husband, and when she did, she loved to entertain in their new home, even larger and more costly than Barclay's.

The evening went as was typical of such events. Music and dancing, though not very lively from Lina's point of view. Fancy food and punch for the ladies, liquor and cigars for the men. Women gossiping amongst themselves and men retiring to discuss business or politics. Lina felt out of place in any group, although she did her best, if only to make the evening go more quickly. Tonight, though, while the ladies were polite when she would join their circle, they seemed to change the subject when she appeared. They turned the discussion to the lovely weather, her charming dress, that delightful new shop, or other meaningless chatter. Lina supposed she and Edward had become the subject of speculation—the Captain and his 'ward.'

Also, everyone seemed abuzz about an announcement to be made that night. Lina heard about it from Mrs. Whittaker herself, or rather, overhead Mrs. Whittaker speaking about it to others, and it all had something to do with whatever was under that conspicuous drape on a long table at the far end of the room.

"Cornelius hasn't told me a thing about it, I swear! Whatever is under that cloth, it's a mystery to me. But I can tell you that it has something to do with Captain Haarten. Oh, here's Miss Clark! Perhaps she knows!"

"Knows what?" Lina asked as she joined the circle.

"Why, what's under there!" said a lady pointing to the drape. "Eugenia says it has something to do with Captain Haarten."

Lina shrugged. "I'm sorry, but I have no idea, either. Captain Haarten hasn't mentioned anything to me. Perhaps Mr. Whittaker is intending it as a surprise for Mrs. Whittaker. Whatever it is, I'm sure we'll find out in due time." Lina tried to sound indifferent, and she made her excuse with the ladies to avoid the subject further. But she found it disquieting that there was a surprised planned, and that it should have something to do with Edward.

As if reading her thoughts, Edward had come upon her unnoticed. "Come with me." Without another word he led her toward the musician's stage. When they reached it, he left her and stepped onto the platform. Cornelius Whittaker joined him, while Mrs. Whittaker came to stand at Lina's side. With a nod from Whittaker, the musicians played a commanding flourish that quieted the room. With the posture of an undertaker, Whittaker stepped forward and spoke.

"I realize there has been considerable speculation this evening about the object to be unveiled. Let us remove that distraction now." He gave another nod, and at the other end of the room two servants removed the drape, revealing a wooden model of a sailing ship, gleaming beneath the candlelight.

"Barclay & Company has secured considerable financing through my institution, Whittaker Blye Banking, for the construction of a new ship, the model of which you see before you. Edward Haarten, principal of Barclay & Company. is with us tonight. I think you all know the remarkable reputation of his firm in general, and the unerring business acumen of the gentleman in particular. Whittaker Blye, and Barclay & Company have chosen this evening to announce the offering of limited partnerships in the venture. I ask that you give your attention to Captain Haarten, so that he can describe the enterprise more fully."

Edward stepped down and crossed the room toward the model. "Gentlemen, we agree that an insufficiency of large vessels in the area is our greatest hindrance to growth. The advent of the steamship may someday signal the decline of the sailing ship, but for now, they are costly to operate, and mostly suitable for coast running. To fully take advantage of our strategic location here at the western edge of the country, we need be dependent on the eastern shipyards no longer. Barclay & Company will build this ship here in California, the first of many such ships to be native born. And with these ships, the largest and finest in their class, we will finally be able to reach the profitable markets of the South Pacific, with a regularity and predictability that no other line, steam *or* sail, can guarantee."

With that there was a healthy but polite round of applause. Lina moved forward with the crowd, hoping to get a better view of the model. It was most impressive, and as she came closer, she noticed the intricate detail with which it was built. People called out questions. "How much'll she hold?" "How fast'll she go?" "Will you captain her yourself, Haarten?" Edward answered them all quickly, and without elaboration. Then someone asked, "What is she called?"

"Carolina." Lina turned quickly to look at Edward, who was already staring at her. "She will be christened Carolina, in honor of my fiancée, Miss Clark." Again, a smattering of polite applause, and a small sisterhood of girls Lina barely knew came forward to say how happy they were for her, and to tell her she should feel honored to be so immortalized. Lina was overwhelmed, which fortunately kept her from having to say anything. She was almost relieved when Edward stepped down to rescue her from the throng. "Now, gentlemen, let us not disrupt this party any further with talk of business." At Whittaker's instruction, the band started playing, and Edward stepped forward to lead Lina to the dance floor. They danced silently, he staring at her, she staring down. To the crowd she looked demure, flushed with emotion.

"I hoped you would be pleased," he finally said.

Softly she answered. "I'm indifferent to the ship, Edward, but if you consider it a compliment, I thank you. It was your announcement about…what you called me. I, we hadn't discussed this yet, not really."

"You conceded the point that evening in the library. This seemed the perfect opportunity. The name, that's a nice touch, don't you think? That should persuade the sentimentalists to invest, I should think."

He's right, she thought. It didn't matter. In fact, it made her escape sweeter, knowing he would be publicly humiliated when he returned from Mexico to find her gone. *What sort of an announcement would he make then?* She smiled at the thought.

"There, that's better. You've a lovely smile, Carolina. And I want everyone here to see you smile."

****

After the dance, they returned to Rincon Hill and retired to their separate rooms. Quietly, she packed the portmanteau, then placed it by the bed. She wanted to be ready to leave the moment Edward was gone, which she hoped would be early enough that the household staff would not yet be about. If that didn't work, then she'd make some excuse. As long as Edward was out before dawn, she would have time to get to the Bantry Bay. So she dressed in her traveling dress, then sat on the bed, fully expecting to sit up all night until she heard his coach pull away.

Suddenly, Lina sat straight up. She had fallen asleep. She fumbled in the dark to the window, and pulled back the drapes. Almost imperceptibly, the night sky was turning grey. It would be dawn within the hour.

Frantically, she stumbled about in the room, aided only by the murky light outside. She found her portmanteau, her coat, and her small handbag. Ready to go now, she opened the bedroom door and came face to face with Mrs. Spear. Lina stood frozen. Before she could speak, Mrs. Spear shoved her back inside and pulled the door closed.

From the darkness of her room, Lina heard Mrs. Spear move down the hallway toward the stairs. Then she spoke. The voice was muffled, so Lina leaned down to listen at the keyhole.

"I'm sorry, sir. Miss Clark has asked me to get her some headache powders. She's not feeling well." Then the unmistakable tone of Edward's low voice, although Lina couldn't make out his words. "Yes, sir. I'll certainly tell her. She'll be as disappointed as you are, no doubt." Mrs. Spear's voice was moving down the stairs, away from Lina's hearing, but she knew the two were still in the hallway. She went to the window and waited. Finally she saw Edward climb in the carriage and watched as it drove away.

Almost immediately, there was a rap at her door. Her heart was still pounding, and she couldn't make herself move until she heard the woman whisper, "Miss Clark, please, let me in." When Lina opened the door, Mrs. Spear swept in, pushing Lina away and closing the door behind them. The two women stood in the dark for a moment before either one spoke.

"It's safe now. He's gone," Mrs. Spear whispered.

Instinctively, Lina kept her voice low too. "What was he doing here? I thought he left hours ago. I must have fallen asleep."

"Yes. The Captain asked that I wake you so he could say his goodbyes. When I came in, I found you asleep." She looked at the portmanteau. "And packed."

"But…" Lina couldn't think of what to say. Everything was all too confusing. Half of her brain was still asleep, the other half scared out of its wits. She felt Mrs. Spear's warm touch on her arm.

"I'm sorry, dear," she said, then with a touch of regret in her voice, she added, "He had me keep an eye out, you know. He thought you might try to leave."

"But you didn't tell him," Lina said incredulously.

"No. But I've told him other things, dear, and I'm sorry for that."

"Then why…"

"It was those trunks of Miss Paul's. When we brought those trunks up here, you asked me something. Do you remember? You asked if I had seen Miss Paul when she was here. Miss Clark, Miss Paul was never here. Captain Haarten had those trunks brought here after Captain Barclay was murdered. He told me Miss Paul had suffered a total collapse upon hearing of the Captain's death, and that he had sent her to the clinic."

New confusion added to old as Lina tried to make sense of this news. The housekeeper kept talking. "I know this is a small thing, this variation in the story. But he's lied, that's for certain. If not to you, to me. And then…"

"Go on, Mrs. Spear."

"Well, I've been keeping an eye on you, like I said. Something just hasn't been right. You seemed worried all the time, preoccupied. I knew Captain Haarten had asked you to marry him. Well, not *knew* it, but, you know…household gossip. But I also could see you weren't happy. I could only imagine he was forcing you into marriage. When I saw the bag you packed, I knew I was right. I don't know what he's up to, and it's probably best I don't. But I won't help him in this. I'm going to help you. What do you need?"

Lina sighed with relief. "Just a carriage."

Mrs. Spear nodded. "I'll arrange for it to pick you up the next street over. Can you carry that bag to there? Good. I'll make certain the staff is busy somewhere else in the house, and then we'll get you downstairs and out the door." Mrs. Spear reached for the door, but then paused.

"I won't ask where you're going. Truthfully, I'd rather not know. But I have to ask. Are you certain this is your only option? There isn't some other way? You know, dear, sometimes the devil you know is better than the devil you don't."

Lina stopped her. "Nothing could be worse than the devil I know, Mrs. Spear. But thank you just the same."

Just after the two women said a hasty goodbye in the doorway, Lina slipped one of Josie's gold pieces into Mrs. Spear's hand. "If he finds out you helped me, you'll need this," she said, then walked off to find her carriage.

Lina arrived at Pier 3 amid the fog of dawn. Riordan was standing on the deck of the Bantry Bay shouting orders and checking his log book as the last of the cargo was loaded, when he spotted Lina.

"Aye, there ya are, miss! I was beginnin' ta think we'd have ta leave without ya. McNab," he hollered, "McNab!"

The first mate came quickly. "Aye, Captain."

"Help this lady on board. Take her and her things below." McNab was leading Lina below deck when she heard the Captain call after her, "I'll be down ta gets ya signed on the log proper like, once we's outta the bay, miss."

The final lines were cast off, and the Bantry Bay began to move into the main channel. The men worked quickly and precisely to bring the sails into line. In front of her, some fifty yards or so, already at full sail and headed straight for the Golden Gate, was a beautiful frigate, clean and polished. The ship looked regal, and seemed to command the other ships to keep their distance. "Aye, now there's a ship. Trim and yar from stern to stem," Riordan mused with a wisp of jealousy as he took the wheel of his own well-worn scow. Then his loyalty and his superstitions got the better of him. He looked at the deck and spoke directly to the ship as though she could hear him. "Now no need bein' jealous, darlin'. I wouldn't trade the Bantry Bay for the Rosalea for all the whiskey in San Francisco."

Part III
The Sound

25

Lina wondered how long she should stay below deck. From her small cabin, the ship seemed to lurch its way to sail, not the graceful gliding motion she expected. The creak of the ship gave her the sense the vessel was on the verge of disintegration. Even the shouts from captain to crew, and the thunder of boots on the deck above made her hesitant to come out from hiding. For hiding was what she was doing, even though she knew it was illogical. Unless she came on deck at precisely the right moment, and Haarten's ship was sailing so close that he could actually see her on board the Bantry Bay, there was no need to stay in her cabin. She had fretted too much about this moment, however, to take even that chance. She couldn't yet believe she was free of him.

When finally she did step out and look around, she saw no other cabins besides this one and Riordan's, so she assumed her presence had displaced the first mate. She wondered what must the men's quarters be like, if this meager cabin was the prize of rank. The room held only one bunk and a cubbyhole for storage. With the door closed, what little room was left would barely be enough to dress. But as a place to sit during the day, away from the business of the ship, it would work fine, with just enough light from the open door to read. She looked about the rest of the lower deck, but from galley to hold she found herself always in someone's way, so she headed topside.

The Bantry Bay was already past the Golden Gate, and there wasn't another ship in sight. Winds were high and crisp, typical of a February morning. She was glad for her cloak as she finally settled in a spot away from the crew. She watched the sailors as they coaxed and fought the

Bantry Bay to full sail. The salt breeze scents, the crack of the sails, every sensation was thrilling. Even sitting, she could feel the strength of the ship as it fought the ocean.

"Ah, miss! You'll catch your death out here!" Riordan had spotted her from mid deck and hurried toward her. "Please, miss, come into the wheelhouse, if ya must be topside."

"I'll b-b-be careful," Lina chattered.

"Ah, see? Already frozen, ya are. Inside with ya, now. No arguments." Riordan took her by the elbow and led her to the wheelhouse. Inside, they each shook themselves of the sea spray and the cold. The captain took the wheel, and Lina sat down on a small stool in the corner.

"There, now. That's better. Though I can't say's I blame ya. It's a fine spot for gettin' a feel for the ship."

"Oh, yes! It's wonderful! I've never been on a ship under sail. Already I see the appeal."

"Well, if yas has never been ta sea before, then ya don't know about the custom."

"Custom?"

With a wink he doffed his cap and made a quick bow. "It's customary the passengers dine with the Captain, ya see. It'll be a grand feast. At least the best to be held on board tonight." Beneath his scruff of a gray beard, he grinned. "But there's only one problem, miss. I don't know who I'll be dining with."

"I beg your pardon?"

"I'm ashamed to admit it, I am, but if ya told me your name when we met, it's lost to me now. And if it was on that paper ya gave that dimwitted boy who told me ya'd booked passage, he lost it. I need it for me log, I do."

"Morgan. Carolina Morgan," she said slowly. Some instinct had struck her as Riordan asked the question, and without hesitation, she gave her maiden name. Morgan was not a name Edward Haarten knew. He would not look for a passenger listed as C. Morgan. She knew little of this Riordan, or who he knew in San Francisco. Until she knew she could trust him or anyone where she was headed, she couldn't afford the risk. But she also realized she had set a course for herself from which there was no going back. *I can't very well tell the truth later, can I? How would that seem?* Still, she had no regrets. Being Carolina Clark had not served her terribly well. Perhaps, she thought, this is a new beginning for a new person.

Lina joined Riordan in his cabin for dinner. It was a modest meal, but the beef was newly butchered, and the bread and greens fresh. "This trip's a short run, but long enough so's we'll not be eatin' like this every evenin'," he told her.

"I certainly hope there was no fuss made on my account, Captain," Lina said.

"A bit, I suspect. The men ain't used to refined company such as yourself." Lina chuckled softly. She couldn't recall anyone ever referring to her as "refined." *Perhaps I'm a different person already*, she mused.

From there on, every turn of their conversation posed an unexpected hazard to Lina. She had changed her name, but hadn't given any thought to what other lies—or truths—she needed to tell. Riordan's questions were designed to draw her out, and when she understood that, she took hold of the discussion.

"She's a lovely ship, Captain. How long have you had her?" The time she'd spent with Barclay taught her that sailors loved to talk about life at sea. She didn't have to worry any more about Riordan's curiosity.

Riordan told his story. He'd left his native Ireland as a boy, to follow the adventure of a sailor's life. In due time, he found himself among the whalers of Massachusetts. A chance to head for the Caribbean brought him on board the Bantry Bay as a hand, later as first mate, and when her captain died suddenly at sea, he simply took over command. "The old dog treated me fair, but he was an ill-tempered sort, without friend or family that any'd heard of. I intended to keep her workin' until someone showed up to claim her, but none did."

"Why did you leave Boston?" Lina asked.

He shifted in his chair uneasily. "Well, ta be perfectly honest, miss, I ran into a bit of financial difficulty, ya might say. I was afraid them what I owed the money to might be coming after me ship. Without clear deed to her, I feared I'd lose her. I couldn't bear the thought of it. So I headed south, around the Horn bringin' them gold rushers. I'd every intention of returnin' after I'd made enough to pay them debts, but, then, other opportunities came up. I started making these here runs between the sound and the Golden Gate. This place we're headed, it's a nice little spot. Good people. We liked it there, so we stayed."

Then he added, "I hopes ya don't think ill of me, miss. I'm not usually a man to run out on me obligations."

"No, Captain. Trust me, I'd be the last to pass judgment on you." Riordan looked at her oddly, and she realized she'd just opened a door for his questions. She quickly closed it again. "You said 'we' Captain? Are you married?"

"Meg's me girl," Riordan said nodding, then he chuckled. "Truth told, she's a might long in the tooth ta be called a girl. She's an old wharf rat like meself. Meg and me been together a long time. Brought her with me when I left Boston, when we decided to drop anchor here permanent like. She runs a sorta tavern, ya might say. Meg offers whiskey and beer, and keeps a griddle goin', with rooms upstairs for boarders. She'll be pleased to put ya up there, no doubt."

"Is that where the other women stay, at that tavern?"

Riordan didn't seem to hear her question. "Sweet Meg's, she calls the place. Kincaid, the gent what has me pass out those handbills, he set her up. He's a real wheeler-dealer, is Martin Kincaid. He's got the millin' operation there, ya see, and it's his idea to turn this place into a genuine town. That's why he's tryin' t'attract females such as yourself. Seems ta think the place'll be more settled-like with women. Wives, babies, well, they have a way of makin' a place civilized."

"Indeed they do," Lina said, half smiling. That was enough to encourage Riordan, and he went on.

"Why, been lots of folks Kincaid's got started up there. Virgil Minifee, for one. He has the general store."

"General store?" *Damn!* Lina thought. She hoped that might be the kind of help this Martin Kincaid was looking for.

"A fine operation it is, too. Then there's Miss Forbes. Kincaid's got her teaching school, though there ain't but a handful of children. And ol' Caspar Mathias, who runs the smokehouse. Kincaid's helped them all. So ya see, Miss Morgan, there's plenty of opportunities for a woman such as yourself."

"But you never answered my question, Captain. What of the other women who've answered Mr. Kincaid's notice?"

"Ah, the others. Yes, the others." Riordan stood up suddenly, then walked to a cupboard, opened it and pulled out a bottle of whiskey and two glasses. "Do ya ever take a taste, miss? 'Cause this might be the time."

Lina looked at him warily, then nodded. He poured the drinks, then picked up his glass and threw the whiskey down his throat. Lina only held hers.

"Those other girls, well, there's only two, besides Miss Forbes, I mean. I hear tell them two got married right off and left."

"But, you told me Mr. Kincaid had work!"

"Now, in fairness, miss, I only told yas that Martin Kincaid was behind that there handbill. The truth is, I didn't rightly know what sort of work there was, I only knew precious few ladies had taken him up on it. It was only after we spoke that I learned there ain't been but the one that's actually stuck it out. And I ain't to be blamed for that, now am I? I'd a told you, I would've, if I'd the chance. But I didn't see yas until this morning when we set sail, and weren't no time then."

"But when did you learn this, Captain?"

"It was Marr what told me. Remember, I mentioned him to yas that day? He's the fella what came with me to San Francisco. When I mentioned to him you'd made inquiries, that's when he told me.

"And why isn't this Mr. Marr here now?" she asked sharply.

"He's stayed over in San Francisco. Trying to land a big contract he is. Now there's an industrious fellow!"

Lina looked into the whiskey glass. She wanted to be angry with someone. With the whole trip ahead of her, she couldn't afford to be angry with Riordan, and regardless, he was clearly ignorant of the situation. Martin Kincaid was still a thousand miles away, and this fellow Marr was conveniently absent. Anger wouldn't serve her. Perhaps the whiskey would. She threw it back, and though it caught on the knot already in her throat, she managed to take it all at once.

Riordan saw something in that swig that made him nervous, so he began to blather on. "And remember, miss. Them other girls, they got married and left, as I told yas. Don't mean there weren't no work for 'em. No tellin' what fine opportunities they passed on for sake of romance. And who knows? Maybe that'll be your fortune too. Find a handsome young buck and put all this worry for work behind you."

"No!" Lina said, and Riordan knew he'd crossed a line. She glared at him until he began to squirm. Then she thumped the empty glass on the table. He raised the bottle but she shook her head. "No, thank you, Captain. I'll say goodnight."

****

Two weeks had not seemed long when Lina first inquired about passage. Two weeks in San Francisco could fly by in the wink of an eye. But as the only passenger on a small schooner, confined mostly to her cramped quarters, there was little to vary her days. The bitter soaking winds of February made being topside unbearable. The single day the sky was clear she tried to spend as much time on deck as she could, but it was a struggle to stay out of the way. But each evening she shared dinner with Riordan, at his insistence, and sometimes afterward, she would accompany him to the wheelhouse.

Lina spent the time with Riordan productively. He was her only glimpse into what lay ahead. Further, given his revelation that Martin Kincaid's offer of employment might be every bit the sham she had feared, she needed to be considering alternatives before she arrived. Every night she questioned Riordan mercilessly. The old man was so consistently kind to her, so open with his thoughts and feelings, so garrulous and so gracious a host, at first she felt guilty about her own lies and evasions. Then she reminded herself that there was every indication her own deceptions were no less than what was on that handbill. Until she knew the truth, she decided she was justified in her duplicity.

What she learned in that first week told her most of what she needed to know. And while in most respects the news was bleak, she preferred it to a surprise. The settlement was tiny—perhaps two dozen people, based on the ones Riordan mentioned by name. In terms of businesses, there were only five the old man could think of, not counting the school. There was Sweet Meg's tavern, but there were few boarders and not enough regular business that Lina could imagine Meg would need her help. There was already a general store of sorts, run by a man named Minifee who, from what she could glean, was doing an adequate job of it. He ran it with his wife and daughter. That dashed her hopes of finding her old familiar work. The smokehouse was another, but a smokehouse hardly took anyone at all to run, let alone extra hands. That left only two. The first was the obvious choice. Martin Kincaid ran a very successful sawmill, and from what Riordan could gather, the man had some money when he arrived, at least enough to bankroll other businesses. If he didn't have a legitimate opportunity already in mind for her, perhaps she could persuade him to let her help with his accounts.

That left only Marr Logging. Marr was the name that came up most often in Lina's conversations with Milo Riordan. Robert Marr had been there the longest. Robert Marr brought his entire family with him. Brothers, cousins—Lina lost track. The loggers who worked for them came to town infrequently, so Riordan didn't know much about them. The timber they logged was far off in the deep forests, and they would often be away for days, even weeks. Nothing could be further from any experience of Lina's. She all but dismissed Marr Logging as having potential for employment, except for one fact—she knew something about the lumber trade. At least she knew enough from her experiences in the warehouse that timber was in high demand in San Francisco, and timber from this area was among the best to be found. Robert Marr had been in San Francisco bidding on a large contract. All this offered enough potential that she could not discount Marr Logging completely. But in the end, it was still Martin Kincaid who offered her best hope in Sleekit.

"Sleekit," Lina repeated the first time Riordan had called the settlement by name. "It's a strange name. Why is it called that?"

Riordan laughed, saying, "You'll have to ask Marr about that." This turned out to be the answer to a good many questions Lina had. How long had the settlement been there? Why there? Who started it? What was the timber country like? What did Riordan know about logging? All these questions were answered the same. "Ask Marr." Lina would have much to discuss with Robert Marr, when she finally met him.

The last full day of the passage saw wind and rain all day, but the weather calmed when evening came, just as the ship entered Puget Sound. Riordan announced it was too treacherous to take the ship in that night, so they weighed anchor. "The place is filled with all manner of small islands, and then there's the loose timbers bobbin' along the shore. No, miss, another night on board, and we'll all be the safer for it."

By the last night, Lina had come to think of the old man as a friend. She was nervous about what the morrow held, but eager, too. Lina and Riordan spent their last night in the routine of sharing dinner, but this time with one glass of whiskey afterward in celebration of the completed trip. When Lina declined another, he filled his glass again.

He considered her a moment. "Have ya figured out what you'll be tellin' them?"

"Telling who? Telling what?

"Them folks in Sleekit, about yourself."

"I don't know what you mean."

"Sure ya does, girl. You've been clever enough to avoid talkin' about yourself so far. This, I'll grant ye, for a woman, is a remarkable thing!" He laughed. "But then, I'm not naturally curious. Other folks won't be so accommodatin'. Other folks is inclined to make up stories when nothin' else is forthcomin'."

Lina let his words sink in. "So you're saying that folks in Sleekit will speculate, unless I tell them the truth."

"What I'm sayin', Lina dear, is that if ya tell them nothin', they'll speculate, and that's a fact. Unless they've been told the story. Whether that story's the truth or no, why, that's up to you. But I'd have a story ready to be tellin' if I was you."

She patted his hand. "It's sound advice, Milo. I take it to heart.

Riordan filled his glass again, then corked the bottle. "Now that's settled. I've one more question, and then we'll go topside. But this one is the hardest for me ta ask."

"Yes?"

"Well, some things *has* made me curious. There was how ya sorta sudden like showed up ta board the ship. And that first day at the docks, well, ya seemed in a bit of a dither over somethin'. I been around long enough to know when a body's in a fix of some sort or another."

"A situation you're familiar with." Lina reminded him, hoping to halt Riordan in whatever direction he was headed.

"Now dearie, I'm yer friend, not your confessor. Let them without sin, as they say, and as I told ya that first night, that wouldn't hardly be me, now would it? No, it's just that, well, if it's trouble, or the law, well, you see, it's just that them people up there are like me own family, and I wouldn't for the world want to be bringin' them any trouble they're not needin' or expectin', if ya grasps me meanin'."

Lina suddenly saw how her lies and his concerns were entangled. She was just as suddenly ashamed that anything she might have done, however unintended, would give this kind man a moment's worry. She thought for a moment and then looked him in the eye.

"Then here's the truth. I came west along the overland trail almost two years ago. Eventually, I found myself in San Francisco working in a warehouse. I traveled with a friend, a woman, who suffered a personal tragedy and now requires care. Those I worked for contributed to her situation, so I chose to leave and come here hoping to make enough to provide for her."

"Ah, now, dear. I didn't mean yas had to unburden yourself just to put me mind at ease."

Lina shook her head. "I wouldn't for the world bring anyone else trouble." She laid her hand upon his arm. "You've been good to me, Milo, more than good, these last two weeks. I thank you for it, and I promise if it comes to that, I won't let anything happen to you or yours."

He patted her hand where it rested on his arm. "Well, I'm glad I got that off me chest. Here now, Let's go topside."

Inside the wheelhouse Lina felt suddenly calm and content. She sat quietly smiling in the corner, and closed her eyes. The long peaceful silence between them was suddenly broken when they heard a low boom. Riordan stepped out on deck, and Lina followed. Far in the distance, she saw a glittering cascade of fire. Another boom, and more shimmering fire.

"Fireworks!" Riordan said with the glee of a child.

Lina laughed. "Does your return always bring out such a display?"

Riordan shook his head, but kept his eye trained on the night sky. "No miss. I 'spects folks are celebratin'. It's official now. Today's the second of March, ain't it? Well, then, Oregon's a state, and Washington Territory'll have to stand on her own. It's a monumental day, miss. Heaven help all us poor souls up here, runnin' from civilization. It's nippin' at our heels, it is."

****

Lina was awake and topside with first light. She was crushed to find a heavy fog bank surrounding them. Frustrated and nervous, she made her way to the wheelhouse where she found Riordan. With one arm pointed forward, he pulled her close to sight down the length of his arm. "There. Right there. Do ya see it?"

"No. See what?" But no sooner had she spoken than she caught sight of a dim light through the fog. *A fire perhaps?* The fog grew thinner, like layers of thick smoke. Dark forested hills framed the background. With every passing second the scene became clearer. Buildings took form. It wasn't a fire but a lantern she had seen, the morning's first lantern light inside a settlement along a muddy shore in a small inlet. The signal fires of Sleekit.

"It's something to see, ain't it? All that green."

Lina would never have imagined trees so tall, so thick, running from the peaks straight down to the water. "All that timber!" she whispered.

"Aye. And open land it is too, to whoever wants to work it."

As they neared the shore, Riordan called for the anchor. "It's time to go, darlin'. Ready?" Lina nodded, and together they headed for the dinghy.

Between Lina's goods and the passengers—Riordan, four crewmembers, and Lina—the small boat was packed to the gunnels. Riordan stood, waving wildly toward the shore, which caused the dinghy to rock back and forth. Lina gripped the gunnels with all her might. She sat on the bottom of the boat, and with all the cargo and people around her, all she could see of the shore was to her left where something moving caught her eye. Creeping slowly beneath the canopy of brush that laced the bank, she thought it was a floating log. Then the log moved out from beneath the canopy into the dim light. It was a long canoe, holding eight men. The men in it were Indians. Then Lina saw another canoe, and then another. She looked over her shoulder toward the Bantry Bay, and saw canoes surrounding the ship. Some, like the first, carried Indians, but others carried white men, and some carried both. Indian and white alike, they all wore rough skins, and the white men had long, dirty beards. Every one of them had come to greet Riordan and the Bantry Bay.

Riordan threw out the line before the dinghy struck the short pier. The man who had grabbed the line had yet to tie the boat off before Riordan climbed out. He gave the boat a good rocking as he did, and for a moment, Lina thought she would fall backwards into the water.

At the last possible moment, it righted itself, but not before she let out a small yelp. Riordan turned quickly.

"Oh, Lina, darlin'! Forgive me! Here, give us a hand." Suddenly, all the men in the dinghy were pulling her up by the arms, raising her to her feet, and pulling her onto the pier. Riordan turned to a woman waiting there, sweeping her in his arms. Sweet Meg was just as Milo had described her. Her faded yellow hair was now almost white, she was nearly as round as she was tall, and she had a girlish, dimpled face and dark, happy eyes. He whispered something in her ear, and Meg giggled as she gave him a little shove. He countered with a quick slap to her backside, and then turned to pull Lina forward.

"Lina, here's the lady I told ya so much about, Miss Meg Fay. Meg, me love, this here's Miss Carolina Morgan, come in response to the handbill."

Lina held out her hand to Meg, who greeted her with a full embrace. "Glad to have you! Welcome to Sleekit! Let's get you settled in. Come on, dear," she said, hooking her arm through Riordan's. "Let's go home."

The settlement was built on this short bluff above the shore, decently out of reach of high tide. But the high ground was only slightly less muddy than the flats below. It took both Lina's hands to keep her dress above the mud. Her shoes couldn't be spared, but she was careful of her step just the same. She noticed Meg, walking ahead of her, wore heavy boots, and her dresses were hemmed to the ankle. *I'll have to get me some of those boots, and take up my skirts as well.*

Sweet Meg's was a plain frame building, stick straight and white all over. An open staircase on the side led to a balcony that rimmed the second story. They stepped through the open doors into dim light, but the smell of breakfast filled the air.

"Miss Fay, I realize you've probably finished breakfast, but perhaps there's something left…."

"No, no, no," Meg patted Lina on the arm. "No leftovers for you! I've plenty of eggs and potatoes, and coffee, of course. Milo, take her things upstairs while I fix her a plate."

The downstairs room at Sweet Meg's reminded Lina of the Golden West, but certainly it was a plain country cousin to its fancier relation. Sweet Meg's was filled with crude, square tables, no two the same.

An upright piano sat in the near corner, and a large black cook stove declared the far corner of the room to be the kitchen. The table near the stove held cluttered pots and plates, with a bucket for washing. With Meg at the stove and Riordan fondly watching her, the tavern had a homey warmth that would never have suited the Golden West, but fit this place perfectly.

Meg brought her food, then pulled up a chair and sat with them. Meg Fay was almost as different from Ada Quincannon as Sweet Meg's was from the Golden West. Meg wore a little paint, and showed just a hint of bosom, but her dress was plain and her manner far homier than Ada's. Indeed, Lina was put more in mind of Greta Olmstead than Ada Quincannon when she looked at Meg Fay. They shared a motherly look, a certain softness to the eyes.

Riordan had been right about provisions on ship flagging after that first dinner. The eggs and potatoes Meg served were delicious, and Lina ate voraciously, though she tried hard to mind her manners. When she had finished, she pushed her plate away and took a long drink of the coffee. Then Meg spoke up.

"Now, Lina. Let's get acquainted. Milo here says you're looking for work."

"Yes I am. I want to talk to this Mr. Kincaid straightaway."

Meg rolled her wide brown eyes. "Hmm. That handbill. Well, I don't know if that'll do you much good, honey. Kincaid talks a better game than he plays. He's getting ahead of himself, if you ask me, trying to turn this puddle into a full-fledged town, although he's pretty much alone in that ambition. But what an ambition! He's done everything he can think of to get this place on the map. Settin' folks up in business," Meg waved her hand to indicate the tavern, "curryin' government men like they were prize bulls, for the promise of the latest territorial boondoggle. Harbors, railroads, military roads. I suspect Martin's the only man who's ever believed a politician! But he's learned a thing or two from them. He's learned how to make a promise he can't keep."

"Now Meggie. Be fair," said Riordan. "Why, every wide spot in the road along this shore is doin' the same. Don't be cursin' the man for tryin' to make sure Sleekit gets its fair share."

"True enough," said Meg. "People around here are no fools, they know big times are ahead. We just have our differences about when and how that should happen."

The conversation stopped abruptly with a thud that sounded like a load of rock hitting wood, followed quickly by a shriek and a cry. Riordan rushed for the door. On the other side, a young woman was down on her knees over a box of pies, pies which now were little more than crumbs and loose apple filling. The young woman looked up as the doors opened, tears welling in her bright blue eyes.

"Oh, Meg! I'm so sorry! I must not have been watching where I was headed. I missed the step. Now look what I've done." The girl's tears trickled down her cheeks as she picked up fragments of the pies. "Oh, mother will have my hide!" the young girl wailed.

"She doesn't ever have to know, honey. Milo, go get the mop and clean this mess up. Jean, get off your knees and come inside. We can take care of this. Why, I'll just buy two more pies! I'll tell your mother they were extra good today, and sold fast."

The young girl's sobs were starting to recede, but a bit of a pout remained on her sweet, tear-stained face.

"Here, now," Meg continued, "Stand up and straighten yourself. Look at your dress, honey, it's a mess. Come inside and brush yourself off."

Lina held the door while Meg brought her young friend inside. "Oh, Meg," the girl sobbed. "I'm so sorry. I promise I'll pay for those pies myself. I insist." She tried to use her hands to brush the dirt from her dress, but with the apple pie filling still smeared on her fingers, she only managed to turn the dirt into a paste that stuck to both her hands and dress. "Oh, no!" she said at the sight of the sticky mess on her pale blue dress, and when her hands went to her face, she smudged her pink cheeks.

"Jean, hold still!" Meg ordered. Jean went stiff so Meg could take a damp cloth to her dress. Other faded spots on the frock, and the childlike way she obeyed Meg's commands, spoke to the fact that this was not the first mess of Jean's that Meg had cleaned up.

"Oh, and I've interrupted your company," Jean said, as soon as she noticed Lina watching them.

"That's not company, Jean. That's Carolina Morgan. She's come from San Francisco, 'cause of that handbill of Kincaid's. Carolina, this is Jean Minifee. Her folks run the store."

"Please, call me Lina," she said. She held out her hand and the young girl took it with a quick curtsey. Their hands stuck together in the apple pie paste, and they laughed.

"That's all I can do for now, honey." Meg said. "Do try to be more careful, won't you?"

"Yes, ma'am," she said softly.

"Now, do me a favor, sweetheart. Take Lina over to Mr. Kincaid's mill. I'd do it myself, but I get so tuckered out on a walk that far. Lina, go with Jean." Then, with a wink, she said, "But watch your step."

****

The town was laid out in a crescent squeezed between the inlet's shore and a thickly wooded bluff, and all the buildings were strung along that crescent. Next to Sweet Meg's and first up from the shore was Minifee's general store. On the other side of Meg's was a small nondescript building Lina decided was the smokehouse. Lina noticed two wagon paths led into town, one from the north, the other from the south. Lina and Jean took a foot path that followed the shoreline south.

"So you've come to find a husband?" Jean asked.

Lina smiled. "I've come because of the handbill, yes, but not to find a husband."

Jean looked at Lina with amazement. "My heavens! Such a long way to come! And here, of all places. Why, this is practically the end of the world! I'd never be brave enough to do such a thing."

Lina looked at the girl. Jean Minifee was obviously a sweet-natured, well-mannered, and very pretty young woman with a lively personality. *And surely*, thought Lina, *two left feet*, for Jean had nearly tripped twice already along the broken footpath they were following to the mill. "How old are you?" she asked.

"Sixteen."

Lina thought about her own circumstances at that age, which now seemed very long ago. "You never know what you'll be brave enough to do."

"I'm to be married soon myself. This autumn," Jean offered with obvious joy. "To Jamie Marr. He's been my sweetheart for ever so long." Her mahogany brown curls, wound in tight ringlets down the back of her neck, bobbed whenever she spoke.

"Yes, Milo told me. He talked so much about all of you, I feel as if I know you already. He told me about you and Jamie. And the Marrs. They're loggers?"

"Yes! Jamie, his brother Robert and their cousin Hugh. It's very hard work, you know, and they're quite good at it." Jean took obvious pride in the accomplishments of her family-to-be.

"So it's not for want of a nest egg that you're waiting?"

"Oh, no. My father wants us to wait until I'm seventeen. Jamie's brother Robert thinks it's a good idea, too. But heavens! I'm nearly that now, and Jamie'll be twenty by then. Why, lots of girls get married younger than that!"

"Yes, but they aren't always the happier for it," said Lina. "I think your families must love you both very much to want to look out for you so."

"I suppose," Jean said with a sign. She stopped on the bank of a stream where it entered the inlet. "I have to get back to the store. Mother will be expecting me. Mr. Kincaid's mill is only a short way up there," Jean said, pointing upstream. "You won't have any trouble finding it."

"Thank you," Lina started walking toward the mill, but Jean stayed rooted to the spot, watching her go.

"Good luck, I guess," Jean said.

"Thank you," Lina said again, waiting for Jean to leave. When she didn't, Lina walked on. Just before the path took a bend, Jean called to her.

"Would you like to take a walk later with me and my friend Millie? We could show you around."

"That would be nice," Lina called back, smiling. She realized what a curiosity she must be in such a small community, particularly to a young girl like Jean. "Come by this afternoon."

"See you then!" Jean cried. Then she ran back toward town.

Lina could hear the whine of the saw blades long before she saw the mill house. Stacks of milled lumber stood amid a carpet of sawdust.

Specks of sawdust floated in the late morning light, and the air was filled with a sweet, woody perfume.

Next to the mill was a clean-looking, well-built little shed with a sign over the door. 'Kincaid Milling Company. M. Kincaid, Proprietor.' She walked toward the office and looked inside the open window, but the room was too dark for her to see inside. She knocked, but no one answered. The shrill grinding din of the saws next door was deafening. Suddenly the saws stopped to expose the sound of a man yelling. "Four more today, Linsen! No less!" Lina heard heavy footsteps headed toward her. She moved away from the door. It was a lucky move, for otherwise Martin Kincaid would surely have knocked her over as he rounded the corner.

"Excuse me!" He said.

"Excuse *me*!" said Lina, stepping back further.

"May I help you?"

"Carolina Morgan, Mr. Kincaid." Lina shook his hand firmly. "I arrived this morning with Captain Riordan?"

"Yes?" Kincaid shrugged.

"In response to your handbill?"

"Oh! Oh, yes! Oh." With each word, Kincaid's pitch lowered. He opened the door. "Please, come in."

The room was dominated by a desk that took more than its fair share of the space. Two cabinets for paperwork and a ledger desk for a bookkeeper were also squeezed in. She glanced at the bookkeeper's desk, and was disappointed to see there were no piles of unposted accounts, nor any paperwork to be filed—in short, no work for her.

Though Kincaid failed to offer it, Lina took a seat. Martin Kincaid was a trim, middle-aged man, dark featured and nearly bald. His face wore a comfortable scowl, as if he was quite used to the expression. He was dressed in a neat grey suit, and an ornate watch chain hung low from his vest pocket. He was not a handsome man, but distinguished.

"Captain Riordan told me you were behind that handbill, and suggested I come to see you straight off about work. That's why I've come, Mr. Kincaid. For work." Lina knew if she had any chance of finding decent work here, it was best to seem eager.

Kincaid sat at his desk, and affected a smile. "Why, that's wonderful, Miss, uh…."

"Morgan."

"Miss Morgan. Just wonderful. Came from San Francisco, did you?"

"Yes, sir."

"And what sort of work have you done, Miss Morgan?"

"I've managed a dockside warehouse. I've kept several stores, done books, inventory, that sort of thing."

"Hmm. Very good. May I ask for whom?"

"Oh, several concerns. Businesses in San Francisco come and go quickly. I'm not certain the names would mean anything to you." She hoped to distract him. "Do you think I might find any work like that here?"

Kincaid's uneasy smile crinkled into a flustered smirk. "Well, to be frank, no."

Lina waited for him to say something else, but he did not. "Then what did you have in mind, Mr. Kincaid?"

He paused a long time. "Laundry."

"Laundry?"

"Yes, Miss Morgan. Laundry. There's quite a need for laundry work here. The few ladies in town take in most of the wash for the millers and loggers, and it's more than they can handle. They make a pretty penny at it, too."

"You're suggesting I take in laundry?" Lina was still amazed that this was all the man could suggest.

"No. I'm suggesting you let me set you up in a business! Something similar to what I've done with the Minifee's, and with Sweet Meg's. Have you met Meg? Oh, of course, you have! Well, then, you catch my meaning. I've had it in my mind for some time that this could be the next business we start here in Pierce."

"Pierce?"

"Yes! I plan to name this community Pierce, after our new President. That is, once the territory officially recognizes it. And to do that, the town's going to need commerce, Miss Morgan, and lots of it! That's what I'm doing; I'm building the businesses around here into a real community."

"And making a nice profit off it, I'm guessing," Lina added quietly.

"Someone has to fuel the engine of commerce, Miss Morgan, and shouldn't they benefit from that? In any event, what I'm proposing is this. Let me start you in a laundry. Inside of three months I can have the whole operation built and ready to open. By then, I hope to have even more young ladies like yourself transplanted here, and they'll be as anxious for the work as you are. I'll make certain you get an adequate wage, and the rest of the profits can go toward paying back my investment. Once that's done, the business is yours free and clear. What do you think?"

"I think, Mr. Kincaid, that's a situation that works very well for you, and not for me. The business would be yours, not mine, at least for a good many years. And your hopes for attracting more eligible females are thin, from what I've heard. That would leave me to do all the work by myself, and then I'd be worse off than the women who are already doing the work and keeping all the profit. And in the meantime, how do I support myself? Three months is a long time, sir. I need work now."

Kincaid leaned back in his chair. "You're right. The arrangement stands me in better stead than it does you, but then, I am the one making the investment, now, aren't I? It's not my aim to amass a fortune just for its own sake, Miss Morgan. I have a longer vision. I see a time in the near future when Washington Territory will be made a state. I want this community to be the one to take the lead, and making sure this is the most progressive settlement in the area is just my way of stacking the deck. That handbill is an honest offer to be part of something bigger than what you've known before. If you're not smart enough to see that, then I'm afraid I can't help you."

"Those are fine sounding dreams, sir," Lina said as she stood. "And I wish you the best with them. But they're not my dreams. Mine are simpler than that. Just a chance to take care of myself and not be beholden to anyone, yourself included."

"If it's a simple dream you want, Miss Morgan, then let me suggest something else. Look around Pierce, and pick out a fellow to marry. There are lots of them. Why, at least five of my men have told me they'd marry the next girl who came. Get married, Miss Morgan. Keep a house, and have children. That will be simple enough, and work enough, too, I imagine."

Lina stood, and then opened the door. "Thank you, no, Mr. Kincaid. That's not part of my dream, either." She closed the door behind her.

On the walk back to Sweet Meg's, Lina considered Kincaid's offer, as distasteful as it might be. Laundry was hard work, she knew from experience, but better than nothing. Still, it would take a lot of shirts to save much to send back for Josephine. It was only her first day here, she reminded herself. *But how many other offers will there be?* she thought. *How long can I afford to wait?*

When Lina told Meg and Riordan of her conversation with Kincaid, there was no problem at all that Meg could see. "Fine, then. You'll work here. On my books. In the kitchen. It won't be full wages, though. I'm afraid there's not that much to do. But it'll cover room and board, and help out 'til you get on your feet, and maybe find something more permanent."

That afternoon, Lina kept her promise to walk with Jean and her friend, Millie. They roamed around the bluff above the mud flats, then down along the shoreline. Lina mostly listened, for the addition of Millie Forbes only made Jean chattier. Lina was already taking a liking to Jean, but she was not sure about Jean's friend. Millie Forbes was small and frail. Though her demeanor was pleasant, her face had a sharp, pinched look that contradicted that. Millie freely admitted her age, which was two years older than Lina. Lina could tell Millie used this seniority to domineer her young friend. But Jean had her way of dealing with Millie, too. Whenever the questions became too personal, Jean would change the subject, or say, "Now, Millie, it's only her first day! There'll be plenty of time to get to know one another." Millie was more than happy to talk about herself as well. She was, she admitted proudly, the first of the girls to respond to Kincaid's offer, and by being the first, she had nabbed the plum job of teacher. Kincaid had built the schoolhouse and paid her salary through a contract with the childrens' families. Millie was making a nice little nest egg, and had to account to no one.

She would no doubt need this nest egg. "I'd hoped to be married by now, of course, but none of the men I met when my family moved to San Francisco seemed interested in marriage. So when I heard of Martin Kincaid's offer, I decided I'd try my luck here. I have no intention of ending up a spinster like Aunt Eloise, I can promise you that!"

"And have you found the prospects here better?" Lina asked.

"Well, so far, no. But that could change any day. Besides, I'm picky. I could have married one of those mill hands who are so anxious to get married. Did Mr. Kincaid mention that to you? I thought as much. You were smart to turn that down. They're a lazy bunch, they are. Just looking for some woman to take care of them, that's all. A woman of my background can certainly do better than that!"

Jean made certain Lina had a chance to meet as many of the town folks as possible. First on the list were Jean's parents, Virgil and Esther Minifee, who ran the general store. When Jean mentioned that she had taken Lina to Kincaid's mill earlier, Virgil Minifee said, "Well, did he make you an offer?" as if he already knew what Kincaid's approach would be. When she told him he had, Minifee said, "Well, I'd advise you consider it, Miss Morgan. He's a hard nut, but well-meaning. He's done well by my family." Jean and Millie took her past a cluster of small cabins as Jean talked. They continued south, passing a few tents, then came upon a small but neatly built cabin. "That'll be your house soon, Jean," Millie giggled. "Jean is engaged, you know, to Jamie Marr."

"Yes, Millie, I told her. But that won't be our home. We're going to build our own place. I couldn't live there with Jamie *and* all of them."

"Jean, you're a lucky girl, in case you don't know that already," Millie said bluntly. "That family you're marrying into, they'll be quite well-off one day. Of course, a woman would have to put up with a good deal of trouble. They're all a bit wild, if you ask me. I have that young Charley in my class, and is he ever a handful! But then, you only have to look to Hugh and Robert to see where he gets it!" Then, quickly putting her hand on Jean's arm, she added, "Oh, but not Jamie! He's the nicest fellow you'd ever want to meet. In fact, when Jamie marries Jean, he'll be the last really good available man in town."

"Millie, don't be silly. There are lots of other nice men in town. Dozens of them. Neither Robert nor Hugh are married."

"Oh, those two," Millie complained, "I said *available*. They aren't the least bit interested in getting married. Just like Martin Kincaid."

"That Martin Kincaid gets under my skin," Jean said. "Jamie said he's been hovering at camp all this time Robert's been away. Jamie said he doesn't trust them, but Jamie and Hugh are doing just fine with Robert gone."

"But he is rather handsome, don't you think?" Millie giggled. "And he does own that saw mill and everything." Then Millie asked carefully, "What type of man are you hoping for, Lina?"

Lina had to smile. "Millie, you'll get no competition from me. It would appear I'm the only woman to come here *not* looking for a man. I'm here to make a new start. I'm looking for work."

"Sleekit's a funny place to move if you're trying to avoid men," said Jean.

"I'm not trying to avoid them. I just don't have any interest in getting married. What I need is a job."

"A man *is* a job!" Millie exclaimed, and the three girls laughed.

****

Every day for that first week, Lina helped in the tavern in exchange for room and board. She started with Meg's books, but that took no time at all. She helped Meg make supply lists. She cleaned and swept and washed dishes and helped with the cooking. None of these chores were hard, but they were chores, not a real job. Milo and Meg reminded her to be patient. "It's not yet spring," Meg had pointed out. "When the weather clears, all sorts of things might come up. You never know. And besides, when Milo leaves next week, I'll appreciate the company."

The room Meg offered was sparse and small but suited Lina quite well. Inside there was nothing but a bed, a chair, and a small table where the lantern sat. There was no window, but the walls were crisp white, and when the door stood open, Lina could look out to the sound. But Lina had unpacked nothing. She couldn't shake the sense that she might have to leave soon. She had already become quite attached to Milo and Meg, for they were kind and generous and doted on her. She knew if she did go, she would be sad to leave them.

Between days and evenings spent at the tavern, and afternoons with Jean and Millie, Lina learned a great deal about life in Sleekit in no time at all. "Kincaid can call it a town if he wants, but it stretches the imagination, if ya asks me," Riordan offered. "More like a way station. There's trappers from the mountains. A fair number of farms to the east, but those folks only come for supplies. Indians, from time to time, but they stay to themselves. Me and me crew, we ain't here but more than a week or two at a time. Then there's Kincaid and his mill workers, but that's not a dozen men. That just leaves the Marrs and their loggers, and they ain't here but at week's end, if they come at all."

Once more, the Marrs seemed to play a part in every story Lina heard. The Marrs, or at least Robert Marr, had been in these parts long before anyone else. Jean told her of eleven-year-old Charley, Jamie and Robert's cousin, and a student of Millie's. Charley stayed with the Minifees when his brother and cousins were at the logging camp, and he helped out at the store to pay for his keep. Charley's older brother Hugh was described as handsome and charming, a young man who had apparently made the acquaintance of almost every girl in every settlement and farm around. Jean never tired of speaking of Jamie, of course, and Meg and Riordan confirmed that this was a good match. Jamie was steady and quiet, and when she was with him Jean shed all her nervous, giggly behavior.

Robert, Jamie's older brother, was the hardest for Lina to imagine. At first she thought him to be a man of Riordan's age, or at least Kincaid's. But Millie and Jean were certain he was not so old, and described him as good looking and charming. Riordan and Meg spoke of his silver tongue. Meg confirmed it was most often Robert Marr, not Martin Kincaid that folks went to when they needed advice or help. Jean told Lina the story of her family coming to Sleekit, and how Robert had his men build them a store and a place to live when Martin Kincaid fell short on his promises. She mentioned this was about the time when Robert brought Jamie here, though she didn't say more about that. She did say that at the time, though she was only then twelve and Jamie fifteen, she and Jamie immediately became friends, and that she knew even then she would marry him one day.

All this added up fine, but after their fifth supper together, Meg said something about Robert that conflicted with everything Lina had heard. "He can be the most contrary man I've ever met. He doesn't seem the least bit interested in seeing Sleekit grow, and if it weren't for the fact that having that sawmill here helps him make money, I think he would have run Martin Kincaid off a long time ago."

"Yet he brought his entire family here," Lina said. "Surely he realized that in itself would cause Sleekit to grow."

"He brought his brother here first, then Hugh and Charley showed up," Meg said. "There was some dust-up with his family that left him no choice but to bring them here, but that was all before we came. Mostly, I'd just say he is a cautious man."

"That's probably wise," Lina said.

Meg shook her head and clicked her tongue. "Wise when it comes to business, I suppose, but sometimes he seems almost fearful of the human race. I can't help but worry for him. There's a part of Robert that seems far away."

Later, Lina was washing the supper dishes when the sound of voices came toward them. Men's voices.

"Don't close the kitchen yet, honey," Meg said. "The boys are back." The words had barely left Meg's lips when a half dozen bounding, boisterous men spilled through the tavern doors and filled the tables. "Hello, Meg!" "I'm starved!" "Two beers, here, Meg!"

"Easy boys, easy. One at a time." Meg shoved a skillet in Lina's hand. "Start frying whatever we've got. I'll handle the bar." Once the men had full glasses, the tumult died down. Then the doors opened again, and in came Jean, with a man on each arm.

"Hello, Meg! Did ya miss us?" cried one, a tall, lean, red-headed man with a beard to match. He threw his arms around Meg and lifted her in a bear hug.

"Hugh Marr, put me down!" she squealed while he laughed.

"Oh, there she is!" Jean was dragging the other fellow toward Lina. "This is her, Jamie. Lina, this is Jamie. And this is Hugh."

Each of the two shook her hand smartly. "Pleasure to meet you," said Hugh. "Meg, two beers for a couple of over-worked buckers."

Meg handed the two their beers, then joined them at their table. Lina served the meals to the others. Each of the loggers introduced himself politely, and a couple tried flirting with her. Lina was pleasant, but detached. She kept an eye on Meg, Jean and the Marrs. The two men were in a spirited debate, but Lina couldn't hear their conversation for all the noise in the room. Then Meg waved her over to join them.

Hugh hit the table with his fist. "Jamie, I know I'm right. If we don't break up into more crews, we'll never get that timber cut in time. Then there's that penalty clause."

"We could get Clem to head up a crew," Jamie offered.

"No, he's too new. He's a good man, but he's not ready to lead a crew yet. I've got to do it." Hugh was adamant.

Jamie looked properly concerned. "I don't know, Hugh. We've a payroll to meet next week."

"Just my point, Jamie. If I have to take care of that, then we lose two days with me coming back to town, then back to camp."

"I suppose that's true. But that's the way Robert's…"

"Robert's not here, though. He left us in charge. And I say, to hell with the paperwork. We're loggers, not bookkeepers."

"I can do it." Lina spoke before she realized it. Everyone at the table turned to her. She looked straight at Hugh. "I can do it. I can do your paperwork." Hugh looked at Meg, who was already nodding.

"It's true, Hugh. Lina had a lot of experience doing that kind of thing. She's a whiz with accounts."

Hugh's eyes brightened, but Jamie wasn't as sure. "Now, just a second, Hugh. I don't know. Hiring someone new, someone we don't really know." He looked at Lina with an air of apology, shrugging his shoulders.

"Well, I know her. And Meg knows her." Jean said.

"That's right, Jamie. She's been working for me all week, and she's more than able." Meg looked at Lina and smiled.

Hugh persisted. "Look, Jamie. It's just this one time. She looks honest enough, and if Meg and Jean vouch for her…."

"But Hugh, you remember Robert said that he didn't want anybody but you or me to carry that payroll packet to camp."

"What he said, cousin, was that he didn't want any of the *men* to carry the packet. Didn't want there to be any reason to tempt any of them. But he didn't say anything about somebody else."

Jamie had to smile. "Now you sound like Robert, twisting the meaning to suit your purpose! You know good and well what Robert would think of a woman carrying the packet."

"Robert doesn't ever have to know, does he? He's not due back for another week, as I count it. By then, the deed'll be done, and we'll have that much more timber cut. Why, he'll be proud of us!"

"Hmm." Jamie kept staring into his beer.

Hugh thought for a moment, then said, "Look, never mind the reasons. It wouldn't matter what Robert said. If we took a vote and he was outvoted, well, then, that would be the end of it."

Jamie grinned. "Since when do we vote on anything? It's always up to Robert. He's in charge."

"When he's here. So, the way I see it, when Robert's gone, it's up to you and me. Or are you always going to let that big brother of yours tell you what to do? And you a man about to take a wife? How's that look?"

"Seems like there's always someone telling me what to do. If it's not Robert, then it's you, or…" Jamie looked at Jean, who smiled sweetly. "Alright, then," he said with a reticent sigh. We can hire Miss Morgan for a day to handle the books."

Hugh let out a whoop and sprung to his feet.

"But only for a day, Hugh. Only for the one day." Hugh was not listening. He took Lina's hand and shook it vigorously.

"Congratulations, Miss Morgan, you're the newest employee of Marr Logging Company."

"Oh, thank you! You won't regret it, I promise! Just tell me what to do and it's done."

****

When Hugh had explained the job to her, Lina was beside herself with delight. It was a simple matter. Hugh showed her how to distribute the pay and gave her the books. The steps he showed her were simple, but he showed her many times. Lina assumed that despite the fact that this was his idea, he harbored his own reservations about her. She was patient with his attempts to explain and explain again what she understood the first time, and promised him she wouldn't let him down.

Hugh was not the only one with reservations. When Lina returned to Sweet Meg's a short time later, Meg pulled her aside.

"Now, honey, if you think this is more than you want to take on…"

"Not at all!" Lina said. "I've done this work before."

"It's not that what has me worried. It could be dangerous. It doesn't happen often, but men have been robbed on that road more than once."

Lina hadn't counted on that concern, but she didn't say anything for fear that Meg would try to talk her out of the work. She so desperately wanted to try this. She had been longing for a chance to see more of the country than just this inlet, and in particular, she was very curious about the Marr's logging operation. She knew nothing about the work, and figured if she could only learn, perhaps she might find a job in it for herself. *Better than laundry*, she thought.

"Do you know how to use a gun?" Meg asked.

"A rifle."

From behind the bar, Meg pulled a small pistol. "It's old, and it hasn't been fired in ages. But I keep it clean and loaded, just in case. You know, with Milo gone so much…"

"Thank you. And I promise, Meg, I'll be careful."

Until the men returned to the timber two days later, the little settlement was a busy place, most particularly Sweet Meg's. Meg insisted on fixing a decent meal for Jamie and Hugh, and she invited Jean and Lina to join them. Young Charley joined them too, for he never left their sides when the men were in town. Lina liked them all immediately, as different as each was. Hugh reminded Lina of Henry in his bumptious energy. But he was handsomer, and his bright red hair and beard were striking. Lina quickly saw that Jamie was the thoughtful one. He was the one who tried to include everyone in the conversation. He refused to let Meg wait on anyone, and he cleared the table when the meal was done. Except for answering Lina's questions, he said little during the meal, but whenever Lina looked up toward him, she caught him smiling and attentive to whoever was speaking. Charley was all boy—a gawky mass of freckles and white blonde hair whose growing frame could not keep from moving constantly, including squirming in his chair and playing with his food. But he was bright and polite and happy to be among his family, listening to their news and eagerly sharing his own.

"I was fishing this week, Hugh! Me and Jimmy…"

"Jimmy and I, Charley," Hugh corrected.

"*You* and Jimmy? Oh, right. Jimmy and *I* went up to the grove, but we didn't catch anything. We found a raccoon nest, though, and some bear tracks! We're going back next…"

"You be careful up there, young man!" said Meg. "A young boy can get into an awful lot of trouble in those woods."

"Yes, ma'am. Anyway, Hugh, I thought maybe you and me…you and *I* could go up there and I'd show you!"

"Sure, Charley. Sure. In the morning. First thing."

Charley's joy was quickly interrupted as Meg asked him, "How's your lessons?"

"Oh. Well, I suppose good enough."

"Good enough? Hmm. Well, what say you and your brother take a look at your lessons before you go off on this bear hunt."

It was clear from Hugh's expression that, like his little brother, he preferred the bear to the books. But he took his responsibility to heart. "Meg's right, boy. Let's check out those lessons tonight. Then tomorrow, the bear!" And they both laughed with anticipation.

After dinner, Charley and Hugh left for their cabin, and Jean and Jamie went for a walk. Lina washed the dishes while Meg sat next to Milo, who was leaning back in his chair, quietly snoring.

"They're very nice, Meg. Just as you described them."

Meg beamed. "They're nearly like my own. It gets quite lonely here, particularly when he's gone," she said, looking over at the sleeping Milo. "That Hugh and Robert, they go at it sometimes. Two more stubborn men I've never known. But it's good for Robert. He needs someone to challenge him! He has his way too often." She laughed.

"Good for Jamie too, I should imagine. For Hugh to push him, I mean," Lina added.

"Yes. Very clever of you to have noticed that. Jamie's the dearest soul on the earth. But he's too eager to please sometimes. Hugh is a good influence on him, I think. He needs to learn to think for himself, not always for Robert. Even if he's wrong."

Lina was silent a moment, then said quietly. "You know, this Robert is beginning to sound like a bit of a bully."

"Oh, don't think ill of him from what I said," said Meg. "He's, well, he's… he's got a bold nature. He's been taking care of himself and Jamie for a good long while. He has his own way of doing things, and he never doubts he's right. But he's a good man, and he loves all those boys dearly."

26

Sleekit was stirring from beneath a blanket of morning fog. The Bantry Bay was a sleeping sentinel in the calm waters of low tide. A single flicker of lantern glow from Sweet Meg's kitchen fluttered like a waking eyelid. The door to Minifee's store opened with a yawn.

When Esther Minifee stepped outside, broom in hand, she didn't see the small canoe silently slipping along the banks. When Millie Forbes rounded the bend toward the small schoolhouse, she didn't see it either, nor did she see the three men inside, wrapped tightly in furs against the dampness. As the two women stood on the store's small stoop, they were too busy chattering to notice the canoe pull up to the banks and deliver a passenger. A man stepped out, shedding his fur wrap to reveal a surprisingly civilized black suit coat. He grabbed a small satchel from the hull of the canoe as he spoke briefly to the other men in a tongue neither Esther or Millie would have understood. Then he waved goodbye as the canoe shoved off.

Robert Marr took long, even strides across the mud flats, partly because it was his nature to take full advantage of the economy of movement that his tall, muscular frame afforded him. In part, too, after two day's travel in the canoe the stretch did his legs good. But this morning, most particularly, he was feeling an urgency to start the day. He had a lot to do and little time in which to do it. His business in San Francisco had not gone well, so he had returned sooner than planned, taking any conveyance he could. The last two days felt like eternity as old friends among the Nisqually slowly paddled him back to Sleekit. Now that he was here, he would have to spend much of this day with

Martin Kincaid, giving him the bad news about the contract that would not be coming their way. He dreaded the meeting, and decided to begin the day with a decent breakfast at Meg's, where he could catch up on any news he had missed in the weeks he had been away.

"Robert!"

Marr heard his name, and something inside of him flinched at the shrill chirp of Millie Forbes. Instinctively, he put on his best smile and walked toward the two women. *Thank heaven Esther is there as well*, he noted as he came closer, all smiles and waves. He considered Esther Minifee a level-headed and even-tempered woman. Millie Forbes, on the other hand, was as annoying as a sand flea, and the only reason he could imagine that Jean chose her as a friend was the notable lack of alternatives. But his proper Scottish breeding taught him to treat the two women equally.

"Good morning, Robert," said Esther. "How was San Francisco?"

"You're home early, aren't you?" Millie asked at the same time. "Jean told me that Jamie said you weren't due until next week. Didn't things go well?"

Robert ignored Millie's interruption, choosing instead to answer Esther. "San Francisco? That city is but a cold gray memory when I can return home to find the morning sun in two such lovely faces." Esther Minifee just chuckled at his charm, but Millie fairly swooned. "I'm just on my way to Meg's to catch up on the news. That is, if there is any." He was immediately sorry he asked. The two needed no further cue to share what they knew. He stood, smiling, and apparently listening, but not really. The conversation flitted from one topic to the next, and most of the time he didn't catch who they were talking about, or why he should be the least bit interested. He settled for just smiling, and that seemed enough. He had just heard Millie say something about Kincaid's handbill, when another familiar, but this time, welcome voice drew his attention.

"Marr! You're home!" Riordan was coming toward him from Sweet Meg's. He threw his arm around Robert's shoulders. "Ah, it's good ta see ya, me lad."

The smile on Robert's face was genuine this time. "Riordan, you ol' reprobate! How are you? I'm headed to Meg's. Care to join me for a little breakfast?"

"I've disappointin' news on that front. Meg's feelin' under the weather, and so all I can offer yas is a cup of coffee." Then Riordan added, with a wink and a whisper, "Or a drink."

Robert laughed. "No thanks, Milo. I have a lot to do. I'll just head to the cabin, then."

"Oh, heavens, Captain! I hope Miss Fay isn't suffering!" Millie gushed.

"Is there anything I can do, Milo?" Esther asked.

"Thank you kindly, ladies. No, just a bit o' the gout. I suspect she'll be up and about by mid-day. But I'll send your regards."

"That's dreadful, Captain. Simply dreadful! Why, my aunt Eloise suffered from the gout so terribly, they almost had to amputate her leg!" As Millie droned on, Robert stopped listening again, for something had distracted him. A woman whose face he could not see stood against the railing along the upstairs at Sweet Meg's. She was combing her hair, her face intriguingly hidden. He knew he hadn't seen her before, for he would have remembered hair that color—a strange, lovely color somewhere between red and gold. For a moment he watched the smooth movement of her hand pulling the comb, and the way the curls sprang back to shape no matter what discipline the comb tried to impose. He thwarted an impulse to ask these folks who this newcomer might be when he realized any questions would only prolong the ladies' interminable conversation. He couldn't afford to waste any of this day.

"If you'll excuse me, folks. A busy day ahead. Milo, my best to Meg of course, and as Esther said, if there's anything I can do, you'll send word, won't you? Good man." Then Robert Marr headed toward his cabin.

****

Lina would leave nothing to chance when it came to performing the job Hugh had given her. The loggers had left three days before, and yesterday when the small ship brought the payroll from Olympia, Lina had come down to take possession of the packet personally. This morning she had risen early to set out for camp, even though she would arrive hours before the men would return. On a horse Hugh left in town for her, and with the ledger's he'd given her tucked in her bag along with Meg's gun, she headed out.

When Lina arrived the place was deserted, and she was surprised to see there was little more to the camp than just a few tents and bedrolls clustered around the remnants of a morning's fire. The tent at the far end was slightly larger than the rest, and with its flap open, she could see a crude table inside. She went in.

Other than the table, there was nothing there but three bedrolls. On the table, two ledgers like the one she carried rested beneath a lantern. Lina picked them up. One was a record of supplies ordered and received. The other was hard for her to decipher, but seemed to track the work they'd done and the timber they'd produced. She lost track of time as she pored through the books. Lina learned a great deal about the Marrs' operation—how much food it took to feed the men, what supplies they used, where everything was purchased, and how much it cost. So engrossed in the books was she that she did not hear the sound of the approaching horse, nor the crunch of heavy boots just outside the tent. She only looked up when something blocked the opening to the tent, obscuring all light within.

In surprise, Lina slammed the ledger closed. A man stood before her, his face lost in the shadow he created. But she could clearly see he was tall with a strong build. Her heart beat quicker as she tried to remember where she had left Meg's gun.

The man stepped toward her, and light came back into the tent. From the expression on his face, she had startled him nearly as much as he had her. "Who are you, and what are you doing here?" he said slowly, his voice deep and resonant.

She stood up and took the offensive. "I might ask the same of you, sir."

"Me? You are the intruder."

"So you say. Yet you offer no introduction."

"A man does not need an introduction in his own tent!"

"He does, if no one there knows him."

"Madam, I am Robert Marr."

She swallowed hard. Somehow, she knew this was true. There was something about his bearing that fit perfectly with everything she had been told. He had a sense of power about him, and he was handsome too, she had to admit, with a full head of dark curls and striking blue-green eyes. His voice had a polish that conflicted with the rough flannel shirt and cord trousers he wore.

"Prove it, sir."

"I beg your pardon?"

"I'm here on the business of Marr Logging, at the request of members of the Marr family. If you are who you say you are, you wouldn't want me to share that business with a stranger, would you?"

"What?" For a moment, Robert was stymied by her impudence. "See here, miss. How do you know that these "members of the Marr family" are who they say they are?"

"If they're frauds, they have the entire town of Sleekit fooled, including Meg Fay."

"You know Meg?"

"I do. I'm a boarder of hers."

"Since when? I don't recall…"

Then he *did* recall. The woman on the balcony. He circled behind her to confirm it. There it was, that hair, twisted in a single braid behind her back. "Ah yes…" he said, as all the pieces fell into place. The woman. Kincaid's handbill. Riordan's mysterious passenger. He laughed.

"What do you find so amusing?"

"Well, miss, I imagine that I know as much about you as you do about me. You came here from San Francisco with Riordan. You would have arrived—let me think—about ten days ago. You came because of that handbill of Kincaid's?"

"That proves nothing. Anyone from around here might have figured as much."

"Very well, then. Ah! You came to the Bantry Bay in San Francisco dressed in your best finery. Riordan wondered about you from the start. He told me so himself."

"A nice story. But I've only your word about Riordan."

"Alright then. You've no doubt become acquainted with Jean, if you're staying with Meg. Jean, no doubt, introduced you to my brother, Jamie, and my cousin Hugh. And I'll bet all the money in that cash box that you're so careful with—you see, I know about that—all that money, that it was Hugh's notion to hire you for the payroll, so he could work with the crews. Am I right?" He grinned with satisfaction.

Lina nodded reluctantly.

"Well, there's no need for you to stay. Those boys'll be heading back any time. I'll handle things from here."

Lina didn't move from her seat behind the table. "No, sir. I'll stay."

"Oh," he said, "I see. Well, let me at the cash drawer and I'll give you what my cousin promised you. How much?"

"That's not it."

"What else then?"

"It wouldn't be right, Mr. Marr. I had an agreement with Hugh, not you. If it's all the same to you, I'll wait until Hugh and Jamie return, and then I'll go."

"And if it's not all the same to me?"

"I'll stay anyway." For a moment, he just stared at her, considering his options. As if reading his thoughts, Lina added, "You can put me on that horse, but I won't ride out."

Robert shook his head. "Suit yourself." Then he came toward her, took her by her shoulders and gently pulled her from the chair. "I have work to do," he said, sitting down.

Lina went to the tent flap and looked out, hoping that Hugh and Jamie might be coming up the road that very moment. But the road was empty. The air outside had grown chilly. Lina rubbed her hands together, and looked back to Robert Marr, who was paying her no notice.

"Would you mind if I sat here while I wait?" she asked, pointing to one of the bedrolls at her feet.

Robert nodded toward the one on the opposite side of the tent. "Sit there. It's Hugh's. You're his guest."

"Thank you," Lina said. Another long silence passed, until Robert Marr closed the ledger.

"What's your name?"

"I beg your pardon?"

"Your name! You have a name, I suppose? Now that you know mine…"

"Carolina Morgan."

"Morgan. You're a Scot, too, then?"

"A Scot? Oh, well, I suppose. I don't really know."

345

"Well, *I* know. The Morgans—they're McKay clan, if I remember. Northern highlands." He opened another ledger book.

"It doesn't mean a thing to me," she said. Shifting uncomfortably on the bedroll, she tried to show her indifference by keeping a watchful eye outside.

"Really? And Riordan was under the impression you were an educated woman…"

She turned sharply, and said, "And Riordan told *me* that you were…"

They were interrupted by the sound of men's voices. Lina sprang to her feet just as she heard Hugh call her name.

"Lina? Are you there? Hugh came bounding in the tent, a big grin on his face. Then he saw Robert sitting at the table. "Robbie! Well, uh, you're back early! Good to see you! Uh, well. So. So, I suppose you've met Lina, then." He struggled to be casual, but Robert would have none of it.

"Yes, Hugh. I've met Miss Morgan. We've spent the better part of the last hour together. She's been a revelation."

When Hugh looked to her, Lina said, "I told Mr. Marr that I was here at *your* request. That's all. I'm afraid he figured out the rest. A clever man, your cousin." The description was not meant as a compliment, a point not lost on Robert. "But I also told him I wouldn't leave until *you* told me to. I work for *you*."

Hugh was at a loss for words, and Jamie seemed unable to offer any help. He shrank back behind Hugh, who shuffled uneasily.

"Hugh," said Robert. "You're the boss. May Miss Morgan leave now?"

"Well, as long as she's here, Robert, don't you think she could do the paymaster's work? I don't see what harm there'd be in that…"

"I think we can handle our own business, Hugh."

The obvious tension between them made Lina uneasy. "Gentlemen, I have no desire to create problems. Just give me my pay, and I'll go."

As Hugh and Robert locked eyes, Jamie went to the cash drawer and removed the two dollars Hugh had promised her. "Come on, Lina, I'll see you out," he said as he handed her the money.

He held the horse as she stepped into the stirrup. "I'm sorry, Jamie," Lina said. "I guess I should have gone when your brother told me to."

"You did fine, Lina. Don't give it another thought. Those two butt heads so often, it's become a habit. If it hadn't been this, it would've been something else." He gave her a reassuring smile. "Get going. You want to be back to Meg's before dark."

On her ride back to Sleekit, Lina thought long and hard about whether she should have ever accepted Hugh's offer. After looking over those ledgers, she was even more convinced that the Marrs' operation was her best hope of work, but what hope would she have if she had angered Robert Marr, or set him and Hugh seriously at odds. Yet if she hadn't taken the offer, she wouldn't have had this chance to prove herself, at least to Hugh and Jamie, and to learn enough about the work to see how she might be helpful. In the end, she suspected Jamie was right. If it hadn't been her, Robert would have found something else to be angry with Hugh about. Now that she had met Robert Marr, she understood why Hugh would take such a risk. Hugh was just a young man itching for experience. *If Robert Marr is as smart as folks say,* she thought, *he would take advantage of all that enterprise.*

****

Lina tried to give the two dollars she'd earned to Meg, but Meg would have none of it. Riordan would be sailing in a few days, and Meg kept saying she ought to pay Lina to stay, just for the company. So Lina kept her money, but it didn't seem worth the trouble to send such a paltry sum with Riordan to deposit in Josephine's trust. Instead, she decided to send some of Josephine's jewelry with him, hoping he could get a fair price and put that in the bank.

She had brought her portmanteau from her room down to the tavern, and was laying out her cache of Josephine's belongings, looking for the strand of pearls she had in mind. The table was covered with dresses, baubles, and the books from Barclay's library. Meg and Milo sat at the table with her. Meg was admiring the pretty dresses when Robert came through the door.

"Robert!" Meg said. "What brings you to town?"

"I heard Milo was set to leave in a few days, and I have a list of things we need." He handed Milo a piece of paper. "Good morning, Miss Morgan."

"Mr. Marr."

"A bit of spring cleaning?" he asked.

Lina didn't answer, but Meg did. "Milo's going to take some things and try to sell them for her in San Francisco." Lina cringed. She suddenly realized that giving Robert Marr the impression she was desperate for money was not to her advantage. But it was too late now.

"What's this?" Robert picked up a book. "Emerson, eh? You like Emerson, do you?"

"I haven't read it."

"Well, if you're in need of some money, I'd be willing to buy this from you."

"It was a gift from a friend, Mr. Marr. I have no intention of selling it."

"That's a pity. Well, if you change your mind..." She finally looked up at him, and saw he was smiling. The derision and the patronizing manner she thought she would find there were not, and she smiled back. She had to admit it was difficult not to return a smile that inviting. Then in a flash the moment was gone. Robert said, "You're an odd one, Miss Morgan. First Meg's, then the camp, and now this? I'm getting the impression that you'll do anything for a buck."

Robert Marr would never understand why this woman didn't find his little joke amusing, but he knew immediately by her expression that she most certainly did not. He knew enough to cut his losses, though. "I'm off to find Charley. Perhaps I'll be back after supper." Then he left.

****

Thwack! Crack! Thwack! Crack! Thump! Thump! The wood splintered in two then was flung into the pile. Over and over, Robert Marr split logs into firewood. He loved the chore, for it reminded him of how far he had come.

When he first arrived in the northwest more than ten years before, he was as green as the hills. Nothing his father had told him, and certainly nothing of his life in Montreal, had prepared him for what he found. The world here was rough and raw and demanded hard labor of a man. Robert Marr's hands might have been soft, but they were willing, and his mind was eager. For if his merchant family's upbringing had not prepared him for the labor, it had taught him how to seize an opportunity. He saw that opportunity here, in the endless acres of unclaimed timber. He determined he would stay and make his fortune, and with the help of those who had always called this place home, he learned what he would need to survive. In those early days, he took every opportunity to better himself, and he remembered this evening how a simple thing like chopping wood had been a part of that.

Since he first took axe in hand, he had loved the feel of the heavy tool, like an extension of his own arms. He had studied the skill of other men who used it well, and he had practiced until he had the same skill. After years of logging, he prided himself on his abilities. He took the same care with firewood that he did with felling big trees. The axe must be struck in just the right place, a decision made in a split second; the axe adjusted just a hair, so it would land precisely where he wanted it. He made a personal challenge of the task. With each tree, he would guess the number of strokes it would take to fell it, and try to better that. He nearly always could.

He liked the muscle the work gave him. He liked to feel the strength of his own body as he worked. In the beginning, he would swing until his arms ached, and then swing some more, to remind himself he had strength in reserve. Often, he would lose himself in the rhythm of the work, as he had now. His body, once started, could work without thinking, freeing his mind to focus on other matters, or on nothing at all. It felt good sometimes to think of nothing but the pendulum of his arms, and the sound of the blade burying itself in the wood. *Thwack! Crack! Thump!*

This evening, Robert's mind would not go blank, hard as he might try. The crews were dangerously behind. *Too many new men, that's the cause of it.* They had hired several men in the last month, inexperienced but strong and sturdy. They were getting the hang of the work, but it was too soon to leave them on their own. Each day he and Jamie would each lead a crew, and when Hugh was finished with his other duties, he would join them. There was never enough time for Hugh to take another crew. Only just enough time to fill in here or there where an extra hand was needed.

Hugh. Whenever Robert thought of him, he struggled with his feelings. In some ways he felt closer to Hugh than Jamie, for Hugh was much more like him. Energetic, ambitious, and adventurous, both of them. They shared a disdain for authority, too, but when Robert was the authority, that was a different matter altogether. They might argue, but in the end, Robert always won. *It has to be that way*, he thought. *Someone has to be responsible. Jamie understands that. Jamie, who never gives me a moment's worry, or a word of argument. He understands. Why doesn't Hugh?* Robert raised the axe again. *Thwack! Crack!*

Hugh shared Robert's determination, too, and because of it, Hugh never gave up on an idea. He had already brought up the subject of Lina and the payroll again. Hugh started by hinting, then turned to suggesting, then needling, and finally to haranguing Robert, to the point of outrage. They had only just had another row on the matter this very evening when Robert, in a fit of frustration, came outside to chop wood, and to block the subject from his already harried mind. *Thwack!*

But it hadn't helped. Robert only heard his own arguments over and over again in his head. He had no desire to have a stranger involved in their business. Particularly not one of these flighty women Kincaid was shipping in. Their relationship with Kincaid was built on a tenuous compact, but at the heart they were rivals. *Perhaps this woman has loyalties to Kincaid. How can I know?*

That was the other piece. Robert was against this plan of Kincaid's to bring women here. *Better those women learn sooner than later what a harsh place they've landed in. If I help them, it'll only delay the inevitable.* The loggers understood the uncertainty of this life. He had made sure of that. The men had other prospects, at least, and if the contracts stopped coming, or the weather kept them out of the timber, the men would get by somehow. He was doing this Miss Morgan a favor, he reminded himself, by not giving her false hopes.

Then the words Hugh had spoken to him that evening filled his ears again. "This isn't what I came here for, Robbie," he had said. "I came to do a man's job. If you keep me cooped up, I'll die." They had made a pact, the two of them, when Hugh had arrived almost three years earlier. Hugh would act as a sort of manager. True, it meant he would spend less time with the crews, but they had agreed on three years. By that time, Robert thought the business might have grown enough to hire someone to handle the paperwork, as Kincaid had. But though they'd had success, Robert said the business couldn't yet afford it. Besides, he thought, the arrangement was working well enough.

It was working for Robert. *But for Hugh?* No, Robert was forced to admit, not for Hugh. This meditation on his own beginnings only reminded him of what Hugh was missing, of what Hugh so desperately wanted to be a part. *It's hardly fair to him, when he's done all I've asked of him, and more. What if something happened tomorrow, and he never had the chance?* Something could happen, Robert knew. In the blink of an eye, everything can change. *Thwack! Crack! Clunk, clunk.* He laid down the axe, took another drink of water, and went back inside the cabin.

Jamie was making supper for the four of them. He had always been the best cook of the lot, even as a boy. "Does Jean know what a prize she's getting in you, Jamie? A handsome, hardworking young man, and the best cook for ten miles?" Robert was trying to lighten the mood.

Jamie just shrugged his shoulders. He tried to remain neutral in these family debates, but privately he took Hugh's side in this, because he knew Robert. If Robert made up his mind, nothing would change it, even if it should. To Jamie, that was just bad thinking, no matter who was right or wrong.

Hugh sat sullenly with his back to the door, pretending to read in front of the fire. Charley sat at the table looking over his schoolwork. Robert took a seat next to him, peering over his shoulder at his sums.

"Charley, I think it's about time we went fishing again. Next Friday, you could skip school, and come up to the camp."

"Sure, Robert! That would be grand, wouldn't it Hugh?"

All three of them looked toward Hugh, who never wavered from the book in front of him. "Aye, Charley, grand."

"Will you be coming back to town for me, then?" the boy asked.

Robert put his arm around Charley's shoulder. "No, I'm going to ask Miss Morgan to bring you."

"I guess that'd be okay. She seems nice. But why is she bringing me?"

Robert looked at Hugh as he gave Charley his answer. "Because I'm going to ask her if she can help us out—for a day."

Hugh looked up quickly, hope in his eyes. Robert's smile confirmed that hope.

"Good," said Charley. "You can use the help. Maybe someday soon you'll let me help you!"

Robert laughed. "It appears the deck's stacked against me, Charley. But you? Not just yet, lad." Then he spoke to Hugh. "You've earned the right, Hugh. I don't know how often we can hire Miss Morgan, and I make no promises. If she doesn't work out, then that'll have to be the end of it, until something else can be arranged. But there's no harm in trying it—once."

Hugh only smiled, resisting the urge to gloat. Jamie was grinning from ear to ear as he set a pot of beef and potatoes on the table. "You'll see, Robert. This is the right thing to do. It'll be the best thing for everybody. I think you'll like Lina, once you get to know her."

"It's not a matter of liking her," Robert said stubbornly. "It has nothing to do with her at all, as a matter of fact. As I've told you both before…"

There was too much talking and commotion for Robert to be heard. Charley was trying to squeeze between Hugh and Jamie to reach the stew pot. "My turn!" he demanded, but Hugh ignored him.

"Jamie," Hugh said. "On Friday, let me have a crack at that stand you were telling me about. I'm sure I can get through it if I have Clem."

"Clem?" Jamie said. "Well, of course you can, if you have him! He's our best! No, cousin. You can take Clem next time."

"Next time? I haven't said there'll be a next time!" Robert hollered. Charley continued to eat, and Hugh and Jamie continued to make their plans. None of them was paying Robert the slightest attention.

✳✳✳✳✳✳✳

Young Charley Marr could not have been happier. Today, he was away from his teacher's demands, from Mr. Minifee's chores and Mrs. Minifee's sharp eye, and he felt fine indeed. He was riding up to camp, without a care in the world. He watched hawks soaring above, listened to the wind through the trees, and imagined that grand adventures waited just beyond the next bend. Best of all, he would spend the night at the camp with his brother and his cousins, and that was more fun than anything he could think of. Charley was so excited at the prospect, he could not sit still, nor keep from chattering.

"I think I'll be a topper," he said to Lina out of the blue.

"A what?"

"A topper. That's the fellow who gets to climb to the top of the tree and cut it off. A fellow's got to be good at climbing to be a topper, and that's me!"

"Sounds dangerous."

Charley thought on that for a moment, then rejected it. "So what if it is? I'm not afraid. Why, I bet I could do it today. Climb, that is. I don't imagine I could cut trees—not yet. But pretty soon."

Lina smiled. "You're very eager to work, Charley. But I suppose that's to be expected. Those cousins and that brother of yours make it seem quite wonderful, I suspect."

Charley smiled, eyes wide. "It *is* wonderful."

Lina looked around her. They rode through a dense covering of tall spruce and fir that sheltered them from the brisk wind of early spring. It had sprinkled earlier, but now the sky was clear and the sunlight that found its way to these depths glistened in the drops that clung to every drooping branch. The air was heavy with the perfume of the forest, and all around them, the woods sang with life. "You're right, Charley. It is wonderful."

After an appreciative silence, Charley said, "Besides, seems everyone around Sleekit has a job, except me."

"Your job is to go to school."

"You sound like Robert," Charley said, shaking his head. "I wish I could see what the point of all that schooling is."

"I wish I'd had more schooling, Charley. It makes you better able to take care of yourself."

"You didn't have much schooling?" he asked her. Lina shook her head. "Well, then, that's my point! You take care of yourself, don't you?"

Lina laughed. "Charley Marr, you'll drive me to distraction! I can see where that mind of yours is headed, but you're wrong. I've had to work since I was your age. I'm lucky, I suppose, because numbers come easy for me. I didn't need school for that. But I wish I'd had it, just the same."

"Why?"

"So I could know more about the world. The world's a very big place, Charley. You don't know what might be out there for you."

"Now you sound like Hugh. That's what he said to me before we came here to be with Robert and Jamie."

"When was that?"

"When Father died. I was eight, I think. Mother died when I was born, so I don't remember her. When Father died, Hugh said we could either go back to Scotland to our grandparents, or come to live with Robert and Jamie. I didn't care, but Hugh wanted to come here very much. So we came." Then, rather proud of himself, he added, "So you see, I *do* know something about the world. I've lived in Sleekit, and I've lived in Montreal, and I might have lived in Scotland, too, if we hadn't come here. Can you say as much?"

"Well, I've traveled across the country, walking beside a wagon. I've crossed mountains twice as tall as these, and passed through great deserts. I've seen giant herds of buffalo, and rocks that look like buildings. I've met Indians, and soldiers, and men who hunt for gold. So yes, Charley, I can say as much."

Charley nodded. "Just like I said. You did all that, and school didn't have a thing to do with it." Lina grinned. Then Charley changed the subject. "Maybe you should tell Robert you've done all those things."

"I'm not sure your cousin Robert is much interested in anything I have to say, much less some boring story."

"No, Robert wouldn't care about the stories. He tells better stories than those. Oh, sorry. No offense."

"None taken."

"But if he knew you'd done all those things, maybe he'd hire you like Hugh wants him to do."

"Now how do you figure that?"

"Well, Hugh wants to do things Robert says he doesn't know enough about to do. But how's a fellow supposed to ever learn, if he doesn't get a chance?"

"There I agree with you, Charley."

"So, it just seemed to me that if Robert knew about all the things you've done, he'd see that you know what you're doing. And then he'd hire you, and Hugh could get his wish." Charley grinned. "Then maybe someday, it'll be easier for me to get *my* wish."

Your receipt

Items that you checked out

Title: Breed
ID: 32417043611696
Due: Sunday, March 03, 2019

Title: Brood
ID: 32417044742763
Due: Sunday, March 03, 2019

Title: The appetites of girls
ID: 32417051794129
Due: Sunday, March 03, 2019

Title: What lies west :
ID: 32417051188215
Due: Sunday, March 03, 2019

Total items: 4
Account balance: $0.00
2/10/2019 3:25 PM
Checked out: 4
Overdue: 0
Hold requests: 0
Ready for pickup: 0

Thank you for using the bibliotheca
SelfCheck System.

"Charley, *I* wish it were as simple as that. I don't want to meddle in family business. That's between Robert and Hugh. But if you think it'll help, I'll tell Robert anything he asks about."

When they arrived, Hugh was waiting for them. "Hey, Hugh," Charley called as he clambered down from the wagon and ran toward his brother. "Did you know Lina's killed buffalo? And that she traveled with the Army, and panned for gold, and…."

"Whoa there, Charley," Lina said. "You're not remembering those stories right."

Hugh laughed. "Fine, Charley, fine. You can tell me all about it later." Hugh affectionately held the boy in front of him, hands resting lightly on his shoulders. "Everything's laid out for you in the tent. The men'll be back around sunset. Jamie, Charley and I, we're heading out for our favorite fishing spot, as soon as the day's done, so we won't see you again. But Robert will be coming to see you get back to town safely."

"He's not going fishing with you?" Lina asked.

Hugh hesitated. "Well, um, no. He *says* he wants to spend the night in town, but to be honest, I think he's just a bit nervous about leaving you to get back to town so late."

Lina looked at Charley again. "I see. I guess he doesn't have any reason to think I can make it on my own, does he?"

"See? I told you, Lina," Charley said.

"Told her what?" Hugh asked.

"Nothing, Hugh. Really. You two go on, now. I know how excited Charley is." Lina watched as the two hurried down the trail racing each other, until they disappeared beyond the bend.

Just as Hugh promised, the men returned late that afternoon. They were paid and long gone, and Lina was checking her figures, when Robert Marr entered the tent.

With no other greeting, he said, "So, you're finished, then?"

"Yes," she answered, offering him the ledger. "You'll want to check my work."

"That'll have to wait," he said. "There's only about an hour of daylight left. We should leave now."

Spring was warming the days, but they rode with the setting sun. Lina felt the last of winter's chill, and pulled her wrap tighter.

"Another hour and we'll be there," Robert said quietly.

"I'm fine."

"Used to the cold, are you? Where was it you said you came from?"

"Missouri. Yes, there's likely snow on the ground back there right now."

"I come from Canada. Montreal. I imagine there's snow there as well. To be honest, I don't miss it."

"The snow or Montreal?"

"What?"

"I meant, do you not miss the snow, or not miss Montreal?"

"Come to think of it, neither!" he laughed. "You? Do *you* miss the snow? Do *you* miss Missouri?"

This time, Lina laughed. "Neither." They shared a brief smile, but soon lapsed into another silence, this one more expectant than awkward. Finally, Robert spoke.

"You know, Miss Morgan, I should be quite put out with you."

Lina's back stiffened. "Why?"

"You seemed to have put all sorts of notions in Charley's mind. About not needing school, that is."

"Charley has notions enough without my help. I promise, I did my best to change his mind."

"With your stories about your trip west? Miss Morgan, you've got a lot to learn about what not to suggest to an eleven-year-old boy." He chuckled softly, and she felt more at ease.

"I probably do, at that. But I did my best."

"Charley spent a good part of the afternoon bending my ear about you. He wanted to make certain I understood you had all sorts of adventures, and probably knew a lot more than I gave you credit for. He said you wouldn't brag on yourself unless I asked you about it. So, I guess I'm asking."

Lina shook her head. "I'm sorry he bothered you, Mr. Marr. As you know he's nearly as determined as his brother to come work with you. You don't have to ask, just because Charley put you up to it." Lina hesitated, but then spoke again. "But I do want to say something. I think you and I, well, we sort of started off wrong, and I suppose I'm to blame for that. I shouldn't have been so stubborn with you that first time at camp. Refusing to believe who you said you were, well, that was silly. At least it seems silly now. But I very much wanted to prove that I could be trusted. I realize you might not want me here, or need me for that matter. But if you ever should, I mean, even once in a while…"

"Miss Morgan," Robert interrupted. "I didn't ask because Charley put me up to it. I asked because I want to know."

"Oh, I see. What would you like to know?"

"Why you're here."

"You mean, why I came here?"

"No. I know why you came—because of Kincaid's offer. But you didn't like that offer much, did you?"

"Well, it didn't seem the best of prospects."

"So the answer is no. It's not for Kincaid's offer that you're still here. That alone speaks to your common sense. You do chores for Meg, for which you get only room and board. And I've been plain enough about our interest in hiring you. You've probably looked around at a few other places, but found there isn't much else in Sleekit that folks need doing. So I have to ask myself, Miss Morgan. Why does a woman with no imminent prospects, and apparently no familial ties, stay in a mud trap such as this? Why not move on, try your luck somewhere else?"

Lina thought hard for a while. She hadn't considered that option, but there it was. Sure, she might fall back a bit in her position. She might have to spend a little money to relocate again, but what if there was a better prospect out there? She had heard talk about other settlements along the sound, several much bigger than Sleekit. But as she thought about it, the reason came to her. "I like it here," she answered.

"You do?" Robert seemed shocked. "Why, in heaven's name?"

"Why? Don't you like it here? Isn't this better than Montreal?"

"I'm asking you."

"Because it's better than any place I've been. Folks are nicer. It's, I don't know. It's just that…well, it may sound strange, but I feel… I feel at home here."

Robert looked at her and smiled, and the smile stayed with him long after he had turned his attention back to the road. Nothing more was said between them until they arrived in front of Sweet Meg's. Robert pulled the team to a stop, jumped down from the wagon, then came around to help Lina.

"Thank you, Mr. Marr. I'm sure you would have rather stayed with the others."

"To tell the truth, I'm looking forward to the relative comfort, and tonight the rare solitude, of the cabin. I'll join them tomorrow."

"Still, I thank you for the kindness. Goodnight."

"Miss Morgan?" he said as she started to leave.

"Yes?"

"Don't you want your pay?"

"Oh, yes! Of course. Thank you."

Robert handed her the money. "Listen, Miss Morgan. I don't want you to think I don't appreciate your good work. I do. It's just that, well, this is a hard business, and we can't afford to make commitments we can't honor. I've made promises enough as it is." Lina expected yet another reminder that Marr Logging wouldn't be hiring her. Then Robert said something unexpected. "I can't offer you anything regular, mind you. But if you're agreeable, we might call upon you from time to time to help us. From time to time, you understand."

"I do understand. And I would very much be agreeable to such an arrangement."

"Well, then. Fine. That's fine. Then I'm sure we'll be seeing one another soon. Until then."

"Until then." He had boarded the wagon, and was just turning it around when she added, "Thank you."

With his back to her, riding away, a wave was his only reply.

****

Robert joined his family the next day, as planned, but only to bring them back to town. "There's too much to do to be idling about up here," he said. "I've made plans, and there's much to be done." Riding back to town, he told them of his change of heart regarding Hugh. "It may be a busy year, boys. I suspect we'll see more settlers moving into these parts, which means building. Folks will be needing lumber, which means Kincaid will be getting richer. Why shouldn't we have a piece of it? More settlers mean more ships too, of course. Ships will need cargo to fill empty hulls. Before winter comes again, I expect a lot of changes around here. We might as well start planning for them."

The boys were enthusiastic about this news, but every time their exuberance rose, Robert was quick to remind them that all this just meant more work. "Hugh, you've still a lot to learn about heading up a crew. But I guess you'll have to learn it as you go. And Jamie, that means for the time being Hugh gets the best men. He'll need the help. You'll have to work harder with the others. Teach 'em what you know, Jamie. That's what I'll be trying to do with my crew. They'll catch on. It will slow us down at first, but it's the only way to get more done in the long run. I see that now. And Charley, you'll have sacrifices to make, too. Hugh won't be there to look after you, to make sure you tend to your lessons and mind the Minifees. We'll all be depending on you, boy. Yes, there'll be sacrifices to be made all the way around. Jamie, you'll no doubt have less time to spend with that sweetheart of yours. So get working on that cabin right away, if you expect to be able to finish it before the wedding."

By the time Robert was done making sure everyone understood the sacrifices that would be called for, the high spirits were kicked right out of them. Once back in town, Hugh and Charley couldn't get away from the cabin fast enough. Robert started to protest, reminding them yet again of all the work ahead. "We should get started now," he said, sitting at the table with papers and maps spread all about.

"Robert, it's just one more evening," Jamie said, as his cousins bounded out the cabin door. "They're off to have a bit of fun. Me too, for that matter."

"Jean, is it?" Robert asked. "Ah, you're right, of course. Go off, then, and have your fun. I expect I'll head over to Meg's in a bit myself."

As Robert gathered his papers, Jamie started to clean up. A small dingy mirror hung from a single nail above the wooden bowl. As Jamie shaved, he watched his brother in the reflection. Robert stacked the papers, carefully reviewing each one before he put it in the pile. He was a study in concentration. Jamie admired that in his brother. Once possessed of an idea, Robert would be the last man to give it up.

"What was it, Robert? What made you change your mind?"

"Change my mind about what?"

"About letting Hugh work. About trusting him."

"I've always trusted him, Jamie. That's not it. It's just that I needed Hugh to do other work."

"But now you don't?"

"I won't lie. If I had my way, we wouldn't be trying this yet. Not just yet."

"Then why?"

"It was something that Miss Morgan said."

Jamie chuckled. "Lina? What could she have said that we haven't been saying for months now?"

"Oh, she didn't talk me into it. That wasn't it. No, I asked her why she stayed here, with no prospects for work. She said that she wanted to stay because she *liked* it here. Simple as that."

Jamie turned, wiping his freshly shaven face with a cloth. "And that made you change your mind?"

Robert leaned back into the chair as Jamie took his clean shirt off the peg on the wall. "When I came here, I came because I knew it was where I belonged. I know that sounds odd, but it's true. You don't remember, of course, but when I was a boy, and father returned from his trip out here, he came back with the most fantastic stories. Trees hundreds of feet tall. Dark, misty islands in deep waters. A whole world painted in deep greens and dewy light. A world peopled with Indians, trappers, mountain men, sailors—incredible characters. Somehow I knew this was the place for me. I suppose I took advantage of Father's love of the place, otherwise, he'd have never have let me leave school. But he wished me well, and sent me on my way. It was rough going, but I've never looked back.

"With Hugh it was different. Hugh was always a sort of laggard. He's smart as a whip, but he never did well in school. Uncle Malcom had him in line for the finest positions the Hudson's Bay Company had to offer, but none of that seemed to interest him. When he showed up here, I didn't expect him to stay. But stay he has. I wondered why, until Lina Morgan answered the question for me. Hugh *likes* it here. I must admit, he seems more dedicated in this endeavor than any I'd heard of before. He deserves his chance, the same as I had mine."

Jamie had finished dressing while Robert talked. He thought for a while when Robert finished, and then spoke.

"Robert, do you remember why you came to Uncle Malcom's to bring me here?"

"Of course. Malcom Marr was a brute and a bully, and would have ruined your life. Besides, you were my brother! My only family, once father died. I wanted you with me."

"Uncle Malcom would've ruined Hugh and Charley's lives, too. I'd been living in that house a long while before you came. I saw what he had done to Hugh. Hugh would have given anything to leave."

"I suppose he would have."

"So with people like Hugh, getting away from a place can be just as much of a dream as coming to a place, like it was for you. Lina Morgan's like Hugh. I don't know much about her, but I have a feeling she came here, not so much expecting to find something as to get away from something. That she found something here, that Hugh found something here, something they like, why, that's a surprise they didn't expect. You expected to find happiness here. They didn't. In a way, that makes them particularly dedicated to making a go of it here, don't you see?"

Robert nodded. "I do now."

"Goodnight, Robert," Jamie said as he headed toward the door.

"Jamie?"

"Yes?"

"What about you? What makes you happy here?"

Jamie smiled wistfully. "Me? Why, Jean, of course." Then he left.

****

It was mid-March in San Francisco, and the bustling town was just emerging from the cold, rainy winter. Commotion was everywhere, particularly along the waterfront. Ships were readying to sail on journeys too arduous for winter, and returning from the ports of the southern hemisphere where winter would soon begin. And Edward Haarten was prepared to make the most of every shipment coming in and out of port. He stood on the deck of the Rosalea as she sailed into the bay that morning, feeling as lighthearted as he knew how to be, surveying the thriving Gomorrah before him.

When affairs at the Rosalea were settled and the first mate had been given his orders, Haarten headed home. His arrivals were always unexpected, so while the household was generally ready to receive him at all times, Jackson was still unprepared to see him coming through the door. Had he all the time in the world, Jackson doubted he would ever be prepared to tell Captain Haarten the news he had waiting for him.

"Good morning, Jackson, it's good to be back," Haarten said when he met him in the foyer.

"Yes, sir, very good to have you home, sir," Jackson was frantically trying to collect his thoughts and choose his words. "Uh, excuse me, sir, but I…."

Haarten sighed. "Jackson, I'm certain there are many household details that need my attention. There always are." Haarten collected his seaman's case and headed toward the study. "I don't have time to meet with every member of the staff. Have Miss Clark bring all the matters to me in an hour." Haarten stepped into the study.

He had barely situated himself at the desk when he looked up and saw Jackson standing in the doorway. "Yes?" Haarten asked impatiently.

"Sir, it's Miss Clark. She's not at home. In fact, sir, no one has seen her since you left, sir. We've been frightfully concerned some misfortune befell her, particularly since Mrs. Spear disappeared that same evening." Jackson proceeded to recount all known events to the Captain. That Lina had returned from the party, went to her room and was never seen again. That no one suspected anything until the next morning when the maids told him the housekeeper was missing. That when he sent a girl to Lina's room to tell her about Mrs. Spear, the girl found Lina gone as well. The authorities had been summoned, and a brief investigation held, but they found no trace of either woman, nor had any unclaimed bodies appeared in the interim.

Edward slowly sat back in the big leather chair as Jackson spoke. He lit a cigar and listened. *No, no trace and no bodys*, he thought, *nor would there be. She wasn't dead. She's escaped. Or thinks she has.*

"Thank you, Jackson. Please send word to the detective in charge. I would like to see him as soon as possible."

The detective had little more to offer than what Jackson had recounted. One woman had been spotted leaving the area that evening in a hired carriage, a carriage which was also seen later that night in the vicinity of the docks, but only briefly. *She's clever,* thought Haarten. *She used the opportunity of my distraction to her advantage, and she knew she'd have time before I could begin to look for her.*

Haarten spent much of the next two weeks using his usual moles and agents. He sent his spies to check Lina's few acquaintances and the places she frequented, but learned nothing. He told them to get a list of every ship that had sailed that night and for the next several days, but the list was long and the ports where she might be by now covered the globe. It would be months before some of these ships would return here, if at all, and it would take some time for him to check each one.

All this he did as circumspectly as possible. Publicly, he played the role of the concerned betrothed, fearing the worst but bravely continuing the search. After his return, many of his society friends called on him, or sent their concerns by way of letter. To anyone who asked, he simply told them that the police were continuing their investigation, and he was hopeful that there would be good news any day.

People disappeared all the time in San Francisco. Some were waylaid, others murdered, and a few were shanghaied. But these things rarely happened among the prominent citizenry, so Lina's disappearance was the subject of considerable speculation before Haarten returned. Some men thought she had deserted the son-of-a-bitch, while others thought she might have run away with a lover. Some ladies spoke in hushed tones from their own fears, that she had been violated, then tossed into the bay and washed out to sea. But after Haarten returned and all his social acquaintances had extended their sympathies, they soon began to avoid the subject altogether in his presence, out of a genuine sympathy for his loss. He seemed so preoccupied now, and certainly bereft.

Haarten's only bereavement was at the loss of attention he was able to pay his first love, his empire. Each day that he learned nothing more of Lina's whereabouts made him increasingly angry with her, and himself. He should have known she would try to leave, but he never expected it would be so soon. A plan of escape takes time, and he had only told her of his trip a few days before departing. So in order for her to manage such an escape, she would need assistance. Undoubtedly that was the role Mrs. Spear had played. But he was no more able to learn of the housekeeper's fate than Lina's.

So Edward Haarten's efforts to find Carolina Clark became a part of his routine. In between his morning lists, his afternoon errands and his evening socials with business associates, he kept a constant stream of underlings searching San Francisco for any trace of her whereabouts.

27

Despite its disorganized appearance, its near isolation, and its lack of recognized legitimacy by any but those who inhabited it, this place into which Lina had stumbled, this settlement called Sleekit, was indeed a community with all the customary rituals. Its inhabitants and neighbors with their sometimes contradictory backgrounds and predilections of nature had come together and, already in their brief collective history, established an aggregation of traditions that suited them just fine. For one, the wall of Minifee's store served as the local newspaper, where notices of all sorts—births, weddings and deaths, a horse for sale, a note left by someone passing through hoping it would be spotted by someone they were looking for—were nailed right to the clapboards. Then there was Martin Kincaid's horse, which he kept in a stall at the mill. The horse was available to anyone who needed him, provided they dropped two bits into the box outside. But of all the curious Sleekit customs, to Lina the most curious was Sunday service.

The one institution that Martin Kincaid had been unable to establish was a church, though he had offered to build one. He told the locals that because it was a church, he would ask no interest on the loan, only their names to a contract to help pay back the cost over time. He felt he'd been more than generous in his offer. The townsfolk laughed in his face.

So Sunday service came to be held at Sweet Meg's, a setting which necessitated certain informalities. Tables were shoved to the far corner, and all the chairs were lined up facing the bar, which served as the pulpit. Services would begin whenever folks arrived, but rarely before late morning. Meg played the piano, with enthusiasm if not proficiency. She knew a few hymns, but her religious repertoire was limited, so often she just played a favorite ballad. No matter, for it was the consensus of the congregation that a voice lifted joyfully in any song was just as much praise to God as any hymn.

There was no shepherd for the flock. After the music, someone would stand before the gathering and read from scripture or perhaps just say a few thoughts. Anyone was welcome, but there were regulars. Already twice, Lina heard a farmer named Harris. He more lectured than preached, on the growing "Indian problem," as he called it, but he did weave in some Bible passages. He was not a favorite, but the congregants seemed to tolerate any opinion, however ill-conceived or poorly delivered, as long as it was brief. Martin Kincaid was a frequent speaker, and his lectures always had the same theme—thrift, industry, and God's bounty. But the best speech Lina had heard so far came from a trapper whose name she never learned. He told a long story about being up north, where he encountered a gigantic grizzly. He described the beast in fervid detail, gave drama to his narrow escape, and peppered the rest with digressing references to other exploits. He finished by saying, "It was a mighty humblin' experience, let me tell ya, and I just wanted to thank God for letting me slip outta the varmint's clutches."

This particular Sunday was the first it had not rained since Lina came to Sleekit. The prospect of a sunny day had everyone planning on a picnic after services, Lina included. Jean had asked her the day before, and Lina said yes for several reasons. She said yes to the chance to see more of the country around Sleekit. She said yes because she liked Jean, Jamie and Hugh. All were easy and pleasant company. Millie, frankly, she could take or leave, but Jean liked her, and Millie was mostly tolerable when in Jean's company. And Lina said yes to the picnic because of Robert. He had made her a vague offer of future opportunity, but nothing else had been forthcoming. She worried he might have forgotten, or perhaps had only made the offer as a polite gesture. She hoped to have a chance to speak with him, thinking that might prompt him to hire her again. At the very least, perhaps if he got to know her a bit better, he might be more likely to think of her as someone upon whom he could count.

The services that day were well attended. The beautiful morning invited everyone out. The room was warm. Two older men sat in the back quietly snoring, a sound that made Lina just a little drowsy herself as she listened to Martin Kincaid drone on about the merits of diligence and hard work.

He finished and returned to his seat. Lina hoped that would be the end of it, for she needed fresh air to rouse herself. No sooner had Kincaid returned to his chair, however, than Robert Marr walked to the pulpit. He laid a small blue book on the bar and opened it. He scrutinized the page, and then, looking to his audience, he spoke.

"I read this last night, and I thought I'd share it with you. It's by a fellow named Wordsworth, oddly enough. William Wordsworth. It's a poem." Some men grumbled, but with a smile Robert continued. "Now, it's a short poem, boys, I promise. Then we can go out and enjoy this beautiful day." He began to read.

> *"It is a beauteous evening, calm and free,*
> *The holy time is quiet as a Nun*
> *Breathless with adoration; the broad sun*
> *Is sinking down in its tranquility;*
> *The gentleness of heaven broods o'er the Sea;*
> *Listen! the mighty Being is awake,*
> *And doth with his eternal motion make*
> *A sound like thunder – everlasting.*
> *Dear Child! dear Girl! that walkest with me here,*
> *If thou appear untouched by solemn thought,*
> *Thy nature is not therefore less divine:*
> *Thou liest in Abraham's bosom all the year;*
> *And worship'st at the Temple's inner shrine,*
> *God being with thee when we know it not."*

He closed the book and walked back to his seat. Meg struck up a final hymn, and the choir joined in. But the only music Lina heard was the echo of that poem. She wanted the room to be quiet, hoping that in that stillness, she might still be able to hear those words. Even now, with Meg playing in the background, the memory of that reading was more beautiful than any song she could remember. Lina had tried to appreciate the poetry she borrowed from Barclay's shelves, but the meaning was always beaten out by the rhythm, the phrases strangled by the form. Robert Marr read this poem so smoothly, so naturally, its meaning came alive. His words seemed to reach out to her, to assure her, as if he had intended them just for her, yet she knew he did not. Still, as the poem had said, God was sometimes with you when you did not know it.

Suddenly, the service was over, and everyone was standing. Jean tugged at Lina's arm. "Are you ready, Lina? Get your basket." Meg had prepared something for her to take so she wouldn't have to inflict her own meager cooking on her friends. She found the basket and walked outside.

The rest of the group was already assembled into two wagons. Robert sat on the buckboard of the first wagon, and Jamie and Jean were piled in the back with the food. "Oh, Lina!" came Millie's shrill little voice from the next wagon. "Oh, Lina! Won't you ride with us?"

Jean leaned over and whispered to Lina. "Millie's trying for Hugh this month!" she giggled. "I think she's hoping you'll keep Charley busy. Do you mind?"

Lina just smiled, and walked toward Millie. "I'd love to," she said, as Hugh helped her in. Millie sat next to Hugh on the seat. "I'd sit back there with you, but I've never grown accustomed to riding like that," Millie said over her shoulder. "But I figured you'd have no problem, what with all that way you came, on the trail, I mean."

Lina rolled her eyes at Millie, but didn't count on Charley noticing. He giggled, but she changed the subject. "Are we going very far?" she asked him.

"Not far," said Charley, "A couple of miles, maybe. It's pretty. There's a stream, and it makes a pond in this one place. And there're lots of animals there, too!"

"What kinds of animals?"

Charley leaned closer to avoid his brother's hearing. "Possum, raccoons, beaver, those kinds. It's my favorite part of going there."

"You like the animals, do you?"

"Oh, yes! I love to watch them, see how they live, watch them eat." In a whisper, he added, "I feed them. Robert tells me not to. He says it's not nature's way, but I do it anyway. After we eat, and everyone gets

sleepy, I go off by myself. If I can, I sneak some of the food to them."
He was grinning. "You won't tell, will you?"

Lina answered with a wink. Charley seemed satisfied.

The picnic spot was just as Charley had described. About a mile
and a half from town, in a part of the woods Lina had never been,
beside a stair step stream, in a grove of small woodland trees hidden
within the deeper forest. Through these thinner trees, the mid-day sun
dappled the rocks beneath them, making them warm to the touch. The
sound of cool water was an invitation to linger.

It fell to the ladies to set out the meal, while the men retreated
from sight. Lina helped Millie and Jean spread some blankets, and
then unload boxes of chicken, biscuits and other morsels from Esther
Minifee's kitchen, including one of her popular apple pies. Just out of
view, they could hear the men laughing amid the splashing of water.

"What are they doing?" Lina finally asked Jean.

"Swimming."

Millie giggled. "Not just swimming!" She leaned forward, and with
a wide-eyed whisper, added. "They like to go swimming in the all-
together!" She giggled some more.

Jean blushed. "Millie, you don't know that. You haven't seen them,
have you?"

"Of course not! Have you?" Jean shook her head, her eyes wide,
too. Millie continued. "Tell the truth, Jean. Aren't you just the teensiest
bit curious?"

"Heavens no, Millie! What would make you say such a thing?" The
poor young girl could not possibly have blushed any redder.

"Well, you *are* going to marry him, aren't you? Don't you sometimes
wonder…." Millie was not quite sure what it was she wondered, but
she wondered, and she supposed all girls did.

Jean smiled, "Well, perhaps. Just a bit." The two broke into more
giggles.

"How about you, Lina? Aren't you the least bit curious?"

"Not in the slightest. I already know." She had not meant it as a
revelation, just a simple statement of fact, but when the girls stopped
giggling she noticed the look of shock on their faces, and realized she
had said more than she needed.

"When? How? Where?" The girls clamored for more. Lina decided there was no reason to lie about Ephraim.

"I was married. Back in Missouri. He's dead."

"Oh, you poor dear!" said Millie. "I had no idea. How you must grieve. But what was it like?"

In that instance, Lina ached to burst the bubble of Millie's romantic notions, but the Marr men were returning. Jean quickly changed the subject. "Anyone hungry?" she called to them. The men answered by sitting down on the blankets, hair still dripping from the swim, and plunging into the feast.

Soon it was the lazy part of the afternoon, the hour of the day when time floats slowly on breezes that whisper and carry the sweet musk of the woods. Charley had wandered off, to be with his animals, Lina assumed. Robert was stretched out on a rock and deep into an afternoon nap. Jamie and Jean sat close and shared a private, sweetheart talk. Millie chattered to Hugh, who looked toward Lina with the eyes of a trapped animal. She chuckled as she leaned back against a tree and closed her eyes, content to listen as their chatter mimicked the trickle of the nearby stream. Before she knew it, she was lost in a light sleep.

She did not nap long. When she opened her eyes, she saw the others dozing where they had sat. Jean was curled up casually against Jamie's arm, a contented smile on her lips. Hugh slept on the blanket in the sun, snoring lightly, as did Millie, who had an unbecoming bit of drool on her lips. Robert was nowhere in sight.

Lina rose quietly. She thought this might be her chance to find Robert, to talk to him, so she walked toward the stream. But soon she was lost in discovering the wilderness around her. She had been raised where rivers ran flat and still, and the woods brimmed with maples, oaks and elms. Those rivers had seemed big, those trees tall and thick, and the hills of Missouri had always broken the horizon and filled her youthful landscape with the promise of something beckoning just beyond. But this place made those horizons, those thick woods and wide rivers seem humble. Today, for the first time she was in the forest, beyond the vague boundaries of Sleekit, and now she noticed the small, subtle differences of the place. She listened to birdcalls she had never heard before and the sound a stream makes when it dances down rocks. She marveled at the trees that filled the forests, not just the mighty fir and spruce that dominated, but the sycamore and aspen that filled out the spaces in between. The wildflowers too, seemed larger, and more vibrant. And under the canopy of the trees, there were ferns, some as tall as she, standing lush, heavy and fertile in the deep shade.

She had walked as far as the pool and had seen no sign of Robert. By then, finding him didn't seem to matter as much. All her sense of urgency was far away, and for now it was enough just to be a part of this place. This was an ancient world. The rocks on which she sat as she dangled her feet in the pool were gray-black, solid, eternal—not the chalky limestone of Missouri, or the desert's sandstone. This stone was hard and true, like the Sierra Nevadas had seemed to her at first, until she saw the tailings, the crumbled rock, and the silt that signaled their sure decline.

"Have you seen Charley?" Lina hadn't heard Robert come from behind, but somehow, his soft voice so blended with the music around her that she was not startled.

"No," she answered over her shoulder. "Not since I fell asleep."

"Off feeding those animals, I suspect," he said.

She smiled. "You're not supposed to know about that, you know."

"Ah, don't worry," he said, as he stretched out on a rock next to her. "A boy ought to have some secrets from his family, don't you think?"

"Mmm. I suppose so." She was content just to sit there, slowly waving her feet through the ripples of the water, listening to the birds and the breezes. Robert said nothing to break the serenity.

When she looked at him, he was propped up on one elbow with his long legs stretched out before him, eyes closed but his face turned skyward, letting the dappled sunlight warm him. He was the very picture of contentment.

"I liked your poem very much," she said.

"Hmm?" He said, not moving.

"Your poem? This morning at services? I liked it very much."

He raised his head and smiled. "Oh you did, did you? I'm glad."

"What was the line?" she asked. "About the mighty being?"

"*Listen! The mighty Being is awake, and doth with his eternal motion make a sound like thunder - everlasting.*"

She thought through the words. "I hear that," she said. "I hear that 'sound like thunder'."

He raised himself up to look at her. "What do you mean?"

"I hear it. Here. In this place. This spot. The road to camp. Along the water. I hear it everywhere around Sleekit."

He looked up the mountain, deep into the forest. "You should hear it up in the high country," he said, lying back again.

With calculated intent, she answered. "I'd like that, very much. Perhaps, next time you send me to camp, I could come with the crews to the timber. Into the mountains…"

She wondered if perhaps he had heard her, or if he had fallen asleep again, for he said nothing for a long while. Then, without opening his eyes or showing any other sign of life, he let out a long sigh, and spoke. "Miss Morgan, I will give you this much. You are nothing if not tenacious."

"Well, I only thought…"

"I know. You only thought if you mentioned it, perhaps I might be reminded."

"Yes."

"Very well, then. Consider me reminded. And please don't bother to do so again. I won't forget." He had never moved, never so much as fluttered an eyelash during the entire exchange. His talent for tranquility amazed Lina, who had always considered herself a bit fidgety. "But as to the high country, I should be honest with you," Robert said, slowly sitting upright. "If you ever do come to camp again, I can't have you going off with the crews."

"Why not?"

"It's a business we're running, Miss Morgan. A visitor would just be in the way."

"A *female* visitor."

He shook his head. "Any visitor, Miss Morgan, who is ill-prepared for the wilderness. And yes, before you start arguing with me, I know all about your talents. Charley has told me all about your westward adventures. You are not wholly unprepared, I'll grant you. If it's any comfort to you, I'd sooner it be you than Jean or Millie Forbes. But I can't afford the risk. There's no reason for me to."

"Except for the everlasting thunder."

"I beg your pardon?"

"From the poem. The mighty being and the everlasting thunder? You said you could especially hear it up there."

"Well, Miss Morgan, that's true. Perhaps *someday*, someday mind you, you'll get to hear the everlasting thunder up there. But not yet."

"I won't stop asking, you know," Lina said with a grin.

"I've no doubt about that," he said, chuckling. "You're a sleekit lass, for certain."

"What do you mean?"

Finally, he sat up and focused his attentions on her. "Do you know why this place is called Sleekit?"

Lina shrugged. "No. It sounded like an Indian name to me."

He shook his head. "It's Scottish," he said.

"Really? What does it mean?"

"Sly, cunning. Like that." He thought for a moment then chuckled. "A while back, Kincaid came into Sweet Meg's with another one of his grand ideas. He wanted to name this place after our illustrious new President. Thought that would, oh, I don't know, make the place a real town or something. Maybe make the President grateful? Who knows? It seemed a silly idea to me at the time—still does. I told him he couldn't possibly think of changing the name of the place! Well, he was quite shocked at this, because, you know, he believes he's the one who created this place, as if it didn't even exist before he showed up. It certainly did exist. To the Nisqually, the Duwamish, all the tribes of course. I don't like his presumption. So I told him the place was a sacred Indian place called Sleekit. I told some nonsense about what it meant, like 'home of the sacred one' or something. Gave him a bit of a lecture about hallowed ground and all that. Sent him off into the night mumbling to himself, I'll tell you. A grand sight it was. I didn't think anyone else at Meg's took it seriously. Never thought of it again. But the name seemed to stick. And I can tell you, I was feeling more than a wee bit sleekit that night." They both grinned. "That's what I meant. As my father might have said, "You're a sleekit lass, you are.""

Suddenly they heard a shrill scream, abruptly ended with a muffled thump, just out of sight. "Charley," Robert whispered, and was off in a dash. Lina started to put on her boots, but grabbed them instead and tried to follow him, barefoot, along the stream's rocky bank. When she caught up with him, he was bent over the young boy who lay unconscious beneath a large tree.

"Charley! Charley!" Robert was yelling and shaking the boy, trying to wake him, and although his voice was strong and calm, Lina could see the worry in his expression.

"Don't shake him," she said calmly, thinking of a broken neck, but not saying the words. Just then, Charley opened his eyes, although he seemed disoriented. There was a large gash above his right eye, a smaller one above his lip, and now blood was pooling in his eye and running into his mouth. Charley was suddenly aware of the blood, and panic came into his eyes.

"What's the matter?" he said. "Am I hurt bad?"

"No, Charley, no." Robert said, letting out a sigh. "You fell."

Lina said, "Here," at the same moment she reached under her skirt and tore a strip off her petticoat. "It's not as bad as it looks, Charley," Lina said calmly. "A cut on the head bleeds a lot, because the skin's so thin there." Then she smiled, and added, "And in your case, because your head's so hard." Charley smiled.

Lina reached over to the stream and dipped the torn muslin in the water. Then she started wiping blood from Charley's forehead.

"Charley," Robert asked calmly. "Don't make any sudden moves, but do you think you've broken anything, boy? Anything hurt?"

Charley seemed to be taking an inventory, although he stayed very still. Then, cautiously, he wiggled his legs and moved his hands just a bit. "No. I don't think anything's broken. I'm a little dizzy, though."

Just then, they heard the voices of the others charging up the hill toward them. "Charley?" hollered Hugh. "Charley? Robert? Where are you?" Hugh and the others called out as they came closer. Hugh was the first to reach Charley's side. "What happened?"

"I was climbing that tree, to look into that nest up there. I don't remember what happened, exactly. I must have lost my grip or something." Hugh gave him a quick smile, then anxiously looked to Robert, who, with nothing more than the right nod told Hugh everything was fine.

Finishing the unspoken thought between them, Robert said, "But we should be getting him back right away. He needs to rest, and we'll need to keep an eye on him."

Jean and Millie headed back down the hill to gather the picnic things, while Jamie and Hugh went to fetch the wagons. Lina took one last bit of the muslin she'd torn to make a quick bandage for Charley's head. "Now, don't you look the adventurer!" she smiled, smoothing his hair from his forehead. "You'll have quite a tale to tell your friends, won't you?"

"Well, I would, if I could remember any of it," he said smiling despite his swelling lip.

"Ah, Charley," she said, holding his hand. "You're a Marr, after all. You can come up with a tale, I have no doubt."

Robert laughed. "Charley, I think she has us figured out, eh? There's no fooling *her* anymore."

When the teams got back to Sleekit, Robert and Hugh took Charley straight to their cabin, while Jamie deposited Millie, Jean and Lina at Minifee's. "I hope Charley's alright," Jean said.

"Oh, my heavens, yes!" Millie said. "I'll excuse him at school, of course. Tell Charley not to worry, I'll send his lessons home to him."

"If there's anything you need, or Charley needs, just let me know," said Jean to Jamie. She gave him a quick kiss. "I'll let you get back to him. I know you won't be happy unless you do."

As he climbed back into the wagon, Lina added, "Yes, Jamie. Please, you know I'll be happy to help any way I can." Jamie gave a quick wave and a smile, and headed home.

****

Word from Robert Marr came to Lina the next morning, by way of Hugh. It was not the word she had hoped for. "Robbie's wanting to know if you would sit with Charley today. Just until we're sure there's no cause for concern." Before she could answer, he added, "Robbie said to tell you we'll pay you."

She was surprised and hurt by the offer, but realized she had no one to blame but herself. *What else could he think, given all we've ever discussed?* "No need, Hugh. I'd be happy to, of course. Anything I can do to help."

Charley woke briefly when she first arrived. "Lina's going to look after you today. Is that alright?" Hugh asked, sitting on the side the bunk.

"Sure." Charley answered. "Can she fix me something to eat?"

Hugh and Lina laughed. "Well, that's a good sign, a healthy appetite," she said. "I would hate to ruin it with my cooking, Charley. I'm really not very good."

"Don't worry," said Hugh. "There's some stew on the oven from last night. Charley's not very fussy when it comes to food anyway," Hugh said, patting his brother's head. "Just as long as there's plenty of it."

Charley ate the stew, and asked for more, and then drifted back into a peaceful sleep. Lina opened the cabin door to let some fresh air in. She had wondered how she might pass the time watching Charley, but as she looked around the room, she could see there was no lack of work to be done. The floor needed a good sweeping, the men's bunks were unmade, there were dishes to wash, and the table was covered with books and papers. She swept, and washed, and made the beds, then turned her attention to the table. The papers she stacked neatly and she gathered the books to return them to where others stood lined up on the mantel. The last in her pile was the book of Wordsworth's poetry that Robert had read from the day before. She settled in a chair at the table and started to read. She liked this poetry. It spoke of the love of nature, and it seemed romantic, but still very real to her. The language was beautiful, and yet the meaning came through clearly. She was still reading when Hugh returned.

"Ah, another bookworm, I see," he said as he closed the cabin door.

"Another? Oh, you mean your cousin, I suppose. But no, not me. I was just curious," she said, closing the book.

Hugh came over and picked up the book.

"Wordsworth again. I take it that little piece of drama yesterday at Meg's made an impression?"

Lina grinned to think about just how strong an impression it had made. "Yes, well, he *does* read it very well. It was quite moving."

"Aye, well, that's Robbie for ya. A bit of a poet himself, in some ways. How's Charley?"

"Fine. He ate all the rest of the stew, and then went back to sleep. He'll be himself in a day or two, I expect."

Hugh smiled. "Thanks in part to you. He told me how well you took care of him when he fell. Robert mentioned it too. It's not often the boy gets the benefit of a woman's touch." Hugh looked around. "Not to mention what you've done to the place! I suppose we could have cleaned up a bit before…"

"No need. I had the time, that's all."

"Well, we've all benefitted from a woman's touch, and we thank you for it. Now, here…" Hugh reached in his pocket to pay her.

"No, please Hugh. I wouldn't feel right. You needn't hire me for this. This was for my friends, not for hire."

Hugh looked at her like he was about to say something. Then he shook his head and smiled. He picked up the Wordsworth and handed it to her. "Then here," he said. "I know Robbie wouldn't mind if you'd borrow this. You'd like to, wouldn't you?" he said with a grin.

"Thank you, yes I would."

She took the book, and spent the evening reading it. The next day, though the Marrs were all away, she went to their cabin and left the book inside on the table, along with another, and a note.

> *Mr. Marr,*
> *Thank you for the loan of the Wordsworth. If it still interests you, it would please me to give you the book by Mr. Emerson you seemed interested in. No doubt you will take more of his meaning than I would.*
> *Carolina Morgan*

The next morning, when she went downstairs for breakfast, Meg presented her with a surprise of her own—a note left by Robert.

> *Miss Morgan,*
> *Thank you for the Emerson. I will consider it a loan, however, for I would not want you to miss the opportunity of its enjoyment. I have taken it with me, but you may retrieve it when you come to camp Friday next to assist Hugh again with payroll.*
> *R. Marr*

****

It was the last frustrating day in a frustrating week for the Marrs. Charley's accident, while minor, had disrupted the careful routine upon which they had come to depend. The crews were being pressured to work long hours to complete the latest contract. They were short on supplies that wouldn't be replenished until Riordan returned from his next run.

At the end of the long day, Robert sent the crews ahead. He knew they had all earned their pay this week, and he didn't have the heart or the strength to work them a minute longer. An hour behind the others, Jamie, Hugh and Robert returned to camp with the wagon full of gear. Lina and the men were long gone.

Hugh fumbled to find the lantern in the dark. They were all three headed to town, and in a hurry to get there. Jamie was going to see Jean, of course. Hugh was looking forward to the sort of small adventure that inevitably befalls a young man headed to town for a drink, and perhaps some cards. Robert only wanted the drink, and a good dinner, and a good night's sleep. He didn't know whether he envied Hugh's energy or worried for his too often cavalier attitude.

Finally, Hugh lit the lantern. The light revealed an unfamiliar sight—order. The place had been chaos when they left that morning. The disarray was more than the usual level of dishevelment the three lived in while at camp. The pace had been so hectic, none of them had kept up with the accumulated scraps and maps and ledgers of a week's worth of work.

"Well, isn't this a pleasant surprise?" Robert said. There was a pile on each man's bedroll. Whatever clothes or gear or other personal affects had been lying about were stacked on top of the blankets, though not very neatly. The work papers were stacked and sorted, too.

While Robert surveyed the improvements, Jamie picked through his clothes, looking for a proper change of shirt, and Hugh gravitated to the table where he found a note.

"I don't think Lina meant to do *us* the favor by picking up in here." Hugh said. "This note says she picked up so she could get work done. I don't think she was pleased."

"Fancy that," Jamie with a wry smile.

Hugh didn't notice. He was still reading. "Hmm. This is interesting."

"What?" asked Robert.

"She's explaining something she found in the books."

"What do you mean, 'found'?"

"An error, I think. I'm still trying to trace her logic. But I think she may have saved us money."

"Really?" said Robert. "Wonderful!"

Hugh kept reading. "Be sure and thank her when you see her at Meg's."

"Thank her yourself," Robert said. "Let's get going. Jamie?"

"I'm ready. Hugh?"

"What? No. Don't wait. I won't be long, but I want to look at this a bit more before I leave."

"I can't believe it!" Robert laughed. "Hugh Marr, the last man to stop at the end of the day? Very well, and high time, I might add! See you in town." Then he left. Jamie followed, after one look back at his cousin sitting alone in the tent, with the books laid out before him.

Once they got to town, Jamie went off to find Jean, and Robert trudged ahead to the tavern. Someone was playing the piano inside Sweet Meg's, badly. It did not matter, for the noise of the banging hammers on strings could only occasionally be heard above the talk and laughter.

There was to be a wedding the next day. Another girl had responded to Kincaid's handbill a week before. This one was more than happy to learn that there were men willing to marry her, sight unseen. So the newly arrived Miss Clara Ferguson, a small, round, plain, but giggly young girl of sixteen, was to marry Mister Clyde Bush, a taciturn man twice her age who worked as a mill hand for Kincaid. The fact that no one knew the bride, nor cared much for the bridegroom, had not prevented everyone who could from coming to Sleekit for the party following the wedding, now that spring was in full bloom. When Robert pushed through the doors of the tavern, men were lined up two deep at the bar, and every table was taken. Back in the corner, Martin Kincaid sat alone, the last of his dinner and a whiskey before him on the table.

Robert sighed, then pushed through the crowd toward Kincaid. He knew if he didn't, Kincaid would find him, anxious to hear how the week had gone. Robert resolved himself to getting that particular conversation over with, if it gave him a seat away from the crowd. He knew he would have to suffer Kincaid's needling inevitably—he always did. He was used to it by now, and he usually got the better of these exchanges.

"Good evening, Marr," Martin said as Robert sat. "So, how far behind schedule are you?"

"Everything's under control," Robert replied coolly. Kincaid chuckled in refute. "I don't know why you take such delight in our failures, Martin. Your success and mine are tied together."

"True enough. But since I'm the one with the burden of the contract, I have more to lose. Like this contract with the territory that you're falling behind over."

"You won't lose. We'll have that timber to you, next week, as promised."

"Marr," Kincaid said, leaning closer, "you're doing an admirable job, but you may be in over your head. Why not just sell the business to me? You'll make a fair sum, I promise. You can still run the operation, for I'll never find someone as good as you to handle it, and I'll pay you a steady wage in the bargain."

"If you think that sounds like a good deal, just because it's been a hell of a week, you're mistaken, Martin," Robert said. "I'm getting something to drink." Robert rose and turned to go. Just then, he saw Lina. She was squeezing her short frame through a crowd of men nearly twice her size, none of whom paid her any attention. As she made her way, she struggled to keep steady the four glasses of beer she carried. She nearly stumbled as she finally pushed free.

"Easy, there," Robert said, catching her by the arm.

She looked at the hand on her arm, and followed it up to the face. "Mr. Marr! Oh, thank you. I'm sorry. It's quite a night, isn't it? Can I get you something?"

"A beer, thank you."

"Take one of these," she said. "I can't recall who ordered them anyway." She laughed as she deposited the remaining glasses on the nearest available table. With a nod, she moved on, disappearing into the crowd.

"Oh, that's right!" Kincaid remarked, when Robert returned. "I heard about your new employee, Miss Morgan. Quite industrious." Robert's only response was his continued smile. "So industrious, in fact, that I won't be surprised if she doesn't tire of working for you and your paltry sums. Change her mind, perhaps, and take me up on that offer of a laundry."

Suddenly, he was reminded of Hugh. *Thank her when you see her*, Hugh had said. Robert looked around for her, but Lina was lost in the crowd. Hugh, however, was barreling through the door. Hugh did not seem to struggle at all to get past the crowd. His eagerness to get to Robert propelled him. "Wait until you see!" he said, when he reached the table.

"Not now," Robert mumbled, but between Hugh's enthusiasm and the din around them, the nuance was lost on Hugh.

"I figured out what she was talking about."

"What *who* was talking about?" Kincaid interrupted.

"Nothing," said Robert, just as Hugh volunteered.

"Lina Morgan. Anyway, Robbie, it seems I'm not as good at this bookkeeping business as you thought. Perhaps it's fate that's relieved me from the responsibility."

"No one has relieved you, Hugh. Not permanently, at least."

"You'll think differently when I tell you what she's done. She went through those supply lists we've been piling up all week, and she looked through all our books, and do you know what she found? We have supplies stored everywhere. By her count, we've got about a week's worth of food stored at Minifee's and Meg's, combined. And Martin here is storing some of our tools. Did you know that?"

"And you didn't mention it?" Robert said to Kincaid, who shrugged and smiled.

"Well, it's hard to say, but we may have enough to keep us going until the next supply run," Hugh continued. "Some axe blades, some rope, not much mind you, but a few things that could tie us over. Timing couldn't be better. I'd say she earned her keep today. Where is she, by the way? I want to thank her myself." He bounded from his seat, and made a lunge through the crowd.

Kincaid burst into laughter. "Well, well. I must agree about the timing. If she's that good, I might have something for her after all. My office fellow, John Harvey, is leaving in a few weeks. This would give Miss Morgan a real opportunity, don't you think?" He grinned at Marr.

"Lina Morgan has better sense than to sell her soul to you." For the first time in a long time, something Kincaid said had struck a nerve in Robert. But it would never do to let him know that, so Robert quickly added, "But she's free to do as she likes, of course." Robert stood to leave. This night, he felt Kincaid had the upper hand, and he was too tired to stay around and be his whipping boy. Then he had a thought that offered the chance for a small bit of reclaimed victory. "Oh, Martin. Coming to the party tomorrow?"

"Of course. Wouldn't miss it."

"Good. Good. Miss Franny Ellis will be there, you know. I'm escorting her. But if you like, I'll let her save a dance for you, so you can try to wheedle business from her father. See you then." He turned and left, but not before he saw the look of irritation on Kincaid's face, and knew he had evened the score.

****

Finally, Robert found a safe corner. The party had been going on all evening, although he had only been there an hour. They would have arrived sooner, but Hugh was late coming back with Franny and his companion for the evening, a young woman named Alice…something. Robert couldn't remember more, but remembered she seemed pleasant enough. But then, most women seemed to fade into the background next to Franny Ellis, an effect which Franny managed deliberately and strategically. Franny was accustomed to being the center of attention, and didn't suffer well occasions such as this when she was not. Franny Ellis was a tall, willowy blonde whose father owned a sawmill like Kincaid's, only much bigger. In fact, Ellis the town and Ellis the man for whom it was named were bigger in every respect than their Sleekit counterparts. Kincaid considered Ellis his primary competition, and the motivation behind his ambition. Ellis did not consider Kincaid, or Sleekit, as competition at all. Robert had met Ellis and his daughter two years ago, and when he saw how easily goaded Kincaid was by anything and everything about the man, Robert invited Franny to a party in Sleekit, solely for that effect. But Robert had to admit, Franny was beautiful and well-educated. She despised living in this backwater, and said so on every occasion. Clearly, as Robert watched her now from a distance, she found ways to make the most of her situation. There she was, in the center of a circle of young women, Jean and Millie among them. She was holding court, and while Robert could not hear their conversation, he knew from the girls' expressions and Franny's beguiling smile that the flock was showering her with compliments and questions of couture. Franny might entertain them this way for hours, if she didn't become bored with it all.

Robert chuckled. It was another reason why he grudgingly liked Franny. She was smarter than most women. *Not in the same way that Lina Morgan is smart*, he thought. *No, Franny is more... a schemer.* He didn't like to admit it, but he knew it was true. Franny was making a calculated play for him. It was not his vanity that told him that, but his business sense. She had her old man's cunning, and she was his only heir. She would be a fool not to consider a man who owned a good business. Martin Kincaid might have been a candidate, if he had been a bit younger and a bit more appealing. That was what made Robert such a good choice. He had just the right mixture of prospects and charm to qualify.

With Franny attended to by the young ladies, Robert had the chance to do some strategizing of his own. Nestled on the edge of the party, generally out of sight among a small stand of trees, he was searching the crowd for Lina Morgan.

"Good evening, Robert," Esther Minifee said, passing by with a heaping basket of bread. "Wonderful party, isn't it?"

"Perfect," Robert said. He gave her a quick smile, and then returned to his hunt.

"I see you brought Miss Ellis again. She's lovely. You two make a handsome couple."

"Hmm," he responded. "I mean, thank you. She's certainly charmed the girls."

"Oh, I think Jean takes to her because she thinks they might be sisters one day."

"What?" Robert asked. The grin and the wink Esther gave him when he looked at her shocked him. "Oh, no. Please tell Jean for me that she needn't invest herself for that reason."

"Whatever you say," Esther said, grinning. "That's what my Virgil said, too, once upon a time. It's what most men say, I suspect, right before they change their minds."

"Esther, have you seen Lina Morgan?"

"Lina? Not for a while. She helped us get ready all day. Probably so tired, she was headed to bed. Why?"

"Oh, just something I needed to ask her."

"If I see her, I'll tell her you're looking for her. I better get this over to the table. Have a good time, Robert. And give my best to Miss Ellis." Esther scurried off.

Damn, thought Robert. If Lina Morgan had gone to bed, then he had missed his opportunity. But then again, perhaps so had Martin Kincaid. Robert had thought all night and again all day about his conversation with Kincaid concerning Lina. Kincaid never missed an opportunity to needle him, but to be fair, Robert knew he never missed an opportunity to respond in kind. Like this business with Franny. Dangling her in front of Kincaid was as good an excuse for inviting her as Robert needed. But something told him that this time, with Lina, Kincaid was not bluffing. And the work would be appealing to Lina. She would be good at it. Too, Martin Kincaid had the resources to pay her more than the Marrs could afford.

When the nagging thoughts from the night before were still with him in the morning, he had taken the time to look at the books that had so impressed Hugh. Things were just as Hugh had described. Robert was impressed at her patience in the detail it took to find the errors, something he sorely lacked. But what impressed him the most was the initiative. They paid her to disburse the pay. Of her own accord, she had taken the time to go through the mess of their books, their notes, their mishandled entries, and see something important. Robert had enough experience with hiring men to know the value of such a trait. Most of his crew—good, loyal, hard-working men—did exactly as they were told, no more, no less. It was what he needed of them, and had come to expect. But every once in a while, a man would come along who gave more than he got. Robert had learned long ago to value such a man, and as a result, his were among the best crews working. In the same way, Robert resolved he would keep Lina Morgan.

He had his doubts that this would be possible. He couldn't offer more money than Kincaid, nor could he offer her work as steady. But Robert's natural confidence convinced him he had more in his favor than against him. Lina Morgan didn't care for Martin Kincaid. She was polite when she spoke of him, but had been blunt about her estimation of his offers. Robert also saw a clear advantage in Lina's obvious fondness for Jean, Jamie and Hugh. Clearly, they shared a growing friendship. If Lina Morgan felt some loyalty to the Marrs, Robert would welcome that as leverage. Finally, Robert counted on his greatest talent—his charm. Since he was a boy, he'd been keenly aware that he could charm his way into, or out of, most situations. His mother, of course, had been an early conquest, but the same could be said for virtually every woman Robert had met since—and there had been more than a few. But it was more than mere flattery or sweet talk, for men could also be charmed, in a wholly different fashion. Robert had long since lost interest in examining this talent. All he cared about at this moment was that charm was his ace in dealing with Lina Morgan. If only she were here.

Robert looked around the square. It was a grand turnout, considering that few, if any, of the guests were there to honor the recently married couple. Robert guessed there might be a hundred people scattered around the muddy center of Sleekit, as precariously perched here and there as the buildings. Robert searched the groups of faces. Then he looked around for Franny. She was still there, in the circle of femininity, on the stoop of Minifee's store. He tried to see the other side of the square, but the fire was burning low, more ember than flame, and the lingering veil of smoke clung near the damp earth, obscuring his view. His attention was drawn to the musicians, as they started another tune. The dancers were on the other side of the fire, too deep behind the smoke to see clearly. Then, from the corner of his eye, Robert saw a flash of two colors—the deep blue of Martin Kincaid's favorite silk waistcoat, and the red-gold of Lina Morgan's hair. They were there, together, moving into the circle of dancers.

He took off toward them, cursing himself for not having taken the time to plan exactly what he would say. He moved to the other side of the square, where he could watch the two as they began to dance. It was a slow, courtly sort of dance, and Kincaid didn't dance well. Robert grinned. *Another factor in my favor*, he thought, but he wasn't so cock-sure of himself right now. For clearly, Martin Kincaid was talking to Lina Morgan about a serious matter. Neither of them smiled, but she seemed wholly caught up in what he was telling her. The dance was over now, but Kincaid was still talking, and now Lina was nodding, and worse, smiling.

Robert moved as quickly as he dared, without seeming to run. *No good to seem too eager*, he reminded himself as he closed in. That was the last moment of strategy he allowed himself. From here on out, he would have to rely on instinct.

The musicians were beginning a new dance when Robert reached them. Lina looked up just as he was reaching for her hand. With a calculated smile, he said, "Pardon me, Miss Morgan, but I was hoping I might have this dance."

"You're too late," Kincaid whispered out of the side of his mouth, away from Lina's ear.

"Am I?" Marr whispered back, and then flashed another smile toward Lina.

"I beg your pardon?" she asked innocently, thinking he had spoken to her.

"I said, 'May I?'" and he took her hand. He was trying with all his might to seem casual, but secretly he wondered if he was too late. She smiled back and their dance began. The tune was a two-step. Robert couldn't have talked to her while they danced if he'd tried, so he gave Lina Morgan the dance of her young life. He was a fine dancer, having been taught well as a young man. He knew the dance was having the desired affect when he saw the smile on Lina's face. *Such a charming smile*, he thought. *And a fair dancer, too*, he noted with some surprise. He would have thought her too serious a girl to be such a lively dancer.

When the dance stopped, they were both breathless. As the musicians struck up a waltz, Robert held out his hand in silent offer, but Lina shook her head. She brought her hand to her cheek.

"I'm afraid you've taken all my reserves, Mr. Marr," she said. "I'm flushed as it is. Another one would surely finish me off." She laughed.

"The flush in your cheeks becomes you," Robert said, but it was not a calculated compliment. He had to admit as he looked into her open, happy face that Lina Morgan was lovelier this night than he remembered.

"That's kind of you," she said, looking up with a shyness Robert didn't expect. "But I must look a fright. I thank you for the dance, but it's been a long day, and I was planning on retiring."

"Then let me walk you back up to Meg's." Robert took her hand. "I was hoping we could talk for a moment." He looped her hand through his arm.

"What did you want to talk about?"

He said nothing until they were out of the dark and near enough to the tavern that the lanterns inside illuminated her face. He would need to see her face, to know what argument to give—if arguments would be needed. But she turned toward the water, and her face became lost in the shadows as she gazed out across the murky pitch of the sound.

"I haven't really given you your due," Robert began, " and I want to apologize for that. Your suggestions, your work for us, well, it's all been invaluable."

"No apologies necessary, Mr. Marr. I was happy to be of help."

"Well, you have been," he said, taking her gently at the elbow, trying to encourage her to face him. When she did, he smiled again. He knew his smile had its effect when she returned it in kind. But he liked to see that smile again, for its own sake. "I, for one, don't know what we'd do without you."

These words had an altogether different effect, an effect Robert was not certain he liked. Lina's smile curled up slowly at the corners, as did the corners of her eyes. She took a small step back and looked at him a long while before she spoke.

"Really? Well, I suppose you would manage. You have before."

"Well, yes! Yes, we did, of course. But I'd like to think we wouldn't have to. I mean, that is to say…"

"Yes?"

"Well, I was hoping you might consider an offer of more permanent work."

"*Might consider*? An interesting choice of words…"

"I simply meant that…"

Suddenly, Lina laughed. Not the sort of coy laugh Robert might have expected, but a full, robust laugh of a woman completed amused.

"I fail to see what you find…" Robert said, trying to sound wounded, trying to recapture the upper hand, which he knew, somehow, he had already lost.

"So you're aware of Mr. Kincaid's offer," Lina said, still chuckling.

"Offer?" he said, trying vainly to affect ignorance.

His efforts only made her laugh more. "Honestly, Mr. Marr, why can't you be direct? Mr. Kincaid made me an offer. You want to make an offer of your own. Why not just say so?"

"Well, because, it's just that…"

"Yes?" By now, he could see she was trying her best not to laugh even more, to the point of biting the insides of her cheeks. In his irritation, he thought for just a moment of forgetting the whole business, and leaving her there in the darkness to have her joke. But he regained himself. If it was the truth she asked for, he would give it to her, and still get what he wanted in the bargain.

"Very well, then," he started, almost yelling at her, as she continued to hold her laughter in. "The reason I didn't just say so was because I thought you might say no. Kincaid told me last night about his offer, although I didn't take him seriously. But then Hugh came in, you see, and started telling me about what you found in the books. And I admit Martin Kincaid can get my back up, so when I saw the two of you talking just now, I decided to make a try. You were right about him, Miss Morgan. He's got no one's interests at heart but his own. And I thought to myself, all day I thought about it, that you could do better than what he could offer."

He had stopped yelling, because as he spoke, he saw she had stopped laughing. Instead, she seemed totally absorbed in his words. He trusted his instincts and continued. Softer now, he said, "It's more than the bookkeeping you've done well. That's what I came to realize, you see. I suppose I just didn't expect that you meant what you said, about really liking it here, about wanting to be a part of this place. I suppose I expected that you'd up and leave one day, chasing the next available dream. A lot of folks do, you know. But you've become a friend, a *real* friend to Jean, and Jamie and Hugh. To all of us." His tone was almost pleading now, and he had her full attention. "I know we can't offer you the money Kincaid can. And it's not the best of working conditions, either. Kincaid can do better, I know. But I was…"

"Yes."

"I beg your pardon?"

"Yes. I said yes, Mr. Marr. I would be honored to work for you. I won't pretend otherwise. I've been plain enough all along about my hope to work for you, so I won't go back on that now, just to take advantage of your…" She let out the last of her giggles. "Your obviously desperate situation."

"Oh, well, it's not so much that I, I mean *we*, are desperate…"

"Never mind that," Lina said. "I won't take advantage of this situation. That was all I meant." She seemed to struggle to find her next words. "I'm…I'm very happy that you've asked. And very grateful, Mr. Marr."

Robert looked down on the young woman before him. How she had managed to turn this entire matter on its head, to make *him*, of all people, become so totally lost in his own argument, and yet to have taken the conquest with such ease, such humor and such humility, seemed to Robert to be the single most surprising conversation of which he had ever been part. "Isn't it time you start calling me by my name? I notice you call Jamie and Hugh by theirs. I hope you'll start to think of me as a friend as well."

"Alright. Robert," she said, and again, "Robert. Thank you, I will. And you must call me Lina."

Tentatively, he reached for her hand again. "The music's starting again…Lina. Would you…"

"Robert? Robert!"

Suddenly, Franny was there, behind Robert. When he turned toward her, Franny saw Lina for the first time.

"Oh! Who is this?"

"Oh, Franny, dear. This is Carolina Morgan. She's just agreed to work for us. Lina Morgan, may I introduce Miss Franny Ellis, my, um, my…" The word seemed to fail him in that moment.

Lina did not wait for his lapse in vocabulary to recover. "Miss Ellis," she said with a polite bob, and a quick offer of her hand. Franny barely took it, never looking Lina in the eye. Robert would have thought nothing of the small slight, for when Franny was determined to be the center of attention, and to have her way, she paid attention to little else. But through Lina's eyes, he saw it for the rudeness it was, and was more than a bit embarrassed for Franny, and himself.

"Robert, you've ignored me long enough! Please, let's go back to the dancing."

"Why, you've been too busy to have missed me at all!" Robert said, trying to make light of her behavior. But Franny was her own worst enemy at times like these.

"Ignored you? Why, I was hoping you'd come rescue me! Every time I'm here, I'm besieged by these simple girls and their incessant questions."

"Perhaps, then, you should stay home, if it's such a bother," Lina said plainly. Franny looked at her blankly, but Robert looked at her with surprise. He could see no evidence of malice in her expression, yet somehow he knew that behind those bright eyes, Lina Morgan had said what others before her had never dared to. He smiled.

"Fine, then, Franny. We'll go back. Lina, come by and see me tomorrow, before we go back to camp. We'll discuss the details then. And thank you," he said as they turned to leave.

They walked together toward the dancers, Franny Ellis pulling Robert closer at the arm. "What did you say that woman's name was? Carolina?"

"Yes, Carolina Morgan. But everyone calls her Lina."

"Lina!" Franny said, with a snicker. "What sort of name is that?"

"A perfectly fine name, I suppose," Robert said more to himself than to Franny. As he walked he savored the word one more time, quietly. "Lina."

28

Lina was happy, as happy as she could ever remember being, even happier than when she was a little girl before her mother died and she fully understood the circumstances of her life. Her concern for Josephine still plagued her. She was sending much less for Josephine's care than she'd planned, but she sent every penny she could. All Lina spent her money on was a dollar a week to Meg, who usually found a way to slip it back to her, and a few dollars now and then at Minifee's for necessities. And with more regular work, she felt certain that the nest egg would now grow. She worried some about doing good work for the Marr's, as she had worried about work always—an eagerness to seem up to any task.

Lina seldom thought of Edward Haarten anymore. She had worried about Haarten incessantly at first. When ships would arrive with mail, she expected a letter. She watched Minifee's wall for a notice of someone searching for a woman. She scanned the face of each person who came to Sleekit, looking for someone familiar, perhaps even Haarten himself.

But in time, with new people in her life and new work to be done, it became ever more difficult to see Haarten as a threat. She imagined— hoped—that he'd have little interest in pursuing her, even for spite. She wanted to believe that he would have no patience for such a ridiculous effort, when he could so easily find another woman to suit his purpose. San Francisco was teeming with eager daughters of ambitious men, and if he did not find one there, Edward Haarten had Barclay's resources at his disposal and the world at his doorstep.

Her new life had indeed made the world seem safer to Lina. Sleekit was peaceful—that was the word that kept coming to her when she thought of the place. San Francisco was noisy, but Sleekit was quiet. In the diggings, she could trust no one, but in Sleekit she felt sure. Westport ran at a frantic pace, or was dead still. In Sleekit, the days had a steady rhythm for which she had boundless energy. In such peace, Lina almost lost the capacity for fear.

On a rainy spring night, Meg and Lina were alone at the tavern. No one had stopped by for an hour and they'd decided to close up and go to bed. Then the sound of heavy boots outside the door drew their attention as two strangers entered. One man was young, perhaps twenty, the other man twice as old or older. They wore the dirt of the road on their simple, homespun clothes. They removed their hats and looked around for a moment before the older one spoke.

"Pardon me, ladies. Name's Holgate. This here's my son. We're heading back to our farm near the White River. Might you have a room?"

"You bet, boys," Meg said. "Two bits."

The older one dug deep into his pockets and came up with the coin. He noticed the pot on the stove and added, "If there's any grub about, we'd be grateful."

Young Holgate finally spoke. "And a beer."

"The meal comes with the room. Supper or breakfast, but not both. The beer is extra," Meg said.

The father searched his pockets again but came up empty. "Just the food, then," he said. They took a table near the door.

"Lina, get the men their meal, please," said Meg. "We're getting ready to close up, so you're welcome to the hospitality, so long as you take it quickly."

Just then, Robert and Hugh appeared. They burst into the room expectantly, looking first at the two strangers, and then to Meg.

"It's alright, boys," she told them. "This here is Mr. Holgate and his son. They come from up by the White."

Robert walked over to the men, and after giving them one last, hard look, extended his hand. "Sorry, fellows. When we saw the horses tied up front, well…we don't get that many strangers in town, at least not at this hour. Welcome to you," he added as they shook hands.

"Thank ya kindly," Mr. Holgate said.

Hugh headed to the bar and poured two beers. "Robbie and I spent the entire evening squeezing every last penny we could out of Martin Kincaid. Such work gives a man a thirst, wouldn't you say?"

"That's right," said Robert. "The best mill rate we've ever had."

"Would you like something to eat?" Lina asked. "Boiled beef and potatoes."

"It's quite tasty," added Meg. "Lina fixed it herself."

"Oh, that's not so, Meg. I just helped."

Meg turned to Robert and Hugh and said, "I'll make a cook of that girl yet. She did most of it herself, and it turned out just fine."

"I'm sure it did," Robert said to Lina. "Thanks, but no. A quick beer, and then we're on our way. But I will buy these two a beer, just to show there're no hard feelings. We can't leave them without something to wash down that fine meal, now can we?" Hugh poured two more, and Robert took the beer to the Holgates' table.

"Thanks," said the elder, without regard to his full mouth. "Say, you folks mind if I ask you somethin'? You had any Indian killin's around here yet?"

"Heavens no!" Meg said immediately. "Why do you ask?"

"We been hearin' rumors. We been down Alki way, and that's all folks are talkin' about."

"What are folks saying?" Robert asked. He pulled a chair up to their table and sat down.

"Well, they say the Indians been raidin' farms up and down the sound. Burning folks out of their cabins, stealing their stock. Some say they figure the Indians are fixin' to run us all out of here. Other folks allow as how they might be plannin' to starve us out next winter."

At the first mention of Indians, Lina had stopped working and listened carefully. She searched her friends' faces for any sign of concern. She saw none, but noticed that both Meg and Hugh were watching Robert closely, whose every muscle was taut as he listened to Holgate.

"I'd warn against spreading idle rumors, friend," Robert said to him.

"You accusin' me a lyin'?" Holgate asked. "Cause if you are…"

"I'm saying folks have a way of letting their imaginations run away with them. You can't trust what people say or do when they're frightened."

"Well, it's the Indians I don't trust." Holgate dunked a piece of bread into the gravy and stuffed it in his mouth. He took one look at the set of Robert's jaw and realized it was time to let the matter go. "Well, anyway, I was just askin'."

That would have been the end of it, had young Holgate stayed quiet. "That's why we stopped here for the night," he chimed in, oblivious to the tension in the room. "Pa was afraid we'd come up on 'em at night, and they'd get the drop on us. Pa says if we can't see 'em, we can't shoot 'em. I guess we'll show 'em whose land this is if that happens, won't we, Pa?" The old man didn't answer. He seemed to sense what was coming. Young Holgate did not.

Robert stood suddenly. He picked up their plates just as the younger was moving for another forkful. "Hey!" young Holgate said as he watched Robert take the plates toward the door. Robert pushed the door open and threw the plates into the dark street. "What the hell did you do that for?" Young Holgate was on his feet now, and ready to take a swing. But when Robert came right up next to him, the younger man backed off.

"Your dinner's waiting for you out there, where you can sleep. Get out. Both of you. Now." He didn't yell, but the resolve in his voice was more threatening than any anger.

"You can't make us leave!" the young man said defiantly. "Pa paid two bits for the room!"

Robert reached into his own pocket. He slammed a coin on the table. "There's your two bits. Now, go." The Holgates took the money and left silently. No one spoke until they heard the sound of the horses' heavy canter fade into the night.

"Good for you, Robbie" said Hugh. "Let me buy you another drink!"

Before he could pour another, Robert said, quietly, "No, Hugh, let's go home. Meg, thank you for the beer." His voice sounded tired, and his face looked suddenly drawn. The men walked past Lina without notice, then Robert turned back just before he reached the door.

Mustering a smile, he said, "My apologies to the cook. No offense meant to the meal, I'm sure."

"None taken," Lina answered him, but they were already gone.

****

"Four? Millie, are you sure you want to bid four again?" Meg asked in frustration. Everyone was frustrated, except Millie and Charley. It was late Sunday afternoon, and the weather had gone chilly again. The ever present rain had kept everyone inside all day with nothing to do, except for Charley who thought the rain a great time to gather worms for fishing. Lina, Jean, Jamie, Hugh, Millie and Meg were crowded around a table at Sweet Meg's. To pass the time, Meg had taught them a card game. It was like whist. Meg had warned that it was rare to bid over three with so many people. But despite Meg's instruction, Millie continually bid four and won. So Millie was not frustrated.

Jean and Jamie were eager to have some time alone before Jamie and Hugh returned to camp the next day. But until the rain stopped, a walk was out of the question. They sat politely and played with the others, but their attentions always seemed to be elsewhere and they lagged in taking their turns. "Listen, you two," Hugh said. "If you're going to stay, at least pay attention." Hugh was antsy, for he hated being cooped up anyplace very long. He was already thinking about the work next week. Robert was gone, and Hugh looked forward to being in charge of the crew. He considered leaving for camp early, but decided he could stay in Sleekit for the chance to sleep in the dry cabin one more night.

Lina had come to the game on edge. When she'd gone to camp on Friday, Robert didn't return with Hugh and Jamie. He'd gone to the high country, they said, and would be back in a week or two. Hugh changed the subject quickly, so she thought better of asking more. But she had mentioned it to Meg, who assured her that Robert did this from time to time. She was still agitated that he hadn't told her where he was going, and she hoped that the table talk would offer an occasion for the subject of Robert to come up, as it almost always did. But not this afternoon. Jean and Millie chattered about the wedding dress Jean's mother was making her. Jean and Jamie cooed on about the cabin he had planned for them. Hugh talked about work and Meg was too busy making sure everyone was playing the game properly to say much else. As in the card game she was playing, on the subject of Robert, Lina came up empty-handed.

Millie had been studying the cards in her hand, and finally answered Meg. "Yes, indeed. I do want to bid four."

"Perhaps we should have played poker, Millie, with the winning streak you're on," Hugh said.

"Play for money? Oh dear, no. A lady doesn't do such a thing."

Lina chuckled to herself, thinking of her own card dealing days in Babel. "We wouldn't have to play for money."

"What would be the point of that?" Hugh said in horror. "Without stakes? No thank you! Besides, what if some of the men were to come in and see us playing poker with girls?" He laughed.

"Is that any worse than this?" Jamie said. He looked nearly despondent. He hated cards and was only going through the motions of playing so he could stay with Jean.

"Then let's talk as we play!" Lina said. "Hmm, let's see. Hugh? Is there anything I should know before you leave for camp?"

"I have a list for you back at the cabin," he answered, as he laid down a card to end the hand. "You can come by later and get it."

"Do you suppose Robert would mind if I borrowed another book?" Lina knew the answer, and wasn't really interested in the book regardless.

She picked the wrong moment to try to start the discussion. The hand was finished and Hugh was tallying the score. "Well, that's that. Millie's won again."

Millie giggled and clapped her hands. "This is fun! Perhaps we *should* be playing for money."

Hugh stood. "I'm done. A fellow has to win a hand every once in a while, just to keep interested in such a silly game." He walked to the door. "Hey, it's stopped raining! And there's still a little light left. Come on, Lina. Let's get you that list."

"That's fine," Millie said, pouting. "The four of us can keep playing."

"I'm sorry, Millie," Jean said. "We've been cooped up in here all day. Besides," she said, turning to Jamie, "*We'd* like to take a walk."

"Come on, Millie," Meg said. "Let me walk you home. The stretch will do these old joints good."

"Oh, no need, Meg," Millie said, looking at Hugh. "Perhaps I could go with you two and then you could walk me home."

"This may take a while, Millie." Hugh said, then hurried out the door, leaving Lina to catch up as she could.

Safely away from Millie, Lina finally said, "You know, Hugh, you might do yourself *and* Millie a favor if you were honest with her. Tell her you're flattered, but that you have no interest."

Hugh shook his head. "I have. It doesn't seem to matter."

"Perhaps she really cares for you."

Hugh laughed hard. "Care for me? No, I don't think so. Oh, Millie's okay, and she's a good friend to Jean. But Millie and me?" He laughed again. "No. I don't think so. She's too much of a gossip for my liking. Any man who marries Millie Forbes hasn't a prayer of keeping his business to himself." They had reached the cabin, and as he opened the door, he turned to Lina and said, "You know that about her, don't you? That if you tell her something, you can bet she's shared it with everyone?"

"I suppose," she said as they stepped inside. "She certainly has told me a good deal more about a lot of people than I care to know. Not that it was all that interesting."

"Then I suppose it won't shock you to know she's told Jamie and me about you being a widow."

"Oh." Lina had not thought of that at the time, but she had mentioned it to Jean and Millie that day Charley had been hurt. Still, what did it matter? This was not a secret she worried about keeping. "No, I suppose it doesn't surprise me. I wasn't aware it would arouse any curiosity." When Hugh said nothing, Lina asked, "Was there something *you* wanted to ask me about it?"

"No, Lina. It's not my business. But I hope you know, as a friend, you needn't be on your guard with me."

"Thank you, Hugh," she said.

He took a piece of paper from the table and handed it to her. Lina looked it over, and found nothing out of the ordinary. "Thanks, Hugh," she said. "I'll see you at the end of the week." She had her hand on the door pull when she turned back and looked at him. He smiled, as if he knew what she was about to ask. "Hugh, why did Robert leave? Where is he?"

He looked at her a moment, then said. "Have a seat. Perhaps there're a few things you should know." She sat down, wide-eyed. "No, don't look like that," Hugh said as he sat beside her. "Nothing bad. Just a bit of history."

"I'm sorry. You don't owe me an explanation. I suppose I was just surprised to find he had left."

"It was sudden. And it's like you said about being a widow. Not so much a secret as something he just doesn't speak of often. Half the answer is he's cruising the timber, scouting new stands. That's what we usually say, and it's true he'll be doing that. But it's not the reason he left. You remember that night those two men stopped at Meg's?"

"The Holgates? Yes, I remember. That's the last time I saw Robert."

"He left first light the next morning. To check on some friends. Indian friends. Some folks he became close to when he first came here. You know, he was just barely grown, then, and he lived with them. So you can understand why when there's talk of trouble between the whites and the Indians, he gets worried and goes to check in on them. He'll spend a few days there."

Lina thought back to her encounters with Indians along the trail. "Those that I saw close up, the Pottawatomi, they ran a ferry. A few folks were nervous, but it was probably the first time they saw one. But the Indians saw white folks all the time, and I guess they weren't nervous about the whites."

"When Robert first came here, there weren't enough whites to cause much concern, for them or for the Indians. Hudson's Bay Company had lots of posts, and they had an amicable relationship with the Indians. Some of them even worked for the Company as scouts or trappers. But the whites stayed near the settlements and the Indians had the rest, and that was that. No one thought a thing about such friendships then. The local tribes are peaceful by nature, and there was plenty of everything to go around. Now, things have changed."

"How?"

"There're more settlers. We started hearing stories about white folks attacking Indians they found on what the whites thought of as their property. Of course the Indians didn't see it that way. And a few of the Indians have fought back. Not many, but enough so that some of the settlers are afraid."

Lina smiled. "And if folks knew Robert was friendly with the Indians…"

"Exactly. Though some do. Most of the folks in town know, and we've had no problems. Some Indians come regularly, to trade. Fewer and fewer all the time, though."

"But if it's not a secret, why didn't he tell me?"

"He wasn't thinking about you, Lina. He was thinking about them—the Holgates. He hadn't planned this cruise, but it gave him an excuse to check up on his friends. That night, on the way home from Meg's, all he said to me was, 'I'll be leaving in the morning.' That's all he had to say. I knew where he was going, and why."

Lina nodded. "Thanks, Hugh. I understand." She leaned back in the chair. "Goodness, I can't imagine what it must have been like for him, a young man coming here, living like that. Has he told you about it?"

Hugh shook his head. "That's his story to tell. I know some of it, but if Robbie wants to share it, he will." He thought for a moment, then said, "I do have a story I can tell, for it's my story. Well, it's a family story, about how Jamie and Charley and I came to follow Robert here. Robert had already been here a while, out to make his own fortune. His mother had passed a few years before. His father, my Uncle James, died, and Jamie came to live with us. Charley and me, and my father. My father and Uncle James might have been brothers, but they were two very different men. Uncle James was a good man, but a dreamer. Not unlike Robert in many ways. My father was anything but a dreamer. He was a stern, hard, practical man. My mother was gone, too. She died when Charley came. I think my father thought it an added burden to have to take care of Jamie. But he took responsibilities seriously. When Robert got the news his father had died, he came back, but it took nearly two years before he got the word and could make it back to Montreal. By then, Charley was still just a wee one, so he didn't suffer much under Father's hand. Me, I was almost too old for him to beat or bully me anymore. Jamie got the worst of it. I did my best to keep him out of harm's way, but I couldn't protect him all the time."

After such a story, Lina was shocked when Hugh suddenly laughed. "You should have seen Robert when he came back for Jamie! Here he was, just barely a man himself. But you'd have never known it, the way he spoke to my father. 'I've come for my brother,' he said, as if that was all that needed to be said. Father was quite one for giving lectures. And he gave one to Robbie that night, that's for certain. He told him he was a fool for thinking he could raise a boy alone, much less in a God-forsaken wilderness. Then he said he didn't know why he would expect anything less of James Marr's son. He told Robert his father was a fool who had wasted his life chasing dreams, and that Robert would wind up the same way, only worse, for he wouldn't have the Marr family money to squander doing it. Then he predicted Robert would come crawling back inside of a year, begging for a good, honest job with the Company, and wouldn't Father have the last laugh then when he told him no. For a moment, I thought Robert might actually hit my father. But he didn't. He took Jamie by the hand, and said that he shouldn't wait for either of them to come back. Then he told him the dreams his father left him were worth far more than the Marr family money, and that someday, when my father was old and alone, he would be sorry he'd never had a dream. Then he thanked me for looking after his brother, and he left."

"Goodness," Lina said quietly. "That's remarkable. No wonder it made such an impression on you."

"Aye, that it did. And Robert's prediction was right. Father died not long after, as bitter and dreamless an old man as ever there was. I didn't hesitate a moment. Charley and I came here to join Robbie."

"Because he was your only family," Lina said.

"No. Because I thought whatever it was in this wilderness that had turned Robbie from a gangly boy into the man who faced my father, I wanted that too. And because I knew I could trust Robbie."

"And you wanted me to know I could trust him, too. Is that the purpose of this little tale?" Lina asked. Hugh grinned. "Well, thank you, Hugh," she said. "I do feel better." She glanced out the window at the waning light. "I better get going. I'll see you at the end of the week." She stood and headed to the door.

"Lina?" Hugh asked. "Didn't you want to borrow a book?"

"Never mind," she said. "I don't need it now."

****

Riordan sailed into the inlet one morning a few days later just as Lina was headed to camp. Even though it had been a short run up the coast and back, his arrival always caused a small uproar in Sleekit, for there would be long-awaited supplies, packages, even letters, and on occasion a visitor. Today, Riordan disappointed no one.

"Ah, me darlins," he said, squeezing the life out of first Meg and then Lina, "it's good to be home." Then he took his welcome from the Minifees and the others who had come down to greet him. "I've all that you've been waitin' for, and then some." Already, the men were bringing the first load over from the ship by canoe, and depositing the cargo on the flats. "Here, now," he said, holding up a large canvas bag, "I've got packages and letters for everyone. Take 'em, Minifee, and see that they get to the proper folks." He tossed the bag to Virgil. "Oh, Lina, dear! I got that bull rope that Robert's been hankerin' for."

"I'm headed to camp this morning."

"Well, then, get some of me men to load that for ya. 'Tis too heavy for the likes of yourself to get in that wagon." Just then, a dinghy came from the ship with a man who was a stranger to Lina, but whose appearance immediately had Meg grinning and waving.

The tall man stepped from the canoe. The brocade of his vest, the stylish woolen cape over his shoulders, even the polish of his walking stick, all were black. So was the small leather bag he carried. "Doc!" Meg cried, holding her arms wide.

The man stepped quickly from the canoe, and in no more than three long strides had taken Meg's hand for a courtly kiss. "Miss Fay, what a pleasure it is! You're looking fit as can be."

"And you, Doc. Handsome as ever!" she said, leaning forward to kiss his cheek. "Oh, Lina. This here is Doctor Maynard, from down south. Doc, this is Carolina Morgan, moved up from San Francisco a few months back."

The man took Lina's hand. "Miss Morgan," he said. Lina was truly struck by the fellow. For such a large, seemingly powerful man, he held her hand gently. He gave her a warm smile as he released her hand. It was then she noticed his china blue eyes.

"My pleasure," she whispered, after he had already turned back to Meg.

"Doc, what on earth brings you so far north? And with Milo, no less?" Meg asked.

"I was looking after some folks. Riordan's was the first ship I could find headed this way. I was counting on finding a way home from here."

"I told him Robert would see he got back somehow," Milo offered.

"Robert's not here," Lina answered.

"No? At camp, then?" the doctor asked.

Lina shook her head. "Cruising."

The doctor gave her a quizzical look. Meg offered the explanation. "Lina works for the Marrs. She was just on her way to camp with supplies."

"A woman in a logging camp?" Maynard said. "And such a lovely one. Wonder of wonders. Well, then, young lady, will you leave a message for him at camp that if he arrives in town before tomorrow, I'd like to see him?"

"You'll stay until tomorrow?" Meg said.

"If you have a room," Maynard said, with a grin.

"For you, always. Come on, let's get you settled in. Milo, make certain Lina has all the help she needs, will you?"

"Is that man really a doctor?" Lina asked Riordan as his men loaded the heavy rope into her wagon.

"Aye, darlin', and a good one, too. Not like that butcher of a barber up in Ellis what passes himself off as a doctor. He came through a year or so ago, during one of Meg's bad spells. He fixed her up good. He made friends for life in us, he did. But then, he's a special fellow, is Doc." The wagon was loaded, and Milo was anxious to join Meg. "Now be off with ya, dearie. You can talk to the good Doctor yourself this evening over supper, I suspect, if you've got any more curiosities."

Lina had no more curiosities, as Riordan had called them, but the idea of having dinner with this intriguing stranger occupied her mind while she drove the wagon to camp. She sometimes missed those evenings in the Golden West, with Barclay and the interesting people who joined him, and thought this evening's dinner might offer some of that appeal.

When she reached camp, it occurred to her that if it had taken two men to load the heavy rope into the wagon, it would be a struggle to unload it alone. She would have to wait for help, which meant she would probably miss the dinner with Doctor Maynard. She gathered up the supplies she could carry and was still in the throes of her disappointment when she stepped inside the Marr's tent. "Oh!" she cried in surprise.

"Ouch!" Lina had not expected to see Robert standing there, let alone lathered like a rabid dog, shaving himself. He had not heard her pull into camp, and the surprise had caused him to knick himself with his razor. "Hello. Damn!" He looked into the jagged mirror hanging on the tent pole to see a small bead of blood on his chin. He daubed it with his finger, and then looked at her again. "What are you doing here?"

"Deliveries," she said. "Welcome home."

"What? Oh, thank you."

She watched him for a moment as he resumed shaving. He pulled the blade across his cheek carefully, and then flicked the soap into a wooden bowl sitting on the chair. "Was there something else?"

"Well, when you have a moment, I could use some help. Riordan arrived this morning. He brought your bull rope."

"Did he now?" Robert's mood lightened. "That's good news, and about time, too. Well, let me finish here, and then I'll help." Lina stood watching. "Miss Morgan? Is there anything else you should be doing besides watching me rid myself of these whiskers?"

"Oh!" Lina was out of the tent in a flash. She had not realized how she had been staring at him until just then. *What he must think,* she wondered as she busied herself unloading the rest of the wagon. She was standing in the bed of the wagon when Robert finally came out. Clean shaven, he still looked disheveled. His hair was tousled, his pants dirty, and his shirt gone, with only his long johns to clothe his torso. And he looked tired. But with little apparent effort, he pulled the rope out of the wagon and threw it over his shoulder to carry it to the tent.

Lina brought the last bundle and set it down with the others. "Have you been back long?"

"No." That he was annoyed was apparent from the tone of his voice. "Why do you ask?"

"I...I suppose I was just trying to make pleasant conversation," she answered.

"Is that so?" he said, and seemed to want to say more. Then he shook his head, and managed a weak smile, saying, "Was there anything else?"

"Well, yes, there was. I was to leave a message for you. Riordan had a passenger. A Doctor Maynard?"

"Maynard?" Robert's tone was altogether different now. "Maynard's in Sleekit?"

"Yes. He asked me to leave word that if you returned before tomorrow, he wanted to see you. He's at Meg's now, and he'll be there until then."

"Wonderful! What lucky timing!" Robert seemed to find new energy in this news. "Tell him I'll be down, but after dark. I need to catch up with Hugh and Jamie again before I leave. They expect me to be here tonight."

"Hugh and Jamie? You've already seen them, then?"

"Yes." There it was again, that tone of irritation in Robert's voice.

"Is something wrong?"

"What?"

"I said, is there something wrong? You've hardly said two words to me since I arrived, except when I mentioned Doctor Maynard. I know I made you cut yourself—and it's still bleeding, by the way—but I hardly think that's reason..."

"Let it alone," he said. Looking in the mirror, he dabbed at his chin with a rag until the bleeding stopped.

"I would rather not leave it alone," Lina continued. "If I've done something, Robert..."

"Very well," he said, tossing the rag into the soap-filled bowl. "Hugh *scolded* me for not telling you where I was going! He said something about you being concerned, or upset, or..."

"Oh, honestly! I was no such thing! I only wish you *had* told me, but he explained to me why you didn't have the chance."

"Oh, he did, did he? What did he tell you?"

Somehow, Lina knew that Robert would not be happy to know the stories Hugh had shared. "He simply told me you made the decision suddenly, the night before you left."

"Hmf!" Robert grunted.

"But now that you're back, you can tell me all about this 'cruising.' I'm very interested, you know. I want to learn as much about logging as I can."

"Aha!" Robert cried. "That's what I suspected. Your stubborn determination to go out with the crews."

"Why, this had nothing to do with that!" Lina was as mad as Robert now. "But since you brought the subject up, it seems odd to me that you accuse *me* of being stubborn, when you're the one who won't consider it, won't even tell me why!"

"Why? Why *should* you go? To satisfy some idle curiosity? For that's the only reason I can see. There's not a single thing you could learn out there that you need to know to do what you're hired to do."

"And what is so wrong with a little curiosity? It was curiosity that led me to look at those books of yours, and save you all that trouble with your supplies. I should think you'd welcome my curiosity."

"Look through the books all you like. Ask as many questions as you need, and I'll answer them. But travel out into the wilderness? Ridiculous. Out of the question."

"You know, I have traveled in the wilderness before…"

"Wagon trains filled with settlers have been coming down that same road for the last decade. It may look like wilderness, but compared with this," he pointed up toward the higher mountains, "it's nothing. There are at least a dozen ways a man can die out there, at the hand of man *or* nature, and he'd never see it coming."

"Well, it's not like I'd be alone. The crews would be there, and…"

"And they have a job to do. And it's *not* protecting you. Besides, it's them I'm thinking of, not you. I have to look out for them. All of them. I can't protect them *and* you, and do a decent job of either. Oh, but then, what do you know of that?" he said, bitterly. "You've got no one to tend to but yourself, do you?"

Lina thought of Josie. *So much for what you know, Robert Marr.* She smiled unwittingly.

"There! You see? The very fact that you find this amusing confirms my intuitions about you not taking the risks of such a venture seriously."

Instantly, her smile vanished. "I don't find this amusing!" she yelled. "Not one little bit. And as to being capable, I wonder how you'd come to such a conclusion, seeing as how you ask so little of me. No one to tend to..." she muttered at the last, as she stormed out of the tent. Robert followed her as far as the opening.

Lina kept talking to Robert, even as she was walking away from him. "No, not like you. You, you have to tend to everyone, don't you?" When she reached the wagon, she turned and saw him there. "I lied before. Hugh told me the real reason why you didn't have time to say anything about leaving. He told me about your friends, the Indians. And he told me about you, and Jamie, and your uncle. It seems you have the weight of the whole *world* on your shoulders. Of course, that burden would be a little lighter if you'd let some of the people who care about you take on some of that load. But, no! That would deprive you of the great satisfaction of taking care of us all! Of handling your family, and this business, and the whole of Sleekit, too. Far be it from me, or anyone else, for that matter, to try to help you out, even a little bit. That's all I was hoping to do, you know, by asking all these questions and trying to learn more. To be a better help to you." She climbed into the wagon and took the reins. "Fine, then. I'll keep my nose where it belongs. I'll make these trips between camp and town, and at the end of the week I'll come up here and count your pennies. That's what you pay me for, and that's what you'll get." She clicked her tongue, setting the team in motion. As she pulled the wagon around to head back down the road, she called over her shoulder to him. "I'll tell Doctor Maynard to expect you later. That is, if being messenger is part of my official duties."

****

Robert arrived late. Expecting him, Meg had saved a meal, but the others had already finished. Lina had enjoyed her time with Meg, Riordan and the doctor. Maynard was a fascinating man. He and Riordan talked of their trip, and Meg asked about Seattle. Martin Kincaid joined them later, but as soon as he was served, Meg and Riordan went upstairs. Lina stayed to clean up and pour the two gentlemen their drinks. She listened casually to their talk of business as she worked. Then Robert arrived. He did not acknowledge her, but went straight over to the table. "Maynard! Good to see you, man! What brings you here?" He pulled up a chair.

As Maynard told him the story of traveling from up north, Lina brought the saved plate of supper to the table. "Here," she said, laying it in front of Robert. "*Meg* saved this for you," she made a point of saying. "Please clear the table when you're done. I'm going to bed. I suppose I can trust you to cover your tab." She didn't wait for his answer. The door gave a small *slap* as she closed it behind her.

"What was that about?" Kincaid asked.

"I haven't a clue," Robert lied, diving into the meal. "Now, tell me all the news."

"News?" Maynard laughed. "What could possibly be new in this forsaken corner of the world. I was hoping you gentlemen could regale me with interesting stories of Sleekit."

Kincaid and Robert both laughed. "Interesting? Sleekit?" Kincaid said.

Maynard looked at Robert. "You're looking fit, Marr. You've been cruising, I understand? Were you successful?"

"Aye," he answered, then looked at Kincaid, cautiously. "Successful enough."

Maynard understood, and asked no more. "Kincaid tells me that business here is booming."

Robert smiled. "It should be a good season. And as long as San Francisco keeps burning down, we can sell them timber to rebuild it. Perhaps you'd like to take up logging again, Doc. I could always use a good man." Maynard laughed. Doc Maynard had arrived in the Pacific Northwest only a few years earlier, and already made a name for himself that had spread far and wide. He was as close to a legend as any living white man in those parts might be. He made his first small fortune by having the good sense to cut four hundred cords of wood, by hand, all by himself. Then, on pure speculation, he shipped it to San Francisco and made a respectable sum. Slowly but surely, he'd been building his fortunes from there.

"No thanks, Marr. I'll leave that to you. No, I'm heading to San Francisco next month, not to sell but to buy. A mill. Or rather, someone to run a mill. So far, no luck, though. Right now, all those folks in San

Francisco hear about the sound is rumor, and none of it good. Cold, and rainy…"

"That's no rumor," Robert said.

"No, but what they hear about this being a wilderness is. We three know this place won't be a wilderness much longer."

"Still, it's no San Francisco," Kincaid said.

"Thank God for that," Robert added.

"Well, you like San Francisco well enough when you visit there," said Kincaid.

"Only for a visit. But not to stay. And I'm in no hurry for boats and wagons filled with pilgrims to come this way and make this place another San Francisco."

Another hour passed in idle chatter, most of it centered on the various fortunes being made or lost by this one or that in the settlements of Puget Sound. Eventually, Martin Kincaid excused himself, leaving Robert and Maynard alone. Robert dutifully cleared the table. *For Meg*, he told himself stubbornly. *Not because* she *said to*. "Well, I suppose I should be heading to the cabin myself," he said.

"I'll walk with you," Maynard said. "I've something to talk to you about."

Robert turned out the last lantern in Sweet Meg's, and closed the door behind him as he followed Doc Maynard outside. "What's on your mind, as if I didn't know?"

"Well, I figured you didn't want to discuss this in front of Kincaid."

"You're right. Him or anyone. It just gets everyone agitated."

Maynard nodded. "I heard from folks down my way that these rumors of attacks have made it as far as San Francisco."

"What had they heard?"

"That some Indians raided a farm along the sound. The way they told it, whole families were slaughtered."

"Doc, you know that's not true."

"And so I told them, but…"

"But what?"

Maynard stopped. "Marr, we both know things have gotten worse, even if it hasn't turned violent yet. Someday, it will, though, and then we'll have real trouble on our hands."

"And you and I will be in the thick of it."

"In the very thick of it." The two men resumed walking. "You know, Marr, if we just asked the territory to help, maybe set up some land just for the tribes…"

"Doc, stop." Robert turned to face Maynard. The night was too deep for either man to read the other's face. But this was an old conversation, so no guesswork was needed. "Doc, I respect you. I respect what you've done for the Indians. Hell, there's not another white man around here who's been a better friend to them…"

"Except you."

"Not even me. You've tended their sick and injured, when others wouldn't. Even doctors and missionaries who are supposed to care for them. And I'm glad for it, glad they trust you. You've been a good friend to them. Someday, perhaps soon, they'll need all the friends they can get. But not the government. They've no friends there. The territory doesn't give a damn about them, and in the end, they'll lie to them. Hell, Doc, they lie to us! Make us promises about railheads and deep-water ports and statehood. What makes you think they won't lie to them, too?"

Doc Maynard had no answer.

Robert sighed. "Doc, you do what you think is right. I won't fight you. But I won't help you. We just have two different ways of looking at the problem."

"And you think I'm wrong?"

"My only quarrel with what you're doing is that you're doing it on behalf of the government. You're trying to mend fences and keep treaties, in the name of the territory. Now, don't argue. You and the Governor, you're well acquainted. Whether he asks you to do his work for him, or you volunteer where you think you're needed, it's all the same. And you think if you can compromise with both the whites and the Indians, you'll have covered your bets. You no doubt think that in the long run, that will help you. But it won't, Doc. When this blows up—and it *will*—the Indians will see you on the side of the white man, and the territory will see you on the side of the red man. You're bound to lose, no matter what."

"And you?"

"Me? I'm not on either side. I'm on the side of peace. We used to have peace around here. I think we still can."

"Did I understand right that you've been out seeing your friends?"

Robert nodded. "There were two men here a while back, spreading those same rumors. I showed them the door. But there was something ugly in the way they talked, uglier than usual. It worried me."

"And?"

"Everything's fine. So far."

They had reached Robert's cabin. "That's good news, at least," Doc said. "Folks down south will be glad to hear that."

"Yes, be sure and tell them, Doc. Tell them they have nothing to fear from these tribes."

The two men shook hands. "Marr, let's hope we can keep saying that for a long time to come." Maynard started to leave.

"Oh, Doc? Did you have a chance to check on Meg?"

"I did," he said. "Don't worry, she's doing fine."

"Good. What do I owe you?"

Maynard waved his hand. "Nothing, Robert. This one's on the house. A fair trade for the reassurance you've just given me."

"You're a good man, Doc Maynard."

"As are you, Robert Marr. Not a very practical man, perhaps, but a good one. Good night."

****

Edward Haarten's efforts to find Carolina Clark had come to nothing. It was as if she had vanished into the ether. There had only been one lead, but it came to nothing. One of his crew had seen a lady fitting Lina's general description pass him on his way to board the Rosalea the morning Haarten left, but all he could swear to was that she had red hair. Haarten was unconvinced. That description could refer to half the tarts in town. But he followed the lead and found out the ship, the Bantry Bay, was headed north. Canada, the Yukon, Russia—no one could say for certain, but all were wildernesses, and hardly seemed places a young woman would set out for alone.

Haarten was lost amongst his logs and ledgers one afternoon when Jackson appeared at the library door. "There's a gentleman here to see you sir. A doctor." Jackson laid a small silver tray on the desk, bearing the man's calling card. "Have him come in," Haarten ordered. When Jackson returned, he opened the door to the library to admit Dr. Josiah Maxwell of the Wilcox Clinic. As soon as Jackson closed the door, Haarten said, "I specifically told you not to contact me. Not here. Not ever. Our business is concluded."

"I know, sir, but there was someone at the clinic asking for Miss Paul."

Haarten felt a stab of fear in his gut, but he kept a cool demeanor for Maxwell. "Who?"

"A lawyer, sir. A Mr. Tunnicliff." The doctor passed Haarten a business card with a shaky hand. "He just showed up, Captain, unannounced. Because you know, sir, had he inquired beforehand, I most certainly would have told him not to come."

"Sit." Haarten went to the brandy and poured the man a glass. "Drink this, man, and calm down." Maxwell did as he was told. "Now tell me exactly what transpired between you and this lawyer."

"Well, this morning, he came to the hospital. I happened to be coming in at the same time, so I asked him if I might help him. He told me that he had come under service to a client who had requested he check in on the condition of one Miss Josephine Paul from time to time, and, if necessary, make certain she was being properly cared for."

"And what did you say to him?"

"Nothing, sir. I excused myself for a moment to collect my thoughts..."

"Quick thinking."

Maxwell smiled. "Thank you, sir. In any event, I came back in a few minutes and told him I'd checked Miss Paul's records and found everything was in order, that all services were paid for."

"Did he ask to see Miss Paul?"

"Oh, no, sir! He hardly came inside the front door. You know how the place is, sir. Some folks just aren't very comfortable in hospitals, and they..."

"Yes, Maxwell. Go on."

"Well, that's it, sir. He gave me that card, and left. Oh, there is one other thing. He told me that if conditions were to change, and Miss Paul did need additional care, that the Clinic was to contact him at that address," he pointed at the card Haarten held, "and that he could arrange for payment through the Page & Beacon Bank."

"Page & Beacon, you say?"

"Yes, sir. I'm sure of it, sir, because I thought, what a coincidence, that was your bank, and...."

"Yes, quite a coincidence, Maxwell." Haarten turned the business card over and over in his hand, absently. "And you're quite sure he told you nothing else? Asked nothing else?"

"Yes, sir. It was a very short meeting."

"You did well, Dr. Maxwell, given the circumstances. Thank you. If this Mr. Tunnicliff shows up again, just continue with what you've already said, and then let me know."

"Oh, I will, sir, I will," Maxwell said, rising. Haarten quickly led him toward the library door.

Haarten wasted no time. An hour later he walked into the lobby of the Page & Beacon Bank as if he owned it, which in fact he did, at least in part. His empire had grown to such an extent that he held large numbers of shares in every major financial institution in California and some outside the country as well. But he had never been inside the Page & Beacon bank before. There was no need. Haarten could always have someone else run his errands. Still, the young man who served as clerk to the president recognized his name. He read the calling card and scurried into an office whose door read "Franklin Greeley, President." Soon, a thin and dour old man emerged, scurrying across the lobby with his hand extended. "Good day, Captain Haarten, sir. It's our pleasure to see you." Greeley led Haarten to his office and closed the door.

"I've long been hoping to make your acquaintance, sir," Greeley said, almost salivating, as he sat behind his desk. Haarten took the chair across from him. "Your reputation throughout the city is renowned, and of course, this institution greatly appreciates your support." Greeley tried to smile. It was not a natural expression for him, but with a man like Haarten, who offered almost endless possibilities for flourishing returns on investment, he would try to seem agreeable. "How may we be of service to you today, sir?"

"I need to know the status of an account opened here by a young lady, a Miss Carolina Clark. I assume you can determine that for me."

Greeley shifted in his chair. "Well, sir, we treat our accounts, *all* our accounts, with the utmost confidentiality. As an investor here yourself, I'm certain you can appreciate the need for this. Strictly speaking, I'm not even allowed to disclose whether such an account exists. I'm sure you understand."

Haarten leaned forward in his chair, and fixed a hard stare on the old man for a long moment before he spoke. "No, Mr. Greeley, I do not understand. Perhaps the bank has absconded with Miss Clark's funds. Perhaps my own assets are not safe here. Perhaps I should consider other investment options."

The warning was clear, and Greeley was frantically trying to think of a way to salvage the conversation. "Let me see what I can find out, Captain. Excuse me." Greeley left the room, and Haarten could hear him talking to the clerk outside the door. Finally, he returned, carrying a small card. "Yes, we have such an account. And the balance of two hundred eighty five dollars represents all deposits made, I assure you."

"I don't give a damn about the balance," Haarten said, further unsettling Greeley who would now do anything to return to Haarten's good graces. "I want your assistance in one thing only. When next a deposit is made, I want the person who makes that deposit followed. Discreetly. Find out who they are and where they go, then send word to me. Immediately. No matter the day or time."

Greeley smiled. This was a curious request, to be sure, but certainly not a breach of any fiduciary confidence that Greeley could see. "Of course, Captain Haarten. You may count on Page & Beacon, sir. I'll see to it myself."

29

Martin Kincaid had the only safe in Sleekit, for the use of which he naturally charged a small fee. It was strong, with a good lock, but small enough that two stout men could have carried it off if they had a mind to. But then, it didn't need to be much of a safe, for few people used it. Townsfolk bartered for goods, and the loggers and millworkers spent their pay quickly. So for the most part Kincaid's safe held only his own payroll, and that of the Marrs. And Lina Morgan's coin purse.

Lina smiled as she lifted the purse from the safe and peeked inside. The two hundred dollars in gold she found in Josie's things was still there, for she had never had to use it, thanks to Meg and Riordan. Soon she would send it and another twenty dollars from working for the Marrs, back to San Francisco with Riordan. She squeezed the soft leather, and the coins made a little jingle.

"That's quite a nest egg you've made for yourself, my dear," Kincaid said. He never left anyone alone with the safe. He watched as Lina inspected the purse's contents. "I had no idea you had done so well working for Marr."

Lina said nothing as she tucked some more currency inside, silently calculating the addition, then returned the purse to the safe.

"Miss Morgan, if you're interested in investing, I could suggest some opportunities…"

Lina laughed. "Mr. Kincaid, you never give up, do you?" Lina left before he answered.

Her other morning errand took her to Minifee's to pick up supplies for Meg. She was hoping to get in and out quickly for there was much to do back at the tavern. The warm weather brought more people through Sleekit, and Meg's was always busy. But inside the store, Millie Forbes was perusing the few yard goods Esther kept in stock.

"I'm sorry, Millie. It's all I have and Captain Riordan won't be bringing any more until it's too late. Oh, good morning, Lina. Is that Meg's list?"

"Good morning. Yes, ma'am," Lina said, handing her the paper. "Good morning, Millie. Making a new dress?"

"Oh, good morning, Lina. Yes, it's for the party in Ellis!"

"A party in Ellis? Someone getting married?" Lina asked just to make conversation.

"Oh, no! It's *the* party. You mean, you didn't notice the handbill?"

Lina stepped outside. There on the front of Minifee's was a large handbill with a picture of an American flag at the top. She read it.

> *To all citizens of Ellis and its surroundings. A celebration in honor of the birth of the Republic. Commemoration of Ellis' new pavilion and flag pole. Oration by local dignitaries. Banquet provided. Musical entertainment. Artillery display that evening. Courtesy Ellis Mills and the Honorable B. Ellis and family.*

When she came back in, Millie had decided on her fabric and Esther was cutting the yardage.

"Well, doesn't it sound thrilling?"

"Yes it does. I'm sure you'll have a wonderful time."

"Oh, but surely you're going too."

"I don't know," Lina said. "I've just now learned about it."

"Well, you should decide soon, dear. You'll be wanting a new dress, too. I expect everyone will wear their Sunday best, in honor of the occasion. Certainly Franny Ellis will."

"It's a picnic, Millie. I won't need a new dress." There was an awkward silence as neither Esther nor Millie would look at her. "What is it?" Then she looked down at her skirt, and suddenly noticed what Esther and Millie and who knows who else must have noticed for some time. Her clothes were clean, but worn beyond reclamation. The dress had been nearly new when she came to Sleekit. But after weeks of hauling supplies to camp and countless nights serving at Sweet Meg's, the stains, the small patched tears and the frayed edges had accumulated to create a genuinely disreputable appearance. And this was the dress she considered to be her *nice* one. "Oh, dear."

At just that moment, Charley came dashing through the door. "Hey, Lina!" he said as he stumbled to a stop.

"Charley, what have I told you about saying 'Hey' "? Millie said.

"Oh. I didn't see you there, Teacher. Hello, Lina."

"Hey, Charley," she said quietly, with a wink only he could see, and that caused a grin to break out across his freckled face.

"Lina," Esther continued, "perhaps Meg could help you, or I might find a few minutes…"

"Thank you, Esther. I'll figure something out. Charley, can you help me take these things back to Meg's?" Before he could answer, she began piling cans into the young boy's arms. "You take these, and I'll take the flour. Thank you Esther. Millie." She leaned down next to Charley's ear and whispered, "Let's get out of here."

"Were they nagging you, too?" Charley asked, almost before they were out of earshot.

"Oh, not exactly. You have to remember, Charley, they mean well. They really do." Charley gave her a skeptical look. "They do!" Then she muttered through a tightened jaw, "I swear, they do."

"Well, if it isn't two of my favorite people!" Meg said as Lina and Charley came through the door. "Here, Charley, you're about to drop those cans." Meg scooped a few out his clutches while Lina dropped the flour sack on the nearest table with a forcible *thud*. "Did you get to Kincaid's?" she asked Lina.

"Yes." Lina snatched an apron off the peg and yanked it around her waist and tied it. With hands on hips, she surveyed the room for a place to start.

"It looks like you got everything on the list," Meg said, watching her carefully.

"Yes." Lina chose the stack of breakfast plates to attack. She started by restacking them, to some purpose that eluded Meg as she watched. Having completed the rearrangement, Lina looked about for a moment. "Water," she said definitively. She grabbed the bucket and headed out back to the rain barrel.

Meg looked at Charley, who just shrugged. "All I know is Teacher was over at the store."

Meg rolled her eyes and nodded. "Here you go, Charley." Meg slipped a penny into Charley's hand. "Thanks for your help. Run along, now." Charley waited just a moment. "Go on with you," she said, patting him on the cheek. "I'll figure it out."

A splash of water preceded Lina into the room when she returned. The bucket swung violently, but she paid no attention to the spray she created or the trail of puddles behind her. She tossed the water into the washing bowl, then started on the plates so fiercely Meg thought she just might rub a hole clean through them.

Meg let her work it off for a few minutes, then took a seat right behind her at the nearest table. "So, what's put you in such a snit?"

"I'm not in a snit," Lina said. The growing stack of clean plates rattled as she carelessly dropped another on top.

"Tsk, tsk," Meg clicked. "That Millie Forbes must have *really* gotten under your skin about something."

"Millie? How did you…" Lina turned around in surprise. "Oh. Charley. Well, no. I can't blame Millie," she said. "It's my own fault. I was embarrassed, but I did that to myself." She held out the sides of her skirt, now splattered with water, which only added to its shabby appearance. "Look at me. I look disgraceful. I can't go to that party in Ellis looking like this."

Meg smiled. "Oh, of course. Millie was over there planning a new frock, wasn't she? Well, then, make yourself a new one."

"I can't," Lina said, sheepishly. "I don't know how. I never learned to sew. I can mend, but make a whole new dress? No, I can't." Then she looked to Meg with hope in her eyes. "Could you…?"

"Me?" Meg said, wide-eyed. "Honey, I can't sew either. But I might have a dress you could borrow."

"What will you wear?" Lina asked.

"Oh, I'm not going. This old leg won't stand for being in a wagon that long."

"Fine, then," Lina said. "That settles it. I'll stay here with you."

"Now wait just a minute, miss. You're going to that party, new dress or not. You spend far too much time working, and saving every penny as if your life depended upon it. It doesn't. You've got to start enjoying yourself, and quit living for tomorrow. This is the only life you've got, you know."

Lina smiled. Josie had said something similar to her, a long time ago. Suddenly, Lina was possessed of an idea. She ran to her room, leaving Meg to wonder what had happened. In no time at all Lina came flying down the stairs, a dress in her hand—Josie's green dress, the one she had sewn her gold into. She held it up at the shoulders in front of her. It was a lovely soft green muslin with small puffed sleeves. "I don't know if it will fit, though."

"Oh, Lina. That's perfect!" Meg said, holding the hem up to get a good look. "We'll make it fit. Esther will help. It shouldn't take much." Then Meg wagged her finger at Lina, smiling all the time. "You see? You shouldn't let yourself get so worked up about small matters. Between us we can figure anything out."

****

Robert took his time making the trip to the grove. Time seemed such a luxury to him these days, he felt almost sinful about wasting it. But the slow ride wasn't a waste of time, he told himself. It was a chance to try to banish some of his worries, forget his responsibilities and to look again at the special splendor of the place, as he had as a young man, what seemed like a lifetime ago. Robert had not been back to the grove since Charley had his fall. The memory sent a quick, sharp chill through him. Charley was fine, just a good knock to the head, but it was a reminder that a place so seemingly safe could still harbor danger.

Charley's fall had bothered Robert more than he wanted anyone to know. He had been Charley once, twenty years ago. He had been the one whose sense of adventure was stronger than his caution. Now he felt responsible for Charley, for all of them. He was glad Hugh and Jamie hadn't been there when he found Charley, lying there seemingly lifeless. What would everyone have thought if they had seen the look of fear that most surely must have been on his face? *Thank God it was only Lina there to see it*. He remembered how calm she seemed to him, and how suddenly calm he had felt then, too. *Thank God Lina had been there*.

He took a different path to the grove this day, one that led him straight to the pool to go swimming. The large boulder jutting out from the side of the water made a perfect partition between the swimming place and the picnic place. He was hungry, but food would wait. He was hot from the ride, so he jumped off the horse and tied it to a place further up the grade where the animal could reach the stream for a drink. "You're hot too, eh, boy?" he said, patting the horse briefly before walking back to the pool. He pulled off his heavy boots, stripped, and dove into the pool.

He loved the feel of the brisk water running across his exposed body, cooling every inch of him. Just as he came up for air, he heard the unmistakable sound of a gun being cocked, and a familiar female voice, saying, "Don't move." He spun around in the water. He wiped the dripping water from his eyes. Standing on the bank, gun aimed more or less at him, dripping wet in her camisole and pantalets, stood Lina Morgan. The clinging wet cotton outlined her figure, a fact Robert did not fail to notice. *And a fine figure, at that*, he thought. *Round where a woman should be round. Strong and firm, too.* He smiled, wondering how long she might stand there before she remembered herself.

Lina laughed aloud as she lowered the pistol. "Meg warned me about grizzlies, Indians and trappers. But she didn't warn me about this."

"Well, you got the drop on me," Robert said, laughing, only his head above the water. "But what did you expect I was going to do to you, from here?"

"I was swimming over there," she said with a nod of her head. "I heard the splashing. I honestly thought it might be a bear. But you're right, of course. If I thought you were a threat, I'd have been smarter to take your clothes than hold you at gunpoint."

"I wouldn't laugh if I were you," Robert said, grinning. "My modesty hasn't been nearly as compromised as your own. Of course, I could even the score by getting out now."

He watched her carefully. She glanced down, suddenly aware of how exposed she was. He expected her to run for cover, but instead she seemed determined not to be the one to back down. She raised the gun again. He could tell it was only a mock threat, but she said, "Come out of the water now, Robert Marr, and it'll be more than your modesty that's compromised."

"With that little pea shooter?" The words had hardly left his lips when he heard the gun go off. "Ping!" went the bullet, as it hit the rocky edge of the bank to his left. Lina aimed well away from him, but she achieved the effect. Robert ducked under the water in a hurry. He bobbed back up and looked over to where the bullet made its mark.

"You'd do better if you knew how to use that thing," he said.

"Zip" was the sound the second bullet made as it broke the water's edge, three feet to Robert's right.

"How good a shot do I have to be?" she asked cunningly, when he came back to the water's surface the second time. "I can wait longer than you can."

"Oh, you think so, do you?" he said. "Tell me, Lina, where'd you get that gun?"

"From Meg."

He chuckled. "I thought so. I gave Meg that gun. And I've never known her to keep more than two bullets in it. Did you load it?"

She seemed to be trying to decide how far she could bluff her way through this. She gave up, lowering the gun to her side. "No," she replied, chagrined.

"Well, then, if you'll let me finish my swim...." Lina stood dumbfounded. "Or would you prefer to join me?"

He noted the too-calm manner in which she said, "No, thank you," and her struggle not to seem in a hurry to move back toward her side of the pond, out of sight. Once she had retreated, he pulled himself up on the riverbank and dressed. "When you're decent, I'm over here by the rocks," she called.

When he reached her, she was sitting on a wide smooth rock with her back to him, shaking the dampness from her long hair. He watched, captivated, as her nimble fingers twisted it quickly and easily into a long thick braid. When she finished, she turned to him, not noticing his stare. "I didn't think anyone was coming here today. Everyone else seemed too busy. I just supposed you were, too."

"I thought I'd come up here for a little time by myself."

Lina was flustered. "Well, in that case, I'll just find another spot." She took hold of her boots and started to pull them on.

"Don't be ridiculous. It's a waste of time for one of us to leave. Say, did you bring yourself something to eat?"

"A bit," she answered.

"Well, then, so have I. Together, we can probably make a nice lunch of it. No reason we can't make the best of this...coincidence." He smiled.

"Besides, you're not bad company, you know." Robert went back to his horse and returned with a small pouch. He handed it to her. "Some jerk, and a few biscuits."

Lina went to her own horse, and took down a kerchief tied to the saddle horn. She laid it next to the bag. "Two apples and bite of cheese."

"Well, there! Between us, we have everything we need." Robert spread the food out on the kerchief. He took out his knife and cut the jerk and the cheese into two pieces. They sat in silence for some time, Robert chewing eagerly at the jerk, Lina nibbling carefully on the cheese.

"It's a nice spot, isn't it?" he said, breaking the quiet.

"Very nice," she answered.

He chewed some more, then said, "Have you been up here since we were all up here together?" Lina shook her head. "Didn't have any problem finding your way back?" She shook her head again. "Didn't have any trouble on the way up?"

"Trouble?"

"Oh, you know…"

"Oh, you mean up here in the *wilderness*?," she said pointedly. "No, I didn't have any trouble."

"You can make fun of me if you like, but you know I'm right."

"I do. I simply think you should give me a bit more credit."

"I give you the credit you earn, which is considerably more than I give most, in case you haven't noticed. When you learn more, I'll trust you more."

"Learn what?"

"Well, you could learn to handle a gun better." He tossed his half-eaten apple on the handkerchief and rose. Walking back to his horse, he reached inside his saddlebag and removed a pistol, which he carried open-handed toward her. "Can you shoot this?" he asked, offering her the gun.

She took it, felt its weight in her palm, turned it over, then, holding the barrel, offered it back to him. "I suppose so," she said. He did not take the gun. "Why?"

"Show me. He grabbed her free hand, pulling her abruptly to her feet. He looked around, then pointed to a tree a hundred feet away. "See that knot, about ten feet off the ground? Try to hit that."

"Look, if you're trying to make some point about me shooting at you...."

"No. No, I'm not. I promise. Just try it."

Lina faced the target and aimed the gun. When she fired, she missed the knot, but hit the tree three feet below the mark.

"Not bad," Robert said. "Here, let me show you." He came behind her, took hold of her arms and raised them level to the ground. He wrapped her with his arms and held her firmly by her elbows. He leaned close to her ear, and spoke in a warm, even voice. "Look straight down the barrel. Aim your sight, here," he said, adjusting her arms. "Now balance it between your hands. Try not to grab the thing too hard. Relax your hands. There, that's it. Now, when you pull the trigger, remember just to squeeze. And don't look at the gun. Keep your eye on your target."

She cocked the gun and squeezed the trigger again. This time the bullet was closer to the mark, but grazed the side of the tree and struck a tree another twenty feet behind it.

"Better!" he said. He still held her arms from behind. For a moment he hesitated. He was aware of her warmth inside his encircling arms. In an instant he imagined that, with no effort at all, he could turn her around, feel her arms around him too, pull her soft lips to his, wrap his fingers in that hair. Then he caught himself. "Once again," he directed her.

Again, she fired, and this time, the bullet landed not six inches from the knot. "That was better, wasn't it?" she said, tilting her head to look at him. He saw an eagerness in her eyes, something that beckoned him. He smiled at her, and he leaned forward for a kiss.

A step back was all it took to break the embrace. "No," she said quietly, looking away with a blush of embarrassment.

"Oh, well, I, uh... are you sure?"

"Of course, I'm sure!" she said.

He looked at her a moment, and then shrugged. "Fine, then." He stepped back casually, and sat down again, reaching for the half-eaten apple.

"Fine? Is that all there is to it?"

"Yes," he said, swallowing his bite. "Isn't it?"

"What on earth would make you think I wanted you to..."

"I *thought* so because I know what a woman looks like when she wants to be kissed."

"And that's what you thought I wanted?" Robert nodded. "Well, it most certainly wasn't!"

"So you said."

"Yes, I most certainly *did* say so!"

"Very well, then. We're back to where we were." He looked around for a way to change the subject. "Care for some more cheese?"

"No." Robert took what was left of her half and ate it in one bite. "Besides," Lina continued, "what sort of man would try to kiss a girl when he already has a sweetheart?" Robert looked at her in total bewilderment. "Franny Ellis?"

"Oh, Franny!" He laughed. "Well, I suppose I don't think of her as my *sweetheart*, as you say."

"Well, I'm sure she would be quite pleased to hear you say that!"

"Hmm. You probably have a point there. Although I've made it quite clear to her on a number of occasions that I don't have any serious intentions where she's concerned."

"And yet you string her along…"

"*String her along*? Lord, what prompted this sermon?" He stood up, and dusted the crumbs from his shirt. "See here, Lina. I'm sorry if I misread your interest. That's the end of it, as far as I'm concerned. I never expected such a reaction. Surely an attractive, available woman such as you has had similar advances before?"

"Of course," Lina said. "Of course! Many times. It's just that, well, you caught me off guard, I suppose."

"Evidently. Well again, my apologies." He looked at her closely for any lingering signs of her anger. "See here, now. This business with the gun, it wasn't a ruse to try to kiss you. I want you to be a better shot. It's important. You're not going to be stupid, are you? You're going to take me seriously about this?"

"I suppose, though I haven't needed a gun yet," she said as she handed him the pistol.

"Keep it," he ordered. "There'll be no arguments. I don't know why I didn't think of it sooner." He looked at her and all he saw in her eyes was her apathy for his concern, and her stubborn determination. "Very well. Don't take the matter seriously. You're so determined to take care of yourself. You're the one who'll suffer the consequences, not me." He picked up his pouch. "It's getting late. I'm heading back to town." Robert didn't wait for her reply. He climbed on his horse and started down the road alone.

****

"It'll just be the five of us," Hugh had told her when he made the invitation. "It seems Millie has wrangled an invitation out of none other than Martin Kincaid himself!"

"Really?" Lina laughed. "She must be beside herself."

"Oh, she is, from what Jean says. I suspect it's because Kincaid wants to make a good impression. I'm betting Kincaid thinks Millie will have the proper manners for that fancy crowd at old man Ellis' private party. A school teacher's breeding, you know."

Lina chuckled. "I'm pleased for her. Sounds like a good match."

"You might be right, at that. Millie will take to all that folderol. Better than Robert will. Franny'll be leading him around by the nose all day, poor fellow. Stuck up there, missing all the real fun."

Lina tried to ignore the thought of Franny and Robert. "It sounds like a fine time, Hugh. Thank you for asking."

"I hear you've a new frock for the occasion? Then I'll do my best to hold up my end. Clean shirt and a tie, how's that?"

When he left, Lina had to smile. *A place so small, even a new dress becomes a topic for discussion.* Now she was glad she had taken Meg's advice and Esther's offer of help. The dress had turned out well, far better than she had expected. Meg had seen it, and approved. "Why, there won't be a prettier girl there, including Franny Ellis herself," she told her lovingly.

When the day of the celebration in Ellis arrived, Lina rode with Hugh and Charley, Jean and Jamie. They traveled with the Minifee's in front of them, and other Sleekit locals in the caravan. There was much singing among the wagons, and the whole trip reminded Lina of the best days on the trail west, when the travel was easy and the mood among the travelers light. As they pulled into the center of Ellis, Lina was astonished to see how many people were there. The crowd no doubt made the town seem much bigger than it was, but she couldn't help thinking what opportunities there were in a place like this. Certainly

Ellis was more like what she had hoped to find in Sleekit. "I suspect there're already near a hundred folks here, and it's still morning," Hugh said.

"And the shops, Hugh," Lina said. "Why, they're all open for business. Those folks will make a pretty penny today, I'd wager."

"Ha. The only person making a penny today is Ellis. Look around, Lina. All those shops, the saloon, the mercantile, the blacksmith, they all belong to Ellis. You think he would miss a chance to make a buck? This is a company town. And Ellis is the company. Kincaid only *tries* to get his hand in everything in Sleekit. Ellis *has* his hand in everything here. It all belongs to him," Hugh said. "*They* all belong to him." He searched over his shoulder, then pointed up a road that led to a large house sitting high on a steep hill behind them, with a commanding view of the sound. "That's *his* house. If that doesn't say it all, I don't know what does." She craned her neck to take it all in as Hugh steered the team to an open spot near the water's edge. "This will be the place to be, come sundown," he said.

With the team tended to, they walked back to the center of town. Ellis had a real square, with a brand new pavilion made from Ellis lumber, of course, and built by Ellis carpenters, just for the occasion. Bunting draped its sides, and sitting beneath its shingled roof, musicians were beginning to gather. Everyone else was preparing the food. Lina guessed every available table in Ellis had been dragged into the open space around the pavilion, as she watched folks piling them high with food. Charley dashed from one table to another, sneaking samples. "Here, boy! Mind your manners. Don't take until it's offered you," Hugh called to him when he saw Charley charming some woman out of a piece of fresh bread. But his admonishment was more formal than sincere, since he just laughed and kept walking. "We won't see him again until nightfall, I suspect. He's like a bird, that one. Eats three times his weight in a day, and never stops moving."

"I think Charley has the right idea," Jamie said. "I'm starved." So the four of them filled plates as soon as they were offered, and found a spot to lay down a blanket and start their picnic. The music started soon after. The sun was warm, there was a breeze to cool them, and plenty of folks stopped by to say hello. The early afternoon passed sweetly. They broke from their conversation when they heard the music stop, then start again with a flourish.

"Heaven help us," Hugh said. "Now come the speeches. This will go on for hours. I'm taking a nap." He leaned back with eyes closed.

"Don't you want to hear them?" Lina watched the crowd move toward the pavilion.

Hugh shook his head. "You go, if you've a mind to."

"Jean? Jamie?"

"No, thanks, Lina. I'm with Hugh on this," Jamie said. "Besides, I need my rest if I'm to keep up with Miss Minifee here, once the dancing starts."

Jean smiled. "Go ahead, Lina. We'll wait here."

Lina moved through the onlookers, trying to get a better view. Peeking over shoulders taller than hers, she glimpsed an entourage entering the pavilion. The stately gentleman in the lead was surely Benjamin Ellis. On his arm was no doubt Mrs. Ellis. Franny Ellis followed, draped on the arm of Robert Marr.

When Ellis stepped forward to the railing a respectful quiet came over the crowd. Ellis looked about the square, then he straightened his posture to its most imposing, stuck his right hand inside his vest, and raised his left. "Welcome! Welcome one and all to Ellis, and to this celebration of the independence of our glorious Republic!" The crowd roared in agreement. With a wave of his hand, he silenced the crowd.

"In only a handful of generations, we have seen the glory that is America. We are a nation destined for greatness. We have thrown off the shackles of tyranny, charted and tamed a great wilderness, and set our people forward into this new world to hasten its growth and prosperity. As the father of this great nation, the magnificent and noble Mr. Washington, said…"

Hugh was right. For what seemed like an eternity, Benjamin Ellis waxed poetic on every ideal and endeavor of the nation, quoting from Washington, Franklin, the territorial governor, some Frenchman, and a few other names that were completely unfamiliar to Lina. She tried to listen, but the words, well spoken though they were, started to run together. She found herself paying more attention to those figures in the pavilion than anything Benjamin Ellis had to say. She could see when Franny leaned close to Robert, and when he seemed to be leaning down to whisper something in her ear. What Hugh had said came back to her. *Well, if she's leading him by the nose, he's a willing beast,* Lina was thinking, when the crowd let out a cheer over something Benjamin Ellis must have said.

"Enjoying yourself?" Hugh had come up behind her.

"You were right," Lina started to say, just as Ellis finished his speech, amid the thunderous applause of the onlookers. The crowd pressed forward, and Lina lost her vantage point. But she caught a glimpse of the Ellis' as they waved to the crowd. She couldn't see Franny as well, but she came forward, too, and Robert joined her, though he did not wave. It seemed to Lina that he looked completely ill at ease. "Good," she said, surprising herself.

"I beg your pardon?" Hugh spoke up to make himself heard above the applause.

"Nothing. Let's get back to the picnic."

"What? And miss the dancing? See now? They're leaving, and the music will start again."

Just as Hugh predicted, the musicians started just as the Ellis entourage began its walk back up the hill. Lina soon lost sight of Robert and Franny in the throng. "We can dance later, Hugh. I think I'd like to sit for a while, in the shade. Shall we find Jean and Jamie again?"

They walked back to the picnic spot, but took their time. Hugh caught sight of Charley for a brief moment, and felt the need to scold him, given the probability the boy had done some bit of mischief he should not have done. "Come back and take a rest, Charley. You can play some more later."

"Resting is for babies," Charley said, but he walked with them nonetheless. Suddenly, he took off like a shot, running toward the picnic spot. "Jamie! Jean!"

"Well, how was it?" Jamie asked, as Hugh and Lina sat down.

"Oh, just as you'd expect, I suppose," Lina said.

"Yes. Boring." Hugh lay back on the blanket. "In fact, it's given me an urge for another nap." He draped his arms across his eyes to shade them.

Suddenly, Charley, who had only just barely come to a stop, was off again like a shot. "Robert!" Charley yelled, bolting toward his cousin.

Beneath his crossed arms, Hugh let out a low groan. "Well, there goes my nap," he muttered, but he did not move. Neither did Lina. It surprised Lina to find she had a lump in her throat at the sight of Franny and Robert together. As she watched them come closer, she was glad for the lump, for it bottled the impulse she had to gasp at the sight of Franny Ellis.

The dress Franny wore was no doubt made especially for this day, and in all the fine dress shops Lina had regularly passed in San Francisco, she had never seen a creation quite like it. The dress was made from flag blue silk. The skirt was an endless drape of scalloped layers, each trimmed in tiny, fine lace of the purest white. The shawl sleeves and a neat little placket in the front of the bodice were broad bright stripes of blue and white. Just for protection from an errant freckle, Franny carried a matching parasol, made of the blue and white stripe. But the touch which made all the difference, which turned the dress from being merely showy to near absurdity, were dozens of tiny red bows all over it. On the skirt they tugged at the upturn of the hemline scallops. They sat like small red birds on each of Franny's shoulders, at the ends of the neckline. As one last show of excess, a large red bow sat dead center atop the parasol.

Charley had caught up with them, and was evidently giving Robert an animated account of his day so far. Robert looked down at the young boy fondly, but as they came closer, he turned his attention to the other members of his family. "Good afternoon!" Robert greeted them with genuine good cheer. Franny didn't look as happy to see them, but she forced a smile nonetheless.

"Good afternoon, Robert. Franny." Jean said, offering a quick curtsey. "I'm so glad you two could join us!" Just then, Jean looked down at Hugh, who had not moved. She gave the bottom of his boot a quick kick. Slowly, reluctantly, Hugh stood up.

"Oh, we can't stay," Franny said quickly. "In fact, we shouldn't be here at all. We have guests arriving." Franny gave Robert a pointed look.

"I insisted," Robert said. "I wanted to make certain the Sleekit contingent was having a good time."

"We certainly are, aren't we?" Jean answered for the group.

Franny gave Jean a weak smile. "Well, I'm certainly enjoying it," she said, squeezing Robert's arm just a bit tighter, and giving him her most adoring gaze. "Did everyone hear Father's speech?"

Jean and Jamie looked a bit embarrassed to tell the truth. They were saved the trouble of answering when Hugh said, "Lina did! She was very excited to hear it, weren't you, Lina?" Hugh grinned from ear to ear when she looked at him.

Damn you, Hugh Marr, Lina thought, but she smiled, "Yes I heard it. It was very….stirring, I guess. At least, the crowd seemed to think so."

"Yes, Father *is* a wonderful speaker. We were disappointed the Territorial Governor couldn't make it. But then, father's very highly regarded, too. He has quite a following here in Ellis."

"Bought and paid for." The words were muttered, but they had escaped Lina's lips before she could check them.

"I beg your pardon?" asked Franny.

Lina looked up quickly to catch the sharp light in Franny's eyes, directed squarely at her. *If she truly heard me, she'll be too much of a lady to call me on it*, Lina thought. She took a chance. "It's quite a party your father's bought and paid for." Lina noticed the corner of Franny's mouth turn up ever so slightly. Her gamble had paid off, but she knew in that moment she would never make a friend of Franny Ellis.

"Why, Jean! You've disappointed me!" Franny said.

"I have?" Jean asked, her brow an instant furrow of distress over the news. "Oh dear! What have I done?"

"You haven't said a word about my dress, and here I had it made just for the occasion." Franny lowered her parasol and twirled. "Well, what do you think?"

For just a moment, no one said anything. Jean was no doubt searching for just the right words. Lina knew better than to trust her luck again, so she stayed quiet. Hugh and Jamie had no idea what to say. It was Charley who broke the silence. "You look like a flag," he said simply.

Simultaneously, Jean's eyes popped wide as Jamie covered his mouth to keep from laughing. "Charley…" Hugh hissed, giving the boy a quick thump on the shoulder.

"Oh, Charley!" Jean said, with a forced laugh that no one believed. "Franny, don't pay him any mind. What do boys know?" She giggled nervously. "Men either, for that matter! It's, well, it's just such a eye-catching dress, Franny. I, I'm at a loss for words."

"Hmm." Franny turned her attention to Lina. "And you, Miss Morgan? You aren't usually at a loss for words."

Lina realized this was the price of her earlier gamble, an extorted compliment. She knew the safest course would be to pay quickly, and humbly. But she couldn't resist. There was something about Franny Ellis that provoked Lina in a way that few people ever had. She resolved to only give partial payment. "Why, that dress is so eye-catching, one hardly notices *you* at all, Franny."

Only Franny understood the insult in the compliment. So the others did not understand the cold look, or the flat, spiteful tone Franny took when she spoke. "And I see you have a new dress, too, don't you? So new you haven't muddied the hem yet. Well, it's a lovely little thing. Simple. Very suited to you. It will make a fine dress for you to work in. And such an appropriate color. Green. Like envy."

"Fran." Robert whispered sharply. No one filled the awkward silence, so he added, "We need to be heading to the house."

"Yes, let's. Good day, everyone." Franny turned quickly and walked away.

Robert watched her for a moment, then turned back to his family. "I hope you have a fine time tonight." Then he followed Franny through the square, but did not hurry to catch up with her.

Jean was the first to speak. "Lina, I'm so sorry. I don't know what prompted her to…"

"I do," Lina said. "But don't you give it another thought, Jean."

Hugh took Charley firmly by the arm and turned him so he could tower above him and look him straight in the eye. "What were you thinking, Charley? Telling Franny she looked like a flag!"

Charley looked up, confused. "Well, doesn't she?"

"Charley, for some people, the truth isn't a valued commodity. Now, the next time you see her, you'll say something nice to her. And you'll apologize to Robert, too." Charley started to argue. "And you'll stay right here, for the rest of the day. No arguments."

Everything felt wrong to Lina. Everyone seemed uneasy, and now Hugh was angry with Charley, for little or no reason. And all because she had lost the good sense to be polite. "Hugh, that's enough. It's not Charley's fault. It's mine. Let's not let this ruin our day. Come on, now. Didn't you promise me a dance?"

The rest of the day went slowly for Lina. Though she tried to keep herself occupied, there was something about that conversation, about seeing Robert with Franny, that would creep back into her thoughts and she would find herself staring and thinking. When evening came, it helped to dance, so Lina danced often. She was dancing with Hugh, but in the growing twilight, every time she noticed the lights from the house on the hill, she slipped into her thoughts.

Finally Hugh gave up. "You don't feel much like dancing, do you?" he asked. She shook her head. "That's alright. I'm getting a bit tired myself. The fireworks'll be starting soon. Let's go find the others." Charley was found with some other boys who had laid their hands on a bunch of small firecrackers. Jean and Jamie finished their last dance, then they all walked back to their picnic spot and sat in silence as the fireworks began.

The show was fantastic, as spectacular as its promise. The barrage was set along the water's edge, and from up on the green, the jewel-like bursts and showers mirrored in the starlit waters below. Lina was enthralled. She had never seen anything so extravagant, so magical. Almost on instinct, she caught herself wondering what Robert's reaction was to this spectacle, and then remembering where he was, she looked up over her shoulder to the house, lit from within. Quickly she turned back to the fireworks and noticed Hugh looking at her. Then, unexpectedly, he gently tapped his finger on the tip of her nose. "Don't worry. Everything's going to be just fine. You have my word on it." Her puzzled expression begged an explanation, but he just grinned and watched the fireworks.

****

As if Benjamin Ellis had timed it so, just after the fireworks had concluded, a soft rain began to fall. Those who lived close enough to make the trip home that night gathered their families, their blankets and baskets and left, the Sleekit folks among them. The rain came in fits and starts on the trip home. Somewhere behind them Lina heard men singing, their words slurred by a day's worth of drink. Charley had fallen sound asleep the moment they left. Jean tried to make conversation for a while, but Lina didn't have the spirit for it. With the cloak of night to hide beneath, she pretended to be asleep. Soon, Jean herself fell asleep.. Jamie and Hugh sat up front and said little to each other as they drove the wagon home.

They all said goodnight in front of Meg's. Jamie walked Jean home, while Hugh took Charley back to the cabin. The tavern was dark, so Lina headed straight for the stairs. As she passed the door to the tavern, Lina heard Meg's voice from within the darkness. "Honey, is that you?"

Lina stepped into the dark. "Yes, Meg, it's me." She could just make out Meg's silhouette, sitting at a table. Meg struck a match and lit the lantern in front of her. Slowly, the light grew to reveal Meg's face, and a half empty glass of whiskey in front of her. "Are you alright, Meg?"

"Me? Oh, I'm fine, honey. I was just sitting here thinking. It was kind of lonely with everybody gone today."

"Well, it's time we both got to bed," Lina answered cheerily. "Let's go upstairs."

"Alright," Meg said. When she stood, she faltered just a bit, and steadied herself by grabbing the chair with one hand, and leaning on the table with the other. Lina step forward quickly, taking hold of Meg's arm. "Oh, it's just this old leg of mine." She patted her right thigh, then took Lina's arm for strength. The two headed slowly toward the stairs. "If I sit too long, or when it's cold or rainy, it gets stiff on me. Been this way for years, ever since that husband of mine broke it."

Lina was shocked. "Riordan broke your leg?"

"Oh no!" Meg laughed. "Not Milo. Oh, heavens, no, honey. Milo wouldn't hurt a fly. No, honey. My husband."

"But I thought Riordan was your husband."

Meg's silver-blonde curls bobbed as she shook her head. "No, honey, we're not married. We can't get married, you see. I have a husband back in Boston."

They had reached the door of Meg's room upstairs, and once inside, Meg released Lina to walk to the table and light the lantern. Her leg seemed better now, so Lina let her walk on her own, although Meg kept her hand on first a chair, and then the bed, as she made her way. Lina stood, dumbfounded in the doorway. With the lantern lit, Meg could see the look of surprise on her face.

"Does that bother you, Lina? Me and Milo not being proper married?"

"Oh, of course not, Meg. No, that's not it. It's just that, well I guess, it's just that I assumed…."

"Sure you did. We don't try to fool anybody, but, it doesn't come up that often, you know, so it's easier to let folks think what they will." Meg could see Lina had questions. She sat down on the edge of her bed, patting the place by her side. Lina sat next to her.

In the soft, warm light of the small room, Meg began. "You knew we came here, Milo and me, a few years back. Milo'd had some trouble back east, some creditors he was trying to stall."

"He told me something of that, when we first met."

Meg smiled. "That he would. He's not a deceitful sort, by nature, and it bothered him to have to high tail it like that. But he didn't tell you the other part of the story. He might have gone without near so much worry, if it weren't for me. He was a regular at a place I ran back there. My husband owned it, but he spent most of his time at the poker table. When he wasn't busy doing that, he liked to come home late and knock me around a bit. Now, don't get me wrong, honey, I wasn't a timid little mouse just waiting for him to take a swing at me. I usually held my own, and I knew enough to stay out of his way. But a girl can't always do that." She sighed, and for a moment, stared into a dark corner of the room. Then she chuckled. "Of course, I wasn't a girl anymore by then. And I confess I was beginning to think that pouring drinks and taking that bastard's suffering was about all life held for me. Until Milo. You know, we were only friends. He'd never said a word to me of any feelings he had for me, although, I must admit, I could tell. A woman can always tell. And I had some feelings for him too, although I'd never said so." She gave Lina a knowing smile. "Well, one night, Milo told me about his circumstances, told me he was leaving the next day. And all of a sudden, I realized how sad I'd be when he was gone. I guess he saw it, too, 'cause it gave him the courage to tell me how he felt, to ask me to go with him. Of course, I said no. I couldn't see how a woman could just up and leave everything, with no regard to her obligations, no matter how horrible they might be. Milo, he didn't try to argue. He just wished me well, gave me a quick kiss on the cheek, and left. I thought I'd never see him again.

"Well, that night, Billy, that's my husband, he came home with a real drunk on, mad as could be. Probably lost at poker or something. Who knows? It never mattered what the cause was, he would take it out on me. That night, I fought back. Took a gun out and held it on him, not that he was sober enough to be afraid. But I managed to hold him off until he passed out. That was all the time I needed. I emptied the cash drawer from the bar, and I left, with nothing more than the clothes on my back and twenty dollars in my purse. I walked down to the Bantry Bay and came on board, and I never looked back."

Lina listened with awe. "You're very brave."

Meg shook her head. "No, honey, I'm a stone cold coward."

"How can you say that? Leaving that horrible man, taking a chance on a whole new life?"

"I'm a coward, honey, because I was more afraid of living whatever was left of my life in misery like that, than I was of starting over. I was more afraid of being unhappy for the rest of my life, than being happy. I was afraid of waking up one day, and thinking why I didn't go with Milo. So I did." She smiled, then changed her tone. "But enough of all this history, honey! Tell me about the doings over in Ellis!"

Lina sat on the edge of Meg's bed and told her of the whole day. She did her best to sound as enthusiastic as she could. She told of the picnic, the dancing, and the fireworks. She talked about Jean and Jamie and Hugh, but it was what she didn't mention that Meg noticed.

"So I take it Robert spent the whole day with Franny?"

Lina tried to sound disinterested. "Oh, we saw them for a bit. He and Franny stopped by to say hello. But I honestly don't know what they did with the rest of their day."

"Probably don't care, either, huh?" Meg asked teasingly.

"Not in the least," Lina said faintly. She was too tired to try to convince Meg of anything, and Meg could see that.

"Well, I'm glad you're home safe and sound," she said. "Without Riordan here, it doesn't seem like home with you gone, too." Meg took Lina's hand and gave it a motherly pat. Lina looked at Meg kindly, then rose. Impulsively, she leaned over and put her arms around Meg, hugging her tightly. She kissed her on her cheek, and whispered in her ear, "I love you, Meg." Then, before her tired tears could escape, she darted through Meg's door, closing it behind her.

****

Young Theodore Colvin was an ambitious lad. He had worked hard to become the fastest rising clerk at Page & Beacon. After long hours and low pay, he'd been rewarded by being made the principal clerk to the President. He was used to being asked to do unusual tasks, but this was the strangest request so far.

That afternoon, a teller had delivered a note to Greeley's office, and a few minutes later Greeley burst through his office door. Colvin watched as the teller looked at Greeley, then pointed discreetly in the direction of a grizzled seaman standing at the counter. The teller returned to the customer, but Greeley nearly yanked Colvin from his desk and into his office.

"Did you see that man that the teller was pointing to? Follow that man, for as long as it takes, until he gets to where he's going. Probably his ship. Then make note of where it is docked, and take that information directly to this man." Greeley handed him the calling card Haarten had left with him. Colvin started to ask, but Greeley gave him no time. He shoved him through the door saying, "Hurry, you fool! He'll be leaving the bank any moment."

Greeley was right. Colvin stepped out and caught sight of the man exiting the bank's main doors. For the next several hours young Colvin followed the old dog through a procession of taverns along the waterfront. Colvin had a drink at the first two, but feared if he tried to keep up he'd be drunk before the man returned to his ship. From then on he simply waited outside.

It was sundown before the old man staggered toward his ship. A few times more he stopped momentarily to banter with a passing sailor, or holler a hallo to a passing lady of dubious reputation. Finally, he stopped at one pier, seemed to gather himself by straightening his cap and pulling at his jacket, and then pointing himself toward the gangplank, went on board a ship. The Bantry Bay, Colvin made note. Pier 3.

****

Riordan stood on deck of the Bantry Bay, bellowing at McNab. "What do yas mean, ya don't know where he went? When was the last time ya seen him?"

"Two days ago, Cap'n. He headed fa dem bawdy houses soon as we docked, jus' lak always. Ain't nobody seen 'im since."

Riordan let out a growl that turned the head of every man on deck. "Awk, man, for all we know, he could be halfway across the Pacific by now, shanghaied." Riordan's agitation was genuine. He'd been sailing with less than a full crew for months. Now he'd lost his second mate.

"But, Cap'n, 'ere's a fella what's interested in signin' on." McNab pointed to a young man standing on the pier below. "Showed up this mornin' lookin' for work, he did. Looks like 'es an able sort."

Riordan motioned for the sailor to come aboard. "You, I hear you're lookin' to sign on as second mate?" Riordan asked

"Aye, Captain. I'm looking. Got any room?"

"That depends, lad. First, I need to know your bona fides. What was your last ship?"

"The Rosalea, sir."

"The Rosalea? Now tell me why a man would leave the finest ship in all of San Francisco Bay for a greasy bucket like this? Are ya a drunk? Tell the truth, man."

"No, Captain."

"A womanizer? Trouble with the law, then?" Both times the sailor shook his head. "What then?"

"The Captain, sir. He's one of them educated types. More interested in the business end of the matter. Don't know the first thing about the sea. He's goin' to get the crew lost or killed, mark my words."

Riordan was skeptical. "What's your name, son?"

"Sullivan, sir. Sully."

Riordan's eyes brightened. "An Irishman, is it? Well, Sully, if you're willin', the Bantry Bay sails for Puget Sound tomorrow at sunset. Get your gear and come aboard."

Sully left and headed straight for the Rosalea, to get his gear. It was waiting for him in the captain's cabin, along with Edward Haarten. Haarten was preparing for the ship's voyage to the Baja at evening's tide when Sully came in.

"I sail for Puget Sound, sir. Tomorrow at sunset." Sully said.

"Fine, sailor, good job." Haarten reached for an envelope on the corner of his desk. "This should help recompense you for the decrease in wages and working conditions."

"Aye, Captain, it's a sorry lookin' vessel. But should be easy duty."

"When you return, I expect a full account," Haarten said. Sully nodded briskly, stuck the envelope beneath his belt, saluted the Captain, and walked out.

30

Lina was eager to put the day in Ellis behind her. Weary as she was when she climbed into bed, sleep didn't find her for hours. She knew she had behaved badly, even if no one but Franny had noticed. It would be easy to make Franny's behavior her excuse, but to be fair, Franny hadn't done anything out of the ordinary, and certainly nothing unwarranted, until Lina provoked her. But what had provoked Lina wasn't Franny's propensity for pettiness. Neither was it her limitless vanity nor even her dismissive attitude, though Lina thought all that had only made it easier for her. No, Lina knew what it was that bothered her. For reasons that passed her immediate understanding, Lina found Robert's choice of Franny particularly irksome. Not understanding Franny, Lina thought that 'poking the bear' might yield some new insight into Franny, and into Robert.

Lina had studied Robert Marr almost from the first day she arrived in Sleekit, even before she met him, so certain she had been that the Marrs would be the key to her survival. Now she tallied up all that she had learned. She scrutinized Robert like her ledger books, carefully checking the columns of his character, the rows of his temperament, searching for the overlooked entry that would account for Franny Ellis.

Perhaps it was the loyalty he displayed so often with his family, with Meg and Riordan, and others. Perhaps he likewise felt a duty to Franny, for some past kindness Lina knew nothing about. This seemed unlikely, for nothing about Franny gave Lina reason to believe Franny would do something out of kindness. *Kindness.* Could that be the reason he tolerated Franny? Robert would never intentionally be unkind to her, no matter how ridiculous or rude she might be. But kindness didn't explain his repeated attentions. Robert was smart enough to extricate himself from Franny's clutches, if he had a mind to. Perhaps it was ambition. She thought of Franny's father, the empire he was building that would presumably fall to his daughter one day. No, Lina discounted that entirely. Robert had his own ambitions. He had no need to covet another man's.

Reluctant though she was to admit it, Lina had to consider this could be simply a physical attraction. Franny was beautiful, there was no arguing. But Lina could find nothing in Robert that led her to believe his vanity was that demanding. Nor could she envision that Franny would be loose with her favors. *No*, Lina decided, *that's the bait on her hook. She'll not give up her virtue without reward.*

Lina summed up all her impressions of Robert and still could not find one good reason why he would tolerate Franny Ellis. Then she added up another column, and realized she had just now named more than enough reasons that Franny would care for Robert. Loyalty, kindness, intelligence, ambition. As exhaustion finally overtook her, she wondered if Franny was aware of any of those virtues, or appreciated Robert at all. Lina certainly did. Perhaps that's why Franny had used the word "envy" to describe Lina. Perhaps it was Franny who was envious of Lina. *How silly…*

****

As Lina came downstairs the next morning, she heard Hugh's voice first, "Robert, I don't see what harm it could do." Standing just outside the door, she could see the center table crowded with all three Marrs, and Martin Kincaid to boot. Kincaid had a stack of papers before him, and Hugh held the account books from camp. Jamie simply stared deep into the coffee mug in his hands. Robert was leaning back in his chair, arms crossed tightly over his chest, shaking his head. "The harm it'll do, Hugh, lies with the risk."

"Risky or not, the time's right for it, and you know that, Marr," Kincaid said, dropping a flat palm over the papers. "A territorial delegation in Ellis—what other opportunity could be as rich as that? Even as we sit here, a small fleet is filling the sound, each ship begging for lumber. Time spent on courting the territory will mean nothing if we don't *show* them Sleekit can produce! You know I'm right. If we don't supply these ships now, Benjamin Ellis will. Is that what you want?"

"Good morning, Lina," Jamie said. He was the only one to have noticed her enter.

"Good morning, Jamie," she answered. "Where's Meg?"

"Gone to Minifee's," Jamie answered. She took her coffee and eggs to an empty table across the room.

"Well, I think we should do it," Hugh said. "Nothing ventured, nothing gained."

"But Hugh," Jamie asked, "Can we afford it?"

Before his cousin could answer, Robert spoke. "You're asking the wrong person, James. Lina?"

Lina looked up in surprise at the sound of her name. In a hurried gulp she swallowed her first mouthful of breakfast. "Yes?"

"Bring your plate over here and join us. We need to ask your advice."

"*My* advice?"

"That's right. Come on," he said impatiently. He pulled another chair to the table, next to his own. Lina gathered her plate and her coffee and came to the table. "Have you been listening to what we were saying?"

"Not really."

"Martin here thinks he and I should go to Ellis next week. There's a territorial delegation coming through, headed for the fort. That much we learned yesterday at the party."

"Much to Benjamin Ellis' regret," Kincaid said, with a self-satisfied grin.

"True enough. Ellis thinks he has these territorial fellows locked up. Martin thinks we need to go to Ellis and sing the praises of Sleekit."

"And I agree," Hugh added. "There's all kind of talk about work the territory has planned. Roads, bridges, railroads, even a harbor! That's the kind of work we need. Big jobs, big contracts."

"It sounds like a fine idea," Lina said.

"I suppose it is," said Robert, "though I'm not convinced you need *me*, Martin."

Kincaid squirmed in his chair. "It pains me to admit it, Marr, but you're the more persuasive salesman. That aside, Benjamin Ellis can hardly give us the boot if *you're* there, can he? What with you and Miss Ellis…"

"Fine," Robert stopped him. "But I can't be in two places at once." He turned his attention back to Lina. "By week's end, the waters will be filled with timbers we've been felling all spring. More than the Bantry Bay or any one ship can hold. Kincaid's sure—we're both sure—that we can sell them to the government on the spot, provided we can load them onto their ships as well. But I can't be in both places to manage both ends of the deal."

"We can handle it, Robert" Jamie said. "Hugh and I can manage the crew and…"

"I know you can," Robert said, laying a confident hand on his brother's shoulder. "It's just that we don't have enough men to do it all. We'll need every hand we have and then some to pull this off."

"Is there no one to hire?" Lina asked.

"A few, perhaps," Jamie answered. "But Robert says not just anyone. Experienced men."

"But not because the work is skilled," said Robert. "It's not. It's long hours of hard labor in cold water. We need men who have experience with the elements. Then, too, we've never tried this before, and we won't know how it's to be done. We need men who can handle themselves in a pinch."

"Trappers," Hugh said.

"What?"

"The trappers! That's it. Remember last week we saw a couple of them passing through when we had the crews in the stand to the north. Old Fournaise, and that other fellow he's always with. We wondered what had them down this way. I'll wager they've heard about the gathering in Ellis. The territory will be after their pelts."

Robert nodded. "Hugh, you've got something there. The trappers would do. But that brings us back to Lina. Can we afford to pay them?"

"It'll be tight, Robert," she said. "How many are you thinking of hiring, and how long do you need them?"

"If we can get them, I need a dozen men or so. For a week."

"Then you'll have to pay them a quarter of what you pay your cheapest man on the logging crew. Will they work for that?"

Robert shook his head. "I won't ask them to."

"What if we pay them another way?" Jamie offered. "The trappers trade their pelts to the government, don't they? They'll have cash from that, and besides, what they really want is ammunition, whiskey, food, boots. And they'll pay dearly for them in Ellis. We've got extra supplies, don't we, Lina?"

"Yes. Not whiskey, of course, but food. Lots of food. We're overstocked. We've got beans, coffee, plenty of cured meat..."

"And when we sell these timbers to the government, we'll have cash to restock before fall!" said Hugh.

Glances passed across the table between them, silent questions as to details overlooked. Finally, Kincaid spoke. "Well, then, there is a plan." He took another sip of his coffee, then stood. "All that remains is to get ready. I'm off to the mill. Lots to do in two days. Good day, gentlemen. Miss Morgan." He tossed some coins on the table and left.

"He's right, boys. Lots to do. Jamie, you get started with the crew. Hugh, take a man or two and figure out what we're going to need to get those timbers loaded. Hurry on, now." Just as the two young men cleared the door, Hugh looked back. "Aren't you coming, Robbie?"

"I'm headed back to the cabin to get ready. I've got to see an old friend." Hugh gave him a quick wave, and ran to catch up with Jamie.

"I should make certain of what we have in the storehouses, if you're counting on making use of it." Lina reached for a rag to clean the table when Robert stopped her.

"There's time for that later," he said. "We'll be spread a bit thin for several days. That means more will fall to you. It'll be dawn to dusk work, and if you need help, you'll be on your own to find it. We won't be able to spare a man. Hugh will be busy with the ships, and Jamie'll be working the crews by himself. You'll need to make daily trips to camp to keep in touch with Jamie, but you'll also need to be here to see what Hugh might need."

"I understand," Lina said.

Robert took a moment, then said, "If this is too much, I understand. Hugh and Jamie, they know they must pitch in when times require. They've signed on for all of it. But you..."

She stopped him. "So have I."

He beamed. "Thank you for that." She smiled, too, until she felt own heart's beat in the lingering silence. "Remember to be careful. There'll be a lot of strangers coming this way. Trappers are a good lot for the most part, but not all of them. They don't spend much time around other folks, and don't know how to behave when they do. Milo will be around, but keep an eye on things here at Meg's all the same. And be doubly careful yourself. That's all."

"Thank you. I will. I promise."

"Then I'll be off."

"You're going to find your Indian friends?"

He nodded again. "Yes, but you know not to mention it…"

"Yes, I know. You think they can tell you something?"

He chuckled. "Lina, Willahe and his tribe know everything that happens within five hundred miles. Why, he's better than Millie Forbes."

Lina laughed. "A remarkable recommendation." Her smile softened as she added, "You take your own advice, Robert. Be careful."

"Thank you," he said, then left.

She watched him go, and suddenly, a deep regret left over from the day before took hold of her. She thought of the confidence in her that he had just displayed, and the concern for her, too. In the face of that kindness, the impulse to rid herself of the regret was too strong. "Robert!" she called out to him.

He turned toward her as she hurried across the bluff to reach him. "Yes?" he said.

"I, uh," she struggled to find the words to start. "I owe you an apology." He looked at her, puzzled. "Yesterday, I, well, I behaved badly with Miss Ellis." He still looked puzzled. "You remember? We were discussing her dress, and…"

"That?" Robert shook his head. "You know, that's the oddest thing. Charley came to me earlier and made a point of apologizing, too. I suspect Hugh put him up to it, for honestly, the boy didn't seem to have any notion why he was apologizing. Can't say as I blame him, either, and I told him so. All he did was tell the truth. Franny *did* look like a flag," he said, trying hard not to laugh at the memory.

"Charley hasn't anything to apologize for, but I feel that I do, Robert. Franny and her family were our hosts, and I was hardly as gracious as I could have been."

"Hmm. Perhaps. I don't recall what you said, to be honest. Although it was clear there was something more to what you two were saying than I heard. But I did hear what Franny said to you. I know that tone well. For some reason, she seemed to want to hurt your feelings in some way. I take it she succeeded?"

Lina shook her head. "No, but she made her point just the same."

"Yes, she's quite good at that," he muttered. "Well, don't give it another thought. You certainly don't owe me an apology. Nor an explanation. I suspect it's Franny who owes you one, though I wouldn't expect it. Just answer me this. Did you have a good time yesterday?"

She forced a smile too broad. "Yes."

"Then that's all that matters. Don't give Franny Ellis another thought."

He left, and Lina once again struggled with the questions from before. Robert seemed to so easily accept that Franny had been the one misbehaving, and yet he tolerated it. As she walked back toward Meg's, Lina realized that of all Robert's counsel today, not giving Franny Ellis another thought would be the one piece of advice it would be difficult for her to take.

****

For the first few days, it was all Lina could do to keep up with Hugh's requests for supplies as he and the trappers struggled to get the loading started. After that, she had to catch up with the needs of Jamie and the crews. All that put her behind at Meg's, too, so she stayed up late each night to finish chores. She was exhausted and a little bit irritable.

Minor interruptions didn't help, but were unavoidable. Today, it had been Millie Forbes. Lina was loading up for camp one last time, looking forward to the end of this busy week. Robert and Kincaid were expected back any time, and Jamie and Hugh reported great progress. Jamie told her they would need nothing more than their pay this last trip, so instead of the cumbersome wagon, she had rented Kincaid's horse and was headed there to load the payroll when she saw Millie scurrying toward her from the direction of the school.

"Lina! Wait, Lina!"

"Millie, please, I'm in an awful hurry to get to camp. I'm already behind. Was there something you needed?"

"Well, I was just wondering if either Hugh or Jamie had heard from Robert…or Martin."

Lina chuckled. "Why do you ask?"

"Well," Millie faltered, "Because, well, it's the school books, you know. The teacher in Ellis offered to send them back with Martin, and…"

"Millie, are you certain you don't have another reason for asking?" She gave Millie a smile to invite her confidence.

"Well, yes, there is, if you can keep a secret!" Millie whispered.

"A secret?" Lina laughed. "Yes, Millie, I suppose if you've managed to keep a secret, then I can keep it for you, too."

Millie looked at her curiously, then dismissed the comment. "It's Mr. Kincaid. Martin," she said. Her eyes danced with the name. "I think I might truly have a beau."

"I'm happy for you, Millie."

"Between us girls, I've never really had a beau before, so I'm not certain. We had a very lovely time at the party in Ellis. The Ellis' have the most beautiful home. Everyone looked so elegant. There were musicians, and we danced! And…," Millie leaned in. "We kissed! When he brought me home. It was a very proper kiss, to be sure. Still," she said dreamily, "it was a very nice kiss."

"Millie, that's wonderful." Lina was fully prepared to leave but as she looked at Millie's hopeful face, she suddenly felt she had to speak up.

"Millie, may I offer some advice?" Millie nodded. "I know you're anxious to see Mr. Kincaid again, but try your hardest to wait until he finds you. If he's brought back the books, he'll come looking for you soon enough. If he hasn't, well, it's a small town. You'll find each other before too long."

Millie nodded eagerly. "Why thank you, Lina! That's very sound advice."

"And Millie. One more suggestion? When you do see him, try not to wear your heart on your sleeve, as you're doing now. Didn't your mother also tell you not to seem too eager?"

Millie's eyes popped wide. "Oh, you're so right, Lina! How did you know? Yes, mustn't seem too eager! Thank you, Lina. I shall go home right now and not move an inch until Martin returns." She started back the way she had come, calling over her shoulder one last time. "Thank you, Lina. Thank you!"

A dozen thoughts occupied Lina as she rode to camp for what seemed like the hundredth time in the last two weeks, and for a moment she couldn't remember which errand she was on. She told herself it was the heat. The mid-summer heat combined with the ever present dampness making for a sultry world that even the shade of the dense forest didn't relieve. She felt distracted, as if she were forgetting something. At one point she caught herself drifting to sleep in the saddle. Perhaps there'd be time to rest when she got to camp, time before the men returned.

At camp, Lina tied up the horse, then took the saddlebag inside the tent. The tent was stuffy but it always picked up her spirits to be there, and she hummed lightly to herself as she began to lay the accounts out on the table and ready the cash in the drawer. Once those were set, she promised herself that nap.

She heard footsteps just outside the tent. She opened the flap expectantly. "Jamie, is that…" was all she managed to say before a man lunged at her, shoving her to the ground inside the tent.

The man reeked of filth and skins and liquor. He stood in the tent opening, looking down at her, a toothless smile behind his dirty beard. "All alone, missy?"

Lina struggled to her feet and backed away from him, but he lunged again, and struck her jaw with the back of his hand. Again she stumbled to the ground. "I'll take that cash ya brung," he demanded, no trace of a smile now. Her face stung from the blow, and her hip hurt from landing against the table when she fell, toppling it to the floor beside her. The saddlebag was knocked to the ground, too, its contents spilled all around her. As the man crept toward her, she scrambled through the mess of money and paper around her until she found what she was looking for. He was reaching for the cash on the ground when the gun went off.

****

It was mid-afternoon when Jamie and his crew reached camp. As the men unloaded the wagon and tended to the teams, Jamie headed toward the tent. He could see Lina inside at the table, her head bent over the books. When he reached the tent she looked up. The sight of the large bruise along her check and jaw stunned him. "Dear God. What happened to you?"

Lina's jaw still hurt too much to talk, and the bump on her head made her dizzy. She pointed toward the corner of the tent where Jamie saw a man. His arms and legs were trussed behind him, and a tourniquet wrapped his thigh. Jamie moved closer and saw the man was half conscious.

"Wanted the cash. Had to shoot him," was all Lina could say through her swollen jaw.

Jamie was stunned. "Shot him? How?"

"This," Lina said, handing the pistol to him.

"Let me see your face. Are you alright?" Outside they heard the men approaching. She stood, then felt a sudden dizziness that caused her sit back down, resting her head in her hand. She could not even look up when she saw two shadows enter the tent, and heard Robert ask, "What is it?"

Some combination of shock and anger filled Jamie's voice when he answered. "This bastard attacked her. Tried to rob us, I guess, and she shot him!"

Robert crossed to Lina, but she was still too dizzy to look up. Besides, she was embarrassed for letting this happen. She figured the man had followed her. She was almost certain she saw him in Sleekit that morning. This was just the sort of danger Robert had warned her about, and she feared she might see reproach in his eyes.

She saw only concern. He took her chin and gently lifted her face toward him. "It's a nasty blow. Are you sure you're alright?" He knelt beside her, then slowly moved her face to the light to inspect every inch.

It was all Lina could do to nod her head. "Just knocked me down. Then hit me."

"Thank God," Robert sighed. "Jamie, get me some water and a rag. Hugh, hand me the whiskey bottle."

"It's gone," Lina answered. Speaking was getting easier the more she talked. "He knocked me and the table over. Everything spilled out. Cash, whiskey, gun. When he reached for the money I shot him. Hit him with the whiskey bottle. He went out cold. I tied him up and dressed his wound best I could. Not serious, just messy." She looked at Robert. "Thank God my hand was shaking or I might have killed him." She smiled, then winced with the pain the smile cost her.

Robert chuckled. He held her hand and stared at her, finding reassurance in her talent to find anything about this horrible situation amusing. "Hugh, get some help and take that piece of dirt to town," he said, looking with disgust at the wretch moaning in the corner. "Lock him in the smokehouse if you have to." Then Robert looked back at Lina. "Let's take you home."

Lina kept reassuring them she was fine, but when she went to climb upon the seat of the wagon, it was clear she was still dizzy. "It'll be too rough for her in the back," Hugh warned.

"Not if I ride with her," Robert said, and so he helped Lina into the back. Robert climbed in beside her. "Would you rather lie down?" he asked.

"No," she said. "Makes me woozy. I'll sit up."

"Then lean against me," he said, pulling her to his shoulder. Lina let her weight fall against him, in too much pain to argue. Robert held them steady with a grip on the wagon with one hand, and his other arm around her. When the wagon reached Meg's, it was near dark. Robert lifted her effortlessly, and carried her up the stairs. She felt small and light in his arms, and she knew there was more to this sense of light-headedness than the bump on her head.

Her eyes were closed with the pain, but Lina heard Hugh holler, "Meg, we'll need your help upstairs." Then she heard voices in a cacophony around her. "What happened? What are you doing? Oh, my goodness! Look at her face! Lina, are you alright? Who did that?" The questions came suddenly and all together, and went unanswered. She felt herself being lowered to the bed, and then she thought she felt warm lips on her forehead, but the sensation was lost in the blur around her. Was it Robert? But now Meg was by her side, and Jean, too. Robert and Hugh and Riordan and the others were somewhere in the distance behind them.

"Get out of here, all of you, now," Meg said. "Leave her to us. We'll take care of her. She'll be fine." Lina knew she would not die, but with the growing pain in her head, she wasn't sure she would ever be fine again either. By the time she could focus again on the room, there was only Meg, hovering over her, wiping a cool wet rag across her tender cheek. "Head still hurt, honey?"

"Mmm." The soft bed in the quiet room, the cool cloth and the soft, soothing sound of Meg's voice were lulling Lina toward sleep.

"Now, honey, I know it's been a hell of a day, but I can't let you sleep. Not just yet. At least for a few hours. You might have hurt your head worse than you think. Drift off to sleep before I'm sure, why, you might not come back." Meg's words were fading, as if she were far away, when Lina felt Meg's hands on her shoulders, and heard her command her. "Lina! Wake up, now. No sleep yet."

Lina forced her eyes open, and smiled. "I'll try Meg. I promise."

"Well, I'm going downstairs to get some coffee, just to be safe. You stay awake until I get back."

The rest of the night was dreamlike, if not dream filled. Despite her promises, Lina could not keep her eyes open long. For a while Meg would wake her every time she dozed, but eventually Meg must have felt reassured for Lina slept through the night.

The next morning Lina woke with a throbbing headache, so she remained in bed all that day, more sleeping than waking, lost in a fitful dream. Twice Meg came and forced her to take some soup. She would have eaten more, but her jaw was still too tender for chewing. The next day was Sunday, and she felt better. She dressed herself, and came downstairs early for a good, hot breakfast, but then returned to her room. She decided against going to Sunday service downstairs. She expected it to be quiet after that, but shortly after the last hymn was sung, she heard folks making a ruckus downstairs. There was a knock at the door, and in crept Millie and Jean, their heads together in conspiracy.

"Oh, my heavens!" Millie shrieked. "Lina, you look absolutely awful!"

"Millie, shush," Jean said. "Lina, I have wonderful news. That horrible man is over in Ellis, in a proper jail."

"Well, that's a relief, isn't it? Thank you."

"No, silly, *that's* not the wonderful news. This is." Jean pulled something from her pocket. "This is for you," she said, placing it in Lina's lap.

It was one hundred dollars cash. Lina looked at the bills and said, "What's this for?"

"You earned it. The man that attacked you was wanted by the territorial marshal for a robbery at another camp. Those people posted a reward, and the sheriff in Ellis gave it to Hugh for bringing him in."

"A bounty?" Lina asked. She looked up at Jean, then back at the money, in amazement. "You were right Jean, this *is* wonderful." She could send all this money to San Francisco. "I must go thank Hugh right away," and she stood to go downstairs.

"You can't." Jean held one hand before her to block Lina's path, the other covered her mouth as she tried to suppress a giggle, but failed. "We have strict orders to keep you inside today."

"Orders from whom?" Lina asked suspiciously.

"From Robert Marr," chimed Millie, but Jean nudged the poor girl's ribs so hard she doubled over.

Jean continued. "From all the Marrs. They have a surprise for you, but that's all I can say."

"Oh, Jean, please tell them it isn't necessary. I'd just as soon be able to leave. I'm tired of being cooped up here. Maybe you could keep me company?"

"Sorry," said Jean, "but if we're going to help, we've got to get busy downstairs. Come along, Millie." She yanked Millie by the hand, and led her away.

Surprises. Lina didn't care for surprises. She couldn't remember ever being surprised and being happy about it. Still, she knew it would be ungracious to stomp downstairs and ruin everyone's fun. But despite her doubts about surprises, Lina grew more curious through the day. She tried to satisfy that curiosity just once, by peeking out the door over the balcony, but the square below was positively desolate.

****

Lina thought she had had all the rest she could stomach, but she must have needed more, for she slept most of the afternoon and all through the night, and never heard a sound. Finally, with more than enough sleep, she woke before anyone else that Monday morning. Still a bit sore, she carefully washed and dressed, then slipped downstairs. She was starving. It had been a long time since Meg had brought her some food the afternoon before, with the same air of secrecy the girls had. She found some bread and cut herself some slices. She wrapped them in a gingham kerchief and walked outside into the cool morning air, just as the first light filled the sky.

It was too early for anyone else to be about, and so she stood outside the tavern, carefully chewing her bread, enjoying her first time out of her small room in days. She breathed deeply and let the crispness fill her lungs. Despite her wounds and aches, she had to admit she felt good—strong, well-rested, and, happy. She looked forward to the day.

To the south, she could just make out the sound of pounding. A hammer against wood. Then silence. Then hammering again. She followed the sound. *Who could be up at this hour, and doing what?* As she passed the Marr's cabin she saw light from within signaling the Marrs were awake. Further south now, past their cabin, and around the bend to where Jean and Jamie's cabin would be. Then the thought struck her. *That must be the sound. Jamie's finally started on the cabin.*

For a moment she believed she was right, as she rounded the bend and saw a cabin where just days before trees had stood. She looked closer and saw it was no cabin. Beneath the eaves, where a cabin would have had one or two windows on each side, the walls were all window from halfway up from the floor to the roof. These windows weren't shuttered on the sides like regular windows. They were hinged at the top, and the shutters stood propped open with sticks. All open as they were now, Lina could look through the building and see the woods behind it. The sound of hammering was coming from within the building, but she could see no one. A lantern lit the inside, heedless of the growing morning light.

She came to the doorway and looked around the single room of the cabin. The room was rich with the smell of fresh cut lumber, and sawdust littered the floor. Sitting in the middle of the floor, his back to her, hammering away at a small table, was Robert. She stood there for some time, watching him work, completely focused on his task. Only when he had finished did he stand up and turn around.

"Well, now, don't you look better!" He laid the hammer down and slapped the sawdust off, then walked toward her, carefully taking her chin to examine her bruise. "Nothing broken. That's good."

Lina lowered her chin, saying, "More embarrassed than hurt, Robert."

"Embarrassed? Why, in God's name?"

"For all the fuss. Really, it wasn't anything."

"You're wrong. It *was* something. Something indeed." There was a tender look in his eyes. "And I, that is we, well, we want to thank you for it. But now you've spoiled the surprise."

"What do you mean? How have I spoiled it?"

"You mean you don't know? You don't see? Good! It's not too late, then! Here." He grabbed her by the hand and ran with her outside, heading back toward his cabin. She struggled to keep up with his long strides, but his hand held hers firmly. When they reached the cabin, he fixed her to a spot in front of the door. "Don't move," he said, then went inside. Lina caught a glimpse of Jamie and Hugh at the table before Robert shut the door behind him. After a minute, the three emerged, Hugh first.

"How can I thank you for that reward money? You've no idea what it means to me." Lina pressed both Hugh's hands between hers as she spoke, then gave him a quick peck on the cheek.

Jamie came forward and said, "We're just glad everything ended well."

Hugh added, " Damn, Lina! Now that you're a bona fide bounty hunter, you won't be looking for a new line of work, will you? We could make you sheriff!"

"And a beautiful sheriff she'd make!" exclaimed Robert. "But no, we're not going to let her find new employment, now are we? Very well. It's time. Boys, run ahead. Holler when you're ready."

With Hugh and Jamie out of site, Lina turned to him. "Robert, really," she started in protest, but he held a finger up to her lips to quiet her. "Now, not another word. You just let us have our fun."

Just then Jamie called out. "Come on. We're ready."

Robert led her back toward the building. This time, when they rounded the bend, Jamie and Hugh stood outside the door, next to a board they had nailed next to the door. Robert led her to where she could read the writing on the board. 'Marr Logging' it read, and underneath, the word 'Office'.

"We decided we needed an office right here in town," Robert said, still holding her hand. "Something a little more substantial than working out of a flimsy old tent."

"And a little safer, perhaps?" Lina looked up at him.

"No, it's not that at all. It's just, well, we just thought…," he trailed off, fumbling for words.

"It was a wonderful thought. But wasn't this the place for your cabin, Jamie?"

Jamie smiled. "There're plenty of spots. And this one was perfect for an office. Close to town, the road and the cabin. And a real pretty spot."

Robert led her inside. There was the small table Robert had been working on, with a chair. There was another larger table, with four chairs. On one wall were some simple shelves, where Lina noticed her account books had already been stacked.

Hugh came in and walked to the other end of the room. "Over here, we'll put a stove to keep it warm in winter," he said, pointing to the hole in the ceiling already cut for the stovepipe. "And over here, a safe." Hugh smiled as he pointed to the opposing corner. "Just in case, you know."

"And with these windows," Jamie walked over, demonstrating the shutters, "you'll be able to see anybody coming, from any direction."

Lina dropped Robert's arm, and moved to the center of the room, pivoting slowly and examining each detail. "I don't know what to say. No one's ever done anything like it for me, ever. Is this what you all were doing yesterday while I was held prisoner?" The men laughed in answer. "But why the hurry?"

"Well, that's other news," Robert said. "The trip to Ellis was quite successful. We've several bits of business for the territory, that'll keep us busy for the next few weeks. You'll be on your own again, for a while, I'm afraid."

"Oh," Lina could not hide the disappointment in her voice. "I'm sorry. I've missed you these last days," then quickly added, "all of you."

"Well," said Jamie, "it won't be so bad. Just a few weeks, Robert guesses. That's all."

That's all, she thought. The last week had reminded her how much she had grown use to seeing them, particularly Robert, every day, and how use to working alongside them and being a part of their lives she had become. It was like she was being punished, although she knew this was not their intent. She had made a stupid mistake, and now she had to pay for it. Still, she recognized the enormity of the gesture.

Looking at Robert, she said, "Thank you," then turning quickly to the Hugh and Jamie, she added, "Thank you all." Grabbing both of Jamie's hands, again she kissed him quickly on the cheek, then moving to Hugh, did the same. She turned to do the same with Robert, but paused for the slightest of moments. He was too tall, but rather than leaning his cheek forward to her, he picked her up quickly, and she lightly kissed him on his left cheek, then whispered in his ear, "Thank you, for everything."

They returned to Sweet Meg's for some breakfast, then the men headed back to camp. Before they left Robert had one more gift. "This belongs to you," he said, placing a small key in the palm of her hand, and gently folding her fingers over it.

"Robert, with all those windows, a lock will hardly keep someone from getting in."

"The bears and raccoons, then," he said jokingly.

Lina passed the day in her new office. She spent the rest of the morning sweeping sawdust and wiping down the woodwork, then worked through the afternoon positioning the tables and chairs in every possible configuration until she found the very best arrangement. She was happiest with her placement of her desk, which faced the door and looked straight out onto the road to camp. All day she kept an eye on that road, hoping one of the Marrs, Robert most particularly, might return so she could show off her work. But the sun was low, she had finished everything she could think of, and there was no sign of them. Hunger was getting the better of her, too, so with one last look around, she closed the door behind her. She pulled the new key from her pocket. For a moment, she stared down at it, resting in her palm. "Mine," she said quietly, with a smile. Then she turned the lock and hurried back to Meg's. She had other business that needed her attention.

With a hold of timbers and furs, the Bantry Bay sat low in the harbor, ready to sail. Riordan would be heading to San Francisco with the early morning tide. The extra men they had hired had all but depleted the Marrs' provisions, and Lina had a list for Riordan that would keep him busy for a week. And she had another, even more important errand for him.

When she returned to Meg's, she hurried up to her room before going into the tavern. Once inside, she opened her trunk and dug among the folds of her dresses until her fingers found the coin purse she had finally taken from Kincaid's safe. One last time, she looked inside. *Nearly four hundred dollars, counting the gold!* She hurried out the door, down the stairs and into the tavern.

Not yet the dinner hour, and already the place was busy. Riordan's small crew was taking advantage of their last chance for a good meal before two weeks at sea. Meg had her hands full keeping up with her customers' appetites, but she chattered happily as she moved from table to table, stewpot nestled in her arm, ladling each plate to the brim. Everyone's attention was turned on the meal, so no one noticed Lina at first as she stood in the doorway, scanning the faces for Riordan's. There he sat, at the table nearest the kitchen, with his first mate, McNab, and another man Lina didn't recognize. She stepped through the door and headed toward him.

"Good evening, Milo," she greeted him, giving him a quick peck before taking the empty chair next to him.

"Ah, Lina. Come to see ol' Riordan off, have yas?"

"Of course. The place just isn't the same when you're gone. We miss you, Meg and I," she said.

"And I the two of yas," he said. "Why, isn't it doubly nice to have two sweethearts to come home to." He gave her a wink, which prompted a giggle from her. "Well, whatever put such a smile on your lovely face, as if I didn't know."

"So you know about the new office?"

"Know about it? Dearie, the whole town's been in an uproar since Robert came up with the notion. Robert's been waylayin' every man who came within ten miles of the place to help him for the last two days. Wouldn't even let 'em come by last night for an evenin's libation.

That's slavery, if ya asks me. This place was like a tomb. Meg ought to demand reparations for the loss of business, she should."

"Oh, shush," Meg said as she came up behind him. "I had enough to do just to feed the crew. And I was happy to help." She turned to Lina. "Well, are you pleased?"

"Pleased? Oh, Meg, it's wonderful! Such a tidy little place, and so convenient. This will make the work so much easier."

"Well, I'm glad for that, but that's not the reason he did it, you know."

"I know," Lina answered softly. "I honestly don't know what to say. It's the kindest thing anyone's ever done for me."

Meg smiled. "That smile on your face says it all, honey. Now be a lamb and help me keep up with these fellows. There're biscuits that need to be passed around."

"Alright, Meg. Just a minute." Lina turned to Riordan. "Milo, can I talk to you for a moment?"

"Of course, dearie."

She leaned closer. "Um, can we step over to the bar?"

"To the bar? Always."

Once behind the bar, she carefully drew the purse from her pocket. "I have another deposit for you. A rather large one."

Milo took the purse and gave it a quick toss to feel the weight of the coins. When it jingled, Lina quickly took hold of his arm and pulled it out of sight.

"Please, Milo. I know I can trust you, but you must take extra care this time. There's nearly four hundred dollars in there. Some of it gold."

His eyes grew wide as he looked back at the purse in his hand. Then, with a quick wink and a nod, he slipped it carefully inside his coat. "Same place, darlin'?"

"Yes, the same place." Lina looked around the room to see if anyone had noticed. She thought she saw the stranger sitting with McNab look her way before he turned his attention back to his plate full of stew.

"Don't give it another thought, dearie. Now do us both a favor and help Meg out. The sooner we get me crew fed and watered, the sooner I can get them back to me ship and out of her hair."

"Of course, Milo. Oh, and here's the supplies we'll need." She pulled the list from her pocket and shoved it into his hand before she headed off to help Meg. Milo read the list as he wandered back to his seat.

"Who was that young lady?" the stranger asked when he returned.

"That lass there? Why, that's Carolina. Lina Morgan. She works for the Marrs. Practically runs the operation, she does. This here's her list of what we need to get for them when we gets to San Francisco." Riordan watched as the man stared at Lina from across the room while he spoke. "Why? What's your interest, lad?"

"Me? No interest?" he said, looking back to his plate.

"No, I'll think not! For didn't you tell me, Sully, you was a married man?"

Sully smiled. "I did, Captain, and I am. But she's a pretty thing. Puts me in mind of my wife, that's all." Sully looked at Lina again, and though Riordan did not catch it, the second mate also cast a quick glance to the bulge in the captain's jacket. "That's all."

31

The pleasing discourse that rose like music from the office cabin had played for an hour when twilight came, and it showed no sign of ending. Hugh lit the lantern in the center of the table, and the gaining light reflected on the faces of the three men and the boy gathered round.

The light spread its warm glow around the room, perfectly matching Lina's mood. It was the end of the work week, and the contracts Robert and Martin Kincaid had secured in Ellis would soon be completed. Lina hoped to spend more evenings like this. She sat at her desk, work spread before her, but it was the men she watched as they laughed and joked, planned and argued, in their familiar way. Her fondness for them was profound. She delighted in the obvious affection they shared, despite the good-natured disagreements that peppered their conversation. She took pride in their accomplishments, as if they were her own. But most of all, she marveled at a joy for life they shared. It fueled their confidence, their determination, and their bond. Unquestionably, they were a family. This was what gave Lina the warm glow she felt—a sense of belonging. For although she wasn't included in the discussion, she felt a part of it. The light from the lantern shown most intensely on these men, but Lina happily abided in its reflection.

So alike, in so many ways, she thought, and yet each his own man. Jamie was their center, his quiet, accepting way providing a haven for each of them, in the storms of their own making. Hugh was their vigor, the one whose fierce drive questioned and provoked. There was an energy in his every movement that revealed the self-assurance and appetites of a young man who saw only opportunity. *And Charley.* Lina looked at the boy, wide eyes moving back and forth between the three heroes before him, trying hard to earn his place at their table. Charley was the future, nipping at their heels like a pup. Lina smiled. That future would be on them before they knew it, she thought, if a bright mind and an eager heart were any measure.

Then there was Robert. Robert was the intellect, the judgment, the foundation on which they were building their lives. He played so many roles—brother, father, leader, teacher, friend. Whether the others realized it or not, it was plain to Lina that every decision the others made and every action they took carried an unspoken question at the end. *What did Robert think? Would he agree? Would he approve? Did he measure them to be the men they thought they were, or hoped to be?* It was a testament to the ease with which he played his roles that the three younger men seemed sure of the answer. *Yes.* Always the answer was yes.

Yet there was something about Robert that was apart from the others. Even now, as she watched him, his strong face lit as much by the smile he wore as the warm lamplight, talking about the work ahead of them, she saw his heart go out of the conversation. For just a moment, he leaned back in his chair, and focused his eyes not on his family, but on some distant point known only to him. His thoughts were a secret shared with no one. It was then Lina felt her heart go out to him in a way that seemed at once unfamiliar yet as natural as her heartbeat. She could neither name the feeling, nor explain it. She only knew that, in that moment, she longed to call his confession, to have the others fade into the shadows so that she might ask him to share those secret thoughts with her.

Robert's attention was drawn back to the table as the talk grew more animated, breaking the spell of Lina's reverie. Fingering the mugs that held the last of the coffee, Robert listened as the others discussed the work still needing to be done. Hugh was arguing for taking a crew to the high timber, while Jamie favored a little time off.

"That spruce'll be hard to get at in winter. We might need them if that other contract comes through," Hugh argued.

"But we can't get those trees down with the wear and tear we've put on the road and flume." Jamie countered.

"'Then let's start there. Fix the skids, patch the flume, then head to the spruce!" Hugh said.

Jamie sighed. "Fine, but you'll have to do it without me. If I don't get that cabin finished before the wedding, Jean and I will have to pitch a tent on the mud flats. Or bunk in with the three of you. Either way, she'll never forgive me."

"There'll be time to do it all." Robert said. "Jamie, suppose you come with us next week. We'll work on the flume and the skids. Get done what we can. That'll put us on schedule for clearing the spruce. Give us your all this week, and next week, you're free."

"Fair enough, I guess. But no more excuses, Robert. Fixed flume or not, I've got to get started."

"I can fill in for Jamie!" Charley offered brightly. "I could help out a lot, I bet."

Robert laughed. "Charley, I appreciate the offer, but I need you to help Jamie with the cabin. It's a good way to learn to work with your hands. It'll be good practice…for someday."

Charley sparked to the idea. "Really? Someday soon?"

"Someday, Charley. We'll see about how soon." Hugh said.

Charley couldn't hide his disappointment. "I only want to see what it's like up there," he mumbled.

"You will, soon enough," Robert said.

"What *is* it like up there?" Charley asked.

Robert thought for a moment, then said, "Words don't do it justice. A person has to see it for themselves."

A few quiet moments passed before Lina heard Robert ask, "Would you still like to see it?" When no one else answered, she looked up, surprised to find the question directed at her. "Would you like to see it?" Robert asked again. "The mountains. The high country. The crew at work. Would you still like to see it?'

"You know I would," Lina answered.

"Then I know a way."

"Robbie? Are you daft?" Hugh blurted out. "Forgive me, Lina, but it's, well, it's impractical. Tell them, Jamie."

Jamie shrugged his shoulders. "It's up to Robert, but I say she's welcome."

459

Robert said, "The work on the skids, that's just an hour more from camp, but from there she can see some of that wilderness she's been pestering me to see." He turned to Lina. "And we can get you back to Sleekit that evening. You can come later in the week, after we've gotten a good start. That way, one of us can take time to show you around, and answer those questions you'll no doubt have." He broke into a grin. "What do you say, boys?"

"I think it's a fine idea," Jamie said.

Hugh gave in without a fight. He smiled and shrugged. "Sure, why not?"

Charley looked perturbed. "Wait a minute! That's not fair. How come *she* gets to go? I've been around longer. And besides, she's a girl!"

Everyone laughed, except Charley. Finally, Robert replied. "Charley, wouldn't you say she's earned her chance?" He pointed to his own cheek, then gave a quick nod toward Lina.

Charley looked puzzled, then he shook his head. "Oh, yeah. Okay, I get it. I guess you're right. But if I get punched in the face, will you let me go, too?"

****

Robert stressed to Lina more than once before they left that the whole plan depended on how the work went, and that he might send word for her not to come at all. She said she understood, and she did, though all week she dreaded each hour ahead as holding the possibility for disappointment. But with each day that no word came, she reveled in the time behind her, and the approaching Friday morning.

She left before any soul stirred in Sleekit, on Kincaid's rented horse. She used the now familiar trip to try to remember all the questions she had, all the reasons her curiosity was piqued about the high country. Robert had also made a point of saying that if the trip was possible, he wouldn't know until the last minute which of them might be there to take her. Yet as she formed the questions in her mind, Robert was always the one she imagined asking.

As she drew near to camp, she heard the whinny of a horse in the clearing ahead. She urged the nag forward. *You've made me late, you silly beast*, she thought. *He's there, waiting for me.* "Robert?" she called as she came into the clearing, her words betraying her hope.

She gasped, and pulled the horse up short when she saw who awaited her. Sitting on the ground, next to his horse, was an old Indian. His hair was long, thin, and white as snow. His face was like leather—mellow brown, worn and wrinkled. His eyes were dark yet as calm as a clear sky. He didn't seem startled by her, nor did he move even slightly at the sight of her. He looked at her almost as carefully as she looked at him, frozen as she was atop her horse. They stared at one another for what seemed an eternity, when finally he smiled. Nervously, she smiled back.

"Hello," she said softly.

"Ha-lo," he answered.

Pleased with this progress, Lina felt more at ease, though she stayed on her horse, erring on the side of caution. "Can I help you?" she asked.

The old man looked at her, then simply and clearly, he said, "Marr man."

Spoken as it was, the words had no meaning at first. "Mormon?" was all Lina could contrive.

The old man understood the distinction. He shook his head, and slowly and deliberately responded, "Marr man."

"Oh! Marr!" Suddenly, the truth struck her. This was one of Robert's friends. She climbed off the horse and came toward him. *Damn, what did he say the man's name was?* She struggled to remember as she approached him slowly, smiling all the way. She sat on the ground across from him. Hesitantly, she tried her best recollection of the name she had heard Robert speak only once. "Willa...?" she asked, pointing to him.

"Willahe," he nodded.

"Willahe," she said, then pointed to herself. "Lina."

"Lie-nah," he said, stretching out the syllables in his musical tongue, until the name was almost unrecognizable. She nodded. His eyes studied her carefully. "Marr klootchman?" he asked.

"I...I'm sorry, I don't know what that means," she said. "I don't know what you want. Oh, dear." She looked around the clearing. "Marr

461

man. Here soon," she said, praying that would mean something to the old man. "At least I hope so," she said under her breath.

They sat across from one another, grinning like two idiots. Lina's smile was forced, trying to convey a sense of calm. The old man's smile was of perfect contentment. Lina felt anxious. She was no longer afraid of the Indian, but the whole business of the two of them sitting there, grinning at one another, was disconcerting to say the least. "Food!" she said suddenly. "Or water. Perhaps you would like something to drink?" She started for the tent, hoping to find something. Just then, she heard the old man say in a lively voice, "Marr man!" She turned around to see Robert riding toward camp. She was so relieved by the sight of him she came running toward him, chattering the whole way.

"Robert! Thank heavens. He was here when I got here. It's your friend," she said, panting.

He chuckled. "Yes, I know. Willahe!" He bounded off his horse, and in two quick steps, took hold of the old man's arms in welcome. Robert spoke to Willahe in his native tongue, as easily as if it were his own. Lina could only guess the conversation, which, once past the greeting, seemed to turn suddenly serious. Robert asked questions, and the Indian answered. Willahe looked worried as he told a long story, interrupted only by Robert's quick questions. Robert's expression soon matched the old man's. When they were done, Robert looked to Lina, but said nothing.

"What is it?" she asked.

Robert didn't answer. He turned back to Willahe and asked some more questions. Willahe looked at Lina and smiled, then nodded. Then he said something Lina recognized. "Marr klootchman?" he asked of Robert.

Robert laughed. "Wakeh, Willahe. Wakeh klootchman. Nika tilacum." Then he headed for the tent. "Come with me," he said as he swept by her.

She followed him. Inside, he was pulling the blankets from the bedrolls. "Here," he said," throwing them to her. "Roll these up." She stood there, dumbfounded, holding the blankets, watching him as he rummaged through the tent.

"He's come for blankets?" she asked.

"Blankets? No, but we'll need them," he said without looking up. "Did you bring any food with you? Ah, here it is." He held up a bottle of whiskey. "What about water? You did bring water with you, didn't you?" He turned around. "Say, get started on those blankets! Now, a note. I need to leave a note..." He muttered to himself as he searched through a small stack of papers. Hurriedly, he picked one, scribbled something on it, and then stuck it through with the nail that held the mirror hanging from the tent post.

"Robert, you're not making sense," she said, but she dutifully rolled the blankets. "Food, water, whiskey, these blankets? You're giving these things to Willahe?"

"No, we're taking them with us."

"Us? You're going with him? But I thought we were going..." she started, then felt ashamed. Surely, whatever assistance Willahe needed was more pressing than her tour of the timber. "Of course, we can do that another time..."

"Oh, you'll get your outing. Just not quite the one either of us imagined. We're going with him to his longhouse. His son's wife is having a baby, and it's not going well. He's come looking for help. He asked for Doc Maynard, but I'm afraid he can't afford another day to Seattle and back. I offered him our help."

"Our help?" She shot a quick glance toward the tent flap, aware that Willahe was only a few feet away, then she whispered, "We're not doctors."

"That's a luxury he can't afford right now." He stopped what he was doing to face her. "Look, Lina. I know this is asking a lot. The truth is, Willahe has no one else. Most of his people are gone. Smallpox, skirmishes with other tribes, or just scattered to the four winds. Willahe's wife died last winter. The family he has left, two sons and his grandson, are hunting and won't be back for days. There's no one but Willahe, the mother and her small daughter. He's left the mother alone with her little girl. Can you imagine how frightened she is? She's been in pain for a day, and still the baby hasn't come. If we don't go, she *and* the baby might die. I can't have that." He took the rolled up blankets from her. "I'll understand if you can't go. But I must. And I'll have to take your food and water." He tucked the whiskey bottle under his arm, and left the tent.

Lina followed him outside, where he was tying the bundle to his horse. Willahe had already mounted his horse, and was waiting patiently. "I've helped with a baby before," she said quietly.

Robert turned to her. "You have? You know how it's done?"

"I've helped. That's all. I was there. I held the mother's hand."

"Then will you come? Please? You can hold the mother's hand again, if nothing else."

With a small, nervous laugh, she said, "Very well. But who will hold *my* hand?"

"I will," he said, grabbing her hand and giving it a quick squeeze. "Now, then. What else might we need?" he asked.

"I suppose you have a knife with you. Bedding, hot water, knife. That's all I remember."

"Then let's go," Robert said. They mounted their horses.

"You know, Mr. Marr, this is really more of an adventure than I planned on." Lina was trying to keep the mood light, if only for her own sense of calm.

"Well, I suspect you're up to it, Miss Morgan. Who knows, this might just be providential, you coming here today." Then they were off. The old Indian led the way, followed by Robert, and Lina behind, all headed toward the mountains along a slowly rising trail that led away from all that Lina knew as familiar.

****

Lina had so long waited to see the deep wilderness, and as she looked around her, she could see its presence already. The stand of trees through which they rode was thicker than the woods between Sleekit and camp. Instead of the white light of day, a bright green glow lit their way. The whole world was green, for even the rough brown bark of the towering trees was speckled with gray green moss, and the forest's carpet was the cool green of soft ferns. She couldn't feel even slightly disappointed that the day had taken this sudden turn from the planned. Ahead waited a young woman who desperately needed help, and though Lina felt humbled and more than a little afraid, until she faced that crisis, this was the chance she had been given and she was determined to take in all she could.

Climbing up the trail toward the crest of the ridge, they rode through a narrow track of trampled ferns and moss. Riding ahead of her, Lina could only barely hear Robert and Willahe talking. Their voices were like a whisper next to her ear. Except for the occasional scamper of some creature deep in the undergrowth, the only sound Lina heard came from the sway of the lush boughs far above her, moving with the breeze. The quiet of the place was stunning.

She reckoned they had been riding for more than an hour when Robert stopped his horse. Willahe, in the lead, continued on. When Lina caught up, she asked, "Is something the matter?"

Robert shook his head, but held his finger to his lips. He didn't move. Long still moments passed before a small bird's cry broke the silence. Robert's every muscle relaxed. "Good. We can go now."

"What was that?" she asked softly.

"We're coming to the clearing. Willahe went ahead to see if it was safe. For the next hour or so, we'll be traveling in the open. If we had time to spare, there's another trail through the trees. This way will save us two or three hours."

"What is there to fear?"

"Do you remember those men who were spreading word of Indian problems? We're crossing an open valley farmers sometimes use for grazing. Folks around here worry when they see Indians on the move, even an old man like Willahe."

"But surely, if he's with you..."

"Being with me won't be a favor to him, any more than his being with me. And having a white woman with us only makes it worse. But Willahe's call says there's no one about."

"That whistle?"

Robert grinned and nodded. The trail took a turn, revealing spackled sunlight peaking from behind the curtain of dark firs. The clearing was ahead, but there was no sign of Willahe. They moved the horses up the trail, closer to the light, when suddenly Lina heard a voice right next to her.

"Klahowya, Lina?" She let out a little gasp, before she realized they had come upon Willahe, who perfectly blended in with the deep shadows and the rough brown trunks of the trees.

"He's asking how you are," Robert said.

"Tell him I am fine, thank you."

Robert answered for her, but she felt certain he must have said something else, for when he was done the two men looked at her and chuckled.

"He apologizes for scaring you. He said if you want to rest, we should do it now. No? Very well, then. Let's get going."

When at last they emerged from the woods, Lina looked across a long valley with a small river. A meadow filled with summer wildflowers covered the hills on both sides, but to the south the meadow gave way to more trees that hid the river for a short distance, until it burst forth into a long narrow lake. Had that been all Lina saw, it would have been enough. The land was lush and green and peaceful, just as she had imagined. But far to the south, there rose a mighty mountain like no other Lina had ever seen. It stood tall, broad, and alone, separate from the mountain ranges all around them. Even on a warm day like this, its peak was blanketed in white. Despite a nearly cloudless sky, the mountain had gathered a mist about its pinnacle that suggested something brooding. As they moved down the meadow, Lina couldn't take her eyes from this beautiful, fearful peak.

The river was wide but shallow, so the crossing was easy. On the other side, the old man picked up the pace, and they moved quickly back up the valley toward the trees. With one quick look back over her shoulder, Lina tried to press the sight of the valley, the lake, and that magnificent mountain into her memory as they slipped inside the deep forest once more.

Lina wondered how long before they would reach the longhouse. The very word made Lina curious, but remembering what waited for them there made her anxious. The quiet woods offered no distractions from her thoughts. Suddenly, the harshness of the wilderness that Robert had cautioned her about so many times seemed everywhere. This mysterious forest, the wild unseen animals that lived there, the storm brewing around the mountain, the nameless, faceless people who lived in that valley and threatened them in unspeakable ways, these were the dangers she had once dismissed. She would never dismiss them again. But at this moment they paled in comparison to the longhouse. She imagined the frightened woman inside, struggling to give birth. She tried to remember all she could from that night on the trail. Her knowledge was meager at best. She said a quick, silent prayer that she would keep her wits about her and figure out what to do when the time came, and that Robert's hope for providence was not unfounded.

Halfway down the eastern face of the second ridge, they came to the longhouse. At first Lina saw only another simple cabin, but as they came closer, she could see it was much longer and lower to the ground. This was no simple building. The masterful joinery of the timbers could be clearly seen at the longhouse's corners, and around its doorless entrance.

Willahe hurried inside as quickly as his ancient legs would carry him. Robert jumped down and nearly dragged Lina from her saddle. "Gather the supplies," he commanded, then he followed Willahe, running.

Lina untied the bundles then hurried toward the longhouse. At the doorway, she stopped. The inside was so dark compared to the bright day behind her that she couldn't see a foot beyond the threshold. Slowly, her eyes distinguished a soft column of light spilling across the floor ahead of her. She heard Robert's voice, then a woman's moans. Cautiously, she entered.

Every step down the narrow center of the longhouse was an effort. Lina clutched the bundles close to her breast like a shield. To either side, she could barely see there were recesses, like stalls in a stable, only larger. The rooms of Willahe's lost family, she thought. She was struck by the hot, stale air of the windowless place. It smelled of smoke and sweat and food. She could barely breathe. She walked toward the sound of Robert's voice and the column of light. A few steps closer and she could a see the light came from a hole in the roof, and beneath it were the remnants of a long-dead fire. Robert and Willahe were in the next stall. Between them, stretched on the ground, her head in Willahe's lap, was the mother. Curled up at her grandfather's knee was the small girl Robert spoke of, not more than five years old. Her eyes were wide, and she held one finger in her mouth. The other hand clutched the old man's leg.

"Lina, this is Hotassa," Robert said. She knelt next to him, and took Hotassa's hand gently.

"Hello," Lina answered. The word came out a tremulous whisper. She could just make out the woman's face. Hotassa's eyes were drawn and weary. Her long, black hair was drenched in sweat and matted to her scalp. Yet despite her condition, she wore a look of serenity. Lina took reassurance from that.

"She says she still has pain," Robert said. "This seems good news to me. As if the baby is still trying to be born." Lina nodded. "But I'm afraid she's so weak," he continued, looking at Hotassa, "that she hasn't the strength for it."

Just then, a dreadful moan rose from within Hotassa as her limp body curled helplessly with the contraction. She whimpered through the course of the pain. Robert reached to support her slim shoulders. Willahe muttered as he stroked her brow. Lina gripped her hand. As she watched the young woman's pain, Lina's mind raced. *What could it be? Why couldn't she deliver this baby?* Almost as quickly as it had claimed her, the pain released Hotassa, who fell back into Willahe's arms. Carefully, he lowered her to the floor.

"I've an idea," Robert said. "Breech births. The baby gets turned around wrong. It's the only thing I can think of. Here, let's spread these blankets out for her. God, what I wouldn't give for more light." He laid one blanket on the floor beneath Hotassa. The other he laid across the woman's legs.

"You're going to…?"

"I have to. I suppose a midwife would be more proper, but it's not that simple. I need to be able to tell her what I'm doing, and what I need her to do, you see."

"Of course." Lina felt relieved.

"Here, now," he teased, "you're not off the hook so easily. I'll need water. Outside, below that tree line to the south, there's a stream. Go and fetch…"

"Robert, should she be here?" Lina asked, nodding toward the little girl.

"She won't leave her mother. I tried to get her to go outside, but she wouldn't. She told me her grandfather said to stay until the baby comes, and she won't do otherwise."

"What's her name?"

"Haide."

"Ask Haide if she would go fetch some water for her mother. Tell her we need her help."

Robert smiled. "Haide, iskum chuck pe mama." The little girl did not move. "Iskum chuck, Haide. Hyak." The little girl looked at her grandfather, who with one nod sent her scurrying outside. Hotassa opened her eyes again. "Mah-sie," she said hoarsely.

Lina looked to Robert. "She said, 'Thank you.'"

Lina sat beside Willahe, Hotassa leaning back against them both. Lina laid her hand on Hotassa's belly. She felt a tremble in Hotassa's weak muscles, then a different sensation, faint but distinct. "Robert!" she whispered. "I felt it move!"

He smiled. "Good! Well, then, let's see what we can do."

"Let me give her some water, first. Look how parched she is." She held the flask to Hotassa's lips. "Water," she said, then looked to Robert. "Tell her I need her to drink."

"Tell her yourself," he said, smiling. "Chuck."

"Chuck?" Lina asked. He nodded. "Chuck, Hotassa. Chuck." Hotassa complied, and raised her head just enough for Lina to pour cool water into her mouth.

Robert spoke to Hotassa, then beneath the meager privacy afforded by the blanket, he began. At his touch, Hotassa flinched a little, then nothing. Lina looked to Robert. His eyes were closed, and he worked with near stillness, while unseen fingers searched for answers.

"There!" he said suddenly. He spoke to Hotassa, and then to Lina. "We were right. It's turned around."

"Can you...?" Another contraction gripped Hotassa. As the young woman rose with the tensing, she whispered something. Lina knew what she said by the fear in her voice. It was a plea. Lina looked to Robert, hoping, but he shook his head. "Not yet," he sighed. "She's got to push. Hotassa..."

"Robert, I don't think she has anything left in her to push." Lina looked him in the eyes and saw him searching her face for the same answer she had looked for from him. *Isn't there something else we can do?* Lina held Hotassa close until the pain receded. Then a thought came. She wasn't certain it was right, but it was all she had to offer. "I remember this fellow back home whose mare had a hard time foaling. He said the horse wanted to lie down, but he couldn't let her, because the foal was twisted up, wouldn't come out right." Robert looked at her, not understanding. "Maybe it's not the baby that needs help. Maybe it's Hotassa."

"Are you suggesting she stand?" Robert asked.

"Well, maybe not stand," Lina said. "But perhaps, if we could get her more upright, it might be easier for the baby to drop on its own."

Robert turned to Willahe, and explained Lina's idea. The old man nodded, then spoke to Hotassa. She nodded once, then struggled to lift herself, but it was no use. She slid back down.

"You're going to have to lift her, Lina. You and Willahe. Can you manage?" he asked.

"Yes."

"And hold her. She's dead weight, you know, and I don't know how long you'll have to hold her."

"I can do it," she said, trying to sound calm. "Just tell me when."

"The next time." Robert spoke to Willahe, who nodded. Lina and Willahe, in unspoken agreement, each slipped their arms behind Hotassa, and let her arms drape limply across their necks. The three of them sat there, not moving, waiting for the next contraction. Lina's clothes were drenched, and her arm felt clammy where she held Hotassa around the waist. Sweat ran down her face and stung her eyes, but she didn't move an inch. Just the effort to breathe seemed to be wasted if she wasn't ready to help Hotassa.

The contraction came. With the first sign, Lina gripped Hotassa, and felt Willahe do the same. They pulled her upright as far as their strength would allow. Robert struggled to grab the baby. "Almost! Just a bit more." Hotassa moaned, and struggled for air.

Lina planted her feet firmly beneath her, and with teeth gritted, pulled as much of Hotassa's weight on her as she could. She grunted with the effort, but she had Hotassa firmly. At that moment, Hotassa's moan coiled into a full-throated cry. Her body shuddered. Lina looked to Robert. He slumped back. "Damn," he muttered.

She watched his face in the dull light. He shook his head, seemingly lost as to what to do next. His uncertainty surprised Lina, but didn't unsettle her. She knew without hesitation he was on the right course. Her faith in him was complete. When he looked at her, she tried to reflect that confidence to him. "Just give it time," Lina said gently. "Do you need water?" she asked. He shook his head.

Time stopped again as they waited for the next contraction. Lina felt a spasm of her own. The muscles in her arm were tiring under the strain. She tried to relax them, but couldn't without quivering. She would not be seen to tremble now, no matter what, so she did her best to ignore it. She listened to her own breathing, making sure it kept an even pace, as slow as she could manage. She gave into the bothersome sweat, and dabbed her forehead with the sleeve of her dress. She reached across and blotted Hotassa's drenched forehead too.

The spasm grabbed Hotassa, and this time, there was no mere moan, but a deep, endless wail. The pain hit her with a force that used all her reserves. More quickly than before, Lina and Willahe lifted Hotassa and held her. Lina closed her eyes. All she heard were the muffled sounds of human strain, until she heard Robert speak. "Here it is!" he cried. Lina's eyes flew open. In his hands, he held a baby boy.

With Hotassa's weight against them, Lina and Willahe folded beneath her. Hotassa sobbed, but smiled, as she looked at her child. "He's not breathing," Robert whispered to Lina.

Lina lifted the tiny creature from Robert's outstretched hands. Her recollections of Greta Olmstead's midwifery were returning. She ran her finger inside the baby's mouth. In reflex, he gasped. Then the gasp became a cry. Robert looked at Lina as if she had performed a miracle. She laughed with relief as she started examining the child. He seemed weak, no doubt from the long birth, but otherwise healthy. "See to the cord," she said, "and give me some of that water. Let's clean him off."

When they had finished, Lina took the child and laid it in his mother's arms. Hotassa looked at the infant and smiled. "Tocanum," she said, running her slim fingers over his tiny features. She pulled him to her face, softly kissing the small head already covered with thick black hair. Lina watched as Hotassa held him there, soaking up the very essence of her baby. Then she took Tocanum to her breast. Almost at the same moment, young Haide returned, bucket in hand. Seeing the baby, she dropped the bucket and ran to her mother. The three of them, mother, son and daughter, curled up. Haide jabbered at her mother. Hotassa answered in a gentle tone, while Haide listened. Then, after a nod from her mother, she cautiously stretched her small hand toward her brother. At the touch of him, she smiled.

"Let me see to her," Lina said to Robert. He spoke to Willahe, and the two men left the longhouse. Lina did her best to clean her, while Hotassa inspected the baby's miniature hands and feet. All the while, she smiled. When Lina finished, she sat down next to Hotassa, and took her hand. "Chuck?" she asked. It was all she knew to say.

Hotassa nodded, but this time Hotassa took the flask and sipped by herself. She handed the flask back to Lina. "Mah-sie," she said. "Mah-sie."

Lina smiled. "You're most welcome." She looked down at the baby's puckered face, still blotchy from birth. He was fast asleep. She took his tiny hand in hers, when suddenly, even in sleep, he gripped her little finger. She tugged at it gently. "Strong," she said to Hotassa.

"Strong." Hotassa mimicked the word, but she understood.

Suddenly, the longhouse seemed too still. Lina needed to stand, to walk outside, but her arms and legs were trembling. She pulled herself up and staggered to the doorway. She took a deep breath, and then another, until her legs felt like they would hold her again. When she thought she could walk without falling, she headed toward Robert.

"How's Hotassa?" Robert asked when he saw her coming.

"Fine, I think." She felt too exhausted to say more.

"And the baby?"

"Fine."

"The new grandfather and I were just celebrating. Care to join us?" From half-opened eyes, she caught a whiff of whiskey. Robert was offering her the bottle they brought with them.

She recoiled at the smell. "No, thank you," she said. He pulled the bottle to his lips and took a swig, but the scent still filled her nostrils. A wave of nausea struck her, but just as she thought she might be sick, it left. Her stomach was empty. They had not eaten all day. She felt tired. She was looking for something to rest against when she tottered slightly. Robert grabbed her arm.

"Say, are *you* alright?"

"I'm fine," she said, but she let him help her sit down. "I think I just needed the air. It was so close in there."

Robert laughed. "Hot, you mean. Yes, not the most favorable conditions for childbirth, but we managed, didn't we?" He laughed again. "A hell of a job." Willahe laughed, then spoke. He motioned toward the longhouse, then back toward the mountains. He said that word again, "klootchman," and Lina knew he was speaking of her.

"Willahe's offering us a place to stay for the night. He thinks maybe you should rest. He says you look worse than Hotassa." Robert found that amusing, but Lina did not.

"No. Please. May we head back?"

"Are you certain? Willahe would feed us well. He's got fresh venison and we'd get a good night's rest…"

"No! I mean, I'm sorry, Robert. I don't want to seem ungrateful. But do you think we could make it back to Sleekit today? I really would like to go home."

"Of course. I didn't think about that…that you…well, yes, I can see now. Of course, we'll leave right away."

"I'm sorry, Robert. You probably think me a ninny. It's just that, I guess this has taken more out of me than I knew."

"No, you're right," he said, reassuring her with a light hand on her shoulder. "We'll leave at once. Here, let me help you." He led her to the horse and helped her mount. He spoke to Willahe, then the two of them went inside the longhouse. Waiting, Lina leaned against the horse's neck. She nuzzled her cheek to the soft, warm coat, and closed her eyes. A breeze against her damp clothes soothed her. She felt as if she could sleep there for hours. When she opened her eyes, Robert was securing the bundle to her horse, and Willahe was tying something wrapped in a skin to Robert's saddle. The men spoke words of parting, then embraced.

"Are you ready?" Robert asked her. She nodded, and with one last clasp of hands, Robert left Willahe. He mounted his horse and started back toward the ridge. Lina turned her horse to follow, when Willahe came along side her. She looked down to see him grinning at her.

"Mah-sie, Marr klootchman. Mesika skookum, skookum tumtum okoke sun. Saghalie tyee klose nanitsh mesika. Nika kumtuks. Saghalie tyee wauwau nika."

"I don't…"

"He thanked you. He said you were strong today. Strong, and brave. He said God would take care of you. He knows, he says, because God speaks to him."

Lina offered Willahe her hand. "Mah-sie," she said.

****

A shadow from the afternoon sun started down the eastern ridge just as Robert neared the crest. He turned to watch Lina, her horse following his like a pack mule, with Lina the lifeless burden. A stiff wind beat her tousled hair against her cheek and blew dust across her face, but she gave no notice. "Let's stop a moment," Robert said when she reached him. He offered her the flask of water. She took a long drink, then cupped her hand and took more. She splashed the cold water on her face, and then wiped it across her brow, her cheeks, and her stinging eyes.

Robert climbed down from his horse. "That's it. You look awful. I don't care how badly you want to get back today. We're stopping for a while. You'll rest, and you'll eat something."

Lina lacked the energy to argue. Limply, she let him help her from the horse. He held onto her until she stood steady on her own. Taking her by the hand, he led her to rest upon a fallen tree lying near the trail.

"Willahe gave us this venison." He opened the skin he had tied to his saddle, then took his knife and cut off a long strip. "Here." She looked at it wearily. "No arguments. Eat some." Then more gently, "Please. A bite or two."

She started gnawing on the dried meat. The first swallow was difficult. "Water," she whispered. He handed her the flask, then cut some venison for himself. Another bite, and another drink, and Lina felt some strength return. "It must be getting late," she said.

He looked up. "This time of year, it doesn't get dark until late. We *should* have plenty of light…."

"Should?"

"Saw some clouds to the north," he said, turning back to her. "Hard to tell which way they're headed. That damn mountain…"

"The big one I saw this morning? I noticed clouds then."

"As did I. You never know with that mountain. The Indians call it Ta-co-bet, `the place where the waters begin.' It's the place where storms begin, too."

"If you're worried, perhaps we should get started." She tried to stand, but he put his hand on her shoulder to stop her.

"I'm not half as worried about those clouds as I am you. We won't make it back if you're not up to it. Are you sure?"

She smiled. "Yes, I think so. I feel better. Really."

"Good. Then take a few minutes more and eat. You'll feel better still." She obeyed.

He sat down next to her. In the silence between them, he studied her openly for signs of weakness, then looked at the sky, then at her again. Dutifully she took one last swallow of jerky, chased it with a gulp of water and handed the flask back to him. "There," she said, forcing her best smile. "Much better. Ready to go."

As they moved down the hill through the forest, the light turned a sickly yellow green. Lina looked up. The clouds above her were thick, some dripping down to the highest treetops. Then, with no warning, the wind came roaring up through the valley and into the forest around them. The tall firs moaned against its force. A sharp clap of thunder in the distance split the air. Lina's horse pulled back, but she held her to the trail.

"We may have ...," Robert started, just as another crack of thunder came, and the skies opened. The rain fell in torrents. The forest offered no shelter. Lina looked up again, and now the sky was black. Rain struck her face like pebbles. She covered her head with her arm to tent her vision, but the rain still blew into her eyes. She heard a crash in the forest to her right, and the sound of wood splintering. She could just make out Robert ahead of her through a veil of rain. She urged her horse to keep moving. Then came another thunderous crack, this time to her left. She thought she saw something hit the forest floor. Her horse flinched. "Whoa!" she cried, praying the animal would listen to her and not instinct.

"Lina!" she heard Robert call. She looked ahead but didn't see him. She rode toward the voice. "Robert!" she cried. She was confused. Had she wandered from the trail? Had he?

Then there came a flash of lightning, a clap of thunder and a crack of wood so loud that for a moment it silenced the pounding rain. The terrible noise seemed to come from straight above her. She struggled to hold the horse still. Even through the wind's roar she heard something falling. Above her, somewhere, a great limb, perhaps the top of a whole tree, was falling. She heard the agony of its shredding as it fell against and through the other trees. The falling seemed to take forever. As it came nearer, she could tell it was headed somewhere ahead of her. She closed her eyes as the wrenching sound grew nearer. *Smack!* The fallen timber struck the ground, and the earth thundered back at the sky.

She screamed, and then heard it echo, deep and long. The scream was no longer hers. It was Robert's.

"Aaargh!" She heard him, but still she could not see him. The scream continued downward, like the falling tree before it, then stopped.

"Robert!" Lina jumped from the horse without thinking, and ran straight ahead. She tripped through the undergrowth and stumbled through the mud. "Robert!" she called again. Then she saw the mighty timber that had fallen from the sky. She dropped to the ground, her heart in her throat as she searched all around it. There was no sign of Robert. She looked around. Perhaps the tree had knocked him some distance. The rain made it impossible to see. "Robert!"

"Down here!"

"Robert!" She scrambled over the tree. A few feet ahead was a ledge. An outcropping of rock hid the steep incline until she came right upon it. She crawled out on the rock and looked down. "Robert?"

"Here." Robert lay on the ground, ten feet below her. "I'm alright. At least I think so."

"Can you get up?" she called down.

He tried, but cried out in pain. "Damn!"

"What is it?"

"I think I've broken my arm."

"Stay there." The wind had died down a little, but the rain still pelted her. She looked around for Robert's horse, but didn't see him. Carefully, she led her own horse by the reins as she picked her way down the mud-soaked trail. She started to slide, and only stopped herself from a bad fall by desperately grabbing a nearby branch. Finally, the trail leveled out and she figured she was even with the ledge. She dropped the reins and inched her way over toward where she reckoned Robert had landed.

She found him leaning against a tree, cradling his left arm with his right. "Thank God!" she said. "I thought that tree had…I couldn't see you…I couldn't find you."

"I'm fine. But we've got to get out of these woods. The horses?"

"I didn't see yours. Mine's over there. But we'll do better to walk out. This trail is too muddy for the horses."

"Then let's get going."

Lina led the way, and Robert used her horse to steady himself with his good arm. He kept his broken arm tucked close. A few times she heard him swear. She knew he was in pain, but she kept them moving. When they reached the tree line at the top of the meadow, Robert's horse stood waiting, still spooked from the storm.

"That tree fell right behind me. The horse threw me. I was afraid he'd gotten it." He looked the horse over, then took the reins. "Come on. This rain isn't letting up soon. There's an abandoned shack down by that lake. I've used it before." With only one good arm, he struggled to mount the horse. They headed down the meadow.

When they found the cabin, it was clearly long abandoned. Lina wondered how much shelter it might offer, for there was a considerable hole in the roof. Still, it was a welcome sight. Robert tied the horses to a nearby tree. He opened the door and looked around. "There's no one here. Get inside."

The hole in the roof proved a blessing, for it admitted the light as well as the rain. There wasn't much to see inside. There were no windows, no chimney, and only an old dead stump to serve all the purposes a table and chair might. Small streams of water traced across the dirt floor, leaving only patches that were even close to dry.

Robert left her for some minutes, then returned with an armful of fir branches. "Here, shake these out over there, where it's already wet. We'll cover the floor with them. Better than sitting in the mud." He left again.

She did as he asked, but when he returned with their blankets and provisions, Lina said, "Let's see to that arm first," She took the bundles from him, then laid out their meager inventory. The venison, two flasks of water, a kerchief that held an apple and some now soggy biscuits she had brought from Meg's that morning, a bottle of whiskey, and two blankets, even more rain-soaked than the biscuits. She took the blankets to the corner of the room and wrung them as dry as she could.

"What are you doing?" Robert asked, still standing in the middle of the room, cradling his wounded arm with his good.

"A sling," she said. "For your arm."

"Don't use that. We'll need that to dry off, and get warm."

"Without a fire?" she chuckled.

"I can make us a fire. Later."

"Everything's wet!"

"I wouldn't be much of a woodsman if I couldn't make a fire in the rain, now would I?" Robert smiled. "But I doubt we'll find much to burn. I'll wait until it's dark, when we need it."

"All the more reason to see to that arm now."

"It's fine."

"Fine, and yet broken, eh? Yes, just fine. Really, Robert, don't be foolish. Let's have a look at it." She came up beside him and started to reach for his arm. Instinctively he pulled back, in anticipation of the pain, but the sudden jerk made him wince despite his caution.

"Damn," he yelled.

"I don't think I can hurt you any worse than you hurt right now." Gingerly, he held his arm still and she gently ran her fingers along his forearm, feeling for breaks. She felt his hard muscles tensed against her light touch.

"Ouch!" he cried, when she touched a spot close to the wrist. "Damn."

She felt the spot again as he held his breath. "Not broken, maybe. At least not all the way through. Maybe you cracked it. Hmm." She turned her attention back to the room, trying to puzzle together a method of dealing with his injury. In the corner a wooden slat hung loose. She grabbed it and with all her strength pulled it free. She set it across the stump and, holding it with one hand, she used her boot to break it in two. "Still," she said as she looked at the two boards, "I'll need something to bind it…"

Robert interrupted her thoughts. "If the rain would just let up, we could make it back to Sleekit, though we'd be traveling in the dark. I'm guessing the worst of the storm is over."

"And what if it isn't? Don't you think we've pushed our luck enough for one day?"

"True," he grinned. "But it's just that, since you didn't want to stay at Willahe's…I just assumed you prefer, for whatever reason, to not have to explain to anyone…well, most ladies would prefer…"

"Oh," she said slowly, as she grasped his meaning. "Well, that's very gentlemanly of you, but I'm more concerned about your arm. Say, can you take off your shirt?" she asked.

"I suppose…" he halted.

"Well, try. And turn your back please. I think I've figured something for that sling."

He did as she asked. With his right hand he began to unbutton his shirt. Behind his view, Lina slipped her hands beneath her dress and untied her petticoat. It fell to her feet, nearly as soggy as her dress, the hem thick with mud. She gave it a good snap, sprinkling water all about. She watched as Robert slipped the galluses from his shoulders, then struggled to pull his shirt from his trousers. He tried to slip his broken arm from the sleeve, but grunted with the discovery of yet one more restriction.

"Let me help you," Lina said. She came behind him and took the shirt at the collar, slowly pulling it off his back as he let his injured arm slip out. The wet shirt stuck to the union suit he wore beneath. She gave the shirt a shake, then tossed it on the drying blankets. He watched as she stood, figuring out what to do next. "This would be easier if you were sitting," she said.

"This will be easier if you'll give me that bottle first."

"What? Oh, yes. That's a good idea." She uncorked the whiskey and handed him the bottle. He took one long sip, and another quick one. She pointed to the stump. "Sit down," she said. As he sat, he eyed her suspiciously. "Don't worry. I'm just going to put on a splint, and then we'll get that arm in a sling. It's all I can do. I'm sorry." She took the petticoat in hand, and began by shredding the muddy, ruffled hem.

"That petticoat…" he said. "I see a ragged edge on it already. Is that the same petticoat you tore to bandage Charley that day he fell?"

"Yes."

"How fortunate to have worn that one today. I suppose I'll have to see you get a new one."

She tore the edges until she had a large square. "I wore it today because it's the only one I own. So, yes, I suppose I'll be needing a new one."

"Only one?" he said, as she took the hem pieces and began tearing them in strips. "I thought ladies had trunks full of such things." He grinned.

With one quick pull the fabric ripped in her hands. "Only ladies like Franny Ellis." She gave him a pointed look. "Most ladies have better things to do with their money."

"Like you?"

"Like me." As she tore the next strip, she noticed a small tremble in her hands. It spread to her shoulders, where her dress cloaked her in cold dampness.

"Here," he said, offering her the bottle. "This will warm you."

"I'm fine."

"Ha! Now who's fooling themselves? Drink it. I need your steady hand for this work."

Reluctantly, she took the bottle and lifted it to her lips. As quickly as she dared, she tilted her head and let the whiskey fill her mouth. She held it there, then swallowed. The liquor was strong. Her mouth flew open and she coughed a bit, but the smoky taste warmed her as it went down. "What is that?" she gasped.

"Scotch whiskey," he said. "Better than that rot-gut you've had before."

"More of a kick, you mean." She coughed once more. "Very well. Ready?"

"Don't you suppose I ought to keep that bottle? I might need it."

"Yes, you will. This will hurt, no doubt."

He took it from her, and after one more swig, nodded. "Ready."

Lina knelt beside him, and held the two slats along the length of his arm. She took the first torn strip and tied the splint in place. He winced as the pressure built, but she continued, tying a second, then a third, and finally a fourth strip the same way, until the splint was secure. When she had finished, she stood up. "That's the worst of it. Now the sling."

Just then, a gust of wind rattled the shack. Lina went stiff at the sound, then let out a long sigh. "That storm. It came up so suddenly. So much different than the usual rains," she said as she folded the large square of muslin.

"Like I told you, up here storms come off that mountain with a fury. But you didn't seem too ruffled by it," he said, watching her closely as she moved next to him. She draped the cloth over his chest, then down along his left arm.

"That falling tree frightened me. What a horrible sound." She pulled the sling gently beneath his wounded arm, moving slowly and minding not to upset the splints.

"In the timber, that's a sound no man wants to hear. The men hear that sound, and everybody runs. A timber, even a branch, falling from those heights can kill a man."

She rested her hand on his shoulder as she secured the sling. His body felt cool to her fingers. His skin responded to her warm touch with a tiny quiver. She felt a rush of warmth engulf her. *The whiskey, no doubt*, she thought. "Well, my respect for your work is renewed. You've given me one more reason to worry about you…and the men."

As she pulled the corner of the sling behind his arm, she leaned over his shoulder, their cheeks nearly touching. "It's as I warned you," he said. His words, so close to her ear, were soft and deep. "There are all sorts of perils up here." She felt a lightness in her head, and a quick stutter to her heartbeat. *The whiskey*, she told herself again, trying to remember what her fingers should do next. With a quick shake of her head, she adjusted the sling into position.

"Yes, you warned me," she said, stepping back. "There, see how that feels."

Robert ran his good hand over the sling. "Fine. Better. Thank you."

"Now, you should have something to eat." Lina moved back to the blanket. "Give me that knife of yours."

"It can wait. Tend to yourself."

"I'm fine."

"You're cold. And are you certain you didn't hurt yourself?"

"Not a scratch."

"Well, you're dripping wet. And exhausted. I can tell. Rest for a while. I'm going to check on the horses, now that you've freed up my good hand." He gave her a smile as he walked out the door.

Lina lay back on the blanket. Robert was right. She was tired. She closed her eyes for what seemed like only a minute. When she opened them again, she faced the warmth of a small fire in the middle of the room. Robert sat next to the fire, watching her. There was no more rain coming in through the roof, and no more light either. Night had come.

"How long have I been sleeping." Lina asked, sitting up.

"An hour. Maybe more."

She stretched her back. "Hmm. Thank you for that. You were right. I was tired."

"And hungry?"

"Starved."

"Help yourself." All the foodstuffs were still on the blanket, neatly cut up. Robert had somehow even managed to dry out the biscuits a bit. She took a slice of apple. "A regular picnic, eh? Like that day at the grove," he teased, but as soon as he said it, he thought better of it. That had been a good day that ended badly.

"Yes," she said, smiling. "Though I recall nicer weather." She finished the apple and started on some venison. "How are you feeling?"

"Fine. The food helped." Robert held up the whiskey bottle. "So did this. If you want any, I suggest you take a drink now. I plan on using this to get me to sleep. With this arm, I don't see any other way. So forgive me in advance, Miss Morgan, but I'm about to get good and drunk."

"You're welcome to it," she said, and took the flask of water instead. She moved closer to the fire. She shuddered in its warmth. "Mmm. Feels good. I still feel soaked." She reached behind her and untied the ribbon that secured what was left of her braid. She untwisted the remaining coils, then with her fingers she combed through her tangled hair. Once loosened, she shook it before the fire, relaxing with the flame's growing warmth. She looked up at Robert, and caught him in a deep, almost transfixed stare, watching her work. She blushed, but Robert couldn't distinguish it from the heat of the fire upon her cheek.

He checked himself, and turned his attention to the venison. Quietly, he said, "I want to say thank you—and I'm sorry."

"For what?"

"Thank you for coming today. Sorry that it wasn't what you hoped."

"I'm glad I came. I'm only sorry I gave out at the end. Once it was over, I realized how scared I'd been. If I had stopped to think about the consequences of what we were doing, I don't know if I could have done it. So I just set my mind to being certain we were on the right course. I wouldn't let myself consider anything else. And I never doubted you, and so I never worried."

"I understand. At first, I assumed I was on my own to figure out what to do. I only thought about you as there to help. But you did more than that. And when you told me to be patient, I thought, she's right. She's got good judgment. If she thinks everything's going to be fine, that's a good sign. I wouldn't have wanted to be there today without you." He took another drink. "Still, I know you wanted something else from the day. I just never understood what it was."

"I don't think I knew. I do now, though." She looked into the fire. "Sleekit's the first place I've ever lived—ever—that I felt like I belonged. But Sleekit wouldn't exist if it weren't for the wilderness around it. These forests and mountains are what feed it, what makes it what it is. I didn't feel like I would ever really know Sleekit until I saw this."

He smiled as he stretched out, leaning on his one good elbow. "There's so much more. I had it in mind to take you to a place not far from here. A waterfall, in the most beautiful little valley you've ever seen. A waterfall one hundred feet high. In spring, when the river runs high, the valley roars with its thunder. Yet there's a softness to it. The spray comes down like a lace curtain blowing in the spring breeze, changing from moment to moment. At the right time of day, the mist makes rainbows that span the whole depth. Rainbows so close, it's as if you could reach out and touch them. I swear there's no greener place on God's earth. Of course, in winter, the falls freeze. Long, fragile columns of ice. It's as though time has stopped and you can see the single moment when the water tumbles toward its destiny."

"It sounds perfect," she said, eyes closed.

"Nearly so," he said.

"Nearly?"

"There's an echo." As he struggled to sit upright, his face twisted with his own discomfort. "Never cared for that echo. It's a...lonely sound." Suddenly, his voice lost the energy that had, only moments ago, so entranced her. He reached for the bottle again. For long moments, the only sound in the cabin was the crackle of the fire.

Lina stared into the flame. "Hotassa was so brave. And she trusted us completely with her life and her baby's life. I've never known such trust. Was it simply that she was too tired, too desperate to be afraid we might fail her?"

Robert shook his head. "No. You're right, they are very trusting people. Even after being betrayed time and again. It's one of the lessons I take from them. After all that has happened, they still believe their god acts with purpose. What happens is what is meant to happen. To them, events are neither good nor bad, simply part of the natural order."

Lina looked down. "I haven't had half the misfortunes they've had, and I can't trust like that. Only myself."

"And me," Robert said matter-of-factly. "Didn't you just say you didn't doubt me today?"

"Yes," Lina said, surprised at the revelation. "Yes, I did."

"There you have it. It's a start." He took another drink. "And I trust you, Miss Carolina Morgan." Just then, they heard the deep rumble of thunder in the distance. "'Listen! The mighty being is awake, and doth with his eternal motion make a sound like thunder - everlasting'," Robert quoted.

Lina laughed. "You remember it still?"

Robert smiled at her oddly, and looked deep into her eyes as he finished the poem. "'Dear child, dear girl, that walkest with me here, God is with thee when we know it not.'" Lina felt suddenly weak under his gaze. She shivered, and had to look away.

"The drink is getting to you," she said. "Eat some more."

"Nope. Ate my fill while you slept."

"Then I'll have some more." She nibbled on a biscuit. "How do you come to know Willahe?"

"I met Willahe when I first came here. My father sent me to him." Her puzzled expression urged him on. He settled in with a quick shot and another bite of meat. "My father had come here years before, when he and his brother, Hugh's father, both worked for the Hudson's Bay Company. Two very different men, my father and Uncle Malcom. Malcom was a born company man. Strict, demanding, very formal.

My father wasn't. He had an adventurer's heart, but he also had a wife he loved more than life. And two small sons. My mother…" He sighed. "She was a good soul, but not strong. She depended upon him for everything. He could never quite still his restlessness. When I was ten, the company offered him a place on an expedition west. Reluctantly, my mother gave her blessing. He was gone a year."

Lina watched his mood change as he told the story, from the light of his father's joy, to some darkness not yet spoken. "My father wrote wonderful letters." He laughed. "I wore those pages to rags, reading them over and over. The world he described! The beauty of the sound, the gigantic forests, the game, the mountains. Right then, I set my mind to coming here one day."

"That must have pleased your father."

"I'm not certain," he said quietly. "Mother took ill while he was gone, and died shortly after he returned. I'm sure he must have felt responsible, though I never heard him say so. He spent his last years buckling down and providing for me and Jamie. I saw the life slip from him day by day. Then what did I do? I came here, leaving him to care for Jamie by himself."

Here then, she thought, is his darkness. "He loved you," she offered. "He wanted you to have your dream. I suspect the only thing you could have done to break his heart would be *not* to follow that dream."

"Hmm. Maybe. Still…" Robert looked at the bottle. The whiskey was almost gone. He took another drink. "So, that's what I meant when I said father sent me to Willahe. Father said he would teach me everything I would need to know to survive, and he did. Willahe took me in like a son. I lived with them for nearly two years."

"What did you do when you first came?" she asked.

"I learned to trap, hunt, cut timber, fish, things second nature to Willahe's people. How ridiculous I must have seemed." He laughed. "I was a boy. All I knew of hunting was the park in Montreal where I once hunted deer. And I'd never done any hard work. Those first months, at night I was so tired I'd fall asleep without eating. But I loved it. I knew instantly why my father was enthralled. I wrote him every chance I had, sharing what I learned." Robert looked at Lina thoughtfully and said. "I suppose you're right. He *was* pleased. His letters back to me told me so."

"Of course he was," Lina said softly.

"When I had figured out that I might support myself by logging, I came down to the inlet and built the cabin. You see, I wanted to live in this beautiful wilderness, but I wanted to make my fortune here, too. I figured if I could make a success of it, I could prove to Uncle Malcom that father's folly, as he used to call it, wasn't a folly at all."

"Well, at that, you've certainly succeeded."

"Yes, but I find it odd. If my father hadn't died, Jamie wouldn't be here with me. If Uncle Malcom hadn't died such a miserable old man, Hugh and Charley wouldn't be here. And without them, I wouldn't have succeeded at all."

Lina shook her head. "Things just would have been different, that's all. You'd have been a success, no matter what you set your mind to."

"Thank you." He looked at her through eyelids heavy with fatigue and whiskey. "And what of you, Miss Carolina Morgan?" His tongue was heavy with the whiskey, too. "What brings you here to the ends of the earth? Why does such a clever, pleasing young woman leave San Francisco and come to Sleekit, of all places?"

"To make a better wage."

"So you've said. Come now, is that all?"

She desperately wanted to say more, and while her trust in him grew by the moment, her trust in herself was waning. In that moment, when the question hung between them, she knew she would happily forget everything else that had ever mattered to keep the world just as it was. To stop time, like the frozen waterfall he spoke of, and stay here in these woods, with the rain's constant music behind them and the warm embrace of the fire between them. To answer his question might break the spell. Yet with each bit of himself he had revealed, the spell had only deepened. She felt she had to try to answer in kind.

"I traveled west with two people I met in Missouri. A fellow named Henry, and a woman named Josephine. It was of mutual benefit. They wanted to go west, and I needed to leave Missouri. They each had their dreams. I left because my husband had died, and his creditors were taking his business. I had to start over—somewhere."

"And your traveling companions, what became of them?" Robert asked, his words slightly slurred.

"Henry got into some trouble on the trail, so he took off. Josephine always intended to go to California, and since I didn't care where I went, I traveled with her. We ended up in the diggings. We ran a camp store. Then the company we worked for offered us jobs in San Francisco."

"A wonderful town."

"For some, yes. I made good money there, though it cost dearly to get by. But Josie and I made new friends, and we got on for a while." The story, so far, had been easily told. The facts Lina had omitted had not detracted from the truth. She paused to choose her words carefully. "I had a chance to go to a school. I had always wanted to go, you see, and my employer made it seem as if I would be getting a real education. The kind I imagine you had. You know so many wonderful things— all those books you've read. That's what I wanted. But it turned out the school was just a finishing school. Social graces. Sewing lessons. Posture. Etiquette." Lina made a face, but Robert's laugh surprised her. "Why is that funny?"

"Just the thought of you..." He stopped himself. "It's not that I don't think of you as a lady, Lina. Just not that sort of lady. Full of silly airs."

Lina chuckled. "I wasn't very good at it. I was very unhappy."

"A terrible waste," he said gently. "You'd have done quite well at study."

"Thank you," she said, a bit embarrassed. "So I left the school, but when I returned, Josie had taken ill."

"I'm sorry," he said.

She thanked him with a wistful smile. "There's nothing to be done for her but see she's cared for. So I came here. My options had run out in San Francisco. I needed work, and I thought this seemed as good a place as any." She smiled. "I'm lucky it turned out to be much more than that." She studied his face, and was taken by the empathy she saw there. His usually bright, clear eyes were made more green than blue in this amber light, and seemed to hold not only her gaze, but a view of his own past. "It seems we both know something about living with difficult decisions," she said.

He nodded. "Yes, but, there's a difference. I came here to follow a dream. To be sure, the dream has changed, but it's driven me. The dream wasn't about sacrifice, either. Your dream is. To sacrifice yourself for your friend? No, that can't be it. You have a dream, some ambition, don't you? Something just for you?"

"I don't think about such things."

"You should. It's healthy. Besides, I suspect your friend would want that for you. Didn't you just say as much to me? Those who truly love us want for us what we want for ourselves. If you don't know what you want, what do you suppose your friend Josephine would want for you? Eh?"

She could not speak. The answer, as it came struggling to the surface of her consciousness, confused her. She knew what Josie would say if she had ever met Robert, if she had ever watched Lina with him. Josie would have seen right through Lina's denial, and pushed her toward happiness. But Josie wasn't here now, and because of that, Lina could not, would not admit to the longing she so suddenly now realized she had for this man. There was no reason to speak it, no point to it. There was nothing to be done to make it real.

"It's enough, for now," Lina said. She looked away from him, for she swore he was on the verge of seeing the truth in her eyes. "And you?" she asked, trying to sound casual. "Have you fulfilled all your dreams?"

"Not at all! I have big ideas. To be the biggest and best logging operation on the sound, with contracts from the Klondike to California."

"Now you sound like Benjamin Ellis!" She laughed.

"A man could do worse," he said, drinking the last of the whiskey.

"Maybe that explains…" Lina started to speak, but caught herself. *Maybe that would explain Franny,* she had started to say.

He grinned. "Ah, I see. You wonder what I see in her, I suspect." Lina only shrugged. "You're not alone in that."

"It's none of my concern." She hoped he would let the subject drop.

Robert sighed. "I know. Franny can be a handful. But I confess, as much as I love this life, at times I miss something of the culture I was raised with. Franny and I share that. We are both out of our native-born elements here. I'm just more at ease with this life than she is. I think she finds comfort in me for that reason. And strangely, it pleases me to be a help to her that way. "

The fire had almost burned itself out, and there was nothing more with which to stoke it. Lina studied Robert's face in the waning light. She was certain the thought that had him now distracted was of Franny Ellis, and it seared her heart. But she forced herself to look at him, hoping it would make her own regrets easier to tolerate.

"It's getting late, don't you think?" she said, standing. "The blankets are dry. Your shirt, too. Stand up and let me help you on with it."

Robert looked at her sheepishly. "Do you suppose I have to get up?" He held up the empty bottle in answer. "I don't think I can right now."

"Very well," Lina said, smiling. She knelt down next to him and helped him slip his arm out of the sling. Gingerly, she slipped a shirt sleeve over first the wounded arm, and then the good one. As she pulled the collar forwarded, he turned to her and said softly, "Do you remember that day in the grove when I tried to kiss you?"

"Yes." Lina held the sling as he returned his arm to its cradle. She summoned her courage and looked into his eyes.

He leaned closer. "If I'd kissed you then, do you suppose we would be good friends, as we are now?"

She turned all her attention to the buttons of his shirt. "I suppose not," she said, with a sadness in her voice she hoped he didn't hear. Then she stood up. All that remained of the fire was embers, and the room was dark as pitch. "Good night, Robert," she said as she stretched out on her blanket on the other side of the coals.

"Good night," he answered. She turned her back to him. When at last he started to snore, she turned onto her back and stared up into the darkness above her. Her mind replayed every moment of the day, lingering somewhere between joy and despair. The perfume of the fir branches and the soft sound of rain outside filled her senses. She felt as if she was buoyed on a cloud, yet somewhere beneath something prodded and nettled her, body and spirit. The last of her energy was spent, and soon she fell into a deep, fitful sleep.

32

"Two hundred eighty-nine."

"Mmm."

"Two hundred eighty-nine."

"You just said that one."

"Sorry. Three hundred thirty-nine."

"Yes."

"Three hundred and fifty-nine."

"Right."

"Four hundred ninety-two."

"Four hundred *ninety- two*? Are you sure?"

"Oh, right. Four hundred twenty-nine."

"Good."

"Six hundred and thirty-nine."

"Don't you have five hundred thirty-five?"

"Oh, yes. First, five hundred thirty-five, and then six hundred thirty-nine."

"Yes, that's right." Lina waited. "Robert?"

"Oh, let's see. What was the last one?"

"Six hundred thirty-nine."

"Six hundred thirty-nine, then six hundred forty-four." Robert sighed. He shifted in the chair, and focused anew on the paper before him. Robert was no good for work with the crews now. His injury wasn't serious, but a month was needed for it to heal fully, and more time before he would have the full strength of his arm. For a few days, Robert had tried going to camp, but with nothing to do, he felt restless and in the way. He spent more time than he should at Sweet Meg's, until he saw the effects of the drinking. Riordan was away, so there was no one to gossip with, and everyone else had work to do. So finally, he had come to the habit of spending the day at the office with Lina. She was no more easily distracted from work than anyone else. After the first day of what she had called 'frittering my time,' she put him to work. This day, he was helping her check a list of numbers, a tedious chore he found nearly impossible to focus on.

"Haven't you found your error yet?" he asked.

Lina only barely looked at him from the corner of her eye, a sly smile on her face. "What makes you so certain it's *my* error?"

He chuckled. "I stand corrected. But whoever's error it is, you haven't found it yet?"

She shook her head. "Next entry, please."

"Six hundred thirty-nine."

"That was the last one."

"Oh. Then it's six hundred forty-four."

"Ah! There's one. It should be six hundred forty."

"A difference of four? That's what all this fuss is about?"

"Ssh. Let me figure." She scribbled on the page. Numbers appeared and were scratched out. "No. I'm still off by twelve board feet."

"Twelve board feet? That's what we've been counting? Twelve board feet isn't worth mentioning! Please, Lina. This is agony. Can't you just...I don't know. Add twelve to something else and leave it at that?"

"Agony?" She looked up suddenly. "Are you uncomfortable? Is it your arm?"

"No, it is not my arm! Stop fussing."

"I'm not fussing."

"I'm sorry. No, you're not fussing. But it's not my arm. It's the tedium." He laid the papers on the desk, and leaned back in his chair. "Please. A spell. I beg you."

Laying down her pencil, she said, "Yes, of course. A rest would do us both good. Coffee?"

"Thank you."

She took a cup from the small shelf by the stove and filled it with coffee. "It's cold."

"No matter."

She set the cup before him, then wandered back to the open window that faced toward the water. Her hands on her waist, she stretched her back. "It does feel good to get up and move."

"I marvel at you and the patience you have for this work."

"Mmm, I suppose, though it comes easy enough. But yes, it can be tedious. It helps when the rewards are great. Like here." She moved back to her desk, and handed him the ledger she had been checking. "Look at the account of those deliveries to Kincaid." Robert looked, but her point eluded him. "Kincaid's been overcharging us on his mill rates," she said.

"What?"

"Don't misunderstand. I've no proof he's doing it deliberately, though I wouldn't put it past him to take advantage of any situation."

"You're not being clear. Has he been cheating me or not?"

"That's for you to say. But we've been overpaying. See here? His rates went up. And here as well. And again here. But each time the rate's gone up, Kincaid's charged us the new rate for the timbers you'd delivered the day before. He might not have milled them until the rate change was in effect, but that's not the contract as I understand it."

"No, it's not." Robert was listening more carefully. "Rate's at the time of delivery."

"But when it favors him, when the rate goes down, he follows the contract. Either way, he's ahead."

"So you think it's just sloppy bookkeeping."

"On my part, yes. I should have paid attention. But then there's this. The increases anticipate large deliveries. So if his bookkeeper's sloppy, he's been lucky about it."

Robert stared at the paper and chuckled. Lina watched with surprise as the chuckle turned into a full laugh. Robert tossed the ledger on the desk.

"So, you're not mad?"

"Good Lord, no. Kincaid's clever, but I've known him long enough to keep an eye on him. No, no one to blame but myself. I'm in charge, after all." Still, he laughed.

Lina shook her head as she sat back down to work. "Now it's my turn to marvel at you. I'd not be that charitable about the loss. But you act as if you had all the money in the world to waste."

"Well, not all the money, but more than enough, I suppose."

"Hardly. I know your bank balances right enough, and you're doing well, but…"

"There's more. More money, that is."

"More? What do you mean?"

Robert slowly sipped his coffee. "I have, that is *we* have, Jamie and I, what our father left us."

"An inheritance?"

He nodded. "Oh, it's not a fortune by any means. But I suspect there're several thousand dollars waiting in that Montreal bank."

"Several thousand dollars?" Lina was aghast. "Why, Robert! Don't you know what that could mean for you and Jamie? And this business! Robert, you could do so much more."

"I know. But, I hate to touch it. After father died and I brought Jamie here, I thought it best to leave it, just in case. When Hugh and Charley came, I thought what if we all need it? Of course, I'm sure Hugh and Charley have their own nest egg. If my father did well by us, just imagine what old Uncle Malcom must have left them!" He laughed.

A studious little wrinkle crossed Lina's brow as she asked, "Do you still feel as though you can't use that money?"

"I've been thinking about that." he said, leaning forward. He placed the coffee cup on the desk beside her. He stared at his hand as his fingers worried the edge of the desk. "Since that night coming back from Willahe's. Do you remember? I told you I wanted the biggest and best logging operation along the sound."

"With contracts from the Klondike to California. I remember," she said softly.

"That started me thinking about plans I'd made years ago. Hiring more men. Starting another camp on the east side of the mountains. Maybe even starting our own mill. To hell with Kincaid, eh? Of course, labor's scarce, but that's changing every day. And if there were more men, the demand for lumber would naturally go up. More men, more families, more cabins, more stores, and all the better for Sleekit."

Lina beamed to see him so enthused. "You must do it! Put that money to work where it'll do the most good. Not some musty old bank in Montreal. Right here in Sleekit!"

"Well, there's still much to do before we'd be ready. I'd need time to figure out the details for all these ideas."

"Time is what you have in abundance now," she said. "Perhaps this injury could be a blessing, if you make good use of the time it's given you."

She could clearly see the excitement in his eyes, yet the light flickered as his practical side rose to the fore. "It seems rather indulgent, though, doesn't it, when there's so much real work to be done?"

"This work is as real as any other, and it's work only you can do. If not now, when will you have the time?" When he didn't answer, she added. "Robert, you said before, one never knows what tomorrow brings. Isn't that reason enough?"

With a quick nod, he said, "Indeed it is. It's settled, then. I'll ask Jamie, but assuming he has no objections I'll start tomorrow." He looked up at her and gently took hold of her fingers. "On one condition of course. You'll help me?" he said coaxingly.

"Of course," she whispered. "Nothing would please me more."

"Good," he said, as he released her. He stood to leave.

"Wait. If I'm to help you tomorrow, then we must finish this today." Like a school marm, she tapped the ledger before her with her pencil.

"What? Oh, yes! I almost forgot. Of course." He took his seat next to her, and picked up the papers. "Where were we?"

Lina sat. "Six hundred forty-four, I believe."

"Right. Then it's six hundred fifty-four."

"Next."

"Six hundred seventy-seven…."

****

Robert resolved to wait before he talked to Jamie of this plan. He wanted to have everything figured out first. All he had now was a list of scattered thoughts stored over the years. If he were to do this properly, there must be a logical course of action. Whatever the current balance of the inheritance was, it was modest. They couldn't afford to squander this opportunity. So to prompt his memory, Robert decided to spend the next day with the crew, making literal note of old ideas, as well as a few new ones. No reason not to make the list long, he decided. There would be time later to sort it out.

He also spent some time in physical labor, as best he could. Secretly, he harbored the hope that he'd be able to return to work within a few days. It seemed easy at first, and a welcome sensation, when he worked with an axe. But he grew tired within minutes, and worse, his arm throbbed with pain. So he stopped. If he worked too hard today, there would be no working tomorrow, and he'd only prolong his agony.

At the end of the day, he was too excited about this plan to wait any longer. When they made their way back to camp, Hugh and Robert found Jamie already in the tent, cleaning up and changing his clothes.

"I'll be ready to head to town in just a minute," Jamie said when he saw them, even as he struggled to button his shirt.

"I wasn't going back," Robert said. "In fact, I was hoping to have supper with the two of you, and a good long chat."

"Oh." Jamie's hurried pace suddenly stopped, mid-button.

The disappointment in Jamie's voice was evident. Robert looked at his brother, who seemed reluctant to speak. Robert looked to Hugh, who seemed to have an answer, but was clearly waiting for Jamie to offer it. When he did not, Hugh spoke up.

"He's off to work on the cabin."

Robert looked at Jamie. "Do you mean your cabin? For you and Jean?"

Jamie nodded. "I only have about a month, but I think that should be enough time, if I spend some time each morning and evening."

"Enough time? Jamie, you can't possibly go to town, work all night—in the dark, no less—and then come back here and work a full day! Why, they'll be nothing left of you for poor Jean to marry!" Robert laughed, but he was alone. Hugh was uncharacteristically silent, and Jamie seemed downcast.

"What choice do I have, Robert? We've got to have some place to live. We can't bunk in at our cabin, and there's no room for us at Minifee's."

"What about Meg's?" Robert offered.

"I thought of that," Jamie said. "But I promised Jean. I *promised* her." He let out a sigh. "She hasn't asked for much. Just this."

"I'm sure she'll understand," Robert said.

"I hate that she would have to." Jamie kicked the ground in frustration. "It's my own fault. I missed a dozen chances. But there was always something. We've been so busy. And then, well, of course, no one expected you to get hurt…"

Robert put his hand on his brother's shoulder. "Jamie, I'm ashamed of myself. Not only had I completely forgotten, I've added to your delay. I've put you in a terrible fix."

"No, Robert. It just turned out this way. And I don't see any way around it." Then suddenly, he brightened. "Unless?"

"Unless?"

"Unless you think you're feeling up to coming back to work? How did it go today?" Jamie got his answer from the silence that came from both Robert and Hugh. Hugh looked away, but Robert just shook his head.

"I have an idea," Hugh said. "Robert could build the cabin."

Jamie shook his head and said, "No, it's my job. Regardless, Robert's not up to it. He just said so."

"You're having to do Robbie's work. Seems only fair that he should do yours, as best he can," said Hugh.

"I *am* up to it," Robert said. "I can't swing an axe all day, but there's other work I can do. It'd be good for me. This sitting around is only making me weaker, if you ask me. A bit of good hard work is just what I need."

"By yourself?" Jamie said, shaking his head.

"Charley can help," Hugh offered. "He'd love it. You know he would."

"Splendid idea!" Robert said. "Jamie, you can come down in the evenings, and do a bit of work, and that way you'll be keeping your promise to Jean. We might not finish the whole cabin, but I can promise you we'll have enough keep the rain off your heads."

"Robert, are you sure you don't mind taking this on?"

"Mind? Of course not! In fact, let's head back tonight. You can lay it all out for me, what you had in mind. By tomorrow night, I'll have it started. Let's go."

Hugh stopped him. "Robbie, you said you had something to talk to us about?"

"Oh," Robert said. He had almost forgotten his own plans. For just a moment, he let himself feel disappointed. Then he shook it off. He looked at Hugh and Jamie, and smiled. They were no longer boys but they depended on him still, to carry whatever weight he could. Smiling, he said, "It'll keep for another day. Come on. Let's all go."

****

When Robert told her about his promise to Jamie, Lina wanted to ask about the work he had planned for himself, but she stopped herself. The disappointment was in his eyes, even though he seemed genuinely eager to start on the cabin. She was disappointed too, for she had looked forward to helping him.

The building site was not far from her office, around the bend and just out of site. As the first day passed, she listened to the sound of hammer on nail, of saw through wood, as a measure of progress, but those sounds were few and far between. She had no notion of how long such a job should take, but she wanted Robert and Charley to finish quickly so Robert could return to his own plans. When he was healed, Lina knew he would be swept up again in the daily demands of Marr Logging. If he missed this chance, he might never make time for another. She fretted on that all the first day, and by evening, she was determined not to let that happen.

She decided to help, certain that another pair of hands would make all the difference. On the second day, with a basket lunch as her ruse, she came to the site to see what she might do. Progress was slow. Robert and Charley were only as far as laying down the floor joists. She watched them work, unnoticed. Charley tried to hold the long board steady while Robert nailed it in place. It was a struggle. Charley was not strong enough, and the board wiggled with nearly every blow Robert struck. He would stop, and Charley would right the board. Then they would try again.

"The floor looks small," Lina said. She walked up, carrying the basket.

Robert looked up, then returned to his hammering. "It always looks that way. But it'll be big enough."

Charley saw the basket and came over to Lina the second Robert drove the nail home. "What'd ya bring?"

She handed him the basket. "See for yourself." She walked over to Robert as he was slowly standing, his back stiff. "Show me around."

"There's not much to show," he said. "It's just one room. The chimney will be there," he said, pointing with the hammer. "The front door, here. And a window here. It's the same as the cabin we live in now."

"How long did that take you?" she asked.

"A month. But I was working by myself. I have Charley, here." He looked over to see Charley digging through the basket, eating everything he found. "Hey, now. Save some for me!"

Lina could see that Charley was probably little help at all. And with Robert still injured, if the first cabin took a month, this one might take three. So she came back the next day, and the day after that. She told Robert she had a few hours with nothing to do, but she didn't tell him she was up early and working twice as hard to find those hours. There was little she was skilled enough to help with, but she did what she could. She helped Charley carry the lumber, and she fetched tools and held boards steady. Hard as they worked, their progress was slow, and they were spent by the end of the day. They worked almost until the light was gone, and Charley would start grumbling about being hungry. Meg fixed them supper, but as soon as the meal was done, Robert and Charley headed home. Meg sent them off with leftover biscuits for breakfast, and a motherly admonishment to get some rest.

"No need to worry about that," Lina said, as she carried the plates from the table. "They're bone-tired. For that matter, so am I. Good thing it's a slow night."

"That won't last long," Meg answered, as she walked toward the bar. "Milo will be back tomorrow. I can always feel it in my bones. His crew alone will liven the place up." Meg poured a short beer. "This'll help me rest." She took a sip, carried the beer to the table, and sat. "Why don't you join me?" With a wink, and a nod toward the beer, she added, "Might do you some good."

Lina thought for only a moment. "It might at that," she said. With her own small glass of beer, she sat down with Meg, "I ache all over, but it's my feet that have my tired," she said as she started unlacing her boots. "I guess I've gotten spoiled, spending so much time sitting at a desk all day." She pulled off her boots and wiggled her toes, then took a sip of the cool beer. "Only two years ago, I was walking halfway across the country. Now I'm quite the lady of leisure!"

"Aren't we both, now?" Meg said with a mock air of elegance. The two of them giggled, then after a proper clink of their glasses, each took another sip.

"Well, it's leisure no more. On top of everything else that's coming our way, there's the wedding," Lina said.

"That's the good stuff, honey. The sort of day that it doesn't seem a chore to get ready for, don't you think?"

Lina sighed. "I do think so. But it's been hard to remind myself of that this week."

"Because of the work on the cabin, you mean?"

Lina nodded. "Robert's promised Jamie to build this cabin. He feels responsible for keeping Jamie from it. He shouldn't, of course. Lord knows, there've been other reasons why it wasn't done before now, not the least of which is probably that office they built, just because of me. Now there's no choice but for Robert and Charley to do it. And me to help. Precious little help that I am, or Charley either, though it's dear to see him try so hard."

"But as you said, honey, Robert wants to do it. And what else would he have done with this time?"

"That's just it, Meg. He was all set to work on these plans he has."

"Plans for what?"

"Oh, to expand the business, hire more men, I don't know. I doubt he knows himself, except that he's had ideas for years. There was always something to keep him from it. That's why this turned out to be such a blessing. He was all fidgety and sour over being hurt. But then he told me a little about his ideas to grow the business. I convinced him he should take this time to figure those things out. I was going to help him. He was so looking forward to it! But first he wanted to talk to Jamie. Then, the next day he came in and said he was going to build the cabin. I could see he was disappointed, though he'd never say so. I suppose it's just the way it is, but it seems unfair that just as he was about to do this, once again he had to put someone else's wants before his own." Lina was tired and frustrated, and was hoping for Meg's sympathy. But when she looked at her, Meg was smiling. "What's funny?" Lina asked, more than a little annoyed.

Meg finished the beer. "I was just thinking. You seem more put out by this delay than Robert does. Like it was *your* plans that have been put off."

"Not at all!" Lina protested. "It's simply that... I only wanted to help Robert. He's done so much for me and..."

"Fine, fine. I understand. It's for Robert. Very well, then. I have the answer, if you're interested."

"Of course I am!"

"Everybody around here tries to do too much on their own, and forgets they have neighbors who'll help, if they'd only ask. And that includes you, Lina dear. Now, I know Robert says they can't spare any men, but there are other men around here. If I'm right about Milo coming home, his whole crew can be pressed into service in a day or two. Until then, we just have to find some other fellas to give Robert and Charley a push. Of course, it would be nice to have some experienced hands, like Kincaid's mill workers, for instance. Lord knows he'll never turn loose of them. But if we think about it..."

"Yes, he will, Meg. I know just what'll make him turn a few men loose."

The next morning, Lina was out the door first thing and headed to Kincaid's mill. She knew she would find him as she did, hunched over his desk, counting receipts. She didn't bother to knock when she entered.

"Good morning, Miss Morgan. Come to get the latest invoices?"

"I'll take them sir, lies that they are, but that's not what I've come for."

"Lies? Whatever do you mean? Marr owes me every last dime."

"He does not, sir. You've been playing fast and loose with your mill rates. I've been working on the proof of it, and I almost have it, too. Although I suspect you don't need to see the proof. I suspect you know good and well what you've been doing."

He leaned back in his chair, and folded his arms across the silk vest of his gray suit. "I don't know what you're talking about," he said slyly. "But you said you'd come for something else?"

"I have. I'm taking four of your best men. For at least today, and perhaps tomorrow. I was just hoping you'd point out which men are the best carpenters of the lot."

"You're *taking*? You're not asking, you're just taking." He snickered. "Forget for a moment that I have no idea *how* you think you're "taking" them. Indulge my curiosity, Miss Morgan, and tell me *why* you need them. Marr short-handed again?"

"Yes, in a way. But not at the camp. Robert and Charley are trying to build a cabin for Jean and Jamie by themselves, and at this rate they'll never get it done. So I'm taking four of your men to help."

"Why on earth should I help? If young Marr has neglected his duties..."

"Jamie has not neglected his duties. It doesn't really matter that the cabin hasn't been built yet. The fact of the matter is, this is where we are, and this is what needs to be done. And just so you don't feel too abused, you're not the only one who'll be offering support. Meg's waylaying Milo's crew when they get back tomorrow. But we need good carpenters. That's why I'm here."

"Well, it'll cost you, Miss Morgan. If my men aren't working in the mill, they still need to be paid."

"And you shall pay them."

"Now stop right there, young woman. You may be able to bully me, in the spirit of community, a spirit of which I myself am a great advocate, as you well know. And no doubt that's why you're taking advantage of this situation. But you'll not abuse me of a red cent. If it's Marr work they'll be doing, it's Marr money they'll be earning."

"And so it is. I suggest you use the extra money you've stolen from Marr Logging regarding those mill rates. You know I can prove it. It'll just be a bookkeeping chore. One which, in order to correct, will distract both our operations from business and will no doubt cost us both the same sum in time spent when all is said and done. What you've managed to shake out of our pockets a nickel at a time will probably just about equal what it costs you to pay those men for a few days. If it's not, you may take the time to figure out what those costs are, and bill me. But be careful, Mr. Kincaid. I will need to see detailed receipts. Now, if you'd be so good as to show me the men I can take with me?"

Kincaid sat belligerently locked in a stare with her. Then he stood abruptly, pushing the chair back from behind him with a terrible clunk. He stormed past her, out the door. As she followed, she heard him calling out. "Damn it! Conklin! Bass! Abbott! Mathias! Come here! Where are you? Bass? Man, get over here. I need you four! Damn it!" In a few moments, the four men appeared, following Kincaid. He marched past her where she stood by the door. As he passed, he hollered in her direction, "I'm going with you. To make certain my men are only working on the cabin, and are not otherwise being taken advantage of."

When they arrived at the cabin, Kincaid didn't wait for instruction. "You four, get started on this side. Over here. Marr? Do you have tools enough? All these fellows will need tools! Conklin! Go back to the mill and bring back whatever you can find."

Robert looked up when Kincaid began yelling at him. He left his place at the framing and came forward to Kincaid. "What's this about?"

"Blackmail!" Kincaid answered.

"I beg your pardon?"

"Ask her," Kincaid said, with a sharp nod over his shoulder. "She's to blame for this." Then he went back to directing his men.

Robert walked toward Lina, but before he could speak she said, "I was afraid we wouldn't get this done before you ran out of time. Meg says Riordan's men will be here in time to help you tomorrow."

"And Kincaid's men? Blackmail?"

She grinned. "I confronted him about those mill rates. He knew I had him dead to rights."

"Inspired!" he said, laughing. "Well, let's get to work, then, before Kincaid decides to build it his way."

By the end of the day, most of Sleekit was working on the cabin or helping in some way or another. Virgil came, proud to be a part of building his daughter's first home. Kincaid had rolled up his sleeves and taken hammer in hand personally. Meg and Millie came with food. In only a few hours' time, the scant boards Robert and Charley had managed to pound together in two days had been transformed into the skeleton of a cabin. The frame was up on all four sides, and the base of the chimney work was laid. There were no walls, doors or windows yet, but there was no mistaking it was a cabin.

Late in the afternoon, Robert came up to Lina and took her by the arm. He led her to stand squarely in front of the cabin shell. "Well, what do you think?"

"It's simply amazing! You were right. It already looks bigger. I can start to imagine what it will be like. And look at Jean." Jean stood inside the frame of her new home. "She doesn't have to imagine it. She can see it all, don't you think?"

"I do. And I think we had best hurry, or she'll start pinning curtains to the studs, for want of windows." They laughed, and then Robert turned to her. "Meg told me this was all your idea."

"Well, she lied to you then, because she convinced me we could find enough help. You're not angry?"

"Angry?" He chuckled. "Why do you always suppose I will be angry with you?"

Lina thought for a moment. "I don't know. Perhaps just remembering, when I first came…oh, never mind. You're right. I shouldn't presume. But this time, I thought, well, that perhaps you wouldn't want the help. That you'd see it as…" she hated to use the word.

"As charity?" he finished for her. "No, if it were for me alone, perhaps I might. I suppose I have that much pride. But this is for Jean and Jamie, and I welcome the help."

"It's what we do for the people we love," she said, then quickly added, "Jean and Jamie, I mean." She turned to watch the men at work.

"A lesson to be learned there for all of us, I suppose," Robert said. "We should have this done in another day or so. Which will still leave me time before the wedding and my arm's fully healed to do a bit of that planning we talked about." She looked down shyly. "Meg told me you mentioned that as well. This cabin, that was for Jamie and Jean. But that thought was for me. Thank you."

"You're welcome," she said quietly. "Well, it looks like the men could use their boss."

"Yes," he chuckled. "That's what I've been elevated to, thanks to the addition of the crew."

"Just as well. It's what you're good at, figuring out what everybody else should be doing," she teased.

"Except for you," he said, teasing her back. "You, Miss Morgan. I wouldn't presume to tell you a thing."

****

Meg was never wrong when it came to Riordan's arrival. The Bantry Bay sailed in the next day, but too late in the day to press the crews into service. Riordan promised them for the following day, and Robert agreed that would be enough to finish the project properly. Robert bought Kincaid and his men a round of drinks at Meg's that night, to thank them for their help.

Nor had Meg been wrong about Riordan's arrival livening up Sleekit, though it was more than the presence of his unruly crew. Riordan brought a handbill, as he announced that evening, "of partic'lar interest to any person named or working for Marr and Kincaid," which included nearly everyone present. The notice told of a large contract to begin soon. The specifics of the project were not to be revealed, the notice said, until the bidding session, to be held in San Francisco in about a month.

The opportunity fit perfectly with the circumstances. Robert had already determined that his plans for the business could only be realized with one big contract from outside the territory, something that would earn a reputation for Marr Logging. The men and equipment, those he could buy. But he had already figured he would have to go to San Francisco and spend time learning about the city, and where such a contract might be found. He hadn't figured when that might be, and honestly found the prospect of spending two or three months away from Sleekit harder than it had ever been in the past. Now that wouldn't be necessary.

It was decided that Robert would go, leaving Kincaid to manage the current contracts, and Hugh and Jamie to mind the crews. Robert could stay for the wedding, but would have to leave the morning after, if the Bantry Bay was to make it to San Francisco in time. Everything seemed perfectly timed. Even the occasion of Riordan hearing of the contract seemed extraordinarily lucky. A man approached him on the docks, he said, with the handbill, almost as if he'd coming looking for him. "Said he wanted to make sure all the timbermen around Puget Sound got word of it."

Suddenly, between the wedding and Robert's trip, there weren't enough hours in the day for anyone. Charley was pressed into extra service at the Minifees. That freed Esther and Jean for the wedding, with Meg's help. Jamie and Hugh devoted themselves to the timber. Robert had blissful permission to plan his trip to San Francisco, with Lina's help. They started with the notice Riordan brought back. There was no contractor's name printed on the handbill or any other detail, except the address where the bidding would be held.

"That's a meeting hall," Lina said. "I know that place. Not far from the waterfront. Heavens, they must be expecting a lot of bidders if they're renting out a hall!"

"That's right. *You* know San Francisco. What do *you* suppose this might be?" Robert asked.

"A factory of some sort, I would guess. New factories were springing up like weeds when I was there. But I suppose it could be for some large public building. Perhaps even a house."

"All that makes a difference, you see." He walked over to a corner where she kept their maps. He searched until he found the one he needed, then brought it to the table, unfurling its curled edges. Robert pointed to a spot on the map. "Different trees are best for different uses. Now for instance, there's the Sitka spruce. The strongest wood, good for heavy construction. The best stand is up around here. The hardest to cut, and the most expensive to get to the mill. That'll make a difference in the bid." He pointed to another spot. "The red cedars are here. Western hemlock, here. Each has its purpose. And its challenge."

"Take the map with you," she offered, "so you'll know."

"I know," he said with a grin as he rolled the map and returned it to its place. "That much I know by heart. But the rest...." He shook his head. "Well, I guess I'll just have to figure it all on the spot, depending on what the job is. A job like this, though, a big job, well, it has to be right, or we could win the contract but still lose our shirts."

"The contract can only be for a few things. A factory, a house, perhaps a city building. We can figure some of this before you go. That way, you won't have to guess."

That was the help he needed. Robert knew what it took to get a job done, in terms of time and men. But what those men would cost him, what the tools and equipment would cost him, he had always left to Hugh, and now to Lina. They spent the day figuring out all the possibilities they could imagine. The work they shared made them both more light-hearted. While they were diligent in their preparations, the conversation often meandered. As Robert asked about San Francisco, Lina shared more stories of her life there. She assiduously avoided certain events, but there seemed no harm in talking about the work she had done, the shops she knew, the little moments that were her fonder memories.

Lina no longer tried to conceal how much she enjoyed Robert's company, but she was pleased to find he seemed to genuinely enjoy hers as well. With little effort, she could make him laugh in an easy sort of way that pleased her enormously. It pleased her, too, that every topic of discussion seemed to elicit from him a story. They found they shared small experiences as travelers west. Though miles and years apart, they still shared a similar journey. Robert had come west as an eager adventurer, and Lina as a reluctant transplant, but they had both grown tired of the same dried beef and beans, both earned their fair share of blisters, both knew what it was to be so tired you didn't notice a midnight rain until you woke the next morning to find yourself soaked.

When the day's work was done, and even the stories had exhausted themselves, they would sit together in the quiet evening lamp light of the office, waiting for Hugh and Jamie to come at day's end. Unaware, they became comfortable in that routine in no time. So comfortable, in fact, that Hugh couldn't help but remark on it. "Quite a scene of domesticity," he said, entering the office. "You two look as comfortable as a pair of old chairs."

With two days before the wedding, Lina hurried out of Meg's before she could be stopped. Meg was ordering Milo's men around, making them scrub the place down like they did the deck of the Bantry Bay. Anyone foolish enough to venture within twenty yards of the place was conscripted. Lina left because she hoped to reach the office early for this last day with Robert. The day after the wedding, Robert would leave for San Francisco, and be gone for nearly a month. When he returned, he'd go back to the mountain. If the trip proved successful, the work might keep him away for weeks. Lina was keenly aware how precious this last day was.

Robert had already come and gone. He left her a note, saying he was heading for Ellis to bring Franny back for the wedding. She would be staying in a room at Meg's. He also said they would be taking their time coming back, but they would arrive before night.

"Franny," she whispered sharply. Franny would be here for two whole days, and at Meg's, no less! There would be no avoiding Franny on Sunday, of course, but there was tonight, and all day tomorrow, and tomorrow night.

And what of this ride? Lina's heart ached at the thought of the two of them alone together. Whatever would they talk about? Where were they going? The trip she made with Robert to the longhouse meant a great deal to her. She had spoken about it to no one, other than what Robert had told the day they returned. It was a special memory, and something she cherished as shared only between them. She tried to take comfort in the fact that Robert and Franny were only off on an afternoon's ride. Those places that had become sacred to her—the woods beyond the camp, the valley with the lake, the abandoned cabin—were too distant to be their destinations. Then, she remembered the waterfall Robert had spoken of so intimately. Suddenly, these tortures she was creating for herself overwhelmed her.

"Enough!" she said aloud as she tossed the note down on the desk. She left, and ran back up the path to the tavern, and to Meg.

"Meg, what needs to be done?" she asked as soon as she came through the door.

"Honey, what are you doing here? I thought you needed to…"

"As it turns out, there's nothing more to be done there. So, tell me what needs to be done here."

"Oh, golly. Everything! I have some baking that could get started. The rooms upstairs need to be cleaned. Cases need to be brought in from the back. Where would you like to start?"

"It doesn't matter," Lina said. "As long as I'm busy."

****

So far, the outing had gone well. Robert admitted privately to a certain reservation about seeing Franny. He had been perturbed with her earlier this summer. Something about being unkind to Lina and Charley, although now the details escaped him. They didn't matter.

He knew Franny well enough to guess at the details. But when they were alone together, he found Franny was for the most part a different person. Certainly more agreeable, if a little too interested in herself for his taste. But today, Franny was in a fine mood. When he collected her that morning, he'd suggested a ride straight away. Franny seemed eager. She sat beside him, seemingly comfortable and happy, despite the fact she usually complained to Robert about such long wagon rides. She was far quieter than usual, but every time he looked toward her, she met him with a dimpled smile. When he made a comment, or asked a question, her responses were affable. The sun was high, it was a glorious day, and they had a basket of food with them. Soon, he would be lazing by the stream under the cool shade of the grove, his belly full, and in the company of a beautiful woman. Robert felt content.

As they ate, Franny became more talkative. In fact, she hardly ate a bite, but played with her food as she talked. "Is everyone ready for the wedding?" she asked him.

"Nearly so, I think. I've been trying to stay out of the way."

"I'm excited to see Jean. I only hope there's something I can still do to help her."

This surprised Robert. He couldn't remember Franny ever eager to be of assistance before. "That's very kind of you, Fran. I'm certain there's plenty still to do."

"I'm happy to help," she said in a honeyed tone. She watched him eat. She smiled. She nibbled on the food. She watched him some more, then quietly and deliberately she spoke. "Robert?" She cast her eyes down demurely, then raised them up with precise calculation and looked at him shyly through long lashes. "Robert? Why did you stay away so long?"

"I…I didn't. Did I?"

"Yes," she said, sorrowfully. "It's been ages since I've seen you."

"Oh, well… It's been busy here, you know. Several jobs in the works. We had to build a cabin for Jamie and Jean. Then, of course, with my arm broken…"

"Your arm? Broken? When? How?"

"Oh, yes. That. I broke my arm." He held it forward and twisted it back and forth, flexing its strength for show. "It's right as rain now."

"You poor dear," she said, as she inched herself closer so that she could take his arm gently in her hands. With just the right mix of intimacy and propriety, she ran her hands along his forearm. "Did you hurt yourself working?"

"No. I was caught in a heavy storm in the range to the east. The horse threw me, and I fell down a ravine."

"But that's a day's ride! You were stranded out there in that wild country? Hurt, and by yourself?"

"Not by myself. Lina was with me."

"Lina? What was *she* doing there?" Franny spoke before thinking, and revealed more of her feelings than she intended. But Robert didn't notice.

"I'd taken her on a tour, of sorts. Around the operation, into the forests. We got stuck in a storm. It was an awful mess." But he laughed as he remembered it.

"Really?" asked Franny, an edge to the question. She would have asked more, but she wouldn't give him the satisfaction of knowing she cared. Then her tongue momentarily got the better of her. "Why in the world did you take her? She's your bookkeeper, for pity's sake."

"I argued against it for a long time. Well, then, she…let's just say she earned the right. It was a simple trip, but the storm came at just the wrong time. So we ended up staying in an abandoned cabin."

"Overnight?" The outburst was evident, but still controlled.

"Now, Fran," Robert grinned. "Is this jealousy I see in those blue eyes?"

"Jealous? Perish the thought, Robert Marr. But, that sort of compromising position isn't good for the reputation. Not hers, if that's an issue, but certainly not yours! I should think you would consider such things…"

"Fran. Franny. Fran," Robert said, trying to interrupt her. He was seized with a thought and was no longer paying attention. "Franny. Forget that. It was nothing. I was hurt, we were both drenched with the rain, and just happy for the shelter. No one here thought a thing about it, and neither should you. Wait. Listen to me. There was something… that reminded me, of something I wanted to ask you."

Suddenly, Robert had her full attention again. Gone was the pout that had appeared from nowhere only a moment ago, and returned was the sweet smiling face of this morning's ride. "Yes?" she asked.

"I wonder…have you ever thought?" He leaned closer, but did not take her hand, she noticed. "There's this place I thought you might like to see. About ten miles from here. It would be a bit of a journey, but it would be worth it. This beautiful waterfall, it's beyond description. It's a special place to me, and I…I would love to show it to you."

Franny looked confused, as if she hadn't understood a word he said. "A waterfall?" she finally asked, dimly.

"Well, it's not just the waterfall. It's a special place…"

"Oh, Robert!" She laughed lightly. "A waterfall? Why, I've seen a waterfall before! There's one near father's mill. Why would I tramp into the wilds just to see a waterfall? It sounds like a good deal of trouble to me."

He suddenly realized he wasn't surprised at all by her response. He smiled and said, "Yes, you're right, Fran. It does sound like a good deal of trouble."

"Was that it, Robert?" she asked. "Was that all you wanted to ask me?"

"Yes. That was all."

"Oh." Franny tried to fill the silence between them. "Would you care for some more chicken?" she asked.

"What? No. No thank you." More silence, until finally Robert spoke. "Franny?"

"Yes?"

"Would you mind terribly if we headed back to town? I, I have some chores to do before the wedding."

"Yes," Franny said. "We should be going." She quickly started to gather the remnants of their picnic. "I should check on Jean as well."

They rode back to Sleekit in a hollow silence that was easier than talking.

33

"Why, Miss Morgan, you look so lovely today, if I didn't know better, I'd swear *you* must be the bride." Hugh watched as Lina came down the stairs the Sunday morning of Jean and Jamie's wedding.

"Hugh, what a lovely thing to say! And I'm sure every other girl you'll say that to today will think so, too," Lina said with a grin. She wore a blue dress she bought in San Francisco—one of those Edward had insisted she buy. It was a simple dress in a lovely soft blue that favored her. Millie had helped with her hair, and between them, they managed to twist it into a braid Lina was sure Josie would have been proud of. She was in uncommonly good spirits, too, owing to the day's occasion. There would be no regular church this Sunday. Too many folks wanted to witness this momentous event, so the ceremony would be the service. The occasion seemed more than joyful enough to qualify.

Hugh looked fine himself, in a simple grey suit. Charley stood with him, wearing Hugh's borrowed tie. "Charley, you look quite the young man." Lina reached down to straighten the tie as Charley squirmed. "Where's Robert and Jamie?" she asked.

"I'm here, but the groom's still at the cabin." At the sound of Robert's voice, Lina looked up with a big smile that froze once she saw him with Franny Ellis. Franny, as always, was beautiful. Her pale grey dress was remarkably demure for her usual taste, but it was as becoming as ever. Robert looked happy enough to be the groom himself. "Good! Most everyone's here." He looked at the three of them, then abruptly looked at Lina again. "Lina, you look very nice."

"Thank you," she said, trying to catch any reaction from Franny out of the corner of her eye.

"Hugh, would you mind if Franny sat with the three of you?" he asked, but gave no chance to reply. "Are we ready to start?" he asked, looking all around the room. "Fine, then. I'll go get Jamie!" He left, bounding back across the mud flats toward the cabin.

In an awkward silence, Hugh led them to their seats. He placed Franny on one side of him, Charley on the other, and Lina on the end. Lina wished there was even more distance, but Franny seemed not to notice her at all.

Sweet Meg's was filled to the brim with well-wishers, and those who had come, as always, for the party to follow. Meg played the piano as folks found their seats. When Robert and Jamie finally arrived, with Riordan right behind them, the crowd grew quiet. Lina marveled at how self-assured Jamie seemed, more so than his brother, who, for once, appeared a bit overwhelmed.

When Jamie suddenly looked toward the door, the crowd followed his gaze. Jean Minifee stood framed in the doorway, her father and mother by her side. The gangly girl was no more. In her place stood a beautiful young woman. Her silky brown hair was braided and wrapped tightly on the back of her head. Her grandmother's lace collar only made her long neck more graceful. Her pale yellow dress set off her soft complexion perfectly. And the smile she wore was all for Jamie Marr.

Esther gave Jean a quick kiss, then went to her seat. As Virgil escorted his daughter to the front of the room, Millie came forward to stand up with her friend. Most eyes watched Jean as she entered, but Lina watched Jamie, and she could see Robert and Hugh were watching him too. Jamie wore the same smile that Jean wore, and he never took his eyes off her.

At the pulpit, Virgil gave his daughter a long look, then a quick kiss, and joined his wife. Riordan began. "Dearly beloved," he proclaimed, "we are gathered together in the sight of God."

Lina heard nothing of the ceremony. She was lost in her own thoughts as she watched Jean and Jamie. *Happiness should always be as simple as that. Pure, unafraid, true. That's what I want. To be that happy.* Then her eyes shifted to Robert. *That's what I want,* came the thought again, but this time it stayed as a lump in her throat, as if she had said, not just thought, the words. Josie was there in those thoughts, too, with a long-ago asked question. "What do you want for yourself?" Josie had asked her a dozen times. Her eyes still on Robert, at long last the answer came. *This is what I want. He is what I want. Oh, Josie! Now that I know, what am I to do? There's nothing I can do.*

With tears welling, Lina looked back to Jean and Jamie just as the vows were over and they shared their first sweet kiss of union. The crowd crushed together around the couple, and Lina was relieved to find she was not the only one in tears. Everyone was kissing and hugging, crying and talking all at once. Lina finally reached Jean. "Oh, honey, you're beautiful," she said. "The most beautiful thing I've ever seen."

"Yes. Mother did a wonderful job, didn't she," Jean said, looking down at her dress.

Lina shook her head. "No, honey, not the dress. It's you that's so beautiful. Deep down inside beautiful." Then she turned to Jamie. The moment was overwhelming, so she settled for giving him a big hug and a kiss on the cheek. "I'm so very happy for you both," she finally managed to say. Then she made herself busy. She grabbed an apron and said to Meg, "Let's get to work."

The party was everything anyone could have hoped for. There was enough food, music and dancing to feed all appetites. Lina spent the day running between the picnic outside and the kitchen. She needed to stay busy. Every time she turned around, Robert and Franny were nearby. She sought out Jean and Millie, and soon Franny was there as well. Lina was having a pleasant chat with Jamie and Hugh, when she saw Franny and Robert, arm in arm, walking in their direction. She brought food to the tables outside, and there they stood, heads together, laughing.

Twilight was on the square, and the party showed little sign of letting up. There was nothing left to do but come outside and join in the dancing or the drinking or the talking. Lina watched from the doorway of Sweet Meg's. She was tired, and wondered how soon she might sneak upstairs and be alone. Before she noticed, Franny was beside her. Lina looked for an escape, but Franny spoke before Lina could flee.

"It was a sweet little wedding, don't you think?" Franny asked.

"Yes," Lina answered impassively.

"Jean told me about the cabin, and what you did to help Robert get it finished. Manual labor! Such commitment to your job."

Lina knew then there would be no graceful exit, but since they were alone, she also decided there was no need to be gracious, either. "It wasn't for my job I did it. It was for my friends. Perhaps you don't have friends, Franny, but that's what friends do for one another."

"Oh, I have friends. Jean, for instance. After all, wasn't I the one who helped her today, making sure her hair was done right, her dress just so? Wasn't I there at her side on such an important day? Why, we're almost family. Whereas you, well, forgive me, my dear, but you clearly lack the breeding to be that kind of friend."

"And what would you know about my breeding?"

"I know what I see. You work as a clerk, in a logging camp, of all places. And you work and live in a saloon! You've no family, no station in the world. You performed manual labor, for heaven's sake, building that cabin. No true lady would callous her hands like that. And worst of all, you have no regard for propriety. That trip you took with Robert? He injured himself being kind to you. Then you were alone together, over night, without a proper chaperone."

Lina laughed. "Robert told you about that, did he?" She took some satisfaction in the fact that this bit of news had obviously irked Franny.

"He told me he indulged you in a whim, and wound up hurt, both his person and his good name. What sort of friend does that? If you don't care a whit for your own reputation, you might have thought about his."

Lina shot back. "If you knew Robert as well as you pretend, you'd know he doesn't care about such things."

"I don't think you know Robert well enough to know what, or *who*, he truly cares about."

Lina was tired of this exchange. It had given her just the excuse she needed to leave the party. She resolved to say nothing more, and took a few steps to leave.

"Did you see the ring Jamie gave Jean? It's a precious thing. Small, but dear. It was his mother's, I understand." Franny stepped closer, and leaned in to whisper in Lina's ear, "I told Robert not to worry. *We* can use my grandmother's ring."

Lina didn't look back. She simply stepped off Sweet Meg's stoop and walked through the crowd, across the square, and out of sight.

Content to have removed her from the party, Franny quickly went off to find Robert.

Neither knew Meg was standing in the tavern, watching the exchange between them. She followed Franny, for she knew the girl would lead her to Robert. She wanted to talk to him, too. By the time Meg found Robert, Franny had already captured him. They were deep in conversation, and Franny hung on his arm like a wet towel.

"Good evening, Meg, my darling," Robert said as she approached them.

Meg was not smiling. "Robert, I need to speak with you. Right away."

"What about?" he asked.

"It's important, and it can't wait. Your friend here will just have to do without you for a while," she said. Robert looked at Franny and shrugged. Franny put on a bit of a pout, but as soon as they were gone, she wandered off to find someone to gossip with.

Inside the tavern, Meg went to her usual table. She patted the chair next to her for Robert to join her.

"It's Lina." Meg started. "I'm concerned about her. I saw her leave the party. Something upset her."

"She's just tired, I expect. We've been so busy lately."

"Then why did she head south, and not just go upstairs? No, something's wrong, I'd bet my life on it. She's been frantic for days. Inventing work around here, like she wanted the distraction. And then…"

"Yes?"

"Well there's your friend, Franny."

"Franny?"

"I saw them. Talking. Neither one seemed very happy. That's when Lina walked off."

"Franny," Robert sighed. "Perhaps. But, Meg, what can I do? If she hasn't confided in you, what would make you think she'd confide in me?"

"Because I have a hunch that whatever it is that's troubling her, it has something to do with you."

"Me?" Robert struggled to think of what he might have said or done to upset Lina. Beleaguered, he shook his head. *There was no telling. With a woman, the possibilities were endless.*

"Please, Robert. Find her. If she doesn't want to talk to you, at least you tried."

"Very well, Meg. For you," he said, giving her a kiss on the brow as he stood. "Do you know where she went?"

"The office, maybe?"

Robert nodded, then headed out the tavern door. The office made sense. He was leaving in the morning. Perhaps she had thought of some last minute detail. That would be like her.

****

Feeling she was about to burst, Lina had headed to the office without thinking, but when she arrived, she knew exactly why she had come there. This was her place. Here, she thought she could calm herself and rid herself of this anger. Then she lit the lantern and saw how wrong she was. Everything in the room, every chair, every scrap of paper, every board in the walls, reminded her of Robert. Her anger dissolved, replaced by sadness deeper than any she had ever felt, even deeper than her thoughts of Josephine. Along with the sadness came a surprising bit of self-pity, along with frustration, regret, and loneliness so profound it frightened her. And all this, she reminded herself, because she had let her feelings for Robert confuse everything. Now, fresh among her pains, her earlier anger was returning. She was angry with cold and callous Franny, who it seemed would soon have what Lina so wanted but would never have. For long minutes she paced the floor, half-crying, then denying the tears, then a sudden fit of temper where she looked for something to throw. She wore herself out, and finally she collapsed at her desk and indulged her tears. She was nearly done when Robert arrived.

"Lina! You're missing all the fun!" he said, bounding into the office. If Meg was right and there was a problem, he was counting on being able to easily cajole her. "Lina?" he said again. He expected her to turn around, but then, almost imperceptibly, he saw her shudder, heard a long sigh, then a quick sniff. The realization that she was crying, or had been, made him uneasy. Scraped knees, wounded pride, even the grief of death, these he knew how to speak to. *Heaven knows what makes a woman cry*, he thought. *Usually the smallest things*. Perhaps it was just the day, he hoped, and this mood would soon pass with some quick but careful attention.

"What?" She straightened her shoulders, and quickly dabbed the end of her nose with her kerchief, but she didn't turn around.

"Now, now," he said, coming closer behind her. "Why are you crying on such a happy day?"

She lowered her head, and turned away to dab the last of her tears. Then, looking up at him with a forced smile, she said, "Oh, I suppose it's just a sentimental day."

Robert chuckled. "Sentimental? You? I've never known you to be much for sentiment."

Wounded, she rose from the desk, and retreated from him. "I can be just as sentimental as the next person!"

"I'm sure you can," he said soothingly. "And it *is* a special day, isn't it? Unusually sentimental, I suppose. I know *I'm* feeling sentimental. I've had a long time to consider this day, but still, here it is! Little Jamie, a married man." He watched her the whole time, hoping she would turn and smile, and this would all be over. "I know how pleased our parents would be today," he added, quietly.

"Yes, I'm sure they would," she said perfunctorily, and still she did not look at him.

"But I must admit, I'm a bit surprised at you. I mean, sentimental over a wedding." Lina finally looked at him, showing an expression of complete puzzlement. "Jamie told me you've made yourself clear on the subject of marriage. That you have no interest, I mean," he said. Lina continued to stare, but there was something in her eyes that began to make Robert nervous, which only made him talk more. "I can understand that, what with your earlier marriage, and all."

"What does that have to do with anything?"

"Look, I'm just trying to help," he said defensively. "Meg thought something had upset you. She saw you talking to Franny, and well, I know you've had words with Fran in the past, so I thought that might be the matter. I came to see if I needed to apologize for something Franny said. But just now it occurred to me the wedding itself might be

517

the reason. That perhaps, today of all days, you might be feeling, well, rather sad. Grieving, perhaps."

The look of pained empathy Robert wore made her laugh. She was glad he had said something this ridiculous. Almost at once she felt better. "Lord, no! Is that what you thought? That I was mourning? No, Robert, that's not it."

"Oh, well, then. Good." They stood facing each other, awkward in the silence. Robert was the first to speak. "Although, you know, you should consider remarrying. You shouldn't be alone, you know. Nobody should."

"Ha!" she said, her frustration at the breaking point. "Well, it always comes back to that, doesn't it? I've been hearing that from everyone I know for the last two years! Love and marriage, the quick fix for what ails you. That's what everybody says, once they're the ones in love. It all seems like a fine idea to you, too, now, I suppose, what with your engagement to Franny and...." Then she stopped. She hadn't meant to say it, hadn't even wanted to think about it. But it was too late.

"My *what*?" he asked, head cocked to one side, eyes wide.

She pulled her shoulders back, and spoke slowly, trying to keep her composure. "Franny just told me. And yes, you're right. I did have words with Franny. Silly words that I immediately regretted. You have nothing to apologize for. And you needn't think that'll be a problem in the future. I simply work for you, and I give you my word that from now on, I'll be as pleasant to Miss Ellis as can be. And once she's your...once you're...married..." Lina forced out the words. "Once you're married, I will make every effort to...get along. So let me be the first to wish you all the happiness..." She thought this last bit might make her façade more convincing. She was wrong. She choked on the words and had to turn away.

She looked back when she heard him laugh, full and long. "Franny told you we're getting married?" Lina gave a quick nod, and Robert laughed again. "Lord, that woman has one hell of an imagination!" he said, rolling his eyes. When he looked at Lina, he couldn't help but notice the sorrow that had been with her since he had arrived was slowly lifting.

Their questions came overlapping. "You mean, it's not true?" she asked, her voice belying her hope, just as he said, "So you believed, her?" Then quickly, he answered, "No, of course it's not true!" just as she was saying, "Why wouldn't I believe her?" To stop the tangle of words, he took her hands. "Lina, I can't believe you'd think I'd actually marry Franny Ellis! I mean, Franny!" He couldn't stop chuckling.

Lina was looking down to where his hands held hers, lost in the warmth of that simple touch. He saw her expression, and a new thought came to him. "Lina," he said, almost afraid to ask, "did that… did what Franny told you…was that what…? Meg thought whatever was troubling you had something to do with me. Is that what's wrong?" She looked down, afraid to let him look into her eyes. He took her chin in his hand, forcing her to look at him. "Did it…did it hurt you, the thought that I would marry Franny?"

This was the time, she knew it. At this moment, she could say something clever to make Robert Marr think whatever she wanted. She could dismiss the whole notion as evidence of his vanity, or a romantic delusion the result of the day. She could, if she wanted, forever put a barrier between herself and Robert he would likely never cross again. But this time, finally, she said no to all the denial of her own dreams. Summoning all the courage she had, she raised her head, and looking him straight in the eye, said, "Yes. It hurt me that you might marry… anyone."

"Really?" he asked, in total surprise. Hesitantly, he brought his right hand to her cheek, as if to study her face for the truth.

"Truly," she answered. She brought her hand up to where his fingers touched her cheek. Then he smiled, that wonderful smile of his, she thought, and leaned toward her. With no more prompting than the soulful look on her face, he brought his lips to hers. This kiss, a first kiss, did not demand, but asked. This was a kiss soft and warm, reticent and hopeful. This was a murmur of a kiss, a prayer of a kiss. A taste of a kiss, tenderly savored. A kiss for a moment, and for a lifetime.

Their lips parted slowly, and Robert searched her face for a reflection of his delight. He found it in the blush upon her cheek, and the tender touch of her fingers on his. Robert smiled, and started to take her in his arms. Just then, a voice outside stole the moment.

"Robert? Are you in there?" It was Franny. They broke their half-embrace quickly. When Franny Ellis came to the door, she looked as if she expected to find she was interrupting something. "Robert," she said, her dimples poised for him, and her sharp glance trained on Lina, "it's getting late. Would you mind seeing me to my room now? The party's all but over, and besides, I hear we'll need to be up early to see you off." Then, as if taunting them, she added, "Unless you two have something you need to finish here?"

"Nothing at all," added Lina. "I was just getting a few things ready for his trip, but that's done now. I'll wish you both a good night," She went out the door and disappeared into the night.

****

Lina almost missed the send-off. She overslept, and when she woke, she felt groggy and disoriented, like the world around her had changed. Then she remembered it *had* changed, and why, and she leapt out of bed, dressed, and ran to the dock, just in time.

When she arrived, Robert was saying his goodbyes. A kiss for Meg, a handshake for Kincaid, a hand through Charley's rumpled hair. But no Franny or Hugh. There was no time to wonder why. Lina hugged Milo and wished him well, then hoped that Robert would come to her. He did. He said goodbye to her last.

"I thought perhaps you weren't coming," he said. "That maybe…"

"I overslept," she interrupted. "I…found it difficult to sleep last night."

Robert grinned. "As did I." He turned his back to the others, and said quietly, "You and I, we have much to talk about when I get back." Lina noticed something of a question in that declaration.

"Yes. I'd like that," she assured him.

Then he took her hand, almost as if he was about to shake it, but at the last moment felt some daring and, impulsively, gave her a quick peck on the cheek. "For luck!" he said, and then he and Riordan headed to the Bantry Bay. The folks of Sleekit waved goodbye until the ship was so far from shore that faces on deck were no longer distinguishable.

In the first days of Robert's absence, Lina had little trouble keeping occupied. The week passed as always, except often, out of nowhere, there came the memory of a kiss. But always, after that moment of reverie, Lina would fix her determination anew to refrain from dwelling on the implications of that kiss. All thoughts, she reminded herself, were only speculation until Robert returned. At first, she could successfully pretend that Robert was merely up with the crews. But when the men returned from camp at week's end, her delusion crumbled as she knew it would. With Jamie and Jean together now, Lina was left with Hugh and Charley for dinner company at Sweet Meg's, themselves a reminder of Robert's absence. To make matters worse, someone was always mentioning Milo or Robert, speculating where the Bantry Bay might be, or supposing how Robert's luck would fare.

The second week Lina began to wrestle with her own part of the talk Robert had promised upon his return. For if that discussion did take the course she hoped for, and now began to believe might be true, she must make a choice. She could go on as before, hiding from Haarten, working to provide for Josephine, and never tell Robert any of this, or she could confess everything. To continue on as before would spare him the worry, she defended, and not ask of him something she felt she had no right to ask. But it also risked everything. Inwardly, she feared that if his feelings were not as strong as she hoped, her dilemma might be reason enough to lose whatever chance she might have. Most of all, she hated the notion of deceiving him any more than she had already done.

On the other hand, telling him the truth offered the hope that he would somehow, miraculously, fix all her problems, as he so often did with others. At the same time, it pained her to think of herself as a problem for him to fix. If she believed he acted toward her out of pity or obligation, she knew she would never trust his feelings for her. More than anything, she needed to trust that. And there was ever the chance that he might be so angry with her for hiding the truth from him, he would never feel the same. So neither choice seemed satisfying, or offered any certainty of outcome. Finding no clear answer, she pushed the worry, like she had the speculation, as far back in her mind as she could. She found herself stuck—neither free to be happy, nor capable of abandoning all hope of happiness.

The third week of Robert's absence took her attention away from her own concerns to those of another—Meg. Lina came downstairs one morning and found the kitchen cold, no friendly smells from the stove, no welcoming sound of chatter within. She stepped outside for any sign of Meg, then checked the shed out back. Suddenly, a sickening feeling filled her stomach. She dashed back through the tavern and took the steps to the second floor two at a time. "Meg?" she called as she knocked on the door, not waiting for an answer. The room was dim in the early morning light. "Meg?" Lina could see Meg's form beneath the covers, but she saw no movement. She could not tell if she was still asleep, or… Her heart quickened. "Meg?" Lina fumbled for a match to light the lantern. In the soft, coming glow, she could see Meg was lying on her back, eyes wide open. "Meg?" she said softly, as she gingerly laid her hand on Meg's forehead, hoping to find it still warm.

"I'm not dead," came the answer in a hoarse, whispered tone. Meg's blue eyes blinked slowly, and her breath came in labored spurts.

"What's the matter?" Lina said, feeling Meg's cheeks.

"Just the same old afflictions." Meg used all her air for that one sentence. Her chest pulled high again with new air as she readied herself for the next. "I get this way sometimes." Then she coughed, a brittle hack that rattled her whole body.

Lina slipped her arm beneath Meg and held her around the shoulders. "Try to sit up," she coaxed. "It might be easier to breathe." Even as she struggled through the cough, Meg nodded, and tried to use her own strength to sit. Lina tugged at her shoulders, and with much effort on both their parts, Meg finally managed herself into a more or less upright position. She started to speak, but Lina stopped her.

"Don't say anything for a while. Breathe in deep, and slow."

Meg shook her head. "Hurts…down deep," but she tried to do as Lina asked, until finally her breathing came a little easier.

"Can you sit here for a bit?" Lina asked. "I'm going to make some tea. I think that would make you feel better, don't you? Your lips look parched, and the room is chilly this morning."

Meg managed a weak smile and a nod. Lina hurried downstairs to light the fire in the stove. The process of making the tea became an ordeal. She broke two matches before she could get the fire lit. The kindling refused to burn properly until she spent precious moments blowing lightly on the small flame. The kettle was dirty, and had to be washed. The water seemed to take forever to come to a boil. She sloshed hot tea as she headed back to Meg because her hand was shaking. She stopped herself at the bottom of the stairs. *Calm down,* she admonished herself.

Meg sat and sipped the tea, and Lina watched with relief as some color returned to Meg's cheeks. Lina had to take the cup from her twice when a wave of coughing struck her, but this time the fits did not last as long. When the last of the tea was gone, Meg handed her the cup and smiled.

"Relax, honey," Meg said. "You look scared to death. I'll be fine."

"Yes, you will. Because I'm staying with you to make certain of it."

Meg shook her head. "I need to sleep this off. Doesn't make much sense you sitting here...watching me sleep."

"And what good am I when I'll be worried about you? No arguing. I'm staying." Meg started to speak, but it was clear talking was still a struggle. "You've been sick like this before?" Meg nodded. "Do you know the cause of it?"

Meg nodded again. "My leg."

"Your *leg*?" Lina asked. "Meg, that doesn't make sense."

"Doc...says it's 'cause I don't... get around too good. Can't... clear my lungs, I guess."

"What does Doc give you for it?"

"Tonic. Tastes like the devil, but makes it easier." She coughed a little. "Behind the bar."

"I'll get it," Lina said, "and I'll make you another cup of tea to chase it down. And then you're getting some rest."

The old woman did as she was told, but not before extracting a promise from Lina not to spend the day at her bedside. Lina would leave, but only if Meg consented to another sitter in her absence. When Meg was asleep again, Lina ran to Jean and Jamie's cabin. She found Jean working inside, bustling with a newlywed's pride and energy.

"Oh, Lina! I'm so glad you've come calling," Jean offered, standing in the open door.

"I can only stay a moment. I've come for a favor." Lina stepped inside. She looked about and realized she had not seen the place since the couple had made it their home. The small cabin was spare, but homey. The room seemed larger for lack of many furnishings, but Jean had brightened the place with some wildflowers set in a jug in the middle of the table. The room was spotless, owing no doubt to the work of the broom Jean still held in her hand. The morning light streamed in through the window and gave a sparkle to the settling dust. Jean was, as usual, smudged with dirt from head to hem, yet she beamed with delight. For just the briefest moment, Lina was aware of an envy she held for Jean's circumstances. *A home of my own.* She let it pass. There were more important matters on her mind. "It's Meg."

"What's wrong?"

"I don't know exactly. But she says she gets this way sometimes. She hasn't the strength to get out of bed. She has a horrid cough, and…"

"Oh, the pleurisy," Jean said matter-of-factly. "She's had it for some time. Doc Maynard's given her something for it. Did she tell you?"

"Yes. I found her laudanum."

"Is it helping?"

"It seemed to. But I hate to leave her alone. She seemed so…so frail."

"Oh, Lina," Jean said, setting the broom by the hearth. "Did it frighten you?" Lina nodded. Jean took her hands. "Meg always comes around. It just takes a few days' bed rest. That's all."

"I was to go to camp today. Would you stay with her? I would feel so much better knowing you were there."

"Of course. I'll be around within the hour. Can you wait until then?"

Lina nodded. "Thank you, Jean."

Jean came as promised, and Lina made her trip to camp as quickly as she could. She told Hugh and Jamie about Meg, but they offered her the same assurances that Jean had given. Meg's illness was a matter of routine, and while everyone showed concern, no one but Lina felt there was reason to worry. A few days bed rest and plenty of tonic, and she would be fine, they promised. On the way back to town, Lina tried to take comfort in the fact that those who knew her longer weren't worried. Still, she was pleased to return to find Meg awake and looking better, owing to some stewed fish Jean had made for her.

Lina stayed close by the rest of the day, watching as Meg slept off and on. As day turned to dusk, Meg was resting easier, and Lina was beginning to believe that everyone might be right after all. She napped a while, but when she woke to find the sun had set and the room was now dark, she had a fleeting wish for her own bed. The straight-backed chair was certainly no substitute. She listened in the dark until she heard the sound of Meg's slumber, then she stood, her back stiff. With caution she moved through the dark toward the door.

She opened it to reveal a beautiful, moonlit night. The moon was behind the tavern, casting the upstairs balcony in shadow. But just beyond the balcony railing, moonlight filled the open space of the mud flats. The serenity of the night cast a spell over her. For a long time, she stood, as still as the night itself, gazing on the deep dark quiet of the settlement. Even the tide was tranquil. The water rippled in and out along the shore with no more than a murmur. The air was calm. There were no other lights, no one about, not even a gull's cry to break the night's perfect silence. After a time she felt more certain of the stillness, and stepped out on to the balcony to lean against the rail.

She looked along the shoreline again, then followed the tiny ripples of the sound to the west, to places even the moon could not illuminate. To some place where, she prayed, the Bantry Bay was sailing home. So much worrying she had done over the last few weeks, while Robert was gone. *Yet what did it matter, after all?* She turned her head back to the room, until she heard Meg slumbering. Meg's illness had scared her. No matter what assurances others had given her, she understood how easy it was to lose those you love. She thought back over all those who had come and gone from her life in the blink of an eye. Some gone for good. Her mother, her father, even Ephraim. Others beyond reclamation. Henry. Josephine. Now, too, perhaps Robert. She wanted to believe, as she looked up into the clear, star-filled sky, that she would not lose him. She leaned out over the balcony's rail to try to catch some of the moonlight on her face, but it was beyond reach. She held her hand outright, letting her fingers play in the white light of the moon. It seemed as if she could just touch it, nearly hold it. But it vanished the minute she pulled her hand back. A whispered moan escaped her lips, finally breaking the stillness of the night.

****

Meg had improved enough that Lina felt she could sleep in her own bed. She woke to the sound of a soft tapping on her door, and someone calling her name. The voice was Meg's.

"Lina, honey, wake up. It's late. We need to get busy."

Stiffly, she moved to the door. There, on the other side, stood Meg, fully dressed.

"Meg? What on earth are you doing? You shouldn't…"

Meg held up a hand. "I'm better, and there's too much to do to be lazing about."

"Do?" Lina squinted into the morning light.

"They'll be home any day. I can feel it in my bones. Oh, dear. Let me sit here on the bed while you get ready. Come on, now. Hurry, honey. Half the morning's gone."

"If you need to sit, perhaps you should still be in bed," Lina said, although she had already started to dress as Meg had ordered.

"Staying in bed won't do me a lick of good now. I've had my rest. That's what it usually takes. Guess I let myself get run down, and the old body just makes up its mind to take a rest, whether I like it or not. I'm still a little weak, but that comes of staying in bed too long. So let's get busy, and I'll feel better. We'll start by firing up the stove, and opening up the kitchen. I've gone four days without a customer. About time to bring some business through the doors."

The two women worked together for the rest of the morning. Meg managed a few chores, but she was at her best directing others anyway, so for the most part she sat at a table and supervised Lina's efforts. Lina started the fire and Meg started a roast boiling and then wrote out a list for Minifee's, while Lina started cleaning. That morning the whole tavern was swept out and washed down. Meg finished the roast then started on bread and baked an apple pie, as well. "It's Milo's favorite, you know." Charley brought supplies from Minifee's and Lina stocked the kitchen and the bar. They stopped long enough for a quick bite to eat, which reminded Lina that sleep was not all she had deprived herself of while Meg was sick. Then the dishes had to be washed, so Lina started in again.

"Just finish those, we'll be done. I can't thank you enough for all you've done for me. Not just today, I mean, but while I was sick. Guess I gave you a bit of a scare, didn't I?"

Lina smiled. "More than a bit. Although I don't know why. Everyone said you would be fine."

"And so I am." Meg stood. "Let me see now," she said, turning a slow circle to survey their handiwork. "Everything looks just fine. I'd say we're ready for Milo."

"And Robert," Lina added without thinking.

"Hmm. Yes. And Robert." Meg looked at her with a strange smile.

"What is it?"

"Tell me, honey. *Are* you ready for Robert?"

"I suppose. There's not much at the office that's lacked for his attention while he's been gone."

"Except you."

"Pardon me?"

"You. You've lacked for his attention. You've been out of sorts since he left. And honey, if you don't know what's bothering you, then I do." Lina looked at her, puzzled. " You're in love with him, simple as that." Lina picked up the broom and started sweeping the already swept floor. Meg indulged her for a moment, then continued. "There's no shame in it, Lina. Nor harm, near as I can see, which is exactly what has me so perplexed about why you're fighting this so."

Lina kept sweeping, but finally she answered her. "Meg, I care for Robert, and maybe, just maybe, he might care for me. But love?"

"Lina, put that broom down and listen to me. I know you as well as anyone here, and I know Robert Marr even better. So don't be telling me I can't trust my own eyes. Honey, you just light up whenever he's around. And Robert, he's always looking for you in the room, always mentioning you when you aren't there. He has a way of looking at you that's different. It's tender-like. And besides, didn't he kiss you just before he left?"

Lina's jaw dropped. "How did you know?"

Meg grinned. "I didn't, until just now. But it wasn't hard to guess. It's why I sent him after you that night. To give him a bit of a shove. You too. I wasn't sure what would happen, but I hoped. Then, the next morning, when Milo was getting ready to shove off, and we all came down to say our goodbyes, I watched the two of you. I saw the way you looked at him. And he at you."

"Oh goodness! Do you think anyone else noticed?" Lina slumped into a chair next to Meg.

"What if they did?"

"It wouldn't be right! I mean, there's Franny, and…"

"Oh, to hell with Franny Ellis!" Meg looked her straight in the eye. "Didn't you wonder why Franny wasn't there to say goodbye that morning?"

"Yes, but I guess I thought they might have said their goodbyes earlier. In private."

"Oh, they said their goodbyes but not that morning, the night before, right after you came back from the office. And it wasn't in private. They stood right there at the bottom of the stairs. I was here inside the tavern alone, and I heard them."

"Meg! You shouldn't have…"

"They shouldn't be having conversations like that where a body can hear them! I didn't sneak up on them, after all. And I can tell you this. Nobody yelled, but it was mighty clear to me that Robert was very unhappy with her. I guess whatever she said to you really got his dander up. Then she seemed to be accusing him of something. Did she catch the two of you?"

Lina shook her head. "No, but she might as well have. I can only imagine what she must have thought when she found us there alone."

"Well, neither one of 'em was a bit happy. There was no sweet send-off, I can promise you that. And I heard him tell her that Hugh would take her back to Ellis in the morning, and then she said "Tell him to be ready at first light!" Then she stormed up to her room and he left. So I don't think you have to worry a bit about Franny Ellis. And about time, I say! Never did care for that one."

Lina couldn't help but smile at the thought of a triumph over Franny, even if she hadn't been there to witness it. But she was still not persuaded. "Meg, it was just a simple kiss, after all. Just one kiss."

"It might have only been one kiss, but that look in your eye says it was no simple kiss."

Lina looked into Meg's eyes as she searched her own soul. "No," she whispered, finally. "No simple kiss. At least not for me."

"And not for him either," Meg said, taking her hand.

"Oh, but Meg, it doesn't matter if you're right. I can't promise him anything. Not now, not yet. It wouldn't be fair. I have…obligations."

"I know. Milo told me. But he didn't know exactly what those were. Would it help to tell me about it?"

Lina thought for only a moment then shook her head. "No. I wish it would, but there's no one who can help me."

Meg looked puzzled. "Hmm. Well, perhaps I was wrong after all."

"Wrong about what?"

"About your feelings for Robert. If you care for him, don't you trust him?"

"Yes, completely, but…"

"And wouldn't you want him to come to you if he needed help?"

"Of course, but…"

"Then you should go to him with this whatever it is that has you so weighed down with worry."

"And give *him* cause to worry? That wouldn't be fair to someone you…you care about."

"You have this all backwards, Lina. Whatever this situation of yours is, you figure it's standing between you and happiness. But from the way I see it, if you'd just trust yourself, and trust Robert, you could have all the happiness you want. It's not the *thing* that's keeping you from happiness, it's accepting what it means to love someone. Someone to share burdens or happiness with. Someone to share a *life* with."

Lina looked at Meg and was suddenly overcome with love for her. Meg was a mother to her, more mother than even her own had lived long enough to be. Thinking back on their months together, Lina knew that was how Meg had come to think of her. All she had done for her, all she had given her, all they had shared, was what Lina had always missed. She felt a wave of sentiment rush over her, and tears came to her tired eyes. She reached over and wrapped her arms around Meg. She hugged her close for a long time. "Thank you," she whispered. "I love you."

She felt Meg's lips brush her cheek, and her hand pat her head. "I know," Meg whispered back.

At the end of the day, Lina headed for the office. If Meg was right, and Robert and Milo would be back soon, she needed to catch up on matters that had fallen by the wayside during Meg's illness. But Meg's counsel didn't leave her. As Lina walked across the flats, a sudden brisk breeze blew in across the water, reminding her that summer was all but over. Time was slipping by so quickly. Her mind jumped randomly between all her memories of the past two years. Weeks and months had rushed past her as swiftly as that breeze, yet hours and days had crawled at a snail's pace. It seemed only yesterday that she had left Missouri, but a lifetime since she'd seen Robert. And like that sudden breeze, a wave of longing for him came over her, and now, she did not fight it. She let the yearning flow through her.

She sat at her desk and sorted through some papers, remembering when she first came to Sleekit, and how hard she tried to earn Robert's trust. In that she knew she had succeeded, despite any other doubts she had. She treasured that trust, yet as Meg had said, Lina withheld her own trust in him. If he knew, would he be as hurt as she would be? Of course. Robert, who made it his business to help anyone who asked, would not understand, even if she had what she believed were the best of reasons. Suddenly, the whole matter was as clear as day. She would tell Robert about Josephine, and Haarten, too. And she would tell him as soon as possible after he arrived.

But tell him how, exactly? She sat back in her chair and stared out the window. "Robert, there's something I haven't told you," she said aloud, to see how it sounded. *Too ominous*, she thought. "Robert, there's something I need to tell you." *Too desperate..* This was going to be difficult. She tried again. "Robert, I need your help." *Yes, that was it. That was the place to start.* "Robert, I need your help," she said again, and then fell silent as she began to put the remaining pieces of the conversation together. She sat there lost in the imaginary discussion until well after dark.

****

Lina woke the next morning to a drizzling rain, which brought disappointment. Most likely, even if Milo had made it as far as the sound, he would not come into port in this weather. Yet just as she was donning her shawl and readying to dash across the muddy Sleekit square to the office, she heard a long, low call in the distance, muffled by the sound of the rain on the roof. She opened the door to her upstairs room and looked out to see the Bantry Bay moving like a ghost through the watery mizzle. She scrambled downstairs as fast as the slippery steps permitted.

"Meg! They're here!" She burst through the door, her eyes searching the room until she saw Meg at the stove.

"I know, honey, I know. I've started breakfast. Milo'll be hungry."

"Are you coming?"

"You go ahead. Get the boys. This damp hurts my leg …"

Lina ran out before Meg could finish. She dashed toward Jean and Jamie's, dodging puddles along the way. She pounded on their door. "Ship's in," she called. Not waiting for an answer, she continued her sprint up the path to the Marr's cabin. Hugh opened the door just as she reached it. His red hair was tousled, and his braces still hung at his sides. He chuckled as he tucked in his shirt.

"Charley's still dressing. Go on, we'll be right behind you."

Lina spun on her heel and headed back toward the square at a full run. She reached it just as a dinghy pushed off from the Bantry Bay. She watched it slip through the misty waters, and by the time she could see it was Milo and Robert sitting inside and surrounded by cargo, Jean and Jamie, Hugh and Charley had arrived, all waving and hollering their hellos.

"Aargh! It's the devil's own weather today," Milo said, the first one out. "I told them men to leave off with the rest of the cargo until later. Ah, Lina, darlin', it's good to see yas," he said as he hugged her.

Then Robert stepped out, and his family hurried forward to welcome him. She wanted to run to him, too, but her feet wouldn't move. She contented herself with watching him. He smiled broadly and embraced each of them in turn even as they bombarded him with questions. With his arms around Jean, Robert looked up to see her, and she felt her heart flutter. Then Hugh's voice rose above the commotion.

"Well, Robbie. Are you going to leave us all in suspense? How was the trip?"

"Give him time to catch his breath," Jamie said. "And let's get out of this rain."

"Meg has breakfast started," Lina heard herself say.

"That sounds fine," Robert said to her. "Let's go to Meg's, and I'll answer all your questions." The small swarm pushed forward. Still she could not move, but just as they passed her, from within the crowd she felt a hand take hold of hers. Robert's hand. She looked up to see him smiling down at her. The whole exchanged happened in a matter of seconds, yet to Lina it was the most perfect of moments.

Then another hand reached for her, and pulled her back to awareness. "Lina, dear. I've something for you." It was Milo. She felt Robert's fingers release hers reluctantly as the throng pushed forward to Meg's.

"Now where did I put it?" Milo patted his old tattered jacket and thrust his hands inside his coat. "Ah. Here 'tis," he said. He took out an envelope and handed it to her. "Someone brought this to the ship in San Francisco."

The writing on it said, "Carolina Clark, Sweet Meg's Tavern, Sleekit, Washington Territory." As she stared at it absently, she mumbled, "Thank you, Milo," then, still staring at the envelope, she heard Robert calling.

"Are you two coming?" The others were already inside, but Robert stood waiting for them. Quickly, she slipped the letter in her pocket, and she and Riordan hurried on to Sweet Meg's.

Once inside Meg's, they found a room of expectant faces. When Meg saw Riordan, she rushed to him. "Oh, it's good to have you back, old man!"

"Ah, dearie. I've missed you," he said, giving her a kiss. "Mmm. What's that I smell? Bacon? Why, yas fixed me breakfast, ya have!" He started for the stove, but Meg pulled him back.

"Not so fast, mister. There's food for everyone. But not until Robert says his piece."

"That's right, Robbie. We're all starving, so be quick about it," Hugh said.

As they looked at him, Robert seemed somber, almost sad. Lina's heart sank, but before Robert said anything, Jamie laughed. "We got the contract, didn't we?"

"What do you mean?" Robert asked.

"You're a terrible actor," Jamie said, "You try this ruse every time. It never works."

Robert gave up the pretense, and grinning from ear to ear, he threw his arms wide and announced, "Yes! We got it!"

Everyone let out a cheer and began hugging each other furiously. "Well," asked Jamie above all the confusion, "what is it? What's the job?"

"A ship!" Robert exclaimed. "The largest schooner ever to run the Pacific Coast. A nice, fat contract. Should keep us busy for months. But it's a tight schedule, and there's a lot to do. We have to get started right away." He looked at Jamie and Hugh. "I've already spent most of our advance."

"The contract comes with an advance?" Hugh asked.

"You've already spent it?" Jamie asked at just the same moment.

"Yes. Two thousand dollars." Hugh gave a long whistle at the impressive sum.

"What could you have spent two thousand dollars on?" Lina asked.

"Supplies, mostly. And some advances to some new men. I managed to hire a few away from those California lumbermen."

"How much is the whole contract?" she asked this time.

Robert laughed. "Ever the good bookkeeper. Look here, I know we'll have to tighten our belts, but only for a while. I promised we'd have the first load of timbers to San Francisco in a month. Once they're there, we get another two thousand. And so forth until the job's done. All done, it's twenty thousand dollars! Can you imagine? It's a fortune! It'll be enough to do all the things we've been planning to do!"

Lina smiled. She knew, if no one else did, that this was what he had hoped this contract would do—allow him to build his dreams. She beamed with happiness for him. "You're right," she told him. "It's wonderful. We'll just tighten our belts, if that's what we have to do."

"Thank you," he said quietly to her. Then to the crowd, he said, "I suppose it's a bit early in the morning to have a proper toast. So coffee will have to do." He picked up a mug and held it high until all the others joined him. "To the benefactor of our celebration. A man whose foresight, intelligence, and good judgment precipitated his selection of Marr Logging as timber suppliers. Friends, I give you, Captain Edward Haarten."

Lina's mug hit the floor with the clatter of tin, just as the others were taking their sips. Lina looked down at the front of her dress, now drenched with spilled coffee. She looked at the tin mug twirling across the floor until it came to a stop. She looked at the puddle of coffee on the floor by her feet. Lina looked at all this, but recognized nothing but the one word that had stopped everything. Finally, she heard Meg's voice come through the fog. "Lina, did you burn yourself?"

"What? Oh, no." Somehow she managed to answer. "How clumsy of me. I'm so sorry. Here, let me clean this up."

"Never mind, honey," she heard Meg say. "Get that dress off. Run upstairs and change."

Thankfully, the celebrations continued, and no one noticed her walk, dazed, out the door and up the stairs. When she was safely inside her room, she wrestled to get the envelope Milo had given her out of her pocket. She tore the envelope open so quickly, she almost ripped the letter in two. She started reading, and with the opening words, a trembling coursed through her. She stood rigid in the middle of the room.

> *My dear Carolina,*
> *If this letter reaches you, then I have found you*
> *at last. I look forward with great anticipation to your*
> *return. Do not hesitate, my dear. You have been gone far*
> *too long, and it is time now to return. Those here who*
> *care about you suffer for your absence. It would only add*
> *misfortune if those there who have come to care about*
> *you should suffer as well.*
> *E.H.*

That it was a threat and an ultimatum was clear. Lina could practically hear him saying the words. But the full nature of the threat escaped her until she walked back inside the tavern. Then she saw it right before her. Everyone was eating Meg's good food, laughing and joking, floating on the promise of their good fortune. What pleasure it gave her to see their easy happiness. Yet she recognized in that moment that these people who had become her family would be Haarten's weapon to extort her into returning. He would harm them, somehow, through this contract with the Marrs. The thought of it sickened her, the thought that something might imperil the life they had worked so hard to build. Worse still was the realization that, although Haarten might be the instigator, if anything were to happen to destroy this happy scene, it would be because of her.

She almost ran back upstairs, but Robert saw her. "Lina, come join us!" Robert pulled a chair next to his own, and held it for her as she sat. "Meg, another plate, please! Charley, more biscuits?"

The young boy reached his hand into the basket. Hugh reached for one as well, even though he was more attentive to the papers in front of him. "Robbie, this is a tremendous amount of timber he's asking for. And all from the most remote stands. Clearing it will take a while. Are you sure we can meet the schedule?"

"It'll be tight, but I know we can, Hugh."

"Did you bring me anything?" Charley asked, his mouth full of biscuit.

"I did! Your very own knife."

"Really?" Charley's face lit up. "Where is it?"

"It's in my satchel. I'll give it to you when I take you to camp later. That's right, Charley, my boy. As of today, I'm putting you to work."

"Hurray!" Charley shouted, jumping out of his seat. "No more school!"

"Wait a minute!" Hugh said.

"I said I'd put him to work, Hugh. I didn't say there'd be no more school. He can help Lina with supplies. And perhaps we can take him to camp part of the week. We'll see what can be done. But he's earned it, Hugh. It's time. This project could be the beginning of great things for this family. He should be a part of it." Robert took one more gulp of coffee, then he stood. "Now, we best be off. Today's going to be the first of many busy days. Charley, go down to the dock and get my satchel. Take it to the cabin, and I'll meet you there." Charley was out the door like a shot. Robert laughed. "See that Hugh? Such energy! We'll make good use of that."

Hugh rose. "If he doesn't wear us all out. Come on, Jamie. Robert, should we wait for you?"

"No. Go ahead. I promised Charley the knife, and then I want to take these papers by the office. Lina, will you come with me?"

"If you need to hurry, you could just give them to me now." For weeks Lina had longed for a moment alone with Robert. Now, all she could think to do was to put it off as long as possible.

"No, I'd like to talk to you now, if I could."

Lina followed him obediently. As they walked toward his cabin, she was grateful that all he spoke of was how he came upon the knife he was giving Charley. She smiled and nodded, and avoided looking him in the eye. Charley was delighted with the knife, real buckskin with a carved handle. Robert told him he won it playing poker with a pirate, though Robert told Lina on the sly he simply bought it from a street peddler. The knife became legendary in Charley's eyes. "Now run along and catch up with Jamie and your brother. Tell them I'll be at camp mid-day."

Robert said nothing to Lina on the short walk to the office. She unlocked the door, and hoped he did not notice the small tremor that caused her to fumble momentarily with the key. Inside, she walked straight to her desk and took a stack of papers she had been saving for him.

"Here, you might want to take a look at these right away," she said.

"Lina, I thought perhaps we should …" He reached for her hand, and she let him take it, but nothing about her bearing encouraged more. "I thought we should have a talk, you and I."

She looked down to where his hand held hers, transfixed by the sight. She was already aware of how few of these moments there would be for them, and the fact that he had no idea of that at all made her feel dishonest in even permitting it now. But she couldn't help herself. Finally, she mustered the strength to look into his eyes. She was right to struggle with the act, for those eyes seemed to watch her with a delight that swelled her heart to bursting. "Yes, we should. But can it wait?"

"Wait? I suppose. It's just that…I've wanted to speak with you… very much…since that night…"

"Yes," she interrupted. "I know. But, you…you need to get to camp. Perhaps later, when there's more time and…"

"Of course. That makes a good deal more sense." He gave her fingers a squeeze, then released her. "This evening, then? Might I have permission to call on you?"

She knew he was teasing her with this formality, even flirting with her, and she hated it. She hated it because there was nothing she could respond in kind that wasn't the worst sort of lie. But she summoned a smile and said, "This evening would be fine."

"Wonderful! Until then. Oh! I nearly forgot. Here's a list of supplies I've brought back. Take a look to see what I've overbought, and what we still need. You'll know best. And take a look at that contract. See what you think all this bloody work is going to cost us, and how much we might actually make. I have some plans for the profits," he said, winking.

"Of course."

"Do you know Haarten?"

The question stunned her into confusion. "I'm sorry? What?"

"Haarten. This man who's given us the contract. I just wondered what sort of fellow he is to deal with, that's all. He seems to be well-heeled, and everyone in town appears to know him. But he's a hard man to read. I just thought if he's that well known, perhaps you'd heard something of him when you were in San Francisco."

She framed her response carefully. "I think it's fair to say that he's known to be single-minded when it comes to what he wants."

"Hmm. He struck me as a hard business man. That's good news. I prefer a man who's steady at business. Well, I'm off. Until tonight?" She nodded weakly. He turned to go, and just as she thought her heart was in the clear, he turned back, and with a light, familiar touch, leaned down and kissed her. It was a short, soft peck that took her completely by surprise, a fact that registered delight in his eyes. He laid his hand on her cheek. "Goodbye," he said softly, then left.

****

Lina sat on the stoop of the Marr's cabin, waiting for Robert to return. She trained her eyes on the path that led to camp. She had been there already for some time, watching that path, but her real attention was turned inward to her own sad thoughts.

She knew from the moment she read Haarten's letter that the timing of its arrival and the awarding of that contract were not coincidental. Lina knew Haarten well enough to know that with all the resources at his command, he was more than capable of planning and carrying out such a scheme. She had rested in Sleekit too easily, felt too comfortable within its shelter, and had too quickly believed she was clever enough to escape without a trace. For a while she tried to think of what might have happened, what trail she might have left, or who might have come through here who was working for him. But the 'how' of it didn't matter. Haarten knew where she was, and now was brandishing his long reach. His scheme would work. Lina knew when she saw the Marrs sitting happily at Meg's that she would have to leave. All that remained was to concoct a story, and plan the departure.

Then, that afternoon, Robert had kissed her, and when he left, she was too heartbroken to speak. If only she had told her tale before he took that liberty. So much time had passed since their first kiss, she had almost forgotten the sweetness of it. But now it was fresh in her mind, and its tenderness tore at her heart. She was frightened because she knew that if Robert saw in her any of the longing or regret she was feeling, he might try to persuade her to stay, or worse, unwittingly force her to reveal the truth. And to tell him what she now so clearly saw as a betrayal of his trust was too much for her to consider. So Lina sat and waited on Robert's stoop, watching the fading sun, and the now shadowy path to camp, forging within her the resolve to do what must be done.

Then Robert came into view. He was alone. *Thank God*, she thought. For a few agonizing moments she watched him, unnoticed, and thought to herself that these were the last few minutes of her only happiness. He emerged from the shadow of the tree line and, looking up, saw her. He smiled. Lina rose to meet him.

"This is a pleasant surprise! I supposed you would still be at the books. Or am I late?" he said when he reached her.

"No, I…I wanted to catch you as soon as you got back."

"Is there something wrong?"

Lina didn't answer. Instead she asked, "Jamie and Hugh?"

"They're behind me. Stayed to finish a few things. I was…" he grinned, "eager to get back to town."

Lina looked away. "I need to talk to you. It's rather important."

"Then there is something wrong. What is it?"

He took her shoulder and gently turned her toward him. She had to look at him, she knew, so she envisioned the face of Edward Haarten, and so was reminded how important it was for her to stay true. Now she could look at Robert with a steady gaze. "Nothing's wrong. But something's happened."

"Tell me," he said plainly.

Lina drew a deep breath and began. "You remember I told you of my friend, the woman I had come west with?"

"Yes, I remember. Josephine, wasn't it? You said she was ill. Oh, Lina, has she....?"

"No. In fact, the letter I received says she's much better."

"But you don't seem as happy about it as I would have thought."

"The letter was from the clinic. Josephine can be discharged at any time. She wants to return home, to St. Louis, but there's no one to take her there. No one but me, that is. You see, she *is* better, but not well enough to travel alone. I feel I owe her that much."

"Of course. It's only right you should feel that way." Robert looked at Lina and nodded. "So that's what you have to tell me? That you must leave?"

"Yes. As soon as possible."

He was quiet for a while, then said, "How long will you be gone?"

Lina went blank. Since she was not really planning this trip, she had not considered that detail. "I, uh, I don't know, actually. Some months, I should think."

"But surely you'll be sailing? I mean, I would just assume you'd be taking the sea route. Much quicker. You can go all the way to New Orleans, and then up the Mississippi..."

"I suppose you're right."

Another long pause, then Robert said, "When will you leave?"

"Tomorrow, if I can arrange it."

"Tomorrow? But, that doesn't leave any time for...Lina, I've just returned. I had hoped..." Robert stepped forward and reached for her hand, but she recoiled.

"No. Please don't."

She had wounded him with this rebuff, she could tell. But he remained constant in his questions, and even in his tone with her. "How will you leave so soon? Milo said it'd be at least two weeks before he left again."

"I hoped I might find a packet out of Ellis. Please, Robert. I have to leave. And because I can't offer you any assurances of when I'll be back, I think it's better if we leave matters between us as they were. I'm sorry." She turned to walk back toward Meg's. She could not bear this conversation another minute. One more question from him, one more look of tenderness or hurt in his eyes and she was sure to lose her resolve.

"Wait!" She didn't turn back, but she did stop. She heard the cabin door open, then in a moment shut again. He came around to face her. "Here," he said softly. In his hand he held the copy of Wordsworth she had borrowed from him so long ago. "Go on, take it."

She took the book. Absently, she ran her fingers lightly across the gold leaf on the binding. "Robert, I can't take this," she said.

"Of course you can. You might enjoy its company on a long voyage." He reached out his hand and laid it on the book, very near her hand. "But you'll give it back when you return."

She looked up suddenly to see his smile, and tears came to her eyes. She did not fight them, but did not give into them either. Robert saw her tears, and his hand slid down to gently grasp her wrist. "Lina? You *are* coming back, aren't you?"

This is the worst lie of all, she thought. For one last indulgence, she took hold of his hand. She clutched it, trying with all her might to burn the sensation into her memory. "Yes," she said hoarsely. "Now please. I must go."

"I understand," he said.

She had started to leave again, but turned back one last time. "Robert? I haven't mentioned this to anyone else yet. I wanted to…to tell you first. Please don't mention it. Let me say my goodbyes in my own way."

He nodded his promise, and she turned back toward Meg's, leaving him standing in the road, the evening light all but faded from the day.

****

In all this misfortune, Lina found one piece of luck. A Canadian lumber schooner was leaving Ellis for San Francisco the next day. Hugh had mentioned the fact in passing one night at dinner. This was Lina's only bit of relief, this promise of a quick departure. There were still goodbyes to be said. And Meg would try to wheedle an explanation. She had hoped the explanation she gave Robert would serve. But talking to

Robert had taken all her strength. Just before she reached the tavern's door, she stopped. The tavern was filled with revelry. Hidden in the evening shadows, Lina watched Meg at the bar, talking to Milo, holding his hand all the while. The old couple seemed happy and content, and Lina didn't have the heart or the strength to disturb that.

"Afraid to go inside?" said a friendly voice right at her shoulder. Hugh had walked up on her, unnoticed.

"What? Oh, Hugh! No, just too tired, I suppose."

"Tired? Well, then, yes, don't go in there. There's too much celebrating tonight. Why don't you go upstairs and rest a bit, then join us later?"

"No. I...I can't. I have too much to do."

Hugh looked at her quizzically. "You're not working tonight, are you? Heavens, lass. Give it a rest from time to time. You're making the rest of us look bad, you are!" He laughed, but he noticed Lina seemed a world away.

Suddenly, she looked at him intently. "Hugh. I need your help."

"Of course. Anything."

"Take me to Ellis. At first light. Can you do that?"

"I...I suppose. But why? If it's about those supplies, it can wait a few days."

"No, it's not that. Please. I can't say anything more." Hugh didn't look appeased. "If you insist, I'll tell you what I can in the morning. But not now. Please, Hugh. It's very important."

"Of course I will."

"And say nothing to anyone. Not to Meg or Milo. Or to Robert. Don't say a word to Robert."

This seemed only to pique Hugh's curiosity more, but he asked nothing else. "First light," he answered with a nod.

Hugh was as good as his word. The next morning, Lina waited for him by the railing upstairs, with her two small bags beside her. Hugh came just as the sky was turning ash gray with the morning light. Silently, they loaded the two bags into the wagon, then pulled away from Meg's. Lina expected a barrage of questions once they were out of Sleekit, but Hugh never said a word until they reached Ellis.

"Where do you want me to take you?" he asked finally.

"The dock," she said. Hugh didn't seem surprised. He pulled the wagon to a stop near the pier. He unloaded her bags, and helped her from the wagon. Then, looking around, he said, "I suppose you haven't had time to arrange for passage. Would you like me to find the captain and…?"

"No. I'll be fine Hugh. You go on back."

But he stayed. "So, you're going back to San Francisco?"

"Yes. A friend of mine needs my help. I've told Robert all about it. He'll explain. But right now, Hugh, I must hurry."

"Just a moment, Lina. Look, I won't ask too many questions. But two days ago everything was fine, and now you're heading back to San Francisco. You've told Robert you're going, but for some reason, you don't want him to know you're leaving today. I assume nobody else knows either. What would you have me say to them, then? Are you asking me to tell them I don't know where you went?"

"No, Hugh, I would never ask you to lie for me."

"I would, if it would help." He said it so quickly it surprised her. She would have expected his defense of the truth to his family, not this sudden display of loyalty to her.

"No," she said softly. "It's not necessary."

"And should I tell them you're not coming back?"

She could tell from Hugh's expression this was no idle speculation on his part. Somehow, he knew.

"I don't know I'm not coming back. I…I just don't think it will be possible. Is that a lie, then, Hugh? If I told them one thing, that I hope is true, but in my heart, believe another thing to *be* true? Please, tell me Hugh. Because I really don't want to lie to them. And I don't want to hurt them. Please, Hugh? Do *you* know?"

He looked at her, then answered. "No, Lina. I don't think it's a lie. But if you're leaving, you'll hurt them anyway. Wouldn't telling them the truth be better?"

"No," she answered. "No it wouldn't. It would only cause more hurt. To someone…to all of them, who deserve better."

"Then so be it." He took her hand and kissed her lightly on the cheek. "I'll not volunteer we had this conversation. But if I'm asked, Lina, I won't lie to them. I'll tell them I don't think you're coming back."

Lina squeezed his hand. "Fair enough. That's all I can ask. Thank you, Hugh. For your help. For everything." She felt a lump in her throat as the first trace of bitter tears came to her eyes. "Now, please. Go. You need to get to work, and I need to get on board."

He left without another word. She watched him until he was out of sight, as if she were watching her life in Sleekit disappear from view. When he was gone, she swallowed hard, and turned her mind and all her energy to putting that behind her. She would need all that, and more, for what was waiting for her in San Francisco.

34

Robert stood in the middle of the office, completely lost. His eyes scanned the papers strewn before him, but nothing looked like the contract. He shuffled the papers for what was surely the fourth time, but still no luck. The problem was that nothing was familiar. The realization prickled him. *Since she took over...*"

But Robert wouldn't let himself think of her. Instead, he blamed this all on Hugh. Robert needed him now to manage the business again. But Hugh had disappeared the same morning Lina had, although to say he had disappeared wasn't exactly true. Robert knew where he was. Jamie had told him that first morning. "Lina's gone. She left notes for everyone. Meg found them. I went to find Hugh, but he'd left a note as well. Said he was going cruising for those stands we'll need for the Haarten job."

At the time, Robert's mind stuck on the news of Lina. He took for granted that Hugh would be back in a few days. But now ten days had passed, and while Hugh sent word he met up with the crew working on the east side of the mountain and would be staying there, that was a day's ride for Robert. Right now, with the pressure of so big a contract, he couldn't afford the time away. So he sent word for Hugh to come back at once. *He should have returned by now*, Robert thought, shuffling the papers yet again. In his haste and impatience, a pile he had already sorted fell to the floor. Robert stood in the middle of the confusion, scanning the litter for any sign of the contract. "Damn!" he said as he scuffed his boot, tossing papers in the air.

"Hello, Robbie." Hugh stood at the door.

"Hugh! Where the hell have you been?"

"I sent word. You must have heard, or you wouldn't have sent for me."

"I mean, what's taken you so long? I need you here."

"Apparently," Hugh said, looking about the room.

"Don't be clever. I'm looking for the Haarten contract."

Hugh stepped into the room, then calmly reached down among the scattered sheets and picked out one. "Here," he said, handing Robert the contract.

Robert snatched it from his hand, and quickly scanned it. "Good," he said curtly. "Now, help me straighten this mess while I tell you what I need." Then he looked to Hugh. "Lina's gone," he said.

"Yes, I know."

"You do? How…? Oh, it doesn't matter. But if you knew, you should have known I needed you here."

"You've made this mess. You fix it."

Robert gave his cousin a sharp stare, but acquiesced. "Very well," he said as he recklessly bundled papers. "But take notes of what I need."

"What *you* need. Take note yourself, Robbie. I'm not your bookkeeper any longer." He turned for the door.

"Look, Hugh. We're stranded high and dry until she gets back. Someone has to maintain order until then, and the job falls back to you." Hugh stood steadfast. Robert's temper soared. "Now, look here, boy! We've got a lot of work ahead of us. I suggest you bear a hand to the job ahead. Take a seat and get busy!"

Between gritted teeth, Hugh said, "I will. I will." Then his patience broke. He turned and hissed, "Like hell I will!" at the same time he drove his fist into Robert's jaw, sending his cousin tumbling back against the wall. Robert was dazed more by the surprise than the blow. Hugh was too, for he kept looking between his fist and Robert's face. Finally, a sheepish grin came to him. "Damn, Robbie. I'm sorry, but that felt good. Are you alright?"

"Yeah," Robert said, rubbing his jaw. He struggled to get his feet underneath him.

Hugh extended his hand and helped Robert to his feet. "You wondered how I knew Lina was gone," he said quietly. "I knew because I took her to Ellis the morning she left."

"You? But why…"

"I met up with her the night before. She asked me to meet her before dawn and take her to Ellis. She insisted I not ask any questions, so I didn't. It was only when we got to Ellis that I knew she was leaving."

"Well, there's a note for you, probably waiting at Meg's or Jamie's. Explaining she has to help a friend in San Francisco get back to St. Louis. She'll be gone for some time. She left messages for everyone… nearly everyone. Meg and Riordan. You and Charley. Jean and Jamie."

"Not you?"

"No. I saw her that night, too. Probably right before you did."

"And she didn't tell you she's not coming back."

The words hit Robert harder than Hugh's fist. "No! In fact, she said quite the contrary. I lent her a book. She promised to bring it back when…" Stubbornly he continued. "No, she's coming back."

"No, she isn't Robbie. I called her on it and she all but admitted it. That's why I didn't come back right away. I told her I wouldn't lie to you, but I knew she didn't want me to tell you she wasn't coming back. So I took the coward's way out and stayed away."

Robert shook his head. "This makes no sense," he said softly.

"Doesn't it, Robbie?" Hugh asked. "It doesn't make sense to *me*, but I thought it might make sense to you."

"Why should it?"

"Before you came back, Lina was fine. Very much looking forward to your return, in fact. Then you came back, and within a day's time, she's gone. Now you tell me you alone talked with her about her leaving. If you can't shed some light on all this, who the hell can?"

"Are you saying *I'm* responsible?" Robert yelled. "Ridiculous! She was fine when I left her!"

"Was she?" Robert looked away. "This news should've been reason for her to be happy. She wasn't happy when I saw her. Was she with you?" Reluctantly, Robert shook his head. Hugh paused before he spoke. "Tell me the truth, Robert."

"Truth?"

Hugh moved in closer, nearly nose to nose with his cousin. "Perhaps this story about a friend was just a ruse. Perhaps there was another reason she left." He looked Robert squarely in the eye. "You haven't been dangling that girl, have you? Leading her on? Robert Marr, the great ladies' man wouldn't take advantage of...." Hugh never finished the sentence. This time, it was Robert's fist that found its mark on Hugh's jaw. It was the better blow, and Hugh fell harder.

When Hugh came out of his daze, there was no penitent face above him. Robert was still angry, but calm. "Is that answer enough for you?"

Hugh nodded, then held out a hand. Robert grabbed it, and pulled Hugh to his feet. Warily, and nursing their wounds, both men slowly took a seat at the table.

"Well, then. Robbie, the whole silly mess makes no sense. If there's nothing between the two of you..." Hugh looked up at Robert, who suddenly looked away. "Robbie?"

Robert took time before he spoke. "It happened the night of Jamie's wedding. She was upset. Meg sent me to see what was wrong, and well, one thing led to another, and..."

"I thought you said...."

"No! Nothing like that! I simply mean, Franny told her a lie, that we were engaged. I told Lina the truth, of course. She seemed so pleased to hear it wasn't true...."

"So you kissed her," Hugh finished, shaking his head.

Robert nodded. "So I kissed her," he said with a sigh.

"And I'll bet I can guess the rest. It wasn't the usual sort of kiss, was it? Not a Franny Ellis sort of kiss, I'm betting."

Robert shook his head. "No I suppose it wasn't. But it was just one kiss. Then Franny showed up, and Lina left."

"So that's why Franny was so eager to get back to Ellis," Hugh said.

"Yes. I think it's safe to say we won't be welcomed in Ellis any time soon."

"But Lina didn't know that, did she? Maybe she thought you were playing fast and loose with her, even if you weren't."

Robert shrugged. "I don't think so, Hugh. She saw me off, and everything seemed fine between us, even if we couldn't really talk. Somehow, I don't think it was the kiss, or Franny or anything like that that scared her away."

"Well, Robbie, perhaps you didn't make this mess after all. But I still have a feeling you're the fellow to fix it." Hugh stood and walked toward the door.

"Where are you going? We've got a lot to do."

"You're right about that," Hugh said. "That's why we're going to Meg's."

****

Lina spent only the first day of her voyage locked in her cabin, crying miserably. It exhausted her, but fatigue drove out memories and dulled the pain of her loss. After that one day, all that was left was a single consuming thought—confronting Edward Haarten. She didn't strategize or even envision any outcome but one. She had turned her back on Sleekit, and surrendered. But with nothing to lose, nothing more he could do to hurt her, she wondered what would he say to her, and she to him, when she finally came to him, conquered to conqueror.

The moment she arrived, she headed straight for the house on Rincon Hill. She didn't wonder if Haarten was in town. He would be there, waiting for her, knowing she would arrive that day, on that ship. Fear and knowledge were his weapons of choice.

Jackson greeted her at the door as if she had only left for a morning's walk. "Good day, Miss Clark," he said as he opened the door. She entered and Jackson quickly reached for her cloak. "I'll tell the Captain you're here."

"Don't forget her bags, Jackson." Lina turned to see Edward Haarten at the library door. Lina looked into his eyes, ready to meet whatever she saw there, a satisfied smirk perhaps, or even a hint of anger. But there was nothing in those dull, grey eyes. Edward turned and went back into the library.

"Yes, Jackson. My bags," she said distractedly. Lina followed Haarten, closing the library's doors behind her.

Haarten stood behind his desk, more attentive to the papers in front of him than to Lina. "You made very good time, my dear."

"As I'm sure you knew I would. But why wouldn't I? Your threats ensured my urgency."

He looked up suddenly. "Threats? Nonsense. I simply reminded you of the consequences of your actions. I thought you understood that before. Plans had been made, commitments given. I had staked a good deal—more than money—on the future of which I had made you a part. Far too much to let it go simply because you had a change of heart. That letter was the consequence of the decision you made to leave. With it, I wanted to make certain you understood what the consequences would be should you decide to stay."

"A threat, just as I said," Lina retorted. "But what if I told you your threat was meaningless, that I don't care one whit what happens to anyone in Sleekit?" She tried to sound indifferent.

"Surely, my dear, you do realize how much I was able to learn about your circumstances up north. I know you were working for the Marrs, and knowing you, you've been an asset to them. You're diligent enough to feel some pride in that. That's your strength. But I know your weaknesses, my dear. You love the work too much, and would have appreciated the opportunities too much, not to feel some allegiance toward them."

She broke right in. "And if I do stay, what assurances do I have that you won't harm them anyway?"

"Why? What have they done to me? Nothing of course. I'm quite certain no one lured you there, and I'm reasonably certain they had no knowledge of the circumstances of your departure. Besides, while I could always find another supplier, they're a competent firm, and I need the ship built."

Lina repulsed at the sense of resignation that was coming over her. Weakly, she spoke. "You're still planning on being married, then?"

"I told you, Carolina, I had taken my time finding the best person to serve as manager of my household, and I determined that person to be you. Nothing has happened since you've been gone to change my mind. Now that you've returned, the matter is not only decided, the course is set. I have started the preparations for the wedding. But all that can be taken care of tomorrow. For now, I have appointments." He picked up some papers, folded them crisply and slipped them inside his coat. As he left he said, "You'll find your room just as you left it. I'll be back this afternoon. You'll remember dinner is at seven, sharp. You can begin tomorrow on the matters needing attention. I'll make a list for you."

That was their only discussion. Beginning the next morning, Haarten behaved as though Lina had never been gone. He had his morning meal, left her with a list of household chores, and was off on his day. Lina went to the library with Haarten's list when Jackson arrived with breakfast. He placed the silver tray on the desk. "Thank you, Jackson," Lina said.

"Anything else, Miss?"

"I didn't see Mrs. Spear yet. Would you please ask her to come see me?"

"Mrs. Spear, miss? Didn't Captain Haarten mention it? Mrs. Spear's left the household, the same night you…."

"Oh." Lina had almost forgotten Mrs. Spear's hand in her own escape. She was glad she forgot, for it had kept her from accidently betraying that knowledge. "Did she find other employment?"

"I don't know, miss. Once I told the Captain of her disappearance, he never mentioned her again. Of course, we did not ask."

"Of course." Lina hoped the story was true. If Edward knew Mrs. Spear's part, no telling what might have become of the poor woman. "So no replacement has been hired?"

"No, miss. The Captain said that would be up to you…after the wedding."

"I see," she said, scanning the list Haarten had left her. The list itself was evidence that no one was attending to the household. Lina shook her head.

"Um, begging your pardon, miss. I was wondering if you had plans to leave the house today."

"I'm just looking at the Captain's list now. Yes, there are a few errands."

"I could have some other member of the staff take care of those, miss."

"Thank you, but that's not necessary."

She noticed his discomfort. He shifted his feet ever so slightly, and he clenched his hands in front of him. "Well, then, miss, what time do you expect to go?"

"Within the hour, I suspect. Is there some reason you ask? Can I attend to some other errand for you?"

"Oh, no, miss! Nothing for me. But I was wondering miss, how long you expect to be gone."

Then she understood. She laid the list on the desk and looked at Jackson, feeling sorry for him. Jackson was too old and docile to be much of a watchdog, but his loyalty to the household made him the best candidate.

"Jackson, I'll leave in an hour. Have the carriage brought around for me. I'll be gone until early afternoon. When the Captain asks, tell him I went only to those places related to this list. That *is* what this is about, isn't it, Jackson? To make certain I don't try to leave again?"

"Oh, no miss! I'm sure it's just because Captain Haarten has missed you so and…"

Lina nearly laughed. "Thank you, Jackson. I tell you what. I'll keep you informed as to my comings and goings. I won't put you in that position with your employer. My employer, too, for that matter," Lina finished with a chuckle.

"I'm sorry, miss," he offered quietly as he shuffled from the library. Lina waited until he left then perused the list. Gone were the important business matters she used to attend to for Haarten. No trips to the warehouse, the docks, the suppliers. These were just household chores and shopping lists, the sort of errands which had always been the housekeeper's purview. Yet for each errand, Haarten had carefully penned a specific instruction. *Have a strong word with the butcher about the quality of his meats for the beef has been fatty and tough as of late. Visit the dressmaker and order new uniforms for the cleaning maids. Their black frocks look disreputable and totally unsuitable for the standing of this household. Find a new laundress, one who can be trusted, for we are too often missing bed linens and such.*

The list of chores was mundane, to say the least. But the chores themselves were hardly the point of this exercise. Of course Edward would be keeping an eye on her. This list told her as much. Here was a test of her willingness to do as she was told. He knew she disdained scolding others for their performance, particularly over seemingly petty infractions. It would be a test, too, of her patience and her ability to turn her talent for detail to managing the household, instead of Barclay

& Company. She sighed. Once, she had loved the challenges of working for Haarten. Of course, that was before she had come to understand what it meant to truly be a part of building something. Before Sleekit, and Robert.

She pushed that thought from her mind as she left the library. If Haarten was going to be keeping an eye on her, then she had to take advantage of every small opportunity that came her way. Poor Jackson would likely reveal to his employer that she had figured out Haarten's plan. In the future, Edward might insist she not leave the house unaccompanied, or worse, have her followed. So today, she would do everything on this list just as Edward asked. But she would also find time for one errand of her own. *It might be my last chance*, she thought, as she headed for the front door and the waiting carriage.

****

Sylvester Tunnicliff graciously ushered Lina into his office. "Miss Clark! What a pleasant surprise. I wasn't sure whether we'd ever see one another again."

"Thank you, Mr. Tunnicliff. Yes, I had some matters that took me away from the city for a while. But I'm back now, and I've come to check on the affairs I left in your custody."

Tunnicliff took some papers from inside his desk. "I made a note of my contact with the Wilcox Clinic staff every month to make certain Miss Paul was being properly cared for. A Dr…where is it?" He pushed his spectacles to the tip of his nose and scanned the paper. "A Dr. Maxwell is the attending physician. The most recent inquiry was last week. I am assured Miss Paul has not lacked for proper treatment."

Lina hesitated, then asked, "Mr. Tunnicliff, did you actually see Miss Paul?"

The bald little man was flustered. "Well, ah, no, not actually. I, I took some initiative. I would have contacted you for permission, but that was quite impossible, as you know. You did not leave word as to how you could be reached. I gave the matter considerable thought, but it seemed…"

"What is it, Mr. Tunnicliff? What is it you've done?" Lina asked anxiously.

"I...well, I went there once, myself. A dreadful place, as you know. Not that they don't appear to be providing adequate care for the inma... patients. But, still, the poor wretches. It hardly seemed fair to the poor woman, in such a state and all, to have strangers about, and so I located a woman to keep an eye on her. A woman whose husband had come to me over some debts owed. She works at the clinic. The family is quite strapped for cash, so I proposed something to benefit all. For a small sum, she takes special care to keep an eye on Miss Paul, and is to apprise me of any situation she considered to be a demonstration of lack of care. She is far more qualified to make that assessment than I. So we had an informant, and did not have to raise suspicions by my regular inquiries. And they had extra income for their family."

"You don't have to explain any further, Mr. Tunnicliff. I quite understand." Lina had come hoping perhaps the lawyer had done her dirty work for her. How could she criticize him for not having the stomach to do what she herself could not? "A wise decision." She took the papers he had laid before her on his desk. "Now, there is another matter I need your help with."

"Yes?"

"I'd like a will. I don't have much, but I want to make certain that if anything happened to me, any assets of mine are used to continue Josephine's care."

Tunnicliff laughed. "What a remarkable coincidence!" Then his tone grew more somber. "I'm sorry. A coincidence yes, but also, I suppose, a sad irony."

"I don't understand."

"I came upon it after you left." He opened the desk drawer and took out another folder. "It's also a will. I had forgotten all about it." Lina opened the folder and read as far as the first few lines. "That's right, Miss Clark. When I first met Miss Paul at the Golden West, she hired me to draw up a will for her. And in it, she left everything to you."

Lina smiled. "Well, that *is* odd, isn't it? I suppose this will is immaterial now."

He took it from her and tucked it neatly back in its folder. "Still, I must keep it, miss. It's the law."

****

Time seemed completely disjointed to Lina. Was it really only a month since she was in Sleekit? Had she only been in San Francisco for a few days? As she went about her day, she would often see something that would cause her to think, "Oh, I must tell Robert about that." When reality came rushing back, she'd feel sick in her head, her heart, and her soul. The tedium of her days now sometimes made her feel as though she had only dreamed her life in Sleekit.

Thinking of the future caused Lina a tremendous sense of dread and despair. It seemed an endless forever, with nothing to relieve the disconsolation, nor break the dull pattern. Daily she was being folded into the rhythm of Edward Haarten's habits of a lifetime. In the morning, they rarely crossed paths. When he was in the house, he was in the library always, and never to be disturbed. At twilight, the doors to the library would open and Lina could enter, if there were demands of the household to address. Once supper was served, there were to be no more demands. Lina and Edward took the meal together in silence, and then she would accompany him into the library. He insisted on her company, yet rarely spoke, for he didn't like to be distracted from his reading. After an hour, she would be free to excuse herself and go to her room. He came upstairs precisely at midnight. This, then, was her life.

When she allowed herself to think on that future, she believed she might go mad. A true madness, like Josephine's. She might simply wake one morning, months or years from now, and have forgotten everything that had ever brought her happiness. She imagined herself a phantom wandering the halls of the house, screaming as if in eternal agony. The suffering in Lina's heart tore at her soul. Dwelling on the past brought a peculiar kind of pain, but dwelling on the future brought something more akin to terror.

Then one day, at the end of that first week in Haarten's house, she stumbled upon the cure for her melancholy and fears. Haarten's coach had taken her on a path that passed near Telegraph Hill, that place that once had been a solace to her. The minute she saw the place again, she commanded the driver to take her up the hill, and when the coach had gone as far as it could up the steep drive, she told him to wait for her. She jumped out and finished the ascent on foot. She stood at the crest of the hill a long time and felt once more the cool, clean breezes that smelled of possibilities. Suddenly, more happy memories than she knew she possessed came rushing forward. Memories from childhood, from the trip overland, from the Golden West, and most especially, of her days in Sleekit, came flooding in, and carried her away on a tide of her own tears. She wept inconsolably, yet with a decided purgative effect. For once the tears abated, the callous she feared was slowly covering her heart since she left Sleekit was gone, and she felt possessed of a most remarkable feeling. Happiness. The source of the happiness was simple and suddenly revealed. Somewhere near the end of the outpouring of her grief, she had a thought—that no matter how sad, how bleak she might feel, as long as she was here doing as Haarten expected, she was still in her own way cherishing those she loved. She kept them safe, and ensured their continued peace. Josephine would have the care she needed. Robert would have the success he dreamed of. Everyone in Sleekit was free to prosper. It would be what she could do for them, and what would always keep them close to her.

The hill was a haven for these thoughts. For her to succeed, she would need to remain stoic around Haarten and in his house. But here, she could allow herself a benediction of memory. So she planned that every day she would come here for an hour, or five minutes if that was all that was allowed her, and indulge herself in her memories of happiness, and in the comfort of her sense of purpose. She would bring with her some beloved volume from Barclay's library. *Or the Wordsworth*, she thought, remembering Robert's precious parting gift to her. *Yes, that would be just the thing.* As Robert had used the poetry in lieu of scripture that long ago Sunday in Sleekit, she would use it to invoke her memories and to reaffirm her resolve.

****

The leads Robert held for his quest were few, and fewer still those that could be counted on to be true. This alone should have made him pessimistic, but his need for answers only added to his already fixed determination to find Lina.

After Hugh's return, when he had finally been convinced there was more to Lina's departure than the simple explanation she had offered, Hugh led Robert to Meg. "I should have made her tell me," Meg said, shaking her head. "Right before you came home, we talked." At that point, Meg stopped, and gave Robert as hard a look as he could ever remember. "I asked her, straight out, about her feelings toward you. And yours to her."

"See, Robbie," Hugh said, "I told you this has something to do with that kiss."

"Ah, yes, we talked about that kiss," Meg said.

Robert shook his head in confusion. "What's that have to do with her leaving? And does *everyone* know about that kiss?"

"I didn't. Until now," Riordan said, leaning forward. "But this conversation's suddenly considerably more interestin'." Meg gave the old man a gentle slap to the head.

Robert ignored them. "What did she say about…her feelings?"

"I think you know what she said," Meg answered. "That's why it puzzled me when she said nothing could come of it. She said… how did she put it? That she had obligations. That's all. She said there was nothing I could do to help." Meg looked pointedly at Robert. "I said she should go to *you*. I told her the two of you wouldn't find any happiness until she put some faith in you. And she listened. If you ask me, she planned to tell you all about this, this obligation. But she didn't get the chance before that letter arrived."

"Well, we know now what it was," Robert said. "Her friend was the obligation."

Hugh shook his head. "She told that to Meg *before* she got that letter. It can't be the same obligation. Something else happened."

"Even so," Meg added, "It doesn't explain why she lied about not coming back."

"Hmm. I wonder if any of this has anything to do with her changin' her name." Milo asked.

"What?" Robert, Hugh and Meg all asked at once.

"Sure. Didn't I tell ya, darlin'? Ah, well, I forgot meself until that letter came with a different name on it."

"She changed her name?" Hugh asked. "Why?"

Milo shrugged. "Didn't offer, and I didn't ask. I didn't know the lady well enough then."

"She lied about her name, too," Robert said quietly.

"And another thing!" Milo added. "It struck me as queer that a lady of her stature came here needin' work."

"What does that mean?" Robert asked.

"Sure, and I told you about that. This I remember as clear as day, I do. You and me talked on deck the night after she booked passage."

"I remember something about this. A conversation about lace knickers, as I recall. 'A woman of means' was how you described her."

"Aye. That was herself."

"*Lina*? That was Lina?" Robert said in amazement. "I'd forgotten all about that."

For the next hour, the four of them pieced together every scrap of information about Lina Morgan they had between them. A woman of some means, who came needing work. A woman who had come overland, with strangers her only companions. Some time spent in the diggings, then time spent in a warehouse in San Francisco. A school that had been less than she had hoped for. A friend named Josephine she was obliged to care for, and money she sent back to San Francisco regularly. A bank where Milo deposited the money. And a letter from San Francisco that changed everything. These scraps offered little to go on, but they would have to be enough.

Still, as Robert and Milo sailed toward San Francisco, it troubled Robert that he couldn't tell what of this was real. She had lied about not coming back. She had lied about her name. What else about Lina was a lie?

When he said as much to Milo one night, Milo's response was immediate and direct. "She's a fine woman. She's smart, and she has a good heart. She cares for all of us, like family. And she loves you. You know those things to be true, don't you, lad?"

Robert thought for a moment. "Yes. I can believe most of them," he said, smiling sadly.

Milo shook his head. "All of 'em, lad. If you doubt her feelin's for ya, ya only need look at her leavin' to know it was no easy task for her. Didn't me darlin' Meg tell ya herself? Whatever lies there is, she had every intention of tellin' ya all that was troublin' her. That's more important than whatever puny prevarications she might've told. That she was ready to trust ya, me boy, ready to turn to you for help. That's what you'd best remember when you find her."

Robert considered the point for a moment, then smiled. "Milo, how'd a crusty old salt like you get to be such an expert on matters of the heart?"

With simple certainty, Milo answered. "I'm an Irishman, lad."

When they arrived in San Francisco, Robert implemented the only plan he could come up with. The one thing Robert felt certain was true was the work Lina had done in San Francisco. Lina had said it was a warehouse and Robert decided on this point to believe her, for he could see no reason for this to be a lie. With countless warehouses to check, Robert started at the first one nearest the dock, and went down the waterfront to each one in succession until the day was over. He had been at his search for three full days when he had a break. The foreman at the warehouse didn't recall her, but as he was leaving one of the dock workers stopped him.

"I remember her," the man said. "She was the boss here for a few months. Been a year since she left. Just up and gone one day. Never heard about her again."

"Do you know anything else about her? Where she lived, perhaps?"

The man shook his head. "Sorry, bub. Never knew a thing about her. 'Cept she didn't take nothin' off nobody. The men here didn't care for her. They was robbin' the owner blind, but she put a stop to that."

"The owner! Perhaps he would know something about her."

"Sure, but I don't think you'll be getting' anything out of him. Barclay's dead."

"Barclay? As in Barclay & Company?" The man nodded. "The same that's owned now by Edward Haarten?"

"The same. But I doubt Haarten'll know much. He's not the type to take much notice of his workers."

Robert didn't care. It was too rich a coincidence that the very Edward Haarten with whom he had a contract, the very same man he had planned to visit before he left San Francisco to give progress on that contract, might know something of Lina. If the man himself didn't know, perhaps he could suggest another lead. Robert wasted no time. He asked directions of the foreman, and arrived at Rincon Hill late in the afternoon.

Jackson opened the door to an unfamiliar face. "May I help you, sir?"

"Is Captain Haarten about?"

"No sir. Were you expected?"

"My name is Robert Marr. I have a contract with the Captain, and I happened to be in San Francisco on other matters. I thought if perhaps he were here, I..."

"I'm sorry, sir. Do come in." Robert stepped inside and looked about the hallway as Jackson shut the door behind him. "Captain Haarten is due back within the hour. I cannot promise you he will speak with you, but if you have business with him, I know he would want me to make you welcome. Please follow me, sir." Jackson opened the wide paneled doors of the library, and motioned for Robert to enter.

"Please make yourself comfortable, sir," Jackson said. "Over there." He indicated a chair next to the fireplace, which Robert took to mean he should not feel free to wander about the room. "Would you care for something, sir? A whiskey, perhaps?"

"No, nothing. Thank you." Jackson nodded, and closed the doors behind him. Robert looked about at the impressive library. The books intrigued him with their titles on botany, navigation, and geography. But the butler had made his point, so Robert resisted the urge to peruse. After some time, Robert decided a drink sounded like just the thing after all. Since the butler had offered him one earlier, he saw no problem in helping himself. He sniffed the contents of two bottles, then chose the whiskey. He carried the glass to the chair and settled in.

Beside him on a table were more books. He looked down the stack at the spines, and found each was a book of poetry or essays. It seemed someone had gleaned all the literature from the dusty shelves and given them refuge here. Then, the word on the spine of the last book in the stack caught his eye. 'Wordsworth.'

Robert shuffled through the other books to get to that buried book. At first he thought it an uncanny coincidence, but there was no mistaking it now. He knew the familiar places where he had worn its corners and burnished its edges with his fingers. This was *his* Wordsworth, the book he had given to Lina.

"Mr. Marr?"

Haarten came through the doorway. He paid no notice of Robert's interest in the book. He walked directly to his desk. "I did not expect you today. Is there some problem with the contract?"

Robert didn't answer. He was looking at Haarten, stunned. For just a moment, he thought to blurt out all the questions running through his mind. Yet he stopped. Haarten was staring at him expectantly. Robert tried to size up the man in that moment, for some instinct of caution came over him. "Single-minded when it comes to what he wants," was what Lina had said when he asked her if she knew of Haarten. He remembered now. That she knew him better than that was clear, now. This book was evidence that she had been in this house. She might still be in this house, he suddenly realized. Yet he could not put all the pieces together, not with Haarten standing there, waiting for him to say something. Asking Haarten if he knew Lina might be the final step in finding her. Or it could be the worst mistake he could make.

Robert held the volume of Wordsworth casually in one hand as he stepped forward to shake Haarten's hand with the other. "No, sir. No problem at all."

"Good," said Haarten. "Then why are you here?"

"The opportunity presented itself. I came back in search of more men. With this contract you've given us, and a few other jobs the company picked up in my absence, I can afford to take on a few more workers. As long as I'd come this far, I thought it opportune to come tell you we're making good progress."

"Hmm. Well, as long as you're here, can I offer you a drink? Ah, I see you have one. Then I'll join you. Sit down, Marr."

Robert settled into the chair behind him as Haarten walked to the mantel to pour a brandy. "I hope you're not overextending yourself, Marr. I presumed that my job would command your full attention."

Robert still held the book in his hand. He would not let his eyes be drawn to it, but he passed his thumb lightly across its cover as he spoke. "Oh, it does, Captain, I assure you.

"Good."

Robert watched Haarten carefully as the man returned to his desk. Haarten sat, opened the humidor on the corner of the desk, and took a cigar. He tilted the open humidor toward Robert, who shook his head. Haarten struck a match, and slowly puffed the cigar. Robert was suddenly aware that Haarten was watching his hand as it fondled the book. With a casual indifference, Robert returned the book to the top of the stack and picked up his drink. "Your health, sir," he said, then took a sip.

Haarten puffed on the cigar until a thick cloud of smoke hung in the air between them. "I presume given your remote location, it's difficult to find good men."

"Yes. Labor is in demand, as you know. And people aren't easily persuaded to relocate to a place so remote. I find that those who do, however, are the happier for it."

"Hmm. Happy. But are they prosperous?"

"Prosperous enough, I suppose."

"A modest goal, Mr. Marr," Haarten said disdainfully. "But you're right. Labor is in demand. Nowhere more so than in San Francisco. I, too, have had to go to great lengths to find just the right person for a particular position. Very recently, in fact." He sipped his brandy, and Robert thought he saw a hint of a smile at the corner of his lips.

Robert watched the man in front of him carefully. He took a moment before he answered. "Give me someone who wants the job, who loves the job. I'll teach them the skills. Or they'll teach themselves. Such a person will stand by you for a lifetime."

Haarten's eyebrow rose slightly, and he leaned forward. "I take it that you have strong allegiances to your people."

"I do. Not unlike at sea, I suspect, Captain, I depend on everyone who works for me. Sometimes for my very life."

Haarten set his drink down. "That's the difference between us, Mr. Marr. I do not depend on my crew for my life. They depend on me. It inspires them to do their best for me, and if they forget that, I feel no remorse in reminding them. Obligation, Mr. Marr, is a great incentive for allegiance."

Robert took a long sip of the whiskey. "As is freedom, Captain Haarten."

Haarten sneered. "Freedom is an illusion, Marr. We are only as free as the obligations that bind us. Contracts, responsibilities, indebtedness, these are the boundaries of our freedom."

Robert looked into the man's hard eyes. "A good point, sir. And a lesson, I suppose, to be careful with whom we enter into such obligations." Before Haarten could respond, Robert rose. "I've no doubt taken up enough of your time, Captain Haarten. And let me reiterate. You have my full attention, sir. In fact, I can safely say I will hardly think of much else in the days to come. Good day, sir."

****

"Good morning, Jackson," Lina said as she met him at the bottom of the stairs. "I see the Captain has left. Did he say when he would return?"

"Late this afternoon, miss."

"Thank you. Please have some coffee brought into the library. I'll be working there for the next hour before I leave for my fitting."

She was trying to make herself feel at home here. When Edward was out of the house, she was permitted the use of the library. She liked the room. Despite the fact that Haarten had tried to make it his domain, it was still the room most like it had been when Barclay lived here. She sat at the desk and opened the drawer that held the household account ledger. Lina had a stack of bills to pay before her errands that day. Most were routine, and she worked through them quickly. Then she came across a statement that didn't look quite right to her, a minor bill, but it caused her to flip back through old payments looking for a duplicate. That was when she noticed the payment to Dr. Josiah Maxwell.

Lina remembered the name as the man Tunnicliff mentioned from the Wilcox Clinic. What she noticed next was the amount. One hundred dollars paid on the first of September. It seemed a paltry sum. Surely Josephine's care at the clinic cost more than that. She flipped back again, to August, and there, again, was another payment to Maxwell, in the same amount. And two more each for June and July. She tried to remember when Josephine first went to the clinic. *Shortly after I left for Miss Ward's*, she decided. She turned far back in the account book. There, in mid October, was a payment to the Wilcox Clinic, for one thousand dollars. Now she moved forward through the book. She found an identical payment of one thousand dollars for each month through March. But in April, payments to the Wilcox Clinic disappeared, and were replaced by the smaller sum to Dr. Maxwell.

A knock on the door broke her concentration. "Your carriage is ready, miss," Jackson said. Lina had completely lost track of the time. She closed the account book and returned it to its place in the drawer. Then, just before leaving the library, she remembered to take with her the copy of Wordsworth. If she could finish her errands in time, she intended to make the trip to Telegraph Hill. With the book tucked neatly under her arm, she hurried outside and into the waiting carriage.

Her principal errand for the day was another in a seemingly endless line of fittings for her wedding dress at the shop of Madame Bonaface. Madame Bonaface was, to Lina's thinking, a silly French woman whose total lack of organization and discipline left her shop in a constant state of disarray. Despite all these fittings, progress on the dress was slow. Early sessions were only to discuss the design and establish the form. Haarten had given Madame Bonaface 'suggestions' as to what the dress should be like, and because Lina didn't care about the dress, Madame Bonaface ruled supreme in that discussion. Then cutting the pattern had to be completed, and only last week had the dress begun to take shape. It seemed to Lina there was much left to be done, but Madame Bonaface always dismissed her concerns with an annoying giggle and a wave of her hand. "Eet eez art! Art must not be rushed!" was the Madame's answer for everything. Behind schedule as they were, Lina realized that meant she would likely be there all day. The prospect distressed her, for it would afford her no time for her private outing, and leave her exhausted and ill-tempered.

When she arrived, one of the girls informed her there would be no fitting that day, because Madame Bonaface was suffering from some indeterminate malady. When Lina suggested they proceed without her, the young girl became insistent. "Madame has left strict instructions. She is to be present for all your fittings. She says Captain Haarten would want it so," the young woman said. "Please, miss. There is nothing for today. We will send word when Madame is ready to see you again."

Lina left the shop, uplifted by the release from duty. She would have to pay for it later, she knew, but not today. Not this morning, so unusually pleasant for mid-autumn. Gone were the characteristic fog and damp breezes. The rains would come soon, but today the air was warm, and the skies clear. Lina ordered the carriage in the direction of Telegraph Hill.

When it reached its destination, the carriage pulled to its usual spot near the mid-point of the hill. Lina had never minded walking the rest of the way, and she usually had the entire hillside to herself. Only two times she had been here, within this very week, in fact, she had noticed another carriage waiting in the same place hers had stopped. At the time she had lamented the fact that her solitude might be interrupted by a stranger, but she had never encountered anyone else. Today, when she saw the same carriage there, she assumed she would not be interrupted this time.

She was wrong. As she crested the hill, her eyes went toward the spot she had declared her own—a near level place beneath one of the few scrub trees on top of the hill. Yet beneath that tree she could see there was someone standing—a man, his back toward her, dressed in a fine, dark suit. She stopped and reconnoitered, then chose another spot a little further down the side of the hill from where the man stood. She turned and walked toward the chosen spot when she heard her name.

"Lina." She stopped, but then continued, sure that it was just some trick of the ever present wind. "Lina," the voice spoke again, and this time, she froze. She was sure it was a trick now, for that was the voice she so often summoned from memory in this place. It was Robert's voice. She turned to look behind her, and there he was. The man who stood beneath her tree, in her spot, had turned to face her. This was no trick of the ear, nor no conjured memory. Robert Marr stood there, smiling at her, as if it were the most natural thing in the world.

She didn't know what to do. But when Robert took a step toward her, instinct told her to run. She dropped the book without realizing it and, gathering her skirts in her fists, started down the side of the hill.

He was on her before she took more than a few fleeting steps. His hand grabbed her arm, and spun her around. "What's the matter? Where are you going?"

"Away!" She said, struggling for release. "Away from you. Before anyone sees us. Before…"

"Before what? Before you have to explain yourself? Before I make you listen to me?"

"Yes. Before either of us says a word."

He surprised her with his sudden, easy smile. "Too late," he said. "We've already spoken. Might as well finish it now." He eased his release on her arm, but as soon as he did, she made another move to escape him. This time, when he caught her, he grabbed her with a hand on each arm. This time, she knew, he would not let her go.

The futility of the struggle left her weak. Her shoulders sagged, and her head dropped. "Please, Robert. There's nothing to say. If you've come to find me, you have. If you've come to confirm the fact that I lied to you, I suspect you know that by now. If you've come to upbraid me for my lies, then do it and be done. But I have nothing to say."

"Nothing?" he said, shaking her just enough to cause her to look up at him. Her eyes were rimmed with tears, but otherwise they were lifeless, hopeless. "Lina, I don't want to upbraid you. But I do want answers. This makes no sense! Yes, I came here to look for you. I found you, too, and in the last place I might have expected—Edward Haarten's house! Why is that, Lina? What on earth were you doing there? What of this friend you were coming here to help?"

"I lied to you, Robert. About many things."

"But why?"

"It was easier. A lie is always easier to tell than the truth." She laughed sardonically. "That's what I've learned, Robert. It's quite easy to do. I've been doing it for a long time."

"Then I should think you'd be better at it," he said. "You don't lie well, my dear. It shows in those lovely eyes of yours. That night you told me you were leaving, I saw the truth, but, I wouldn't let myself believe it. But when Hugh told me, I knew I had fooled myself into believing you were coming back."

Lina sighed. "Hugh told you, then."

"Yes, and thank God he did! Thank God all of them sat me down and forced me to realize the truth. That something must be wrong for you to leave as you did." His voice softened as he continued. "Just when I thought you and I..."

A tiny gasp escaped as she felt her throat tightened, and her tears well again. "Please, Robert. Don't speak of that. It's too difficult for me." She was truly begging him now.

"Why? *Why?*" She kept her head down, and he leaned in close to her, trying to will her to look at him.

"Because...I'm going to marry Edward Haarten!" She blurted it out, and achieved the desired effect. Robert's eyes went wide, and he released his hold on her. She steadied herself for his fury, but only silence followed. Finally, she looked up to see him staring at her in disbelief.

"You don't love him," he said. It was not a question.

"I.."

"Don't even try it, Lina. I told you, you're no good at lies. You don't love him. If you did, you would have found a way to tell me so. A liar, perhaps, but a coward? No, not you. No, there's something else you're not saying. Why would you ..." Suddenly, he looked away. His voice turned into a whisper, and he seemed to speak to himself. "Oh dear God. Obligations."

"What?"

Robert stepped away as he spoke, looking into the air as he looked into the past. "I came to Haarten's house a week ago. I came there on a lead, looking for you."

This time it was Lina who grabbed Robert by the arm. "Oh, Robert! You didn't ask him about me, did you?"

"No. I started to, but something told me not to. I found the Wordsworth. Ah, here it is." He picked it up and dusted the dirt from the cover. "This book was sitting in that library where I waited. Funny, isn't it? Had I not lent it to you, I wouldn't have known you were there. But I found it, there in the library, just as Haarten entered. We started to talk about those who worked for us. How we felt about them, how we dealt with them. At the time, I wondered if he knew I was looking for you, yet nothing he said was direct. I'm certain he has no reason to think I've found you. Yet he let me know, I realize now, that you have some obligation to him. That's it, isn't it?"

"Yes," she said.

"What is it?"

"It doesn't matter. Please, Robert. I'm begging you. I have no other means of persuasion. Please, you should leave here now and return to Sleekit, and forget you ever found me."

"I can't do that—not while you're afraid of him."

"For myself I'm not afraid," she said. "But I fear what he might do to those I care about."

"Your friend?"

"Among others."

"Who?"

"Robert, please. If you force me to say more, you'll take from me the last bit of happiness I can ever hope for."

"Happiness? You don't look happy to me!"

"If I'm not, it's because you're here!"

"I make you unhappy?" he said, stunned.

"No. Never. But you being here, asking all these questions. That makes me unhappy. Don't you see? As long as I could come here, and sit quietly on this hill, and read those damn poems you love, I had peace. I could sit on this hill and remember you. I could imagine what you might be doing, what everyone in Sleekit might be doing. And I would be happy, knowing you were happy and safe. But now you're here, and to tell you more means you might not be safe, any of you." She started to sob as she spoke, and with each new word the tears fought for release, until finally, she could no longer keep from weeping openly. Weak, she slumped to her knees and buried her head in her hands.

Robert knelt in front of her. He gently pried her hands away, and when finally she looked up, he said softly, "Well, then, your imaginings were all wrong, don't you see? For since you left, none of us have been happy." He touched her cheek to brush back a tear. "Least of all, me." He smiled. "Lina, I never had the chance to tell you, that night you told me you were leaving, what had been in my heart for weeks to say. You were all I could think of on that trip, Lina. You, and that kiss. I missed you the moment we left, and I only missed you more as the days went by. I'd wanted to kiss you for some time. But you always seemed too distant. Yet despite that we became friends. Good friends. True friends. And then, when we finally did kiss, well, as I had time to think of it, it seemed the most natural thing in the world. We belong together, you and I, Lina."

"Robert, please.."

"Let me finish. You say you've become accustomed to lying. It seems to me your lies aren't as bad as all that. Why, didn't Meg tell me you planned to tell me something, to trust me with some secret? It wasn't in your heart to lie to me then. And you won't lie to me now, just as I can't lie to you. I love you. That's the only truth I know that matters,

Lina." He moved his hands to the sides of her face. "Now tell me *your* truth Lina. Do you love me?" Then he kissed her.

His kiss, this kiss, demanded, did not ask. His lips took hers fully. He breathed her air, gave her life and took it back. His hands pulled her to him, the full length of her. She felt swallowed by his strength, his desire. His arms pulled her shoulders to him, pulled their very hearts together, beating one against another. Those arms held her firmly, insisting on an answer, pleading for an answer to him. She pushed against his shoulders, bracing herself, sheltering herself against the wind behind them. Suddenly, she reached around him, pulled him toward her, and with her kiss gave her answer. She thought he could not hold her closer, but when he felt her arms encircle him, he gathered her even tighter in his embrace.

Lina clung to Robert as if her life depended upon him, as if those arms enfolding her were her only protection against the world she feared. But finally, slowly, he pulled back, bringing his two hands to the side of her face once more. "Tell me, Lina. Do you love me?"

She looked deep into his eyes, and a small smile came to her lips. In a whisper, she answered, "With all my heart."

"And do you believe that I love you?" he asked.

His eyes seemed to plead for her faith. "I believe you," she whispered. "But Robert, it's not as simple as that." She wanted to smile but tears welled in her eyes, and her throat tightened.

He took her hand and held it between his two hands, next to his heart. "It is," he said, giving her a calm, confident smile. She knew then that she could deny him nothing, and that whatever else came as a consequence, she would tell him the whole truth.

He led her back to the spot under the tree. They sat on that hill, overlooking the bay, and Lina began her long story. She told him everything. The story told in full explained so much of her to him. When she spoke of Josephine, Robert could clearly see how her affection for her friend had grown, despite her natural uneasiness with attachment, and in that, he felt a kinship with her. When she spoke of times long before those with him, when she had turned her back on chances to have someone else take care of her, he understood why she felt so strongly the need to resolve this matter with Haarten by herself.

She told her story looking away from him. Focusing across the bay on the play of the light on the water made it easier not to search his face for one expression, only, she feared, to find another. Her story told, she finally turned to him again. The look of penitence on her face was sincere. "I'm sorry...."

He stopped her with just a shake of his head. Then he smiled, and asked, "What can I do to help?"

Her relief made her smile, but the day had taken its toll, and her voice was frail and lifeless when she answered. "Nothing." She sat by his side, his arm behind her on which to rest, his shoulder on which to lean.

"Lina, if it's merely a matter of Josephine's care, I could pay...."

"That's just it. It isn't merely a matter of Josephine. Not anymore. Not since you came back to Sleekit with that contract." He looked at her, puzzled. "Robert, don't you see? I'd been able to provide for Josephine, and Edward figured that out, somehow. Lord, I would love to know how he found me!" she said, her energy returning. "But that doesn't matter now. When he learned I no longer needed him to take care of Josephine, he found another way. Your contract. He'll ruin you through that contract, somehow, if I don't marry him. Make no mistake, Robert. He will do it. He's done it before."

"Let him, then. I don't need his bloody contract."

"It's not just the contract. He'll ruin *you*, Robert. He'll find a way to make it look as if you've defaulted, and before you know it, he'll own Marr Logging. What's left of it, that is, after the lawyers and the creditors have picked over the carcass."

"I still say, let him. I can start over."

"And what of everyone else, Robert? Must they all start over? Everyone in Sleekit depends on you. It's not only you who will be ruined."

He chuckled, then kissed her lightly on her head. "You give me too much credit, my love. There's more to keep Sleekit alive than our little operation. But what of it? What can he take? A few saws and axes? Fifty pounds of beans? A couple of wagons and a few horses? He's welcome to them. Land? If there's one thing that we have in abundance, it's land. Why, I was thinking of staking another claim. Did I tell you? I learned an interesting fact after Jamie and Jean were married. The government let them claim another three hundred twenty acres. Seems there's an added benefit to being married," he said, smiling down at her. "No, as long as I have my life, and," he took her hand, "those I love about me, there's nothing Edward Haarten can do to me."

"If you must be a part of this, then so be it," she said. With the newness of the physical expression, she slowly, hesitantly, reached up to lightly touch his cheek. His hand came to hers, tenderly pressing her palm to his lips. "But I'll not drag the rest of them in as well. I'll only go if you and I can figure something out to stop him." She turned to face him as she had so many times in the past. The look in his eyes was the same—calm, confident, fearless. "But I've turned it over and over in my mind, and I don't know what can be done. Edward holds all the cards, as far as I can see."

"But what about what you can't see, my dear? I suspect that any man this duplicitous has more trickery going on than what you know."

The whirlwind of the last two hours had swept the memory of the morning from her mind, but now she remembered. "This morning!" she said. "I came across something odd in the payments to the clinic, but then I had to leave quickly, and, well, I completely forgot it until now."

"Odd?"

"Well, yes. He stopped paying last spring, or rather he's paying someone else. I'm worried. Perhaps Josie's not being cared for, even though Tunnicliff assured me the clinic said everything was fine."

"You haven't gone to see Josephine yourself?" She shook her head, and the pain the question brought was apparent. "Would you like me to check on her? I know it's difficult for you, if for no other reason than I'm sure Haarten must have cohorts there. I could tell them I was her brother, or make up some other story. Perhaps I could even get in to see her."

"Oh, Robert," Lina said, thinking of the horrors that were her only memories of the place, "I couldn't ask that. You don't know what it's like there."

"I know this is something I can do for you, that you can't do for yourself. Please, Lina. Let me do this. And while I go to the clinic, you can look through those books." He grinned. "After all, you *are* very clever. I'm sure you'll be able to find something that might help."

She looked at him a long time, and found in his confident expression a reason to smile. "Alright," she said. "But go to Mr. Tunnicliff. Tell him I sent you. Ask about the nurse he hired, and he'll know I sent you. Perhaps she'll be able to answer your questions without you having to go there yourself."

"I'll go tomorrow." They both smiled, but he had questions of his own to ask, questions more difficult to voice. "How long before...."

"The wedding?" Lina shuddered at the word. "Only a week."

His eyes betrayed his worry, but he mustered a reassuring smile, and said, "Well, that'll have to be enough time. What will you be doing?"

"Preparing for something I pray will never happen," she said. "There's a great deal to do, and he'll expect me to do it."

"So you'll be out of the house?"

"Almost daily, I suspect."

"Will it be possible to meet again?"

She shook her head. "It'll be dangerous to contact me. Most of the servants are on watch. There are very few places in the city where Edward doesn't have agents." Then she smiled, as she remembered one place she knew Edward Haarten wouldn't think to look. "The Golden West. The tavern where Josie and I lived. Edward sold the place, and whoever owns it now is surely no friend of Edward's. Meet me there on Monday, four o'clock. And if anything should happen before then, contact me through Tunnicliff. He can get word to me. Edward might find it strange, a note from Tunnicliff, but I can come up with some plausible story for it."

He turned toward her, and smiled. "There, now. We have a plan. It might not seem much of a plan, but it's a beginning, isn't it? The first step to a way out of this." His finger caught hold of a single strand of her hair, broken free by the breeze, and he smoothed it back from her worried brow.

"Oh, Robert," she sighed once more. "I only hope you're right."

He took her hand in his. "Understand, Lina, despite what you said, you're coming home with me. Even if we don't learn anything that will help us, we're going back to Sleekit, you and I. Nothing else matters. You will not marry that man." As they leaned together, their lips met in one last, lingering kiss.

35

Well, it's been long enough, Lina thought as she saw her smile in the mirror the next morning. She felt giddy. She could think of no other word for it, but it was a sensation she honestly didn't remember having ever experienced before, this particular lightness of heart. She felt distracted and pensive all at once, and she reveled in the feeling. But going down to face the staff, this smile wouldn't do at all. No one in the Haarten household ever appeared this happy, so this smile would only raise eyebrows. She was grateful it was only the staff she would have to face. She had stayed so long in her room this day she was sure she had already missed Edward. With Edward, such a smile might raise more than eyebrows. It might raise questions. So she banished the smile from her face and went downstairs.

It had been her hope to spend the day with those books that had so intrigued her the day before. But she had scarcely begun when Jackson interrupted her with a note from Madame Bonaface's shop asking if she could come for her fitting. Just as she had dreaded, she would likely now have to spend the day away from the house. Edward would no doubt be back by the time she returned. But the fitting could not be avoided.

As she was donning her cloak to leave, she said to Jackson, "I know you'll be certain to let Captain Haarten know where I've gone. Please tell him I may be late returning this afternoon. This is likely to take some time."

"Yes, miss. But he also asked that I tell you he very much wants to speak with you this evening. He said to tell you he wants to discuss the wedding."

She took a carriage to Madame Bonaface's shop, where she gave direction and made decisions with authority. By the time she left, the dressmakers were in a flurry of lace and white satin. When she paid Madame Bonaface a healthy sum, the woman fawned over her, and complimented her on her choices and sense of style. Lina had to laugh, remembering the total ineptitude which she had always displayed under Josephine's tutelage. She was only slightly more adept now, and she knew Madame Bonaface thought so, too. But the money was enough to prompt the dressmaker's unending flattery. She thought, *This is what Haarten really buys with his money—indiscriminate respect..*

On the ride back to Rincon Hill, Lina caught a glimpse of Telegraph Hill from the carriage. She summoned the memory of Robert's words to her the day before. *A beginning*, he had said. *A first step to a way out.* She found hope in those words, and in the fact that Robert was, perhaps that very day, talking to Tunnicliff or the nurse, learning something, anything, that might change the course of events.

Edward's notion to spend the evening discussing the wedding had not been an idle one. After dinner, when they retired to the library, Lina retreated to a book immediately. Edward, however, was determined to engage her in conversation. He asked about the wedding, the reception, the dress, even the household, and each time she gave him a quick, cursory response, maintaining her attention on the book before her. Finally he asked quite pointedly, "I understand you spent the day at the dressmakers. But didn't you also have a fitting yesterday? Is there some reason you're spending so much time away from the house?"

His tone was sharp and direct. Lina looked up and saw in his face that there was no question about it—Edward was suspicious. Carefully, she calculated her response. She closed the book and spoke.

"So I had planned, but at the last minute, it was cancelled. Honestly, Edward," she sniped, affecting a tone for his benefit, "I really am losing patience with your Madame Bonaface. If she isn't wasting *my* time and *your* money talking rather than making this dress, she's taken to bed with some imagined affliction. Yesterday, her assistant sent me away, claiming Madame was ill. Today, I went back and put my foot down.

After all, the wedding's only a few days away, and there's so much to do!"

"Quite right, Carolina. You mustn't let subordinates get the better of you. People in our position are always targets for those who think we have more money than sense. I'm glad to see you're learning to be firm with them."

"Oh, yes," she said, "I'm learning a great many things." It was a private joke, but it made her feel better about listening to his insults and disparagement of others. "But all this delay has put me behind in my household work. I was wondering," she asked, trying to sound casual in her interest, "Will you be working here in the library tomorrow, Edward?"

"Yes," he responded absently.

"And Monday? Will you be here, too?"

Haarten laid his work down on the desk. "Is there some reason for this interest in my daily routine?"

She answered carefully. "All these preparations have left me feeling tired by the time evening comes. I hate to disturb you when you're working here in the day, and I…" She was suddenly inspired to try a ploy that had never occurred to her before. "I enjoy spending time here after supper." She managed a smile. "So I hoped to be able to catch up on my work, and still preserve my evening time…for you." She dared to look up at him, and was surprised to find him smiling.

"I shall be here in the morning, but the afternoon you are free to work here. Monday, I will be away all day. That should give you ample time to catch up." Edward rose from the desk and came to stand next to her chair. He was rigid and tense, but he spoke softly. "Carolina, in a matter of days we will be married." She could tell this was not a conversation Edward Haarten held easily. His words came haltingly, but to his credit, he kept his eyes on her the whole time. "It pleases me to see that you're beginning to enjoy my companionship." He stepped toward her, reached down and took her left hand by the fingers then brought them to his lips in an awkward kiss. She sat dumbfounded by his words, and even more so by this simple act. She pulled her hand away from him when the kiss was completed, but immediately regretted it. Any trace of warmth left his eyes. "You find that unappealing?"

She shook her head. "Edward, it's only that, well, our relationship has always been straightforward, and of a business nature. Even this marriage seems more a business matter than a personal one. I suppose I always assumed it would stay that way."

"And did you assume it would stay that way after the marriage? Did you assume you would share my house, but not my bed?"

It was a shocking and direct question from this man whom she had never before heard express an intimate thought. The question made her blush. "No, Edward. I assumed it would be a marriage—in that way. It's you who has never shown the slightest interest in such matters."

He gently but firmly pulled her up to stand next to him. "Then let me do so now." He pulled her to him, and kissed her. His kiss was insistent, but not cruel. She returned the kiss, only because to give him nothing might add to any suspicions he might still have. Haarten made no other move, not to take her in his arms, to embrace her, nor to press his passions any further. She was thankful, for it made the kiss endurable. Edward seemed pleased to have any response from her at all. When he pulled back from the kiss, he was smiling. She took the chance to seem coy.

"Goodnight, Edward," she said, eyes down. She left him standing alone in his library.

****

Time crept in a painful way between Sunday and Monday afternoon, when she was to see Robert again. Lina and Edward spent Sunday evening together in the library, where Lina subtly tried to bore him with the tiniest details of the wedding. He maintained more curiosity than she would have guessed, but in the end, she wore his patience down. When they were talking about matters that he seemed to care about, such as the cost of it all, who had been retained for what service, and which of his important friends had accepted or declined the invitation, he was attentive. When she regaled him with the cut and cloth of the dress, the wisdom of choosing one pastry over another, or the decorations for the house, he lost interest. Just when she thought he would excuse himself, however, he changed the subject to the running of the household, and here, Haarten won, for he had no end of suggestions, directives or admonishments for her. She listened carefully, even took notes at times, and limited her responses to a simple, 'Yes, Edward,' or 'Whatever you wish.'

Monday Edward lingered about the house until mid morning. She had to confine herself to her room so as not to seem too eager for him to leave. When she finally had the library, she instructed Jackson to have the carriage ready at four o'clock. Then she locked the library door, sat at the desk, and went to work.

Lina began with a list of all the payments she could find attributed to the Wilcox Clinic, including those made separately to Dr. Maxwell. Payments to the clinic began the prior autumn, with a thousand dollars, and were made monthly. In April, the smaller payments to Dr. Maxwell began, and continued until shortly before she returned. If they continued thereafter, Edward was paying them from a different account. It was odd, no doubt, but she couldn't decide what significance any of this had. She went back through the books again, but found nothing else.

She was also curious to get some idea of what might be her entire debt to Haarten. She held no real hope to be able to pay it, but she wanted to know. She already could count more than seven thousand dollars. The only other significant expense was the tuition to Miss Ward's school. She turned the pages back to August of the previous year, to find one payment to Miss Ward of five hundred dollars. In September, she found another for the same amount. She found another in October, and then something else caught her eye. A draft had been written to an undertaker in late October. Then she remembered Barclay, and the bittersweet sadness that always accompanied his memory came over her. She pressed on through the books making note of the rest of the payments to Miss Ward. Her total was now nearly ten thousand dollars. *It might as well be a million*, she thought. She went through the book one last time to make sure of her sums. That was when she noticed a second draft to the same undertaker, this one in mid April.

There was no time to consider the meaning of this. Jackson knocked on the door. "Your carriage is out front, Miss," he said.

Lina slipped her notes inside her pocket and left. She let the carriage take her only as far as Portsmouth Square, on the excuse of doing some marketing. She walked the rest of the way. When she came around the corner and saw the Golden West, she beamed. She knew she would find no familiar faces inside, but from the outside the place had not changed a lick. She took one more precaution against discovery, to come in through the kitchen as she used to. She would get a peek at the tavern's main room before she entered. None of the kitchen staff even noticed her as she walked through. From the kitchen door, she saw Robert immediately, sitting at the private table she had shared with Barclay and Josephine many times before. She walked quickly toward him.

She surprised him, coming from the back as she had. He rose immediately when he saw her, and took her hand as she came to the table. He smiled, but his tone was reserved as he spoke her name. "Lina."

She assumed he was being wise to keep this distance between them, as much as she wished he could take her in his arms as he had before. "Would you like something to drink?" he asked, but she shook her head. After waiting all week to see him, she hardly knew where to begin.

"It's so good to see you," she whispered, trying to find a shared sentiment in his eyes, but instead, he looked sad and distant. "I was nearly late, I was so lost in looking through those books." She took the notes from her pocket. "I'm not sure what any of this means, but perhaps between us we...."

She thought he was reaching for the paper, but he took both her hands, and held them tight. He was searching her face, and it was obvious he was looking for words. She had never known him to be at such a loss, and almost laughingly, she said, "What is it, Robert?"

If anything, his face grew darker, and her smile vanished as he squeezed her hands again. "Lina. I'm so sorry." Robert looked briefly down at where their hands were joined, hoping for mercy in quickness, he said, "Josephine is dead."

He knew full well this would be hard for her to hear. He was prepared for tears, even for screams or moans. Lina didn't seem like the fainting type, but even that he half-expected. He didn't expect this long, long silence. There were tears brimming in her eyes, but she never lost her composure. She just seemed completely absorbed in her thoughts. He could stand it no longer.

"Lina? Are you alright?" he asked. She nodded.

Robert could clearly see the acceptance on her face, but her eyes were nearly vacant. He waited for her to come back to him, to the moment. "Lina?" he said, firmly but softly, and he gave her hand a tight squeeze. Lina's first response was to grip his fingers tightly, to blunt her pain like a patient under the surgeon's knife. Then she started taking deep breaths, letting the air out slowly. The careful breathing made her relax enough to speak. "I'll take that drink now, please."

Robert signaled to one of the girls. "Some water for the lady."

"No," Lina interrupted, "Whiskey."

"Whiskey," he concurred. A glass was delivered in short order. Lina took one quick sip, then slowly poured the rest down her throat, and waited for the liquor's warmth to pass before she spoke again.

"Tell me what you learned," she said, too matter-of-factly.

"Look, Lina. Perhaps it would be easier if we left here, took a walk...."

"No," she said. "I'll be fine. Please, Robert." He looked at her, still unconvinced, but she swayed him with her tone. "Please?"

"I found Tunnicliff. He told me all about this nurse. I found her just as he said I would. Her name is Alice Feeney. She lives in those encampments they call Happy Valley." He snickered. "What a name. It's squalor, pure and simple. Not even as good as a tenement."

"Yes. Mr. Tunnicliff said she and her husband had debts. That's how he met them."

"Well, her husband's left her. She's got four small children. They were all there, covered in filth, hunger in their eyes. My heart broke for her. I asked her about your friend. I told her Mr. Tunnicliff had sent me to hear for myself how Josephine was fairing. From the moment I mentioned Josephine's name, the woman was terrified. She stuttered and stammered, and when I tried to calm her down, she suddenly broke down and confessed. She'd lied to Tunnicliff. She wasn't a nurse, but only an orderly, so there was nothing she could do for Josephine's care, except keep an eye on her. But she remembered when she passed. Last April, of consumption. She was there the day it happened."

"Oh God." Lina choked at the thought of her friend's fate. "This is too horrible. In that awful place, and sick..."

Robert stopped her. "Don't think on that now. There's more to tell. I asked about Josephine's mental capacity, but she said Josephine had never been a patient in the hospital's mental ward. And though she couldn't say for certain what the listed reason was for her admittance, she was quite certain Josephine was in the ward for consumptive patients."

"But why didn't she tell Tunnicliff?"

"The money. She knew if she told Tunnicliff that Josephine was dead, he'd stop paying her."

"But I saw her with my own eyes. She was deranged," Lina said.

"Mrs. Feeney promises that wasn't her. She did say, however, that Josephine insisted everyone refer to her as Mrs. Barclay. That was the only madness Mrs. Feeney saw, and she thought that harmless enough, so she called her that. It evidently bothered the doctors a great deal, however."

The story Robert told fit with what she had learned from Haarten's accounts. A payment to an undertaker, in April. Josephine had died in April, just as Lina was finding a home in Sleekit. Lina felt a choking in her throat. Guilt, sadness, regret, and despair came upon her at once. She wanted to fling herself upon the table and wail, or pound it with her fists, or go screaming from the building. But she couldn't forget that she still had to be mindful there might always be someone near who worked for Edward Haarten. At the thought of him, all other emotions were suddenly gone, and only a searing sense of hatred filled her.

"He killed her," Lina said, flatly.

"But Lina, the nurse said...."

"Don't you understand? Edward put her there and left her to die." A realization struck her, and she whispered from behind the hand that came up suddenly to cover her mouth, "I could have done something. I came back in November! I didn't leave until February. I could have done something, if I'd just been a little braver or cleverer, I could have learned all this for myself. Oh, my God."

"Stop it!" he hissed, snatching back her hand, yanking her arm so she was forced to look at him. "I'm sorry, Lina. I'm terribly sorry she's dead. I'm terribly sorry to have upset you, but I'm glad you heard it from me, not some stranger in that hospital. And you've nothing to feel guilty about. Nothing! There's more to this story than we know now, but whatever it is, you aren't responsible, do you understand me?" He yanked her by the arm again, but though their eyes connected, she didn't answer. "You do realize that Haarten has one less claim on you now. There's nothing to keep us here. Please, Lina. Come back to Sleekit." His eyes implored her. "Come home."

She looked at him in total disbelief. "I can't go back," she said, then added urgently. "But you have to go. You have to leave right away!"

"What are you talking about? I'm not leaving here without you!"

"Yes. You have to. What if I'm right? What if Edward did this horrible thing deliberately, maliciously? He could, you know. He's clearly capable of it. I won't risk someone else I love because of this."

"Why would Haarten harm me?" Robert asked. The whole notion seemed preposterous to him.

"Why would he harm Josephine? God only knows, but he did, didn't he? She's dead, isn't she? That's all the evidence I need."

"Very well! If Haarten's such a dangerous man, then I'll be damned if I'll leave you here by yourself! Living under the same roof with him!"

"Edward won't hurt me."

"How can you be so sure?"

"I just am. That's all I can say."

"Well, that isn't guarantee enough for me."

"Well, it will just have to be!" Lina jerked her hands away from his. She tried to remember how it felt to be truly angry with him. Seeing him here now, it was so hard to remember that time, but anger would make this easier. "Robert Marr, you're going to listen to me. They'll be no arguments and no further discussion. This isn't up to you. Leave here, go back to the Bantry Bay, and tell Riordan to sail for Sleekit. If there's anything to be done to stop this, then I promise you, I will. I'll do whatever I can to keep from marrying Edward, short of murder. And if I can, I'll come back to Sleekit." This next was the hardest. "But if there isn't a way out, if I haven't come to the ship by Friday evening...."

He looked at her in horror. "Then *what*, in God's name? Are you telling me you'd actually *marry* this man? Lina, don't be stupid."

"I'm not being stupid. I'm being practical." The look she gave him was so cold, so distant, it frightened him. "Now, go," she commanded him.

Robert had his own resolve. "You can't make me leave."

Lina stood. "You're right. But if you make any attempt to interfere, to contact me, or confront Edward, I swear to God I'll marry him. You'll leave me no choice." He wore a desperate look, but she was too determined to be softened by it. She turned to go.

"Lina." She heard him rise from his chair, then walk toward her until he stood in front of her. Gone was the pleading look. What she saw now in his eyes was hard. "I know you think that if you marry Haarten, it'll be some sort of noble act. Perhaps you even think it will absolve you of something. But this isn't noble, it's selfish, in the worst possible way. It's a denial of everyone that's important to you. No one who cares about you wants this. No one will be better off for it. That mountain back there, why, it's only so much land, in a place filled with nothing but land. I could lose it all tomorrow, and I'd have no regrets. But this, missing this chance with you, that I would regret. Forever. And you'll be miserable, which is the worst crime of all. If Josephine was as much a friend to you as you claim, then you'll honor her. You won't let Edward Haarten, or anyone come between you and your happiness."

Something about his words was so familiar to her that for a moment Robert thought that puzzled look on Lina's face meant she had changed her mind. But she had not.

"I have to handle Edward in my own way, Robert," was all she said.

"I know. Well, I can't promise you I'll stay to watch you do this. Riordan wanted to leave Thursday. I guess I'll tell him," he paused, "it's time to go."

"Do as you must," she said. She left through the kitchen as she had come.

****

It was nearly the supper hour by the time she returned to Haarten's house. She didn't know if Haarten was home, nor did she care. She came through the front door and walked straight up to her room. She closed the door behind her, locked it, and then began to undress, although it was only dusk. Shortly, thereafter, just as she finished changing into her dressing gown, Jackson knocked on the door.

"Miss? Are you alright, miss?"

"Yes. Please leave me alone."

"Is there something wrong, miss? The meal's on the table, and the Captain is asking for you."

"Tell him I'm not feeling well. I'm not hungry either. Tell him I just need some rest. I'll see him tomorrow." Lina heard the man's hurried steps pass along the hallway, and down the stairs. Shortly she heard the familiar sound of heavy boots quickly taking the stairs, followed by another knock at the door.

"Carolina? Are you ill?" It was Haarten.

"No, Edward. Please. Just let me get some rest."

"If there's something wrong…"

"Nothing is wrong!" she yelled. Then she stepped closer to the door. "Please, Edward, just let me rest." She tried to make her voice sound soft and pleading, to give it the kind of fragility he might expect of a woman, and to hide the anger she felt. It seemed to work.

"Very well. Rest. But if there's anything you need, call for Jackson. Or one of the maids."

"Good night, Edward." She heard his heavy stride walk away. Finally, she had the solitude she'd so desperately wanted since leaving the Golden West. But the solitude offered her no solace. Instead, it allowed a rush of memories too painful to bear. Lina collapsed onto her bed and cried, muffling her moans among the bedclothes until she exhausted herself into sleep.

In the middle of the night, she awoke. Her face felt hot and puffy from her tears, and her mouth was dry. She lit the lantern, then found her way to the washstand. She took a cloth and carefully wiped her cheeks and cleared her eyes, then for good measure, reached her hands into the cool water and splashed it over her face. She was beginning to feel better, but only just.

As she dabbed her face dry, she walked towards the window. Outside, the world was nearly dark, with only a few scattered lanterns to give the city any light at all. For such a busy, bustling place, San Francisco seemed cold and empty at night. Though her tears were dried up for now, thoughts of Josephine stayed with her. It had been more than a year since she'd seen Josie, but Lina had always believed there would come a day when she would see her again. Many times Lina had sat in this house and missed her friend. Many times, too, during happy moments in Sleekit, she missed her. Now she was no longer missing Josephine—she was mourning her.

Somewhere, probably on the outskirts of the city, Josephine no doubt lay forgotten in some unmarked grave. Lina never held much store in commemorating the dead, but somehow she felt Josephine was owed a proper service. Despite all her frailties and flaws, Josephine was, after all, a devout Catholic, in her own peculiar way. *Josephine would have liked a service*, Lina thought. *Well, then, by God, she'll have it!*

Lina turned the wick up on the lantern, and filled the room with warm lamplight. She opened the trunk where she kept her most valued possessions, including Josie's Bible. Lina took the Bible, then reached for the lantern and brought both to the small dressing table that sat before the window. Against the high windows with their heavy draperies, the dressing table made a fine altar.

Lina sat at the table, searching her memory for the right passage. Her own knowledge of scripture was meager. It held only a minor place in her life as a child, and none at all since she had grown. She couldn't think of any passage save the Twenty-third Psalm which she had ever heard read at a funeral, and that seemed too sad. Then she remembered the story of Ruth. The story of Ruth had made an impression on her as a small girl, for there were so few women who had their own stories in the Bible. Lina knew the story well enough to know of a passage that fit this occasion.

Flipping quickly through the Old Testament, she found the Book, then skimmed the lines for the passage. Tracing her finger along the small print, trying to cipher the sometimes strange language, she finally came to the passage she wanted. Aloud, but in a whispered tone, for fear someone might overhear her, she read.

> *And Ruth said, Entreat me not to leave thee, or to*
> *return from following after thee: for whither thou goest,*
> *I will go; and where thou lodgest, I will lodge: thy people*
> *shall be my people, and thy God my God. Where thou*
> *diest, will I die, and there will I be buried: the Lord do so*
> *to me, and more also, if ought but death part thee and me.*

Lina began to weep for Josie again, not the same sort of mournful wails that buried her in sleep earlier, but something more bittersweet. *We went together, and we lodged together, and more, didn't we Josie, dear?* As she read on through the Book's verses, she could almost chuckle at the notion of Josie gleaning in the fields of corn, as Ruth had. *No, nothing so menial for you. But Ruth's got nothing on you for constancy. Never was there a truer friend.*

Lina kept reading the Book of Ruth, but as she moved further into its passages, she found her thoughts were more on Josie than her reading. Her fingers fluttered the corners of the pages absently as she read, when she noticed something pressed between the pages. It was a thin onionskin envelope. There were no markings on the outside. Lina opened the fragile envelope, and gently tugged at the page inside. It pulled free, and Lina unfolded it carefully, then held it close to the lamp to read the fine writing. It was not Josephine's hand that had written this. She skimmed the words which seemed to have no meaning. She started over, reading carefully now, and by the time she reached the document's end, her jaw hung open. Suddenly, she began to laugh, until she caught herself, remembering both the hour and the place. Had anyone been sitting across from Lina, they would have been amazed at the transformation in her expression. Where only moments before there had been tears, now her eyes were filled with light. She held her hand over her mouth to muffle the sound of her voice as she said, once more, "Good girl, Josie. Good girl!"

****

"Good morning, Edward!" Lina was downstairs the next morning before Edward. She made sure of it. She felt well rested, and made certain she looked it before she left her room. She was halfway through a large breakfast, and was busy making notes for her day when Edward entered. He was obviously shocked to find her not only awake and up, but so chipper, for he stopped at the door and watched her, astounded.

"No need to ask how you're feeling. This is good news." He took his seat, and let the servants bring him his morning meal. "I had no idea you weren't feeling well. You should have said something."

"I'm feeling fine, Edward. Really." Lina grinned.

"Then all you needed was a little rest, I suppose."

"Yes. That must be it." Lina laid her cup down, and stood. "Well, Edward, I'm off. Lots to do today. I'll see you this evening." She left without his answer. She took Haarten's carriage as far as Portsmouth Square, then dismissed it, and walked straight for the office of Sylvester Tunnicliff.

"Good morning, Miss Clark! What a pleasant surprise! I do declare, you look in much finer fettle than the last time we spoke."

"I am!" Lina said cheerfully, as she took her seat.

"Then I take it that all went well with Mr. Marr's inquiries?"

"Yes, Mr. Tunnicliff. I sent him to do what neither of us was brave enough to do. I sent him to find out what he could about Miss Paul."

"And what did he learn?"

"That she is dead."

Tunnicliff was stunned. "Miss Clark! I...I had no idea! Oh, my deepest sympathies! When did it happen? And why didn't that blasted Feeney woman...oh, forgive me...I feel just awful..."

"Please, Mr. Tunnicliff. There's no point in blaming yourself or Mrs. Feeney. I know who is to blame, and I'm taking steps to deal with that. It's another matter that's brought me here today." She sat up straight, and laid her hands carefully in her lap. "I have need yet again of your services. Frankly, sir, what I'm going to ask you to do isn't at all a complicated legal matter. The thing is either true or it isn't. But if it's true, it will prompt a good deal of work over the next week. You've proved yourself trustworthy in the past, and that, as much as your legal expertise, is why I'm here today. And as an incentive, I've brought you this." She took a piece of paper out of her bag, and handed it to him.

He unfolded the paper. It was a draft for one thousand dollars. "Why, of course, Miss Clark," he grinned. "Anything you need!" He laughed.

Lina laughed, too. "Very well, then." She opened her bag again and pulled out the document she found the night before and laid it before him. As he began to read, she said, "I have every reason to believe this document is real, that it is just what it appears to be. You will recognize the names, I believe." Quickly, the lawyer looked up at her over his glasses, then, as quickly, back down to the paper. "So, tell me, please, in your judgment, that document, in combination with the one you already have, do they mean what I think they mean?"

"Well, miss, it's difficult to say. Probate matters are often among the most complicated of legal issues. It might, then again, it might not."

"But it should be enough to raise questions, don't you think?"

Tunnicliff grinned from ear to ear. "At the very least, Miss Clark."

"The only hitch to this plan, Mr. Tunnicliff, is that you absolutely must have the answer for me by Friday. Any later than that, and I'm afraid the news won't do me much good, one way or another."

Tunnicliff shook his head. "Still, miss. It's a very short time. There's no way you can extend the period?"

"No, sir. On Friday I will be marrying Captain Edward Haarten."

Tunnicliff was stunned. "But, but Miss Clark! Then by Friday, all this will be immaterial, will it not?"

"Yes. This is why it's so important we get busy today." Lina looked him in the eye. "Will you do as I ask? Will you help me?"

"Of course," he told her. "Where do we begin?"

****

"Um. Hello! Hello? Can anyone hear me? Oh, drat. What's the word? Ahoy! Ahoy the Bantry Bay!" Sylvester Tunnicliff called from the dock below. "Anybody aboard?"

Riordan knew the look of a lawyer when he saw one. Lawyer or banker, could be either, he thought, as if there were any difference. *Trouble, that's what they are.*

"Aye, state your business." Riordan called brusquely from the deck.

"I'm looking for a Mr. Marr?"

"Never heard of 'im."

"Are you certain, sir? It's quite important. Mr. Marr came to see me about a...," Tunnicliff looked carefully around him, then tried to whisper, "...a Miss Clark? Carolina Clark?"

"Well, why didn't yas say so, ya witless man! Come aboard. Himself's here, he is!"

Just then, Robert appeared on deck. "Tunnicliff!"

"Relax, Mr. Marr," Tunnicliff said, recognizing the concern on Marr's face. "Everything is fine with the lady. At least, there's some hope that it might be."

"What is it?"

Tunnicliff looked around once more. "Perhaps there's some place we can talk privately?"

"You can share anything with Riordan here that you'd share with me," Robert assured. Tunnicliff looked at Riordan, who wore a look of insult moving to outrage at the lawyer's insinuation.

"Oh, no!" The lawyer laughed nervously. "No, it's not you, sir. It's just that Captain Haarten *does* have quite an influence around these parts, as you can imagine. I'd hate for us to be seen or heard by others."

"Come below, then." The three men went to Riordan's cabin. "Milo, whiskey," Robert said, knowing what would loosen the lawyer's tongue. With the glasses poured, he continued. "Tunnicliff, you're making me nervous. Get to the point."

Tunnicliff finished the shot in one gulp. "Well, I've come at the request of Miss Clark, herself. I am pleased to say the lady has taken me into her full confidence, and entrusted me with quite a charge. Quite a charge, indeed."

"What exactly has Lina entrusted you with?"

"The whole story, sir," Tunnicliff answered, and punctuated it with a wink. "And she has a plan that she believes will extricate her from her obligations at week's end."

Robert beamed. "Wonderful!"

"But she was concerned about the timing. I am to tell you she's very hopeful she'll be able to set sail with you on Friday, but you gave her to believe it was your intention to leave on Thursday."

"Oh, hang that! I'll wait for a month of Fridays, if that's what it takes."

"I wish that were all it was." Tunnicliff glanced from the bottle on the table to Riordan, who trained a suspicious eye on him.

"Here," Robert said, pouring another shot.

"Thank you, sir." Tunnicliff took another drink. "It's just that, well, I'm not certain I'll be able to accomplish what she needs by then, in order for that to be possible. And I would feel dreadful, after all this business with Miss Paul, to further disappoint Miss Clark. I'm rather fond of her, you know."

"So am I," Robert said with a grin. "But damn it, Tunnicliff. I understand now why lawyers charge by the hour. You need to be clear. Will Miss Clark make it or won't she?"

"Well, sir, I'm hoping there's something you might be able to do to help with that."

"Drink up," Robert said, "and start talking."

****

Only two days left, and Lina had nothing left to do to prepare for the wedding except ride herd on the household staff. Haarten continued to treat her with kid gloves. Sometimes his tone made her think he considered her a china doll, about to break, as she must have seemed the night she came home feigning exhaustion. At other times, he seemed to regard her with general suspicion, as if he couldn't believe his plans were going so smoothly. Whatever the cause, Lina always treated him the same. She smiled in his presence, was always pleasant but not fawning, and she kept busy and out of his way when possible. She kept him informed of every monotonous detail of the wedding. She followed any instructions he gave her completely and unequivocally. She tried her best not to be alone with him, except when the servants were about, to avoid any intimacy. Once, however, he caught her unawares, and actually asked permission for a kiss, so she allowed it. Afterward, when she was alone, she thought Josie would have understood this perfectly. Because of Robert, Lina now understood what a kiss could mean. Haarten's kiss was so much less, so without feeling, that it cost Lina nothing to give it.

Lina refused to believe the plan she'd set in motion would not bring the hoped for result. "But even if Robert leaves before this is over," she reminded herself, "I can always go home to him." She imagined herself arriving in Sleekit, to find him waiting for her with open arms and that radiant smile. *Please, God,* she thought.

The day before the wedding, true exhaustion struck her. That evening, Lina felt as if she might not survive the final few hours of efforts required of her. So she considered it a blessing when a dinner invitation for that evening was suddenly canceled. Mr. and Mrs.

Cornelius Whittaker had invited them over for a large celebratory gathering of all of Edward's business associates and their wives. But at the last possible moment, Cornelius Whittaker sent a note to the house canceling the party, due to the sudden illness of Mrs. Whittaker. Edward was noticeably put out, but Lina was wonderfully relieved. She had just finished dressing and had opened the door to come downstairs when she met Edward standing just outside with the news.

"Oh, well, I hope it's nothing serious," she said politely.

"It's terribly rude of them, but I suppose it can't be helped." Edward seemed less than convinced.

"Please, Edward. Don't be angry on my account," Lina said, though she knew her feelings were far down on the list of Haarten's considerations. "It's for the best. I have a dozen things to do before tomorrow."

"Carolina, one moment." He held his hand against the door, firmly but not insistently. She pulled the door open and let him pass before her into the room, but she kept the door slightly open, as propriety dictated. "There's no need for concern, Carolina," he said softly, looking down at her as he stood close to her.

Lina took a step back and said. "I know, Edward. I'm not afraid of you."

He looked her up and down, then quietly said, "You never were, were you? Not like most people." Haarten seemed to tense suddenly, and he took a few steps away from her and further into the room. "I've brought you something. I suppose this was yours, by tradition, a long time ago. Frankly, I didn't trust you enough to give it to you until recently. But I've come to believe you mean to stand by your word." He awkwardly thrust a hand forward, where a small box rested on his palm. "Here."

She took the box, then opened its stiffly hinged lid. The box held a beautiful ring, encrusted with small sapphires and set in the middle with a magnificent diamond. The setting was filigree, an impressive piece of workmanship.

"Oh my, Edward," she said, overwhelmed. "It's lovely."

"It was my mother's," he said simply. "When I was a young man," he haltingly began, "my mother didn't want me to leave for a life at sea. I suppose that's what mothers do—tell their sons not to leave. I left under rather strained circumstances with my father, as well. My mother gave me this piece before I left. 'Just in case,' she said. I suppose she meant just in case I should ever need the money. I never did. It seemed fitting to give it to you. As an engagement ring. That *is* the expected thing, isn't it? And from one's mother, that's traditional, I understand."

"Yes, very traditional," Lina said, still looking at the ring in its box.

"I can only assume, it must not have meant very much to her, or she wouldn't have given it away."

Lina looked at Edward with one final rush of compassion. "Oh, Edward. You're wrong about that. I imagine this ring meant very much to your mother. Otherwise, she wouldn't have given it to you as a keepsake."

"Keepsake?" he asked, bewildered.

"Yes. Your mother may have given it to you as a sort of insurance, I suppose. But she may also have given it to you as a reminder of her. Just in case you would need one. That would be very like a mother, too."

"Oh," he said, surprised. "That hadn't occurred to me."

Lina closed the lid to the box, then looked Edward straight in the eye. "There's another possibility for 'just in case.' Perhaps she meant it for you, just in case you should ever find someone you wanted to spend your life with, someone you could truly love." She held the box toward him as he had given it to her, resting flatly on her palm. "It's not too late, Edward. You could still find someone who would mean something to you, and who felt the same for you. You could have that kind of happiness."

Edward's grey eyes went cold. He waved his hand in a quick dismissal. "You're making too much of this, as usual, Carolina. The ring is simply part of what's expected. Take it in that spirit. Nothing more." He left abruptly and shut the door behind him.

Lina changed into her dressing gown, and asked Jackson to send a tray up with her dinner. She had nothing more to say to Edward, and with the party canceled, Lina was anxious to get her personal preparations underway. Tomorrow would be a busy day.

First Lina packed. She had two very different trips to pack for. In keeping with the recent fashion of the newly rich, Edward had planned a wedding excursion, really just a thinly disguised necessary business trip to Mexico. Lina, of course, had no intention of going, but she did accept it as a possibility. For her other trip, the trip she planned with all her heart on making, back to Sleekit, she needed very little. By the time she went to bed, she had two large steamer trunks crammed with fine clothes she hoped never to wear again, and two small satchels crammed with all that she brought with her from Sleekit.

When she woke the next morning, her first thought was "Twelve long hours." She quickly ran her schedule for the day backward through her mind. The wedding was scheduled for six o'clock. Madame Bonaface and her ladies were due at three o'clock to help her dress. By then, she should have attended to all the downstairs arrangements. The wedding would be held in the long parlor, set up as it had been for Barclay's Christmas party, with all the doors opened wide to create a ballroom. Nearly two hundred guests were expected. She would have to start checking these details by early afternoon. Although she clung to the belief that the wedding would not go as planned, she still wanted to make sure that it had all the appearances of perfection. *That'll only heighten the effect*, she thought.

But that still left six long hours to fill. She dressed and went downstairs for some coffee and something to eat. She was delighted to learn that Edward planned on being away all day. Jackson was more than a bit embarrassed when he said, "I believe, miss, the Captain said it seemed only proper that the bridegroom not see the bride before...." He blushed rather than finish the thought.

An hour later, Lina was alone, enjoying the delicious bath she had ordered. She let the warm, sweet-smelling water relax her, make her sleepy, even dreamy. *A bath is a wonderful thing,* she thought. *It cleans you when you are dirty. It soothes you when you are tired.* Her mind drifted back to that indulgent soak at the Golden West the night she and Josephine came to San Francisco. As she trickled the soft water from the sponge down her face and neck, she remembered that she had never felt so in need of a bath, nor so completely indulged by one. *A bath can put you to sleep, or wake you up*, she thought, recalling the cold water baths at Meg's. As she moved the sponge along her arms and shoulders, she shivered just a bit at the memory of a bath on a brisk spring morning in Sleekit just after she arrived. Now, here in her room,

591

she enjoyed the most indulgent bath of her life. More extravagant than the luxuries she'd enjoyed at the Golden West, the soaps, the salts, were all of the finest sorts, and there were maids available at her beck and call for the satisfaction of any whim. Only now, she longed for Sleekit. For the cold mornings, and the days without sunshine. For all the places that she had come to know as home. The tavern. Her little office. For the people so dear to her. And for Robert. She closed her eyes and she could see him, and hear him, so clearly. Unaware, as she thought of him, as she dreamed of him, she slowly drew the sponge down her thighs and along her legs.

A knock on the door brought her back to the present. It was Jackson. "Miss? A gentleman just left a note for you."

Lina was already jumping from her bath and scrambling for her dressing gown when she said, "Just slide it under the door, please."

Frantically, she tore open the envelope and pulled out the single sheet.

> *Miss Clark*
> *I have confirmed the information you requested. If you have no objections, I will be returning at half past five this afternoon. Mr. Cornelius Whittaker and Mr. Franklin Greeley will be accompanying me.*
> *ST*

****

The caterers and the florists came much earlier than Lina had expected them. Within an hour of her bath, she was downstairs directing the arrival of food and flowers. The household staff stood at the ready, awed by her command. She gave specific directions on how the buffet would be laid out, where to place the flowers, how the rooms were to be arranged. And for good measure, as she handled these matters, she was ever on the watch for small, overlooked details. When she saw crooked candles in the chandeliers, she ordered them straightened, although it meant moving all the chairs from the parlors to make room for the lowered chandeliers. When she noticed a spot on the windows or the brass or the wood, she ordered them polished. She directed one poor maid to simply start dusting, and when she had finished dusting everything she could think of, she was to start over.

By three o'clock, the house was ready. The buffet held the largest, most elaborate array of foods Lina could find. She ordered all the silly dishes she had seen served at other elegant houses, like horrible, salty caviar and pasty, bland goose liver. She included pounds and pounds of choice rare beef, a stuffed goose, and a roast pig. She followed the meal up with dozens of fancy pastries filled with rich cream, and for good measure, made sure there were no less than six dozen bottles of the finest champagne on hand. The ballroom looked like a spring garden. Although it was nearing winter, the whole room was filled with dozens and dozens of creamy white roses, grown in the southern climes of California and shipped here at great expense. The flowers were gathered with broad bands of silk in an off-white tone that matched the petals. The same silk was used to festoon the room, using not just ribbons, but whole bolts of the luxuriant, expensive fabric, shipped directly to Haarten from the Orient. At one end of the room, where the ceremony was to be held, the chairs were already set up for twenty-four musicians, a small orchestra Lina had assembled from the area, all of whom would be paid a handsome price for their services.

When she was certain all the details were attended to, once more she went to the library, and once more she took out the household account book. She wrote drafts for the caterer and the florist, paid them, and dismissed them. She wrote several more drafts. She looked at the balance in the account, and smiled. She wrote one final draft, then folded it, and slipped it into her pocket. Then she asked Jackson to call the staff into the library.

"I just want you all to know how much I appreciate everything you've done for me in the past few weeks," she told them when they finally assembled. "I'm sure it's been difficult, but I hope that this will make up for that." She walked along them as they stood in a row, and handed each, in turn, a draft for one hundred dollars.

Next, Madame Bonaface and her assistants arrived. Lina led them to her room, and allowed them to fuss over her for the next two hours. Priority was given to two young women who were put in charge of fixing Lina's hair. They made little clicking noises with their teeth and tongues, and gave little shakes of their heads, as if pronouncing the task impossible. But they went about their work, and eventually, one of them held the hand mirror out to Lina for her approval. Her curls were piled as high as she had ever worn them. In the reflection, Lina marveled at the construction. The girls had braided her hair, then braided the braids, then wound the whole mess in some secret way that gave her hair a sort of woven look. She found it both intriguing and preposterous. When she smiled, it was out of amusement, but her attendants took the smile for approval. "Fine," Lina giggled. "This is just perfect."

Next came the dress. Lina didn't so much wear the dress, as the dress wore her. The dress was taken off the form with tender, loving hands, while Lina was jerked and moved into place. The dress was held steady while Madame Bonaface and her ladies threaded Lina's legs through the waist and her arms through the sleeves. She was ordered not to move until the dress was secured, then she was lectured in the proper way to move in the dress, how to handle the dress, how to breathe in the dress. Then final adjustments were made. After all the endless, tedious fittings, Lina couldn't believe Madame Bonaface still insisted on putting in a tuck here, taking out a stitch there. But she allowed herself to be poked and prodded this final bit before Madame Bonaface herself declared the ensemble complete. Lina turned to look at herself in the full-length mirror. "Slowly! Slowly!" Madame Bonaface chastised her as she started to move. Lina didn't recognize herself. Her hair piled high made her neck look long and graceful, particularly accentuated by the dress' straight neckline. The fitted bodice and the full skirt were made of a fine off-white silk, but the dress was overlaid with a drape of ivory lace that softened her every curve. For her veil, there was a matching piece of lace which Madame Bonaface was anxious to attach. But for Lina, the veil would have been just that one detail too much, too close to her worst fear.

"I'll have someone help me with that later." Madame Bonaface was shocked at the suggestion that her grand veil might be thrown on at the last minute, but Lina was insistent. "Here," she said, thrusting the final payment into her hand, "thank you. You did a lovely job. You may go." Once paid, Madame Bonaface gathered her flock and left. Edward Haarten passed them as he entered the house. It was an hour until the wedding.

At half past five, Lina, still in the cloister of her room, ran toward the door when she heard the sound of someone arriving downstairs. But before she emerged, she heard Jackson speaking with the minister and the musicians, who had arrived at the same time. She closed her door and stood in the middle of the room, waiting expectantly for another knock at the door to come any moment.

By a quarter of six, everyone in the household was on edge. Haarten was up and down the stairs bellowing to the servants, Jackson in particular. "Why haven't any guests arrived? You haven't received a word from anyone? Are you positive?" The servants were trying to look busy, and to keep out of Haarten's way. In her room, Lina was pacing, waiting for Tunnicliff's arrival. He was already fifteen minutes late. Finally, she could stand it no longer. She threw open the door, and came downstairs in full wedding regalia. Lina could hear Haarten upstairs, still bellowing at Jackson. She slipped into the library, where she could look out the windows for any sign of Tunnicliff. She stayed with her nose pressed against the glass. It was nearly six o'clock before a carriage pulled up to the house, and Lina recognized Tunnicliff's bald head emerging from the coach. She opened the library door, where she ran smack into Haarten, bumping him so hard he grabbed her by her shoulders to steady them both.

"Carolina! What the devil? What are you doing down here? And where are the guests? They should have started arriving an hour ago. Did you make certain the invitations were correct?" Edward was completely befuddled by the chaos of the household.

"Yes, of course, Edward. Now, if you'll excuse me," she said, trying to get past him in the doorway.

It was not until then that Haarten had a good look at her. He held her away from him at arm's length. "Well, I must say, you look very nice. The dress turned out magnificently. You should be proud of yourself." Then he grinned an unbecoming grin, nearly a leer, and said, "But isn't it usually considered unlucky for the groom to see the bride before the wedding?"

"Yes, Edward. You've no idea how unlucky," she grinned back. "Now please. Wait for me here. I have a surprise for you. That's what this is all about. Please?" But she gave him no time to answer. She simply shoved her way past him, and closed the library doors behind her.

Lina moved in front of Jackson, and opened the door herself. On the step stood Sylvester Tunnicliff, and behind him two men. Lina knew Cornelius Whittaker, and she assumed the lanky, prunish man with them was Franklin Greeley. "Come in, gentlemen. Do come in."

Tunnicliff entered timidly, but the two bankers behind him did not. "Miss Clark," Franklin Greeley began immediately in a hushed, almost funereal tone, "I'm so very sorry to disturb you at a time like this. But this fellow here, Tunnicliff, insisted that you wanted us to do this now. I kept asking for assurances...."

"Oh to hell with assurances!" barked Whittaker, bullying his way to the front. "It's our money, isn't it? Don't we have the right? Now where the hell is Haarten? I demand to know! If you think you can hide him, Miss Clark...."

Tunnicliff spoke for Lina. "I assure you, Mr. Whittaker, Miss Clark has no interest in protecting Captain Haarten."

"That's right, gentlemen. Quite the opposite. But first, I must ask you to wait here, please," she said, leading them into the front parlor where the minister and the musicians awaited the ceremony. "Give me just a few moments, and then you can have all the time with Captain Haarten you like." She left Whittaker and Greeley looking awkward as the only two guests in the big room. The men stared at the minister and he stared at them, as she led Tunnicliff back into the hallway.

"Can you tell me what you were able to learn?" she asked.

"All I can tell you with any certainty is that the matters concerning the estate will be enough to accomplish what you want. Of course, if this whole matter goes to court, I cannot promise the outcome."

Lina smiled. "That's fine, Mr. Tunnicliff. You've done a wonderful job. This will be enough. It'll just have to be. Did you bring the documents?" He handed her the papers. She took them, then headed toward the library. She gave a quick look back over her shoulder to Tunnicliff, and said, "Wish me luck!" She went into the library to face Haarten.

Haarten was standing by the window. "Take a seat, Edward," she said flatly. He did not, and instead stepped closer to her.

"Carolina, I demand to know what's going on. That sounded like Whittaker out in the hall. Is it? If the guests are arriving, then we should...."

"The guests aren't arriving, Edward. I don't think there'll be any guests. I suppose you can ask your friend Mr. Whittaker when you speak with him, but I have a feeling it's for the same reason he canceled last night's party."

"*What* is the reason?" Edward roared in total frustration.

"This," she said plainly, handing him one of the papers Tunnicliff had given her.

Haarten took the paper. It was Josephine's will, naming Lina as the sole beneficiary of Josephine's worldly goods. Haarten read it with interest, and she noted a flash of anxiety on his face, but when he was done, he tossed it on the desk nonchalantly.

"Why should this be of interest to me?" he asked.

"Tell me, Edward. When did you plan on telling me Josephine was dead?"

Until that moment, he hadn't been sure she knew. He calculated how much of the story to tell her at this point. If this was her only concern, perhaps not much truth at all.

"Soon, I promise, my dear. It's just that I knew it would be a terrible blow, and I wanted to save you the pain until...."

"Until when, Edward? Would you have told me tonight, on our wedding night? Or maybe when we were in Mexico? A month from now? A year from now? When, Edward? Please tell me, when would have been a *good* time? When you were sure you could have gotten away with her murder?"

Haarten was genuinely shocked at the accusation. "Murder? How dare you accuse me of such an act! She died of consumption, simple disease, nothing more."

"I accuse you because it's true. You put her in that horrid place and you left her to die! That's the act I accuse you of."

"I put her there because she was delusional! Out of her mind, clearly. It seemed to me the charitable thing to do."

"Yes, I'm quite certain that's your idea of charity. But charity for who? Certainly not Josephine. Certainly not me. Charitable to you, only. It saved you from an unpleasantness. If something doesn't please Edward Haarten, he bullies it or manipulates it until it is as he thinks it should be. And if that doesn't work, he simply banishes it from his sight. Tell me, Edward, did it cost you even one hour's sleep, what you did to her?"

"What I did *for* her, was more than she deserved. You're the one who ignores an unpleasant truth, Carolina. You want to believe something noble of this woman, but I assure you, there was nothing noble about her kind. She was an opportunist of the first order. But whether you agree with me or not, it hardly matters now." He looked down at the will lying on the desk between them, and sneered. "As to what this has to do with the present, I'm not sure. If you think simply because Josephine is dead, that your obligations to me have ended, let me remind you of the contract I have with the Marrs."

"Oh, don't worry," Lina said with a smile. "I haven't forgotten that contract. But I thought you might find the will interesting, particularly today of all days."

Haarten made the mistake of snickering when he said, "If this is your idea of a dowry, a whore's meager fortune...."

"Use that word again about Josephine, and I'll forget the promise I made to myself not to kill you!" she spat. Her temper caught him by surprise. "Read this," she said, handing him the second document.

This document made the whole situation, suddenly, nauseatingly clear to Haarten, but he reread it several times to make certain there was no misunderstanding. The document he held in his hands was a marriage license, legalizing a marriage in early September of the previous year, between Captain William Barclay and Miss Josephine Paul.

"It's a forgery. It must be," he said hoarsely, desperately.

"I'm happy to say it isn't. I've had it verified. But then, I suspect you know something about forgeries, don't you Edward? I assume the will you had entered for Barclay's estate was a forgery."

"You can't prove that!" he said sharply.

Lina was amazed at how calm she felt, finally. "Probably not. But I won't need to. Others will be only too happy to prove it, I imagine. And it makes an excellent motive for murder, don't you think?"

"Quit saying that!" he screamed at her. She had never seen him so enraged. "Why would you think I could have someone murdered? What have I ever done to lead you to believe I was capable of that?"

Lina laughed. "You make some strange moral distinctions, Edward. Extortion, forgery, theft, all these are acceptable, but I'm to think you incapable of murder? Why?"

Edward looked at her, dazed. "I've done nothing wrong! I've taken nothing that wasn't rightfully mine. The forgery, as you call it? All I'll admit to you is formalizing what had always been the understanding between Captain Barclay and myself. Blackmail? Your debt to me, Carolina, is very real. I offered a way for you to repay that debt, and you accepted. Nothing more. And theft? How can I steal what was mine to begin with? Barclay & Company is mine, by rights. I wasn't about to let that woman keep it from me!"

"And so you killed her!"

"No! For the last time, stop saying that!" For some odd reason, Haarten seemed sickened by her accusation. "I only wanted to keep them apart. Just long enough for Barclay's fascination to wane. I knew it would. I'd seen it happen a dozen times before." Haarten looked down at the license still in his hands, and aimlessly walked toward the desk. To himself more than Lina, he said very quietly, "But it didn't play out the way I planned."

She knew if she was ever to get him to tell her the truth, this was the moment, but the confession would have to be coaxed out of him gently. Despite everything, she had little leverage to force him to give up his secrets. "What didn't?" she asked softly.

"What?" he said, sinking into his chair at the desk. He opened the humidor and took out a cigar, but did not light it. Instead, he twisted it back and forth between his fingers, and studied it closely as he slowly spoke. "I only meant for her to leave. But I knew she wouldn't, no matter what I might offer as an incentive, as long as you were close by. That's when I thought of sending you to school. It seemed such an obvious plan. Even then, I thought of asking you to marry me. I knew you had the talent to be the kind of wife I would need, if only you had a little more polish. Sending you to Miss Ward's resolved both dilemmas. Once you were gone, and Barclay was at sea, I came to her and told her Barclay had sent me to tell her he was through with her. She laughed. She told me then that she didn't see how that was possible, since they'd been married just before he left. I didn't believe her. I thought she was bluffing, of course, or mad. But she wasn't to be swayed, so then I thought a simple monetary incentive would be enough to convince her to go. She only laughed more." He paused, his brow wrinkled. Clearly, he still couldn't believe Josie hadn't taken the money.

"But you must understand," he continued. He leaned forward in his chair, and spoke as persuasively as he could. "She really was quite out of control. She made all kinds of wild accusations, threats. I couldn't have her speaking to Barclay again. I didn't know what else to do. So I had her taken to the clinic. I only thought to keep her there until I could make certain Barclay wanted nothing more to do with her."

"How in the name of God did you expect to do that?" she cried. "He loved her, you fool, and she loved him!"

"You don't know Barclay like I do. I've worked for that man, by his side, managing his business, for years. He was as changeable as the weather. I told you his interests in women waxed and waned. And so did theirs for him. This wouldn't have been the first time Barclay found a woman he thought he loved who then proved to be inconstant or unfaithful. It never took him long to recover from the blow. He always seemed to quickly find another object for his amorous tendencies."

"But he didn't believe you, did he?" Lina said. "Oh, my God, Edward! You didn't, did you?"

"What?" he said, seeing the absolute horror on her face. "No! Of course not! I told you, I am *not* a murderer. And I certainly would *never* have murdered Barclay! Of all people!" he wailed. Then, in a whisper, he said, "I was closer to that man than any other person I've ever known."

"Then what happened?" she said, almost afraid to hear the truth.

This next part of the story would cost him, Lina could tell by the way he struggled to form the words. He looked away, and saw that day again in his mind. "When he returned," he said slowly and softly. "I told him right away. As soon as he came here from the ship. He seemed in high spirits, and I didn't like ruining his mood, but it had to be done, before he went looking for her." He paused, reflecting. "When I told him, he said almost nothing at all. He was shocked, more shocked than I'd ever seen him. He slumped into this chair." Haarten laid his hands on the arms of the desk chair, and looked around him, as if he saw Barclay there, instead of himself. Then he looked up at her again. "I, I left him here. He asked me to, so I did. I went down to the warehouses to work, but I'd not been there an hour when Jackson sent word to me to come back right away. When I returned, he took me to Barclay's room." Still in total disbelief, he said, "He'd shot himself. Upstairs, in his room."

"Oh, no," moaned Lina.

Haarten continued. "Jackson's a good man. He knew just what to do. He locked the Captain's bedroom door, made certain no one in the house had heard the shot, then sent for me. Something like this could have serious implications for the Company."

"To hell with your precious Company! The man was your friend, or so you claim!"

"He *was* my friend! And I certainly wasn't about to have his reputation tarnished with something like this! And over a...." He didn't finish when he saw the fury in her eyes.

Lina stared him down, until he could look her in the eyes no longer. "So you told everyone he was murdered," she said, finishing Barclay's sad tale. She had been standing across the room from Edward, fascinated by his wholly changeable demeanor, one moment defiant and defensive, the next nearly meek and apologetic. Now she walked toward the desk, took the front edge with her hands and asked, almost pleadingly, "But what about Josie, Edward? With Barclay dead, what difference did it make? Why not just let her be?"

"Because!" he roared, rising to his feet. "Because she kept insisting they were married! I didn't believe her, I couldn't believe her! But if I'd let her go, she'd have pursued it, and that would have ruined everything!"

"Ruined what?" she said.

"What I'd worked for my whole life. Barclay was nothing more than a speculator when I met him, rich through inheritance, but with an uncanny eye for opportunity. He could turn a dime into a dollar with almost no effort. But he was a wastrel, his money spent as soon as it was made. That he had any fortune at all is through *my* doing, *my* hoarding his money, *my* investments, *my* work for this Company. Barclay had no heirs, and he treated me as a son. His fortune, his company, his property, they were mine by rights, and I'd been planning on them from the beginning. Do you honestly think I would have given all that time, all my hard work, for nothing?"

Lina could only look at him now with abject pity. "Well, Edward, it seems it *has* been for nothing. These papers have seen to that," she said, lifting the two documents from the desk. "You see, right now, my lawyer, and your cronies Mr. Whittaker and Mr. Greeley are waiting outside. They've seen these, you see, and they're of the opinion that you've been using Barclay's funds illegally. They presume, probably rightfully, that as Barclay's widow, his estate would have passed to Josephine, and through her, to me. Don't you find that funny, Edward? I certainly do. Neither of us knew it, but had we been married today, you would have landed exactly where you wanted."

"I still will," he said. The familiar Edward Haarten was returning. "I can dispute these claims, easily enough. And who do you think will be believed in the end? Someone like myself, with connections throughout the city, or an inconsequential person like yourself."

"I wouldn't count too heavily on those friends of yours, Edward. If the Whittaker party last night is any indication, your so-called friends are deserting you like, well, forgive the obvious comparison, but like rats deserting a sinking ship." She chuckled. "That's my only regret. I *had* hoped to publicly humiliate you, with all of San Francisco society in attendance, but it seems they didn't have the stomach for it. Oh, well. This will have to do. At least I know Cornelius Whittaker is out there, fit to be tied." She came next to him and opened the desk drawer. "In any event, perhaps you'll win, perhaps you won't. I do know this." She threw the household account book in front of him on the desk. "You'll find no resources here to help you. There isn't enough left in there to keep you in brandy and cigars for a week."

"There was fifty thousand dollars in that account! You've been stealing from me!" he yelled indignantly.

His outrage made her laugh. "Really, Edward, you're not thinking clearly. It's so unlike you. As I told you, Mr. Whittaker and Mr. Greeley are under the presumption that the money is mine, as part of the estate. But even if that turns out not to be the case, you yourself gave me open access to this account, remember? So regardless of what's proved about the wills, I can hardly be accused of doing something wrong, can I?"

For a moment, he could not believe she could be this clever. Then he remembered something, and with a sneer added, "That's only a small part of what I have at my disposal, you do realize that, don't you?"

"Well, I realize you have other monies, some of which I'm sure will never be found. But I also can guess that Mr. Greeley and Mr. Whittaker, and some of their other friends in business around town are already taking a very active interest in your affairs. I can only imagine what other questionable deals they'll uncover. It'll certainly be enough to keep you tied up in courts for some time, if not sent off to prison, where belong!" She reached once more into the drawer and took out the small, hinged box. With a light toss, she dropped it on top of the account book on the desk. "Here's your ring, Edward. Maybe, after all, this is the 'just in case' your mother meant."

She was done with him, finally. She picked up the two documents from the desk and started toward the door. With her hand on the knob, she heard him bellow one last threat. "Don't forget your friends up north, my dear! I can still ruin them! And I'll do it, too, just for the spite of it!"

Looking at him over her shoulder, she said, "No, Edward, you can't. You can't hurt any of us anymore. Goodbye." She opened the library doors, and left, closing them behind her and leaving Haarten alone. She walked into the parlor where Greeley and Whittaker stood in nervous agitation. "Gentlemen, he's all yours," she said with a smile. The two men stormed past her, opened the library doors, and went inside. From behind the closed doors she could hear Whittaker's muffled tirade, and Greeley's stuttering apologies. She never heard a sound from Edward Haarten again.

Tunnicliff was waiting for her when she entered the hallway. She threw her arms around him and gave him a kiss on his cheek. "Oh, Mr. Tunnicliff! Thank you, thank you, thank you! You've done everything I could have asked! I'll never be able to thank you enough!" She would not release him, and though he enjoyed her attentions, Tunnicliff began to squirm a bit in embarrassment.

"Well, to be honest, Miss Clark, I'm afraid I can't take all the credit."

"Oh, but you should! You should! I would never have been able to do this without you!" she said, giving him one last peck.

"And Mr. Marr," Tunnicliff added.

"What? Who?"

"Mr. Marr. He has everything to do with this. I went to see him right after you came to me with the marriage license. I knew my meager reputation in this city would not be enough to accomplish what you wanted. Oh, I could do the legal inquiries, but you wanted me to besmirch Captain Haarten's reputation. I'm afraid nobody would pay much attention to a small-time lawyer such as me. They'd question my motives, right off. And my credibility. But you told me this Mr. Marr was a man of business. I hoped his reputation, and at least his acumen, would be sufficient to make the necessary inquiries. Plant the seeds of doubt, as it were. And you needed everything done in such a short amount of time, well, I couldn't think of where else to turn. You know better than I do, Miss Clark, how Captain Haarten seems to have a finger in every pie in this city. So I went to see your Mr. Marr. I know you told me not to speak to him about this matter, but I felt I had no choice. I needed someone who was an ally of yours. So I told him about all the information we needed concerning the Captain's business dealings. It turns out he was the perfect person to help. He has business dealings with Haarten, did you know that? Oh, of course you would. Well, but it was clear he had no loyalty to the man, so I gave him the job of speaking to Mr. Haarten's business associates, spreading those seeds of doubt, while I verified the legality of those documents. By the time I could confirm their authenticity, he had spoken to enough bankers and suppliers around the city to create quite an air of suspicion about Haarten." Tunnicliff smiled. "I gather your Mr. Marr can be quite persuasive."

Lina beamed. "Yes, yes he can."

Tunnicliff smiled sheepishly. "Miss Clark, at the risk of being presumptuous, it's fairly clear to me how Mr. Marr feels about you. So it shouldn't surprise you that when I called on him, as you asked, to verify when he intended to leave San Francisco, he assured me he would...how did he put it...? He would 'wait a month of Fridays if that's what it takes.' I believe you'll find that ship waiting for you, although Captain Riordan did warn me that the tide goes out at eight o'clock."

Lina was frozen to the spot. "But...," was all she could manage to say.

"It's seven o'clock now, my dear," Tunnicliff said. With that, she was bounding up the stairs. "I'll have my carriage take you!" he called to her, just before she shut the door to her room.

Even on the way up the stairs, she was struggling to get out of the wedding gown. Once inside, she nearly ripped it from her body, and tossed it in a crumpled heap on the floor. Waiting for her, regardless of the outcome of this day, was another of Madame Bonaface's creations. It was designed to be a bride's traveling dress, simple, but elegant, in her favorite shade of green. *Perfect*, she decided, as she fumbled with the hooks and buttons of the skirt and blouse. Once dressed, she grabbed her two small satchels, and started downstairs. "Oh!" she said suddenly, turning back to the room. When she came out again, she headed down the stairs and straight for Tunnicliff, still waiting in the hallway.

"Here," she said, thrusting the will and the marriage license into his hands. "Hold on to these, Tunnicliff. Be prepared to use them if necessary." She looked over her shoulder to the library, doors still closed. "Though I have a feeling it won't be." She gave him a quick kiss. "We'll be in touch!" she said, as she grabbed her bags and flew out the front door and into the night.

36

On the ride to the waterfront, Lina leaned intently at the window, making agonizing note of every purchase made of time and distance. She hollered up to the driver more than once to hurry, but he didn't hear her amid the clattering of hooves and creaking of wheels. Nor would it have changed their pace, for the uneven cobbled streets could only be maneuvered so fast, and crowds near the waterfront soon made the way impassable.

Lina opened the carriage and stepped out the moment it had slowed enough to do so. She didn't hear the driver call out to her. "Miss, your bags!" She threw herself into a sea of humanity, carriages, and cargo. She darted among the crowd, and more than once had to turn around, finding her path blocked by a pile of trunks, or a driver struggling to keep his team under control. At last she broke free from the tangle, and stood apart to look for Robert. The crowd was thick, and she felt herself jostled in every direction. *Tunnicliff said he would be here,* she reminded herself. Yet with each passing second without success, she felt the knot in her stomach tighten against nagging worry. Had she missed him? Did he change his mind?

Then she saw him. She watched as he moved among the carriages, searching the face of each new arrival. He was not more than twenty paces away from her, yet he didn't see her. He searched, not frantically as she had, but with an urgent determination. She bore secret witness to the concern and intent on his face. *He would have come for me, no matter what,* she now knew, a realization that filled her with a calm and quiet joy. And she somehow knew, too, that it would always be that

606

way. Robert Marr—the truest man she had ever known. She silently pledged to be as true to him.

He turned and saw her just as that lovely thought had brought a smile to her. He stopped, and as the smile broke across his own face, his arms opened wide. She pushed toward him through the crowd, her pace quickening with each step until he took her in his arms. Neither said a word as she clung to his neck. She might have happily stayed there, but she felt him sigh deeply and then he let her go.

"Milo's fit to be tied. He wasn't as certain as I was of today's outcome, and he's nagged me all day to come find you and drag you back here." He held her face for an instant and looked deep into her eyes. "But I knew you'd be here," he said. Then he looked around. "What, no bags?" They were found standing in a pile next to several others, where the carriage had stopped. He grabbed the handles of both with one hand, and with his other, grabbed her. "Let's be off, then."

Twilight had all but faded by the time they reached the Bantry Bay. When Lina saw Milo, she threw her arms around him and hugged him tight, delighting in the musky mix of familiar smells. He hugged her back, then sighed. "Ah, it's good to have yas back, dearie. Meg'll be so pleased you're comin' home."

"I'm pleased to be coming home, Milo. More than I can say." She was suddenly so overcome with happiness that she threw her arms around him again and, squeezing him as hard as she might, kissed him on the cheek repeatedly.

Riordan nearly toppled as she did so. "Here, now!" He tried to sound stern, but his chuckling betrayed him. "None of that. We've got a ship to get underway. Marr, take the lady below, if yas please, and get out her out the way until we're under sail."

"Come on," Robert said, grabbing Lina's hand and leading her below.

They inched their way down the small flight of stairs into full darkness. Lina heard Robert open the door to the captain's cabin. He stepped inside to light the lantern. Lina quickly followed him, both of them still laughing as they had been all the way down the stairs. When he closed the door behind him, though, the laughter faded, and an expectant silence eased into the space between them, made more intimate by the warm, dim flicker of the lamplight.

Lina spoke nervously. "Tunnicliff told me what you did for me. Robert, I.."

"Don't ask me to apologize for going against your wishes, Lina. You shouldn't have expected anything less, you know. If you thought I was capable of just sitting by, waiting, hoping for the best, you were wrong."

"I don't know what I expected, but I know I would not have you any other way."

He reached for her, and she offered no resistance at all. This kiss was the first release of long-anticipated desire. The pain of denial gave way to the pleasure of fulfillment as their embrace intensified. She responded when his hand slowly moved down the small of her back across to her thigh as he pulled her closer. At the same time his other hand glided upward along her bodice. A jolt went through her when she felt his warm, strong hand over her breast for the first time.

Suddenly, both his hands withdrew from their caresses, and returned to her waist. Holding her at arm's length, he pulled back from their kiss to look down on her. Her smile was affirming, but still he cleared his throat, and said huskily, "Miss Clark, I think it's only fair to warn you that if you value your modesty, it's best I go."

Lina stepped back. "Yes, I suppose you're right," she sighed. She walked toward the cabin door and put her hand on the knob. With her back still to him, she turned the latch of the door, and locked it. "But I don't care," she whispered. She turned to face him, and for just a moment, she sensed a bit of surprise on his face. But when she walked back toward him, he simply smiled, and took off his jacket. He held his hand out to her, pulled her closer and kissed her slowly, while his fingers reached for the buttons on her blouse. Her breathing was uneven, and the slight touch of his fingers made her feel warm and lightheaded at once. The blouse was undone, and he gently slipped it off, then pressed his lips down the side of her neck, and along the line of her shoulders to the strap of her camisole. She closed her eyes and felt herself float.

Robert stood back again, smiling at her, as he reached for the buttons on his own shirt. So much of this was new, Lina hardly knew what was expected of her, and the blood rushing through her made it difficult to think. But on instinct she moved his hand aside and began to release the buttons herself. With the top buttons open, she could see a trace of dark curls stretched across his broad chest. She let herself dare to reach up and touch him there, to lay her hand so close to him, to feel him so alive under her touch.

"I can feel your heart," she said in whispered amazement.

"You are my heart," he answered. She slipped her arms around him as he leaned forward to kiss her.

Bang! Bang! Bang! The door to the cabin shuddered under the weight of a heavy fist. "Marr? Are you in there?" Riordan bellowed. "All hands on deck!"

Robert and Lina stood frozen in their embrace. He placed a finger to his lips to beg her silence.

Bang! Bang! Bang! "Marr, I know you're in there, ya cowardly son of… Get your worthless self on deck this minute, before I come in after yas! There's a storm a brewin' and I need yas topside! Now!"

As Lina looked at Robert, she saw the inner struggle. Finally, he sighed, saying, "I…well, he's short a man."

Bang! Bang! Bang!

"Coming!" Robert yelled. Frantically, he buttoned his shirt, then grabbed his jacket. "I promise, I'll be back just as soon as I can. I'm… God, I'm sorry, Lina. You've no idea. But I've got…"

She smiled. "Go," she said. "I'll be here."

He grinned, then gave her a quick kiss, and then a longer one for good measure. In his hurry, he struggled with the lock on the door, then flew out, still putting on his jacket. "Damn you, Milo! I'm on my way," she heard him call as he left.

Lina shut the door behind him, then turned and looked around the small cabin. Robert's bag sat next to the bunk. In a moment of pleasant surprise, she wondered if Robert had brought her here fully intending this to be a cabin they shared. She blushed. She had never been the object of a seduction before. Nothing she had ever shared in any intimacy with Ephraim Clark could have even remotely been described as such. She decided she should probably be shocked, but she had to admit she liked the notion.

Her eyes fell upon the modest little bunk. *Small for two*, she thought, giggling. She was suddenly aware of how strange this all was. Here she was standing, half-dressed, waiting for Robert to return. *Waiting for a lover*. But what was expected of her in such a situation? Should she dress again, so as not to seem too eager? *Too late for that*. She had already declared her eagerness, and rather brazenly, too. Perhaps then, she should undress completely, and crawl into the bunk and wait for him. That seemed entirely too bold. Besides, in just a few moments alone with him, he had shown her how the prelude to the moment had its own allure.

She wondered how long she had to prepare for Robert's return. Riordan could clearly be heard topside, shouting orders. She slipped her blouse back on to keep the chill off her bare shoulders, but decided, under the circumstances, to leave it unbuttoned. She was still feeling chilly when she remembered Milo's whiskey was hidden in the cupboard. She poured herself a short drink and had started on a second when suddenly she felt quite warm indeed. She crawled into the bunk and pulled the blanket up around her. With the whiskey beside her and a dreamy smile on her lips, she settled in to wait for Robert.

The lantern had long since burned itself out when the knob turned on the latched door to the cabin. The door rattled softly against the lock, then a voice whispered, "Lina? Are you awake?" Robert listened but heard nothing on the other side. Lina barely stirred as she thought she heard footsteps fading into the distance, then she fell asleep again.

****

"Robert!" Lina began calling his name as soon as she rushed through the cabin door the next morning. She woke in a frenzy of need. She remembered the heady evening she might have had, had she not let the whiskey rob her of the opportunity, and she was highly agitated with herself. Even worse, she woke with a momentary panic that somehow she had dreamt much of what had happened between her and Robert, and for a split second imagined she was, instead, on the Rosalea with Edward. She knew better immediately, of course, but the thought left her heart racing, and all the more eager to find Robert.

"Robert!" she called as she trotted up the companionway to the deck. She looked all around, and while many of the hands were on deck, there was no sign of Robert. Her flush of enthusiasm pushed all reason out of her head. She could not even think of where to look for him. Then she saw Riordan in the wheelhouse. She dashed across the deck and up the steps to him.

"Milo! Have you…"

"Aye, there she is. And about time, too! Well, the galley'll be emptied by now, dearie."

"I'm not hungry. I'm looking for Robert. Have you seen him?" she asked, even as she looked through the views of the wheelhouse for him.

"Hmm. I have. The man was in a black mood earlier."

"Really? Why?"

Milo looked at her askance. "Are yas standin' there tellin' me you've no idea?"

Lina turned around, slowly. She gave Riordan an innocent stare, but the hawkish look he gave back broke her façade. "I suppose I do," she said quietly.

Milo laughed. "Ah, I thought as much. And I'm proud of yas, I am. No matter his intentions, that Robert Marr can charm a lady right out of her britch…er, that is to say, her morals, quicker'n…well, that's not to say I know such a thing to be true. I mean, not from personal experience, just what the man's told…Oh sweet Mary…But you know it's true, Lina darlin'. He's…he seems the sort who could…if the lady were willin'…not to say you were willin', darlin'. I mean, a fine young woman as yourself knows how to handle herself…I mean, handle such advances…that is, if advances were offered. Oh, damn it all!"

Lina swallowed a laugh. "I think I know your meaning, Milo. And yes, I think I know how to handle myself."

"Well maybe so, but I'd have no part of takin' chances. That's why I done what I done. Why, somebody had to show they had good sense! And I make no apologies for me actions, neither. 'Twas wrong of him to get ahead of himself, and I told him as much this mornin'. That explains that foul mood of his, no doubt. I'll wager it's been a while since anyone's given him the sort of scoldin' I gave him this mornin'."

Lina stood slack-jawed. "Milo, do you mean to say you were…" She struggled to think of the phrase. "Protecting my honor?"

"Aye! That's it exactly! I was protectin' your honor! And who better, I asks? Why, don't me and Meg think of you as our very own? Herself would have me carved from gut to gullet, she would, if I did any less.

You're deservin' of a proper declaration of intentions, same as any lass."

"Milo," she said softly, her hand drawn to her heart. "That's the dearest thing anyone's ever done for me!" She planted a kiss on his grizzled cheek.

"Here now! None of that," he said, though he was smiling the whole time. He pushed her to arm's length and looked her straight in the eye. "That was last night. But I'll not be spendin' the whole voyage keepin' the two of yas from playin' patsy. Go on, now and find him. And figure out what the two of yas is goin' to do."

"That's just what I came to do! Where is he?"

"Ach. Where did the man go? Ah, there he is! Comin' out of the hold. Robert Marr!" Milo boomed. Robert looked up, and Lina thought she saw a frown cross his face when he caught sight of her.

She hurried down from the wheelhouse toward Robert, smiling as she approached him. He seemed to feign indifference, not only by his expression, but by his whole bearing. "Good morning," he said dully.

Lina ploughed ahead. "Good morning. I've been looking for you everywhere since I woke. I couldn't wait to talk to you."

"Hmm," he said. "Well, what is it? I promised the steward I'd help him and…"

"Milo promised me we could have some time to talk. Alone."

"Oh, did he now?" Robert said with a scowl toward the wheelhouse. "How very kind of him. And of you, too. To make time for me." He sat on a hatch cover and crossed his arms over his broad chest. His pose seemed sullen, yet Lina could only smile.

"I can see your feelings are hurt," she said sweetly. "I do apologize for that. For last night, I mean," she added in a whisper.

"I've no idea what you mean," he said.

Slowly, Lina sat down next to him. She could tell there was some fence mending to be done before anything more passed between them. "Of course you know what I mean," she said softly. "You've every right to be annoyed with me. When you left, you were expecting….well, a very different sort of evening than what you had, I suspect."

"Hmm," he said, not moving an inch.

"And I expected it, too." She dared to lay her hand on his arm. "Welcomed it, even." He looked down at the hand, and then to her face. "I didn't change my mind....about wanting that, I mean. I did. And I do," she added, with just enough of a blush that she saw a light come to his eyes. "But I took some of Milo's whiskey for the chill, and then I fell asleep. I'm sorry. I had every intention of waiting for you."

"I did come back," he said. "But by then, the cabin was dark, and it was too late, all thanks to Milo there," he said with a sharp nod toward the wheelhouse. "It was his ploy to keep us apart. He said I was taking undue advantage of the situation. Had me convinced you might think the same. Sat me down this morning and preached to me about my 'intentions.'"

Lina chuckled. "Oh, I know very well what your intentions were." She found she liked it when he seemed slightly shocked by what she said. "But maybe it was for the best. There's something I forgot to tell you last night, and when I remembered this morning, I thought perhaps it was just as well we didn't...that we waited."

"Then tell me quickly, for there's something I want to ask you."

Lina reached deep within her pocket and pulled out a small, folded piece of paper. "Here," she said as she handed it to him.

"What's this?" She waited for him to read the paper. "Lina? This is a bank receipt!"

"Yes, I know," she said, hardly able to contain her delight.

"It's made out to Marr Logging, and it's...it's..."

"Five thousand dollars!" she said gleefully. "I deposited it in a bank in San Francisco. It's yours."

"But how? Why? I mean, it's written from Haarten's bank account." Suddenly, his face darkened. "Lina? You didn't steal this, did you?"

She burst out laughing. "Not at all! It's the money that's owed you. That's about right, isn't it? I tried to guess what sort of costs you had already incurred. I hope I was close. But I knew you'd never see a penny of anything he owed you. It was only fair. You've earned it."

"But how is it that you could write this?"

"Edward gave me access to the household account. It took a bit of effort, but I think I managed to spend every last dime in it."

"Well, well, well," Robert said, still holding the draft before him in amazement.

Lina put her arm in his. "I hope there might be some left over for you to start those plans of yours. You've given me my dreams, and I just wanted to help give you yours. Nothing would make me happier than to see you make those plans come true. And the sooner the better."

"Hmm," he said, carefully slipping the paper inside his shirt. "Do you mean that?"

"Of course!"

"I wonder…" he said. "Even if it was something done, well, suddenly? Without a plan of any sort?"

"Of course, if it's what you truly wanted to do," she answered.

"Then…" He looked at her doubtfully, "No, never mind."

"No, tell me! What is it?"

With a dare in his eyes, he said, "Marry me."

Her answer came as sure and steady as her own heartbeat. "Yes. Of course."

"Now."

"Now?"

"Now. Today. This minute," he said, grinning. When surprise left her speechless, he laughed. "That's what I wanted to ask you. I had every intention of asking last night, if Milo had given me the chance. I wanted to see if it was possible for you to do something impulsively. If you'd let your heart win out over your head, just for once. But I suspect it's only natural for a woman to want to plan something as important as a wedding."

"No! I mean, yes!" She shook her head as if to straighten her words. "I mean, no, I have no interest in planning another wedding. So if you want to be married now, I say yes."

"Truly?"

She drew her arms around him and kissed him. "Besides," she said, looking up to see Riordan trying hard not to appear to be watching them, "as Milo said, it's a long trip home. He'll be worn out if he has to spend all his time protecting my virtue."

****

"Meg, we're home."

Lina stood in the doorway to the tavern, watching Meg fix breakfast. The morning was overcast, and the light inside was dim, but already the inviting scent of bacon and biscuits filled the air.

Meg turned around, smiling broadly, but saying nothing at first. She did not seem the least bit surprised to see Lina standing there. Meg crossed the floor and took Lina in her arms. "Oh, thank God, honey. I prayed everyday they were gone they'd find a way to bring you home."

Lina held Meg tightly, treasuring the reception. "It's good to be home," she answered. Then she pulled back. She looked into her friend's warm, smiling eyes. "Meg, I'm so sorry if I caused you any worry. I should have at least explained why I had to go."

Meg put her hand to Lina's lips. "I don't want to hear it. Not right now, anyway. It doesn't matter. Maybe someday, when the men are away and there's just the two of us with time to tell stories that don't matter anymore, stories just for fun. All that matters now is that you're home, safe and sound." With a grin, she added, "And happy?"

"Very happy."

"Well, then! I guess that means you and Robert have set things right between you?"

Lina nodded. "That, and more. We're married, Meg. Milo married us."

"Bless my soul!" she said, throwing her arms around her again. "And where is Robert? I need to give him a kiss, too."

"Off to find Jamie and Charley to share our good news."

Meg beamed. "Well, there's good news waiting for him there, too. Jean and Jamie have a baby on the way. Should be here with summer."

"Why, Meg! That's wonderful! Robert'll be thrilled."

Meg nodded. "Jamie's so proud of himself he's about to bust a button. Poor Jean, though, she's been sufferin' with it. She'll be fine in another few weeks. Oh, I just remembered!" Meg giggled. "I wasn't to tell you. Jean's planning a big to-do tonight. She wants to have everyone over for supper. Wanted to make a real family affair of it. I promised her I wouldn't say a word until they could tell you themselves."

"Supper? Tonight? But how did she...?"

"Know you'd be here? Like I told you before, honey. I felt it in my bones you'd be home today. Woke up with it yesterday as sure as anything. And I knew it would be a good homecoming, too. See? Don't ever doubt what you feel deep down in your bones. Leastwise, I don't."

****

The supper Jean served that night could not have been more perfect. Even her temperamental stomach ceased to bother her for the evening, but it slowed her progress through the day, and made the meal later than planned. No one minded. It left plenty of time for talking about the new baby, and the plans Robert had for using Haarten's money to grow the business. No one asked Lina about the circumstances of her leaving, or how she came to return. She suspected Robert of conspiring with his family to that end, but she didn't care. She enjoyed the evening on its own terms, not as a reunion or an absolution, but just as a simple gathering of the clan.

Lina did feel a particular obligation to Hugh, however. When he stepped outside to get more wood for the fire, she followed. He looked up and saw her approach as he was stacking the firewood. "Better get back inside, Lina. It's starting to rain, and you're without a wrap."

"I'll be fine. A little rain won't hurt me. I wanted a word with you, Hugh." He stopped his work and looked at her. "I feel I owe you an explanation…" she started to say.

"No, you don't."

She put her hand on his arm. "Yes, I do. I asked you to lie for me, Hugh. That was wrong, and I'm sorry."

He shook his head. "But I didn't lie for you. I just waited a few days to tell Robbie the truth. Who knows? Perhaps it's better I did. If I hadn't let him stew in his own juice, he might not have come to realize how much he missed you. See, that's the funny thing about the past, Lina. You can't change it. And if you could, perhaps things wouldn't have turned out the way they did. The way they should. I understand why you feel as you do, maybe even why you have some regrets. But as for me, whatever happened, I wouldn't have it any other way," he said.

She smiled. "You might not remember, but you told me once, it seems like a long time ago, that everything would turn out alright. Do you remember?"

"I do. I was right then. And I'm right now. Don't you know that yet, Lina? I'm nearly always right." Lina laughed. "Now, that's settled," he said. "Let's get back inside and have a nice dinner and finish figuring out how to spend that money you rescued for us, and when it's all over, you and Robbie can go back to the cabin and get accustomed to your new home."

"But you and Charley..."

"I'll be up at camp, and Charley'll be staying with Jamie and Jean. Just for tonight, Lina. We'll figure out how we'll all manage together later. Just consider tonight....a wedding present."

And with that, the matter was settled. After the meal and a few rounds of drink for the men, Robert and Lina returned to the cabin. Hugh had made sure there was a fire ready for them. The place never seemed homier. That night, within those cabin walls, Lina felt a peace and a comfort she had never known before. "Home," she thought, as she drifted about the small cabin, fingers lightly touching the books on the small shelf, the rough plank table and the soft blankets. "Home," she thought, as she joined Robert in bed, and where later, in the darkness, in the midst of their playful passion, she heard herself laugh—a rich, happy kind of music. It was the way Josephine would have laughed, she realized, and the memory warmed her heart.

The next morning, Lina woke early, content but still unsettled. She slipped from the bed to dress herself, then lit the stove for coffee. She had not been about long when Robert woke, and sat up in bed.

"What has you up so early?" he asked, rubbing his eyes, and stretching. Lina just smiled.

****

As Hugh came down the road from camp, he met Jamie coming out of his door. "How's Jean this morning?" he asked.

"Tired, but better, I think. Do you suppose this will last until the baby comes?"

The two talked as they walked toward the office, but as they approached they saw the door already open. Hugh took off at a trot toward the door, with Jamie right at his heels. Then they heard the laughter. As they entered the office, they saw Robert looking at papers spread before him on the table. Coffee cup in hand, one foot on the chair, leaning forward, he was still chuckling. So was Lina, who was bustling about the room collecting the stray pieces of paper that seemed to be everywhere. Lina saw the men first. "Good morning!" she said, cheerfully.

"I didn't expect to see you two here today," Hugh said.

"Well, where else did you expect us to be?" she said, giggling.

Robert grinned, looking at Lina, "She insisted that this is what she wanted to do today." He shook his head in wonder. "Can you believe it?"

"Oh, I know it must be hard for you to imagine I could resist your considerable charms," she said, coming over to give him a kiss on the cheek. Then she stuck some papers in his hand. "But these are all the chores that need attending, and from the looks of this place, we're not back a moment too soon. All that talk last night about new hires, new work, well, it's put me in a frenzy to get busy. So, if you gentleman will excuse me, I need to get started."

"Come on, boys," Robert said, "We can tell when we're not wanted. Let's get on the road. We've a busy week ahead of us."

Lina looked to Robert suddenly. "Will you be staying at camp all week?"

Robert smiled. "Not this week. Not just yet. This week, I need to keep close to town."

Lina blushed, but answered boldly. "Yes, you certainly do," she said.

Robert gave her a quick kiss and then started to follow Hugh and Jamie out the door. Hugh and Jamie walked off ahead of him, but Robert paused for just a moment to look back at his new wife through the open door. Lina didn't see him. She had already turned her attention to the task at hand. Robert smiled as he watched her take the books to her desk, open them, and with a small curl of contentment on her lips, pick up her pencil and start to work.